Dido: Death is now a welcome guest.
When I am laid in earth,
May my wrongs create
No trouble in thy breast.
Remember me, but ah! forget my fate.

Libretto by Nahum Tate for
Dido and Aeneas by Henry Purcell
from *The Aeneid* by Virgil

Remember Me...

MELVYN BRAGG

SCEPTRE

First published in Great Britain in 2008 by Sceptre
An imprint of Hodder & Stoughton
An Hachette Livre UK company

1

A CIP catalogue record for this title is available from the British Library.

Hardback ISBN 978 0 340 95121 7
Trade Paperback ISBN 978 0 340 95122 4

Typeset in Minion by Hewer Text UK Ltd, Edinburgh
Printed and bound by Clays Ltd, St Ives plc

Hodder & Stoughton policy is to use papers that are natural, renewable
and recyclable products and made from wood grown in sustainable forests.
The logging and manufacturing processes are expected to conform to
the environmental regulations of the country of origin.

Hodder & Stoughton Ltd
338 Euston Road
London NW1 3BH

www.hodder.co.uk

IN MEMORIAM
L.R.

PART ONE
MEETING

CHAPTER ONE

She was silhouetted against the log fire, sitting on the floor, her legs drawn elegantly to one side, her right arm as it were a prop, in her left hand the cigarette. When Joe saw her as he came, nervous through loneliness, into the grand drawing room of the riverside house, he went across to her tentatively but immediately, perhaps already sensing a fellow loneliness, captured by the dark silhouette, darkened further by the deep purple dress she wore, which, he would learn, was her only good dress. He was attracted across the quietly convivial room full of strangers by the sadness of her isolation and the space around her.

There was the mystery of her, from the beginning, the difference about her. Joe would often come back to that first image. It was not love at first sight. It proved to be not much of a conversation. He wanted to tell her that she looked like the engraving of Shelley in his book of the poems, but he could not summon up the nerve.

They smoked. He poured her a glass of red wine from the cheap bottle he had brought. He never could remember much of what they talked about but he always remembered not telling her, not then, that she looked like Shelley. Even many years later when it finally proved to be the time to tell her story, their story, to their daughter, to tell it in full as far as he could, it was this picture of her to which he returned, the silhouette, which made him want to cry out again for the violent death, the wounded life. He could find so much, fathomless, which came from that first accidental encounter. He did not know then that like him she was still numb and lost in the aftermath of a love which had taken almost too much to bear; he did not even sense that, and as for the rest she was and in ways remained as unknown as an undiscovered planet. Whereas before her, from the first he felt transparent; he believed she could understand everything about him. To the end, he held onto the conviction that she saw right through him.

The party went on around them but it was as if the volume had been turned down by someone aware that the two of them needed all the silence and stillness they could get to nurse the feeble pilot flame of this slight encounter. Nothing should have come of it. They were not meant to meet, he never felt that nor did she, nor did they pretend. But for a splicing of accidents they would never have met at all: and yet, given the way this unsought fragile conversation was to wrench their lives, mark, brand and gut them, it came to seem impossible that their life could have been lived on any terms other than those to be set in motion in these unplotted moments. A million taunting reasons never to meet each other. Trajectories in different quarters of the universe. The worlds of their deeper past so far apart. All they had to build on was the temporary companionship of strangers. But the pilot flame stayed alive, that night, in the week before Christmas, in the rather run-down Victorian manor house by the Thames just outside Oxford, leased by American art students, log-lit, candlelit, everyone shadowed, the flickering lights stroking a glass or revealing the sudden fullness of a glance across the room.

In the early days, Joe had liked to dwell on the high odds that led to their meeting. It lent the glamour of the miraculous. Even sticking to the narrow window of that evening, so many exceptional factors had been required. She had stayed on in Oxford rather than return to France following another bitter exchange of letters, so bitter that for the first time in her life she would not spend that season in her own country with her own family. Jonathan, one of the Americans in the art school, had taken pity, knowing, as they all did, what had happened between Robert and herself, what a cruel breaking apart it had been, and though this friendly soul did not know the worst of it he knew enough to seek her out and persuade her to come to Shillingford that evening where there was to be a gentle party for the left-outs and leftovers. Several students from their art school had missed her over the past weeks, he said. She was persuaded partly out of her good manners, partly because

4

the American was kind; mostly, though, because the family she worked for was on holiday and the house was cold and its emptiness intensified her dread.

On that evening, Joe had been standing in front of the Oxfam shop in Broad Street wondering whether to go back to the library for a last couple of hours. For the first time he had stayed on at the university for an extra week. The excuse was that he needed to catch up on his work, but a stronger reason was that he was reluctant to go home to Wigton and see Rachel, whom he still loved, as happy now with someone else as she had been for so long with him. The Oxfam window could trap him. One late afternoon he had been convinced that Rachel would come to see him and he had gone to the station and waited until the last train arrived and departed and still he sat on the station bench as if he could will her to appear before him. On the way back that night he had stopped in front of this Oxfam shop, bewildered with his need for her, and looked at the rows and rows of second-hand paperbacks, attempting to staunch the bleed of hopeless passion by trying to memorise the titles and authors.

Roderick called him from across the street, clipped military syllables cracking through the icy air. Off to some party, sure Joe would be welcome, just grab a bottle at the off-licence next to the bus station. An American GI met at a concert, very bright, at the Ruskin School of Art. Party would be full of arty types but could be fun.

Yet that was no more than the tip of it, Joe would think later. He could so easily have walked back by the High Street and not the Broad. He could have stayed in the pub for another drink as he very nearly did. She could have changed her mind about the invitation as she had so often done about others in the past few weeks. Roderick might not have spotted him across the street. He could have said 'no'. She could have been in another room and not silhouetted against the log fire. Someone else could have been talking to her. The possibility of their meeting could be sliced so thin it would disappear altogether like the thought of parallel lines meeting only in infinity which had once made him giddy. He could still sweat at the thought years on. What if he had missed her? If destiny meant anything surely they were destined not even to know of each other's existence let alone to meet, and yet out of this would come an embrace to the death: so perhaps, he thought, later, chance was their destiny.

It seemed very difficult to ask her name. 'Natasha,' she said and waited, but Joe took time to enjoy the name, the charm of those three syllables falling like quiet notes in a Romantic sonata, a name unique in Joe's personal experience and pronounced in a silver-toned English which managed to sound both pure and foreign.

'French?' he guessed.

The response was a barely perceptible smile.

'Joe,' he announced.

'That's American. GI Joe.'

'No it isn't!' He spotted no playfulness. 'Joe's plain English.' Once again the brief smile across features as pure and foreign as the accent. Again she waited. 'It's Jewish, to be fair,' he said. 'The coat of many colours.'

'That's Joseph. I prefer Joseph.'

His aunt Grace, who had aspirations, had wanted him to be called by his 'full name'. 'Call him Joseph and he'll get Joe,' she had warned, 'and Joe's common.'

'Joe it is, then,' said Sam, his father.

'Natasha's a great name.'

'It's not good enough for my aunts. But my mother was bohemian.'

Joe held tight to the fistful of questions her sentence provoked. It was as if there were a bowl brimful of mercury between them and he must not spill it. Bohemian!

'Thomas Mann wrote a novel about Joseph,' he said.

'I've read only *Death in Venice*. I must go to Venice. I must.'

He caught something of urgency, even desperation, but it was too remote a cry to do anything but hear and faintly register, and again be excited by the foreignness and want for more, try to fix her face despite the failings of candlelight.

'It did not get much further,' he told their daughter, 'and some of what I remember could well have been drawn from later encounters, or be made up, or be misremembering, or come from the desire to please you. But she always called me Joseph.'

—◊—

Joe stayed the night. He was given a bed in a large room with two double beds. Don, the blond American painter who seemed to be in charge, was in the other bed.

'Natasha Jeanne Prévost,' said in answer to Joe's question. 'She's been at the college for years. She's an enigma.'

Joe wanted more than that but he did not know what he was looking for.

'If you concentrate,' said Don, after a long pause, 'you can hear the Thames out there. Just close your eyes – that strengthens your hearing – and listen. Out there.' They listened. Joe thought he heard something but he may have been trying to oblige his host who had so easily and generously offered the bed. 'I used to imagine the Thames to be such a big river, when I read about it back home,' Don said. 'Something like the Mississippi. I couldn't believe how small it was when I saw it. But now I think it's a big river again because of the artists and the history. Does that make sense to you?' Joe wanted to think it through and say something which sounded intelligent, as if Don were an examiner. 'I'll open the curtains,' said Don. The moonlight lit up his nakedness: he was built like a boxer, Joe thought, not like an artist at all, a light heavyweight at least, and unashamed to stand ivory-white nude before the big window, which he opened. You yourself could be a painting, Joe thought.

Don went slowly back to his bed. The moonlight was a shaft between them and now Joe could hear something in the distance.

'It's the weir,' Don said. 'A boy was drowned there last fall. Another boy tried to rescue him and he got in trouble but they pulled him out in time.' Don paused. Joe liked these pauses, they implied deeper meaning. They introduced a grain of drama. 'What would make a boy risk his life to save another boy?'

'You just do it, don't you?' Joe said. 'You just – do it.'

'I see that,' said Don, in a rich American tone that reminded Joe of so many films and because of that made Don instantly familiar, friendly, to be liked and trusted. 'Instinctive heroism. Dying for your comrade in arms.' Again the pause, but the distant drama of the weir, the few glasses of wine, the newness of it all were making Joe sleepy, keen to burrow into the bed, squirrel down and defy the winter air. 'Deeper than that,' said Don, 'it must be the love that the Bible says passes the understanding of women. Women don't do what we do. For other women. Men can love men, don't you think so, Joe?'

'Yes.' He thought of one of his friends at home in Wigton of whose adolescent friendship he had been so jealous and he thought of James, so discerningly understanding, with whom he had shared a room in his first year at Oxford. 'I'm sure they can. You can even put your arm around their shoulders. I used to do that.'

'And when you did that, was it a sort of love you felt, do you think? Would you call it that?'

'I don't see why not,' said Joe. 'There's got to be lots of different sorts, haven't there?'

'But the intensity of voluntary love – not family – voluntary, is that always the same? Man or woman?'

This time the pause came from Joe and it lengthened into silence and the soft purr of his sleep.

—ɯ—

Natasha always slept with the curtains open. She preferred the night.

She had come home the moment Jonathan had offered her a lift. The party had filled in time but there was nothing to keep her there. The art students, the genteel young English, had been discreet; the older Americans more awkward but then Natasha suspected they might be a little ashamed of what Robert had done to her. She had invited Jonathan in for a polite coffee but he had to pack, he said. Paris tomorrow and then Berlin with his sketch pad as a cover. After all, he said in his slow delivery which had always amused Natasha because she could never quite work out whether it was a heroically corrected stammer or a sly means of commanding and controlling the fullest attention, artists had long been anonymous in European capitals and he wanted to spy on the existentialists in Paris, sketch out the culture of the Cold War in Berlin, stitch the two together and see if he could place the piece in the *New Yorker*.

As he drove away to his digs in Walton Street he wished he had not mentioned Paris.

Natasha lodged in a tall, Georgian house in the Banbury Road and the three flights of stairs to her attic room were steep. She ought not to have felt so very weary after such a small effort, but when she closed the door of her room behind her she could have collapsed. She sat on the edge of the bed to undress and the clothes lay where they dropped.

Her portrait of Robert was where she had left it and full on to the moonlight. She should get out of bed and turn it to the wall but in the secrecy of the small room she could study it. It was unfinished. She could see its technical shortcomings. Unlike Robert, the other Americans and most of the English, Natasha had come to the Ruskin without any formal training beyond a modest talent encouraged by one of the nuns who had taught drawing at school. But the portrait had a strong look of him, Robert himself had admitted that and he was even more critical than Natasha herself. Sometimes, he said, technique can get in the way. The perfectly crafted thing can be perfectly dead. An ounce of true innerness can be worth a ton of accuracy. Better not to finish it, he said, this is as good as you'll get.

He was the best artist in the Ruskin, they all said as much. He had picked her out, the real one, he had said, not like the others. Though she had been burned before and though she knew he was careless of women, she became his wilful accomplice. He had released her, thrillingly, from her self-imprisonment. She had surrendered to his promises and been helpless when they were broken, brutally broken. She had felt herself break with them. If she looked long enough, hard enough at the portrait maybe she would understand and begin to find a way out of this darkness. Her watch told her she had been in her room for less than ten minutes. It already seemed half the night and yet she wanted only to be here in the slow time of her lair, humiliated, hurt, adrift, looking for a place she could neither see nor reach.

She had called him Robert in the French way. At first he had liked that; then he had come to hate it. Perhaps she ought to have dropped it sooner and not teased him. He did not like being teased but she liked the reaction it provoked and the animation of anger. She brooded on the portrait, looking for explanations, looking for comfort. The faint light enriched the painting, she thought. She looked at the dark window panes that needed to be cleaned. Beyond the window were slated

9

rooftops and below it the garden adjoining other gardens, winter dead, sealed in the city of learning sunk now in sleep inside its beautiful and ancient walls of scholarship. Robert had involved her in that, too, with Jonathan, and a few American academics who threw around their ideas with a vigour that could make Natasha want to applaud. That group had gone out of her world now. Save for Jonathan, none of them had been seen since Robert had left her, without warning, just a note, a note, not even a letter.

She turned away from the portrait, put her face to the wall and huddled under the bedclothes, legs drawn up to try to squeeze out the misery by going back to unthinkingness, rocking herself slightly. There were no resources left. Misery was in every cell. Misery was her condition. It was beyond pointlessness now, even more than before. She wanted sleep. But even there, he would be waiting.

—m—

Joe walked quietly even though Don's loud snoring signalled deep sleep. Odd it did not wake up Don himself, Joe thought: he had been disturbed awake by the dawn light through the open window and the snoring had made it impossible to go back to sleep. It was an entertaining noise, though perhaps just for a short time. Don lay splayed on his back, mouth gargoyle open, blond hair mussed over his forehead, somehow incongruous that he was snoring, too young to snore.

The drawing room was a mess and Joe was glad to tidy up, to earn his stay, take away the glasses and wash them, empty the heaped ashtrays, clean out the grate. He liked being in a room so uncramped: it emanated ease and quiet wealth.

'Coffee?' Don was in the kitchen. Joe had put on the kettle for tea but he complied.

'Thanks, yes. Toast?'

'Sure. You done all this?' Don indicated the wine glasses washed and dried and set out neatly on the kitchen table. 'That's Northern British, isn't it? Like your accent. Not really English at all.'

Joe was unaccountably nervous and he did not know whether to be flattered or piqued.

'You guys are Celts,' said Don, 'so it isn't your fault.' He paused. 'You have a nice smile.' Joe felt it slide off his face. Don laughed and handed Joe the coffee. 'Let's go look at Ole Man River.'

They took the bus into Oxford at midday and Don insisted he came to see the poky, raffish Ruskin Art School tucked away in the back of the Ashmolean Museum. The American walked through the museum as if he owned it, Joe thought. He himself felt it was a waste not to examine some of the paintings and statues especially when he was with a real artist who could tell him about them, but Don ignored everything.

Don had produced Natasha's address and after a pie and a pint in the Lamb and Flag, Joe went to her house which was just a few hundred yards away. He had known since he left her that he would seek her out; their loneliness was a mutual field of force. As he walked out into the grey, low-cloud winter afternoon, enjoying the bite of the cold, he sensed that she would be there waiting for him.

The shrill doorbell startled her awake but she would not go down. It would not be Robert and she wanted to see no one else. When she was sure the visitor had given up, she did go down – to the kitchen where there was food. They had asked her to give the house 'a good clean' while they were away and they would be back in two days. She would start after a cup of coffee. But after the coffee as she looked through the window it began to snow and the prettiness of it, the lingering flakes of white, the sweetness of the snow, the pure white life in those unstained innocent flakes made her cry and cry so hard she could do nothing until night came back.

Their daughter wanted to know more about Shelley. Joe could recite a few lines and recall some of the life, but it was how he looked that she wanted to know. 'Hair swept back,' he said, 'far too long for the close-cropped male of post-war England and the style gave the poet a feminine look and Natasha's hair was swept dashingly from her face in a similar manner. A broad high forehead. A strong nose, the "Bourbon nose" she was to call it. Face rather long and pale with a look of distinction in the slim lips and the eyes, just a little large, but so

voluptuously and teasingly expressive. Even against the fire in silhouette, the candlelight had given me glimpses of the eyes and it was most
likely,' he said, 'that it was what I saw there which would one day lead
me to a life I could never have dreamed of.

'But there were other photos from around that time,' he said, 'and
sometimes she doesn't look at all like Shelley. There's none of that
romantic brooding. She's just smiling, so lovely, clear-eyed.'

He did not tell her that a disturbing dream had returned since he had
begun to write, which had recurred often in his adolescence. In it he
saw a dam which he had built across the river with other boys when he
was seven or eight. In the field beside the dam a girl was buried, a girl
he had somehow murdered, a girl he recognised. The field was always
empty but he knew that one day they would arrive and dig her up.

Nor did he tell their daughter that he had sought out photographs
recently as a preparation for this telling. They were in a drawer at the
bottom of an old linen chest he used for storing finished work. He had
not seen them for decades. There were packets of them. Some neatly
labelled by Natasha, others not as neatly by himself. After just a few
minutes, a look at the merest fraction, he had put them away. They
were unbearable. Her look of such life.

CHAPTER TWO

He bought winter roses, deep red. Seven. The man in the market threw in the extra one for luck. The boy looked so spry, so clearly, eagerly, nervously on the gad. Joe walked through the near-empty, pre-term Oxford streets not sure whether it was better to hold the flowers down like a walking stick or up like an umbrella. He alternated. The deep red flowers were like a torch that late slate January afternoon, under the frozen busts which guarded the Sheldonian, past Trinity and Balliol, colleges now as familiar as Wigton pubs, names warm to him at last, in his final year. He turned to pass St Mary Magdalene's of the incense and the chanting in Latin and then the Martyrs' Memorial calm in stone where a few centuries ago red torches had burned men alive for their faith, and he headed for North Oxford and fabled dens of inimitable Oxford dons, including the two at whose house Natasha was the au pair. The Ashmolean was to his left, the Lamb and Flag pub, soon to be their favourite, to his right. On his rose-bearing journey to Natasha through the cold streets, he felt open, free, unencumbered.

His return to Wigton for the Christmas vacation had been under-mined by sightings of Rachel. He decided to leave it early to come back to Oxford. To study for Finals was a good excuse, but there was also the tug of the thread of contact with Natasha from that first and only meeting. It had held through the cold break in the North and grown stronger in imagination. A phone call to Don had confirmed that Natasha was still in Oxford and had been ill over Christmas with 'something like influenza, more a depression, I'd guess'. When he pressed the bell he put the flowers behind his back.

This did not deceive Julia, who smiled but did not comment. Her smile widened when she took in his outfit: he had bought himself a canvas jacket with a fake fur collar and a pair of light brown cords, thin-ribbed and tight.

'He looks about sixteen,' said Julia later in the drawing room to Matthew, who was almost through his annual Christmas read of the whole of Jane Austen. He did not look up. 'Like one of those town boys one sees on Saturday nights on the way to the dance.'

'And very nice too,' said Matthew, his head determinedly bowed.

'Oh, I agree. But for Natasha? Surely . . . ?'

'He can't be worse than Robert.' Still steadily moving through the prose, he added with precise dismissive conviction, 'Robert was a shit.'

'I disagree,' said Julia. 'He was a predator like a lot of men of his type at his age. He wanted an affair and then he would move on, he is a sort of sexual nomad. It was quite obvious to me.'

'From what I gather,' Matthew uplifted his head for a moment or two, 'he gave wholly the opposite impression to Natasha.'

'She always expects too much,' said Julia. 'And she is an adult.'

'I'll stick,' said Mattthew, 'with shit.' And his eyes returned to the pages of *Sense and Sensibility*.

Julia picked up her copy of *Death on the Nile*.

Her accent, like that of her husband, was careful, clear, academic in its exactness, eschewing 'upper' but espousing pure. They would have wanted the approval of Jane Austen. Julia looked the part, Joe was to think, as he got to know her, extremely pretty, plainly served, morally earthed, amused.

'May I ask your name?'

'Joe, Joseph, Joe. Richardson.'

'I presume you are a friend of Natasha?'

'Well . . . not really . . . We've met. Once . . .'

'She's at the top of the house, the room on the left. Come in.' She stood aside. Joe blushed as he revealed the flowers. Noting this, Julia said, 'What lovely roses. I'm sure she'll approve.' He was nodded through.

'I noticed that *Lady Chatterley* was sticking out of the pocket of that dreadful jacket,' she said. 'Rather obvious.'

'Or merely coincidental,' said Matthew, and read on.

—⟋⟍—

'I've never been in an artist's studio,' said Joe.

The bed was unmade as he thought it should be. The floors were bare boards, quite right, and clothes were not in a cupboard but hung on a rail in full view. There were saucers used as ashtrays and paint brushes sticking out of coffee mugs. There were two old easy chairs, one of which looked very unreliable. The sink was stashed with unwashed dishes. The day was darkening and the light was on. The central bulb was bare. Best of all, Joe thought, was the easel, on which was a canvas barely begun. None of the paintings stacked around the easel or on the walls was framed and Joe was soon to be told that none of them was finished.

To Joe the room was exotic. There was even a sloping ceiling. And Natasha fitted the part; a black dressing gown, sloppily tied, no slippers, cigarette, trying to force the stalks of the seven roses into a hastily rinsed milk bottle. Three was the limit. She snapped the stalks off the remaining four and put them in a coffee mug next to the brushes against the bare window. The milk bottle went on the small table beside her bed, displacing the plate bearing the half-eaten sandwich. Joe had never seen flowers look so artistically arranged.

'They look great,' he said, 'don't they?'

Natasha drew the dressing gown around her as she sat down and turned on a small red-shaded lamp which stood on the floor. In the ruby light the studio, Joe thought, became a set.

'Look,' she said, pointing to the mug of amputated roses next to the window. 'They transform the balance of the whole room.' She turned. 'And those three . . .' She looked at the three blood-headed roses in the milk bottle, arrested, for a moment, by the fact of them. The velvet heads still upright, green stalks in clear water. She could understand why painters would want to capture them though still lifes were not for her. 'Yet you think – they're dying. Once they are cut they begin to die,' she murmured.

The soft rosy light from the lamp had recaptured some of the silhouetted beauty he had nursed throughout his absence. When he had come into the room he had been rather thrown by her pallor, the sweat-flattened hair, the listlessness. Now that very evidence of illness, softened and made beguiling by the low seductive light, attracted him afresh, gave him an impetus of concern.

'Don said you hadn't been well.'

'Did you see Don?'

'No. I phoned him.'

'You spent that night at Shillingford?'

'Yes. He put me up. It was very good of him.'

Natasha smiled at the tone: so innocent. But did that mean it was to be believed? Joe felt the appraisal.

'I like that,' he said, pointing to the portrait of Robert. 'I really like that.' He fixed his gaze on the portrait, trying to squeeze as much out of it as he possibly could. Natasha glanced at him as he stood unawares, and caught her first glimpse of an energy and an intensity which had so comprehensively drained out of her.

'He must be a friend,' said Joe, and there was an intimation of jealousy. 'A good friend?'

'He was.'

Natasha went across to the bed and sat against a heap of dented pillows.

'Not any more?'

She looked at him and for a moment or two everything was in the finest balance. She thought she might throw out this unfeeling stranger in his stupid jacket or just cry: but she could not impose that on him. The three roses stood between them.

'There's some wine in a bottle by the sink,' she said, eventually, and Joe was relieved, though he did not know why. 'Use teacups.'

He washed them carefully, delighted again, and sat on the armchair nearest the bed. They smoked. For some time Natasha said nothing. She had pulled up her knees and wrapped her arms around them, the motion of smoking being the only movement. She wished he would go away. Tiredness was pulling her into unconsciousness like a relentless undertow and she did not want to find the means to resist it.

Joe had felt a strong scent of danger when the portrait had been discussed. It was better to say nothing. It was as if Natasha had imposed on him a sudden glimmering of wisdom. Before this encounter he would have rushed to fill every void with words. Now he sensed that he scarcely existed for her and that realisation made him breathe softly, stay still, just stay. Staying was the best he could hope for.

She looked around for the saucer to offload the collapsing column of ash and noticed him.

'Why did you come?'

'Don said you hadn't been very well.'

Why had Don not come? Or any of the others who were in Oxford over Christmas? But these were weary questions, not seeking an answer. She thought less of herself even for letting them crawl across her exhausted mind. She was truly glad they had not come. She wanted none of them. But this stranger who had walked in, why had he come? Was it not just naïf, unthinking, without a history? Or had she been made sentimental by the gift of the blood-headed winter roses?

'Thank you for the roses,' she said and in such a way that Joe stood up to leave.

He tried to think up a telling, witty last line, but blurted out,

'It would be great to see you again. We could go to *Wild Strawberries*. Ingmar Bergman. I get two complimentary tickets because I review films for *Cherwell* – it's the university newspaper. Same time tomorrow?'

He would spend some time throughout the rest of the evening burning with retrospective embarrassment, closely analysing those clumsy sentences and finding every single component wrong, wrong, wrong.

Natasha made a small gesture with the cigarette. Contempt? Tiredness? Certainly it said, 'Please go.'

He closed the door quietly and though a burden was lifted from her when he left the room, there was also the faintest regret, for his openness, the excitement he tried to conceal with such limited success. That truly terrible jacket.

She took the flowers across to the bin beside the sink but then decided to keep them. Watch them die.

The smell of them brought no memories, filled her with no sweet sensation of that natural benediction which came from herbs and flowers. Freshly cut lavender was the only potion which could move her. There was that photograph of her mother holding a large bunch of lavender, smiling over her shoulder, dressed like the peasant women in

Provence before the war. Natasha looked at it only rarely. It was too hard.

The sink was such a mess. She turned on the unreliable hot water tap, and looked around for washing-up powder. She had let the place go. As the water ran, she began to tidy up, slowly, moving like an old woman, prepared to quit at any time.

Much later, when she was brooding yet again on their beginnings, she came to believe that Joe's first awkward visit may well have helped save her.

CHAPTER THREE

'Just as shiny-faced,' Julia reported, 'and still that dreadful jacket.'

'I must,' said Matthew, who was preparing himself for *Emma* which he always kept until last, 'catch a glimpse.'

'You must. I have never seen such an appalling garment.'

'I meant of him,' said Matthew. 'Dick?'

'Joseph she calls him.' Julia frowned. 'Joe is much more appropriate.'

'How would you defend that?'

'You know perfectly well what I mean.'

Joe was relieved that Natasha's room was tidier. The more he had thought on its bohemianism, and he had thought of their meeting constantly, the thinner the scruffy glamour had worn. Disorder excited him but only in small doses. There were still the unfinished canvases and the easel, the unorthodox wardrobe and what he had named 'the forbidden portrait'. It was still properly artistic, he thought, a real studio, but no longer a mess. The bed was made. The seven roses were reunited, all shorn now, in a large jam jar beside the tubes of paint.

He had taken down the number on the phone in the hall on his way out the previous evening and called just before lunch to leave a message that he would be there at five. To be fair and give her the chance not to be there? Or pretend not to be there? Or be there? In those first days Joe had not much of a clue as to what he was doing or why. He was like a puppy dog in a wood, blundering after scents which might be dead, might not, just enough to keep it keen. He had small expectations.

Natasha noted that she was pleased to see him. For the company, for the gust of life that came through the door, for the smile which so

19

openly liked her? It was a brief and superficial stroke of pleasure, like a flat stone merely skimming across the surface of a lake. Yet she was honest enough and so acutely attuned to her own depression to notice and to register this positive effect of his presence and be grateful.

'Feeling better?'

She nodded, not wanting to disappoint him.

'You look better.'

A long woven wine-coloured skirt bought in the market in Avignon, a clean white shirt open at the throat, a thick college scarf draped as a shawl, the lightest rub of lipstick, the pallor softened as her back was to the window.

'Which college is that?'

Natasha looked at the scarf as if surprised to find it there. 'Roland gave it to me,' she said and shook her head.

'Who's Roland?'

'You are nosy.' The flickered smile only partly reassured him. She drew deeply on her cigarette and Joe reached for his own. She exhaled the smoke evenly, in perfect lines, Joe observed, like those sharp rays of light that shot down through a mass of cloud, staircases to heaven they had been called, staircases to her lips. He smiled more broadly, encouraged by the warmth which was in him, which came from the force of attention he was paying her, though from a distance, still circling.

'Roland is the janitor at the college. He finds lost property in the museum and after a few months he gives it to us. Jonathan says that Roland gave him a packet of contraceptives just before Christmas. One had been used.'

Joe kept his mouth shut and blushed. In the Ashmolean Museum? Where?

'I've got the tickets.' He patted his jacket pocket, unsure why he needed the reinforcement of mime. 'It starts at six-ten.'

'Six-ten.' She repeated the numbers mockingly, and waited.

'We'll miss the trailers.'

'I see.'

'Which I like. I like trailers . . . usually . . . Not always.'

'Six-ten. Now it is five-fifty-two.'

She stood up and Joe's heart leaped to see her stand, again silhouetted, this time against the window which brought in the last light from a dying winter sun. He saw that she was wearing leather boots.

'You look like a Cossack,' he said. 'Have you read *The Cossacks*? I think it's his best.'

'You are funny,' she said and Joe felt complimented by the first warmth in her tone.

In the cinema Natasha used the celluloid-lit darkness and the comfort of the thin audience to float, to be borne up above the pain, to let the images on the screen give her just enough of a drug to stir into the painkillers taken before Joe came, to numb the ravenous grief. Occasionally her attention would be caught by the adolescent girls in the elaborate white dresses of a distant time, and memories of photographs and of her own childhood would surface to remind her of past losses, missed chances of happiness; or the bewildered expression of the old professor would be transferred onto a recollection of her father and the world of the film would become a dream, welcomed because it eased the pressure of grief at what Robert had done. Without finding the opportunity to object, she was guided to a small restaurant that Joe and Roderick used occasionally. It was cheap but the crisp tablecloths were in a red and white checked pattern and she could see the place was well cleaned. The woman who served was Spanish. On the walls were the accoutrements of matadors and two posters of the Bull Ring in Seville. There was a guitar hanging next to the door to the kitchen. It was the most sophisticated and romantic restaurant that Joe knew.

Natasha's sweet smile as she sat down at a corner table – the place was quite full but this table was produced like a special treat – confirmed to Joe that he had made the right choice. The waitress came and with a flourish she lit the thick red wax-dripped candle stuck in the dead bottle of Mateus rosé. She stood back, her native costume enlivened by the glow, and bowed her head slightly at Joe's beam of applause.

'Bravo!' said Natasha, and the women held each other's gaze for a moment and then, in a slightly different tone which appeased and convinced the waitress, 'Truly: bravo,' Natasha repeated and held out a cigarette to the candle, twirling it slowly in the yellow flame. An understanding had been reached.

After the paella – they had only one course and Natasha scarcely ate – and house red wine, two glasses for Joe, one for Natasha, he sat back proprietorially with coffee and a cigarette, glowing with hope.

'My father teaches . . . like that old professor in the film.'

'My father wanted to be a teacher,' Joe said. 'A village schoolmaster.'

It was as if she had not heard him.

'He is ill now,' she continued. 'He has been made ill!' The snap of the sentence alerted Joe to instant concern.

'I'm sorry. What is it . . . ?'

She shook her head, chiding herself, not Joe. 'The film you made with your friends. Was Ingmar Bergman your inspiration?'

'It was a bit of a failure really,' Joe murmured. Somehow – he could not work out why – she put a new and testing perspective on what he had done. He had hoped she had forgotten his nervous boasting on the way to the cinema. 'We thought it was existentialist.'

'What do you know about existentialism?'

'English existentialism.' He tried to grin. 'We put jokes in. They didn't come off.'

'You should see your expression.'

Joe looked around as if for cover.

'You are so disappointed. Like a little boy. About your film.'

'That's what I'm going to do,' he said, provoked to boast but avoiding her mocking eyes. 'I'll make a film. I'll do it one day. I'll get the bill,' he said and Natasha regretted her teasing.

'We must share.'

'No. My treat.' Natasha reached out as if to restrain his arm from going to his wallet. 'No. I'm flush.' He looked around for the waitress.

'She is in the kitchen,' said Natasha. 'It is not normal for a woman to be the waitress in a restaurant like this.'

'She told me about that. Her husband's a better cook, she said. And he never wanted to be a waiter. She likes doing it: she says she couldn't

22

do it in Spain, but I don't know. They met in Seville when they were at school. They left because of Franco. She's called Carmen – like the opera. That's how she tells you – "I'm Carmen-like-the-opera-in-Seville." She once said she was my Spanish mother!'

'You know all about these people,' Natasha said. 'That is good.'

'Well,' Joe threw an explanation over his embarrassment, 'Roderick and I have been here a few times.'

'You make it sound like an excuse. Not everybody who comes here will be interested to know what you know. And you know much more. Don't you? Why is that?'

'My mother and father . . .' He changed his mind and said no more.

As they were about to leave, Carmen came to the door with them. To Natasha she presented a small-faced white carnation. To Joe she said, most solemnly and in a stage whisper, with a possessive hand on his arm, 'She is grand, Joseph . . .' And looked deeply into his eyes.

Grand? Missing its Spanish meaning, Joe rather jibbed at the word. Grand was nowhere near right. They went out into the cold.

'I can walk by myself from here.'

'I'll set you back.'

' "Set" me?'

'Take you.'

' "Set" is better. But no. Please. And thank you for a lovely evening . . . Please.'

Suddenly she had to go. The front of manners fell away. Weariness engulfed her.

She left him and he watched her walking through the yellow pools of lamplight along the empty Oxford pavement, the clicking of her boots finally fading away and still he stood for some moments, relishing her absence.

He was confident that they would meet again: she had already become such an essential presence in his life. He would make it happen.

Over the next few days she would not see him.

'I'm sorry,' said Julia, 'but she's not at all well.'

All the more reason to see her, Joe thought, all the more reason to be with her.

'I'll take those up to her.' Joe handed over the six red roses. 'You're very sweet.'

He did not want to be sweet but let it pass.

'Will you tell her I'm asking after her?'

'Of course.'

They stood as if they were on a vital narrow bridge challenging each other to see who would give way first. Noises of children from within the house settled the matter.

'They're back from their grandmother's,' said Julia. 'Peace is at an end. I must fly.'

Although she shut the door gently, she had a twinge of conscience as if she were unfairly shutting it in his face. She was starting to like him although she thought him unsuitable.

'He does seem devoted to you. I might even say obsessed,' Julia said to Natasha as she picked up clothes and tidied up the room which had soon subsided into slovenliness. 'He's very sweet,' and she added, with emphasis, 'he's becoming a limpet.'

Natasha looked at her and said, 'Please keep the flowers. I can't stand them.' The little outing with Joe seemed to have accentuated and not eased the remorseless gnawing on her wound. The glint of light that evening had been extinguished minutes after she had left the restaurant and she found herself at once utterly consumed by her loss. She knew that Julia was being kind but she wanted Julia gone. She needed all the space around her to be empty to cope with these relentless surging tides of darkness.

'I'm exhausted,' said Julia. She and Matthew had come together to listen to the headlines of the news on the radio, to have a final (and in Julia's case her first) drink of the day and to discuss what, as atheists, they liked to call their parish notices. 'One doesn't anticipate the au pair becoming more of a burden than the children she has been employed to help organise or the house she is supposed to keep clean.'

'Natasha is not one of nature's skivvies,' said Matthew, taking care not to over-soda the whisky.

'I appreciate that.' Julia filled up her tumbler with a quantity of tap water guaranteed to drown the modest tot of scotch. The coal fire was low but still warm; the yellow side lamps threw cosy shadows across the well-proportioned room; the few paintings and the regiments of read books were a reassurance of arrival. Academic North Oxford was Julia's Arcadia.

'We are in *loco parentis*,' said Matthew, removing his spectacles to mark the end of another day's hard reading.

'Others did not think as we do.' Julia had protected him from Natasha's more lurid stories of a bleak life below stairs as au pair to other Oxford intellectuals of modest means who aspired to the pre-war luxury of servants through the cheap and exploited labour of young foreign girls 'learning English'.

'That makes it all the more incumbent on us,' said Matthew.

'Quite frankly I'm worried about her,' said Julia. 'She's been in Oxford for ages. She won't take any of the exams at the Ruskin. She shows no ambition and no sense of direction and the small sum she gets from her parents barely keeps her going.'

'Her parents are a mystery,' said Matthew. 'Now and then there's a sighting . . .' He fished out what would be his last cigarette of the day. 'And now there's this new chap.'

'He is much too young for her. Excuse me, I must go up and see her.'

Natasha was asleep. Julia looked at her for a while. She had no truck with any form of divination yet she stayed for some time and wished that by thought alone she could help and heal Natasha, and feared what might happen to the self-hugged, pallid, foetal figure so desperately asleep in the narrow bed.

The college library was open until midnight. Joe was making notes on an essay which he should have handed in the previous term. He had promised himself that after Christmas he would drop everything (save the film criticism) and work flat out for Finals. Exams were the point of being at Oxford, he told himself. That was what the scholarship was for. It was a matter of pride. It was a question of honour. To show them.

He had been asked to discuss the effect of the French Revolution on Ideology in British Politics. He was trying to make himself familiar with the principal characters for his essay. Already met in school were Hazlitt and Wordsworth. Now there were new heroes, Tom Paine and Charles James Fox, a new villain the younger Pitt, and the disturbance of Edmund Burke. What Joe really wanted to write was that it was a tragedy that revolutionary ideas did not flower in a Britain in which many of them had been seeded.

He had looked out a copy of *The Prelude* and found the passage in which the young Wordsworth and a pro-revolutionary officer had been walking in the countryside. They had come across a 'hunger-bitten girl' who 'crept along' leading a heifer.

> . . . at the sight my Friend
> In agitation said, ' 'Tis against *that*
> Which we are fighting . . .'

When he had read that at school, Joe had immediately and passionately transferred the image to the lanes around his home town, an area still mired in Victorian rural poverty. He saw it where he was and that one image called out his most generous feelings every bit as much as the following lines served as a clarion call to arms.

> I with him believed
> Devoutly that a spirit was abroad
> Which could not be withstood, that poverty,
> At least like this, would in a little time
> Be found no more, that we should see the earth
> Unthwarted in her wish to recompense
> The industrious, and the lowly Child of Toil . . .

He still felt the words as a song in his mind, as an anthem, even a creed.

Until he came into the arms of Oxford, he would have argued that to be the inheritor of the French Revolution which had blown up privilege and sanctified equality would be a far, far better thing than to be the subject of what in England at that time was still in style and social order a feudal system. But now he himself was privileged and a price was demanded and part of that was to see early views as naïf.

Head bowed over the desk he now argued for the superiority of English moderation despite the repressive acts which made it very like a tyranny.

Perhaps because his heart was not in it, his concentration was patchy. He had been at the desk for about three hours. He took a break for a breath of air and a cigarette and he strolled around the shadow-cloaked quad. In that cloistered darkness he felt a bliss of certainty and calm. Everything was so good. Thoughts of Natasha displaced scholarship. He was at the beginning of the adult adventure, in Oxford, fired up with life. He wanted to race around to make her see him, but he forced himself back into the library.

Over the past year he had fallen behind in his academic work and accepted that the duty of hard reading was waiting for him. Now was the time. What did the world have in store for someone from his common background, just another scholarship boy who had somehow managed to clamber aboard Oxford, if he failed the crucial final exams? What did acting and writing and making an existentialist film matter compared with Finals which could take him he could not define exactly where but on some safe and desirable path in this new world to which he had gained access. If he fell out of the race now – what waste! What shame! And what would there be to do?

Yet lash himself as much as he could, the taste for it, the love even, was diminished. Natasha was now his chief subject and study and her banishment of him was hard to bear. Every day's rejection turned the screw tighter.

He scarcely knew her. He ought to pull himself together. It was the masculine approach, it was the sensible approach and it took him nowhere. She had made him realise the hunger of his loneliness.

He would not let her go. He had been caught and he had wanted to be caught. The tug grew more insistent the more he saw of her. He could not give up. And yet he would not have described what he felt as love, not yet, not like the ever-aching, carnal, lust-twinned love he had known for Rachel.

As he sat in the library with a few others equally roped to the oars as the final examinations reared up in an uncomfortably foreseeable future, thoughts of Natasha, vague, indistinct, but relentless, drew him further and further away from the effect of the French Revolution on Ideology in British Politics or other tasks in waiting: the influence of Aristotle and Plato on the Italian Renaissance, or the tragedy of Dido in *The Aeneid*, Book Four, which luckily he had studied at school and learned chunks of by heart. After less than an hour he surrendered, closed the books and left them there for the morning. They could not, as so recently they had done, take over his life, or not now, which ought to have been disturbing. Yet as he walked through the perfect Jacobean college quadrangle, there was elation, and an undefined freedom.

It was about a mile and a half to his digs out of the centre of the city along the Marston Road. He enjoyed the night walk in the frosty air. He liked the thought that he was the only human being walking down the curving lane of Holywell, imagining himself a Jude the Obscure, barred, bricked, out walking alongside the high wall of Magdalen College, picturing the herd of college deer asleep in its silvery park. He loved to see the running of the deer. He was the sole traveller to pass the mediaeval, singing tower on the bridge and he stood there a while looking down on the water, somewhere between striking a pose and relishing the solitary present.

Then he was out of the enchantment of the university and into the swathes of semi-detached houses which shored up the city, home of legendary Oxford landladies like his own, Mrs Harries, who had told Roderick and himself on their arrival that she would 'brook no nonsense'.

Walking often lifted his mood. There was a settlement inside himself which came from steady solitary walking, a physical clarification that could exercise its way to an experience of happiness, a rhythm which could reach into a reservoir of calm. It encouraged thought. He could understand why Wordsworth liked to compose his poems while he was walking, the beat of the heart, the breath of the stride, the beat of the line.

By the time he put the latchkey in Mrs Harries's lock his anxiety was dissipated. He would find a way to meet Natasha again. Whatever she did, he would not let her go.

CHAPTER FOUR

Their daughter wanted to know precisely when they had fallen in love. Joe wanted to find a dramatic moment. Something wild and romantic, to smile over and cherish, a gift to one who had suffered so much, a light in the dark inheritance. Most of all she needed something to smile over, to remember fondly, to see her parents as young, younger than she was now, in Oxford as she was, wonderfully in love then, everything finally worth it because of that. Joe was tempted. Julia had later described what he did in those early days as 'a siege' and been quite funny about his brazen dogged unsnubbable visits, sometimes two, even three times a day. But that was not enough; that did not deliver what his daughter needed. Roderick could tell funny stories about covering for Joe when, as the love affair developed, he failed to turn up at his digs and Mrs Harries went 'madly puritanical'; but that was later. It was the beginning she longed to know about, the seed of it, as if so much that was to happen would be understood and could be forgiven if only their beginning could be claimed as pure and marvellous.

He would retell the story of first seeing her beside the fire. He would tell of his first visit to her mother's 'artist's studio' and elaborate on its garret bohemianism, its thrilling resemblance to the studio of Modigliani which he'd seen in a French film. He would describe the first meal and even point out the little Spanish restaurant. But falling in love had happened without Joe recognising it. Perhaps he was still nervous after Rachel. Perhaps he wanted it so much that he dare not look it fully in the face. Or he took his cue from Natasha, who was distant in those early weeks, as if seeing him short-sightedly.

It was Natasha who controlled those days. Joe sensed that to crash in would be to destroy whatever small connection had been made. She was so far away from him. Her eyes were sometimes kind, sometimes teasing, but mostly they were clouded in concentration on herself, straining to combat and vanquish the reality of her abandoned state. They were eyes that wanted no one to look at them because they feared the pain would be too clear and too shameful. Only later did he realise that he had seen her always in those early weeks through a veil of pain. They were eyes that could seem to want to be closed in peace and for ever and whose expression, when Joe did catch it unawares, sliced to his heart.

He had to wait some time until he knew for certain they were in love, he said, because of your mother. It was not the beginning that mattered. But she would not be deterred and he did his best. He could joke that this older, more distinguished and experienced Frenchwoman of a mixed European ancestry simply did not recognise the obstinate country courtesy of the Northern grammar-school arriviste. There was even some pleasure to be had as Joe played up the story of the rustic lump and the courtly lady and there was a truth there. But he knew it was a waste of time to look for truth in the beginning.

Many years later he made a radio programme called *Not One Truth*. There was religious truth through divine Revelation, the truth in the genes, Galileo's truth that the book of the universe was written in the language of mathematics, the truth of the historical method, Keats's 'Beauty is truth, truth beauty', truth as relative, as analysis, as physics, as reason, as fiction and finally as unknowable. The routes to private truth were no less numerous. Yet a single answer was always longed for by those, like their daughter, who thought all life would be made understandable if only they could see and hold the one key.

The start of the love that came to lock together Natasha and Joe in a dance of life and then of death had to come from her. Joe was willing. At that stage in his life Joe was longing to fall in love, it was a condition that had recurred after Rachel and more than likely it was the lack of response from Natasha in those first weeks, her very emptiness, which spurred him on and gave him courage. Had there been resistance perhaps he would have fallen away quite soon as he had done during the past year on his few tentative forays back into the ring.

What he tried to tell their daughter was that Natasha had no wiles, she had no agenda, she had no English baggage of 'placing' him. When she gave him her attention she possibly saw a rather blurred young Englishman who had loomed out of an undergraduate Oxford she scarcely knew, and certainly not in young men such as Joe. There was from her no categorisation after the English fashion. In that undemanding ambience, Joe's confidence grew.

'What did Mum think of you when she first met you?' He had an answer to that yearning question only years later and even then he was sure that he knew it only in part. 'Not much, at first,' he said. 'She thought of me very little at first and in the landscape of her mind I was way in the background, I was that small figure in the far distance only there to prove a point about perspective. I don't know if she thought of me at all then.'

From the beginning, Joe was eager to spend his energy on her as recklessly as a rich suitor lavishes gifts, but it was better than that, Natasha thought, because he did not give any signal she could recognise of looking for a reward. Now and then he attempted a kiss but proved too shy. Once or twice she caught him looking at the bed with a cautious hope, easily deflected. What he seemed to want was to look after her. Her only previous experience of that was deep in the unwanted past, two loving friends of her mother, ages ago in Provence.

But this was different. He was younger than her, she felt safe in that, as if the age gap was a sure layer of security, enabling her to control him, and yet he as it were 'mothered' her. Even fussed over her. He took her to London to see *West Side Story*, recommended by James, a friend, a classical scholar who had become bored with Classics and left the university more than a year ago. They had continued to keep in contact. He bought the train tickets, pre-planned the day in some detail, went to a small Italian restaurant in Hampstead (also recommended by James, who lived there), clucked over their poor seats in the half-empty matinée and stealthily stole to better seats after ten minutes or so, using the pretending-to-go-to-the-Gents' manoeuvre. He even asked her if she ought not to be wearing a coat in this weather! She did not have a coat. She only just prevented him from buying some hideous garment in the January sales. She insisted on the adequacy of her old

31

black leather jacket and soon he took a liking to it. Very gradually his attentions, for they could be chastely and rather formally described in that word, began to touch feelings in her she had thought dead.

'Your mother trusted me, I think,' Joe said to their daughter, 'that was the heart of it. And she was right.' He paused and sought to engage with the look in his daughter's, her mother's, eyes. 'And she was wrong.'

—⁓—

Joe introduced them with pride.

'David Green – David knows everything about who's who in Oxford; Natasha Prévost.' He had described her to David at length one evening in David's enviable Georgian rooms in St John's Street.

Joe had chosen the bar of the Randolph which David liked and which for Natasha was conveniently across the road from the Ashmolean. To Joe it suppurated exclusivity and made him uncomfortable but his determination was that David and Natasha know and like each other and if it had to be the bar of the Randolph then that was the price. It was not part of his experience, a clubby male bar casually crowded with the latest inheritors of Brideshead, informal in expensive sports jackets, cravats and cavalry twill trousers.

David watched him go across to the bar with what Natasha construed as a possessive amusement.

'He is your marionette?' said Natasha.

'He is yours,' said David.

She liked his boldness. David Green was rather large, constantly in movement as if physically uneasy but the movements seemed choreographed; his hair black and long, his face generous and expressive, mouth thin, vivid, rate of speech rapid, emphatic, punctuated by giggles which Natasha came to delight in.

'Let me say this at once,' said David, 'while Joe's at the bar (I know you prefer Joseph). He described you perfectly but what I had not been prepared for was a certain hauteur which makes you rather nearer my class than his although I do know they order things differently in la France.' He pronounced 'la France' in the French way.

Natasha was yet some time away from being fond of David and he had moved too fast on a first encounter.

'*Je m'excuse, mais* in France we do not fly to conclusions with so little proof.'

'Ah! *La logique française.*'

'Non. Good manners, *anglais.*'

'Touché.'

'Joseph is very fond of you.' Natasha looked at him steadily. 'He is not difficult to impress.'

'His unguardedness, which I love, and his defencelessness may be a little more seductive than you imagine.'

'Seductive? I don't think so.'

'I am probably wrong. I'm told I make rather a habit of it.'

'Told?'

'People!' He waved his hand at the early evening crowd in the bar. 'Critics.'

'Are you on the stage?'

'Ah!' said David, relieved at Joe's arrival. 'The drinks.' For Natasha and himself halves of bitter, for David a cocktail.

David sipped at the cocktail almost distastefully. Joe was to realise that David did not really enjoy drinking and his aim was to avoid being an outsider by imbibing steadily but as little as possible. As he sipped, an action which necessarily gave him pause, his eyes swivelled around the room and lit up at several recognitions which his eyebrows and the ends of his otherwise occupied lips acknowledged; the manoeuvre was done with some speed so as not to appear rude but it was clear to Natasha that there was a greed or more like a need for it and that softened her towards this otherwise swashbucklingly dominant figure.

'You've caught me out,' David said, reading into her glance. 'My little weakness.'

'You enjoy it,' said Natasha.

'That's the only point in having a weakness.'

Natasha nodded in recognition at the effort that David was making.

'He was a star, you know,' David said, waving both hands as if he were about to transform Joe into a Hollywood icon. 'They made a film

33

and Joe wandered around looking significant although we could never quite fathom what he was being significant about.'

'Alienation,' said Joe, promptly, quite enjoying the role into which David had cast him.

'Much better if it had been about class, and your exile from your class,' said David. 'Alienation is far too European and middle class for you. Joseph and I went on the Ban the Bomb march together last Easter,' he said to Natasha, 'with the jazz bands and Bertrand Russell, with vicars and MPs and playwrights, all very English, very village English, like a garden fête, and the conversation among the under-graduates in the evenings would often revolve around this word "alienation". I thought they should stick to class. Now there's a subject.'

'You see yourself as his guide, don't you?'

'I,' said David, giggling, 'am his Virgil, guiding him through the Oxford circles of hell.'

'This is a very boyish hell, David.'

'So it seems this evening. You should see them scent blood and bay at the sound of breaking glass – Evelyn Waugh is reliable on that.' He paused. 'Let me tell you something.' Another mite of a sip and a rapid smile from those long curvaceous lips and he leaned forward, voice guarded. 'In my first week here at Oxford, four of us met in my rooms for tea. We had never met before. Each of us had been to a different public school. In less than an hour we discovered that we knew about sixty people in common – in their case often sisters and cousins but in all our cases friends we'd met through school chums or at London parties or wherever. It's a caste . . . England is a hierarchy of courts and clubs and this handsome cadre may be tolerant and amused by the Joes of this world but, as a group, they do not rate or like or understand his world. Individuals can be an exception, of course.' His smile melted Natasha's resistance. 'But Joe's background is very foreign, slightly threatening, coarse, and less attractive than, say, that of any roughneck from the old colonies. He is, unfortunately for them, English, and being at Oxford theoretically one of "them" but he is clearly not, until he converts and adopts their religion, but even then . . .'

'Why should Joseph need a guide to that?' Natasha asked. 'And how can it matter? Class is of no importance in the real world.'

'Of course you are right,' he said, and changed the subject.

Soon David left, all but danced away, full of beaming affection for both of them, his drink barely touched, on his way to the first of three parties that evening. Natasha and Joe soon followed. She too had scarcely touched her drink.

Natasha had to be back by seven to babysit the three Stevens children; Joe went to eat in college.

When he came back the children were headed for bed. The boys were aged eight and six, the girl four. Joe's contribution was to romp with them and make them too excited to want to go to bed. Natasha sent him down to the kitchen, with which he was now quite familiar. He made a pot of tea and read more of *Justine* while he waited.

'David's great, isn't he? And it doesn't show but he knows a heck of a lot.'

Natasha was drawn in. Joe could sense it. He sat as still and alert as a hare, all but trembling at this particle of slight but crucial development. She offered him a cigarette and let him offer her a light.

'I think he is a good man,' she said, exhaling the perfectly even column he could never quite match. 'But . . . horribly nervous.' Which is why I can trust him, she thought.

'Nervous?' Joe shook his head, plunged in. 'David Green goes to more parties than anybody else in Oxford according to *Parson's Pleasure*. They poke fun at him sometimes.'

'He needs those parties,' Natasha said. 'He likes you.'

'I like him. He got me the job on *Cherwell*. We met at the party after the film preview and he asked me back to his rooms. We talked until about five o'clock in the morning. About everything. He says he talked about the Old Guard and I talked about the New Wave! He asked me if I wanted to be the film critic for *Cherwell*, I said if he thought I could do it, and that was that! He's in with everybody.'

'Is he?' Natasha kept her tone neutral. 'I like him,' she said.

'That's great! I could see he liked you. He's the first of my friends you've met. They've all been yours so far. And I bet you'll like Roderick and Bob as well.'

'Are you making me part of a family, Joseph?'

'Why not?'

His cocky look was flirtatious and Natasha felt as if she had been touched gently on the cheek. For the first time Joe felt that he was more than just attendant on her.

'You have kind eyes,' she said. The compliment disconcerted him. For a moment he did not know where to look. He was not used to it. He could rarely if ever remember his mother paying him a direct compliment. Yet there was a subversive feeling of pleasure. What if she were right?

He knew he ought to return the compliment and he wanted to but it was too difficult. She had the loveliest smile he had ever seen.

'You told David a lot about yourself that night in his rooms.'

'Yes.' About Rachel, of course. And the pub he had grown up in. His parents. The small town of Wigton. His friends back home. His ambition to make films. Much of which he had repeated over the past weeks to Natasha.

'He would want to know everything about you,' Natasha said, quietly, 'I can see that.'

'He talked to me about himself as well,' said Joe, 'it wasn't just one-sided.'

Natasha waited. Joe was a little reluctant. Had it been confidential? But then, nothing should be kept secret from Natasha.

'One thing that will surprise you,' he said, dropping his voice. 'He isn't really English. His father is German, was German, was killed in the war but before that he got his mother and David out, because she's Jewish. They have well-off relatives over here and they pay for his education.'

Natasha took another cigarette.

'Poor boy. German father. Jewish mother. English public school. And now, Oxford.'

'He did say he was got at a bit. But he joked about it.'

'I see. So he is taking his revenge now, in a most intelligent and very risky manner.' She laughed to herself. 'I like David. He is daring them.'

A few days afterwards, in the mid-afternoon, when the children were being taught at their respective schools and Matthew and Julia were doing research at their respective colleges, they made love. It took Joe by surprise.

In fact, when it became clear that Natasha would go to bed with him Joe panicked. He went downstairs to the lavatory where he tried unsuccessfully to pee. Back upstairs he suggested a glass of wine 'Before . . . before . . .' Natasha poured half a teacup for him which he knocked off like beer. He was too nervous to notice her mood, too fearful of fatal failure, consumed wholly by the desperate hope that it would be big enough, that he could last long enough and she would not laugh or be disappointed and leave him. What he had been male-groomed to think he wanted most about a relationship he now wanted least. She stripped, without coquetry, and slid into the rickety bed. Joe tugged at buttons, cursed socks, hesitated at underpants. She was French. She was an artist. She was unknown.

It was impossible to talk to their daughter about any of that, out of which, a few years later, she was created. Memories of their early frequent love-making came back unsummoned. They seemed so innocent; too innocent, it was to prove. It was an innocence that stoppered curiosity, baulked at unfettered sensuality, left questions, over time, to fester. But for now, for some years, it was enough, it was the physical seal, and it was sweet and loving.

Joseph was to be trusted, she told herself. He was like one of the village boys she had played with in La Rotonde, the brother of Martine her best friend, an open-faced, cheeky, sure-grounded boy, guileless, she thought.

Joseph would not harm her.

Robert had to be annulled. All he had done and not done had to become the past in her body as she so longed for it to be in her mind. She had to be brave: and to be brave, again, as his urgent but boyish love-making threatened comparisons with Robert. Yet, she thought, Joseph would carry no danger, Joseph could be controlled.

That night, after he had gone, that first night, Natasha felt the possible dawning of a new life. She lay in her room in the dark and, unusually, turned on the radio, found a performance of *Fidelio* and let herself be dissolved into it.

Joe skimmed the ground as he went back to Mrs Harries's. He had not realised the burden of the emptiness. Natasha gave him everything and he felt almost mad with it. He would move in with her. They would never be parted. There was a new world now, a world fulfilled and for ever with Natasha.

Natasha stood in her black dressing gown at the window. Her feet grew colder on the bare floorboards. Darkness outside, darkness in the room, afloat on the genius of Beethoven. She smoked and peered intently through the glass, seeking to order her thoughts and feelings and take on this tide of energy which Joseph brought to her. This love, this new beginning which would not be denied.

CHAPTER FIVE

Jonathan came into Natasha's room like a man condemned.

Joe was there. He had become a fixture after their first coupling. For Joe such love and sex meant marriage and despite the moral straitjacket of Oxford, England in 1961, he had decided a semblance of that could start now. Matthew and Julia had become resigned to the rattle of the rickety bed late at night, followed by Joe thundering down the stairs to race back to his digs. 'There are several reasons why I ought to disapprove, but I find that I don't,' said Matthew.

'Natasha is almost normal and occasionally even cheerful, which is a miracle,' Julia said, 'so what can one say? You can smell it on them.'

Jonathan too was to report that he could 'smell it on them'. He thought of waiting until Joe left but soon realised that Joe would never leave him alone with Natasha.

He would accept nothing to drink.

Natasha and Joe looked at him expectantly.

'I come bearing a message,' he said, slowly, eventually, reluctantly.

They waited.

'A friend,' he looked at Natasha pleadingly, then at Joe without success, then at the ceiling. 'A mutual friend of ours – that is Natasha's and mine – is back from abroad and would like,' one final pause, one more moment in which the bad news was not yet delivered, 'to see you . . . Tomorrow . . . For a drink . . . In the White Horse . . . At one.'

Natasha went still. Joe tried to read her expression but failed. She wanted both of them to go. The news came as an act of aggression. Now that she and Joe were lovers she had begun to believe the affair with Robert was buried, or at least beginning to retreat from her present mind and move into the past, be anaesthetised, to be coped with. But how could it be? It roared back through her. She made such a taxing effort to reveal nothing of the turbulence of her feelings in front of the two men that she felt dizzy with the strain of it.

'Natasha?' Joe's voice came from far away. She could not open her mouth to reply in case a cry came out of it and she did not want him to hear that. She just wanted both of them to go away.

'I'll leave.' Jonathan heaved himself slowly to his feet. 'Don't shoot the messenger. I told him to phone but he point blank refused. He said that either Julia or Matthew would answer and they were not reliable. He said something more colourful than that but "not reliable" covers the case.'

He went out in silence and his deliberate tread on the stairs accentuated their own continuing dumbness.

Joe's gaze sought out the portrait of Robert. 'You don't have to go,' he said.

She did. She had to go whatever the consequences.

'I shall just see him this last time,' she said.

'Not if you don't want to.'

Natasha looked at him with such complexity in her expression that Joe stepped back. He felt hit in the solar plexus by this. From somewhere, though, from stubbornness and the certainty and power of happiness, he recovered. 'You meet him at one. I'll turn up at two.'

Again she looked and this time Joe knew she was pleading with him and he knew he ought to give in and make it easier for her, but he stood his ground.

Robert looked older than his portrait, darker and more thickset. Joe had not anticipated that. It made sense of course – he had been a GI and put in military service like so many of Joe's contemporaries, an experience he regretted that he had missed. There was something else, Joe thought; a worldliness, the feeling that if he had not done it all, he had done a good deal of it and from the way he gave the once-over to Joe, he knew a greenhorn when he saw one. Natasha introduced them, without apparent emotion.

Natasha was dressed in the Cossack style Joe most admired. There was a Paisley neckerchief and a broad silver-looking bangle on her wrist and her face was without pallor – from her time with Joe? From this reunion? Her beauty winded him. He pulled up a chair in the quiet corner of the pub Robert had chosen.

As Robert had just returned from Spain Joe had thought he might crash in with Orwell on the Civil War or Picasso's Spanish influences or was he for or against bullfighting. As Robert was an American Joe had thought he might ask him about the new young President Kennedy or the Arms Race. As Robert was an artist he had thought to ask his opinion of Van Gogh or Pop Art. He had also rehearsed other options. None now seemed appropriate. That the two people before him had been physically locked together was something he had to block out. This man was a visitor, maybe a guest, just passing through.

'Natasha tells me you're a film critic.'

'Where do you come from?'

'The South.'

'I thought so. *Gone with the Wind*. It's a great accent. Tennessee Williams.'

'And what's your accent?'

'I'm from the North.'

Robert nodded, uninterested.

'Well now. We got each other just about taped. I'm a Southerner. You're a Northerner. You English get an accent and that's all you need. Right?'

'Not really. Not always. Not necessarily. There is something in what you say.'

'I'm relieved to hear it.'

Joe laughed. The drawl was so attractive. So was Robert, he conceded. The black leather flying jacket was glamorous and indicated a style and experience way beyond Joe's reach. His thick black hair was too long by the Oxford undergraduate standards adopted by Joe, who had come to the university sporting just such a rock and roll cut. A fear of nonconformity had led him to be shorn. He liked the way Robert looked. Robert, he thought, would court nonconformity.

'Try one of these?'

Robert offered Joe a Camel cigarette. He lit an extra one in his own mouth for Natasha and passed it over to her. Joe's stomach clenched and he tried not to look as she put it in her mouth. The shock of fury and jealousy wiped out all sympathy.

'How long will you be here?'

'Now that depends.'

On what? Too obvious.

'Did you do much work in Spain?'

'That depends on what you call work.'

Joe's temper was unsuccessfully bridled.

'I would have thought it was obvious enough. Work's work, isn't it?'

'Depends again.'

One more 'depends', Joe thought, and I'll be allowed to blow up.

'You mean work doesn't necessarily need to have an end product. I see,' Joe said. 'You can think, or just dream, I suppose, if you're an artist. That can count.'

'On the button.'

The patronising tone was like a jab to the jaw. Joe came back.

'What sort of art do you do?'

'You could call it a kind of Abstract Expressionism.'

'But what do you call it?'

Natasha laughed, a small, quiet laugh, but unmistakably a laugh which to Joe sounded like applause.

Robert looked at Joe as if he were about to hit him.

'Natasha and I were engaged in a private conversation.'

Joe stubbed out the Camel and took out one of his own.

'What I am saying, Joe, is why don't you just hurry along and leave us be?'

'Why don't you?'

Robert had trouble keeping calm. Joe leaned back a little; out of range, he hoped.

'What about tonight?' Robert said to Natasha, deliberately cutting Joe out.

'Tonight,' said Joe, 'we're going to see the new Fellini at La Scala.'

'We could have a meal together,' said Robert, looking intently at Natasha.

'I've got the tickets,' said Joe, 'and booked a restaurant for afterwards. Spanish.'

Robert turned slowly and said with measured sweetness,

'Why don't you just fuck off, sonny boy?'

That was the uppercut. Joe was unprepared for it. What did you do when somebody told you to fuck off? In Wigton you would be expected to fight. But in Oxford? And with an American?

'I have to go,' said Natasha. She stood up as she spoke the words and held out her hand to Joe.

For a moment he could not believe he had been chosen. Then he too stood. Should he say something? Surely he had to say something after being sworn at.

'I'm late,' Natasha said to Joe and her hand drew him away.

This time it was Robert who laughed.

Later Joe thought of the many cutting, devastating comments he could have made. Sentences that would kill. But he had said and done nothing.

Natasha scarcely spoke as they went back to the empty afternoon house where she sped upstairs, took off her clothes and made love to Joe more furiously, more fiercely than she had ever done before, murmuring 'Joseph' which profoundly moved and inflamed him.

They sat back against the pillows for some time in silence, a blanket shielding them against the cold which was mitigated only slightly by the two-bar electric fire. They were in a sweat of satisfaction.

'Do you think I was a coward?'

'I thought it was bold of you to come to the pub.'

'Did you?' Joe was relieved.

His simple-seeming question sought out more comfort.

'Yes.' She looked around for the saucer and found a resting place for her ash on a heap of butts.

Joe waited in vain for more. He was reluctant but determined to face up to his failure. 'When he told me to fuck off. Shouldn't I have hit him?'

'Why should you do that?'

'I don't know. But I felt as if I should. And,' he pushed on, 'when I didn't, I felt that I'd been a coward.' Further. 'I've been a coward before, so I recognise it.'

'Oh, Joseph!' Natasha leaned across and kissed him on the cheek; the blanket slid down and he saw her breasts. 'You are not a Sicilian. My honour was not at stake. Nor was yours.'

'But it felt like that. And I just walked away.'

'It was I who walked away. You came with me.'

'That's even worse.'

He spoke so gloomily. Natasha was moved by him as she had never been. She stubbed out her cigarette, did the same with his, and eventually, more quietly, they made love again. When they had finished, Natasha held onto him, her own courage strengthened. Both his strength and his weakness could nourish her; already she saw, valued and loved that.

'He is a cruel man,' she said.

Her face rested against his throat. She did not want to look at him while she said what now must be said whatever the consequences. The sentence put Joe on alert. If Robert was a 'cruel man', why had she gone with him? Why had she done that fine painting of him? Surely a work like that had to come out of deep feeling. Didn't all great art? Why had she insisted she had to meet him?

'At first I didn't realise he was cruel.'

Joe tried not to get tense. This was fair enough. He had told her about Rachel. Somehow he had to keep Robert out of this bed, this room, see him as a figure in her story only.

She had to risk telling him. He was serious and deserved the truth.

'I ought to have told you sooner,' she began, 'but I thought Robert was gone for ever . . . Perhaps it would have made you less . . . determined . . .' She paused and it was as if every pore in her body was sensitised to the slightest tremor of retreat on his part: none came. She concentrated and tried to speak evenly.

Robert, she said, had pursued her for more than a year. Or, she thought he had. There had been other women; his friends said that he treated the women in the Ruskin School of Art like his personal harem. But Natasha had kept her distance, partly to show that she was not a member of the harem and partly because she knew that she must not trust him.

But he had 'captured' her: the word was emphasised. She wanted to live with him, he said he wanted to travel the world with her. He would be her twin soul in the pure pursuit of painting. She fell under his spell.

He began to neglect her. That was bad enough. Then he told her, with increasing bluntness, that she was not sufficiently passionate as a lover. She discovered that he told others this too. He further humiliated her by publicly turning his attention to a young English rose who had drifted into the Ruskin from a finishing school in Florence. There had been a scene after a life class where he had told her, loudly, in front of their friends that she had to leave him alone. Finally, she said, very quietly, there had been her attempts to win him back, even pleading with him. He had gone to Europe, to get away from her, he said, although she did not wholly believe that.

She did not tell Joseph about the still-unhealed wound of failure nor of the scarcely bearable pain of that rupture. It was, in any case, impossible to describe. That a separation could cause such insistent physical agony . . . that it could go on, and on, through the day, through the night, a malign infection occupying every moment, crushing her with the awareness of her own failure, leaving her with a weight of misery and loss she thought that she would never be able to shift. Nor had she been able to do so – until she met Joseph. He dissolved in a pride of love for her when she said that: to be of such importance in her life, to be of such use.

'When you met him, I knew if I walked away with you, he had lost his power over me. You have freed me from him.'

And then she fell silent, fearing that his love for her might now be fatally impaired by the confession, fearing it the more because this young foreign implacable suitor had become so swiftly the keystone in the building of her new life.

—ɱ—

Joe let a silence help him absorb both her story and what he could breathe in like air itself, her continuing distress. He felt that he had been admitted to the deepest and most private corner of her soul. He could feel what it had cost her to make that confession and the love that was growing for her was now steeled with an all but worshipping admiration. Insofar as the confession could be uttered in a neutral manner, it had been. There was no sobbing, no self-pity. She had offered him the freedom to walk away.

Pity, engulfing pity was what Joe felt. But responsibility as well. She had put herself in his hands and that was a sort of real love, wasn't it?

And as for the pain of it, he felt it pass into him from her, he felt some of the weight of it light on him and he was glad. It more strongly bound them, that he could bear some of her pain. In those moments the love which had grown in the vague blind ways of inexperience and impatience, as much in the fear of not succeeding as by the usual rules of desire, took on the possibility of a new dimension, of sharing pain and truth and of being open to the understanding of what was most intimate and perilous about the nature of someone else.

Joe lay there after her challenge, her confession, and wave upon wave of warm feelings swept through his body and his mind with a certainty of exhilaration twin to the surge of sexual fulfilment. If he knew anything at all in this tidal rush then he knew he would never leave her, nor she him.

CHAPTER SIX

'I think you may prove to be very lucky,' David said. 'She'll lever you away from that charming but clinging background of yours and set you free. I see you as a pair of refugees, exiled from your own countries, out to find a new life. I'm rather pleased with that!' He giggled and his brief intense look as always made Joe feel uniquely appreciated.

They were in the Cadena, fashionable with the artistic and intellectual crowd, taking mid-morning coffee and biscuits which David, plumping out, ate instantly. Joe sat back. David cast some sort of spell on him; in his company he felt cradled.

'May I?' He took one of Joe's biscuits, swept his eyes around the room, ceaseless searchlights, spotting and docking, and then returned his gaze to someone who, for a short time, would be his plasticine. But also someone he respected, puzzled over, wanted to befriend. 'Not that there's anything intrinsically wrong with your clinging background,' he spoke through the biscuit, 'on the contrary,' a wistful smile, 'everything you tell me about it makes it sound enviably desirable but you have to let it go now or you'll end up going back there as an outsider, a schoolteacher or something, very nice too, but I think you can do something other, not better, "other". To me Natasha proves it. Your interest in her, to use an anaemic word for the PASSION of it!' a sudden loud ear-catching laugh, 'is telling you what I am telling you. She won't let you go back.'

Joe laughed. It was such rubbish. He loved David's company. For a moment he was tempted to tell him that the clinging background was the setting for two recently written short stories, which had driven him straight back to his childhood in that far Northern town so exotic to David, so magnetic to Joe. But the writing had to be kept secret . . .

A few days later, Roderick and Bob, friends he had met in his first week in Oxford, were introduced to Natasha, also in the Cadena. She had heard much about them from Joseph: Roderick, who, like Joe, was reading History, was from an army family, lean-jawed, square-shouldered, in all things brisk, very like the heroes in Joe's boyhood books on public schools. Bob more languid, owlish, the swotty boy who surprised them all in those school yarns which had been magical kingdoms to Joe. Bob was a zoologist and a fanatical fisherman. Both, Natasha noticed, appeared more relaxed and self-possessed than Joseph but clearly all three were fond of each other in that understated English way she liked.

Afterwards, they were unreservedly complimentary. Nor in private did their opinion veer from this.

'They're so different, it makes a kind of sense,' Roderick said as he and Bob killed the final hour of the morning in the King's Arms. 'I must say I feel rather responsible – hauling him off to that Christmas party.'

'She is,' said Bob, his hesitation down to a scientist's care with fresh evidence, 'both delightful and very intelligent. Not, I suspect, a common combination. Half of bitter?'

'She is,' said Roderick, when Bob returned from the bar, 'somewhat older.'

'Possibly a touch more than somewhat.'

'No bad thing,' hurriedly added.

'On the contrary,' Bob began the lengthy process of filling his big pipe. Roderick waited for more but more was not forthcoming. Bob was fully engaged with his pipe and would be for some time . . .

In their late-night drawing room, the children fed and finally bedded, Julia and Matthew sat down with their books and drink. The house shivered a little as the single rickety bed two floors up strained at the demands being put on it.

Matthew glanced at the ceiling.

'Yes,' Julia drawled, thoughtfully. 'He can't seem to leave the poor woman alone.'

'Perhaps . . .' Matthew paused entirely for effect, 'she enjoys it?'

'I sincerely hope so,' said Julia and took a sip of her watery whisky, 'if only to drive out Robert.'

In the morning break in the life-drawing class, Don and Jonathan came out for some air and to lounge against the great columns at the entrance to the Ashmolean. Americans appropriately framed in the neo-classical architecture of imperial power. Both enjoyed their awareness of it and took a mental snapshot for memories back home. They smoked American cigarettes, Lucky Strike.

'He told me,' said Jonathan, in slow awe, 'that he thinks she should have an exhibition and he'll organise it.' Taking his time, he drew every particle of the smoke deep down into his waiting lungs.

'He's certainly changed,' said Don, with some regret.

'So,' Jonathan struggled to reach the next two monosyllables, 'has she.'

'Not as much as him. It's blast-off.'

Jonathan nodded and once more appeared to attempt to suck through the whole cigarette in a single inhalation.

'She's on the rebound,' Don said. 'Dangerous.'

'Maybe,' said Jonathan. He looked across to the Randolph Hotel, and observed the scurrying grey figures in the bleak English winter light. He wanted to distance himself from Natasha for whom, when she had become, as he thought, free, post-Robert, he had felt an unmistakable pang.

'She'll be too complicated for him,' said Don and ground a wastefully big stub under the heel of his warm American boot. 'And he needs time to play around.'

Joe's essay on the impact of the French Revolution on English thought in the 1790s had been thin. He had read it slowly because it was also too short but a chill had soon settled in his mind as the intensifying boredom of Malcolm Turney, his tutor, had transferred its force across the short space between their armchairs. It was the final tutorial of the morning, the noon-to-one slot, never an easy posting with lunch in the offing. Turney on his third tutorial hour of the morning was aching to get on with his own work in the afternoon, already switched on to it, lending a mere fraction of his mind to the present, a trick he could also manage at the concerts and operas to which his cultivated Italian wife zealously drove him. Joe had begun to follow the panic-fashion of

49

getting up very early on the day of a morning tutorial and finishing the essay by relying on the drive of the deadline, collapsing arguments into lists and filling with waffle the gaps left by inadequate preparation. Oxford, Roderick maintained, was a world leader in the higher waffle.

Turney let him endure a serious interval of silence after the final blustered paragraph and then opened up and spared him nothing. It was quite merciless. Joe did not have the guns to return fire and he was honest enough with himself to give up the attempt early on. When it was done, the tutor glanced at his watch. There was still twenty minutes to go. He would steal ten.

'Sherry?'

Joe accepted the unexpected treat with suspicion. They sipped.

'If you want a decent degree you'll have to pull your socks up. You know that.'

'Yes.' The sherry felt strong. He was suddenly tired from the frantic morning.

'My guess is that you've already decided against trying for a first.' Turney sank his face behind long steepled hands. 'Making a film, writing for *Cherwell,* that sort of thing.'

Joe nodded: it was a reprieve of sorts.

'You mustn't let it drift too far, Richardson.'

'Sorry about that.' He indicated the sheets of paper now on the floor.

'More or less a waste of time for both of us.'

'I agree.' Joe thought this owning up was rather man to man and felt somehow enhanced by the exchange.

'Mrs Harries has laid complaints against you, I'm afraid.'

The floor would not open up and let him disappear. He wanted to look away but found his gaze locked onto the eyes of a man who was not giving him an inch.

'I am your moral tutor as well as everything else.'

'I know,' Joe agreed eagerly, appealingly, he hoped.

'Mrs Harries is a much valued landlady and servant of this college. She reports that despite clumsy attempts at a cover-up by Roderick, you have not spent the night there on, she reports, at least three occasions during the last week alone.'

A response was clearly called for and Joe found none.

'I presume it is what I guess it is.'

'Yes.' The syllable crawled all the way up a long dry throat, over a barely living tongue, fell lamely through crumpling worried lips and scarcely made the short distance between them.

'Is she up?'

'No.' Joe felt more confident in denying that she was at the university which would have been more serious: there was even the bud of virtue in his denial.

'Town girl?'

'No.'

'For pity's sake, Richardson!'

'An art student.'

'Ah!' Turney swept the sherry down. 'What do I do with Mrs Harries? The college cannot afford to lose a landlady with her length of service and she's hopping mad.'

'I'm sorry.'

'Joseph.' Joe felt the Christian name like a blow to the back of his neck. 'This is a moral matter. If you continue to flout the rules I will have little option but to send you down. Expel you. For a few weeks at least and at a most inconvenient time. You could miss Finals.' Turney looked at his watch.

Joe was stunned. To be expelled from Oxford was to be eternally disgraced, to let down his schoolteachers, to expose his parents to public shame, to find himself among the damned.

He tried to swallow but his Adam's apple had trebled in size.

'Don't be an ass. Bluff out the weekends, Saturdays only, Friday in extremis, a trip, a visit, but through the week you belong under the roof of Mrs Harries.'

'Thank you.'

'I'm fining you ten pounds.'

'Thank you.'

'That was a lousy essay. Beta minus.'

'Thank you.'

'Lunch.'

—ɯ—

After lunch Joe took to the Parks.

Walking alone had been a first resort for years now, ever since the breakdown in his early teens when the rhythm of it, the daring to face himself in solitude, the immersion of himself in nature had eventually worked some calming, ordering magic. Walking alone was by now a compulsion in times of anxiety.

The Parks were all but deserted on the pewter-grey winter afternoon. His breath pushed out a plume almost as dense as the exhalation of a mouthful of cigarette smoke. He walked across to the river and followed it until he came to the round pond on the perimeter of the Parks where he found a bench, took out a cigarette, opened his pad and began to write down the pros and cons of his present situation. But sitting down was no good. Nor did the usually so helpful listing of pros and cons apply to his case now. He could not even construct one of those timetables of his days which used to come so easily and which were useful, like a rope rail to help the haul up steep stairs. Monday 9– 1: Italian Renaissance – revise Guiccardini; 2–4.30: English History notes; 5–7: more English History; 9–11: if not out, back to Renaissance or practise for French and Latin papers. And so through the week he would attempt to go, as if he were on an assembly line, steadily shifting the work. The very making of lists had once been a sufficient jump-start, commandments to himself, both energising and reassuring. But on that day on that freezing bench in cold weather in the Oxford Parks they seemed a waste of time. He abandoned the attempt and walked on.

He crossed the bow-backed bridge and turned onto the path in the fields. It was more countryside here, an echo, a relation of the country-side which in those adolescent walks in the far North he had found healing. Not that he was as distraught as he had been then, nor was he full of nameless fear: but he had been jarred by Mr Turney, jangled by the harsh tone of a man he respected and a man who had proved over the last couple of years to have his best interests at heart.

What was his course of action? It was hard to think without pen and paper. But the seat by the pond had proved no sanctuary. He had to let the encounter into his imagination and hope that thinking on it in the steady beat of the walk would resolve it as sleep sometimes resolved it. Although he did not realise this until later, the encounter with Natasha had released and focused a spring of energy which had catalysed his belief in himself. The walk was now no more than a nod to his past; redundant. It was with Natasha that he would shape his world.

Natasha was now so important in his life that everything else had receded. She was like a hand that could block out or reveal the sun. Friendships that mattered to him still mattered but they had been moved aside; the academic work that he enjoyed was still there to be enjoyed but now it was at arm's length, even though Finals were less than four months away, and he ought to be winding up, he ought to be dominated by a routine. Now it was Natasha that fed into all that he did.

He liked the film reviewing now because Natasha came to the cinema with him. He was trying to persuade the editor of the university newspaper to let her write about art. He was sure she could do it. He wanted to help her do her exams once and for all. She had failed to pass them in previous years only because she had failed to work, he was convinced of that. He had found a school report, 'Livret Scolaire', from the Institut Notre Dame at Meudon in 1953. Dissertation Philosophique: first in the class. Mathématiques: second. Sciences Physiques: fourth. Sciences Naturelles: third. 'Très intelligent.' 'Bon travail . . .'

What had happened? When asked, point blank and bluntly, she smiled and turned away. When asked again, she merely shook her head. 'Some other day,' she said. 'It was so long ago.'

'But you will take these exams this time.'

Natasha pulled a face but she could not resist his bounty of help.

'If you say so,' she said, to please him, which it did.

He wanted to persuade her to do enough paintings for an exhibition. He could organise it, he said, in that unused room next to the Junior Common Room in the college. He wanted to make sure that none of the men at the Ruskin moved in on her. He wanted her to shine, to throw off all melancholy, to be seen as glorious as he knew she was. He wanted nothing but to be with, to serve, to please, to impress, to be fascinated by Natasha.

So on a walk aimed at divesting himself of thoughts of Natasha in order to put the rest of his life in order he strolled along the banks of the icy river thinking of nothing but Natasha. He stopped to look at an

53

English winter through the bare-ribbed trees, the dull and frosty landscape, the canopy of low grey cloud, the narrow leaden lustreless river and the white sun, which reminded him more than anything of the Northern winter, a sublime contradiction, an ice-coloured sun. Natasha ought to be here to see and paint this.

In the past he had been able to force himself into a working pattern at will. That capacity seemed to have gone, a slave to any whims of feeling for Natasha. She had led him outside, above, his old imperatives. For instance, what steps was he taking to get a job? Now was the time the Oxford Appointments Board summoned the stately businessmen of England to occupy the better hotels and vet future managers; now was the time the Civil Service beckoned, the professions called, the job-fat world out there held its arms open to embrace the products of that small privileged Oxbridge band who were ready to take their influential place in the nation. Joe had to make himself interested. He had no clue what he wanted to do: writing short stories and making films were not on the careers list. Natasha wanted him to dare to be an artist. But how would they live?

He walked back to his college briskly, nothing accomplished, happy.

Evening, and they were in bed together, reading, smoking, drinking coffee. A curtainless window framed a crescent moon sliced clearly in the black icy night. Joe was in a bliss of bohemianism.

It was the constancy and the ardour, both, Natasha thought. He gave her no time to question, no room for retreat, no excuse for refusal. Whenever she saw her, he smiled with warmth and open love and he saw her at every spare moment. The memory of Robert was inexorably being erased by the pressure of Joe's attention. It was so ardent it made her smile when she saw him, smile in prospect and smile at the recollection of their meetings. He bounded up to her. He embraced her the moment they were alone: embraced? Hugged her as if for dear life. He had schemes for her. He made her laugh and with a transparency which touched her heart. To Joe she was strange, unique, irresistible.

Over the next few weeks, when they were not at the cinema or extravagantly in 'their' Spanish restaurant, they sat side by side prop-pillowed in the single bed, Natasha reluctantly working for her exams, Joe more enthusiastically for his. Spans of time in which an observer might have predicted a long and settled, a calm and equal life of books, loving silences, enduring companionship.

The room was sprucer now. Joe liked it tidy and tidied up when it was needed, which was less and less often as Natasha kept it cleaner. Half the table had been declared his desk. The sink was not allowed to host dirty dishes for more than a few hours. Joe replenished the jar with flowers as soon as the imminent death of the current bunch could no longer be ignored. There were shillings at hand for the meter. Joe was in no doubt that they could live together in that attic room for all time.

It was there that he learned the outline of her life. She told him in one swoop like a confession. She told him that her mother had been a scientist and a bohemian who admired Georges Sand. She had insisted on going back to work too soon after Natasha had been born and as a result, weakened, had contracted pneumonia and died. She told him she was an unwanted child, accidentally conceived ten years into a blissful marriage. Five years later her father married again – Natasha did not know the precise circumstances but coloured the event darkly. This stepmother had persecuted her relentlessly, sent her to a succession of punitive convent schools, had three children of her own who were allowed liberties and privileges denied her, and tried all she could, as Natasha saw it, to cut her off from her father.

In adolescence her hated new mother had sent her to a psychoanalyst for no good reason and then let her leave home to live with an elderly cousin who Natasha said had used her as an apprentice housekeeper and gave her no time to study for her baccalaureate, as a result of which she failed. She went to Switzerland to work in a ski resort for some time until she took ill with a deficiency in the adrenal glands. Her father then arrived and in effect saved her. He was a teacher in Provence, his own father Italian, his mother Provençal; her own mother too had mixed parentage, a French father, a mother from Latvia, and beyond that a genealogy which spun from the Baltic into Russia.

Natasha had come to Oxford to stay with an old colleague of her father's and her first return to France was so unhappy that she came back to Oxford and here she had stayed, as an au pair and a student, for eight years, returning to France in the summer and at Christmas for visits which were invariably distressing. Finally, this last Christmas, she had rejected them. She wanted never again to go to a home where she was never wanted.

When she finished it was as if thunder had rolled through the room and demanded a silence succeed it.

'Over the years,' he told their daughter later, 'all this would be unravelled and dissected and assume meanings different from those ascribed by Natasha on that night of revelations. But then it was received as given, whole, gospel, her testament.'

Joe fed on her story with every grain of his imagination. His sympathy for her was unbounded and unleashed. She was a heroine in a novel, forever unjustly treated, forever baulked by misfortunes not of her making. She spoke of these trials in a quiet ferocity of tone which gripped him, the anger and the hurt, the shame and the bruises were so deep. Some American soldiers had come to the house as the war was ending and she had sat on the knee of one of them and sang a song for him and her stepmother had sent her to her room without supper after they had gone, punishment for promiscuity. When she went to the lavatory to pee she had to hit the side of the bowl for no sound of splashing must be heard. None of the other children was sent away to boarding school. She had run away three times and each time her stepmother had come to see the nuns and told them to be harsher with her, that she was fatally exhibitionist, bohemian, it was in the blood. Her story mesmerised him.

Joe saw the young girl, alone, rejected, humiliated, unwanted, crushed, and his love for her strengthened by the day: the worse news she brought him the greater his love until it grew to a flood which he was certain would sweep away all her grievous past, all that persecution. He would take care of her.

On the last day of term, just before the Easter vacation, he proposed to her and moved in.

CHAPTER SEVEN

'I do believe he believes he has moved in permanently,' said Julia.

'I met him this afternoon on the stairs.' Matthew gave her his full attention, laying aside *Such Darling Dodos* and lighting a cigarette. 'He offered to pay rent, which I thought commendable.'

'And?'

'Julia!'

'I would have accepted.'

'Turney speaks quite highly of him.'

'The children tolerate him rather well. Except for Peter, who appears to be jealous.'

'Nine is a difficult age.'

'Can you truly remember?'

'Precisely,' said Matthew. 'A visit to the pantomime on Brighton Pier. The Principal Boy was love at first sight. A *coup de foudre*. The usual long-legged shapely young girl of course, but to me an apparition of sexuality. Perhaps it was the doublet and tights. Disturbing and confusing, but inexplicably exciting and indubitably sexual in nature. That was for my ninth birthday.'

'Goodness me.'

'The eroticism of pre-puberty is understandably under-researched.'

'I suppose we just accept him.'

'Out of term time,' said Matthew, 'yes. When term recommences, no.'

'Did you tell him that?'

'It seemed rather early. The vac. has just begun.'

'I will have to tell him. You're such a coward in these matters.'

'The critical point,' said Matthew, his hand holding the cigarette as elegantly as all other unconscious imitators of Noël Coward, 'is that Natasha is beginning to look happy. Rarely a satisfactory word. But here it fits perfectly.'

'I still have anxieties.'

'Yes?'

'What if he wants to marry her?'

'Ah.' Matthew took his time. 'I hadn't considered that.'

—〰—

'Why do you want to marry me?' Natasha spoke softly, looking away from him. They were packed together in the single bed, books propped on knees, bared black windows rattling cosily against the excited wind.

Joe wondered why she was asking.

Because I love you, he wanted to say and had done and would again but not again now; her tone was too thoughtful for that, she needed a more deliberated answer. But other words failed him. He loved her, that was all in all. They had made love. They should get married. But there was something serious in her voice and in that simple question a warning, which he could not quite fathom, that he ought to take great care. To remain silent would be to allow her to doubt his feelings. Yet they had been so quickly fixed into stone certainty. He had to say something! Why was 'because I love you' not enough? He could just say it again, perhaps he should say it again and then again and again until she was forced to accept it.

'You told me,' she said, kindly lancing the silence, 'that your mother and father waited for more than three years and "saved up" – that was it? – and courted each other to make sure.'

'They did.' Joe eagerly embraced the chance to speak. 'Most people back home still do. One man's been courting for seventeen years. They go for a walk every Sunday after evensong. He's a cobbler. He says he wants to be sure.'

Natasha smiled but kept to her purpose.

'Why aren't you doing that, Joseph? Why aren't we courting?'

58

'I'm at university,' he said, promptly. But that was an excuse. It was Natasha, Natasha, not Oxford. It was nothing to do with the university, he thought, when later, as always, he picked over their conversation.

Again she smiled, again she held her peace, but his answer helped her. To Joseph, she thought, university was a foreign country. The old order held no sway. You could begin again, and, if you were bold, reinvent yourself. This is what she assumed Joseph wanted to do. For Joseph, she thought, it was not so much liberty as opportunity. In this transaction he felt that he need obey few of the old rules. No one was watching him, no one who mattered in his past. He was an explorer in a newly discovered land not understanding much of the language of the natives yet but seeing in their difference from his own tribe a chance to slip off the old skin. She appreciated that. She liked that daring all the more because it was hedged about with anxieties. That made it harder for him. That would make him stronger. Already she knew him well, she thought, as clear as he was foggy, as cool as he was hot.

'We too have times for courtship, where I come from,' she said. 'And in Provence it is in all the classes of society.' But not in Oxford, not on this island of exile, she thought to herself and smiled that inward smile whose last and smallest ripple would appear faint as a will-o'-the-wisp in her eyes and tantalise him.

'Why wait?' Joe strove to sound plausibly mature, all aspects examined, soundings philosophically taken. 'If you're sure, why wait?'

How are you sure of it? How are you ever sure?

She returned to her examination book which plodded through the history of Impressionism; it was a way to end the conversation without causing any offence. He would not give up, she knew that, and it brought a pressure to bear which she did not like, the urgency, its unrelenting nature; and yet, to be wanted so much, to be loved . . .

Why wait? He seemed to be making such a difference to her life. Wait for what? More proof, of course; her eyes picked listlessly over the pedantic 'explanation' for the rise of Impressionism and for Joe's sake she stuck at the task. It meant so much to him that she pass these silly exams. What did exams have to do with any life worth living? Of course they would enable her to graduate from the college with the normal certificates but they meant little to her; time spent painting and talking, most of all being free to think and dream, that was the life that mattered. She wanted to discover how to live fully, seriously, and now perhaps happily.

He shored her up here in her studies as steadily as he did in the careful, innocent, unlearned physical attentiveness which had already begun to repair what had seemed her irreparable failure with Robert. But why, she could still ask herself, should Joseph be more enduring, more steadfast? He was much younger than Robert, younger than her, younger than all her crowd. Sometimes he looked like, sounded like a boy, among these men, especially the Americans, so many toughened by military experience, long studies back home and hard pay-your-way work: but there was something in him that she trusted above them.

Suddenly, into the bookish silence, Joe sang. He sang very loudly, pretending he was still reading, pulling out all the Elvis Presley vibrato he could summon up, especially on the last two lines, every word in them drawn out with throat-swollen intensity:

> It's now or never,
> My love won't wait

'Love' was held high and long until breathlessness.

Natasha wanted to say, 'Keep quiet, they'll hear you all over the house.' He had been impassive over his book while the song erupted into the room. She loved the incongruity of it, the bit of madness that made her feel safer.

When the air had settled, she said,

'That is "O Sole Mio".'

'Not any more,' said Joe, still at book. 'It's "Now or Never". Elvis the King has claimed it. Droit de seigneur.'

Natasha turned to him quite abruptly and stared hard at him, the rather faded blue eyes searching to force him to open up to his deepest truths. She had to know. It was a look which sought to find his soul and hold it. Could she trust him?

Joe tried to meet her gaze and succeeded for a while. What did she want him to feel? What could he return to a look as intense as hers? He felt nervous, he felt that he was being scrutinised beyond his capacity, plumbed too deep. He wanted to hide so as not to be found out. There was a physical sense of weakening: what could he give? Finally, his eyes dropped back to the book and he said nothing.

'I was on a boat in the Bay of Naples one night,' she said, 'a warm night in summer and across the water some people in another boat started to sing "O Sole Mio", then others, then those in our boat, until it seemed the whole of the Bay of Naples was singing "O Sole Mio". We had lanterns even though the moon was up.'

Joe envied that moment. There was an easy and simple richness to it that seemed a life away.

'Why do I want to marry you?' he said, eventually. Because you made so little fuss about making love? Because you are always here now when I call? Because you are enigmatic and I don't know you but there's something I know I can do for you? Because I feel set and grounded and I can see a wonderful life with you, a life which will take me to where I would never have dreamed of going without you but I want to go there? And I can't leave you alone. And all I can do is persist. But he said none of that.

'I want to marry you,' he said. 'That's it.'

Later when he thought back on it, Joe wondered if he had under-estimated the gratitude he felt from that so easily forfeited gift of sex. Sex which in his generation and class and reckoning had to be paid for, in marriage or in guilt. Perhaps it was her sinless easiness which overcame him. She wanted no return and yet she had resolved the greatest problem of his physical life. She had given herself wholly and trustingly and thereby he was honour-bound; she had made no demands and so the responsibility to her was doubled. It was an arrangement; he need never again ache and long for sexual love. Life was now unencumbered, the point and curse of life was taken care of. It would be deeply unjust, unchristian, to some extent unthinkable, to enjoy sex and not to want marriage as the consequence. She must love him to do it so soon and with no demand on him.

More than thirty years later it was hard to explain how important that might have been at the time. Yet he came to think he had exaggerated the gift of sex. The truth was that he loved her in ways he did not know then nor would he ever fully know what this 'love' was, where it came from, why it sealed him to her and why it could not prevent destruction. So sex was not the essential thing, but what a line was crossed, what a key to life was given when that first awkward but unfussed coupling was accomplished. Now he thought that the key had been her erotic Frenchness, the lure of the older woman, so foreign to his past. She was as much imagination as flesh.

'But Marriage,' an incredulous daughter asked, 'so soon, after just a few weeks, you only turned twenty-one, why Marriage?' 'Because Marriage then for me in the world of my youth was the goal, the pinnacle and the end of waiting, and of wanting. Marriage for me and for millions like me was the happy ending of the first chapter. Marriage was bold, it was a public declaration, it was manly and honourable. It staked a sole claim. It was the end of adolescence. It was the mark of manhood. The real adventure started here. It was the biggest statement of life on your own terms that you could make. And Marriage meant that the world could be shown how much your mother and I mattered to each other and that, then, mattered.'

Yet these explanations, however hard they try to root out the morals and imperatives of the time and of the man he was then, however much through hindsight as well as recollection they reason through the need he felt, are beside the point. Reason was not present. There was a falling like gravity, the compulsion like gravity, that surge of feeling too deep to excavate, known by the fortunate and unfortunate alike who have no choice, who believe even briefly that they have found all that completes them in another person, who are impelled into love by forces they do not and do not want to understand, and Joe was of that self-selected tribe.

To Natasha, he later thought, it may at that time have carried little if any of that burden or that resonance. There was an imbalance which would be reversed, cruelly. Moreover, Joe came to believe that sex was never the determining matter for her that it might have been for him. She gave it to him as comfort perhaps because he comforted her. She would never give herself to anyone else and she never did because she knew that would hurt him. To Natasha sex was not the centre: trust was the centre; trust and freedom, perhaps even faith although she believed in no God.

—⚭—

Yet what he could see now as he looked back was the sense of his own selfish certainty; it was blind to her needs. He assumed that as the force of his certainty was so unquestioning and permitted to be such, then she must share it. He had no idea that he might be taking advantage of her pain or ripping her out of a womb of slow healing or unthinkingly imprinting his ways and wants on someone all but destroyed, someone who would cling to him for life and, having found a support, stay for that support, expect it, rely on it, have their love moulded around it.

The more he thought later about Natasha and himself, in those first months, the more ashamed he grew that he had taken so little trouble to find out more about her. Yet how could he have done that? What she told him was enough and good enough. He made no effort to question her, to discover what lay behind the acceptance of his occupancy of her small room, of sex with her, of his directives. He believed her words.

For Natasha it was a little like walking in her sleep. Actions were pursued. Steps went in a known direction. The greater part of her was bound and isolated in a secluded, shrouded life of her own. But there were moments when she saw him clearly, when she felt his love for her and she could sense there was a life to be had, perhaps even a life knowing happiness.

'Should I marry him?'

'You must decide for yourself,' said Julia. 'I like him. So does Matthew.'

'He is young.'

'Yes. And there are great differences between you. But there we are.' Julia smiled. 'You certainly seem much happier now that he is on the horizon.'

'Do I?' Natasha looked away and Julia thought how beautiful she looked, and fragile, her face seen through a faint gauze of cigarette smoke. 'I shall write to my father,' she said.

CHAPTER EIGHT

The heart of it is shame. That is what he wanted to tell his daughter, but how could he convey it without running into an excess of self-reproach or falling into the arms of self-pity? And you tried not to pass on your burdens to your children, not to saddle them with your debts, or brand them with your mistakes. If he told her that since her mother's death shame had all but crushed him, had been the weight to be shifted before anything could be done, then what would that serve? What would it mean? That he was making excuses? That he was apologising yet again?

He saw the truth of it when the depression came back – shame reappeared as clearly as the mark of Cain. The shame had poisoned him, but it was a poison he deserved and his system learned to live with it though at a price. Shame was a weakener of life, a permanent wound, and to try to conquer it he had to race headlong into activity, the more intense, risky and distracting the better. Silence fed the shame as did solitude. Yet he craved both.

He would have had to say to her also that a life of sorts can be lived with that condition. There can be friendships, there can be work done, there can even be spans of happiness now and then, but any dwelling on that past summons up the shame and he could not leave the past alone. He could not pass this on to her just as he could not be at any peace with her mother, not until he had served his time, the life sentence.

'I am coming across to London for a conference which is fortunate,' her father replied. 'Therefore I can come to Oxford to see you to discuss the matter. I will telephone you to tell you the time of arrival of the train. We could meet at the railway station . . . ?'

Natasha was there early, clutching his letter like a card of identity. She was dressed in her Cossack outfit. Had her father noticed such things, had he not still been a little annoyed at being required to use a break in the conference for this errand, had he wanted to respond to her fully, or be tender, he would have been touched by the earnest hope which seemed to tremble on her features like broken sunlight on still water. Her longing for his love, even for a token of his love, was barely containable.

'Ah! Natasha,' he said when he reached her on the platform. He put down his briefcase and laid his hands on her shoulders and for a moment looked at her. Sweetly? Steadily? She could not tell. Then he kissed her first on the left and then on the right cheek: lovingly? A vertigo of confusion threatened to take possession of her as her childhood engulfed her in those two dry kisses. Yet she loved him and could not and did not want to stop herself loving him and despite everything that had happened and not happened between them she held to a conviction, a faith, that he loved her and also through her the wife he had so worshipped and so cruelly lost.

'We could go to my room first, I thought,' she spoke in French, 'it's the quietest place.'

'First, no. First I will take a look around Oxford. Your mother and I went to Cambridge for one summer before the war. We never came to Oxford. We intended to. Now I will "stroll around" ' – he broke into English – 'with you.'

He took her arm and the dry touch of the kisses faded away. To be on his arm, daughter and representative of mother, as they walked up from the station into the university city was a double pleasure which fed so richly her long-starved affection that she would remember for always that hour, just the two of them, just walking through Oxford, she on his arm. She let nothing diminish that hour. It was a phial of great happiness.

He had looked through a brief history of Oxford and he commented on the architecture, on the names of the colleges, produced references to eminent Oxford scholars from the past, delighted in the Radcliffe

Camera, talked of the camera obscura and of St Peter's, was impressed at the sight of the Bodleian Library, compared it to the Bibliothèque Nationale and other libraries back to Alexandria. By the magnificence of Christ Church he was '*étonné*', by the haughty spires of All Souls he was '*enchanté*'. Natasha was relieved to become the visitor, he the guide and she wanted Joseph to be there both to listen to the easy learning of her father which on so many subjects over the years could mesmerise her into a kind of adoration and to contribute, as he surely would have done, being, as she had found out, such a proud tenant of the university.

'To conclude – the Ashmolean Museum,' he said, 'where I believe there is a marvellous Uccello.'

She did not take him to the painting school. Term was finished. It would look dingy. And she did not want to draw the attention of this scholarly man to her life as a student of painting. Much as she wanted it she knew that even if it found his formal approval it still represented a sad lapse from the academic honours he had hoped for and she, in his version, had flung away. And had he come to the small painting rooms she sensed that in his presence she might have agreed with him, that they were a portrait of her failure.

'Cambridge is more beautiful,' he concluded as they approached the Stevenses' house. 'But Oxford has more character. Thank you for giving me the opportunity to see it.'

He was rather portly and by the time he reached the top of the stairs he was catching his breath.

Natasha's studio was stunningly tidy.

'A garret,' was all he said, after the briefest of glances and appeared to give it neither another thought nor another glance.

'I was hoping you would offer me English tea,' he said. '*Merci.*'

'I thought you would enjoy it,' she replied, shyly.

Natasha smiled at this evidence of their closeness and they sat down at the table with the crockery borrowed from Julia and the plum cake baked by Julia. He had two cups of tea and two slices of cake and from the intensity of Natasha's concern he could have been taking the holy sacraments.

He wiped his lips with a pristine white handkerchief, glanced at his watch, sat back in the chair, and fixed her with a concentrated but not unkind look.

'So what is all this drama?'

She smiled, reminded of old times when he had called her into his study to deliver warnings and propose logical and apparently effortless routes out of her failures and confusion. But now she was a woman and it seemed that her father had not registered the change. So she smiled out of the sense of liberation.

He frowned, but let it pass. Sometimes he did not like to look at her too directly: the resemblance to his first wife in aspect and gesture could be too strong. And he felt that she not so much looked at him as searched his face looking for resemblances to herself.

'Is it serious, this proposal of marriage?'

'Joseph is very serious.'

'But so sudden? And you say he wants to be married soon?'

'He is impatient.' She withdrew from him a little, letting Joseph into her thoughts now, not letting the searchlight of her father's presence eliminate all other shades and figures, and she repeated, 'He is impatient. But he has reasons. He will need to find work after July and that will not be in Oxford. If I am to live with him he says we must marry. I understand that.'

It was the first time she had said out loud that she would 'not be in Oxford' and for the first time she felt apprehensive about where he would take her. She made herself put it aside.

'I am helpless,' he said and this time she smiled broadly. There was no one less helpless than her father. He understood and nodded his appreciation. 'But this young man – who is he?'

'He is waiting to meet you.'

'Tell me about him.'

And so, carefully, without gloss, Natasha sketched in his character. She made a fine case for him, referred to the little she knew of his ordinary background in the far North of England, dwelled rather heavily on the scholarship which she knew would impress, mentioned the reviewing and the acting and risked the existentialist film he had made. Her father laughed at that, an amused laugh, she judged.

It was not a long story, not a long life. She told him nothing that most mattered to her.

Then, out of nowhere, it seemed, came a question which, looking back, she knew she could never have put in any other context; a question which, as it was uttered, seemed to carry a terrible weight of longing.

'For how long did you know my mother before you proposed to her?'

Would he reply or, as so very often, ignore what did not suit him?

'I fell in love with her the instant,' the word was explored and repeated, 'the instant I saw her.'

And following that, a pause in which she scented the romance of her parents, seen through two photographs, one of her father when a young academic, the air of distinction already there, she thought, and so confident, in his first university post, the other of her mother smiling over her shoulder in the lavender fields. Her association with the photographs, her love for them, flooded through her.

'And Mother?' She was bold.

'Ah!' He smiled, Natasha's smile. '*Afterwards* she said – "just the same for me", but not at the time!' He laughed. 'She was from a superior family, you know, but she was intellectual and a little bit bohemian and so! I had to wait. I had to prove myself. Ha!'

Could he not say more? Could he not use the eloquence he had used for the Oxford buildings to tell her what her mother was like? What she was really like, then, at Natasha's age, how she spoke, what she enjoyed, what she read, how that famous bohemianism had been expressed, and above all what they had meant to each other. Could he not, for once, tell her? Why could he never tell her and not even now?

'You are like her,' he said, abruptly, 'in many ways.' He stood up. 'Where is this young man?'

Natasha would not cry. She too stood up.

'In the Randolph Hotel. He thought we could have tea.'

'Tea! Again?' He looked at his watch. 'Is this hotel near to the station?'

'It's on the way.'

'Very well. More tea! He is a true Englishman.'

He turned to go and she followed.

Joe had made every attempt to look the part. He wore the clerical grey suit bought by his mother at the outset of his voyage to the new world, the uniform of acceptance. But he decided against the waistcoat. In that at least he acknowledged the first budding of an uncommandeered self. White shirt, college tie, black shoes polished to his father's standards, spectacles lodged in breast pocket ready to be whipped out should they be required, a fresh packet of cigarettes and even a clean handkerchief.

The Randolph Hotel was chosen because it was the best. It was also the most expensive. Joe's finances were at their outer limit. He had always been thrifty and with holiday jobs, the occasional lobbing in of a gift from his father and the careful husbandry of the grants – from the state and from the college – he had managed well enough. The only clothes he had bought which cost more than a couple of pounds were the fake fur jacket, rarely worn now, the whipped cords and the black shirt and zip-up boots which he had bought for the film. He drank little; cigarettes were cheap. The libraries supplied the books; those purchased were sixpence each, paperbacks from Oxfam. The only extravagance was the Spanish restaurant but even there Natasha now insisted on paying her way. His parents had sent him seventy-five pounds for his twenty-first birthday the previous autumn and thirty-five pounds were still untouched.

But there had been the outings – London for *West Side Story* – there were the flowers. Money like much else in his life over the past few months had somehow slid into another dimension, not as threatening as it had been, no longer the tyrant, rather companionable, more Natasha's style. He must never borrow, debt was the slippery slope; but the fear of it was receding as skins began to be sloughed off in this new world. It was, in many ways, the old world, the ancient culture of privilege and advantage. He was beginning to be changed and this rendezvous in the aped grand-country-house drawing room of the Randolph Hotel, where tea would be served as by a butler and maids in the stately homes of England, was a proof of that change.

He fretted, he wished there was a proper table with hard-backed chairs and not these overlarge chintzy armchairs, too deep, too comfortable, too far away from the inconvenient low table, but that was the way it was and so he sat on the edge of the seat.

He had ordered the sandwiches and cakes and scones in advance, despite the barely perceptible demur of the young waiter: it would speed things up.

But when Natasha and her father arrived it took him several agitated minutes to fail to secure the attention of the demurring young waiter who seemed intent on rendering Joe invisible. Joe was up and down like a yo-yo but tea came only when Natasha caught the young man's eye: her disdainful look restored his sight.

'I will try the cucumber sandwiches. Let me see if they taste like Cambridge.' Her father's English was lightly accented and confident. Joe had been mugging up his French but that one sentence let him off.

The two of them watched him eat the tiny, quartered white-bread cucumber sandwich.

'Excellent,' he judged, 'exactly the same.'

He ate nothing else.

Not until the fiddling with the cups, teapot and hot-water pot and milk or lemon and sugar and would you like a scone were dealt with could Joe feel that the real conversation could start. But who would start it? And was it a conversation or an examination?

'Why is this hotel called the Randolph?'

'I don't know,' Joe said.

Dr Prévost looked disappointed.

'There was no King Randolph. No?'

'No.'

'A duke?'

'I don't know,' Joe said.

'Maybe a very rich man,' he mused, 'who wanted to perpetuate his name. That is not uncommon. But not so common with hotels. Not in France. In England?'

'I don't know,' Joe said, miserably, 'sorry.'

'It is not important. Natasha tells me you are a student of History?'

'Yes.' Joe made the word sound as neutral as possible.

'Do you begin with the Greeks or before the Greeks with the Babylonians and the Egyptians?'

'That's more Classics,' Joe said, grimly holding onto his disappearing nerve, 'that's Ancient History.'

'But it is History.'

'In Oxford, History is divided: the History I do is Modern History.'

'Only Modern History?'

'We start in AD 412.'

'I see. When the Roman legions withdrew from Britain.'

'Yes.' Relief. Perhaps the siege would be lifted.

'The Dark Ages.'

'Not altogether Dark,' Joe ventured. 'At least not over here. We have the Lindisfarne Gospels and *The Anglo-Saxon Chronicle*.' He warmed up a little putting up a defence for the English who had not been attacked. 'There's Beowulf. All the work that King Alfred did in Winchester . . .' What else?

'But compared with the Arabs it was the Dark Ages. The Arabs are very interesting at that time. Especially how they translated the Greeks in medicine and mathematics and in philosophy.'

'We don't learn about the Arabs,' Joe conceded. Then he rallied. 'We concentrate on Europe. Well, Western Europe. Mostly Britain. England, really.'

'And America?'

'You can take America only as a Special Subject.'

'Modern History but not America?'

'Not on the main syllabus. Most people don't do it. I did the Italian Renaissance.' Joe was dismayed that it sounded like an apology. Surely everybody knew that the Oxford history course was the Best in the World.

'*Les anglais.*' Dr Prévost shook his head, then took pity. Skilfully he found some common ground in the French Revolution.

'You were excellent,' Natasha said to him afterwards. Joe was not convinced. Nor did the word 'excellent' do anything save make him feel ungraciously uncomfortable. 'He said you were "*un jeune homme très sérieux*".' That was better, much better. It was the first time he had been called 'serious' and though he thought it funny (it must have been the whipping out of his spectacles when they talked of Robespierre) he was flattered. But '*jeune homme*'. He was aware that he was thought too young for Natasha, too young for marriage and he objected. Plenty of men in Wigton were married by twenty-one. Princes had been betrothed at twelve years old. Young love? Popular songs and ballads described little else. And what about Romeo? Twenty-one was not young and young was not a drawback.

Joe had insisted that Natasha alone take her father back to the station; he thought he knew what it meant to her. He ate a few of the tiny sandwiches and a couple of cakes before asking for the bill to which he added a scrupulous ten per cent tip.

'He knows a lot,' Joe said, that evening, as they sat in the Lamb and Flag, two halves of bitter on the wooden-topped table between them. 'But if you teach History every day I suppose you're bound to know a lot.'

Natasha could not resist.

'He teaches Chemistry and Biology,' she said and went on, forcefully ducking any response, 'he's always known about everything. Did you like him?'

'He's impressive, isn't he? He knew far more than I did about the French Revolution.'

'He is French, after all.'

'But he didn't study it, did he? And I've been writing essays about it for weeks. Not good essays, but still.' He struck out with precisely what she wanted to hear. 'It was good to see you with him. You looked very happy.'

Natasha smiled, full of pride. That he had been so bowled over by her father, that her father on the way to the station had been sincerely complimentary about Joe as a '*vrai*' young Oxford scholar, meant much to her. She had united these two men, acting independently. It brought about a momentary equilibrium and even the possibility of a future in which all could be fulfilled.

'He has no objection,' she said and raised her glass. '*Salut.*'

She did not want to tell him the whole truth. It was important for him not to be entangled in the web of her background; she wanted a new start; Joseph's ignorance of her past had to be preserved. Nor did she let the afternoon be stained by how it had concluded . . .

They had arrived at the station too late for the train and though there was only an hour to wait for the next London connection, her father's agitation at the compounding consequences of broken engagements soon eroded the goodwill brought on by the architectural beauties of the university and the encounter in the Randolph.

As his temper sharpened Natasha's past clawed at her and she was immersed in the fears and guilts and second guessing of her distraught childhood. Although he said little explicitly, indeed grew more and more silent as the hour deepened, Natasha felt the heart of this beloved father close against her yet again. Her stepmother – who, he told her, was among other objections suspicious of the urgency of this marriage, a suspicion shared by the aunts who also wanted to know why a Frenchman was not good enough – was invoked as always as the avenging sword of rectitude.

Natasha, who had bloomed in that brief time alone with her father, withdrew, became angry in return, suppressed it, hated herself both for feeling it and for suppressing it, finished side by side with him on the bench, both of them intense in silent longing for the arrival of the train to Paddington. His attempt at a reconciliation as he kissed her goodbye was not hollow but it was not enough. She stood on the platform until the train was out of sight.

For the first time she was glad that it was a weekday and so Joe had to be under the morally correct roof of Mrs Harries.

Just before he left he said, 'Your father didn't look ill. You said he was ill.'

Natasha flushed but kept her tone steady.

'He is in a good phase,' she said. 'They come and go. We were fortunate to see him in a good phase.'

'We were,' said Joe. 'You look a bit like him, not a lot, but a bit, there's no mistaking it.'

This time she blushed with pleasure.

—⟊⟊—

Joe would still find time whenever he could, which was now less and less often, to go for a walk in the countryside around Oxford. It was there that he found the head in a ditch. It was slightly bigger than life-size, dull grey stone, heavy as Joe discovered when he hauled it out and, he thought, splendid. Classical, bearded, the nose half chopped away, a boxer's broken nose, it reminded him of busts he had seen in the Louvre or more recently outside the Sheldonian Theatre. He looked around like a thief but no one was there to detect him.

Staggering into Oxford he felt like some mythical wretch fated to carry the lump of stone for eternity. His hands were scraped and sore and subject to cramps. His shoulders and his arms ached. Yet to abandon it would be to give in. Besides it felt lucky.

It would be perfect in Natasha's studio. He had seen classical busts in paintings of artists' studios and this could begin to enhance what he saw increasingly as 'their' studio. More than that, as he struggled to carry the stone down endless winding English roads and along leaf-tunnelled lanes, he felt like a Viking at some great Trial in the Sagas. It was a Trophy. Rescued for the Fair Natasha. A proof of love. A prize, the head of her deadliest enemy, a stone god of art, and he a Sisyphus reborn as he sweated fantasies until he turned into the long but final road. But instead of his taking it on its last triumphant lap, up the stairs, to its true destination, Julia, who was in the hall, demanded that he bring it downstairs to the kitchen so that they could all examine it.

'More nineteenth than eighteenth century, I would say, an imitation of an imitation of perhaps a Roman imitation from the Greek,' Matthew asserted when the stone thudded onto the kitchen table, 'and therefore of little real value. The fashion on the great estates, especially, I suspect, those of the nouveau riche around these parts, was to pop classical-looking busts on top of every available high wall. Did you find it near a wall?'

'Yes,' said Joe, his arms tingling with lightness, 'but there were no busts on the wall. I looked. And it had been in the ditch for some time: I cleaned it up.'

Matthew considered the matter: that estate, he knew, was run-down, perhaps unoccupied. Julia and Natasha waited for his verdict.

'Strictly speaking you ought to report it to the police.'

'They have quite enough to do,' said Julia.

'Quite. There's some law of "treasure" one ought to know about,' said Matthew, looking to Joe who shook his head and sank a big mouthful of tea. Could he will Natasha to understand this was for her? For them? He tried, he concentrated.

'I like it.' Natasha smiled at all of them. 'Joseph's head. It will bring luck.'

'It could stay here,' said Julia, 'as a reminder of the two of you. It would look perfectly in place in the drawing room.'

'I knew Julia would get her hands on it,' said Natasha, later. 'I could see from the way she looked at it. You carried it all that way for me, didn't you?'

'We can claim it back when we settle down.' He was disappointed, unreasonably, he thought, Julia had been good to them.

But somehow they never did claim it. It stayed in the house in which they had met. After her death it was occasionally referred to. He let it stay on, somehow wanting it to be there, a presence there cast in stone, and not until the Stevenses finally retired and moved to a smaller home did he take possession of it and pass it on to their daughter who had heard the story several times and liked it that her mother had christened it 'Joseph's head'.

Dear Mam and Dad,

Sorry for not writing last week. I've been trying to catch up on work for Finals. They're only six weeks away now but I find it quite hard to concentrate. Still, I'm sure I can work here better than anywhere else. After all, it's purpose-built for the job!

I'm spending some of the time encouraging Natasha to get enough paintings together for an exhibition. The bursar says I can have a room in college for three days at five pounds a day and we're sure we can cover that at least. She is a wonderful painter and the exhibition will consist of what she calls 'monotypes', thickly textured prints over which she paints. There's a very crude first 'pull' which she transforms: it's great to watch her doing it. She's never had an exhibition and I've never organised one and so it's fingers crossed! She's studying hard too for what are called the Cambridge Exams (I don't know why), but she'll walk it, she's amazingly intelligent. I'm sure you'll both like her very much. Did I tell you she wrote poetry?

Well, I proposed to her and she accepted. I know this will be a bit of a shock but I've no doubt she's the one. And I want to get married as soon as I've taken the exams. The reason for this is that we could have our honeymoon in the summer and I could get back for work – whatever that turns out to be – in September. I've put in for some jobs – the WEA, Marks & Spencer, the BBC and ICI. If the degree is OK I could stay up and carry on studying but my tutor says it would be better to get out and see a bit of the world and come back to university only if I really felt like it. I rather think he'd like to get rid of me and I don't blame him! Anyway, there we are. I'll give you more details when I know about them.

You really will love Natasha and I'm sure she'll get on very well with both of you. Thanks for the ten pounds, Dad. It was a real help.

Yours truly, Joe

PS I met her father three days ago. He's a teacher. Natasha said he was in favour. Her mother died just after she was born.
PPS We'll be married in Oxford. Natasha wants that.

In the kitchen of the pub, last embering of coal, late at night when all the customers and helpers had gone, Sam and Ellen, finally alone together, tried to address their son's letter. Sam folded a corner of the page and closed *The Third Man*.

It was he who broke the silence.

'Do you think I should go and have a talk with him?'

'He's twenty-one,' said Ellen and looked again at the letter.

'Things can get out of proportion when you're cut off.'

'I hoped he might get back with Rachel at Christmas. You could tell he was keen. I still speak to her when we meet. I always thought they might get together again.'

'He's always needed somebody . . .' Somebody strong, Sam wanted to say, somebody to counteract the yield and history of that seven-year, over-protected, semi-orphaned war childhood with his mother. He needed somebody who would face him up to life . . .

'He's out of your reach now, Sam,' she said.

He has been for a while, Sam thought, but not when it came to the business of right and wrong and the employment of common sense. He could still have an impact there and Joe knew it and was perhaps avoiding him on that account.

'He'd have come home if he wanted to talk it over,' said Ellen. 'He would have brought her to meet us if he'd really wanted us in on it. But he's made his own mind up.'

Each year he seemed more foreign now, her son. Each year he went further away, despite his loyalty, and she saw him circling further and further, in the distance, from her, from the town, from his past. She envied with all her might those of her friends lucky enough to have children who stayed near by, sons who did not want to leave or soar, a family intact: what could be better than that?

She put the letter on the table, closed down the fire and went to bed, slowly up the stairs, feeling old.

'She sounds very talented,' said Sam. 'A poet.'

CHAPTER NINE

Natasha's garret had become the setting for a cottage industry. The monotypes, most of them framed by now, so dominated the small space that it was difficult to move without disturbing a finished work of art. Those unfinished were under the bed. There was a circle on the floor near the middle of the room, like the space left clear for a fire in primitive times or the meeting place for a powwow: this was where Natasha sat and worked, like a shaman with her own spirits, studying the first pull of the monotypes and then working on them with oils. In the last days before the exhibition she was enraptured in concentration.

She was moved that Joe had initiated it, not only in steaming ahead with this undreamed-of exhibition but in his constant, pressing, warming admiration for her work. Instantly he saw in her the true heir to all the painters he liked. Soon after that first visit to her attic room he had launched into a rhapsody about the 'real' paintings he had seen in Paris, especially those in the Jeu de Paume, so enthusiastic and proprietorial that she did not at the time want to spoil it by confessing that she too, who had lived in Paris for many years, knew those paintings and indeed had, in a depressive state, after considering herself an academic failure, been inspired to try painting after seeing there the work of Van Gogh, reinforced soon afterwards by seeing *Lust for Life*. The tragedy of Van Gogh, the mind-catching power both of his painting and his notebooks, had met her need to go as far away as possible from scholarship.

Now the imperative to mount an exhibition at such speed had, for the first time since that adolescent escapist desire, called fully on her resources.

What emerged were paintings which disturbed and intrigued those who knew how to read paintings. Her modest technique was not exposed by works founded on clear and heavy shapes of thick paint; her individuality was unloosed in archetypical images. Circles would metamorphosise into faces, sometimes several as in one large vivid yellow-orange face filled with egg shapes, like cells in the brain, the cells themselves hinting at other even more elusive faces. Menace and darkness prevailed: there was no redemption. It was as if her fears had at last found expression outside herself. The most literal was a picture of a realistically painted naked body, but blue-winged and falling away from the sun: Julia pointed out to Natasha that this was surely Joe's body. Natasha merely smiled. Enigmatic images crept through the heavy textures of paint, a new world arrived in that small room, a world which sometimes dismayed Natasha herself, sometimes made her want to destroy everything. But a stronger impulse would not let her surrender and Joe fortified her. He was in a trance of excitement.

He sought out Jonathan.

'They gave me a good discount at *Cherwell* for an advertisement,' he said. He had hoped they would do it for nothing, not only because he was a contributor but because he had wheedled a promise for a review by Natasha of a book on Le Corbusier. So she too surely deserved a favour. The business manager, who was reading Politics, Philosophy and Economics with an eye on the City, had been immovable. *Cherwell*, he said, had to break even.

'I need posters.'

'Posters?' It was then, Jonathan reported, that he realised Joe was serious.

'Yes. Where do you get posters?'

'I'll make them,' said Jonathan. 'How many?'

Joe had no idea. He sipped at his half of bitter, keeping his head clear for afternoon swotting. They were in the Eagle and Child, the Bird and Baby to old hands, among whom Joe was now beginning to count himself. His involvement with Natasha had not only healed the loss of Rachel, and put in motion a passion and a friendship which were set to deepen beyond the horizon, it had put him at ease with himself, as if the invisible but effective armour of apprehension was no longer necessary.

That outsider sense of lurking in the tolerated margins of privilege was disappearing. The anxiety about 'doing the right thing' began to abate. The fears that there were better ways of behaving than those he had been taught, different ways of phrasing that he would never get the hang of unless he abandoned his former self and became a class mimic were fading. With and through Natasha he sensed that another way was opening up involving neither imitation nor embarrassment. It could be the entry to a world built equally on his past and her vision, free, unbound; and for a time it seemed possible. The great exhibition was the first public proof of this.

'Forty posters,' Joe said, eventually. 'One – no, two – for the *Cherwell* offices, one for the Union, one for the Ruskin, two or maybe three for Wadham, thirty for other colleges, and what's left over for any of the art galleries in Oxford that will let you in. There's the Bear Lane for one, we went to an exhibition of watercolours there last week – Geoffrey Rhodes, one of Natasha's teachers.'

'I'll do fifty,' said Jonathan, seeing his days and nights totally requisitioned by this mere undergraduate's enthusiasm.

'By Friday?'

Jonathan sipped very slowly at his pint and then said,

'Chriiiiiiist! . . . OK . . . Consider it a tribute. To Natasha.'

Joe sought out David and found him asleep in the college garden, under the big copper beech tree, lying flat on his back, a white handkerchief across his face, white shirt uncharacteristically unbuttoned at the neck, tie slid down, black trouser legs crossed at the ankles revealing black socks in black shoes, black jacket folded as a pillow. Joe hesitated for a moment or two and then nudged him on the shoulder. David woke and gave Joe a beatific smile.

'The sunlight,' he said, 'dappled through the copper beech leaves, gives you a sort of halo.'

He made no attempt to sit up. Joe sat down, awkwardly cross-legged, beside him.

'Sleep is the best compliment one can pay to the traditional Oxford summer luncheon,' David said. 'Salmon, cucumber, salad, a punnet of strawberries and cream of course, but the Pimm's they insist on drinking! It tastes like lemonade which I love but then the gin hits you. Why do the English have to fill themselves up with alcohol to enjoy life? How are you?'

'Natasha and I went to a press launch at the Bear Lane Gallery,' Joe said. 'We should have a press launch for her exhibition.'

'I agree,' said David, who enjoyed remaining recumbent, looking up beyond Joe through the sunlit leaves, 'but it would be a mistake to call it a press launch. Far too pretentious. You'll only get *Cherwell*, *Isis* and the *Oxford Mail* anyway, and that's if you're lucky. Call it an opening. No one can object to that. You'll need wine. In London they have champagne for this kind of thing. For this you must get the cheapest white wine it is possible to buy and make sure it is stone cold so that all the taste will be driven out. This will be seen as appropriate. Don't offer any other drinks *at all*: far too bourgeois. They should be grateful for the white wine. I will underwrite this. A friend of mine buys wine regularly, I'll enlist him; he's a rather louche and extravagant aristocrat and the wine merchant will wish to do him a favour. You can often get a discount even on the dirt cheap.'

'I can pay,' said Joe.

'I'm sure you can,' David smiled again, 'and I hope you will. When I say underwrite, I mean that after you have paid for the framing, and for the cost of the room, and the advertisement in *Cherwell* – you should have asked me about that, the editor is a good friend – I will submit my costs before Natasha takes home the sack of gold.'

'She's not doing it to make money.'

'I am absolutely certain that profit has occurred to neither of you. Nevertheless.'

'What about the glasses?'

'The college bar will loan us the glasses. I'll ask my scout to serve the wine. I'll tell him half a glass max at a time and not to hurry. He'll relish that. He comes from a rationing age and thinks wine is too good for us anyway. They are there to look at the paintings and, one hopes, buy them.'

Natasha invited David to help her with the pricing. He arrived with a packet of small circular red stickers.

'These will indicate "sold",' he said. 'Stick them on immediately and take the painting off the list.' From the moment he came in the room, his probing, restless eyes swung their glances between the paintings, appraising, checking, picking.

'Joe's making the list.'

She had offered him a glass of red wine but he preferred a glass of water. It was a warm May evening, the window of her room wide open, a fine flowering bringing in perfumes from the Oxford gardens.

'Joe is hopeless about pricing,' she said.

'And you don't care.'

'I don't want the prices to be foolish.'

'I,' said David, 'am a connoisseur of the prices of paintings I cannot afford. These, though, present a problem.' Without looking at her, he said, 'These are very good, Natasha, and powerful. I am surprised.'

'Should I be pleased or offended?'

'Now, now.'

David was looking at the painting of Icarus. He saw the closed eyes, the fall of the head (so clearly Joe), the resignation of the boy who flew so close to the sun that his waxen wings were melted and here he was poised in that caught crucial moment for the death drop to earth. He saw the violent – some might say too violent – yellow of the sun – but more than that he saw the black strokes and rages of darkness coming up from the earth waiting to claim the life which had tried to defy it.

'That,' he said, 'should be Not For Sale. It is always rather stylish to have at least one painting with the sticker NFS. It adds a little mystery.' He paused and turned and looked at her full on. 'And you should keep it,' he said, 'unless you want to give it on loan.'

'To you.'

'Who else?' He looked again and said, 'Better if you keep it. Now! We are dealing with nervous friends with little money who will want to buy to support you. Therefore a few of the small ones at seven pounds ten shillings, rather more for the rather more affluent friends at ten pounds, and then throw caution to the winds, move to fifteen pounds, and for better ones, and some of the bigger ones – twenty-five, one or two at thirty and forty. Perhaps even a fifty-pound jewel. Let's work out which. What fun!'

Joe was high; somehow the energy which he gave Natasha and her exhibition fed rather than tired him and he was working harder for his

Finals than either he or his tutors had anticipated. Certain expenditures of energy, he thought, energy for someone you loved, for instance, instead of exhausting you seemed to recharge you. His trusted school-boy lists reappeared, the underlinings in red ink, sometimes twice, the culling of twelve reasons for an event to six to three, and more importantly the drawing of connections between one period in history and another. Yet it was still not the same as it had been before he met Natasha; still he felt rather disconnected and he would dream of being pushed onto a stage having forgotten all his lines. The conviction that Natasha had to be supported, unstintedly and constantly, tested him in new ways. But the exhilaration of this unpremeditated life made by the two of them lit into him and he loved the flame.

'It's a pity that we do not possess a car,' said Julia. She and Joe were alone in the kitchen. Matthew was still at his college. Natasha had gone back to the Ruskin to work on what she promised would be the final two prints and the children were in the sunlit garden. Tea had been poured, there was bread, strawberry jam and half a sponge cake.

'Matthew walks everywhere, I have my bicycle, cars are useless in Oxford. No one actually needs one. Help yourself, please. The cake was baked yesterday. It needs to be eaten.'

Joe obediently reached out for a second slice.

'Take a big one,' said Julia and watched while he did. She waited until he had bitten off a self-conscious mouthful. 'We think that you have been very good for Natasha,' she said. 'Her whole attitude has changed. It would not be true to say that she is a different person but, as Matthew put it, you have drawn out the positive and quelled many of the negative aspects of her personality. We can't quite work out how you've done it.' She had considered telling him, plainly, that she had until very recently thought him unsuitable, but he looked tired. Even the rather cheerful remark she had made seemed to stump him.

He tried to take refuge in another bite which went down the wrong way but produced a merciful coughing fit. The subject was closed.

'He simply ignored what I said.'

'Perhaps,' said Matthew, 'or more likely he was overcome with shyness. It sounds as if you delivered the compliment rather forcefully.'

'He wanted to know if we could recommend someone with a car to help shift these wretched works of art to Wadham.'

'Wretched? Unfair. You have not seen them.'

'It is that which arouses my suspicion.'

'You read too many crime novels.'

'Don't be absurd.'

Roderick found the solution.

'Bob, you and me, four or five trips each, carry the things, what's wrong with that?'

So they did. The little procession of three undergraduates walked backwards and forwards between the college and the house of Professor Stevens several times, bearing paintings. Roderick looked approvingly at the final stack in the college room which had no history of being an art gallery.

'Quite an effective operation. Drink?'

'There's one more,' said Joe. 'She's working on it now. I said I'd collect it at about seven.'

'Time for a quick one, then,' said Bob who, like Roderick, was determined to treat Joe to a drink for having helped him.

'They have to be hung by ten tomorrow morning,' Joe said as they congregated around the bar. 'Could you tell Mrs Harries I'll be legitimately late?'

'She won't buy it for a minute. Good luck. Here's to the exhibition.'

The three glasses were raised in a ragged salute.

'I deliberately,' said Bob, after a deep sip had left him with a white froth moustache, 'tried not to look. Far better to see them in situ.'

'Gawd, suddenly it's "in situ",' said Roderick. 'Is there no end to the man's talents?'

'She writes poetry as well,' Joe said. 'I wanted her to use lines from it underneath the paintings. She doesn't believe in titles. She says that English people in particular read the title more carefully than they look at the painting.'

'Fair cop,' said Roderick, 'that's me.'

'I like a title,' said Bob, taking out the pipe and the tin of Bruno and beginning the slow charging; Roderick offered Joe a Disque Bleu. 'I like to test my idea of what the artist says it is with the artist's own idea.'

'Natasha says the point is the painting. Not how anyone describes it – not even the artist.'

'If it says it's the Battle of Waterloo that could be quite important, couldn't it?' said Roderick. 'Imagine the confusion to all parties if it turned out to be the Battle of Blenheim.'

'I grant you historical paintings,' said Joe.

'And portraits? Terrible rumpus in France if Louis XIV were mistaken for Louis XV.'

'Portraits I'll give you.'

'Landscapes? You wouldn't want to think that Holland was Norfolk, would you?'

'Landscape, OK,' said Joe.

'Still lifes? Apples is apples, and if the artist wants to say *Apples* he should be given the benefit of the doubt, surely?'

'Still lifes – oh, shut up!'

They looked on as Bob put a well-flamed match to the little haystack of tobacco. Joe felt overcharged with happiness.

Natasha had taken it out of the house and back to the art school because she could no longer bear Joe's puzzlement bordering on impatience that it would not 'come out'. She was convinced it was the best work she had ever done even among this sudden dynamic flurry which had produced more and better work than ever before.

It was the biggest. There was a woman, naked, thrown diagonally across the piece, legs stretched apart in agony or desire, it was difficult to decide which, breasts definitely modelled on her own as was the ghost-like face, hair swept back from the forehead, eyes slanted to one side, transfixed. But by what, Natasha wondered, and why? The rest of the painting would not emerge. Thick black stabbing strokes, small images which could be imps or homunculi, two big claws reaching up on either side like a dark comment on the shell from which Venus arises but here undoubtedly about to close over her and claw her down, annul her. Natasha had explained to Joe, in answer to his persistent questions, that she painted from ideas more than from the run of the paint, and that the ideas were often never resolved. At its best this gave a power of ambiguity which was compelling. But this one? Standing in the poor light of the Ruskin life-class room, alone, given special permission to stay late, she stared at her work, troubled that she could not resolve it, her mind beginning to panic with the effort of trying to find a way to make it work, make it satisfy some notion, even if only half understood, which would give her ease.

She became aware that she too, in this cluttered gloaming of easels and the picturesque detritus of painters, was being stared at. She let it go on for a few moments and then, although it was a very unwelcome intrusion, eventually she turned.

It was Robert.

'Leave it,' he said. 'It's as good as you'll get it to be.' He came forward, looking intently at the painting. Natasha refused to shrink away from him as her instinct demanded. He had been drinking: she feared the mood it could generate. 'Jonathan told me you'd been doing new work.' He stopped, looked for another moment or two, said, 'The misery's done you a service. I should get a credit.' He laughed, turned to her and held out his arms. She stepped back.

'Come on.'

In the poor light, his American maleness, black leather jacketed even in the summer heat, black hair, thick, oiled, big hands, 'farmer's hands' he called them, the Southern tone which could cross so quickly from comfort to menace; she had to be brave to face him.

'I don't want to see you, Robert.'

'But you can't help it. Here I am. Wholly visible.'

'You've been trailing me.'

'Clever girl.'

'You are wasting your time, Robert.'

'I don't believe so.' He took a step nearer to her and she did not step back. His breath smelled rich with whisky. 'I came to take you for a drink.' The room seemed smaller now. The museum around them had long ago closed. The dead objects in the galleries would hear no cries. 'Let's go. We're good together. We're both a bit mad, Natasha. Let's go now!'

'No.' Natasha tried to breathe evenly. 'I will not come with you of my free will, Robert.'

The answer made him pause. Then he smiled, a broad, white, even-toothed smile, threatening.

'Do you think I would take you by force?'

Natasha did not reply but her bravery was revealed by a steadiness in her look which held his eyes and took the sting out of them. It was he who looked away.

'I'm sorry about all that, Natasha. It was wrong. I regret it, believe me.'

But she had found strength in silence.

'It wasn't good. I've had time to think about that. I behaved badly.' He turned back to her, the threat now a plea. 'But why don't we just, make it up, here,' he looked at the floor, 'right now, right here.' Still no answer. There was the threat of tearfulness in his voice which gave her hope. 'I was a fool, Natasha. Maybe I ran away because I was afraid to be so hooked. Well, it didn't take me far, did it? Here I am again, just as hooked.'

She would have to leave the painting on the easel. That would be no hardship. It was not ready. Perhaps it never would be. She walked away suddenly, quickly, without gesture, without looking back.

Had she turned her head she would have seen him looking closely at the painting, in one hand a cigarette, in the other the brush which Natasha had just put down.

She went out into the air, cool, clean, able to be free of him, she thought; the act of leaving had been done but much more than that she had felt no love for him, and no hate, only that he was an obstacle, in those moments, between herself and Joseph, an obstacle she had cleared. Now she had to see Joseph; her heart lifted, her step lightened, she loved him.

Joe thought the Post-Mortem was best of all. The exhibition had opened on Thursday. On Wednesday night, starting at ten, they had hung the paintings. Joe had no idea this could be such a lengthy and fastidious business. His notion was that you knocked in the hooks, strung the paintings, popped them up and that was that. But to Frances, her best girl friend at the Ruskin, whom Natasha had enrolled for her 'perfect taste', and Jonathan who somehow just turned up, it was a conference and, it seemed to a sturdily patient but increasingly weary Joe, an unnecessary, addictive drama, the longer drawn out the better for those involved. It went on and on and on. At first he acknowledged and saw that improvements had been made but quite soon he concluded it was the law of diminishing returns but kept that to himself. He arrived at his digs at 2.30 a.m. and Mrs Harries woke up and woke up Mr Harries to inform him for the umpteenth time that this was what came of letting his kind into a university like Oxford.

Thursday afternoon was when people from *Cherwell* and *Isis* arrived, and the *Oxford Mail* also sent an unanticipated photographer who made Natasha nervous. Friday was exhaustion for Natasha and for Joe the hurried preparation of an essay for an evening tutorial, a day made more unstable by his inability to stay in the college library for more than half an hour without rushing down to see if anyone had strayed into the exhibition and bought a painting.

Now it was late Saturday morning, Natasha's room, just the two of them, coffee and two copies of an *Oxford Mail* which had devoted a full page and two photographs (one of Natasha, one of Icarus) to the exhibition to which the critic had given high praise. Natasha could not take it in. She had skimmed it twice and picked out 'a true talent although something may be owed to Francis Bacon', 'a rare intensity for one so young', 'the monotype is not a fashionable form but in the hands of Miss Prévost it explores great depths with a very confident technique'. This was so far from where she had been so recently. Was that photograph really her?

'I don't see why he has to mention Francis Bacon,' said Joe. 'All your stuff is off your own bat: that's the point of being an artist.'

Natasha smiled, but now without any mockery or teasing. Joe would race or blunder into the lists for her whatever the merits of the case. She saw him ever more plainly and what she saw, she believed, was someone honest and clever and bold and to be trusted. And as she began to drop her guard, she accepted the love he had for her which flowed towards her ceaselessly, unqualified, and hers for him grew firm.

'Julia came up to talk about it,' she said. At one time she would have added that she did not know whether Julia had come in appreciation of the review or of the exhibition. But a gentler mood, softened by a happy tiredness and the confidence of her success, made her keep the barb to herself. 'She was very sweet.' She had been much more, but Natasha preferred to hug that to herself. The exhibition had given Julia an occasion on which to express her respect for Natasha, and generously to imply an equality which, she sensed, until now Natasha had never thought she accepted. But 'very, very impressive' were the words that remained. 'And Matthew thought so too, indeed even more emphatically. We bought,' said Julia, 'number nineteen. I would have appreciated titles.'

Many people had bought. David, of course, and Roderick and Bob as Joe had expected but for which he was still grateful, Don and more obviously Jonathan and several others from the Ruskin, including Frances and Geoffrey Rhodes, her favourite teacher, Malcolm Turney, with his formidable Italian wife – they had bought 'a thirty-pounder!' said Joe, as had an elderly, willowy, linen-suited acquaintance of David. The Wadham College Junior Common Room Picture-Buying Committee had spent more than an hour scrutinising the paintings and retired for discussions never to return. The editor of *Cherwell* came too late for the cheap ones and muttered that he had to leave early for the office. James, slimmer and less guarded than he had been at Oxford, on the way to becoming a dandy, had come up from London, back to the college which had exiled him, together with a young actor. The actor had bought and so had James. With Bob and Roderick they commandeered a corner of the room for some time until James sensed the moment had come to break it up. Joe watched proprietorially as he went across to Natasha and congratulated her.

Now, in the redoubt of her garret, Joe, with a little flourish, produced a copy of the red-freckled sale list. Natasha looked but said nothing, not wanting to spoil his moment.

'Nearly two-thirds sold! Almost unheard of, David said. And . . .' again the conjuring gesture, this time a sheet of paper covered in numbers, 'after deductions for rent of room, framing, cost of wine, tip to scout, you have a profit of seventy-two pounds and ten shillings. So far!'

'The honeymoon,' said Natasha, surprising herself so much that she felt a prickle of tears behind her eyes, 'that will be for the honeymoon.'

Joe nodded, gravely, and stood up to undress. At last, it registered in some secure part of his mind, at last in her words and in her mood and in the calm of her success, at last he knew that the marriage really would happen and there would be a honeymoon.

—ww—

'It is better,' she said.

Robert had brought the painting to her room and, pretending that Natasha had asked him to deliver it, managed to negotiate past Julia who nevertheless went upstairs to dust the bedrooms on the floor below Natasha.

Natasha looked at it for some time. What he had done was very skilful, she thought, and, she had to admit, sensitive. The work now had a force, and a coherence, though perhaps its ambiguity had gone: this, she thought, was a portrait of a woman unmistakably condemned to darkness.

'It's disturbing,' she said.

'All art should be disturbing.'

For once she thought his Delphic pronouncement rather trite.

'I don't want it,' she said.

'It's the best thing you've ever done.'

'I didn't do it.'

'Undo it, then.'

'No. I don't want it. I'm not her. I don't want to be her.'

'It'll grow on you.'

Natasha shook her head and turned to face him.

'I think I am in love with Joseph,' she said. 'I know he is younger and all sorts of other things, I know, but he lets me love him and I have no doubts about him.'

'You're taking a hell of a risk, Natasha. Listen to me. I've lost. But listen to me. You needn't do this.'

You left me with no option, she thought. Risk was the only way out.

She saw a handsome, talented American man, a master of his world, confident, ruthless, mature, and she knew why she had fallen so deeply for him and why she had become his prey. With Joseph she would not be prey.

'Thank you, Robert,' she said, looking at the painting, 'it's a better painting. But it's yours.' If he did not take it, she would turn it to the wall.

She kept her eyes away from him, knowing that even now, at the last, he had the power to weaken her.

'I'll play the Southern Gentleman, ma'am,' he drawled. 'I'll quit the field.'

He left the door half open and walked quietly down the stairs. Julia nodded with relief and then bashed the pillows with unnecessary vigour.

When she came back the following evening, Joe was sitting on the bed staring at the painting. She had scarcely stepped in when he said,

'Why didn't you show this?'

She looked at it, flinched at the doomed young woman and looked away, her eyes resting on the Icarus painting, again propped up by Joe in a prominent position.

'It's great,' he said, and looked up to smile at her, that enthusiastic, innocent, intelligent smile that seduced her by its safety. 'It's your best. I got out the other,' he nodded to the Icarus, 'to compare. Neck and neck, I think.'

'I didn't finish it in time,' she said.

'Well. It can be the big one for the next exhibition.'

He looked intently once more at the woman so clearly pulled into darkness and fear, so expertly pointed up by Robert.

Natasha for a moment felt that she inhabited him. She could see what he saw, she could feel what he felt, this man to whom she was to pledge her life. She could become him. That would be safety.

Did he really understand? Did he not realise that here, in this picture, it was only one step through the art to the artist? If not, her relief was profound, the liberation from her past like the breaking of psychological chains. What he saw in this painting was not her; he did not see her like that; he did not want to see her like that. That was more than she could have hoped for.

'You look tired, Joseph,' she said, 'why don't you sleep for a little while?'

He nodded, her sympathetic words like a spell.

'It is great, though,' he said.

'I'll wake you in an hour.'

While he was asleep she took both paintings down the stairs to the cellar where she had stacked the unsold paintings after the exhibition.

CHAPTER TEN

'Your mother brought me luck at the beginning,' he told their daughter. 'I think I gave her luck in return. I believe that it does exist. It's like a sixth sense: not uncommon to experience, not easy to explain. Natasha was my good luck, I'm sure of it. Just by being who she was and the way she made me feel about myself – confidence, perhaps, or a useful relaxed carelessness – helped me land the best job I could have hoped for. I was probably the first Richardson to do a job he really wanted to do,' Joe told her, 'previous Richardsons had taken work available, usually at the bottom of the heap, and been obliged to make the best of it. To them, to "love work" would have been a contradiction in terms. To me it was the sun and the moon: it still is.'

Joe had told Natasha that he wanted to write novels and so he needed a job which would give him free time or at least leave him the energy to dig out the time. Joe was a close student of those potted biographies of writers posted on the back of paperbacks and his general impression was that the best thing to do to prepare yourself for literature was to dunk yourself in work often as far removed from writing as conceivable. Be a hobo, a bartender, a lumberjack, a salesman, unemployed, a soldier, a sailor, a waiter, work in a bank, in an office, in an exotic location or, more attainably, be a schoolteacher. He had tried for a form of schoolteaching by applying to the Workers' Educational Association whose purpose was to offer academic courses to working people in the evenings. Joe had told the panel that this sounded perfect for a would-be writer. The day would be free for writing and he could work for the WEA from tea time onwards. He did not get the job.

There were times when Natasha and Joe tried to imagine themselves bumming around Europe, washing dishes, taking any old work, sleeping on warm Mediterranean beaches. It was tempting. They would have lived a dream and that, he would reflect as time went by, could have delivered wholly unanticipated riches.

But Joe was still too provincial, too nervous and too programmed for that. Maybe he could have grown into it. Maybe he would have opted for it had he not so unexpectedly landed a job in broadcasting. Maybe beachcombing would in the end have provided more time, more insights, brought in more of the world.

He had been to two preliminary BBC interview panels and he had made the final short list. He was pleased but Natasha just laughed and said what did it matter, jobs were not important, only art and finding out how to live were important. Her cavalier certainty dispelled his anxiety.

It was odd not to be sick with anxiety as another hurdle approached: anxiety had been his adrenalin. All the scholarship trials had been preceded by severe, even neurotic anxiety and agitation. But she relieved him from that and after spending a night with her he was truly carefree in an empty compartment on this bright May morning, on his way to London for the interview. He read a copy of *The Times* and glanced out of the window as the lush countryside rolled past. He rarely read newspapers. *The Times* had been bought only because he had forgotten to bring the current paperback which was usually stuffed into his jacket pocket; perhaps it was not there because unconsciously he heard his mother telling him not to ruin his best suit.

As the train clickety-clicked over the points, he felt excitement, an excitement wholly fed by the new dimension into which he had been rocketed when Natasha had said the profits of her exhibition were for the honeymoon which meant that she would marry him and the earth did an extra spin. Nothing could be better than life lived on the oxygen of his love for Natasha and now, he dared say it, hers for him. Everything was better, the sky was more vivid and interesting, the fields teemed with sheep and cattle, the Thames was spangled in glittering patterns of shifting sunlight, hedgerows bloomed the blossoms of May: life was music.

His mood could not be punctured even by the devastating smile of the Honourable Nicholas Taunton who was chairing the BBC Selection Board. Joe was to learn that the Honourable Nicholas had a skin so fine that nothing but silk could be endured next to it. The smile said to Joe – truly pleased to meet you but not our type – 'Do sit down and smoke if you wish.' Taunton led with what he thought was a rather good-length question on the implication of the vote of the white electors of Rhodesia. Fortunately, Joe had read the same article in *The Times* as the Honourable Nicholas Taunton appeared to have scanned and his regular sparring with Malcolm Turney enabled him to engage in an adequately robust exchange to the smiling disappointment of the chairman.

Adam Maxwell came next. He believed that the British Empire had been built on rugby as played in the public schools and the universities. Joe was the only one of the final candidates who had played the game. Joe had talked sport with his father and with his friends for much of his life, and Adam Maxwell, who feared that sport might not be high on the BBC agenda, was grateful that the young man put so much vim into their exchange. Mr Plumpton, an alcoholic from Administration in a wide-striped, three-piece suit, a regimental tie and red socks, lobbed him a wholly anticipated package that he lobbed to everyone alike. Why do you want to join the BBC? Which are your favourite programmes? Describe and discuss. What do you think of the objectives of Lord Reith – 'To inform, to educate and to entertain'? What did you most enjoy in your years at Oxford? Joe had been told by the university appointments officer that the point about this package was on no account to seem to be clever. Lob must be met with lob.

Joe quite enjoyed it while observing as much as he could of the over-ornate room, the Board's manoeuvring, the accents of the interlocutors which threw into relief his own Northern burr. He was already putting together a mimicked retelling for Natasha to whom he always reported his adventures of the day.

'You have studied History,' the voice was low, even guttural, but passionate; a different voice altogether, a voice that immediately put Joe on the alert. It came from the only man who had not yet spoken, Martin Abrahams, a heap of thick black hair, an olive skin, heavy spectacles, collar too tight, tie knot too small (like his father's, Joe thought, a hard small knot), a man exuding independence, 'and you have talked about politics and sport and the university activities and so on. But there is always literature. What would you say is the difference between James Joyce and Samuel Beckett?'

Joe took a breath. He had read no Beckett and of Joyce only *A Portrait of the Artist as a Young Man*. But he had seen *Waiting for Godot* and remembered in the discussion afterwards the brilliant analysis of Brian, a young scholar who was now a don. And Joyce's *Ulysses* had been given a reading at the college in play form as *Bloomsday*. Yet he liked the question. The way it was put. Tentatively, probing his own thoughts rather than delivering a hasty summary, Joe began to explore the territory. He confessed his initial bewilderment at Beckett, the slow understanding which came through his talk with others and the growing realisation of the layers of meaning in the pared-down mystery of the piece. Then he talked of how the portrait of the young 'artist' in James Joyce was at once so foreign and yet so autobiographically familiar, especially the religious forces at work. He spoke quietly and, unsure of himself, was always aware of Martin Abrahams, nodding, helping him along. Joe was reminded of Turney, who, when he had clearly done his best in an essay but not got there, would reach out a hand and pull him to the shore.

'Do you write?'

'Yes.' Joe felt the admission forced out of him: it was too public a place to confess that and besides, what value did his writing have?

'Poetry.'

'Used to. At school.'

'Short stories now?'

'Yes.'

'Good.'

'Any questions for us?' said the Honourable Nicholas, who had leaned back with an elegant du Maurier cigarette during the final exchange. 'We've gone rather over our time, I'm afraid. One question.'

'When do we get to know?'

'Good question,' said Adam Maxwell. Mr Plumpton, his bloodshot eyes avoiding contact, provided the official answer.

As Joe left the room he looked across to Martin Abrahams, but he was slumped in his chair, scribbling on the pad provided.

'I found out he was a writer,' Joe told Natasha. 'He writes about modern literature. He was very like the Brian I told you about – the way his mind worked.'

When they met, about a year later, in the BBC canteen, Martin Abrahams said, 'I got you that job, you know. You'd aced the Honourable Nicholas on the Rhodesian thing. Adam had been impressed by the talk on rugby. But Plumpton and more emphatically Nicholas were against. Together they thought they were unstoppable.'

Ensconced now on the payroll, up and running, Joe, though winded, could afford a man-to-man smile.

'But,' said Martin, 'it was the first – and last! – time I'd been on such a selection board. Grace Powell-Hastings was supposed to do it but she had to rush off to the dentist. I was the stand-in. You were number seven, I think. I was bored out of my skull and by then I realised that I did not count for very much with those people. So I decided to count. Like you, I was off their class radar.'

'And,' Joe's throat was now a little dry, 'you picked me.'

'Yes. I picked you!' Martin laughed. 'Do you regret it?'

'No.'

'Good.' Martin nodded. 'Neither do I.'

He took his tray of lunch to an empty table in the far corner.

Luck begat luck like a genealogy in the Old Testament. The luck of the article in *The Times*, the luck of Martin, the luck of remembering what had been said in his college rooms two years before in that discussion on Beckett; but behind it all, he told their daughter, was her mother, who had given him something of the ruling style that was respected in such a forum; she was his true luck, she was his own lady of luck.

'That was what I said to myself, to Natasha and to our friends. And that is what I say to you. And yet, sometimes, I think what began as gratitude and expressed itself constantly did not tell the whole truth. Possibly not the greater portion of the truth. As if I wanted to heap all praise on her, credit any success to her, honour her with the responsibility for any progress I made in order to hold her fast, willing to erase my share, embedding myself in her, to possess her.'

—⟁—

Frances looked at the layout of the Tarot cards with an unease she found it hard to dismiss. This was the third time they had worked out against Natasha: the first time had been of no significance; the second worried her and she had fudged the explanation; this time, as the same end loomed, she took avoiding action and swept the cards into a patternless heap.

'I'm bored,' she said, 'you've been very patient.' She gathered up the cards. 'It's light enough still. Let's go for a walk in the garden.'

Gardens, more like. Frances's house, twelve miles outside Oxford, had been in her family since the early seventeenth century. The severe almost Spartan Jacobean style of the house had resisted all the temptations of progress: there were no eighteenth-century appendages, no nineteenth-century follies and as for the twentieth century, it scarcely showed its head. The only two concessions were the gardens, re-designed in the eighteenth century on the prevailing scientific principles of the day and regarded as the supreme example of that period. And there was a large conservatory, built just after the Great Exhibition but tucked away behind the famous walled rose garden which now contained not a single rose as Frances's father disliked them. The house was not open to the public. Despite swingeing post-war taxation, the rents from the farms on the estate managed to keep it going. These were allied to a spectacular miserliness and a tenacious devotion to the inheritance by Frances's family, a cadet branch of one that had arrived in England alongside William of Normandy.

Frances had taken several of her art-college friends there on more than one occasion but Natasha had been the most frequent visitor. Her father liked to practise his 'awful French' on her. Her mother noted with approval how appropriately Natasha fitted in.

They took the two Jack Russells which bolted across the great lawn and made for Blood Wood yelping with predatory pleasure the moment they struck the undergrowth.

The moon was not yet up, the sky an English soft grey rain-washed canopy of high clouds barely moving, it seemed, and on the ground the silence of a landscape which could appear immovably peaceful, ordered and kind, masking with evening grace a history often cruel and unforgivable.

'You know you're my best friend at the Ruskin, perhaps anywhere . . .' said Frances. They were approaching the lake. Neither had spoken; Frances had been screwing up her courage, Natasha had been drifting into a deeply reinforcing state of contentment. Frances's words brought her rather reluctantly back to the surface of the present. She drew on her cigarette, a small burning spot in the darkening air, like an imp in the night.

Frances said no more until they came to the lake and sat on the steps of the artfully concealed boathouse. Frances too lit up. The lake was glass calm.

'I just want you to be sure,' she said. 'Robert had such an impact on you. I think I know you very well. We have a lot in common, don't we?'

'Robert's gone now.'

'And then Joe came along.'

'Yes,' Natasha laughed. 'And then Joseph came along. And he would not go away! And he did not want me to go away!'

'We all like him, and it's clear what he feels about you; but, marry him? The rebound thing. Now? Why marry? Why now?'

Natasha threw the burning remains of the cigarette into the lake.

'Sometimes I know,' she said, 'sometimes I know nothing.'

She wrapped her arms around her knees and gazed across the water to the twilit beech woods on the other side, gazed intensely as if a voice would come across the lake or a figure rise out of the water and give her the answer, the answer sought by everyone, the single simple answer that ends all questions.

'Why not wait?'

Frances was tempted to reveal the warnings in the Tarot cards which had, among other insights, predicted that after a few years of tranquillity, there would be catastrophe. She believed in the cards, but Natasha, she knew, had no such faith.

'He is so determined,' Natasha smiled, 'there are no shadows around Joseph.'

'Are you sure? I can see shadows.'

'That is his shyness. Or his nervousness. Now and then he is overcome by that.'

'No.' Frances repeated carefully, 'I can see shadows.'

'He is a Romantic and he is a Realist, both at the same time. But more a Romantic. If he were here he would want to talk deep thoughts.'

Frances laughed.

'Yes. It is funny,' said Natasha. 'But it is not funny at the same time. In fact, I love it.'

'Rather earnest.'

'That can be attractive, Frances. Sometimes seriousness is the most seductive.'

'Do you think,' Frances trod with the greatest care, 'he sees you, from his own background, let us say, as something of a "catch"?'

'I am a poor art student whose father is a teacher in France.'

'Is that what he believes?'

'Of course.'

'He certainly proved himself with the exhibition,' Frances admitted. 'I'll give him that.'

'He wants to help me . . . He wants to help me all the time. I think I trust him.'

'Only think?'

'What else is there?'

She looked across the water towards the trees darkening, just a rim marking their tops outlined against the sky: shades of darkness all around. Her landscape. Were there names for all those different shades of darkness?

The nightscape enveloped her and seemed to enter into her mind, seemed in a way to join her mind, to make what was within her part of that which was without. There was no distinction. Her thoughts floated on those velvet shadows, her imagination was calm; the water, the sky, the silence, the grass beneath her, the breath of her life were all one and she longed for this state of pure completion to go on, on, on for all time.

Joseph floated to the surface of her thoughts. After Robert she had begun to drown and she could find in herself no resistance. Joseph had given her another chance, perhaps the final chance. The ripple of that thought disturbed her back into the present and she waited for Frances to say something, to start again.

But Frances left off and after a while she whistled up the terriers and the two women ambled back towards the house, yellow-lit in a couple of windows, a floating fortress of stone, yet solid in the changing times.

'You haven't asked me to be your bridesmaid,' said Frances as they reached the house.

'Can you have a bridesmaid in a register office?'

'Certainly.'

'Frances!' Natasha turned, and with a rare impulsive gesture, took her friend by the shoulder and kissed her hard on the cheek. 'Thank you! That is so lovely.'

In her room later that night, Frances took out the Tarot cards, wanting to break their spell. But she dare not try them again, and returned the mystical, disturbing picture messages to their drawer.

—⟨⟨⟩⟩—

'There was bad luck too,' Joe told her. 'But when you have really good luck then even bad luck somehow works for you. The good luck absorbs it and eliminates the negative.'

Two days before his final exams he found himself covered in small, hard, red lumps.

Glandular fever, the doctor said, hospital isolation room, immediately.

Psychosomatic, said Julia, quite common at Finals.

Unlikely to be psychosomatic, said Turney, not the type.

They are lumps, said Natasha, horrible little red lumps, not imaginary lumps.

A vicar who had suffered and survived glandular fever was his invigilator and brought along the examination papers every day at 9.30 a.m., left for lunch at 12.30 and returned at 2 p.m. to stay until 5 p.m. He sealed up and took away Joe's essays after elaborately licking the thick gum on the envelope with a long doggy tongue. He was a chatty man and the three-hour silences were difficult for him to bear. He was also inordinately fond of hot chocolate and at least twice in every session he would ask Joe if he would like 'a little pot of their first-rate hot chocolate'. Joe always agreed and tried not to look up and catch the vicar's doleful eye, pleading for a little conversation. But three hours for four examination questions were barely enough and although the nurse had provided a solid bed table, lying in bed was not the optimum position for the speed writing required.

It was hot and he kept open the french windows while he swotted in the evening. On three successive evenings his room was invaded by a drunken Scottish anaesthetist who liked to talk about skiing. He never stayed for much more than an hour.

Joe was in there for nine nights. No visitors. The weekend was free of examinations, otherwise there were two sessions a day, up to the last one on the Thursday morning. That was the translation paper, Latin and at least one other language. The vicar announced that he was 'a bit of linguist' and looked over Joe's shoulder quite a lot in that session.

When it was over, the last hot chocolate drunk, the last gum licked, the vicar liberated, Joe felt good. Being so isolated, he thought, had been lucky. It had allowed him to give it his undistracted and best shot. He felt a sweet, healthy tiredness.

It was over at last, the long journey. The slog at school, the harsh self-regulating timetables, the heavy loads of homework, the practice tests, the marks, the memorising, the real tests, the waiting on the results, the scholarship exams, the entrance exams, the weekly, sometimes bi-weekly essays, the cramming and sifting and learning to learn. The education was over. He felt he could float, up to the ceiling, out into the grounds of the hospital, float above Oxford, go to the deep North and hover over his old school, hover over his bedroom in the pub in which so many solitary hours had been spent while his parents worked downstairs; he could float above it and say goodbye, and thanks, many thanks; whatever it was that had set him out and pulled him along was over and the world was beyond examinations now, outside, waiting and unlimited.

He had his lunch and then went for a bath. The lumps were definitely receding. He had overheard the doctor say that he was no longer infectious but still quite weak. Keep him in for another two or three days under observation.

Joe returned to his room, dressed, walked through the french windows and through the sun-filled grounds, walked down Headington Hill and over Magdalen Bridge, walked slowly into the heart of Oxford, the streets now occupied by white-tied, black-gowned undergraduates blinking into liberty. In a state of euphoric dizziness he walked past his celebrating college for luck, but walked on, making for Natasha.

CHAPTER ELEVEN

Ellen bought a new hat. She kept it in its box until a few minutes before she set off for the wedding. Sam wore his 'best suit', seven years in spare service, dry-cleaned. Without consultation, Ellen bought him a new white shirt and a smart tie. She would have enjoyed buying a new outfit for herself but Joe had warned her that very few people would be there because most of them had left the university; it would be a register office ceremony; and the 'wedding breakfast' would be a few drinks in the college gardens, immediately after which he and Natasha would go on their honeymoon. It seemed an unnecessary extravagance – especially as Sam had given her the money for a good suit only recently to celebrate their wedding anniversary. And the marriage was not in Wigton.

It was hard not to be upset, Ellen thought, her heart almost sick with unease, and she flickered through wildly changing moods as the steam engine clicked over the points and drew them south. She had not met the woman who would be her son's wife. There would be no church wedding. No friends there, no crowd lingering at the church door as she and other women had done so many times, ready with the confetti, connoisseurs of a wedding. But, far more importantly, whatever she said in public, she knew that he was too young for marriage. He had not known Natasha for long enough. But it was too late, it was too late, too late, too late, and the words replaced the clickety-click on the rails.

When she got to their small hotel and Joe came round to see them, she discovered that he had forgotten about a wedding cake. At least it gave her a purpose and the next morning Ellen finally hunted down a suitably iced cake, with 'Happy Birthday' inscribed on it. An uncollected cake. The inscription was rather ineptly removed: there was no time, the shopkeeper said, to put on 'Congratulations'.

Sam would glance at her now and then and there would be a faint smile, a little forced, he thought, but he too was apprehensive. Joe's impetuosity was not something he admired. He would have thought more of their son if he had come home with or without Natasha and announced it face to face.

Natasha had gone to London to meet her father and her stepmother. Their parents met at the pre-wedding lunch in the Spanish restaurant. Frances, Jonathan and Roderick, who was to be best man, were there, and the Stevenses, who proved to be invaluable and somehow made it all seem normal and as it should be, happily inevitable. It was 'their' restaurant, Joe told his mother, and Ellen told him it felt very friendly. It felt something like a wedding for that hour or so. Afterwards Natasha went back to the Stevenses' with her parents to be prepared for the four o'clock nuptial and, after dropping off the cake at the Porters' Lodge, Joe took Sam and Ellen on a brisk tour of central Oxford which provoked Ellen to wonder and Sam to an increasingly silent understanding. Joe showed it off, he thought, as if this were now his home, this to Sam forbidding and awesome place. By the time the Richardson family arrived at the Town Hall, at the tail end of an earlier wedding, they were thoughtful, even subdued, each one affected by the complex and powerful atmosphere of the old university city.

Joe and Roderick went into the office to check out the form. As Sam and Ellen waited in the lofty antechamber, he said,

'I'm glad I got to Oxford at last.'

'He invited us twice.'

'He did,' said Sam, 'and he meant it.'

'Maybe we should have accepted.'

'We should've done. But we didn't want to embarrass him. We should have chanced it.'

'He's just the same, isn't he?' Ellen said, rather timidly.

Sam nodded; he had noticed many changes on the surface but time would be needed to work out their implications and time together, a browsing, loose-reined time together, would no longer be available. Already on that day he had noticed his son ducking away, keeping his distance, unkeen to connect. Sam felt a sadness for a long-hoped-for friendship that would now never have time to take root. The boy had been stretched and impatient in his last two years at school and nothing had grown between them nor had the increasingly unhappy returns to a Wigton without Rachel allowed the easy hours together to which Sam now realised he had looked forward and waited for. It would be another path not taken, and here, waiting for the wedding in Oxford Town Hall, he could feel Joe drift out of reach, finally go beyond him, and he mourned the loss.

'It is very good that he is to work for the BBC,' said Dr Prévost to Sam as they walked to the college after the ceremony. 'You see, in France the BBC during the war was absolutely necessary.'

Sam did not have an apposite response and his silence, interpreted as good manners, allowed the Frenchman to go on and enabled Sam to weigh him up. The two men were walking down the sleepy summer High Street side by side, as were Ellen and Véronique (who had complimented Ellen on her hat in such a way as to make Ellen want to throw it away), followed by Roderick and Frances, Bob, Julia and Matthew, two girls from the Ruskin, the Turneys bringing up the rear. Joe looked back as they crossed the road to St Mary's Church.

'We could be leading them to the Ark,' he said.

I wish they'd got married in a church like that, thought Ellen as they crossed over the street. She noticed that it was called St Mary's like their church in Wigton and for a moment she thought she would cry; their church in Wigton seemed so steeped in security.

'The dome is interesting,' said Dr Prévost as they passed the Radcliffe Camera. 'It is probably Muslim in origin and requires great ingenuity of engineering.'

The words and the information roll out in a university, Sam thought, what a life they must have in such a place.

'Evelyn Waugh was at Hertford. He hated the place. He was a terrible little snob. Brilliant writer,' said Roderick as they passed that college: he was determined to impress Frances ever since she had come up to him and said, 'You Best Man, me Bridesmaid. How!'

'It is very good that Joseph is in the BBC,' said Madame Prévost to Ellen. 'We were so relieved.'

'I rather think they'll make a go of it,' said Turney.

'I think they just might make a go of it,' said Julia, 'especially after meeting the parents.'

'The parents, I agree, are not unimpressive. All four,' said Matthew.

'I wish David could have postponed his holiday,' said Natasha as they turned into the college.

'I wish James could be here as well,' said Joe, who beat away any sense of disappointment that they were too few. 'It was good of Roderick and Bob to make an effort,' he said. 'Oxford's dead now that term's over.'

But under a high, unthreatening grey sky, warm enough, a white-tableclothed trestle table set out with sandwiches and cakes, wine and tea next to the copper beech, it became a lively making the best of it, which became making the most of it, an Oxford occasion, to be remembered. Bob had appointed himself the official 'wedding snapper' and was conscientious not only in the taking but in the thoroughness of the taking; the bride and groom, the bride and groom with best man and bridesmaid, the bride and groom with family and best man and bridesmaid, the bridegroom with everyone including Bob himself (photograph courtesy of the college servant who had been hired to dispense drinks) and, at Roderick's special request, the best man and bridesmaid.

The icing on the cake had hardened over the uncollected days, but once cracked open the fruit cake itself was applauded as was the neat brief speech given by Roderick and the elegant words said by Dr Prévost, who came over to Natasha at the end of it and kissed her more tenderly than she could recall, so tenderly that she avoided her stepmother's eye. Joe's speech was unbearably nervous and because of that applauded most warmly. About an hour later they left, a taxi at the gate booked to take them to a 'secret location', which was the bus station. They had half an hour to wait for the next bus to Henley, where they would change for another bus. They went into the Welsh Pony.

It was just after opening time and empty. The emptiness was a relief. Joe appreciated the knowing smile of the barmaid but took the two halves of bitter well away from the bar, into the far corner of the room, against the big window. The late afternoon light illuminated Natasha.

She could not have been more enticingly lit by the best cameraman in films, Joe thought, so bathed in the intense streams of light, so wrapped in it, enthroned in it as the rays burst through the window panes and radiated around her, as if she had for those moments been chosen.

This, he wanted to tell their daughter, was when he fell profoundly in love with her mother. But it would have been thought too late, he guessed, and too difficult to explain how he was so certain. Why so late? she would have asked. What had been his feelings before then? How could he have proposed without being 'really in love'? Natasha was almost like a vision, he would think, even a revelation, but that was too grandiose to pass on and how could visions and revelations lead to what happened? The truth about Natasha would come out slowly and piecemeal.

Perhaps in his nervousness he had needed the few months since meeting her to build up the confidence to realise the finality of it. Perhaps there was something about that particular moment in the corner of the pub next to the bus station that prompted the unmistakable physical sensation of finally, utterly falling, falling into love, the great force of the sunlight, the sense of unique good fortune, the confluence of assured desire and protectiveness. But it was falling most of all, falling for Natasha.

Did she feel the same at that moment? He never did ask her. And how valid or significant was this flood of his feeling if not returned? Was it no more than a stone thrown into space? Was it love of his own love for her?

But most of all he did not speak of it to their daughter because the memory of it led immediately to a much later image of her, towards the end, so worn, so disappointed, frightened, strained, so far from their wedding day; a fall too tormenting to speak of, one which still caused him physically to flinch and turn away his head as if blows were being rained on him, a deep strike of guilt and the unceasing reminder of responsibility, of failing.

'To us,' he said, and raised his glass of beer.

Natasha's smile was shy, unusual for her; in this public place together she felt so rawly married.

'Who did your hair?'

'I'm pleased you like it.'

'It's great,' Joe said. 'It really is dead classy. No question.'

Frances had decided that Natasha must have her hair up for the occasion and the long student locks had been shaped and swept into a high soft curving crown. It made her look distinguished.

'She's what you could call handsome, isn't she?' Ellen said as they sat in the bed at the end of the day and picked their way through the last twelve hours. Sam merely nodded; he was sifting through his impressions with some care. 'That hairstyle suited her well,' said Ellen. 'I've seen it on women at society weddings. You have to be tall to carry it off . . .'

'That dress,' said Joe. 'It's . . . You suit it well.'

It was new, bought with money given to Natasha by her father, high-necked, long-sleeved, in patterns of lilac and cream, and something in the material that floated, Joe thought, bore her up, and again altered her to bring out that which he had not seen before, another Natasha even more mysterious than the woman he knew . . .

—⁓—

'She looked very like her mother,' said Dr Prévost as they walked back to the Randolph from the Stevenses', where they had been offered supper. Véronique held his arm and held her peace; it was not often he referred back to his first wife so directly and it would pass. 'Especially with the hair,' he gesticulated with his free arm, '*comme ça.*'

'She looked well,' was her measured response. I feared she would do so much worse was unsaid. 'He is very young.'

'Professor Stevens speaks highly of him. He says he is a very solid young man, from the North of England and full of common sense. He is exactly right for Natasha. And the BBC!' Again a gesticulation. 'Professor Stevens told me that was a very good thing. No. I am pleased for her.' He patted his wife's hand. 'I am very pleased for her.'

You are very pleased for yourself, she thought, but again an indulgent silence prevailed. She is finally off your hands. And mine, she thought, holding his arm more tightly as they turned into Beaumont Street. Thank God, at last, off mine.

'I talked to Joseph about Africa,' he said as they strolled across the empty road. 'He was very intelligent about the British Empire. The French have similar problems. I invited him to come to Provence for the summer. They do not have much money.'

'But we . . . The arrangements are . . . Would it not be better for them to be on their own?'

'He was very pleased to be invited.' He stood back so that she could precede him up the steps. 'I must ask where this name Randolph comes from. Professor Stevens said he "had not a clue".' Dr Prévost said it in English, the phrase amused him. ' "He had not a clue" . . . !'

The bus stopped just a few yards from the Stonor Arms, the small hotel in the Chilterns recommended by Frances. It seemed to Joe to be more like a house, the house of wealthy people, Joe thought, as he took in the comfortable floral-patterned sofas in the reception area, the dark oil paintings on the wall, the highly coloured rugs, the antique umbrella stand, the sets of antlers jutting out from above the ornately designed fireplace and what he thought of as the rather intimidating welcome from the tall, tweeded owner, whose look seemed to say, 'Newly-weds, ha! I'll be keeping an eye on you two.' Joe was a little brusque in confirming the four-night reservation and Natasha took comfort in this reassuring gaucheness.

Their room, large, two deep armchairs, plumped cushions, old mahogany furniture, heavy curtains, paintings and rugs once again, was the most luxurious bedroom Joe had ever seen.

'Look.' He sat on the bed and attempted to bounce, but sank into the deep goose-feathered mattress. 'A double bed!'

The cases were unpacked, the curtains drawn, the gong sounded for dinner. Joe took off with speed the clerical grey suit put on with such care, wrenched off the tie and watched as Natasha, more slowly, did she know how beautiful she was? undressed and they took possession of the double bed.

'Ah,' said their host, gin and tonic in hand, as they came down the stairs late for dinner, 'our newly-weds! Is the room to your liking?'

'It's fine,' said Joe. 'Thank you. I'm starving.'

'A young warrior,' murmured the host, and Natasha noticed his condescension.

'*Mais bien sûr*,' she said, '*comme tous les vrais anglais, n'est-ce pas?*' They swept into the whispering dining room . . .

—·—

'It was nice of that Roderick and Bob to take us for a drink,' Sam said. They were in bed, too restless to sleep, too full of the day to read.

'Yes.' Ellen grasped at this, as reassurance. 'They're very good-mannered.'

'So he's made a couple of good friends,' said Sam. 'That's all you need. That tutor was good to talk to. So was her father.'

For Sam it had been a day of unanticipated satisfaction. Oxford had taken his breath away: Joe had told him about it but he had never anticipated the impact of the buildings, the gardens and streets, the towers and spires, the variety of colleges. Dr Prévost, Professor Stevens, Malcolm Turney, all had treated him as an equal in conversation and their cast of mind, the way they expressed and commented on even the simplest issues made it a privilege, he said later to a friend back in Wigton, just to listen.

'And Natasha,' Ellen said, 'what did you think of Natasha?' She had wanted to save that question until they were back home when there would have been time to consider. But she could not repress it.

'I liked her.'

'She's not too old for him?'

'They'll manage.'

'Not too sophisticated?'

'Joe can cope.'

'You can't help but take to her,' said Ellen quietly, after a pause, 'there's something about her, isn't there? Something you can't help but like.' But for Joe? What would they have in common, she thought, after they left Oxford, after the attraction of mutual strangeness had worn off? She needed Sam to help her.

Sam nodded but said no more. He had been captivated by Natasha. If he could have found an acceptable way to use the word he would have confessed that at first sight he had loved her. He did not want to examine it now. It could wait, better to wait. But he was utterly captivated by her – the bold smile in her eyes, the high style, the equality of her attention, the way she had immediately called him 'Sam', but something much deeper, a fragile innerness which Sam could sense and wanted to guard, an innerness which to understand would, he thought, be to know something rare.

'I hope he takes care of her,' he said, rather huskily.

'He will.' Ellen was quick to defend. There would be no real talk with Sam about the wedding and so she put off that conversation for the future. She looked over at the chest of drawers where her hat lay as in state, a wide-brimmed pearl-grey creation, which matched the suit, decorated with a broad pink satin band bowed at the side which, the shopkeeper had said, 'threw it into relief'. 'What do you think of my hat?'

'Very nice,' said Sam, scarcely glancing.

'I don't think it was quite right for the occasion.'

'You looked,' Sam said, unusually firmly, 'the bee's knees.'

'I've heard more romantic declarations.' Yet his calm, his contentment reassured her and over time the day clarified and took on a remembered happiness . . .

Joe pounded through the Chiltern Hills scornfully as if proving by the pace his several times expressed view that they were 'nothing like the Lake District'. He and Natasha were out soon after breakfast and onto the paths and bridleways which took them through old woods, up deep valleys rich in forest, onto hills on which Natasha demanded a break while she pencil-sketched a prospect of what she called 'the true English countryside, so green, so varied, and gentle'.

'No wonder your lot came over to grab it,' Joe said.

They stopped for lunch in pubs invariably ancient and oak-beamed in tranquil villages, Ibstone, Turville, Hambledon, and Joe would propel her into the churches or use the afternoon to make for another landmark.

'You have peasant legs,' she said.

'They come in useful.'

In those few days they roved widely over the bow-backed hills, ambled through dappled woods, lay and looked at the clouds and talked profoundly and lightly of eternal questions, made love in forested seclusion, wedded in Oxford and wedded again in those days when Natasha saw him plain and let go more of herself, and Joe was so swept up by her he soared on the upward surge of his feelings, soared and glided, like the hawks.

On the last afternoon they were later than usual and came from Turville Heath down to South End to cut through the Stonor Estate to the hotel. The light was clear and though the sun had gone it was warm. Both of them were tired and quiet.

They went down into the dense woods and came out at a point where the crescent mass of Stonor House lay just a few hundred yards below them and beyond that were the now familiar multiple green undulations of what had become for both of them a countryside of dreams.

Joe stopped and held out an arm to check Natasha. He put his finger to his lips. Then she too heard the drumming sound, the light drumming on the ground and the brushing of the trees like a wind among the leaves and suddenly there they were, led by a magnificently antlered white hart, a herd of deer, racing out of the wood behind the great white hart, twenty, thirty deer, following him into the open down the hill and then changing direction obediently as he swerved to climb again and race into another reach of the woods, into silence.

Joe was taken over by intense and inexplicable joy and Natasha too, he saw, was smiling, fully, no teasing, no mockery, like him, blest.

'That was you,' she said, 'the white one.'

Joe's cup flowed over.

'And you?'

'All of the rest, Joseph,' she said and took his arm. 'I am all of the others. Beware!'

CHAPTER TWELVE

As the car moved across one of the high plateaux of northern Provence, Joe increasingly felt as if he were being seduced by Frenchness and drugged by the voluptuous difference of it all. Then he saw the village, La Rotonde, which appeared at a distance, as if it were an illustration in a mediaeval Book of Hours. That first sight of the village immediately imprinted itself on his imagination.

It rose up suddenly like a double helix spiralling towards a cylinder of stone, a beacon of war, the tower, La Rotonde itself. Lavender fields occupied the gently rising ground which came to the skirts of the village and in fields beyond the lavender Joe could see, and would hear, shepherds with their biblical flocks of sheep and goats, bells round their necks tinkling with a tinny sound like the small bell of the church whose modest Renaissance tower floated above the maze of ascending rooftops. The heat of late afternoon brought a shimmer to the light. Joe felt a brush of Jerusalem, the shining city on the hill, the golden. The steep road up to the village curled round the outside of the rock settlements: once inside, to Joe's pinch-himself delight, there was no space for cars, the streets were too narrow, many of them were stepped, only humans and horses had passage. Cars were parked outside the massive walls.

When Joe got out of the car and went to the parapet to look over the broad, hazy, apparently uninhabited valley with even the tips of other hill villages obscured by the veil of heat, he was transported into the landscape, as he had been on occasions when walking near his home town in the Lake District where also he had been overcome by the feeling that whatever it was that was him had for a moment escaped the skull and joined up with what was before it. The hills, the haze, the heat dissolved all thought and his senses wholly possessed his mind. Maybe that connection with nature, and the disappearance of the self, was the crucial purpose of a life, he had said to her on their honeymoon, just letting go; joining, rejoining, knowing being alive, perhaps this was the soul, perhaps this was the best of it. He had been far too exhilarated by the new freedom of marriage to catch her muted scepticism at the time, her puzzlement at these outbursts of a faith somewhere between paganism and pantheism.

When he walked through the half-ruined fifteenth-century arch into the village itself it was like entering a dream made stone. The narrow streets, more like lanes, twisted and turned with rarely a straight run of more than a dozen metres. Most of these passages were in shadow, protected by the high-walled houses, some of them still farmhouses with the ground-floor rooms used by animals in the winter. There were steps everywhere, staircases of stone, always broken, in romantic disrepair, Joe thought, as in those weeks he clambered over the village, a village in retreat, empty cottages, fallen stones, dereliction. Whichever route he took, he always found his way to the tower, and sat on a heap of stones from which he could gaze downhill into the stony heart of a settlement which had, over centuries, past its martial purpose, slowly waterfallen down the rock in unordered rivulets of habitation, reluctantly leaving the security of the high fortification, wending their way as slowly as they could, the paths twisting and even turning back as if looking over their shoulders.

The place infected him. If he could escape the house even for half an hour he would do so, just to lose himself in it, as if this physical spot was in some way Natasha, but also as if his infatuation with it was of an intensity he could not quite bring himself to show directly to Natasha or feel that she would allow. La Rotonde was always waiting, faithful, attentive to his moods. The villagers took to him, the mad young Englishman forever wandering about in the heat and then pausing, basking like a lizard in the deep sun, or 'in a dream', they said, 'in love', 'a new husband'.

As Joe explored the village in the next weeks, he was to discover several grand Renaissance houses, run-down like everything else, and be surprised by their elaborately ornamented doors, their declarations of old splendour hidden in the modesty of alleyways: somehow that was Natasha too, her splendour hidden by modesty.

The shepherds brought their tinkling sheep and goats through the village. For fresh bread every morning you went to the window of the bakery and the hot loaf was handed over to you as you stood in the street; there was one bar only and all those who drank congregated outside there in the evening while inside you could eat food which was reared or grown around the place. As in the Wigton of his childhood, everyone who passed by nodded to you as a friend would do. The slit alleys made for sudden theatrical exits and entrances and this isolated place bred as it had in Wigton its daily gossip of who had done what, the routines, the similarities, the differences, the remarks closely analysed, the unwearying finely worked chronicle and story of the village.

It was a story which stretched back to the early Middle Ages as the fortifications bore witness. La Rotonde itself was a circular building, in picaresque disrepair, roofless, uncared for. But inside were twelve stone niches, twelve broad seats for the twelve knights who had gathered there centuries ago preparatory to leading their men south, over the mountains down to the toe of Italy and from there east across the Mediterranean to fight for Christ and Jerusalem.

He liked to walk alone, feeling free. Walking with Natasha brought different feelings. He knew that in her heart she responded as he did but for her it was as if there were a constant searching, her eyes not so much looking at as examining the buildings, her preoccupations often beyond him. She liked to take her watercolours up some of the steps and sit there for a morning, transforming the enduring slow time-layered work of La Rotonde, itself become a work like art, into watercolours, quick, delicate, fragile, so easily dried by the sun.

Usually when he went off alone late in the morning, she let him rove. But about a week after their arrival she sought him out. He was sitting in the sun, unusually not reading his current passion, more absorbed by the heavy drug of the sun than by the stories of Chekhov. She appeared suddenly as it were out of the stone, and they moved to the shade against the wall of La Rotonde itself.

They smoked in silence for a while but although she looked out across the rooftops to the already sun-hazed valley, Joe knew that she was looking inwards and waited.

'Véronique told me you were too young and would soon look for others. She said you reminded her of the baker's son training to be a chef.'

Joe waited. Natasha paused, fighting her anger or her fear, letting herself alone take the blow.

'That is what she is like.'

Véronique had been overwhelmingly kind and appreciative to Joe but now was not the time to say so. The quality of Natasha's silence, he knew, was unmistakable proof of hurt.

'She says I am lucky my father likes you.'

Joe knew that it was not the correct reaction, but he felt flattered.

'We had a dog. It was my dog. When I came back last year she said it had been so ill it had to be destroyed. And I believed her! How could I believe her? She never liked it.'

Nothing that came to mind seemed sufficient to be turned into speech, he thought, and she had not come to seek out his opinion, only his company.

'She takes revenge in many ways.'

'She's very generous to me,' Joe said, a sense of justice finding voice. 'Speak as you find.'

'Yes,' Natasha turned to him, 'poor Joseph.'

She moved down a few steps and took out her sketching pad.

'Try to be still and keep your face in one expression,' she said. 'You are difficult to catch.' His face froze in compliance as she worked him onto her pad.

—⟋⟍—

They would go up to the Crusaders' Tower at night. They walked quietly in the dark, picking their way carefully along broken paths, uneven steps, the moon not up yet. They stood in silence, his arm around her shoulder, smoking, looking out across the black hills, into the blank dark of woods. It would be so good, Joe thought, never to move from this spot; just be there for ever.

When they did finally and always reluctantly go down, their way clear now under the moon, they went to the outer wall of the village, a wall built in the time of the religious wars, rearing out of the great rock on which the village had been planted. Certain houses had been built into the encircling fortifications. They had the purpose and the atmosphere of a castle. These houses were war-walled, many-storeyed, bedded into the base rock: one of these belonged to Natasha's family.

'Why don't we stay on and live here?' Joe said, as they lingered to draw out every last taste of the night.

'Could we?'

'Why not? If your parents don't mind us being in the house when they're not here. Or there are broken-down cottages up near La Rotonde. We could rent one of those. Or do one up. That would be better. Our own place. I could teach English somewhere. You could sell your paintings. I could write. A lot of English and American writers came to France to write. When we talked about this before in Oxford it seemed impossible. But this place changes everything, doesn't it? Why don't we just stay? It would be great, wouldn't it? We don't need much to live on.'

'One minute you're so romantic and then you are so practical.' She lit a cigarette. 'But not really practical, Joseph . . .'

'Why not? We—'

'Ssshhh . . . Listen.'

The noise of the cicadas rose and cascaded around their ears like diamond hailstones. They listened, separate but bound in the same spell . . .

'I can't live in France and certainly not here,' said Natasha, firmly. 'We must go now. They do not like us to be out too late. See? I am already following the rules of childhood again. I am already doing what is expected of me. No.'

Joe let it go, but only, he thought, for a while. Why not? It was perfect. Where would they find anything as perfect, anywhere? Oh, it would be such an amazing life, here, the two of them, for ever. 'We should have done it,' he told their daughter, 'we should have found a way, if not there then somewhere else, we should have taken all the risks we could at that time, while we were young and able, and then we might have been safe.'

He followed her into the big, rather daunting house.

—⁓—

'The house came from my mother's family.'

Natasha spoke with reluctance but Joe had waited for an explanation for long enough, she thought. They were outside the bar-restaurant in mid-morning, the only customers. Before them over the narrow street was a small classically modelled square, roofed, pillared, overlooking the valley, used for village gatherings, a place to stand in the shade and look towards the sun.

'It's a big house,' Joe said, cautiously.

'She was from a big family!'

'The flat in Paris was big as well.'

'That belongs to the university.'

'You didn't tell me he taught at a university.'

Natasha hoped someone would pass by. She had known the village all her life and it was second nature to talk to villagers and learn something of everyone's business. But no one rescued her.

'No.' She stubbed out her cigarette. 'He is mainly in his laboratory now.'

'In Paris?'

'No, the main one. In Concarneau, in Brittany. He will go there soon. He always prefers to go there alone. Except when my mother was alive of course. They worked there together.'

'Was he brought up around here?'

It was only fair to answer, but she still had a reluctance, almost a foreboding: better if he did not know.

'Yes, and the first university he went to was Montpellier. Joseph! Enough questions. Since the wedding he likes to talk to you.' She looked mockingly at him. 'You like to listen! And you give him a chance to practise his English.' But she was pleased. Matthew Stevens had given her father a glittering reference which, coming from an academic whom Dr Prévost had discovered to be distinguished, had thoroughly established Joseph in favour.

'Your mother's very kind.' He wanted to talk about her: to pick at it.

'My stepmother.'

'Yes.'

'I am married now. And my father likes you.'

'Neither of them will let me pay for a thing. He won't let me pay our way when we eat at the café. When we went to Avignon she was always offering to buy me things.'

'She wants to prove her generosity in front of my father.'

'You seem to get on with her a lot better than I thought you would. From what you said.'

'Do I?'

Natasha smiled, stood up, and walked up the narrow street, leaving him to follow.

How could she tell him that already she hated being here? That she hated it so much that apart from the time spent with him it was a struggle against the old pressures she had left behind. She had torn herself out at such cost but succeeded and by herself made herself free. Would he understand that? And yet, did he need to know?

How could she tell him that, when she saw him on such a wing of happiness and when his presence had brought her father so much closer to her? Was that not the greatest bonus she could have imagined? How could she say she longed to pack now and go back to damp, alien England, where her childhood could be kept at bay and she would be out of her stepmother's reach? She turned and waited for him. It took some time to pay the patron as conversation was a necessary part of the transaction. But as he came towards her, tanned now, his sandy hair becoming lighter, his open enthusiastic smile all for her, loving the place so much, she thought, I will stay just a little more time for him, just a little more time here before I am, at last, with him wholly free to build my own life.

—⁓—

When what Dr Prévost called 'the children' were alone together, there was a feeling of wildness generated by Natasha. They would leave 'the parents' in the evening after the early dinner if at home and play elaborate games two floors below. François, who was seventeen, like his father in looks but cursed by academic failure and a heavy burden on Véronique; Pierre, fifteen, bright like his father with the looks of his mother; and Madeleine, fourteen, who dreamed of being a ballet dancer, in awe of her older, artistic, exiled and now triumphantly married sister.

They played children's games with children's energy. Joe, or Joseph as everyone called him, was bemused and then elated at this younger immature Natasha, reclaiming a meagerly loved past, he thought, delinquent, in full flow, cheating at table tennis and cards, turning hide-and-seek into a horror movie, seeing who could get around the room without touching the floor, starting cushion fights and then instructing Joseph to organise charades 'the English way', the Stevenses' way, embraced by and embracing her brothers and sister with an openness and passion concealed when the full family was in formal session. To the delight of the younger ones, who had expected an Englishman in a bowler hat with a pin-striped suit, a rolled umbrella and a monocle, Joseph was swept up in the games in this fortress of a house, swept along, too, by Natasha's unbridled new siblings.

'She is making them over-excited again,' said Véronique, of the distant laughter. She had tried hard to block it out with the new Françoise Sagan.

Louis as usual had made a desk out of his armchair by putting a large chopping board across the arms. He looked up calmly from his small fast neat handwriting. Sometimes it annoyed him too.

'It is the holidays,' he said, 'in Paris they have to be so careful. I don't hear them.'

'Natasha offered to look after François if we wanted to send him to London to retake his baccalaureate. The French School is very good in London.'

'That is a lot to ask of her, and of Joseph,' Louis said. 'They have a life to begin. They have to learn how to live together. That can be very difficult.'

But François disturbs you, she thought, and you think his slowness is my fault.

'Natasha is much better than she was,' said Véronique, to please.

'Yes,' his eyes were now on the page, 'this young Englishman will be good for her.'

'He is not like an Englishman,' Véronique murmured, 'not like those we meet in Paris.'

But Louis's attention had returned to the paper he was drafting and Véronique made another assault on Françoise Sagan. Downstairs the challenging laughter continued, even louder, but she set herself against it.

—∭—

Members of Dr Prévost's family came to see them in La Rotonde for tea, bearing gifts. Despite some effort at generalisation, conversation was soon back among the histories of the family and what Joe could understand he could appreciate: just like home, he thought approvingly.

But the visit to the two aunts, the sisters of Natasha's mother, had to be made at their house across country; a long journey, beyond Arles. Joe asked Dr Prévost – he never used the 'Papa' which Natasha suggested – if they could stop in Arles so that he could see some of the places painted by Van Gogh and just stroll around where the great artist had lived.

'Of course! We will leave early. My wife will drive one car and I will drive the other one. You must see the Roman remains. They are very important. In the South there is much to see from Roman times. We will leave the house at seven o'clock to avoid the heat. I have not been there for three years.'

Louis Prévost strode through the city like an emperor but in his case a ruler of information. The Amphitheatre was closely examined, the aqueducts were analysed in detail and praised – 'A reliable supply of fresh water and good engineering are the key to civilisation,' he said. Gradually the family peeled away until only Joseph and Natasha were left with him as he exulted in the architecture, placed Arles in context and in an hour and a quarter delivered the Decline and Fall of the Roman Empire as experienced through this one city in Provence. When it came to Van Gogh he waved a rather punch-drunk Joe in the right direction and invited Natasha to have a glass of *citron pressé* with him.

Joe was disappointed. After the Romans and the atmosphere built up by Natasha's father, his solitary meander, more closely to understand the lonely genius of Van Gogh, fell flat. It was too hot; people were too well dressed; the normality and efficiency of the French squeezed out the frenized, irredeemably unhappy Dutchman Joe was looking for. Even the famous café held no magic. He bought a few postcards to send back home.

The sisters lived together in one house although the married one, Marie-Christine, occupied two-thirds of it with her husband, a lawyer, Yvon; Marie-Françoise had what amounted to a wing of the ample eighteenth-century manor. The de Vivaise family, Joseph was told by Natasha's father a few minutes before they arrived for lunch, had lived there for more than a hundred and fifty years. Sophie, Natasha's mother, had been the eldest of the three girls: there were no male heirs.

From the moment the cars turned through the gates and up the drive, healthy with weeds, flanked by plane trees, Joe thought he was in a film by Jean Renoir. To dispel the daze of being in such unexpected, splendid and unearned surroundings, he kept going an independent line of thought in which he saw it all as a film.

There would be maids at the table, he guessed, and there were (two, one hired for the day), though no butler; there would be cooks (one, permanent, in her seventies), and a gardener, and there was; the woods beyond the gardens would be full of game to be shot by parties who stayed overnight and criss-crossed the corridors between bedrooms; and it would all be too large to maintain, which it was, but its owners would not publicly acknowledge this and behave as if the war, and the economic collapse, had never happened, which they did.

The grounds in which the house was set were an Impressionist's canvas, Joe thought, as in the paintings of Jean Renoir's father, Pierre Auguste, whose works he had studied in those summer weeks in Paris, three years ago. And to complete this scenario, all that was needed was for Jean Renoir, himself an actor as well as director, to appear, that large man, with his kindly ugly face, who played the fool while filled with wisdom and sadness. And he appeared! In the person of Yvon, the bulbous-nosed lawyer, dandruff and all, he appeared, to Joe's delight, and he was remarkably close to the original. He almost shook Joe's hand off and from then on Joe knew that he would enjoy this lunch. When he saw the degree of attention Natasha paid to every word and gesture spoken by the sisters, her aunts, he knew that she, too, was caught up in the day.

The plates and crockery, used no more than twice a year, were Limoges, which passed Joe by but brought a smile of thanks directed from Natasha to her hostess aunt, a smile which acknowledged the quality of the reception given. The glasses were old crystal and after he had accidentally fingernailed one, Joe had to resist pinging them for their remarkably pure sound. The silver cutlery bore the family crest and there were two large art nouveau vases of lilies, the best that the leaking and dilapidated conservatory could supply. Marie-Christine tinkled a small silver bell when she wanted the table cleared. The maids did not always come instantly and Marie-Christine would roll her eyes.

Unlike the conversation in the Prévost gathering where family matters had soon taken the reins, the talk at the de Vivaise lunch, directed by Marie-Christine, whose steeliness it was agreed had 'kept everything together over the years', centred, as good manners demanded, around England and the English.

Like the French spoken by Louis and her sister Marie-Françoise, Marie-Christine's French was clear, unhurried and roundly pronounced, similar to that which had been dinned into Joe at school and been a compulsory part of his history course at university. To his surprise he had little difficulty in joining in, save for mistakes of vocabulary which all around the table were pleased to correct. Most of them were much cheered by this, having braced themselves for an English-speaking lunch. Joe was self-conscious at first, especially as Natasha had always teased him about his French and always spoke to him in English. But Marie-Christine would not have him teased. She acted as his champion. She said 'Bravo!' and 'Bien fait' and 'Mais alors il parle le français très bien, mais très, très bien,' building up his confidence until Joe, fortified by the wine which was modest in portion but high in quality and changed with every dish, brimmed full of social contentment.

'To talk about the English in the French language,' said Yvon, who could not find a signal which would indicate to the new maid that he absolutely needed much more wine than the others, 'is a great joy and a

great revenge, because so much of the English language is itself French.'
He toasted his own observation, finished the St Julien, held up the
empty glass and twirled it round as if a toast earned a refill, but was
obliged to put it down unrecharged.

The English, said Louis, and here his two sisters-in-law, who had
adored him since his marriage into the de Vivaise family, almost
physically bristled with the fierceness of their attention, were the most
strange people in Europe. Three very important things needed always to
be remembered, he said, as he took a sip of wine and then lectured them.
Firstly, the English lived on an island and though this was an obvious fact,
it was a key one psychologically. Secondly, and paradoxically, they had
been invaded by many different peoples. Consequently they had a unique
combination of the Romantic and the German and the Nordic which was
later enriched by exiles fleeing from Europe, so they were not a race but,
much better, a people. Thirdly, to trade, they had to cross the water, so the
English became masters of the seas and peoples from all over the world
knew them and their language and came back to live there and so their
island also became a little world of its own.

Louis took another, a merest sip of wine. 'Louis,' Marie-Christine
whispered to Joe, 'has always known everything.'

'Charles de Gaulle,' exclaimed Marie-Françoise, 'is a great Frenchman.' The table murmured assent. 'But Winston Churchill is a great
man. That is different!' There was, a little to Joe's surprise, an equal
murmur of assent. 'Winston Churchill,' said Marie-Françoise, who had
exceeded her permitted limit of one glass of wine, 'was strong. He
would never surrender. He would fight in the streets. With the cigar. He
is my hero,' she said. 'Natasha has chosen the right country.'

Yvon tried to convey that the wine in front of Marie-Françoise would
be much better deployed in front of him, but the young maid simply
looked away, either unable to read the twitching eyebrows, the barely
concealed winks, the toying with the glass, or reading them in an
altogether different way.

The children, Joe realised later, were impressively and unnaturally
silent, speaking only when addressed and then briefly, muted.
Véronique seemed to be an observer but not so reserved as to
draw attention to herself.

125

'Now,' said Marie-Christine, standing, 'the pièce de résistance.' She took up an envelope, withdrew a sheet of newsprint and carefully unfolded the relevant page of the *Oxford Mail*, given to Louis by Julia Stevens and brought to the lunch for the aunts. 'Look!' she said. 'My English is not my best language – the grammar is intolerable – but look! Louis has told me what it says. I will spare your blushes, Natasha, but we are very proud in the de Vivaise house.'

'Yes,' said Marie-Françoise, loudly. 'Yes! Yes! Yes! We love the photograph of you, we love the Icarus and we hope you will fly better than him.' Marie-Christine tinkled the bell. 'Yvon.'

Yvon stood as the glasses of champagne came in on two trays. He made a short speech, looking directly first at Natasha, talking of her, then at Joseph whom he welcomed into the family as a true Englishman; he touched on the joy that would have been experienced by Natasha's mother and praised Véronique for bringing up Natasha with such success and then he summoned the company to its feet and toasted the new couple and wished them great fortune, great happiness, they were so young. Joe and Natasha, seated, were united in being moved by the kindness and yearning in Yvon's tone and Natasha smiled when, after draining his glass, he whipped around and held out a commanding hand for a refill. It was impossible for the maid to refuse.

After lunch they walked in the garden and Joseph, clasped by the arm of Marie-Christine, was told of the former splendour and told more about Louis and Sophie than Natasha had ever offered. She also explained that French gardens were formal and English gardens were free and now she preferred English gardens 'and they are so much cheaper to maintain'. Natasha, who had been claimed by Yvon, his suit looking frayed in the open air, was guided a little apart from the others and told how much he knew she had suffered but how everything in the past had to be forgotten and forgiven now, it was the only way to live. He gave her a tender kiss on both cheeks and, with tears in his eyes, told her that he had always loved her mother above all others and now she had a duty to be happy for her mother's sake.

At the princely peak of the village, in his favourite spot, on tumbled stones which formed a seat outside the Crusaders' Tower, Joe sat and smoked and made no attempt to sift and clarify the views and impressions and events that spun through his brain. He was more than content, content as never before, he thought, to let life be.

Darkness gathered around the village he would now have to leave. He would carry it with him. Alongside the wall, below him, there were the dozens of tall cypresses which guarded the cemetery and drew the night into their still branches. He could never get enough of this voluptuous place, the shapes, the cones, the helix of the hill leading to the tower; the past, the windings and the stratifications, and now, the place of Natasha who had been changed in his mind so much since coming to France. Her father, the house, the allusion by Marie-Françoise to the title through the female line that Natasha refused to claim. He did not want to raise the matter with Natasha: he now realised that she felt exposed in her own country and he did not want to rub that sore.

He was high above the plain. Perched as a lookout on night watch. So still. The clock tower which Natasha had painted several times was silhouetted against the cloud-free sky.

For a few hours on that morning, as she sat with François outside the bar, Natasha thought she might stay, she painting, Joseph writing his stories . . . And as she walked up the hill to the Renaissance house whose door she wanted to draw one last time, it did seem almost possible. Joseph loved the place so much. But as the morning drew on the impulse faded. It was no more than a dream soon drained away by the wounds of memory.

CHAPTER THIRTEEN

'They are my true parents,' Natasha said, 'my father is my father, but he was so often away and . . . they are my true parents.'

They were lying on a small beach a few miles east of St Tropez. It had been only thinly populated through the day and now as the first cool breeze came off the Mediterranean and the sun began to set, it was empty save for the two of them and a beachcomber with his dog in the distance under the cliff. Joe had gazed on the sea and lay in the sun yet again, despite advice. On this fourth beach day, he was still red, rather prickle-skinned, sore, salted, a little feverish. Natasha, who had taken both sun and sea in a modest habituated manner, was freshened by the breeze and relaxed now after La Rotonde.

Joe waited for her to tell him more. He knew by now that too direct a question about her childhood could halt her for days. He had learned to look away from her when she was in this mood in which he sensed both something dangerous and something sacred.

'Alain was at school with my father,' she said, propped on her elbows, looking out at the Mediterranean, 'and then at university, in Montpellier and in Paris. Both of them set out to be doctors but my father went into research and then . . . Alain stayed here, in Provence, and the only thing about him that is not Provençal is Isabel, whom he met in Paris. She comes from a good family, an only child like you. She was a great beauty – I think you can still see it today, but she won't be photographed! My father laughs at her a little,' Natasha herself laughed as she said this as if remembering the occasions, 'because she loves Radio Monte Carlo and takes so much time to dress, but I know he admires her high style, and after all she is Alain's wife.

'He always says Alain ought to have gone on into research with him but I think he envies what Alain does. My father's father, like Alain, was a country doctor in Provence. He knew Braque. My father calls Isabel "La Belle". She always protests but maybe she doesn't mind. He can do no wrong. In the old days she told us about Paris and the dresses and the parties, but not any more. They could not have children – so she makes a big fuss of the dogs.' She turned to Joe. 'And me. And now you.'

Joe felt blessed. This blind and urgent marriage had proved a magic carpet into lives, places, societies previously beyond his horizon. He had not expected any of this and to absorb it was not easy, it was puzzling, there seemed nothing in his past life that linked to this new world and yet everywhere he was accepted as a natural part of it.

'I like the dogs,' he said.

'That's lucky.'

'Yes.' They were German shepherds. 'I got on their good side as fast as I could.'

'Do you see how special they are, Isabel and Alain?'

'Oh yes.' He meant it and repeated the affirmation. Alain and Isabel Brossart had been emphatically welcoming to him, first at their house near La Rotonde and now here at their house by the sea to which Alain had been obliged to return for a week, giving Isabel the much desired opportunity to have the two young people to herself despite her hatred of the coast in the summer months.

'We must go in,' Natasha said, 'Isabel doesn't like us to be late for *l'apéritif*.'

Joe got up very stiffly.

'Why are you so stupid about the sun, Joseph?'

He shook his head. The beach had been irresistible; warm pure sand which trickled so finely through his fingers, warm blue sea, blue clear skies, sun-filled all day. It was privilege and luxury, it was to his damp Northern-clouded childhood the temptation which had to be taken for it might never come again. Perhaps, Joe told himself, seeking justification, it provoked a deep instinctively compelling sun worship denied for centuries in the weather-beaten North. More likely it began in La Rotonde as a show-off aim to get a tan, surest proof of a holiday

Abroad. Loot. It soon became an addiction. Though pitied by Natasha, warned by Alain – 'speaking as a doctor' – and told crossly by Isabel that it was not at all 'chic', he persisted.

His lips were still a little blebbed. His shoulders had been blistered but had started to peel. From his knees to his shins his legs smarted and at night the pain could be acute but he had stuck at it, waiting for the day when the pink would mature to the oaken brown of the film stars and the playboys.

He hobbled up the beach, past the small restaurant to which Alain and Isabel had taken them on their first night, rather disappointingly it had seemed to Joe at first but the way in which the Brossarts had appeared to own it, the taste of the freshly caught fish, the chef and the patron joining them for a digestif, not a table empty, convinced him that it was, to use one of Isabel's favourite phrases, '*très chic*'. They would go there again tonight. Joe had his eye on the one grand well-ornamented restaurant in the square and he offered to take them all there – his treat – but Isabel said that she would rather starve and besides he was to pay for nothing, he was a guest.

After he had chilled himself in a long cold shower, Natasha rubbed in the cream very gently. 'Makes it worth it,' he said, quoting from some obscure forgotten film and feeling adult, and she liked that. Joe declared himself 'much better' as they sat on the verandah sipping their drinks. All four smoked, the red tips of their cigarettes dancing like wingless insects in the twilight. In the cool approaching dusk, the sea, the mythic Mediterranean, surging and dropping back in the near distance, was the heartbeat of their evenings, Joe thought, its sonorously thrumming base line providing a sound which slowly washed your mind of the sores of the day and said, 'This is what is; live like this.'

The verandah before dinner was the place for the Brossarts to feel close to Natasha. It was as if they wanted to enclose her in a loving ambience which would soothe her as surely as the cream had soothed Joseph.

From these evenings on the verandah Joe would remember sentences, fragments as they looked out to the shore. Now and then there would be arguments and the Brossarts, to Joe's relief, were robust.

Issues of the day blew up, were batted about like tennis balls and then arbitrarily dropped.

'At Cambridge,' said Alain, who dipped in and out of English with dainty self-mockery, 'we would go into a little PUB, and sit with PINTS of beer or throw darts at the BOARD. It was very agreeable. The English know how to enjoy themselves, I think.'

'My parents keep a pub,' said Joe, diving in, but probably they knew anyway. 'For a lot of people it's more a place to keep warm and get out of the house.'

'But that is the genius of the English,' said Alain. 'Everybody is cold. Nobody likes to be in the house. *Voilà!* You invent the PUB. You have a fire and you have warm beer – everything is solved.'

Natasha suddenly thought of the Welsh Pony, of that moment when Joe had looked at her as if for the first time. She looked at him lovingly: Isabel noticed the look and would treasure it.

'Pubs can be chic,' she said, to tease Isabel. 'In Oxford some of them are *très chic.*'

'Oxford! Cambridge! English! The PUBS!' Isabel's voice carried; there were other verandahs at no great distance, but regardless her voice was quite loud, very clear, and the night air carried it well. 'I am fed up with the English. Joseph is different. He is the husband of Natasha. And Joseph is not English. I have not been to Cambridge or to Oxford or anywhere in England and I will never go into a PUB to drink a PINT of beer – the thought disgusts me – but I know who is English – Winston Churchill, Anthony Eden, Charles Morgan, the rolled umbrella and the silly hat – that is English. Joseph is like a Breton. And Winston Churchill, Winston Churchill, Winston Churchill! – we are all supposed to worship Winston Churchill! I am for Charles de Gaulle. And Napoleon Bonaparte!'

'You see how ridiculous my wife can be,' said Alain in that tone which Natasha loved, infinite affection posing as brutal criticism, 'she is uneducated, sadly. She was brought up in Paris society. What do you expect? Listen! Winston Churchill saved Europe from Hitler – is that not true? Joseph, you are a historian – speak.'

'He will be English when he speaks about the war,' said Isabel. 'He cannot be trusted.'

'I think that Churchill—' Joe began.

'I am sorry, Joseph,' Isabel cut in, 'the English have done too many massacres in France and for centuries. At my convent Sister Aquinas was excellent at history. The other sisters said she could have written a book. She said – I am sorry – that the English were Godless and enemies of the Pope. It is better not to be English, Joseph. That is enough!'

'Isabel,' said Alain, raising his glass, 'has spoken.'

But Isabel had not quite finished.

'Véronique,' she said, turning to Joseph, 'she is not French. She was brought up in Lille but the family is Dutch.'

'What is the logic here?' said Alain. 'Logic and my wife are like sheep and goats.'

'Be quiet, Alain. She converted to the faith for the sake of Louis but she was brought up as a Calvinist. They are the worst.'

'What is she saying now?'

'Natasha understands. But, Joseph, Véronique tried very hard. She is now a good Catholic. She did everything to please Louis.'

'Louis has the great skill,' said Alain, 'of making everybody want to please him.'

'I met them together in Paris,' said Isabel. 'I was very young.'

'Eighteen?' said Alain as if claiming a point. 'And the belle of Paris.'

'That is not true, Joseph. Alain exaggerates like other people tell jokes.'

'I have seen photographs,' said Natasha. 'Alain is right.'

'The point is,' said Isabel, 'Louis and Alain – they were such friends. Together they were such good friends, so good and funny with each other.'

'She will soon say she fell in love with both of us.'

'For a few weeks I was in love with both of them,' said Isabel. '*Voilà!*'

'But then I saw that Louis would go so much further, with that brain, and Alain was much more handsome.'

'That is true,' said Alain, 'I can agree with that.'

'Natasha's mother knew both of them too, at that time. She could be serious. Like Louis. And when they worked together in the laboratory and began to make discoveries . . .'

'Very important discoveries,' Alain said, 'work on the adrenal gland. Serious discoveries.'

'They should have had the Nobel Prize,' said Isabel, 'but there is always a prejudice against the French.'

'Marie Curie?'

'Marie Curie was Polish.' Isabel paused for a while. The sound of the sea surged strongly in the silence.

'Your mother gave Louis everything, everything. We were four together,' said Isabel, quietly, and let the words go, as she turned her thoughts back. 'It was very sad.'

'What a brain,' said Alain, quietly. 'Bio-chemistry is his chief subject but physics, biology, history, especially archaeology, art; he speaks German, English as you know, Italian, Spanish and Dutch now because of Véronique; he knows Latin and Greek . . . he is like blotting paper. He reads, he looks up, he remembers!'

'But he is still the Louis I met in Paris, Natasha. And he loves you, Natasha. I know he was not there very much. But still. That is not the most important thing. You are precious to him but also you remind him of Sophie and that must be hard . . .'

'Véronique is formidable,' said Alain, abruptly, 'you would not guess she was Dutch, not for a moment.'

'Alain is sometimes very stupid for such an intelligent man,' said Isabel, and then, carefully, 'but I like Véronique. Now. Time to eat, my children.'

The dogs were collected from the kitchen and it was to them that Isabel directed much of her attention as they sat near the sea and ate fish caught there earlier in the day.

The Brossarts had invited old friends, a couple their own age and their two children, Michel, on his way to becoming a surgeon, who was a little older than Natasha and had known her for years, and his sister Andrée, Joe's age, who was still at Montpellier University.

As usual one or two boatmen came around and asked if anyone would like a half-hour on the sea. Alain encouraged the four young people to take up the opportunity and they went willingly into the rowing boat, lanterns fore and aft.

Michel and Natasha sat together facing the boatman, Joe and Andrée behind them.

Natasha was happy. These days with Isabel and Alain had sealed the new life. Joseph was accepted, and respected. He was a barricade against Véronique, he had become a friend of her brothers and sister, her father and her mother's family and now the Brossarts had all taken to him.

She was greatly relieved. There would be a life. She would paint, he would write and work until they could live by the writing and painting – they agreed it would take time but they were without material ambitions and their heads were full of stories of young artists who had persisted and come through.

It was at this house, in fact on the beach, that Natasha had completed her first painting, a dour study in oil of the cliff which closed off the beach to the east. She had been living with Alain and Isabel then, for some time, after the worst troubles with Véronique and the problems with her studies and her health. Alain and Isabel had a room in both their houses which they called 'Natasha's Room' and no one but she – and Joseph now, of course – was allowed to use it.

The boatman stopped after ten minutes or so, just occasionally touching the oars, letting the little boat sway in the murmuring, swirling water. The lights on the shore were not so very distant but, Natasha thought, it was like looking into another country. Michel caught the keenness of her look and asked her how she would paint it. She reminded him that he had laughed at her first efforts; 'Not laughed,' he protested; 'Yes,' said Natasha, smiling, 'and you were right. You were going to be a great surgeon then,' she said, 'and do you remember Clothilde? Well, she is in a publishing house in Paris now and some of her articles have appeared in magazines.'

Joe tried to restrain his rapid ejection into jealousy but he could not. Of course! Michel was the man she should really have married. They were perfect together. Background, class, country, language, friends. The way she laughed was not how she laughed with him; it was so easily intimate. The music in her voice – was that there for him? Michel was clearly entranced by her, he spoke in a low voice so that Joe would not be able to hear, he leaned close, he steadied her unnecessarily, Joe thought, by putting an arm around her shoulders when the boat was only barely caught by a little breeze, he showed off to her: and she to him, Joe thought.

He tried to continue to answer Andrée's questions about the Royal Family but less and less of his mind was engaged until he felt none of it was. He was blocked out with this almost tearful rage and certainty. She ought to be married to Michel! She would really have preferred to be married to Michel. Everyone in France they had met secretly knew that. He found that breathing was an act he had to think about. While Andrée posed urgent questions about Princess Margaret, his mind which had locked itself in a closed chamber tried to let something penetrate from Andrée. But most of all he had to instruct his mouth to suck in the air, the heavy salty air and then expel it. Yet it threatened to suffocate him. He took off his shirt and sandals and trousers and dived into the sea and swam as fast as he could, swam feeling a fool but swam as he had done in the baths in Wigton, swam to get away from himself.

When he was far enough away he lay on his back, looked at the stars. His marriage was a terrible mistake. They had nothing deeply in common – nothing of the richness she had so instantly with Michel. He turned face down and held his breath, floating like a drowned man. The boat came over.

He would not get back into the boat, swam behind it back to the beach. 'It is the sunburn,' said Alain, when he arrived back at the little restaurant, 'it has driven him a little mad, a mad Englishman.'

'Go, now, to the house,' Isabel commanded, 'here are the keys. Go and change and shower, you must go.'

Despite his protestations, Natasha insisted on coming with him, along the beach, up the steps and onto the narrow path which took them to the house.

'What is it, Joseph?'

'I wanted to swim. I got very hot. That's all. It was great in the water. It got rid of the sunburn.'

'Is that all?'

'What else could there be?'

That was not how Joseph talked. And he was acting as he had not acted before. Alain had told her where to find the painkillers. He took two. They went onto the verandah, still warm, though Joe shivered a little even in his dry clothes.

'We should go in.'

'Let's stay out here. The sound of the sea is . . . you know. Let's stay here.'

A final, an almost convulsive shiver shook through him.

'Better,' he said. He breathed very deeply and again and then again, deeply for the pleasure, for the reassurance of it. 'Sorry,' he said, and reached out in a rather blind way to take her hand.

He is jealous, Natasha realised. I should have been more careful. He is a jealous man. I should have known that before. He is a man of honour. He wanted to fight Robert. He is more foreign now, away from Oxford. I have to understand him, these violent responses.

They were to take the plane back from Marseilles and Alain and Isabel drove them there. Isabel was subdued, as was Natasha. Joe, who sat in the front next to Alain at Isabel's insistence, kept up a cheerful banter with the handsome doctor whose friendship was so light and easy.

At the airport, Isabel took him aside, very deliberately.

'Now, Joseph,' she said, 'everybody thinks you are a good choice for Natasha. So do I. You are young but you are strong. And you love her, that is true?'

She looked at him so intently that Joe felt that he had to blink but to blink would be to let her down.

'Yes,' he said, in a rather choked voice, 'I do.'

'Good. That is good. Now promise one thing. You promise?'

'Yes.'

'You must bring her to us if she is ever very unhappy. Ever. You understand? She must come to us. She is very, very precious to us. Do you promise to bring her?'

'Yes, I promise.'

'Good,' said Isabel; she paused; her eyes, he saw, were moist. She leaned forward, she kissed him on both cheeks and hugged him for a moment. 'Good,' she repeated. '*Alors! Bon voyage* to the two of you.'

PART TWO
TOWARDS AN IDEAL

CHAPTER FOURTEEN

Natasha stood in her black dressing gown, looked through the french windows into the small North London suburban garden and watched the wind move the long tresses of the big willow tree. Sometimes the wind was so low that the delicate branches scarcely shifted, but even in that bare movement Natasha found a warm pleasure; and when the wind rose to lift and sway the elegant green October leaves she broke into a smile at the gentleness of the effort and at a sight so endlessly mesmerising, like waves breaking on a shore.

Joe had left for work half an hour ago; bolted a spartan breakfast, seized a fierce embrace, slammed the door of their downstairs flat and raced through the streets and across the park to the tube. She knew the path he took, it was the first lap of their route into the heart of London.

She wished they lived in the city, but she liked Joe's commanding impetuosity too much to resist his insistence on this remote suburb. They had stayed a few nights with his Oxford friend James and his parents in a house in Hampstead Garden Suburb whose interior displacement of books, good furniture, paintings, things inherited and well spotted in sales in the early days of a marriage, had been comfortably in tune with the houses of her father and that of the Stevenses. James's father knew a local estate agent who, in the spirit of helping a young couple, offered them for a low rent what he considered to be a bargain, in Finchley – two rooms, a kitchen and bathroom on the ground floor with a garden in a 'nice quiet road'. Joe had been ready to accept sight unseen. Natasha had doubts – which had grown – but Joe's carelessness about where and how they lived, though it could also be interpreted as a sort of selfishness, an inattention to her needs and wishes, charmed her. It was what she thought of as part of his innocence.

Now he was gone for the day and his loss sucked the flat into an emptiness which was not lonely, she reassured herself, nor was it sad: he was gone only to return, and with gifts, his talk of the day.

The other fine tree in the garden was a tall chestnut, which, together with the willow, blocked the view of the end and part of the sides of their small lawn and gave the garden an unusual privacy, even shrouded it, an effect intensified by the thick ivy which clustered over the rickety wooden fences. She watched brown and yellow leaves drop from the chestnut, lit her second cigarette of the day, took a sip of the tepid coffee, and decided what better was there to do for the next few minutes than stand and stare and let a happy boredom, a comfortable melancholy, grow into a poem.

The aunts had given them as a wedding present a handsomely bound set of the great French poets and she was reading Verlaine and Rimbaud, the more avidly perhaps because their physical world and the world of their poetry was so far from these regiments of neat, quiet, opaque, moat-gardened, semi-detached English houses standing in obedient formation on lifeless streets.

She had wandered around Finchley several times and acknowledged what she admired as the English tranquillity of it, the order in the shops, the lack of Gallic expostulation, the politeness which she thought verged on indifference. There were no cafés in which she could sit and read or write and the pubs, unlike those in Oxford, seemed forbidding. Natasha had attempted to find some sort of recognition and failed. There was a sense of foreignness here so extremely different to her own experiences of France and Oxford that no comparisons could be plucked at, no threads unravelled what must surely be, behind the gods of tidiness and discretion, a life, lives, equal to those she had known elsewhere. She knew only a morsel of England. This suburb was an England on which she had no purchase. That there were bridge evenings and coffee mornings, choirs, sporting clubs, active religious persuasions, communities of scholars, a subterranean network of associations and all the hobbied clutter of English suburban life was unknown to her, and without knowing how to advance into it, she retreated.

The flat was adequately furnished. She had set up her easel in the sitting room but little painting had been done. Upstairs there was a couple encountered once on the doorstep. The man, very thickset, shaven-headed, brown-skinned, had abruptly announced himself as Felix, an Austrian, an engineer; then he introduced his dark silent companion as Rebecca, a Jewess whom he had met at the engineering company at which he worked.

Later, Natasha told Joe that Felix was certainly German and Rebecca was not Jewish, and besides her hair was dyed black. Joe at first argued – how could she know? – and then he took her word for it. She could see that he was not interested and she let it go. His new life enveloped him completely.

Two things happened. A robin settled on the rotting old bench at the back of the garden. Natasha loved its puff-chested perkiness, that red blaze and proud strut, the eager peck of its head and the sense of lightness. She tried to will it to stay until she had enjoyed all its pert show of life. When it flew away she felt a small sadness.

But then two grey squirrels scampered so swiftly across the branches of the chestnut tree she was beguiled by their graceful urgency. What had brought it on? Were they being pursued? Were they racing back to deposit the plunder of the morning? Was one hunting down the other? Or, like the arrival of the robin and the intermittent gusting of the wind, was it inadequately human to look for patterns and consequences. Things happened. Look at her own life.

She turned to the unmade bed and decided to warm up her coffee and settle there. The flat was cold. It was grey outside. Joe's imprint would still be on the sheets.

Perhaps there was a poem. The surging tresses of the willow, playthings of the wind, the robin and the squirrels, Joseph's absence, the solid broad chestnut sadly shedding its past, the yellow-brown leaves, dead, pocking the lawn in the morning silence of the suburb: all her present life was there.

—ɯ—

The train was already quite full when Joe got aboard in the open heights of East Finchley. London down in the Thames basin was once again braced for the invasion of the commuters as the tubes droned into the metropolitan reservoir of labour. Mostly men, all reading, all silent, Joe included, as he gutted *The Times*, part of his job, to be done before he reached the office. It became more difficult to manoeuvre the large sheets of newsprint as the train filled up, still mostly men, yet more silence, as if rehearsing their prayers or their curses before the offices of the day.

The train seemed to speed up and rattle more loudly when it went underground and Joe ticked off some stations, old acquaintances: Golders Green and Evelyn Waugh; Hampstead Heath and Lawrence, Keats and Constable; Camden Town, Sickert and Dickens; and Mornington Crescent, the title, he thought, of a murder mystery; Warren Street, was that Mrs Warren? And 'Farewell Leicester Square' down to Charing Cross of the road of the bookshops, heaven of a sort. Here he dismounted, walked quickly up the Strand and felt on the way to becoming a Londoner, loving London Town, past the Savoy Theatre of Gilbert and Sullivan, facing Fleet Street, St Paul's beyond, round the Aldwych to Bush House, the BBC World Service, which transmitted trusted news – he never failed to think on this with a childish imperial pride – to more than a hundred nations in their own languages: the truth centre, Joe thought, the Greenwich Mean Time of the honest state of the world.

Every time he went through the modest BBC entrance next to St Clement's, Joe was exhilarated, taken over by the romance of the place, the ambition, the reach, his imagination infested with the thought of sentences and sounds in so many tongues unleashed around the globe twenty-four hours every day. Bush House, as he soon learned, was staffed by exiles from tyrannies, escapees from prisons, refugees from persecution, intellectuals of planetary distinction, a Salvation Army of humanity dedicated to nothing but the truth, to telling it like it was, to slaying the dragon of propaganda wherever it breathed its blighting fire. He always ran up the broad and palatial stairs, too impatient to wait for a lift, as if running to escape the imaginary policeman who would tap him on the shoulder and tell him that his time was up, that he had to get a real job, vividly aware of the belief in these early months that chance alone had landed him in this wonderful cathedral of radio, a place of unique rectitude, this first attachment as a BBC trainee. And George Orwell had worked there.

The meeting of the European Services Unit, to which he had been assigned, began at nine-thirty. By 10 a.m. the agenda had been ticked off, the stories had been decided on and distributed among the five writers. At first Joe ran alongside one of these, like a puppy terrier on a hunt tied to its mother. Only after several trials and errors was he unleashed alone and then on the gentler slopes. Out into morning London or to a library to pursue information, a five-hundred-word script to be delivered at three-thirty and corrected by the Head of Department, invariably to be rewritten by four-thirty and scanned once more and tweaked one final time, deadline five-thirty. It would then be translated into forty-two languages and broadcast over the next twenty-four hours. At first that prospect inhibited Joe to a point of near paralysis and then he became secretly intoxicated at the thought of his words flying all over Europe.

Prompt at five-thirty the walk back to Charing Cross, this time along the Embankment, to see the flowing Thames and feel the ripples of so much of his history. In the distance up river Westminster Bridge, Wordsworth and the Houses of Parliament; down river, wastelands, T.S. Eliot, where once the Globe had stood, and the White Tower of royal tyrannies and tortures, the few Wren and Hawksmoor churches unbombed and St Paul's, God-saved intact. Inside Bush House he was inside a polyglot global orchestra, outside he was in England's great city, a city of singing birds, and bloody acts, and in imagination alive, electric, it seemed to Joe, in every alley, in every square, in every street.

No, when Natasha looked at him sceptically, he was not exaggerating, not about any of it. There was no space for scepticism. No, he protested to her, his reaction was not excessive: this was how it was. Everything was special. Even the Bush House canteen, which was the only feeding ground for all who worked there, held a unique democracy of nationality, class, creed and colour which satisfied Joe deeply. It was the home of the True Word, a resurrected Pentecostal speaking in many tongues. It was high seriousness, he told her, born from a certainty of high purpose, knowing that what was said on the airwaves in London did indeed influence what was thought elsewhere and did affect what was done or could be undone even in the most savage crucibles of struggle. This was the power of the Word, Joe excitedly told Natasha, this was the New Word and like the Old Word, like the First Word, it came out of space, and went into darkness bringing light.

When he telephoned Natasha at lunchtime, as he did every day, and thought of her in the hallway at that payphone, and felt close because he could 'see' every detail, the red and grey squared lino, the chipped banisters of the staircase, the dark varnish on the doors, he spilled over with the news of the morning and the brilliance of those for whom he worked: Konrad Syrop, Ludwig Gottlieb, Tosca Fyvel, world aware and alert to all its nuances of political climate, readers of journals in German, Polish, French, Italian and Czech. Joe could scarcely believe that he was in such company, and every one a published author, he told her, more than once, bookmen all. They were not allowed into the secret of his own writing ambitions but there they stood before him, examples.

He basked in the uninhibited love these immigrants had for England. You must not write about it as a worn-out, merely historical place, they said, entertained by his enthusiasm; this is a fine and free country, this is an important example so many other countries look to. It was as if to them he was an heir to all this and must be well advised of its qualities. They became his wise guardians. His own patriotism was encouraged and justified, by men of harrowing experience and foreign intellectual vigour. He was on ether.

Every two or three days when he thought they needed refreshing he bought Natasha a small bunch of cheap flowers at Charing Cross Station from an old scarlet-faced, multi-layered flower seller, beside whose small stall was a card: 'An Original Cockney Flower Girl'. He tried to protect the offering on the journey home while absorbed in a novel, as the train rattled under the city making for the open air of the northern suburb. He was at once drained by the day and full of it, longing to see Natasha and tell her everything. Sometimes as he came through the door, before he kissed her, he sang out, 'Shantih, shantih, shantih.'

—⟶

He came into the flat, she wrote, 'like a burning bush'. His face had been smacked into colour by the rapid march from the station in the darkening autumn air; his eyes devoured her with delight. Most days she had spoken to no one save him on that one telephone call since he had left the cold flat in the morning. He always made for the kitchen. The two bars of the electric fire in the smallest and warmest of the rooms seemed, she thought, a mere accompaniment to his warmth. He laid his day at her feet, retailing the ways of the world outside to a lover confined, and in doing so the walls of the flat dissolved and Natasha allowed herself to be captured by this bigger picture he brought to her as a tribute which not to receive with pleasure would have been unkind. For it meant so much to Joseph, she saw that clearly. And he wanted it to mean as much to her. Any demur was overwhelmed by the ardour of his reports. These evening disgorgements were, she came to think, in their way, his love letters.

'I would like to show you Paris,' she said one night. She was dreamy-eyed at the prospect of taking him along the Seine, through the intricate innocent Left Bank streets of a curtailed childhood and youth which in truth had allowed her little space to roam, but the vision of the two of them dawdling arm in arm through the city, her city, suddenly captivated her. 'It's something I could give to you,' she said, and saw that he too was ensnared: it was so simple to ensnare him.

Joe was within a moment of reminding her that he had spent weeks in Paris before going to Oxford, that he had raked the museums and raided the churches, that he had sat in a café in the Boulevard St Germain and written – only a letter to his girlfriend, true, but still written in a café like a true French writer, Disque Bleu, cognac and all, and that he had even witnessed in the Bois de Vincennes one night a peppering of gunfire between Algerian rebels and the police. But she had spoken of Paris in a tone which claimed it as hers and just in time he drew back and let it be: and already he anticipated seeing it through her eyes.

'My father has written a letter,' she said. It was a few days old now; she was uncertain what to do about it. 'I think you have made a big impression on both of them, Joseph.' She smiled and he was reassured that she meant what she said. 'I think both of them are anxious to send François to l'Ecole Normale here in London, as soon as possible. It is not working out with him. He is such a sweet little guy. They persecute him! Why does he have to pass exams? Why do they make him miserable? Who cares about exams!'

Her sudden vertical take-off into anger was impressive.

'He wants us to go to see them at Christmas. Why should I go back there? I hate them!'

'Not your father.'

'No.'

'Nor all the others save . . .'

'For Her! But she kills me.'

'We enjoyed La Rotonde.' He had told Natasha at the time that he had found her stepmother sympathetic. And, he could have added, I thought she was perfectly pleasant to you.

'We did. But . . .' Why should she tell him of the wounds that had opened up? He did not deserve that. This marriage in this strange new place was a good start; she wanted to hold onto that.

'You want to go to Paris,' she said, accusingly, forgetting her earlier invitation.

'I could meet your Paris friends. You've said a lot about them. They sound terrific.'

'Yes.' She was suddenly deflated by his clever diversion. 'And they want to see you. Joseph,' she said, and then, taking in a sharp breath, 'I think that I should look for an art college.'

'Why?'

'To keep up with my drawing. You need a life class for that.'

'But you know how to draw. And you were at the Ruskin for years. You can paint here. You can have that front room to yourself.'

She noted the tremor of panic under his voice.

'I could meet other people and painters.'

'We meet people.'

'Your friends.'

'Our friends.'

'People I meet at art college could be our friends too.'

'You write here as well as paint.'

'I could find a college in London and we could travel together on the tube and meet for lunch and travel back together.'

Joe nodded but with no enthusiasm and she knew again that she had hit the nerve of his jealousy. She would come back to this plan, she assured herself, although she wanted to avoid hurting him.

'I bought sausages,' she said. 'They look disgusting but you have said so much about your sausages.'

'Cumberland sausages?'

'These are Finchley sausages. Cumberland was too far to go.'

As they made supper he chattered his way through the day as if nothing had disturbed the evening and she complimented his memory and slyly provoked him to more mimicry. The kitchen table boasted four chairs but two of them had early on been relegated to the cold, heavy and rarely used front room. Joe insisted that the sausages were grilled to the point of Boy Scout charcoal and she stood back, unapologetically amused at his unselfconscious scraping off a layer of the charcoal. There was a small mound of frozen peas and cauliflower bought for want of any more appetising-looking vegetable. They drank water. Joe tucked in as he always did with no other comment than 'This is good.' He accepted two of her three sausages but only after he was convinced when she told him that she had eaten too much at lunch.

'James is coming round tomorrow,' he announced; he had saved this up. 'With Howard. They were at school together in Hampstead. They edited the school magazine there and they want to start up a little magazine.' He pushed the empty plate away and sank the water. 'James wants me to write for it and' – this was the best of it – 'they want you' – he did not say that he had suggested it – 'to design, do a painting for, whatever, the cover *and*' – this was the knockout – 'let them publish your poems!'

Natasha loved him.

'What will you contribute?'

'I don't know. We're discussing it. Film reviews? A sort of diary from Bush House? I don't know.'

'Your stories.'

'Oh no! They don't know I write short stories. Only you know that. Please don't tell them.'

'Let me read them.'

'No. Please. Please don't tell anyone.' He offered her a cigarette as if asking her to sign a treaty. She took it and his panic passed. Soon she would make real coffee and the table would be cleared for writing and life would be almost unendurably perfect. '*La Règle du Jeu*'s on at the Academy in Oxford Street,' he said. 'I thought we might see it again; we could go on Saturday for the five o'clock. Peter' – Peter Mills, a colleague at Bush House, much admired by Joe, another winner of a traineeship, a man whom Joe had seen at a distance at university when he was an unapproachable president of the Oxford Union – 'has invited us to a bottle party in his flat in Paddington.'

'I like Paddington.'

'Because you could just jump on a train to Oxford?'

'Yes.' Her smile was a little rueful. 'And because it is in the middle of London.'

'Peter says it's a hole.'

'Peter is a politician.'

'Peter says what we have here is exactly what we need.'

'How can Peter possibly know that? But he has an opinion. You see – he is already a politician.'

'He will be,' said Joe, rather grimly. 'At Oxford they said he could even become Prime Minister.'

'All your geese are swans, Joe.'

After they had washed up, they wrote. At first, Natasha had employed a second-hand and stubborn typewriter but Joe could not bear the noise of it and had moved to the front room. There was no argument but she had put the typewriter aside after two days. He moved back into the kitchen with her.

This was their best time. The kitchen was small and snug, barely furnished, a haven, she thought. Just them. Joseph worked at a story she would not be allowed to read: she worked at a poem he would nag her into reading aloud. Sometimes he would read poetry to her, Eliot, Yeats, Lawrence . . .

The autumn deepened. There would be many nights like this. They were in a boat, she thought, the two of them, in a lighted place in the dark, drifting purposefully though with no dominating ambition, drifting in the dark of London, of England, of the world itself and sufficient together, she thought, building up the mutual strength which would protect them from all invaders. The silence and the private worlds shared, brought out the best in them, she believed, gradually expelling all that had harmed them, finding and making a unique contentment.

'Read it to me, then,' he said, tired now, past eleven, but not wanting the evening to be over.

'I can't finish it.'

'I know you did something, though. Didn't you?'

'I began to translate a poem of Rimbaud. You remember my father asked you to read to us in English from *Hamlet*? That is why I chose this poem.'

'Go on, then. In French first.'

She smiled at his eagerness, his love, her certain intuition that this, for him, was all that it was and for ever.

> *Sur l'onde calme et noire où dorment les étoiles*
> *La blonde Ophélia flotte comme un grand lys,*
> *Flotte très lentement, couchée en ses longues voiles . . .*
> *On entend dans les bois lointains des hallalis.*

'It's difficult,' she said, 'to find English rhymes.'

They were so close to each other now that he caught in her reading an intimation of the fine shading of regret, that she had stepped outside her own language, that she, who loved to talk and write, was for ever committed now, through him, to a foreign tongue. Though it had been her decision, he could see it as his fault, even his guilt. What a loss, he sensed, a distant chord that would grow in time as he realised that the loss of language was the loss of a world.

'So . . . ?'

> On the tranquil dark water, where the stars drown,
> Ophelia floats white as a lily
> Floats gently, slowly, in her long gown . . .
> From the distant woods you hear the sound of '*les hallalis*'.

' "*Hallalis*" is so good – I can't find a good English word.'

'Why do you need to?'

'It should be "sleep" not "drown".'

'Drown's better,' he said. 'It's beautiful.'

There was something wild in his gratitude, she thought. She must protect him yet let him be free. She looked at him carefully and then said, as if extracting a solemn promise,

'This is it, isn't it, Joseph? This is enough.'

'Oh yes,' he said. 'This is everything. Just this.'

CHAPTER FIFTEEN

In the late December dusk of Paris, seated defiantly out of doors, like many others of their age, at the big café next to the Pont St Michel, they could have been taken for just another couple of students who had spilled down from the Sorbonne at the end of the day to relax and take in the first night-lighting of the city, to postscript gossip to another academic day. But Natasha would now never study in the university so beloved of her father, nor would her half-brother François, she had concluded. Her half-brother sat with his pastis and Gitane, blissfully vacant, exempt from effort by the presence of Natasha. François did not need conversation.

The figures that criss-crossed by, the lights on the Seine and the growls of the traffic were more than enough to line his mind with contentment. He was with a sister he loved and the sole person in his family and among his friends, as she realised, who did not look at him and say in that look, 'Why are you a failure?' 'Why do you not make greater efforts?' 'Why do you so miserably let down your parents and humiliate them?' 'What happened to that Prévost boy?' But Natasha's eyes said, 'I like being with you, François. Just as you are. Let's have a drink or go to a movie and talk, if at all, aimlessly.' To be alone with Natasha was, for this bewildered teenage boy, physically undersized, something strained about his poor skin, to be alone with his bold sister Natasha was a balm and all he wanted was to sit there, time without end, and watch the daylight finally drain away and take with it the unacknowledged welts and bruises of a constantly criticised life . . .

—⧢—

'I am afraid, Joseph, that it will be too hard for you both,' said Véronique. She had waited until Joe and Louis had finished polishing a speech Louis was to deliver in English at a conference in Copenhagen. Louis had gone into the university for a final hour. Natasha was out with François. Véronique pounced on Joseph. They sat in the large, elegantly furnished drawing room – which Louis would it be? he wondered. He saw it as a set more than a room. Gilbert the butler had served them drinks, cocktails, at Véronique's suggestion, hers barely touched, Joe's already all but supped. 'You are just beginning on your marriage and marriage is hard enough without extra burdens.'

'François won't be actually living with us,' he said, encouragingly, wanting to please.

'But Natasha wants him to live near by. She said she thought there might even be lodgings in the same street as yours.'

Véronique took out a cigarette, American, and Joe took this as permission to light up a Disque Bleu.

'François is unfortunate,' she said, 'Louis is so . . . distinguished and from François, the first boy, so much was expected and demanded. And he has been a fool. He will not work. He only pretends to be stupid, I am convinced of that.'

The harshness of the last three sentences embarrassed Joe into an alert silence. Véronique followed suit and for some moments they sat as if each feared to break it.

'England could change him,' she said. 'The English are very practical.' Joe nodded. 'They decide to do something – they go out and do those things.' Joe nodded once again. 'He will be away from . . . us.' She took up her glass and sipped. Joe finished his off, felt urgently that another would ease this tension but did not know how to ask.

'It would be a very important gift to his father and to myself.'

Joe saw his way. He was powered by one of those unaccountable gusts of fearless and often treacherous confidence magnified since he had been sure of Natasha.

'I like François,' he said, glowing in the role of gift-bearer, healer. 'He'll be good company for Natasha. The sooner he comes the better.'

'My husband,' said Véronique, quietly, 'believes that he can find him a place in the Ecole Normale in London, to begin in January.'

'We'll have found somewhere for him to live by then.'

'You are so good for Natasha,' said Véronique. 'We are all very grateful to you.'

Joe's humble smile, she thought, was a touch that of a simpleton.

'It has to be done,' she concluded, and Joe stood up, recognising that the conversation or the audience was over. He sought to formulate some reassuring, worldly, unpatronising parting line, but it eluded him.

Time on his hands! He ran down the stairs and out into the streets of Paris, always choosing the narrowest as he tacked towards the Seine, expecting and so partly seeing a city seething with spectacle, a carnival of vivacious Parisiennes, *Les Enfants du Paradis* . . .

'Did you see *La Dolce Vita*?' said François, out of the blue, as they walked back arm in arm, up the youthful and animated Boulevard St Michel.

Natasha nodded. 'Joseph wrote about it for a new magazine. We disagreed on it. I thought it was fun, but pretentious. Joseph loved it.'

'What tits!' said François. '*Quelle poitrine!*'

He looked daringly at her with a sort of amazement, a wonder that such a bosom should be, that he should have been allowed to see the bosom and that he could admit this out loud to a glamorous woman, even though she was his sister.

'Come to London, François,' Natasha said, and turned her face away a little as his smile conveyed such unbearable relief. 'Come to London with us.'

The following evening, Natasha and Joe walked arm in arm past the *bouquinistes* which after half a dozen previous lootings he had to force himself to pass without a pause, all but averting his eyes as if these trunks of books were ladies of the night to whose temptations he had to blind himself. The nearer they drew to Notre Dame the more resolute was his stride until he felt that he and Natasha were being drawn ever more strongly by invisible beams magnetising the mothy dusk of the evening, being pulled towards the force of faith and sculpture on the spectacular, figure-embossed, twin-towered west front of the cathedral, willed on by its sacred power.

Joseph went into the cathedral as into a meeting with an old, ever-faithful friend. When he had worked in Paris for a few weeks before going to university, Notre Dame had been a prime destination. He loved the crepuscular murmurings of prayers emanating from the small congregation in that vast space, a gallant survival of witnesses, he thought, and the quiet respectful people moving behind pillars, gazing into side chapels, filling the cathedral with an echoed whispering, seeking everything from a rest, or a shelter, to an affirmation of divinity, a miracle. The guiding invisible power was made visible in the vaulting, the rose windows, the testimony of prayer-slaked stone and rich embroidered glass all announcing that this was the true and timeless God's house.

Natasha kept a step or two behind him; this, her childhood faith, and this the cathedral of her city, she now considered to be a museum rather than a House of God and the call to worship in such a place had been repelled long ago. Now its religiosity seemed a dead weight. She was aware of its cultural importance but even that pressed down on her. Quite simply she wanted to be out of this mediaeval candlelit gloom, away from the confession boxes which looked to her like little torture chambers, away from the bleeding Christs and the imploring women of Christ, away from the menace of absolute faith. But she stayed beside Joseph at once polite and intrigued by the drug this seemed to be for him. Where was his mind? she wondered. And yet again, as one sensation after another seemed to possess him, who is he?

'I would like to come to mass on Christmas Eve,' he said, as they came out into the dark city air which to Natasha seemed life-salvingly fresh. 'I won't be able to take a Roman Catholic communion but it would be great to be there. It's so . . .' He paused. He was bowed down by the fact of being in that place with Natasha, on that evening, a pinnacle of privilege.

'My stepmother comes here,' Natasha said, 'usually alone. My father says that he will go but he rarely does. I am like him.'

'So you won't go? How can you not? On Christmas Eve.'

154

'Because of my religion,' she smiled. 'My atheism, Joseph, forbids it.'

'But Notre Dame. The music.'

'The music I can listen to on the radio.'

He took her arm firmly and almost marched her to the east end of the cathedral. 'How can you not believe when you have been in a place like that?'

'I have been in other places, Joseph, and not "believed" in them either. And not expected to believe. Anyway, God is dead, the Catholic Church is too wealthy to be good and most of the priests are corrupt.'

'How can you prove that?'

'My father says that most of them were not good in the war, Joseph. And some were very bad. What did they do to stop the fascists?'

'There's always evil.'

'Not evil. That is a religious word. "Bad" will do. Or "rotten". Or "cowards". Or just men who found a comfortable life in a faith which does not need principles.'

'Here!' he said. 'Look!'

They stood, his arm around her waist, their breath fogging the clear cold air, staring up.

The flying buttresses were lit up and Natasha smiled at the spectacle. This gigantic spider-legged set of stone props holding up the great weight of the east end of the cathedral was, she understood, clear proof to Joseph of faith at work.

'We don't know who built this,' he said. 'Good artisans, that's all. But I think they are finer than all modern sculpture. And they were done out of faith.'

'Where can you see proof of that?'

'Why else did they do it?'

'For a wage.'

'How do you know?'

'For pride.'

'Why not for faith?'

'Perhaps they were persuaded by the propaganda.'

'Did no one have faith? What about Chartres? You can't deny that was built purely because of faith.'

'It was a sort of organised hysteria. They knew no better.'

'Do we?'

'We can doubt and disagree without being persecuted.'

'But do we know better?'

'Yes. We know that God does not send down plagues. Plagues come from viruses. We know that God does not cause floods or famines. We know that if there is such a God,' she turned to him, her face set, '*I* know that if there is such a God I want nothing to do with Him and I will certainly not bow to Him or pray to Him or worship a monster who creates a world like this one.' She paused and smiled. 'Poor Joseph. You don't like this.'

Joe was offended but he was also impressed.

'So what do you believe in?'

'Why do I have to believe?'

'If you don't believe in anything, what's the point?'

'I do not like this word. But if you force me to use it, I believe in you and me, Joseph. I believe we should help François. I believe that some people I have known were cruel and hateful. I believe the world is full of wrong but some right too, but I don't need the pomp of Notre Dame for that. Notre Dame gets in the way. It is too complicated. It is a dictatorship of belief. It takes us up too many unnecessary paths.'

'So the flying buttresses are just an accident?'

'A glorious accident, Joseph.'

'You believe in art, don't you?'

'Believe?'

'So why is the greatest art a by-product of religion?'

'Because what we call art is like the bacteria which will keep alive in anything, no matter what, or when. Art is not belief, Joseph, but it is us, it tells us what we are and what we could be and if it has to feed off religion or atheism, off democracy or tyranny, it will. Art is one of the essential messages we send to each other but we don't know why. We will never know.'

—ɯ—

'I still have an occasional yearning for the certainty and the testing mysteries of religion. At that time I was far nearer the heat of an

156

adolescent infatuation, even a love for it. I thought I had put it aside but it was still raw and Notre Dame murmuring with history and prayer had revived that.

'I did not know until later,' he told their daughter, 'that however much she smiled, your mother's argument with religion was a passion. I did not realise much until many years later. Perhaps this was because we had spent so little time together before the marriage. There was not the time to doubt, the time to pause, the time to look, look away, the time to question and wait for answers. But once our marriage was made, certain assumptions soon set in, with me, at any rate. It was like being mantled in a livery made for you before your time. Marriage was the uniform of your new status. There were fundamental assumptions about Married People, about what they had closed off and what they could take for granted, part of which was that they had somehow come to know everything important, everything worth knowing about each other just by the act of getting married.

'Once you were married you no longer needed to exercise any curiosity because the fact of marriage proved you accepted everything about the other and because of that acceptance you knew everything you needed to know. I am sure now that I was far too bound up with myself and with my idea, or idealisation, of Natasha to take enough care to know more, to probe more deeply. Perhaps there was a suspicion that if I probed too deeply I would find what I did not like, what I did not want to experience. That would be hard and marriage existed to make life easy. Perhaps I suspected already the schisms to come. We are all tempted to see ourselves as prophets in the past. We like to think that our lives are foretold, that a special destiny works slowly through us. It was a culpable failing then not to recognise how serious her lack of faith was for her. I should have teased out the causes and the consequences of her total denial of faith. But I breezed along, we breezed along, Paris, Christmas week, just married, snowed under with good fortune and on the way to the apartment of Maria Troubnikoff, Natasha's closest friend, a White Russian, who had invited other friends around to meet me.

'They seemed so dazzling, maybe because their French was so dazzling and so rapid. They were like starlings. They found out that

I could keep up a little, soon assumed that I could keep up a lot and sped into higher and higher gears of word play and references to French actors and singers and comedians which left me marooned, but contented to see Natasha so brilliant in this company, the language illuminating her character in ways I simply had not seen before. She was the most dazzling of all, I thought, she was the centre of energy; her eyes laughed, her gestures were quick and fluent: she was another self. Her language gave her access to the whole of her life. From that evening I believed increasingly that her exile from the French language left her unbearably lesser and lonely, underlined the loneliness she carried like an inheritance. Language much more than painting was her great love and her great loss. At the time I may have had an inkling that I was somehow responsible for this; now I feel it strongly.

'When they did slow down and include me it was to talk about politics because that was what the BBC brought them. But here I felt even more of a stranger because they were consumed by the Algerian question; the bizarre intellectual alliance between Sartre and de Gaulle, his promises of withdrawal, the influence of Ben Bella's Hunger Strike and the rumours of torture. Apart from floundering in a shallow pool of generalisations, trying to honour the reputation of the BBC by appearing knowledgeable, I had nothing of any significance to contribute and I was embarrassed and consequently frustrated. I remember talking afterwards to Natasha and saying, out of pique, perhaps, that Algeria seemed 'rather provincial' compared with the world-encompassing Ban the Bomb arguments and marches back in London. I remember saying that because she turned on me, scorned the Ban the Bombers, Bertrand Russell and all his tribe of angry writers, described them as fantasists and praised the reality and complexity of the actions and discussion on this French post-colonial debacle. The English, she said, would never mount such a profound debate. I was worse than an idealist, she said, I was a Romantic and they had caused all the problems. I never forgot that. I thought it was brilliant of her to have said that.

'But I did not take it on board. Again, likely as not, I did not understand. I was probably unshaken. Post-war England to me seemed so emphatically to have the high ground in any comparison of national virtue or achievement that her pride in the French way was simply, arrogantly, mistakenly not to be taken seriously. Perhaps it was there that I had the first intimation that I was such a long way from understanding her. Hindsight will be Satan, throughout this account.'

———m———

On Joe's first visit to Paris, made in the months before he went to university, the city had been a living museum. It seemed to him that some of the finest artefacts in the world had been herded up and penned in solely for his education and in that short time he had fed on them at first with indiscriminate greed and then, he liked to think, with more of a gourmet's taste buds, as he returned again and again to chosen sites and picnicked on favourite Impressionist paintings, grazed on grand sculptures, entombed himself happily face to face with inscrutable objects from enthralling but impenetrable ancient civilisations.

This time Paris was a movie. Everything in the riddle of small streets on the Left Bank, streets and alleys which were a direct though hugely more elaborate cousin of the streets and alleys mapped on his mind from Wigton, reminded him of French films. It was as if the very narrowness of the streets, their intimacy, represented his state of mind as they had in childhood and radiated a sensation of security and magic. There was one thin little street which housed seven cinemas. It was like seeing all the da Vincis in the Louvre. He framed shots for his own instant films by making screen squares with his thumbs and index fingers. He thought he spotted a location for this or that scene from the wave after wave of films of the French directors whose work had been thrown onto the shores of his university culture.

Then he saw the photograph of Memphis Slim. It was in a window at the bottom of an excessively narrow street called Le Chat Qui Pêche which led away from the left bank of the Seine. Memphis Slim was a hero. Joe's ambition had been to play the piano like Memphis Slim. Though diffident about declaring his sense of kinship with the blues – if you're white, not all right – it was visceral. When the bluesmen sang

159

and played, the sounds and sometimes the words came out of a soulful darkness Joe recognised and into a light he wanted. At first he thought the photograph was for sale, memorabilia or a promotion for a jazz shop in a city which had embraced black jazz for decades. But it was an advertisement for Memphis Slim. He was in Paris. He would play here, down those steps, in that cellar, first set nine o'clock. Memphis Slim.

Joe raced back to get Natasha . . .

She watched him across the small table furnished with an ashtray and a vase with three red paper roses, gradually becoming as drawn to Joseph even as enraptured by him as he was by the music of Memphis Slim. How could Joseph let himself go like that, so immediately? She had seen it in Notre Dame, she had seen it when they were watching films together. She studied this man, this young husband who could give so much so deeply and she sensed as before that the quick of life had moved out of him and was soldered outside himself, this time onto the sound of the piano player. She recognised his experience of it. She knew what it was to be enveloped by his concentration, sealed inside it, captured by it but a willing prisoner and less and less happy to be free of it.

She glanced around the bare room. About half full, at most. Younger people. The older crowd would come to the eleven o'clock or the one o'clock sets and they would be better, she guessed, for connoisseurs (Joseph, she knew, would not have worked that out). This audience was reverentially young, they could have been in a chapel, scarcely a sound interfered with the music of Memphis Slim. But suddenly there were palms clapping hard and Joe turned to her, eyes ablaze, 'How about that? This is IT! He's a genius, isn't he?'

They had ordered two small glasses of red wine. Natasha had taken a sip and would drink no more. Joe threw back his glass as a Russian would his vodka. He looked around for a waiter, saw one, held up his empty glass like, he thought, an habitué, like, as Natasha thought, a tourist, and then turned back immediately as the heavy bass 'Celeste Boogie' began. They were on the edge of the meagre dance floor. To Joe, this was the key table, the table taken by gangsters and Rita Hayworth, the table to which stars were ushered by an obsequious dinner jacket.

Just on ten, after 'Frankie and Johnnie', in which Joe needed heavy self-restraint not to sing along, after the last rolls of the wrist, the upright man at the baby grand concluded, stood up, bowed, stepped out of the spotlight and walked in the direction of Joe and Natasha.

'You were great!' Joe said. '*Très, très bon*,' in case English was somehow out of order. '*Magnifique.*'

'*Merci.*' The man paused for a moment and offered a small bow to Natasha.

'Would you like – *voulez-vous avoir un verre du vin?*' Joe's request came out of the blue. It surprised him. He glanced around to see if somehow he had become the instrument of a ventriloquist. Memphis Slim?

The man glanced into the now half-lit room and waved; Natasha, who followed his glance, saw a blonde white woman at a table by the wall at the back. He then pulled up a chair. He had come out of his screen, Joe thought, and now they were in Joe's movie.

Natasha offered him a cigarette. Why, Joe said to himself, could I not have thought of that?

The pianist gently prised the packet from her fingers. 'English,' he noted. 'You English?'

'French.' She took the cigarette he offered her from her own pack.

Joe lit up a Disque Bleu.

'*You* French?'

'English.'

'I like that,' said the pianist and in his hand was a heavy silver lighter out of which there torched a flame fit to burn down the jazz club. Joe and Natasha leaned forward for the fire and thanked him.

His drink arrived, unordered. A large Jack Daniels. He picked up the glass.

'What do you say in England?'

'Down the hatch.'

Natasha and Memphis Slim looked at Joe, then at each other, and laughed.

'Down the hatch,' they said, in a ragged unison, and Joe clinked glasses with his hero.

Now what did he say?

'You live here?' the pianist asked Natasha.

'No. London.'

'London's good. Good if you like grey. I passed through London.'

'Did you ever meet Big Bill Broonzy?' said Joe.

He raised the bourbon.

'To Bill,' he said. 'The Man.'

Joe finished off his second glass with a hiccup-inducing gulp.

'Want me to pat you on the back?'

Out of the contorted frenzy trying to disguise itself as nonchalance, Joe shook his head.

'You play beautifully,' said Natasha, drawing him away from Joe, whose blotched hiccuping face looked ready to burst open.

'Thank you, ma'am.'

'Do you,' said Joe, a tormented gasp, 'play the same,' tears in the eyes, 'variations every night?'

'I let it flow, son, I let the fingers do the walking and the music do the talking.'

'That's lovely,' said Natasha.

Joe trusted himself only to nod. But his nod was vigorous. Memphis Slim glanced over Natasha's shoulder.

'Well now, people,' he said. 'My little lady's given me the call.' He picked up his glass, only one modest sip taken, and stood up.

'Will you be here for the next set?'

'No,' said Natasha, even as Joe was swallowing the last hiccup and ready to relaunch his questions. 'We have to eat.'

'We all have to eat. *A bientôt?*'

'*Peut-être. Mais, merci infiniment.*'

'You take care,' he said to Joe. And he was gone.

A few minutes later Natasha manoeuvred Joe into getting the bill, out of the cellar and up onto the street where the cold December air smacked into his face and seemed to wake him from a trance.

'I had to get the hiccups.'

'It didn't show. I'm sure he didn't even notice,' said Natasha, taking his arm firmly and walking towards the nearby Boulevard St Michel. 'He knew you were a real admirer. That's why he joined us.'

'Did he? Are you sure?'

'*Absolument.*'

'That's why he joined us?'

'Of course.'

'He's great, isn't he? Isn't he terrific? Memphis Slim.'

'Formidable,' she said, 'they are brave, these blacks.' She steered him towards a restaurant. 'But we must eat.' She did not remind him that he had ripped her away from a dinner carefully prepared for them by Véronique, who had not insisted and done so with grace, which had left Natasha more admiring of her than she wanted to be.

Joe would not be rushed.

'Let's go and look at the Seine,' he said. 'It is our last night, after all. We can always eat.'

So they strolled under the trees, on the very bank of the river, the lights bobbing in the dark gliding water, calm down there almost under the city. Joe thought he would call his film *Ill Met in Paris*. There would be this brilliant young woman, an artist who had run away from home as a girl and, after adventures only revealed in fragments as the film went on, after rejection and near starvation, after humiliation and poverty which had led her to sleep under the bridges of Paris alongside the dangerous *clochards*, the tramps who found the bridge their only roof, an Englishman, not unlike himself, but an Englishman in a state of existential ennui would be loitering with ominous purpose on the very bank along which they now walked arm in arm, and see coming towards him, this shadow, this dark creature, walking away from the taunts of the *clochards*, and . . .

'What are you thinking about, Joseph?'

'Why don't we live in Paris? You could write and paint here so much more easily. I could write a film.'

'Are you serious?'

'Yes,' he said, instantly.

'Joseph? You have the BBC.'

'But look at Paris.'

Natasha admitted only much later that she too had dreamed of that on their Christmas visit. She knew that Joe could be the catalyst enabling her to come home, to her friends, to her language, to her city. Maria Troubnikoff had told her of a little apartment in her district, very cheap. Perhaps she could get into the Collège des Beaux-Arts, which would please her father.

'There's a BBC office in Paris,' said Joe. Natasha felt a rush of hope. 'Could you work there?'

'I could work there.'

The moment he said that, Joe knew that the bureaucracy would not allow it. He had been taken on by the BBC as a trainee to follow a route laid out for him by them. There could be no other route. Even his short experience of the corporation had given him enough insight to fear the consequences of challenging their plans.

'Are you sure, Joseph?'

She tried to ask it casually. They were nearly opposite the end of l'Ile de la Cité furthest from Notre Dame. The few cars were no more than a pleasant hum over the high river wall. They were alone on this stretch. Joe had been thinking he would have an accordion play over this passage. But Natasha's silence after her question brought something of her seriousness to bear on him. It demanded a truthful response.

'I don't suppose I could get a position right away,' he said. 'To be honest. But later, if things go well, there's no reason I shouldn't try to get a transfer here. In a year or two. I could try then.'

'I can't ask you to promise,' said Natasha. 'A promise can be a curse. But, well, I am glad.' She paused. 'Thank you.'

In the low dabbing light from the widely spaced lamps, he could not see her eyes, but from the tone of her words he saw her expression and was moved by it. He would return: he swore that to himself. He would bring her back to Paris. At times, not on great occasions, just at small turning times, she could pierce him to the root.

He took her in his arms and she clung to him. It was as if they had been lost and now were found but feared that soon they could be lost again. They stood in that tight unmoving embrace a few yards from the river for no more than a minute or two but it seemed an age and when they uncoupled there was a sense of frailty, the one without the other.

'Now we must eat,' said Natasha.

They turned and headed back the way they had come, walking quite quickly, holding hands lightly, and then Joe swung his arm, swinging hers with it, feeling self-conscious even in the semi-dark of a foreign city, but in his mind's eye seeing them there, at large in Paris, the bite of the cold air giving yet more life to their life.

'I would have a song from Edith Piaf over this bit,' Joe said, 'or maybe Georges Brassens would be better. Let's waltz!'

He took her in his arms and he sang '*Sous les Ponts de Paris*' and they waltzed, just a few turns, just a few yards, but they waltzed on the banks of the Seine in sight of Notre Dame.

'You're mad, Joseph,' she said, 'you're completely mad.'

Under the bridges of Paris, they danced on under the bridges of Paris, they whirled, one-two-three, one-two-three, they danced until the cold air tingled in their lungs and they ran out of breath. Natasha loved him singing to her, no one else had ever done that, singing in his English French as they danced that night, '*Sous les Ponts de Paris*'.

CHAPTER SIXTEEN

It was in Cumberland that Natasha understood how different Joseph was. It was there that was planted the seed of what would become her intense study of him.

When the train passed Watford Joe said,

'This is further north than you have ever been.'

Natasha looked out of the window, indifferent to what she thought of as the indifferent landscape. She was insulating herself in fiction. The Stevenses had sent her *A Severed Head* for Christmas, written, they said, by a good friend of theirs, and she had just got round to reading it. The story in the book happily blanked out the story of their journey into Joseph's birthland.

When the train pulled into the metropolis of steam called Crewe Station, he said,

'We are now entering Another World. The North.'

They were lucky, he thought, to be sharing their second-class compartment with just two others, respectable middle-aged women travelling together but mercifully, Joe thought, as absorbed in their books as Natasha and himself. One of them was reading *The Prime of Miss Jean Brodie* and the only semblance of a conversation they had had was when she passed the book over to her friend with her index finger on what was probably a particularly felicitous paragraph. This was read silently; a smile was enough to convey appreciation and approval. Joe was determined to finish *Catch-22* before Carlisle. He had bought it for his father.

When the train stopped in Wigan and overlooked the town, Joe said, fiercely, 'That is as fine a townscape as I've seen. Not just the look of it. What it's been through.'

This time Natasha looked with interest. She saw from the height of the train a forest floor of chimney pots, every one streaming with smoke; she saw what seemed to be miles of identical terraces, small brick houses with small back yards and small front doors opening directly onto ugly narrow streets. The late winter light was already waning and she saw it through gloom and greyness. She saw no one on the streets. It was poor, uniform, dull and, she thought, beyond all aesthetic redemption. What did he mean by 'fine'? But when she glanced at him she observed that he was as wrapped up in it as she had been and there was no irony in him. His voice had been fierce; his look was affectionate. Natasha kept her reservations to herself and plunged back into the more familiar world of Iris Murdoch.

As the train left Carnforth after a brief stop, Joe put aside Joseph Heller's novel, unable to resist the landscape. It was near dark but the big skies and the bare-pelted hills held onto the light and to Joe the slow chug of the train, as it went up the mountain which fortified his home county against the South, was like the overture to a magnificent performance. Seeing how absorbed he was, Natasha tried to see it through Joe's expression which was rapt, as if he were at a film. The hills were smooth, shapely, she thought, but very bare. Now and then a fast-running silver stream slashed through a slender ghyll. There were only a handful of farms, down in the valleys. The sky was cloud-steely, taking no colour from the masked setting sun, but adding, she could see, to the wholeness of this scene, the sense of sombre grandeur, of outpost. He looked at her, and broke into a grin and reached for her thigh, touching it only for a moment so as not to offend the two ladies travelling together to Glasgow.

At the top of Shap Fell, Joe said,

'Cumberland ahoy. Sit back!'

The tons of steel were pointed due north and went steeply down at over a hundred miles an hour as the engine swooped to the plain, swerved on the curved lines through Penrith and full speed across the flatlands to Carlisle.

'I was born here,' Joe said as they stepped onto the platform.

'Home.'

'No. Wigton's home.'

They had less than an hour to wait for the country train to complete the last ten miles of the weary three-hundred-mile journey. From Wigton Station they walked up into the town, in the dusk, passing muffled figures, every one of whom greeted them without breaking step.

Natasha's first impressions of Wigton were polarised.

'You are like a hunting dog, Joseph,' she said, 'one who has picked up a scent and becomes more frenzied the stronger the scent grows.'

True. He was alight.

On Station Road they were passed by a small marching band singing 'Glory Glory Hallelujah' as they returned to the Salvation Rooms after their Saturday night missionary work at the end of Water Street. The main street was poorly lit and all the shops were shut. When they finally heaved their luggage through the door of the as yet unbusy pub, Natasha was met by a flurry of embarrassment, over-attention and offers of provision. They went into the kitchen where an early customer was drinking a pint of bitter. Joseph went into the bar to talk arrangements with Sam. The kitchen, the stranger later explained to Natasha, was the best room in the house; beer a penny dearer, but more of a homely room than a pub. There was also a darts room and a singing room.

'Just for singing?' she asked.

'That's the idea.'

And then a bar – men only. The stranger asked her if she would like a drink but she refused and then felt she had been impolite but could find no words to retrieve the situation.

Others came in over the next hour or so while she tried to eat a meal prepared in the scullery by Ellen. Natasha experienced a rather fearful shyness. The accents were warm, the expressions on the faces were tolerant and cheerful, there was nothing but kindness and yet she felt she was on shifting sands. The very kitchen became macabre, so many smiling faces, how could she judge them? So many kind questions, how could she answer them? So much food to be publicly consumed while others watched, how could she eat? How could she not eat? Joseph seemed oblivious to this public feeding. Natasha saw only certainties, a solidity, a deep foundation for Joseph, a good childhood, she thought, one which was firm, one which she had never had. By contrast it sent her back to her own childhood uncertainties, the unsmiling faces, the lack of solidity. Who was she here, and why?

'I feel awful about it.'

Ellen had ushered Joe upstairs. They stood on the landing.

'Your dad and me thought of giving up our bed,' she said.

Joe was impatient. The Saturday evening hubbub was building up and Natasha was abandoned for the second time; he had seen the worry in her when he had been called out of the kitchen.

'It's terrible.' Ellen's distressed tone commanded Joe's full attention. He looked closely at his mother. Her eyes were strained as if threatening tears. 'Your own son comes to see you with his new wife and you can't put them up. What sort of life is that?'

'It's fine. Honestly. Natasha doesn't mind.'

'How could we put you in the two single rooms?'

'You couldn't. We understand.'

'But, Joe,' she said and reached out to touch his arm as if pleading with him, a gesture he had never before encountered, a gesture which moved him to stillness, to hope it would pass, 'we ought to be able to put up you and your wife and maybe all four of us spend the evening together.'

'You will. We will. We're here for a few days.'

'I'm sorry.'

His eagerness to assuage her pain was the reassurance she had sought.

'Of course we will.'

'There's a lot to catch up on,' he said.

'There is. I'll follow you down. You go back to Natasha.'

'She's been looking forward to this.'

'Yes. You go to her now. You go.'

And still obedient to the commands of childhood, he went down the stairs. Ellen took a few deep breaths. In the bathroom she splashed water on her face. In the mirror she told herself not to be a fool. In her heart she could not stop the burn – of shame? Of loss? It was too hard to distinguish.

Joe and Natasha set off soon afterwards, another journey, this time by car, driven by Joe's Uncle Leonard, now retired, a wise man who saw they needed some peace and saw that they had it as he motored with exemplary caution out of the town, south, and into the hills, to the pitch-black village of Caldbeck in which they had rented a terraced cottage for the week. Joe's polite invitation to stay for a cup of tea was as politely refused and Leonard drove back even more slowly, wanting to draw every nuance possible from their meeting. She was, he thought, difficult to weigh up.

Though Joe lit the fire, already laid, and brought down a side light from the bedroom to replace the glare of the central bulb, though stores had been brought up earlier in the day from Wigton and half a dozen bottles of beer were part of the reception committee, though the radio played Chopin and the room was a haven, Natasha felt depressed. 'I may have caught a cold,' she said, 'what do you say? Nursing? I may be nursing a cold.'

She slept badly and was troubled by dreams and felt out of the reach of Joseph. She tried to find her bearings, with a husband becoming strange to her in this place.

—⟋⟍—

Natasha awoke to the sounds of ducks. She stretched out her hands; his side of the bed was already cold. She felt heavy-limbed but the bustle of sounds coming up the stairs levered her out of bed. She parted the curtains and saw, across the little path which ran by a fast stream, the village duck pond and two small children dressed, she assumed, for church, a boy and a girl, carefully feeding morsels of bread to the strutting, quacking colony of Caldbeck ducks. The boy was nervous; the girl – it must have been his sister – far bolder, taking him by the hand, leading him towards the fat and noisy ducks. Natasha looked on until the father arrival in a dark coat and dark hat and called for the children who came, the boy running, the girl dragging, and went across to a further road which, Natasha guessed, would take them to the tinny peal of the church bell. She wove happy threads of domestic content-ment around them. Soon the ducks ceased to quack. A lady sped down the last lap of the hill guiding her bicycle with one hand, the other holding onto her hat. Natasha's eyes pricked and she felt a rise of enveloping unaccountable happiness as the darkness began to lift. Joseph called for her.

'Thought you'd never get up,' he said and the sight of him blew away any remaining shadows. White shirtsleeves rolled up above the elbow, smuts of coal on his forearms from where he had re-laid and relit the fire, face smiling and ruddy from the fresh air in the handkerchief back garden, hair flopping over his brow, and accent, she noticed, rather broader and warmer. 'Boiled eggs. Toast. Marmalade. You won't want cornflakes. Water on the go for tea. Would madam come this way?'

Still in her black dressing gown, Natasha edged her way around the cluttered furniture in what in daylight seemed an even smaller room than she remembered, and through to a yet smaller space, the kitchen, which with the recently added bathroom constituted the whole of the ground floor.

The table was laid. Joe held out a chair for her and then put a white paper napkin across her knees.

'I do hope the eggs – farmyard fresh and brown to boot – are to madam's liking,' he said. 'Perhaps a little harder on account of the wait while madam proceeded at her leisure down the grand staircase. Shall I butter your toast?'

'There are ducks,' she said, 'out there.'

'I'm very pleased they turned up, madam. Quite expensive, ducks, especially Caldbeck ducks, and not always reliable, but I did want you to start your day with a Cumbrian duck. I owe them half a loaf of bread.'

'It looks a very pretty village – from the window.'

'Positioned for the purpose,' he said. 'Caldbeck is, in my view, the gem of the Northern fells. Once a thriving town, with several grand houses, not least the vicarage, formerly a house for lepers. When we take the air – after madam has performed her toilet, or rather concluded her toilet – she will see the village set in a bowl of hills, an unpoetic soul would call it a pudding basin with Caldbeck happily settled in the bottom of the bowl.'

'What else?' She could not resist his delight in showing and telling her of this place.

'Cald-beck, you ask? Beck is a local word for stream. Cald must mean cold, the Scots, our deadly neighbours, pronounce cold as cald and so do we Cumbrians and moreover it is true, the water is cold, pure from the hills.'

'Joseph!'

'Did you call me?' He held his toast as if it were a baton, waiting to beat out the decisive chord. But Natasha just shook her head. She loved it when he played the fool.

'I thought it would be like Wigan,' she said, 'that smoke, those terraced houses.'

'Knock not Wigan,' said Joe. 'Wigan works for the world we live in.'

They strolled alongside the river which went past the east end of the church. There was sun, weak but sufficient to give Natasha a holiday feeling. She held his arm rather tightly and she could feel a physical uncoiling of tensions in her stomach on this placid early spring Sunday morning, buds just beginning to show, Joseph earthed.

'It is not England here,' she said, 'the mountains are like a fortress.'

'That's what we all like to think,' he said, as he stopped to scoop a few smooth pebbles out of the shallow sparkling stream. 'But it only works for some of the time.'

'It's like Provence,' she said, 'where the peasants never want to leave.'

'You've caught it on a good day,' said Joseph, selecting the smoothest of the pebbles. 'Our biggest export is people.'

'I'll give you Jean Giono's novels,' she said. 'You'll see. He is the great novelist of Provence.'

'Of the peasants?'

'Yes.'

'Like us peasants?'

'Yes.' She smiled and he acknowledged the tease.

He skimmed a stone across the surface of the water.

'Two,' he said, 'not much cop.' He tried again. The stone plopped. 'You try.'

'I can't throw stones.'

'We used to fight with stones like these when we were kids,' Joe said. 'One gang on one bank, another on the other. We would agree a time for a stone fight and turn up and just pelt each other.' He smiled.

'That's where I got this.' He pointed to the small scar trace beside his left eye.

'Fight with stones?'

For a moment Joe felt foolishly heroic. Natasha shook her head.

'We used to bike here from Wigton and go up into these woods,' he waved towards the adjacent hillside, 'the trees were so bushy and close together we could go from tree to tree.'

'Like monkeys?'

'Yes.'

'And you had battles there as well?'

'We built stockades, yes. You would use branches as lances and dig pits and put pointed sticks in them.'

'To maim your friends?'

'We didn't think of it like that.'

'I suppose you did bare-fist fighting?'

'We did. I did. I wasn't very good at it. I didn't like it.'

'Why did you do it?'

'You did.' Joe slung another pebble at the water. A flash of memory, of the sickening fear of bare-fist fights came over him. 'You just did.'

'For honour?'

'That's laying it on a bit thick.'

'It was,' said Natasha, thoughtfully. 'It was for honour. Wasn't it? Just as you were disappointed with yourself when you did not hit Robert after he had insulted you.'

'I should have clocked him one, yes.'

'Clocked?'

'Hit.'

'Why?'

He stopped. He did not want to be reminded of Robert. Even retrospective jealousy was disturbing.

'We are in Sicily,' said Natasha. 'Honour.'

'Corsica!' Joe said. '*The Corsican Brothers.*'

'I begin to understand. There is no café in Caldbeck of course.'

'Of course not.'

'And if there were, women would be banned.'

'Come on!'

'Ceaseless childbearing and the church and enslaved to the house.'
'Tradition.'
'While the men drink in the pubs.'
'Or work in the fields or work in the mines.'
'But later they drink in the pubs.'
'Some of them. There are many nonconformist teetotallers in these fells.'
'I am trying,' said Natasha sternly, 'to build up a picture of your background. This is important for our future.'
'Then we'd best go to Wigton immediately!'
They laughed, and after Joe had made a quick survey, they kissed each other, in public, far too closely, Joe thought, and at far too great a length for a Caldbeck Sunday morning.
'First we must pay the ducks,' said Natasha.

They went to Wigton three times.

Natasha's memories of Wigton from that visit were as of a triptych. The single figure of Joseph dominated one panel; the single figure of Sam the other; and between them, like a crowd moving in procession towards a shrine, the faces and voices of her new husband's old home. It was not unlike a Breughel, she thought.

Once in the town Joseph was like a hound off a leash. He took her into Church Street and pointed out the marvel of a street shaped like a crooked leg and little yards and even smaller alleys off; the pig market in the middle of it where they had stolen in to play hounds and hares and the runnels down to the High Street where they had hidden when the Chair-leg Gang swept down from Bridlefield, running hard and looking for a fight; the slaughterhouse where he had watched the sudden sickening buckle of knees as the gun to the head was fired, and the West Cumberland Farmers' Warehouse out of which came a smell of grain so thick it could have been eaten. And above Eddie Bell's father's shop Eddie had made a gym, he had weights and chest expanders and photographs of Mr Universe papering the wall; Blob lived in this house, Mazza in that, next to Mr Routledge who had led the union at the factory and then notoriously, unforgivably, switched to the management, and Peter Donnelly who had to sleep with all the windows open because of his TB had set up as a photographer at the top of those stone stairs. This was just part of what he told her about one street.

He took her to the bottom of Meeting House Lane to see the Salvation Army Hall whose youth club he had patronised, as he had those of the Methodists, for the table tennis; the Roman Catholics, for the dances; and of course his own church, the Church of England, for the Anglican Young People's Association and the socials. Also in Meeting House Lane under one of the many arches that led off the two main streets was the Palace Picture House in which he had seen hundreds of films.

She was marched the length of slumland Water Street whose heroes and villains and crowded histories of war and peace were unrolled, a scroll of battle and survival. He took her along the Crofts which dated, he told her proudly, from the eighth century and squirrelled her around the wriggling tentacles which stretched out from Market Hill, Birdcage Walk, down Burnfoot, up Plaskett's Lane, and wove her back to the network behind the Parish Rooms. He did not go into the churches and the many chapels but pointed them out, insisting she be impressed by their number and variety.

It was something of a fever, she thought, and puzzled over its intensity. What she saw was a plain little town, not flattered by the drizzle, a place of little colour and animation, dead on the first day they visited, admittedly a Sunday, Natasha thought at first that the deadness revealed its true character.

Until the next day when, shyly, he led her into a yard off Water Street. The cloud was high, light pearl grey, the yard small, empty and surely condemned, Natasha thought, as they emerged into it through a short tunnel. It was, she thought, a pitiful hovel. She felt love for the small boy who had lived in this awful place. Joseph had told her with some regret that it was about to be demolished.

'Four houses,' he announced, looking at her proudly, she thought, and a little fiercely, 'one up, one down, one wash house and one shared WC over there.' He let it sink in for a while. He had discovered that she was as impressed and intrigued by the context of his past as he had been with hers. This both moved and surprised him. Her sense of the equality of their lives had never struck him so strongly and he was grateful. He had never been ashamed of his past but he had never thought he could boast about it. Natasha licensed him to do so and he leaped at the chance. And this hovel, as he saw it through her eyes, this sanctuary as he himself remembered it from the time his father had returned from the war, this place now abandoned was not to be hidden away.

'There was a man called Kettler lived in that house,' he pointed. 'He lived on tripe and beer and never did a day's work. He cadged and odd-jobbed at the cattle and pig auctions and once he drowned some kittens just there. I saved one!'

Natasha smiled.

'There was a girl lived next to us who loved that kitten but I rationed her helpings with it. Why was I so mean? I went to see her with Mam and the cat just before she died. She was only about eight. In a sanatorium. She had TB. There was an epidemic of TB in Wigton just after the war. My mother had it. And though I didn't find this out until I had glandular fever, they told me at the hospital that I'd had it, in 1945. It can't have been much of a dose. My mother never told me and I can't remember a thing about it. But I can remember,' rather reluctantly, 'that WC stank. My mother used to try to keep it fresh. But it stank. There was another girl . . . she went to Germany with her mother. The town was made up of yards like this. We thought they were just great.' He looked around and she lost him for a few moments. The eye of love, she thought.

'I used to have a dream,' he said. 'There was this girl buried in a field I used to play in. It was the girl with TB. I was convinced, in the dream, that I'd murdered her and one day she would be dug up.'

So much had happened here, she thought, so much had happened to Joseph here in this yard and in these mean streets and lanes and insignificant alleyways, so much that mattered so deeply to him . . .

He was infused by it, drunk on it, she thought. Yet it was not just this place, it was in Joseph himself. He had been just as swept up in France, she thought, though she had feared at first that he was merely over-impressed. He had been overwhelmed by the BBC, though that could have been no more than that he was suffering from a kind of vertigo having been rocketed beyond all expectation. And here, in Wigton, though fiercer, it was the same and she saw that he had the energy and the capacity to embrace whatever appealed strongly to him, an un-embarrassed love for what moved him, a love, she thought, unafraid to express itself. This she had never before encountered. His almost shameless, certainly reckless, but wholly genuine embrace of life both puzzled and beguiled her.

—m—

'He's very loyal,' said Sam.

'Why do you say that?'

Sam smiled and let it drift. Both of them knew the answer. Joe had gone to spend time with Alan, his oldest friend, to whom Natasha had already been introduced. Ellen was making afternoon tea – lunch was impossible with the pub's opening hours. She had shooed away Natasha's offer of help and Sam was taking her for a walk 'around the Backs' – along Tenter's Row, over the hill called Stoneybanks to the Swimming Baths, and back up a small hill into Proctor's Row against St Mary's Church.

Sam strolled where Joseph had marched. Sam was thoughtful and measured in contrast to Joseph's gleam-eyed championing. Three times they were passed by men with dogs; on each occasion Sam was warmly greeted and Natasha was swiftly, slyly, appraised.

'Is he like you?'

'You ask some blunt questions, Natasha. Is he like me?'

'Is he?'

'We had very different "bringings-up". Life was just harder in my time. Not that Joe – well, not that Joe didn't have his problems.'

'What problems? Was it to do with being different?'

'Do you think he is different?'

'How else could he have come out of here?'

'More hard-working, I'd say, than different. And determined.' He paused. 'A bit different.'

'What were these problems, Sam?'

Whenever she said his name, Sam felt a weakening. The more so in this case as she accompanied it by slipping her arm through his. She was a little taller than he was, but the reach of their stride was in perfect unison. There was that about her which touched Sam to a tenderness he must once have felt for Ellen, he told himself, but perhaps not even for her. There was some mixture of frailty and boldness in Natasha, as if there were no defences but no fear either and yet she called out for protection. She was a woman you could gladly spend a lifetime getting to know.

'He found things a bit of a strain,' he said, 'at times.'

'The examination work?'

'Not so much that, more what it was leading to.'

'Or leading from?'

Sam nodded. She was always onto it.

'He was a good swimmer,' Sam said, as they passed by the Public Baths, built, she noticed, in the warm sandstone which was, she thought, the best feature of the town's architecture.

'Have I married a hero?'

'You don't have to tackle anybody when you swim.'

'I have not seen him confrontational.'

'Both of you took a lot on trust.'

The drizzle strengthened. As if to shield her from it, he held her arm a little more tightly.

'He often tells me that you could have done what he has done.'

'Does he?' Sam was almost stopped in his tracks. 'Does he now?'

'He says he thinks you're cleverer than him. He also admires you for fighting in the war in the Far East. But he says you can't talk about it.'

'Does he?'

'You seem amazed.'

Sam said nothing but pressed her arm gently; to stop.

'Were you scarred by the war, Sam?'

'Very likely.' He paused. 'Sometimes I think Ellen and Joe had the worst of it.'

'Why was that?'

'You can probably work it out better than I can, Natasha. I haven't got the psychology.'

'You mean you don't want to . . . He's very confident,' Natasha said, and waited to be challenged.

'I'm glad you find him so,' he said. 'I can't give him any maps for where he is or where he's going. Mine ran out long ago. But he'll need all the help going.'

'Why?'

'You know why, Natasha. He's finding places he's no idea of and . . .'

'Yes?' He's about to say, 'He's weak,' she thought.

'He's very lucky, to my mind,' Sam said, most deliberately, eyes straight ahead, 'to have you by his side.'

Natasha was moved. I have found another father, she said to herself. Or rather, I have found Sam, my father-in-law. Joe had to be rooted in Sam, hadn't he? 'Will you tell me about – Burma? It was terrible, wasn't it?'

And Sam told her, freely, as he had never told Joe who, when he learned of it, was both proud of his wife's drawing blood from that stone and envious of her closeness to his father.

A few days later on his people tour, Joe took Natasha to the cattle auction to witness the Tuesday Sale. They sat at the back of the crowded arena, a wooden structure, roof, walls and bare-board seats, a circular central sand-floored space for the display of the cattle. Here beasts turned into money following the chant of the high priest, Josh Benson, auctioneer. His rapid half-sung drone from the altar of his desk summoned the faithful to buy. 'I have ten bid, ten bid, ten bid, ten bid ten, bid ten, eleven, twelve, twelve bid twelve and thirteen, I have thirteen bid, thirteen bid, thirteen bid, fourteen, fourteen bid, fourteen bid, over there fifteen, I have fifteen, sixteen, seventeen, I have seventeen bid, seventeen bid, seventeen, I have . . .'

Natasha was entranced by the sound and Joe directed her to the faces, all topped by a flat cap, real Cumbrian faces, Joseph whispered, some concentrated, some cunning, some nursing pain, but strong faces, he pointed out to her afterwards, faces you saw again and again in the district, careful, world-worn, Northern, Norse, faces of farming men whose way of life had changed so little and stretched back unbroken beyond biblical years. Joseph, she thought, you are a fathomless romantic about your own past.

—m—

'I'm his Uncle Colin.' They were outside the Co-op: Joseph had paused there and for a moment Natasha had feared he might take her in to face more introductions. Instead Colin, to whom he had referred a little and guardedly, popped out, clad in black motorcycling leather. 'I expect he's been trying to avoid you and me meeting up.'

'No I haven't!'

Colin did not take his eyes off Natasha. Always hit them right between the eyes, that was his tactic. He transferred the brown carrier bag to his left hand. 'Stores,' he explained, and held out his right. '*Bonjour*, anyway. *Parlez-vous*. I expect you think Wigton's a dump.'

'Not at all.'

'It isn't a dump!' Joe was indignant.

'Joe always defends the little place,' said Colin, his eyes still 'fixing' Natasha, unaware that this amused her. 'But then he doesn't live here any more.'

'There are very nice people here,' said Natasha and looked at Joseph to release herself from Colin's absurd attempt at a 'spell'.

'They'll be nice to you,' said Colin, 'they know you're here today, gone tomorrow. They can afford to be nice to you.'

'That's not fair!'

'Look at me,' said Colin. 'I've got a lifestyle that's a bit different. Most of them wouldn't know a lifestyle from a turnip. I like soul music. Glenn Miller's the limit for this lot. And television game shows. It's desperate here, mademoiselle, and I bet you won't come back in a hurry.'

'We are in Caldbeck,' Natasha said, helplessly.

'Good God! Has he taken you to Caldbeck?'

'It's a grand little place.'

'You,' jabbed out Colin, at last turning his full-frontal attention to his nephew, 'have sent me neither a letter nor a postcard in more than a year. You've got above yourself, Joe Richardson, and I'm sorry to be the

180

one to tell you. You've lost yourself. *Au revoir*, missus, and all the very best.'

He was gone.

'He was looking for a door,' Natasha said, as they watched him go, 'so that he could slam it.'

'He has his bad times,' said Joe anxiously, a little shaken. Colin could still shake him.

'It can't be easy being a homosexual in Wigton,' she said.

Joe's head seemed to turn in slow motion. To his knowledge, nobody had ever called Colin homosexual. If he himself had ever suspected it, the prospect of his mother's anger, and the iron-bound hoops of Victorian small-town hypocrisy, would have forbidden it to be articulated into thought, let alone spoken out loud, and on the streets and by a stranger to the place.

'Yes.' He swallowed very hard. 'Perhaps you're right but maybe, my mother, her half-brother . . .'

'I won't say anything to Ellen. Sam will know everything of course.'

There began in Joe a slow unravelling and recovering, a path to be followed deep into his childhood, words, looks, actions, suggestions, promises, invitations, to be reviewed: the whole jigsaw to be remade. For years he had denied that Colin, who had tickled him to hysteria and thrown him in the air until he was exhausted, who had sulked over card games and used his superior years and his status as Ellen's half-brother to dominate Joe, had any mark of homosexuality about him. When Natasha said, later and helpfully as she thought, that there must have been both fear and obligatory kinship warmth in his relationship with Colin and that must have shaped some of his dealings with men subsequently, Joseph refused to consider it and she let it pass. He had his own hidden cellars as she had and the doors were best not forced.

There were other shops to go into to meet friends of his who had taken up their family business, Johnston's Shoes, Saunderson's Hardware, Alan at the paper shop, William in the café. Then there arrived a memorable encounter, just before six, with the shops shutting down and the thirteen pubs opening up, Diddler arrived, zigzagging over the pavement, tipsy, from the tips from his jobs around the busy auctions, without his teeth as it was a working day, dressed like the gypsy he was, and one whose day had gone too well, but his gummy smile a beam of joy to Joe.

'Joseph!' He managed to come to a halt beside the Old Vic and used the wall as a prop. His hands had not moved from his pockets. 'Is this the lucky lady, Joseph?'

'It is. Natasha, this is Diddler. Diddler, Natasha. My wife.'

'Well now,' the old man heaved himself away from the wall and appeared to consider which hand to take out of the pocket. The left emerged. 'Congratulations now, missus. There we are. Another Mrs Richardson and may I say if you live up to the boy's mother you'll have nothing to be ashamed of.'

'Diddler and my father were brought up in the same buildings.'

'Down on Vinegar Hill. The council's destroyed them now. But I did well out of that one, Joe, and you and your da helped me with the slates and the lead and all. Still making money while it stays safe in the yard.'

'Joseph has talked about you,' Natasha said, remembering part of Joseph's rhapsody the previous day about this old gypsy as proof of the living archaeology of the town, where ancient scavengers still roamed.

'Has he now? What's he want to talk about me for?'

'He talked about having rides on your cart.'

'The old flat cart. I've still got it, Joe. And I've still got the horses, never fear about that. His father was a little gamecock,' said Diddler, 'frightened of nothing and nobody, Sam Richardson.'

'We went to the auction and into the Market Hall,' said Joe.

'Too dear, Joseph, too dear for ordinary folk. Now then. I know I should be offering you a present, but I made a bad move in the Lion and Lamb. The oldest trick in the world and I fell for it. A market fella out from Hexham way. You couldn't sub me a couple of bob for a day or so?'

'Yes. Here.' Quits, Joe thought.

'That was easily done, missus. If I'd known it was going to be that easy, I'd've asked for five. Never mind. So. Blessings on your house.'

And with a sidestep and a right swerve and a pinpoint forward lurch he left the damp, cold streets and toppled into the warm snug of the Old Vic.

'Sadie will be sorry to have missed you,' Ellen said, 'but they took her into hospital last week.'

'What is it?'

'They can't say.'

The three of them were in the kitchen, uninvaded at this hour. Three regulars kept Sam frustratingly trapped in the bar. In the darts room the Pearson brothers were practising for an evening of challenge games. The lights in the singing room were off, the fire unlit.

Ellen looked at them and saw they were happy. So why was there this tinge of sadness, too selfish to admit? When she and Sam talked at the end of the night, she said, 'We could take a pub down South, Sam, to be near them. Especially when they have a family. We'll be too far away then.'

Sam nodded – Ellen would never move – and went back to *Catch-22*.

They borrowed bicycles and strayed up into the bare hills whose blankness and grandeur, emptiness and splendour of shapes made them such a necessary landscape for Joe. When Natasha, more or less un-prompted, also declared for them and admired them in much the same terms, it was as if a rare gift had been fully appreciated. And she sketched the hills, bold lines encompassing mass, a close-up of a stone wall, a tipple of fell tops running towards the horizon, and clouds. She became obsessed with clouds but never satisfied, even angry at herself, finally, to Joe's consternation, tearing up every one of the cloud sketches.

On their last morning he took her up to the spectacular hidden waterfall on the southern rim of Caldbeck. It was called the Howk. It looked as if a particularly stubborn glacial finger had been so reluctant to be withdrawn north, to be called back by the Gods of the Arctic, that it had gouged out this great raw cleft now deep in woods.

The noise of the waterfall was as thrilling as the sight, Joseph said, and Natasha nodded, once again happy in his happiness. They walked up the narrow slippery path beside the fall and the force of water. At first Joe tried to tell her about other waterfalls described by Words-worth and Southey and the gothic tales set around them. She nodded but did not encourage him. He understood: he too wanted to be alone on this cliff of fall.

Natasha was absorbed in this radiant sight: the white perpetually changing chutes of water, the spray sometimes catching the winter sun through the trees and sparkling with colours, the trees above them, bare-boughed, stripped of all leaves, in mourning. Words were no use, too certain for this unceasing motion of water and light, words would only hold back the flow of these sensations alchemising into imagination, into a dream of life. Did this represent the life she could have with Joseph?

At the top of the fall they looked down at the way they had come. The waterfall hit the black rocks and split into furious strands, foaming between those disruptive obstacles. Natasha put her arm around Joseph's waist and leaned her head on his shoulder. Often enough when the chance arose, they had made love in the open, always instigated by Joseph. Now, having grown so much closer to him on his home ground, it was she who wanted the seal of sex.

But, though he put his arm around her, though he drew her close and kissed her, there was no more. A little later, when they were circling the village for the last time, she thought she understood why it was so. He must have made love to Rachel there.

By indirections, over patient months, she found out that had been the case and she was impressed that he had kept the place faithful to the girl of his youth.

CHAPTER SEVENTEEN

François brought Natasha a project; himself. When she met him at Victoria Station on that smog-stricken late January afternoon, she was first moved to pity at the small slight figure so timidly looking out for her and then, when his wasted face lit up at the sight of her, the pity turned to love. Someone had to love him, had to, she thought, as the nakedly relieved face pressed towards her through the crowd and she felt the imminence of unexpected tears at this trust, this hope, this delivery of himself into her hands. He has never known love, she thought, not the love without question that Joseph gives to me, not the love that is a rock. She would give him that.

In the weeks and months that followed (he stayed for almost a calendar year in London), Natasha dedicated herself to this task. She saw the afflicting effect of her stepmother, she saw the impatient neglect of their father, she saw prejudice and lack of charity, she saw ignorance and lack of understanding. There was something of herself in François. They had tried to box and straitjacket her too; she would never forget that.

She did not calculate the harm that might come to her from going back into a time of her life from which she had jaggedly liberated herself with such a protracted and wounding effort. Joseph offered her a bridge back to her past but it would only serve, she had told herself, for a little while. It would prove her worth to her father and confound her stepmother and indulge Joseph, so dazzled by her old world, so blind to it. But this bridge, she believed, was nothing but a drawbridge, to be hauled up whenever she had a mind. François was a road which drove into the heart of her darkness. To help François thoroughly was to risk reactivating the terrified misery of her childhood and yet she did not hesitate: from the moment she saw him on Victoria Station she reached out to save him.

She watched over him. When he returned in the mid-afternoons from l'Ecole Normale in Kensington, he came back not to his lodgings eighteen doors down the street, but to her, to her kitchen or the garden as spring grew warmer, to tea or coffee around the table or under the willow, to chat for hours sometimes but only rarely about his work, mostly about himself, the story of himself, free at last to tell his heroic anecdotal autobiography, portraying himself as cunning, shrewd, a swashbuckler. Or he would recount jokes, he collected jokes; and then occasionally there would be grandly shallow adolescent generalities about international affairs.

'He wants so much to be like our father,' she told Joseph for whom she assumed François was as inexhaustible a subject as he was to herself, 'he has opinions on everything. Sometimes I suspect he may be parodying my father. No world event can arise without François giving it the benefit of his reflections. They are rarely more than one sentence long but stated with ambassadorial authority.'

Joe soon found that he would unconsciously time these conversations. He liked François and was pleased to be the sort of man who could do such a favour for his wife's family and he was glad, glad and grateful, that, when he thought of Natasha in the cold Finchley flat while he was embraced in work, she was not alone. Yet despite this, there was a little jealousy; that François should now threaten him as the centre of Natasha's attention. He tried to deflect this by reminding himself that brothers and sisters were uncharted territory to him and had their own rules which were part of a wholly different engagement. He suppressed the occasional irritation of envy when he arrived back tired to the sound of fresh voices, unworn by the railroad of daily slog however much he enjoyed it. His work was a pleasure but even work-pleasure could be tiring and that was confusing. Everywhere simplicities were on the retreat. He loved his work but sometimes it took too much and he resented it even though he could not believe his luck.

So sometimes when Natasha talked about François he shamefully counted the minutes until he could change the subject without hurting her feelings or move away and get to his writing. He could see how much it meant to her that François was growing happier and that she was the cause, she was the giver; he could see that it made her bloom, to be the giver. 'He talks about his life,' she said, 'but in such a way that even he must know I know he is fibbing. He does so little, that is the truth. He appears to have no friends. He goes to the cinema. It's good for him that so many French films are shown in London. He's interesting about films – not like you – but from his own viewpoint. The films are always related to his own life. He could be the hero, he derides the bad men, he would not make that stupid mistake, he doesn't believe someone could do that. It's refreshing after all that Nouvelle Vague film criticism. And of course he is always talking about the breasts of the actresses.'

The films were the only part of the deal to which Joe found he rather objected. It was unfair, it was impolite, but he did not like to go to films with both François and Natasha. The two of them went on their own in late afternoons and that was fine. Even when they did go, the three of them, Natasha's attention was not on the film, not on him, but on François's reactions. After *Last Year in Marienbad* for instance, whose puzzle Joe had tried to solve when they came home, he had been irritated that his ideas were so raucously dismissed by François, who was supported by Natasha's teasing laughter.

'It is peculiar what is inherited,' she said. 'We know about my father's memory. Yours is strong too though not in the same areas, more to do with your own history than History. But François's memory is equally formidable. Except it is mostly for jokes. Often rude jokes. Some are quite funny. I can spend whole afternoons with him and most of the time he is telling me jokes. He told me he reads books of jokes, they pass them round in l'Ecole – but his retention of those jokes is phenomenal. So it is there, you see, it is all in place. It just has to be redirected.'

'You sound like your father,' said Joe.

'No! My father only respects certain sorts of knowledge. I respect the mind that can reach out for knowledge. He has never allowed François to have a mind because François does not follow his rules.'

'But you also want François to follow a path he's clearly not keen on.'

'How do you know what he is keen on?'

'He told me once that most of all he would like to drive big lorries,' said Joe.

'They would not let him do that.'

'Why not? Why don't you make him feel it's OK to want to drive big lorries? Would you be ashamed of that?'

'That is unfair, Joseph! That is very unfair.'

'I'm sorry.'

'That is very unfair. And untrue.'

'I'm sorry. Sometimes he looks so lost. Do you think it really helps him to be out of his own country? You've told me how much you miss about France and the language – and your English is wonderful, you've been here for years, you have friends, you have me. He's adrift here, isn't he? He's alone but for us. He's an exile.'

'Exile can be good. You are an exile. I saw that when we were in Wigton. The language they speak, that you once spoke, you no longer speak. The society you lived in is not the society you live in now. Your expectations and ambitions have changed utterly. You have to find new bearings in this new world. Even Sam can't help you. You are an exile in London, it is another country, and it does you good.'

'Does it?' Onto the screen in Joe's mind flowed images of the ceaselessly expanding opportunities and riches of this life, this work, this London, the current pulling him towards strange and unknown seas. 'But I have to do it. Is it the same for François? Does it do him good?'

'It will.'

'Do you mean, you will make it be good for him?'

'Perhaps.' She needed help. 'Do I?'

'Yes,' he said, immediately, and his affirmation, spoken as he looked at her with all the love he could muster, released in her a smile of contentment.

'I cut François's hair today,' she said. 'Would you like me to cut yours?'

'It'll save a bob or two.'

'He has learned to sing "Hit the Road, Jack" in English. You should ask him to do it for you. I know he can't sing, but . . .'

'I'm glad he's here,' Joe said and did not add, 'for your sake more than for his because he gives you a purpose, when I am gone.'

———〜———

'Looking back,' Joe told their daughter, 'roving the city for broadcasting material, and by that token given a passport to enter otherwise forbidden reaches of society, door after door would open. There were treasures, secrets and the flattering corruption of privilege. London began to draw me in, a willing victim, tempting, enthralling, poisoning, transforming. I was half in bondage to it and half the untutored Goth raiding Rome in lust for its loot. I could not wait to get at the city, and work was a carnival.

'The traineeship entailed postings around the BBC and after the World Service I was sent to the Headquarters – Broadcasting House, standing like a battleship in Portland Place in Central London, a bulldog building, shaped to rule the airwaves the world over. My job, in the Features Department, I was told, was to be a dogsbody. Some dogs!

'There was a radio producer who was a poet, for whom I worked on his translation and production of Goethe's *Faust*. Save on production days he strolled in grandly at about half ten or eleven, strolled across to the pub just before one o'clock, strolled back about three, napped, penned, moved off smartly at five-thirty and his fine poems, the radio productions and the translations were somehow hatched in the mellow interstices, and leftovers of earning time. He said, "What are you writing?"

' "A novel."

' "I can't read novels," he said, "too long. Let's go to the George for a drink." These and other of his sayings I harvested for Natasha.

'There was another full-time poet-producer, rather peppery, perpetually sensitive to his inadequate place in the poetic pecking order. There were two historical biographers, a writer of radio ballads and verse dramas in the tradition of Dylan Thomas, who himself had quite recently worked in the department which had commissioned his verse-drama *Under Milk Wood*. There was a diffident, all but blind author who would one day finish the autobiographical fiction of his childhood in a great house in Ireland and see it meet wholly unanticipated success. Finally there were those whose reputation in the war years had forged their names in radio legend, legends that were already, unbearably, fading fast in the glare of television.

'Yet for all their air of the dilettante and their extra-curricular preoccupations, I saw that they were careful men, unsparing in their criticism if the job of creating word pictures was not done with flair and love, meticulous over the beat of a cut on the tape. Sometimes I felt surrounded by fathers.

'All of them were surpassed by their boss, a man of the proportions and the intellectual generosity of Orson Welles, the Big Daddy, magnificent in his command, who held easy rule over these idiosyncratic, often eccentric, sometimes pub-stewed talents, a big, warm, divorced, lonely, puzzled man fatally undermined by the unforeseen gear change of technology. His life's work was bypassed. Radio, which still was dominant among the world's listeners, had lost most of its domestic power. Like a thief in the night, television had stolen away millions of its British congregation, and despite outposts of resistance, these were felt to be the last days of the Radio Raj. The viceroy was redundant.

'He took a fancy to your mother and me and in those months he made it his business to dip us into otherwise inaccessible experiences. We were bundled off to Chichester to see *Uncle Vanya* and dined in a restaurant afterwards with Laurence Olivier. We were taken to meet a retired ambassador in a villa in St John's Wood which impressed me out of my skin but made Natasha laugh at what she called its pretentiousness. I think he rather fell in love with her but oddly I was never jealous. I liked that he liked Natasha. She enjoyed it too, she treated it like a session with foils. Perhaps as he was so old (in his fifties!) and fat, I never dreamed, in the infinite stupidity of youth, that he could ever be competition. Or was I rather intimidated and therefore over-accommodating?

'Your mother was not as interested in my new colleagues as she had been in the epic figures from the World Service. Perhaps François now took up more of the slack. Perhaps I noted it as a first small act of separation. But in truth I scarcely needed her or anyone else as an audience. The work, the life, was more like a dream than a real world and dreams need no greater audience than one.

'For a long time, until habit set in and familiarity dulled surprise, I found it very strange that the work was not hard. Work was supposed to be hard: that was what work was. Work was tough and unfulfilling. Before work "you don't know you're born", the men would say, and therefore school was "the best time in your life". Work was the end of childhood, the end of play. Work was your battle with the world to earn and deserve your place in it. That was your grandfather's world,' he told their daughter, 'and way back down the line into our unrecorded past.

'But this? This was sitting around talking or pottering in the belly of London or playing, in effect, in the studios of Broadcasting House. Because the Radio Raj was closing down, those of us who came in young and willing had the run of the place. We were permissive scavengers. Our juvenile programmes got on the air, heady stuff. Perhaps we were comforting evidence, to be grasped at, to be held onto by the beached survivors, that young people still wanted to work in this medium, that its former glories would not be abandoned. So to be young in radio at that time was Liberty Hall.

'From that blunt-nosed grey building, I caught buses and tubes and walked to record programme material, and the first wave of what London could mean began to break over me. An initial gentle wave by comparison with the engulfment of a few years later, which would unbalance and undermine me, but even in the early days there was the feeling of being exposed to the pull of great tides moving with their own purposes, somewhere out there, in the deep of the city. There was a sense of being in a place of oceanic shifts, which could overwhelm you, of fathomless potential, a place which could disturb and metamorphose you and in which you could lose yourself in the pleasure and the poison of it.'

—◊—

Joe panicked. In a blink of time he passed from calm to fear. He had been detailed to work on local news for a week and the producer had asked him to 'stay on' until 6.30 p.m. and read out, 'live', the short continuity link which would bring the listeners back from the regional opt-out into the national Home Service. Joe sat – alone for almost half an hour sealed in a small windowless basement studio, headphones clamped to his ears, the microphone square before him, the three lines of continuity script on the table in front of him. He knew them by heart; he could not remember a word.

He began to feel that he was moving rapidly out of himself, that his mind was leaving his body. He had experienced this intensely and for long periods in adolescence but for some years now he had been largely free of it and grown bolder and careless and pushed himself further, unfearful, liberated. Now, in this solitary incarceration, it was back, as if an alien virus had somehow slid into that small cell, as if it had been forever lurking but at this time of over-exhilaration, over-confidence and nervousness, had found him at his most vulnerable and reasserted its powers.

Joe wanted to run out of the studio. He wanted to tear off the headphones and go. But how could he? Who would say those words? There would be silence. He would be to blame. And he could not let them down. The big studio clock ticked its relentless Greenwich Mean Time. The programme he was listening to went on, thankfully, but it would soon be over, he would have to say those words. He tried to take a deep breath but his throat was too dry and tight. This thing that was him was unloosed. How could he talk? The regional programme ended. It was him, alone, before millions of the unseen, now. The green light flashed on.

The words were uttered, they got out there, somehow, they were said.

He left the building as fast as he could. It was a spring evening. There was no drama in the sky to match and perhaps ease his fears. Portland Place looked placidly the same. All Souls' Church looked elegantly the same. Yet he walked along plain old Mortimer Street to good old Goodge Street tube station feeling scooped out. He had not the nerve to take the lift down to the tube, so he walked north, up Tottenham Court Road, up to Chalk Farm, passing the purposeful faces of others just going about their business, so calm they all seemed, how could they be so calm?

'I heard you,' said Natasha.

'How was it?'

'You sounded nervous,' she said. 'I would have been terrified.'

'I was nervous,' he confessed, with some relief, although he would say no more and tell her nothing of that.

'François brought some bottles of German beer,' she said. 'For you too. He doesn't like English beer.'

'I'd really like one.'

He went into the garden. François was sitting on a kitchen chair under the willow tree. He waved and smiled. Joe felt a rush of affection for him.

'Thanks,' he said, and raised his glass.

It was still best, they agreed, when they were together, at the kitchen table, writing, or reading aloud to each other, drawing on the apparently limitless oxygen of their love for each other, filling a reservoir of friendship, floating on the deep feelings that flowed between them, set for life.

James's magazine had folded after nine issues – 'They will become collectors' items,' said James, defiantly prophetic, 'they will be seen to be crucially before their time.' Natasha was still working on the poems and translations she would have sent in. She had forwarded some of her work to two other, well-established magazines and their rejections had halted her.

'You just have to keep on,' said Joe, 'they'll get it. And, "Better far than praise of men, is to sit with book and pen".'

'Yes.' It was happiness enough to work on the poems sitting in that kitchen with Joseph.

He was attempting to complete a novel. He had made two starts, failing after chapter two on the first and chapter five on the second. This time he was determined to complete it. Mondays to Thursdays he got up at six to do a couple of hours before setting off for work; Friday was a day off writing; the weekend was his own agenda; writing first, then films, now and then a bottle party. Increasingly they went to see a play for which, it had been broken to him at the BBC, he could reclaim the money spent on two tickets. He began to see the work of his own generation on the stage just as he saw it on the screen.

This novel had begun as a diagram. He had drawn seven concentric circles. When he had seen the diagram he had been flooded, he thought, with insights and inspiration. He was now on chapter three and had no idea where it was going or what he was doing with it. So far Aeneas had made a telling series of moves, so had others, including Lucifer and King Arthur; there was an unknown, perhaps an unknowable dark power within the shadows of the cave in the centre circle. There was a woman faced by seven walls or tests as she, like Aeneas, attempted to move from the outer edge to meet him in the cave. She alone would know how to interpret the shadowed power and discover its secret. Each circle had to represent a key stage in the development of man (all plucked from a book of mythology remaindered in the *Times* bookshop underneath Bush House) and while it was not overtly religious it had the solving of the mystery of meaning as its quest. It was a struggle. It sprawled. It was inexplicably, even mystically, satisfying. It threatened to take over the rest of his life.

'François had a good joke today,' Natasha said, as the clock indicated that the last cup of coffee was due before the reading in bed replaced the writing in the kitchen.

'Not another dirty one.'

'No. And they are not all dirty. They are Rabelaisian. I bought you Rabelais. You should read it.'

'I have.' The stack of classics he had set himself to read in order to compensate for reading History instead of English Literature was substantial. 'Well, I've dipped into it. Very rude. Very gross. Much farting.'

'It was the diet. Like Aristophanes. Beans, my father said. But it's a classic so you don't object.'

'I don't object to François's jokes either.'

'You do!' She was delighted. 'You can be a prude, Joseph, or is it a prune?'

'Neither.'

'Your denial is so feeble.'

'Prune or prude?'

'A man goes to a doctor. He is in pain. He taps his finger on his forehead. "Doctor," he says, "it hurts here." He taps his finger on his heart. "Doctor, it hurts here"; on his left knee, "and here"; on his right knee, "and here. What have I got?"' The sweetness of Natasha's smile inevitably elicited a like smile in Joe. '"You have a broken finger," the doctor said.'

They laughed, though whether at the joke, or her awkward telling, at the happiness it had given to François to relate and Natasha to receive and retell, or whether just at the fact that they were there, the two of them, embarked on a life together. They could never know. Natasha watched him closely, and her heart opened: she really was in love, and she trusted him.

CHAPTER EIGHTEEN

Eventually, he found a postcard in the small town which took its name from the Chateau. It was black and white and the Chateau looked rather gloomy but the mass of it, the splendour of the crescent, the French seventeenth-century power and style of it was unmistakable.

He went to a bar. It was empty. The town, ruled into a perfect grid, was desolate, it seemed, and silent, not in the least 'Christmassy'. Joe had wandered away from the twilit fairy-tale Chateau, found himself at the great elaborate iron gates, pushed on, to explore the town, but found nothing of interest except the postcards. He bought two: one to keep, one for his parents.

The coffee, the waiter and even the Armagnac were scarcely festive. There was much grandeur about the Chateau to which Natasha's father, in his new position as Rector of the university, had the right of access as his official holiday residence, but it felt no more Christmassy than this leaden town. He had thought a Roman Catholic country would make more of the birth of Christ than a northern Protestant people, but not here, not deep in central France.

Joe decided he would not despoil the card. He bought envelopes and notepaper. He lit a Disque Bleu, sipped the brandy. A sudden shot of memory hit him from the time, years before, he had been sitting outside the Café Flore in Paris writing a letter to Rachel. He could still be disturbed by memories of Rachel. He let the memory pass by, not wanting to seize on it, not wanting to revisit a past best buried. This letter was for his father and mother. He had not written to them for some weeks and the guilt, reinforced by a nostalgia for 'over there' which was in equilibrium to his sense of being overawed 'over here', unbuttoned him.

He described the Chateau in detail, the grounds with their two small lakes and carefully ragged woodland in which he had twice gone deerstalking with the men who worked on the estate, expeditions that had ended in a savagely skilful butchering of the deer, the carcass hooked up and hung, preparing for its journey to the kitchens. The formal gardens which once competed with royalty were now, in academic hands, reduced but still resilient in neglect. There were caves in which the estate wine was stored. He told them of the size and number of the rooms and of their bedroom, more like a flat, he wrote, as big as the whole of their flat in Finchley, and they had their own bathroom in which there were sofas, heavy curtains and like everywhere else in the Chateau rich materials, antique furniture, the sense of almost-museum.

In Paris, he wrote, Véronique and Louis had held a cocktail party. André Malraux, the famous French hero-author, had arrived and shaken hands and chatted, though in unrelenting French. Others, probably equally renowned but off his radar, had made courteous overtures of good-mannered inclusion. Gilbert had been in full fig.

Gilbert had driven them down to the Chateau; Gilbert was the butler, valet, manservant, a Breton who had now served nine academic masters and never lost his sense of good fortune – 'I was an orphan,' he would say, 'now look.' François, Natasha and he were in the family car, the others followed in the much grander university vehicle. He told Sam and Ellen that he had introduced his wife and brother-in-law and Gilbert to the pleasures of 'I Spy'. He had been annoyed when François and Natasha cheated. Gilbert played by the rules.

He described what Natasha was doing for François and how much he seemed to have improved while in England. François was to return to France now and finish his studies there. Natasha would miss him.

There followed a eulogy on Natasha. He wrote of her wonderful poetry, her effortless talent for drawing, her ideas for a novel; he wrote about how she made him understand that you could have a life you wanted and not a life that others wanted you to have. He wrote about how funny she could be, how cutting, but also how she appeared to examine everybody and every idea with such seriousness, just as she examined herself, just as she examined him.

She hated newspapers. She had become fond of the radio. He knew that she was not particularly well informed and yet she managed to sound informed or intelligent on everything their new London acquaintances discussed. She could be very direct and personal and even shocking in public. He had told her that her comments on his programmes and on his writing were overly critical, but she had asked him what else should she do? She said so much that made him think. For instance just this afternoon she said, 'The idea of the Holy is gone; and I am glad. You miss it, though, Joseph, don't you? Never mind, there is still the Sacred.' And then she laughed.

Her father, he wrote, had told him some more about her. He had said that her mother's family had owned large properties near Trieste, confiscated by the Communists; that Natasha's title, of countess, came down the female line and that neither her mother nor Natasha had wished to acknowledge it; that the death of her mother, so young and Natasha still in arms, had devastated everyone in the family for years but Oxford and marriage had helped her. Louis, he wrote, gave him a pair of antique gold Venetian cufflinks and Natasha said that was significant.

Joe's letter, which became something of a despatch from the front, wound on to include Véronique, the children, Isabel and Alain who had come as guests, Pierre, the stout red-faced 'keeper of the caves' on the estate who reminded him of Diddler, Gilbert and his unavoidable service, and his own research into who had lived at and visited the Chateau over the years, the statesmen, the men of letters and once, most cherished of all in the town, a royal prince, a Bourbon.

He was tired by the time he had finished. There were now more than half a dozen people in the bar. He put the letter in the envelope alongside the postcard but did not seal it. Having written in such terms about Natasha, he wanted to engineer that she read it. He paid and then hurried back, through the side gate, almost trotting up the great drive, guided by the solid band of ground-floor light in the Chateau, worried that he was late for dinner.

—⚏—

'A house like this needs many more servants,' said Isabel.

'*Liberté, Egalité, Fraternité!*' said Alain.

'Not when you are cold and the food is cold, the rooms are cold and everything is fading away. Look at those curtains.' They were in their suite, a little whisky before bed.

'I like decadence,' said Alain. 'I prefer decomposition. If it were all new I would distrust it.'

'Hypocrite!'

'Speak of yourself. You adore the Chateau. I see your eyes. I see you nod, like this,' he nodded, 'that means – I like it. I recognise this from shopping.'

'It is too gloomy. But it has style. It was a great period for the French.'

'Some of them.'

'Us.'

'Isabel! You are insupportable.'

'Louis loves it,' she said. 'Véronique is uncomfortable.'

'Louis does not notice it. Véronique is always uncomfortable.'

'Alain!' She held out her glass. 'The merest touch,' she said, 'and a single jet of soda.'

He waited on her, as he always did.

'So what do you think?' she demanded.

'Isabel! Not again! Every night – whisky and Natasha. Whisky and Joseph. They are still happy. Is that not enough of a miracle for any marriage?'

'I want your analysis.'

'I offered it to you last night. And the night before. Since then nothing has happened!'

'Is she deeply happy?'

'*Chérie!* That is not a question for adults. You will now ask it again.'

'But do you think she is really happy?'

'I consider,' Alain raised his whisky glass and gazed on it enigmatically, 'that Natasha is happier than I would ever have thought possible.'

'Do you not see the nervousness still, and the sudden disappearance of her personality?'

'Not more than usual. In fact I find Joseph more nervous than Natasha. There is a history to Joseph which he very courageously conceals.'

'What history?'

'I don't know. He conceals it.'

'You talk nonsense.'

'It is the only solution.' He raised his glass in a toast.

'He is much more confident. He is so full of plans now. He wants to write novels, he wants to make films, he wants to conquer the world.'

'You make it sound like a crime.'

'Perhaps it is.'

'Not in the young. And not in the honest heart.'

'Are you sure he is honest? Honest! What does that matter? True. True to Natasha.'

'We have only the moment to judge, my dear: and in this moment – yes. He is true to Natasha.'

'She *is* stronger. Despite having to nurse François.'

'That was a kindness,' said Alain. 'Louis is grateful to her.'

'It was an imposition!' said Isabel. 'Louis and Véronique ought to be ashamed of themselves.'

'François looks better.'

'We'll see what happens when Natasha leaves him.'

'Can we please talk about the cold dining room?'

'No.'

'The horrible wine? The good conversation?'

'Monologue.'

'About Malraux, and the war?'

'No. I was never fond of André Malraux. I must take you to bed, Alain. You are tired.'

'Not so very tired.'

'We are old, Alain my sweet, and not at home.'

—◊—

Louis walked alone for half an hour after breakfast and about three-quarters of an hour after lunch. He did not care much where he walked. The grounds of the Chateau were no more or less inviting than the Boulevard St Michel. He preferred familiar routes so that he could go onto automatic and think. Walking accompanied disturbed him.

Natasha knew this and felt a weight of apprehension when he asked her to join him after lunch. He went, as usual, directly and unseeingly through the formal gardens to the path by the nearest wood which he would follow for the allocated minutes and then turn a hundred and eighty degrees and retrace his steps.

He waited until the formal gardens were behind them. Then he took her arm and a surge of privilege warmed through Natasha, a feeling that she was being given her rightful place, a late but due blessing. It built on that afternoon in Oxford.

'I want to thank you, Natasha,' he began, 'for the care you have taken with François.' He patted her hand and paused and held it for a moment or two while he looked at her directly and she was for that moment healed. 'He is so much more confident. He is calmer. The results are not marvellous but they are better than they were here in France.'

They moved on. Natasha realised that the conversation was over. He increased his pace.

Natasha had wanted to be the one who instigated this discussion. As the silence built up, not a worrying silence but certainly a determined silence, she regrouped. It was not the time for circumlocution.

'I think it would be a mistake for him to go back to l'Ecole in Paris,' she said.

'Why is that?' His eyes were now looking ahead.

'He doesn't want to. He will never be engaged. He only worked hard in London because he wants you to be proud of him. He is not made for your type of work, Papa, and the sooner we let him leave it behind the better.'

'But he has to finish. He has to pass all the examinations. There is no question.'

'He will just get depressed again,' she said, 'and I can't be in Paris.'

'No, no. He is better now. He will take the examinations and then we will have a discussion.'

'With him?'

'Of course.'

'What if he wants to give up all formal education for ever? What if he wants to do something wholly different?'

'That is possible. What, for example?'

Natasha took a deep breath. She had not planned it to come out this bluntly.

'Drive a lorry?'

'That is very funny, Natasha. Good!' He looked at his watch.

'Go in the navy.'

'He will need examinations. And his sciences are not solid.'

'Just travel, around Europe, for a year, to get his bearings.'

'And then come back after a year to begin his education once again? That will be much more difficult for him.'

'But he hates academic work.'

'That can change.'

'Why does he have to change? He is fine as he is. He is kind and gentle, he is helpful and he wants so little. Why does he have to change?'

'You have spent too much time with him,' Louis said, and patted her hand once again. 'My wife said that it would be a great strain for you. She was worried for you and now I see her point of view. So you must stop now, Natasha; you and Joseph have done more than I could have hoped for. François must not spoil your life or your marriage.'

'I loved being with François. I was happy with him. It was a pleasure.'

'I understand.'

'Please. Papa. Let him go his own way.'

'He will. But only when he has passed all the examinations. Then he will go his own way.'

'Please.'

'No more. I am very grateful to you . . . Do you see the gate over there?'

'Yes.'

'That is where I turn back. But we must step out.'

—⚍—

Joe roved under a bright half-moon. The grounds were picked out almost as clearly as they had been on the dawn hunting trips. Now he was alone, walking, smoking, rather cold, having ignored Isabel's advice to wear a coat, wanting in some macho way to impress her, needing to be alone to let in the dislocating largeness of all that was happening to him. Film stars left grand parties and strolled in such grounds with a reflective cigarette, he thought, though usually in a dinner jacket. He had just turned twenty-three but he felt himself in that celluloid tradition of the evening strolling grandee. His sense of the specialness that had been thrust upon him was accentuated by the unremitting attention Gilbert had paid to his wardrobe . . . the clerical grey suit bought for him by his mother and father more than five years ago, his sartorial camouflage for his journey into the interior of Oxford University, had been ironed and brushed and somehow rejuvenated; the clean white shirt had been pressed flawless, as had the college tie – and the shoes glittered, pacing before him, shining black mirrors, reflecting the moonlight.

He tried to impose order and occupy himself by picking out features in the moonscape, measuring them, filing them for later use; but his heart was not in it. The general flux of the life in this borrowed palace, the crystal, the candelabra, the paintings of French victories and French luminaries on the walls, the ancient and studied luxuriance of style unearthed him.

There was a ballooning in his mind and in his body. It was as if both were ready to burst open simply with the fullness of what was happening. The mixture of reality and fantasy, the smiling eyes of Natasha whenever he sought them out, the compliments of Isabel, the gratitude of Véronique, it was as if he had been turned into a different person. He had no idea what he should or could do about it. He had to force himself back into the Chateau.

Natasha was in the chair nearest the bed, smoking, reading. At Joe's suggestion she had begun *The Cossacks* but he could tell, as soon as he came in, pink-faced from the cold air, that she wanted to talk.

'It was fantastic out there!' he said. 'I wish you had been with me.'

'You went so quickly,' she said. 'Sometimes you do. You move from impulse to act with nothing in between.'

'Is that bad?'

'Sometimes.'

Her tone was flat, unusually so, without any of that resonance which made her so alive for him.

He sat down opposite her. He would have liked another drink but to go downstairs in search of alcohol was unthinkable.

'I didn't leave when I shouldn't, did I?'

'No.'

'Nor say anything wrong?'

'They think you are perfect, Joseph. You have parachuted out of the sky like a saviour.'

'Please.' He could not read her in this mood and always feared the worst. 'Don't say things like that.'

'It is true.'

'It can't be true,' he said, firmly, as he thought, drawing a line under it.

'I'm sorry, Joseph,' she said, 'this is very bad of me. I apologise in advance – but I read the letter you have written to Sam and Ellen.'

It was always a little rub against the grain when she uttered his parents' Christian names. But it declared an independence in her that he admired.

'Well?'

He remembered how lovingly he had written of her and waited for the appreciation.

'Joseph.' She took a deep drag on the cigarette. 'You must not send this letter. And you must not say these things. Not to anyone. Please. You must not.'

'What things?'

'Sam and Ellen will not know what to say to me. It will be too much for them. And I like them: I like them to know me as I am, not through *this*!'

'What?' he asked, but he knew the answer.

'Joseph! The boasting. The meaningless title and confiscated property and all of it! I hate it, Joseph! Don't you understand that? How can you not understand that? How can you not? How can you know me and not understand that I abandoned all that many years ago? I am here now because of François and because I see how much you love it and I want to be near my father when he is so benevolent, but I left all this, Joseph. I could not live in this air, I left it to live a life of my own, whatever came of it, of my own, don't you see? I cannot carry all this past with me. I will not. I will not! You must not put it back around my neck!'

'Why do you say that?' He felt a chill from her accusation.

'Because it is true.'

'I'm not a snob.'

'It's easy to be influenced by all this, Joseph. Especially . . .'

'As I'm a peasant.'

'You can see what they have done to François and therefore what they did to me.'

'You told me your father was a teacher. He isn't. You said he was ill. He isn't. You said Véronique was the wicked witch. She doesn't seem like that to me.'

'You have taken me off their hands.' Natasha's tone was bitter. 'They think, they hope, that everything has changed. But my past has not changed.'

'So I'm just somebody who did them a favour.'

'. . . Not for my father, no. I can see that he admires you. And Véronique is grateful for François, although she has learned nothing.' She paused and, for the first time in the conversation, she looked at him without anger. 'Poor Joseph. You are so miserable now when you were so happy a moment ago.'

'I'm perfectly OK.'

'It is better not to mix these things. We shall be on our own, tabula rasa, both, somewhere anonymous, with one or two friends, writing together and reading and talking together. That is all we need.'

'Why do you think I wrote that letter?'

'Because you were proud: of me, and of this borrowed splendour and of yourself.'

'I knew none of this when I met you. You were just lonely and unhappy.'

'And you rescued me!' She smiled, her good humour entirely restored. Joseph's crestfallen expression was too young to bear any more chastisement.

'I didn't set out to rescue you.'

'But you have done.' She stood up and came across to him and pulled him to his feet. 'Don't sulk, Joseph.' She put her arm around his neck and stayed until he felt forced to look at her. And her smile, the sweet, intelligent softness of love in her eyes, the clarity of her as always abashed and seduced him.

'It is a very big bed.'

He looked: the canopy, the curtains, the luxury so inappropriate for them, he thought.

'I liked that single bed in Oxford better.'

'That is inverse snobbery, Joseph.'

'No,' he said, 'it was better.'

Over the next two, the last two days, Natasha was as loving to him as she had ever been. It was noted by Isabel with relief and approval, by Véronique with scepticism, and by the younger children with ribaldry as Natasha declared public tendernesses. But the waters did not quite close over.

On the last afternoon they – 'the children' – went for a walk into the town and then back to the house by the most meandering route they could find. Natasha and François soon dropped behind. Joe liked being left alone with the younger ones. Natasha was not there to tease him and they appreciated his adequate French, indeed they seemed rather astonished by it, that of all people an Englishman had mastered their precious tongue. Joe revelled in these inherited siblings. He had no responsibility for them; he was as occasional as a shooting star and they revered him as the English husband of their artistic and rebellious sister. It was easy to show off and there seemed no harm in it. Joe found genuine happiness in his time with the children. There seemed to be no way to lose, no penalties. He fed them opinions, banalities, elementary historical facts, curiosities from English life and they leaped up like young dolphins, taking the fish every time. In their company Joe re-joined to the family from which Natasha's censure had threatened to sever him.

Natasha and François fell behind and in the extensive grounds they lost contact with the others and made their own way. François was sad and the weight of his sadness pressed down on her.

'You can always come back to see us in London.'

'Maman says no. Enough.' His right hand made a chopping gesture. 'Anyway, you are going to the North now.'

'The BBC is like the army,' said Natasha. 'Now Joseph has to go to the Roman Wall for a few months.'

'I will be near the exams then.' François did not look at her. She felt she was abandoning him and it was insupportable. 'They will be even less inclined to let me go.'

'I'll come over to Paris,' said Natasha, 'I'll come every month.'

'No.' François let his cigarette fall and ground it out. 'They will not like that.'

'Who cares?'

His smile was a reproach. He took her arm.

'Do you remember Papa telling us about the Pétomanes? The men who farted tunes? He told us that his father took him to see them in a circus.'

'Yes?'

'I always thought he was making it up. But it is true! I saw a little film of them. Five of them. Five fat types bending over and farting in tune. They even did the Marseillaise.' He looked at her rather dreamily. 'It was magnificent.'

Joe stood at the head of the grand stone staircase which swept up to the main doors. He felt proprietorial. But when he caught sight of François and Natasha there was a pass of anxiety. They walked together so closely, holding tight to each other, meandering, talking so intensely, so confidentially, so excludingly. They did not look up or look ahead. He was unnoticed. In the twilight they could seem to be clinging together as if each needed the other, just to go forward.

CHAPTER NINETEEN

'Come in and close the door, pet,' he said, 'it's cold outside.' Natasha hesitated. The wind whipped off the River Tyne, whistled in from the north-east and bit through her coat. The unrelenting dourness of the terraced, dark-brick cottages which opened onto the narrow pavement made her apprehensive. The poverty and pinched faces she had seen in the streets which tumbled down from the castled city to the river had moved her but reinforced her sense of being a total outsider. Yet the old man's knobbly face, his smile enriched by the gleaming false teeth, the warmth of tone and the strange reassurance in the word 'pet' drew her across the threshold and straight into what appeared to be both a kitchen and a living area, the two striking features of which were the black fireplace, polished like an exhibit, Natasha thought, and on a table next to it, a television set.

'Sit down, pet,' he said, 'you can have my chair by the fire. Just prod the dog. I'll put the kettle on.'

He disappeared into what Natasha recognised, from her holiday in Caldbeck, as the back kitchen and after prodding the dog which slid off the armchair sinuously as a snake, she sat down; it was very comfortable. She would like a dog, she thought, suddenly back in her childhood when her dog had been her only friend; she would like a dog for company while Joseph strode out to this work of his which took so much, too much, from so many of their days.

'Aa haven't made it too strong,' he said, 'that's an acquired taste. The biscuits were fresh baked yesterday. I've put some toast on. It's starvation out there.'

As far as Natasha was concerned she might have been in a cave in the middle of a mountain somewhere in the weirdness of Eastern Europe.

Yet she felt safe. Even in that short time she was aware of the practice of kindness.

'When me sister lost her man she had a bad turn,' he explained. 'Well, she took it bad, put it that way, pet. She was always bothered with her nerves, that's why myself and the wife (she's doin' her afternoon stint, she'll be sorry to have missed you), that's why we were pleased when she moved in next door particularly since they couldn't have bairns. That seemed to prey on her, you know.'

The lilt and pattern of speech, and occasional words that she did not recognise, wove a spell. His face, she now saw, was lumped by scars, decorated with thin black lines, she noticed, and wanted to ask him about it. This must have been what Joseph had experienced, she thought, this daily, hourly, percolation of affection just in the warmth of the words, this comfort: how lucky Joseph had been, she thought, probably for the first time, how lucky if he had this. She felt unnerved by the instant warmth and by his immediate confession.

'The upshot is she's had to go away. Well, pet, truth to tell, she's been put away.' The scarred face seemed close to instant tears and then the moment passed. 'So we decided to let the house, three months maximum.'

'Three months is all we need.'

'It's the spit of this place but I'll take you round when you've finished your tea. Where you from?'

'France.'

'A long walk home, then.'

Natasha laughed.

'I like it here.'

'Your sentence is only three months, pet.' He smiled broadly, a smile was never far from his lips. 'Most of us up here are lifers. Aa've allus fancied Gay Paree, ooh la la, and French champagne.'

Next door was indeed the twin. After a tender farewell, Natasha, now warm as the toast, spent an hour or so alongside the Tyne, intrigued by the network of steep steps and small houses, the shops and the pubs, the painterly possibilities of the ill-lit streets, the boats in the river, the ceaseless background surging sound of that warm-throated, long-rubbed guttural dialect. She could wander around and sketch. She could get a dog. People on the street, strangers, greeted her already, a stranger. After a few weeks she would walk in the security of kindly acquaintanceships, she thought, and be part of this quayside world.

And how Joseph would like it! It would remind him of Wigton where, she had suggested, unsuccessfully, he ought to set a novel. She had seen a film which was set in the North of England, in a city not unlike Newcastle, and been taken by the physical and emotional similarities Joseph bore to the hero. And she had read about the working-class North being an inspiration to contemporary artists. Here in Newcastle she saw it plainly, far more dramatic, she thought, than its miniature version in Wigton. So she would be helping Joseph go back to his roots without the difficulty and embarrassment which she recognised he might have in going back to his home. And the more she imagined life here, her own life on the quayside, the more she was convinced that she too would love it, she knew she would, it was a real place, it was perfect for an artist. They would adopt a pub.

She outlined this to him as they ate a hushed dinner in the small dining room of the modest Bed and Breakfast to which BBC Personnel had directed them.

The B and B was in a crescent of semi-detached houses in Jesmond, an affluent suburb of Newcastle, cut off from the heavy industrial city by the Town Moor, an urban cordon sanitaire. They had been there for less than a week but Joe had already worked out a morning routine which included walking to work across the Moor. Despite the traffic flow along its spine, the Moor had a residual atmosphere of Northern bleak landscape which he liked. He liked the deep silence of the crescent. He liked the temptation of nothing to do in the evenings but stay in and write.

He went to see the terraced house by the Tyne the following evening. He too was taken by the locality, by the people, by the culture. In the house that was to be let he found much that was familiar but the clear sounds of television sets to the left and right of him raised worries. Perhaps the noise could be lived with. After all he had grown up above noise, the racket of a pub, and at Oxford experienced inevitable intrusion when he shared rooms.

They were all but escorted to the pub on the corner of the street, the King's Head, and Joe decided to drink nothing but Newcastle Brown Ale. It could not have been more friendly and Joe saw Natasha's eyes glitter with pleasure at this rich new discovery. That he worked for the BBC and that she was an artist were facts relayed to all newcomers. Natasha flowered under the chatting scrutiny of interested women and the saucy glances of one or two of the younger men. 'It's as if we have been here before,' Natasha whispered, 'already they have made us feel like their family.'

It was a Friday, pay day, busy, intimate. Natasha, he could see, rode on the crest of it and he thought he understood why. This, she would think, was Joseph's world: this would take him back, slough off the strain of being the new creation of Oxford and the BBC, reconnect him with his past, which as she had said several times, he had to examine as a writer. He saw her eyes gleam with hope, misguided, for as the noise grew and the cheerfulness intensified and the drink began to exercise its grip, Joe realised with a sad but inflexible certainty that it would do him no good.

He would like it too much. He would be putty in their hands, invitations, drinks, friendships – he could see them coming and it would be full of ease but the privacy and the puzzling need of a writer's solitude would be difficult to maintain. Solitude, especially in a stranger, was deliberate separateness, unfriendly. The quayside prospered on community; it needed community. Pulling together was the tribal imperative.

Across the room was a young man, perhaps a year or two ahead of Joe, the sort of young man Joe had always envied. Joe had never had that poise and lack of fret. Handsome, cavalier, out for the night with good mates around the companionable pints which nudged each other on the little table. Joe learned that the gang of them worked in the shipyards together. The young man would look across at Joe now and then and nod, but it was Natasha who drew his more intense and questioning gaze.

The man was netted by her difference. She caught his eye, Joe was watching closely; and her happy openness, her unabashed difference in such company clearly stirred and intrigued the young man. He would be after her, Joe thought, when I was away at work, or even here in the pub, he would be after her; and others like him. He could not bear the thought of it. He began to reason it away. Would Natasha still be as enraptured with the place after a few weeks of this? She would soon find out the limitations of the transitory visitor. Then there was a danger of slumming it, he thought. That would be a good argument. And he would paint the darker side of this glow. Men and women utterly disarming, hospitable to embarrassment, but quick in their quarrels, sharp at offence given or thought to be given, able to bond instantly but also able to exclude and eject just as swiftly.

As they went back across the dark Moor on the merrily lit bus, he articulated none of this to Natasha. It had been a good evening. The pub was well run, the singing at the end had been roof-raising, Natasha had been a princess for that night and she had enjoyed it. He had not the heart to tell her what he thought, not then, not the next day, not until the Sunday when he told her that the landlady of the Bed and Breakfast had a friend a few doors along, a Mrs Farr, widow of a solicitor, who let her upstairs as a self-contained flat. It had been on the market for a while because she was so picky. But for a young man in the BBC she was sure it would be available and most reasonable. Very quiet. Very quiet indeed. No parties. No pets.

It was, thought Natasha, like a tomb.

—⟋⟍—

'I thought she looked starved the moment I set eyes on her,' Ellen said, 'and the cough on her chest is bad. She hadn't taken anything for it. We went straight from the station to the chemist.'

Sam gave her his full attention. Ellen had come back later than expected from her day trip to Newcastle and, most unusually, gone immediately upstairs, without staying to help in the pub. And she had waited upstairs until the place was cleared. She looked upset, Sam thought; and there was some anger and puzzlement. It was rare that Sam felt Ellen out of reach, and outside his understanding of her mood, but this was one such time. When she did come down, he made her a cup of tea and waited, desisting, with difficulty, from the interrogation he felt the need to undertake.

He had put coal on the fire late as it was, partly to give the kitchen more life and partly just to do something to show that a preparation had been made.

'It's bitter over there,' said Ellen, holding the cup with both hands and sipping the tea gratefully as if it were medicine. 'Far worse than here. They always seem to have it colder in the North-east.'

Sam lit a new cigarette off the stump of the old.

'She seemed so sunk in herself,' said Ellen, after a long pause. 'She couldn't have been more friendly when she met me at the station, but I could see she was having to force herself. To tell you the truth I thought that something had gone bad between them.'

Sam was disturbed by this but made no comment.

'We went back to their flat. It's very nice. It reminded me of Miss Snaith's when Joe did the piano lessons. A lot of good old-fashioned furniture and those very quiet colours. The woman downstairs was kindness itself; she put a pot of tea and some cakes on the top of the stairs and just gave a little tap at the door and disappeared. She always does that, Natasha said. But it was cold. Natasha didn't take her coat off. It was bitter. There's a meter to be fed with shillings but you can't always have enough shillings.'

Sam had waited long enough. He spoke as evenly as he could.

'Did you get to the bottom of what was ailing her?'

'It was something inside her, Sam. Way inside her. It was . . . it was as if she was hardly in the room with me. She tried, she's very well mannered, she just seemed in herself, as if the rest of the world was shut out. I can't explain it. But I could feel it.'

'When did he get back?'

'After six.'

Sam reined himself in.

'She just lit up, poor thing, when he walked in but he looked tired himself and wanting to eat and get on with more work. Natasha says he reads all the time when he isn't writing. He said he liked the job, he said it was the sort of job he could do for life.'

'Did you feel anything between them?'

'Just, as if she was far away, looking for a hand, I don't know, Sam. You would have worked it out.'

'Do you think he was looking after her well enough?'

'He's always been very . . . what is it?'

'Concentrated?'

'On himself, hasn't he? You used to say that was what got him through.'

'It's not always the best of qualities when you're married. Especially if your wife's – what would you say she was?'

'I wish I knew, Sam.' She was distressed but strove not to show it.

'They should come back over here,' he said, 'for a rest.'

'They should.' Now at last she looked at him, her eyes filling with tears. 'But where could we put them up, Sam? And how can we look after her when there's everything we have to do all day in the pub? She needs somewhere quiet and a normal life – and so does Joe. He's clashing himself. But what can we do for them here in the pub, Sam? Tell me that.'

Natasha went to the doctor as Ellen had urged her to do and he put her on a course of antibiotics, told her to keep warm, advised regular hot drinks and said that she would feel 'down in the dumps' for two or three weeks.

But the physical explanation was not enough for her. Natasha was driven into herself once more to haunt regions of unhappiness she thought she had escaped; unhappiness and blank apprehension, un-answerable questions infinitely multiplied like images in opposing mirrors. For several weeks she spent much of the day in bed, depleted by the chest infection which cleared up only slowly, fearful of the bite of the hard Northern winter, phone-less, talking to no one, not even to Mrs Farr whose concern brought a tray of tea and biscuits every afternoon but whose manners dictated that she leave it on the landing at the top of the stairs and immediately retire to her own quarters.

Natasha had no energy for drawing and though she continued to read and attempted to write poetry it seemed a doleful business. When Joseph burst in from work her heart lifted, her expression lightened, but he was preoccupied. He delivered his day to her as he always had done but she saw that it was almost as much a duty as a pleasure. There were still the stories, there was still the mimicry to entertain her, but he was turning inward too and even when they shared the table in the sitting room and wrote face to face she sensed that now he would have preferred the solitude in which she had been imprisoned all day. He read furiously, sometimes reading aloud a passage – 'How did he do that?' 'Listen to this' – and his writing consumed ever more of his free time and energy.

Natasha made a literal retreat from the table to one of the two large armchairs by the electric fire where she watched him, his back and head hunched over the pad. How could he be so near yet so far away? He was surely the same Joseph. He still came back to her; he loved her; she trusted him, she relied on him; too much? Was it dependence? Was the need for him too great, more than he wanted to bear? She had to be careful, she decided, as she glanced over to him and tried to stifle her cough.

And then he would look around and grin, or suddenly jump up from his chair and come across and kiss her or, best of all, say, 'What do you think of this?' – and read a paragraph or two which she would praise and only later, a day or two later, find a moment to introduce her misgivings. 'I've already done that,' he would usually say, or, 'That's good. That's really helpful. Thanks,' with a hug and for a while the clouds lifted.

Joe abandoned Aeneas and his journey through the concentric circles of walls. He had managed just over thirty thousand words but as his interest flagged the prose slackened, the pace of writing dragged, the novel ran out on him in his second week in Newcastle.

He began to plan a novel with the title *The Metropolitan Line*. This would be seven interconnected stories, seven characters apparently unrelated, differing greatly in their background and class and position in the city but crossing each other's paths, at first without knowing they were doing so, but, in the end somehow (to be discovered in the writing) seen as bound together. It would be a chance to feed off his excitement at the impact of London, to write about the present, to portray a spectrum of life from the old flower seller at Charing Cross Station to the grandees he had brushed against in Broadcasting House. He could not think of a plot. He did not want a murder or a will or an accident. The plot, he decided, itching to get going, would emerge from the characters. And this time, whatever happened, he would finish it. It would need all the energy he could dredge up.

Newcastle skewered it. Joe's attachment was to the daily local radio programme called *Let the People Speak* and he was being given a drubbing by the small scornful former Communist Arnold Baxter, its editor, whose encouragement to Joe, in an overemphatic Geordie accent, included, 'We don't need Oxford folk to tell us what to do,' 'You're nothing but a working-class rural Conservative in Liberal sheep's clothing – worst of both worlds,' and 'Raymond Williams has already written everything you might attempt. There's no point.' The other two producers, John, a young Yorkshireman who'd served time on the *Manchester Guardian*, and Harold, a local man who'd been lured across to radio from the *Newcastle Journal*, told him to ignore 'the old sod', but as they respected the old sod and conspired with him to make a programme as radical and left-wing as they could possibly get away with, Joe had the uncomfortable feeling that they rather agreed with the old sod and indeed he himself often thought that the old sod had a point.

Joe had sailed along from his adolescence on the comfortable tide of post-war Welfare State Labour. A glimpse of Oxford politics had confirmed his preference for the unexamined certainties of a political position which could effectively be shelved while he got on with his life. Life, for Arnold Baxter, was nothing but politics, hard politics. 'Arnold makes Lenin look soft,' said John. 'I don't know how the BBC lets him get away with it.'

'He wins prizes,' said Harold, 'and he would raise holy hell if they censored him.'

'He'll try to break your spirit,' said John cheerfully, 'he thinks you're a class traitor.'

They were in the pub. At lunchtime they were always in the pub. It was Arnold's parliament. Despite a weak head and a careful budget, Joe felt he had to turn up at least twice a week or the wrath of Arnold would extend to even more corrosive remarks on his character. 'A bloody nancy drink,' he said, when Joe ordered a mere half of mild ale. 'If you can't drink you're no good to me.'

Throughout the time of his attachment, Joe was never sure about Arnold. Was his contempt real, or an act? Did he despise Joe as much as his words indicated or was the tongue-lashing a helpful way to knock a political education into him in double quick time? Or did he just loathe him? There were many clear and discomforting signs of that and, though not unused to being loathed, Joe was thrown. The only way through was to please the man by the work he did but it seemed the man was not to be pleased.

There was a strike in the Vickers Shipyard and Joe was detailed to bring back an interview with the spokesman for the management. John dealt with the Trades Unions, Harold did a 'colour' piece, interviewing the children of the strikers.

Arnold listened to Joe's tape in his small tidy office. Joe faced him across the empty desk. After the tape ended, Arnold let a silence roll in before he pronounced.

'No follow-up questions. No pushing him at all. Did you ask him to show you the disgraceful so-called canteen and the stinking lavatories? No? Suppose he refused? You should have gone there on your own and described them for us. You're a reporter. Report! It's the conditions this is about. They're mediaeval. They would insult a Neanderthal. You let him walk all over you. Maybe we can hack thirty seconds out of it.' He laughed. 'For balance! For the Powers That Be.' His laugh was a bark. 'All you've brought me is the bloody balance.'

There was a pattern. Joe was despatched to talk to a Liberal councillor about the lack of books in primary schools. 'You should have nailed him. He had no case.' He was sent out of the city, deep into the feudal Northumbrian countryside to interview a local Conservative MP who had just been promoted into the Cabinet: 'He pissed all over you.' He talked to a sculptor in Durham whose abstract response to a council commission had inflamed much local opinion, including Arnold's whose aesthetic soul was ambered in Soviet Realism; unfortunately Joe liked the work: 'Christ, we have a bloody pansy on our hands.' He was sent to do vox pops at the Jesmond Golf Club.

In these first weeks the height of Joe's ambition was to earn an encouraging word. He found it difficult to question Arnold's judgements and he was increasingly downcast at his own stupidity.

'The trick with Arnold,' John told him on their way to St James's Park to see the derby match between Newcastle and Sunderland, 'is to understand that he is totally black and white. In everything. Without fail. Workers good, bosses bad; councillors crafty or corrupt; ordinary people who complain about them honest and reliable; business, bureaucracies, government presence in all its forms, guilty until proved innocent; man and woman in the street, soul of virtue; politicians untrustworthy by definition; men in pubs and women who work in canteen, wise and dependable also by definition; revolution merely delayed a decade or so; status quo untenable and unspeakable. That's about the size of it. Takes you a long way if you have the instincts of a dictator and the luck to run a remote and insignificant regional colony at the outer edges of BBC Radio. And of course,' John paused and his tone changed, 'there's his upbringing which was truly awful, beggars belief.' Another pause. 'And his marriage – enough said. And, most of all, Joe, he is a bloody brilliant editor. No question. Just take it on the chin and walk on. You'll learn a lot and what you don't like will drop off when you get out of his range.'

'I'm not sure I want it to drop off,' Joe said to Natasha later that night. They had been to see *This Sporting Life* and Joe had found himself analysing it in Arnold's terms. 'I feel as if I've been sleepwalking about politics.' They were in their sitting room, a last cup of tea, chairs drawn up to the two-barred fire. 'Just taking things for granted.'

'Why not?' Natasha's face was almost ghostly pale. The infection had cleared but, had Joe taken the trouble to look closely, he would have seen the persisting weakness. 'Why not take it for granted?'

'It seems irresponsible,' said Joe. 'Just leaving it to others.'

'We have to leave most things to others,' said Natasha, 'that's how civilisation works.'

'But all of us are involved in politics. Whether we acknowledge it or not.'

'That is your dreadful Arnold talking.'

'He said something like that. But I believe it for myself.'

'No you don't. You just want to please him. Even when he is not here you want to please him. You are practising on me!'

'That's unfair.'

'You want to write novels, Joseph. That is enough. You must leave the politics for others. The BBC is beginning to possess you.'

'I can't just give it up.'

'You must be more indifferent. Like the poet in London who came in to work so late and left so early. Not like Arnold who torments you most likely out of envy.'

'What could he envy about me?'

'Joseph. Sometimes you are blind.'

'I like it here,' he said. 'When I've done the television attachment I'm going to see if I can be transferred back to the North.'

'To play at politics?'

'To do something for the community. I've put somebody like that in the new novel.'

'You'd be frustrated. And how do you know you would be any good at it?'

'You can say that about everything I'm doing.'

'But the writing is what you want to do, it comes out of you, it is your decision taken alone and not influenced by Arnold. Any Arnolds.'

'You'd probably get on well with him.'

'I don't want to meet him. I've seen what he's done to you.'

'What's that?'

'He's upset you. And why? Because he is a bully and you are inexperienced but very willing and therefore easy to bully. I would tell him that if I did meet him.'

'I bet you would.'

He smiled and her returned smile was irresistible.

'I bet you would,' he repeated. He looked at her intently. 'You're very tired, aren't you? And you're thinner.'

'I'm getting stronger now. As long as you stick to what is true in you we will come to no harm.'

'I still want to come back to the North,' he said as he moved towards her.

'You have never left it,' she said, as he kneeled in front of her and began to caress her. 'Perhaps you never will. But you must try.'

CHAPTER TWENTY

'I shall miss them,' said Julia. They had lodged with the Stevenses for three weeks while searching for a place in London. 'The house is less fun. I fail to see why they could not find a place in Oxford. Natasha would love to live here. And the train takes scarcely more than an hour and a quarter.'

'But then,' Matthew attended to the glasses of whisky, 'as he explained, with the tube and the walking at both ends it would be about four hours a day in transit.'

'He could read on the train.'

'He could. But clearly even that was not sufficient temptation. And the journey would not be inexpensive.'

'Kew Gardens sounds perfectly adequate,' Julia conceded as she took the whisky, 'it will give us a chance to visit the Botanical Gardens. Natasha said that rather a crowd of BBC people live there or thereabouts because of its proximity to the studios.'

'In work proximity is all,' said Matthew. 'Here's to proximity.' He lifted his tumbler.

'Joe has the air of someone who gets good luck.' Julia sipped the whisky and grimaced. It was too strong. 'Unfortunately, those are the ones who tend to come a cropper sooner or later. A bit like hubris and nemesis.'

The house in Kew Gardens was semi-detached, built between the wars on the site of a once locally famous orchard. The patch of garden boasted two apple trees and one pear tree. It was just around the corner from the station which would take Joe the few stops to a destination from which he could walk to work in the television studios in the west of London. The house was handy for an elegant Edwardian parade of shops sufficient for all normal domestic purposes, plumped out with a second-hand bookshop, two junky antique shops, a restaurant and a café with tables outside. It was about five minutes from Kew Botanical Gardens and ten minutes from a particularly lush bend of the Thames.

It was Natasha's third English suburb. It never occurred to her to include Oxford. It still took some understanding, so whisperingly tidy, so quiet, hushed by the ubiquitous avenues of trees, so uniform, so organised, so toy-like in architecture, so empty by day and emptier by night; the placid playground, the tranquil shops and the regular dashes of keep-out privet, kilometres of privet, the gardens all tended trim yet unshowy, the suburbanites somnambulistic whether strolling to the tennis courts or strolling towards the river with obedient dogs or strolling towards well-mannered gatherings; such admirable tolerance, such niceness which must, she thought, given what she knew from an often bombastic Joseph of the violent history of England, be a pose: but why? Perhaps, she wrote to Julia, that could be her mission: to uncover the secrets of the English-speaking suburb. Julia could give her tips on how Agatha Christie would proceed. But she took much more notice of Kew Gardens than she had done of Finchley or of Jesmond. For in Kew they bought a house and planted their life together.

To buy a house was something of a shock to both of them. BBC Personnel advised it and a London friend of Louis to whom he recommended that Natasha turn for advice had said, 'In England it is always bricks and mortar.' Natasha was impressed by the man's authority and eased into this unexpected move by the thought that it would please and reassure her father. Joseph was struck with the revelation that paying rent was getting nothing back whereas taking out a mortgage on your own house was both a canny and a morally defensible investment. They bought three bedrooms, two living rooms, one small kitchen, bathroom and cloakroom for four thousand and two hundred pounds. It went through without a glitch. Joe could raise two thousand and seven hundred and fifty as a mortgage against his salary. Louis released a good proportion of Natasha's trust to make up the rest. The trust had brought her a modest income for several years, less than half of Joe's earnings, but it had made an important difference. Now it was depleted but everyone agreed the house was bricks and mortar surety.

The previous owner had died in the house at a great age, leaving behind him slabs of Edwardian furniture, several rejected by his almost equally aged relatives. Because Joe saw both convenience and a bargain, they bought the dead man's bed ('Every bed's a dead man's bed,' he said, 'unless it's new and we can't afford that'); they bought the dead man's three-piece suite, the dead man's dining table and six chairs, his garden tools and two very large prints of battles – Waterloo and Trafalgar – which Natasha thought was typical of Joseph.

The rest of their furniture was flung together from the overflowing cheaper junk shop in the nearby parade outside the station. The shop was run by a curly-haired blond actor and his straight-haired blonde sister, an actress; neither of them regularly employed. The business flourished because of their charm and their guile at offering to clear the heaped remains of domestic imperial days from the Victorian and Edwardian villas of Kew. These were being steadily drained of their once affluent owners and the objects unwanted by relations made good junk for young homeowners.

The novelty of the purchase refreshed the two of them and for that alone Natasha was persuaded that it was acceptable. How on earth they had come to buy a house was wholly unexpected but so was much that had happened since she had met Joseph. But this! Property? How had they become bourgeois? What had they lost? Yet, she reassured herself, they could always sell it. They were not trapped. They were still free. The argument was weak, she accepted that too.

The Thames was no distance and the Thames ran to be painted. She saw it through the work of Monet and as the spring and summer warmed the suburb she felt confident enough to take out her water-colours and found a safe harbour on the towpath beside the wall of the Gardens. The Gardens themselves were priceless. Fenced, patrolled, ordered, deeply secure and full of fantasy, they became a refuge. One penny was the entrance fee and that royally trifling sum clicked you through the iron turnstile into a man-planted Garden of Eden, only two centuries old. The gigantic Palm House and the Temperate House brought exotic and luxuriant plants from the Tropics. The rose garden bloomed in a gentle Englishness she was growing to love. But it was the exotic which most drew in Natasha, the camellias and magnolias, the great planting of giant redwoods, and the Mediterranean garden, and the tall, incongruous Pagoda which always made her smile.

Two sites were special: one was the lake which a pair of black swans ruled with such serene beauty – Natasha could dream on them for hours, finding comfort and endless mystery in their tranquil, stately movement. Then there was the artist of the Gardens, Marianne North, whose gallery of watercolours drawn from her bold Victorian journeys to rarely visited corners of the globe filled Natasha with awe and not a little envy. Would she ever have the resources to be as independent as that? How strong in herself that woman must have been, she thought, and how fortunate – or was it determined? – in the fulfilment of her calling. She would stare for minutes on end at photographs of the dumpy little artist, clothed, bedecked, like Queen Victoria, looking for clues.

She needed refuge in the first months chiefly because of the aeroplanes. When they bought the house they had not taken the planes into account. Soon it was as if they pursued her. The house was under the flight path six miles out from London's Heathrow Airport, and just above them the planes braked and wheeled and made for a runway. Natasha began to fear the planes. 'I keep thinking they are carrying bombs,' she told Joseph, 'I keep thinking they will explode over us. I keep seeing the mushroom cloud.' Though he had the concern to comfort her or try to talk her some way out of it, she knew that he did not really understand.

One night she awoke sobbing and he held her until she was calm, amazed by the force of her distress. He suggested they move house but she thought he did not mean it and saw it as a test. Now he began to ask her about the planes when he came back from work. She construed his kindness as pity and she could not bear that, so it became a task for her, to conquer this fear, to blank out not only the sound but the riot of alarm brought about by the high steel whining sound of the planes braking overhead.

She set herself to work at it, to erase Joseph's pity, and by constant exercise of will she gradually began to succeed. It was tiring. She concentrated so hard through the days that there was in those first months little energy for her own work, but she knew, in some way even more important than proving herself to Joseph, that this had to be survived. It was hard, it took a great deal out of her, but she was encouraged by the belief that she could not have done it before she met Joseph. She drove the fears deeper into her mind, into the pit of her mind, until they lay with the other terrible fears, but, she thought, inert, safe unless unleashed by new monsters.

And in this struggle the Botanical Gardens and the Edwardian parade became her allies, the earthed powers of her daily life, people in shops who smiled at her, the old lady who read the *Daily Telegraph* so intently, chain-smoked and took mid-morning coffee about the time she did, the 'resting' actors in the junk shop, the talkative polo-necked idealist in the bookshop, the greengrocer and the butcher, the black swans and Marianne North's gallery, the ticket collector who was invariably chatty when she stood on the small platform waiting for the tube to take her into London and to Joseph, the lush meanders by the river.

'They seem to have settled in rather well,' said Julia after a day trip.

'And the house?'

'Hideous, but Natasha has made it look rather bohemian. Against heavy odds. She has a touch.'

'She has the gift,' said Matthew, as if correcting her, but refusing to look up from *One Day in the Life of Ivan Denisovich*. He could and had to finish it before bed.

'She tells me that Joseph, as she calls him, had promised her an instant circle of friends from the BBC who also live there. But little sign as yet.'

'Takes time.'

'We went into Kew Gardens. They were breathtaking. She is very lucky to have them. She's made some rather good watercolours.'

'Excellent.'

'But I still feel . . .'

She did not badger him for a response, knowing precisely the peculiar compulsion which could rivet you to finishing a book. But she left her *Silent Spring* unopened and sat back to comb the day and try to dig up clues to explain her persisting unease.

'It was in Kew Gardens that our love for each other grew and was wholly realised,' he told their daughter. 'I now believe that, after a few months, your mother began to feel totally safe and when I imagine her now in that house, in the street and in the Gardens, or by the river and with our friends in those early years, I see how contentment made her beautiful. I look at the few photographs that remain from those days, seeking out shadows but what I see is happiness. I find it unbearable that I destroyed that as on so many days since I am convinced I did. Her smile in the photographs even now so many years later makes me smile in return, as it did many others, just for the life, the wit her eyes conveyed, the shine of her. She told me, "You have infiltrated my heart." Then she would laugh and turn away.

'Kew was where she did her best work, where both of us made a serious start on our journey into fiction. We were full of hope, unfearful of failure, expecting very little, the doing was what mattered, her painting, our writing and reading each other's work; living in the dream, I suppose, of being artists, although I could never find the confidence to describe myself as an artist. Natasha could. Natasha was. There were new friends, there was, there really was, you must believe me, settled happiness and most of all there was, three years after we arrived, you.

'In the English classical suburban reaches of Kew Gardens we played out the parts we were inventing for ourselves. You think you shape your life. Even when circumstances lift you up on a wholly unpredicted tide and deposit you somewhere you'd never thought of, you still think that in some way this was engineered; by yourself. The idea that we are little more than flecks of spray on the tides of time or randomly rearranged particles remains hard to take, however intellectually convincing, as do all other theories proving the relentless demotion, even demolition, of our significance in the scheme of things. But then, young, together, we thought we owned our lives.

'I had not counted on being seduced by my attachment to the Arts Department. After work I still set off back home as soon as I could, making excuses not to join the "one last drink before you go" crowd, eager to be with Natasha and the novel. But in the mornings I was eager, perhaps just as eager, to get to work, to be in the cutting rooms or on location or in a script conference or in the canteen listening to the arguments brought on by the previous night's programmes, programmes which seemed to the producers to be of crucial importance to the mind and spirit of the nation, of the world of mankind itself! For the first time since leaving school and my home town I felt inside a society. Different though it was, hoisted into a new class in one heave as I was, I had been raised up into the mongrel media middle-class club and I was at home.'

—m—

His traineeship was coming to an end. It had been a time without ambition. He had been shuttled around the BBC, 'taught' by being chucked in at the deep end, provided with no lifebelt, and left to the devices of a faith in common sense, talent and proof of both through work. What he might do in the future rarely troubled him. But now the traineeship was coming to an end.

'I have to get a real job in the BBC. It's the only way I can make films,' he said to Natasha. They were in their garden, in the shade of the pear tree, late Saturday afternoon, only a few planes, the arrival routes shared more equally over West London during the weekend, the weekend a prime time for being together. His earnestness made her smile, as it always did, and it slightly annoyed him, but his conviction rather disturbed her.

'You write,' she said, 'you spend hours writing, here, in the evenings, this morning, tomorrow much of the day.' And we are together, bound in word and in deed and in our own private world. 'Isn't that enough?'

'I need a job,' he said, 'I have a mortgage to pay.'

'We agreed we would sell the house as soon as one of us said that.'

'We need a wage coming in. One of us has to work. I can make these films for television, don't you see, as the job I do. It's not films for the cinema but it's films all the same. And films that everyone can see if they want to. They can be good. Two of the television directors I know have gone on to make feature films.'

'You told me they weren't as good as their television films.' The notion of Joe planning to go even further away alarmed her. 'And what do you know about feature films?'

'I could learn.' He smiled at her. 'It's a job, Natasha. And to do that I need to be a producer.' He did not admit the strength of the need for this job, its sudden imperative. This was the world he now so much wanted to be part of, whatever Natasha said or however much he agreed with her.

She did not pursue it. The day was too good to spoil and besides how could he resist? She knew that he had dreamed of heroes and adventures, of happy love and effortless laughter in the Palace Picture House in Wigton as a boy; at university he had discovered cinema and written about it and made an attempt to copy it and since then his enthusiasm had not abated. And now he had the opportunity to make films 'that everyone can see if they want to', he said, meaning back home, meaning back there, for those who thought he had left them behind for something better. How could she, why should she resist him in this? And what would be the use? His fretful, determined, must-succeed urgency was too strong for her.

And yet his decision to go for the post of producer, to get the key to the magic kingdom of film-making and to convince her on that warm healing suburban late afternoon with the evening mapped out and the Sunday promising a day of perfect unity, felt like a warning, that the world out there, his world, was beginning to exercise a fateful magnetic pull, away from her.

Joe sweated out the weeks before the interview for the producer post. He was still a dogsbody. He made tea. He carried props. He was sent on errands at crucial times and so he missed seeing the director for whom he was working set up some of the best shots. He showered the editor with suggestions and learned to live with the punch when they came back rejected. He was keen, he was willing, he was everything they wanted him to be and was unaware that it was not what he did but his energy and passion for the whole notion of the thing that impressed them and even endeared him to them. The breakthrough came when they accepted a suggestion and said he could direct the film. If he got through that, he would be given the job.

It was a film based on two painters in the North of England. One was a coal miner, whose work he had seen when he was in Newcastle. The directness of the work – men crowded at the pit face, men walking along the cinder track pre-dawn to the early shifts, the lights from the silhouetted pit making the telegraph poles look like crosses on the road to Calvary, men in pubs, work-worn faces, exhausted lungs, but no surrender, laughter like small-arms fire all around the drinking trenches. This work reached back into the past of Joe's family and though he understood that his reaction was visceral rather than aesthetic the 'rawness' and 'grittiness' of this subject, as one of the other producers acknowledged, got it through at the programme's ideas meeting.

He vaguely sensed that both he and the painter were being patronised, and yet even if he had been keenly aware of it, the imperative was to get an idea accepted. The other subject was a young woman of widely noted beauty, the daughter of a miner from Cumberland, born quite near Joe's town. She was already a London 'name' with the in-crowd, who paused for a while in their pursuit of Abstract Expressionism and Pop Art and Action Painting to admire and admit her violent disturbed landscapes, which were of the mountains of the Lake District painted as if under the influence of drugs, illness or nightmares.

He would intercut the two films, he proposed; the whole would last about twenty minutes. He put aside his writing to work out the shots, the story-board, the style. It would, he decided, and Natasha agreed, be appropriate to employ a different style for each film. He was so unselfconsciously enraptured, Disque Bleu at the ready, the auteur, that Natasha could deny him nothing and this time she did not tease him, even when he fantasised about the cinematic influences he could bring to bear. The miner would be grainy, Italian Realism, De Sica, an overall sense of dark oppression redeemed by bursts of painting, the night lights at the pit head and the telegraph poles become crucifixions.

The miner's daughter would be lyrical, something of Renoir, a touch of the fantasy of Truffaut, could there be a hint of Fellini? And yet the photography of the mountains themselves (he would ask the artist to take him to her favourite mountain locations to make drawings, on large white sheets, in thick black charcoal which matched her long jet hair) would be brooding, with a *Wuthering Heights* feel to it, Bergman-esque, as would the interviews, not so much interviews as big close-up statements, unsmiling, no ingratiation. The choice of music took him hours but in the end he settled for 'Nimrod' played by the Grimethorpe Colliery Brass Band for the miner and 'The Lark Ascending' for the miner's daughter. *The Miner and the Miner's Daughter*: an uncompromisingly Lawrentian title, he thought. The twenty-minute length was a problem: it could, he thought, be at least three times as long.

He asked Natasha to join him for the filming in Cumberland. They stayed at a small hotel a few score yards from Bassenthwaite, the most northerly lake. On the last night they had a crew dinner. Jessica, the artist, the guest of honour, stick thin, ate little and drank steadily. Joe, unusually, drank several glasses of red wine and was merry. The film was good. The world was good. The world could get no better. Alex Foster, the cameraman, had saved his skin; the reports back from London on the rushes were encouraging, he was in Cumberland and he was with Natasha. Jessica had contradicted rumour and been cooperative and read passionately two passages from Van Gogh's diaries which, Joe thought, slotted in like the final piece in a jigsaw. He was twenty-four, he was a film director, he loved Natasha, he loved the crew, he was in a posh hotel, he was amazed that he was him, here, now, walking on a tightrope to the bar for the last round and not yelling or singing, despite the bells of jubilation pealing inside his skull.

Alex, the cameraman, stayed for a last drink. He had devoted more than usual attention to photographing Jessica, especially in the close-ups. Her wide-boned, taut face, the big dark brown eyes made darker by black mascara, that long crow-black hair, had attracted him strongly and her flirting had stirred anticipation. Though she looked like a chiselled remote beauty, her accent still proudly bore the sound of her Northern childhood and Alex found encouragement in that: earthy.

Jessica had been warm to Natasha from the moment they met. Joe had told her about Natasha's painting and Jessica, in her mid-thirties a few years older and key stages further on in her career, took equality and a painterly comradeship so unpatronisingly for granted that Natasha, who had expressed doubts about joining them on the filming, found her doubts dissolve and even seem a little shameful, having prejudged someone to their disadvantage. Nevertheless she had followed only a small percentage of the filming, preferring to find a place of her own in which to sketch, or to read in the old-fashioned, oak-beamed lounge of the small distinguished hotel.

Joe brought back a double whisky for Alex, a large brandy for Jessica, nothing for Natasha who had merely sipped at her third glass of wine, and for himself a malt whisky, his first, a Glenfiddich recommended by the barman.

'Here's to Jessica,' he said, and accepted her offer of a Black Sobranie.

'Happy days,' said Alex, raising his glass and looking very directly at Jessica, 'but for somebody like you, I expect every day is happy.'

'Why's that?' Jessica took such a pull at her brandy that Joe feared she might want more.

'Artists,' said Alex, shaking his greying head, 'do what they want to do. Result – happiness.'

'You're an artist,' she said, 'are you happy?'

'I just take the pictures,' he said, 'the best that could be said is that it's a bit of a knack.'

'I disagree,' she said, drank again and looked at Joe, who looked across at the barman who understood and brought another. 'Photographers call themselves artists – look at Robert Frank, look at Cartier Bresson. And film cameramen do more than they do. But are you happy? If you are happy you can't be an artist. All artists have to be unhappy.'

'Rubbish,' said Joe. He sipped the elatingly light malt whisky and considered the matter closed.

'It is not rubbish,' said Jessica in a level tone recognised as anger by Natasha.

'OK. We're all unhappy now and then. But to say an artist *has* to be unhappy, how can you generalise?'

'Disturbed might be better,' said Jessica, finishing the brandy as the next arrived on the table, 'or depressed, flawed in some way, or wounded. Or all of them together, most likely. And the greater the flaws and the deeper the wounds the better the artist. Look at Van Gogh. Look at Kafka. Look at John Clare. Look at Nijinsky. Cheers.'

Natasha saw that Joe was drunk. She saw also a stubborn look about him now, a look, she feared, which indicated the clouding of reason through the poison of alcohol.

'Look at Jane Austen,' he said. 'Look at Henry Fielding. Look at Picasso if you want. And nobody said Shakespeare was "wounded" or "flawed" or "depressed". He just got on with it.'

'We know nothing about the private lives, the real lives of those people,' Jessica said, sitting bolt upright on her chair. She looks like a witch, Alex thought, a beautiful wicked witch. 'Whenever we do find out anything about them we always discover that they have been traumatised.'

'Not all.' Joe sipped again: it went down so sweetly. 'Not all.'

'All. All who are any good.'

'What do you think?'

Natasha sought a neutral exit. She rather agreed with Jessica, but Joe was already becoming flustered.

'She agrees with me,' said Jessica and gave Natasha a loving smile. 'But she doesn't want to say so.'

Joe smiled at what he saw as flattery.

'Natasha always says what she thinks,' he said.

'I think,' said Natasha, as truthfully as she could, 'that the roots of all creativity are so tangled and dark that any attempt to identify them, using a single method, is bound to be unsatisfactory.'

'There you are,' said Joe.

'She agrees with me,' said Jessica.

'Couldn't both of you be right?' Alex turned to the bar and pointed to his empty whisky glass and also to Joe's much diminished malt.

'You absolutely *know* I'm right, though,' Jessica said, 'don't you, Natasha?'

'Look,' said Joe, with only a slight slur, 'you are absolutely not right. Not absolutely right. What about cathedrals? They're the best art. Or those Egyptian statues. Whoever was depressed building a cathedral or a sphinx unless he was a poor sod of a slave? Then he was just unhappy with life, full stop. Because he was a slave. Not because he was an artist, which he was. It was being an artist that kept him going most likely, although he wouldn't be allowed to think of himself as an artist, not in those days, poor sod. And was the man in the Lascaux Caves traumatised? That's the question. Was he?'

'Undoubtedly,' said Jessica, enjoying Joe's flailing.

'Tripe. Anyway. Who knows? And who cares? I think his cave drawings are better than Picasso's. Picasso probably nicked them. You all do.'

'Artists?'

'Yes. Look how they robbed Africa. Modigliani. A man in Paris showed me the evidence years ago.' Natasha was puzzled at the surly tone of personal resentment.

'I bet you think women should know their place as well.'

'What place? What's women got to do with it? I like women.'

'No you don't. Not strong women. Not women who argue back.'

'What do you know? Anyway, what's it got to do with art? You just jump about.'

Jessica applauded. 'Come to Cumberland to see the world in a nutshell!'

'Why not? That's what you do, isn't it? Paint these hills to be all hills and all moods and all everything.' He reached out for his second malt and Natasha forced herself not to warn him off it. 'A grain of sand, Jessica,' he waved the malt whisky, 'remember that we see the world in a grain of sand.'

'Blake was a depressive,' she said. 'He was seriously unhappy.'

'For Christ's sake! Was Turner, who is miles better than Blake, was Turner depressive?'

'We don't know enough.'

'That's always your cop-out.' Joe brooded for a few moments but inside the muddied stirrings of his mind the moments seemed an age of contemplation. 'The trouble is you can say what you like because nobody knows and all I'm saying is that the opposite of what you say is just as true like most so-called famous generalisations: the opposite is always just as true.'

'You're unhappy but you won't admit it,' said Jessica, whose slender body was fortified and steadied, it seemed at this stage, by alcohol. She swept back the second brandy.

'Beddy byes?' said Alex, his hopes of a conquest deflated.

'You are very, very unhappy,' said Jessica and she held his eyes in her gaze as intensely as a hypnotist. 'And until you admit it you'll write nothing any good.'

'Admit what?'

The bravado in his tone alerted Natasha.

'Admit it,' said Jessica sotto voce. 'We're twins, Joe. And polar opposites. Admit it.'

'Admit what?'

This time it was more of a plea and Natasha remembered that her best friend and bridesmaid, Frances, now in America, had spoken of seeing the 'shadows' around Joseph and she had dismissed the insight as merely part of Frances's psychic indulgence. But undoubtedly, now, the shadows were gathering over him. He was losing something of himself. It was unlike anything she had seen in him before.

'Confess the suffering. Admit the pain.' Jessica beat her hands on the arm of the chair.

Natasha saw a face of Joseph which was new to her. It had loosened. There was some fear in it and an unmistakable violence. Even his voice had changed, thicker toned, coarser.

'It's not fair,' he said, picking out the monosyllable with great care. 'I mean – it's not true.'

But as he spoke particles of fracturing memories swirled through his mind and he was infested again by the distress of adolescent years when he was imprisoned in panic, distraught, when his consciousness drifted uncontrollably away from his body and took away the life of him, when he saw a spot of light which was him, his soul, his being, hover above him, threatening to leave him for dead.

He thought that had gone for good. Even now it was impossible for him fully to admit to himself, let alone articulate to anyone else, what had been a severe depression, a breakdown, which for almost two years had made him febrile, afraid of solitude, afraid of cracking into a howl of desperation, helplessly isolated in that small town just a few miles away. But how could he call out? Be such a baby. Be such a coward. And who would listen or understand? Time, the shedding of skins through growing adolescent strengths, work. Rachel and now Natasha had cauterised that, he thought, he believed, he needed to believe.

He looked at Natasha, puzzled, holding on, breathing in shallow gasps, mouth slackening: he looked at Natasha for faith.

'I can see . . .'

'No!' Natasha held up her hand to Jessica and pushed it towards her as if she were physically warding off a curse. 'No!' They held each other's look.

Suddenly Jessica relaxed. A sweet and gentle smile transformed her face to innocence. She blew Natasha a kiss. 'Come to my room,' she said to Alex. 'Bring brandy.'

And with another blown kiss to Natasha and a triumphant look at the downcast lolling head of Joe, she left them, quickly followed by a greatly confused Alex bearing brandy.

The barman came across with a large glass of water. Natasha nodded her thanks and indicated he should retreat. She waited for Joseph to look up. She knew something now that she had not previously known about him. She knew the fear that was all but suffocating him. When he did look up, so helpless, so ashamed, she could have wept. This was another Joseph, this was a different man, stripped bare.

CHAPTER TWENTY-ONE

'In the first years, Kew Gardens was very good for us. Once your mother (as I came to think at tremendous expense of willpower) had overcome or repressed the fears triggered by the sound of the braking, descending aeroplanes, she found a mooring safe until the waters rose to a flood. She seemed happier for a longer period, her friends would say, than at any time in her life. The darkness was still in her but because I was away much of the day and because, I now realise, she saved up or at least waited for my return, to talk, to be together, to express all that spirit and vivacity that was hers, I did not see much of the darkness and when it revealed itself as fatigue or a clinging cold or a lustreless depression, I was always confident I could help her through it. I revelled in being able to help her, acting not as the flawed and disturbed man I knew myself to be but as someone whole, strong, further strengthened by helping one who was weaker. And I loved her so much.

'I remember getting off the tube at Kew Gardens and stepping out to get home, longing to put the key into the door to hear her voice and see her walk towards me and me to her, that small hall made a trysting place night after night. We continued to dwell, on one level, in an atmosphere of idealism which, I now think, was not only unsustainable but carried the seeds of destruction within it; for any falling away came to seem to be a fundamental failing of the marriage. Yet one of the most powerful attractions between us was that the marriage allowed and encouraged this idealism, that was at its core, for her always and for me equally in the early years. And it was so good: it was so fine, our attempt to find and capture the best of life.

'We continued to read out passages of our books to each other. We were austere and high-minded in our artistic tastes and judgements to an extent that to outsiders might have hit caricature and been sneered at but to us was the only way to live. Our judgements on events, works, people, were unforgiving and although we disagreed often enough we were together inside our own bubble of exhilarated certainties which, again to outsiders, could have seemed arrogant and foolish but to us were goals to be pursued, truths to be grasped, the world as we found it to be thought through. In this she led.

'There were other levels. Of course. There were two people boxed in together playing Blind Man's Bluff, bumping into the furniture of our old lives, grappling with the stranger who was often more evident than the lover. There were two uprooted exiles. I wanted her to remain my ideal, older, wiser, more stern, richer in history and character: she, I think, wanted me to become her project, younger, apparently malleable, innocent, responsive to guidance. I could make her laugh, both at me and with me. She could always make me smile in admiration.

'Was our high-mindedness merely overreaching conceit? Did it become hubris? It was serious, believe me; it felt real. But maybe it was a fond falseness, tempting nemesis, too long sealed off, waiting to be exposed and crumble in the light.

'We were convinced that reading great literature would lead us to great thoughts and teach us how to write great works ourselves; we, or rather Natasha, had that capacity of the refined intellectual to find in the most mundane exchange a key which would turn it into an abstract discussion. That was what mattered. We enjoyed adequate means and on that basis were mutually unworldly, not contemptuous of but uninterested in a life of getting and spending.'

'It really was like that,' he told their daughter, knowing very well that overemphasis could be counter-productive, but wanting to make sure she knew at least how much it meant to him to tell her.

'At that time we seemed to spin around each other closer and closer in perfect gravity.'

Julia had said on her first visit to Natasha, 'London suburbs are all right for children – they know nothing else – both Matthew and I grew up in a London suburb. But for adults? I think not.' Natasha was pleased as the months went by to discover that her experience contradicted Julia's pronouncement. Perhaps she was reliving a missed part of her childhood. Perhaps, she thought, we all have to spend part of our adult lives filling in the unexperienced but necessary parts of our childhood in order to make us fit for present purpose. There was a feeling of tolerance and kindness in the Kew suburb and something of a child's dream landscape in the exotic amplitude of the Gardens. She drifted through them in the early months again and again, soothed by the fantasies of juxtapositions and lulled into a waking sleep by the eternal flow of the Thames.

She made three women friends, none of whom had an untroubled past, all of whom were in varying stages of quiet retreat, holding on, quick to appreciate Natasha as a soul mate, carefully coming to trust and love her and see that despite her high style, she too had lacunae, forbidden places, had seen an abyss. Through these women a network began to grow. Joe brought a couple of the fabled television people into play, and a neighbouring older sculptor and his wife, a potter, became friendly. The immediate neighbours invited them round for drinks. It was good that they arrived in Kew in a warm spring and set up house in a decent summer when people could move around for tea or more occasionally a drink in gardens which had once been orchards and sit under the fruit trees as the fruit began to move from green to ripeness.

Natasha did watercolours for a while and Joe suggested he ask the local bookshop if he would let her have an exhibition there, but she was not at all enthusiastic. It would, she thought, be too intrusive of her in this community which, she hoped, would eventually become hers. There needed to be caution. Any sort of local prominence would set her apart. And besides, she wanted to write, this had always been her first love, she told him.

She started for the first time to write fiction and put her poetry aside. The time needed to attend to it and the inevitable sinking into herself in order to find the images to meet the sound and the sense she wanted took her on her first constructive journey towards the remote radiation, the fission of her past. She could sit alone at the kitchen table half the day and not write a word and yet feel that the life of the day had been unwasted. She decided to write in English.

To some observers when she came out to shop in the parade or sit and drink a coffee, generally alone, outside the station buffet which opened onto the parade, or when she drifted towards the Gardens and the river, she seemed abstracted, aloof, rather like the black swans, sometimes undrawn by the custom of the small polite passing smile, *nerveuse*, well skilled at concealing the pressures within, ethereal even, but someone looked out for, a remarked-on, complex figure in the easy English suburban landscape.

———⚭———

David had suggested they meet 'just the two of us' before dinner, 'any old pub will do very nicely, pubs have been a conspicuous gap in my life recently'. Joe fussed for a while and then settled for a pub on Kew Green beyond the Georgian church, beyond the picture-postcard cricket pitch. It was still warm enough to take their drinks outside on a deck overlooking the river.

'Long time no see,' said David, hitting the first word with mocking emphasis. He raised his gin drowned in tonic, took a small sip and enveloped Joe in an intense gaze of greeting. He had led them to the edge of the deck. There was only one other table occupied and that some distance away. He accepted Joe's offer of a cigarette.

'I'm glad you're drinking beer,' he said.

'I'm only doing it to fit your stereotyping.'

'Not a bad way to disguise oneself,' said David, 'though not an option for me, I'm afraid. Not in England.'

'No absinthe?'

'Now, now.' He looked intently at Joe, to Joe's flattered embarrassment. 'Rather strained. Be careful. You don't have to do everything at once. Natasha will tell you that. Excited with life. Life good?'

'Life good. You?'

'Agony, but one soldiers on.' He puffed on his cigarette as if he wished he did not really have to smoke. 'Africa is every bit as marvellous as I knew it would be. The people there must be the most charming and luckless in the world. But all one can see in the future are disasters and corruption and rip-offs by Western colonists in new capitalist clothing. It will get much worse. Everyone says that. Everyone who knows. Until the Africans take it in their own hands. And one is helpless. It will take generations.'

'Have you been to South Africa?'

'Inspirational. The anti-apartheid movement is so noble, Joe, it makes you almost proud to be human except that apartheid itself is so despicable it makes you ashamed to be human. I think a lot depends on what's happening in America with the Freedom Movement and Martin Luther King. If he can change America then it will be another shot that will ring around the world. The days of apartheid will be numbered. You ought to be there, Joe, it would open you up.' He smiled, that quick, wide Mephistophelean smile.

'Do you really think so?'

'Oh yes. But do *you* really think so? No. So let me not be tedious about it. Your turn.'

Joe delivered his update as quickly as he could, anxious to ask David more about Africa.

'And the writing?'

'I sent off a novel, to Nelson and Chapel. *The Metropolitan Line.*'

'A distinguished publisher. A perfectly acceptable title. And?'

'After six weeks,' Joe had told this to no one but Natasha, 'it came back with a nice enough letter. Plot too thin, this good, that OK, the other not so good, politics too obvious and an intrusion, cannot publish it as it stands, if you want to discuss further please contact.'

'Did you?'

'No. He was right. It was an effort not a novel. I've started another.'

'Set in the North.'

'Wait and, I hope, see.'

'I can "see" already. Ju-ju. I saw your little film on the two Northern painters. Quite good, I thought. I could have done without the arty bits, the Bergman and Renoir references and such. I rather prefer cinema verité, but this was made with love and well crafted.'

'That was the cameraman. And the film editor. And the programme editor. He polished up the rough cut.'

'Never mind. I saw you in it throughout and it had your name on it at the end. That will do. The overture has been played. The programme's

239

editor is Ross McCulloch, isn't it? He's rather famous. Was it he who gave you your job?'

'Yes.'

'That's a bouquet in itself.'

'It was only because I told him I didn't want to work in television, I preferred radio, but the traineeship dictated I *had* to do some television and I said I would only do an arts programme. It made him laugh.'

'Always a good ploy: laughter puts people off their guard. The Foreign Office ought to run courses in it.'

'He lives near here. He has a big house on the river.'

'I believe I met him once, years ago, at the Partons'. Do you know them? They have a truly astonishing collection of African art. Henry Moore was there. Who else do you see? Who have you met on your metropolitan line?'

Joe was only too pleased to answer and in passing to boast. He told David about Peter Mills, the older trainee, former President of the Oxford Union, and hell bent on a political career; of Edward, a poet, who had also overlapped at Oxford, now running a poetry magazine on the radio; Arthur, again from Oxford, already a staged playwright; Anthony, Oxford yet again, who was surely destined either to storm the West End theatre or just as surely become the rising new British director in Hollywood, and . . .

'Let me interrupt,' said David. 'I presume there are one or two more from Oxford and others from other universities, all met through the media network?' Joe nodded. 'It's what I have christened "generational kinship",' David continued. 'I'm rather pleased with the phrase. You are attracted to each other not through blood or class or even those old school ties but through talent and attitude. These people and others like them will stay with you now for the duration. You knew none of these people when you were at Oxford – not that it matters but I knew all of them – but what is important is that this new medium is bringing about a sort of cadre with connections and recognitions and mutual simila-rities very like the more traditional tribes. What is exciting is that it has suddenly gained a critical mass, like the old aristocracy, the real old aristocracy, though of course not as significant, yet. Fascinating! And, Joe, there you are, caught up in it, and all through no fault of your own!'

'Of yours.'

'Very likely. How gratifying to have one's little theories proved. One can understand why Einstein always had a smile on his face. We must go now. Natasha will think us rude.'

'She's quite . . .'

'Not quite, very, good mannered. Which is one, only one, of the reasons I adore her. Quick, quick! How far?'

'Fifteen minutes if we step on the gas.'

'That far! I suppose the exercise will do me no lasting harm.' He put down his scarcely touched drink. 'It's so good to see you, Joe.'

'And you,' said Joe, with equal warmth.

'Well, that's all right, then. Onward!'

David had brought them James Baldwin's *Another Country* – 'which I cannot recommend highly enough. He writes beautifully and what he says is very important.' Joe felt challenged. 'A friend of mine is trying to arrange for us to meet when I go back through Paris.'

'Paris,' said Natasha.

'Joe's very clever to hide you both away in Kew Gardens,' said David, 'this is where exotic flora grow best, after all.'

—m—

In Oxford there had been one favoured cinema. In London there were many and they could ride the tube to the urban villages of Hampstead, Chelsea and Kensington and right into the dazzle of options in the West End. Their London was first mapped by its cinemas. As the masterpieces from Europe continued to roll in, idols discovered at Oxford and the directors or auteurs made up what was later seen as a golden age – Truffaut and Polanski vied with new films from Resnais, De Sica, Antonioni, Fellini, Buñuel, Renoir and Bergman.

It was at this time that Joe began to appreciate qualities of those shoals of American and English films he had in his youth seen so intensely, carelessly, the 'flicks', and absorbed unselfconsciously. Was he perhaps the more directly affected because of that? He discussed this with Natasha. Perhaps unconscious education was the deepest, the purest. She too believed that primary and self-found images penetrated more strongly when there was no analytical barrier, nothing but the acceptance of pure sensations, a direct feed to the unconscious. Joe saw some truth in that although he thought that in her case exactly the opposite obtained. And critical selection had to come in somewhere. But he recognised that for example the most fruitful factor in what might be called his musical education and certainly his love of music was not the hours spent under the unforgiving tutelage of Miss Snaith, the piano teacher, nor even his attempts at Oxford and since to try to assess the classics. It was those hours, daily, yearly, spent singing in various choirs as a boy, singing authentic plainsong and nineteenth-century anthems, singing psalms and hymns often of haunting melody, but basically just singing, letting the music directly take over his mind without filter and be returned to the air umoderated by anything but a basic, unthinking mechanical skill.

A key to the bounty of their lives in London was the BBC Arts Department's willingness to provide, on receipt of two modestly priced stubs, a full return on theatre though not cinema tickets. It was, as it would continue to be, Xanadu. In one year what they saw included *Uncle Vanya, John Gabriel Borkman, The Father, The Seagull, Six Characters in Search of an Author, St Joan, Othello* and *Hamlet*; they saw new plays by Beckett, Pinter, Orton, Osborne, Arden and Wesker; occasionally they went with new friends and would eat afterwards at the French Club just off St James's, a small, literary enclosure, aristocratically connected, to which they were introduced by Anthony, the television drama director, and his wife Victoria, a painter who became a friend of Natasha. Then back, a race to the underground and to domestic Kew, inflamed.

On nights in they would set aside time to watch television, and Joe became addicted to the drama, often worked on, directed and written by people he saw around the studios, which added a dimension of privilege to the viewing. Joe saw on the screen a British new wave which portrayed much of the society he had left behind. Natasha built up a picture of Britain whose humour and harshness were new to her; dramas whose anger activated Joseph's rage, comedies which would wring him dry of a laughter so infectious that she had to join in however foreign it could all still seem. He identified with so much of it!

At that time his undirected chameleon nature intrigued her. As he reached out blindly for his own voice, the powerful voices of others poached his mind again and again. He would come out of Chekhov wanting to be true and lyrical and tragic all at once; he would come out of Beckett wanting to find the bare knuckle of his prose; he would come out of Strindberg blaming himself for being so lily-livered about basic passions – where was Greed? Where was Vengeance? Where were Lust, Envy, Power, the tectonic plates of our nature? He would come out of Ibsen looking around for the Great Moral Issues of the Day. He would come from the realistic drama on television wanting to join that conquering group of committed social dramatists. He would come out of Shakespeare thinking he ought to give up.

Every writer, on stage, in television, film and novels had a seasoning which Joe saw was their key individuality. He knew that all that mattered in the end was to find a way to express individuality, to give your own unique testament, your mind-print, whatever it turned out to be, otherwise what was the point of writing? But how did you seek it? Did you know when you had found it? And If and When you found it, would it be good enough? The novel he was now writing, set in Cumberland, *The Kingdom Was Lost,* could bring him to a fever of excitement but also to a sickness of anxiety as he wrote and, for the first time, grimly re-wrote, striving to put the sound in his head into words on the paper. He would come to bed late and want to wake her to talk and make love and Natasha knew he needed that.

Natasha seemed to have a much surer inner voice, he thought. There was far less struggle. She had finally decided to take the advice she had given to Joseph and she went back towards her own childhood – not to the roots of it, not to the private pain, skirting that pain, but to the time of the aunts, the breaks in the clouds when they took her up. She wanted to write about Isabel and Alain but they were too dear to her; she feared that she would hurt them by writing about them in the rather mocking way in which she described the provincial unease of her aunts. She laid a melodramatic plot, the preventable and deceitfully reported death of a child and the ending aimed to shock.

She was unlike Joseph who was sometimes all but overcome with agitation to be published. Let it take its time, she thought, let it grow. And she told herself that writing in English helped. It made her think harder. That was good. It gave her a distance from the wholly French and familiar material. Joseph helped her whenever she asked for help. The pride he took in her work never faltered.

CHAPTER TWENTY-TWO

Joe got the job but, as if to show him that this would make his life tougher and not easier, Ross made him sweat. He was now in the ring equally with the established producers to get his next commission. He was told that Borges was too intractable; that King's College Choir was too familiar through its Christmas carols; that Graham Sutherland was too obvious and Maria Callas too dangerous. He became desperate and suggested Elvis Presley and the White Takeover of Black Music. This was considered to be outside the programme's brief. He wanted to suggest the new sound, the city sound of British music, the Beatles, the Stones, but he did not have the nerve. Yet it was a new pulse in the land.

Joe sensed it, like others, like swallows sensing the time to fly south. It made him want to dance. It passed Natasha by. The music did not make her want to dance and Joe discovered, by omission, how much over the last few years he had missed dancing. Yet he could always be persuaded by what she loved. He deferred to her taste almost invariably. When they went back to Paris, she took him to club-cafés around the Sorbonne or in the narrow streets of romantic entrapment on the Left Bank and there they drank wine while the confident heirs of Brassens and Brel, of Piaf and Greco sang their poems accompanied by an acoustic guitar or an accordion. They embraced their audience with effortless ease in the balladeer music and words that were in proud direct descent from the mediaeval troubadours of old independent Provence, now melded to the body of France. Joe was taken over by them.

On his return from their holiday in Paris he suggested a film on French Chanson which was accepted. Natasha was proud of her country's songs, moved that Joseph should want to make a film about them and excited to spend ten unexpected days in Paris with him and the crew in a hotel in the Rue Jacob. She went to the 'concerts' in the cafés but on most of the days she met her friends or made for the Café Flore to write in public like a true Parisienne. Though he was studying she sought out François and encouraged him to play truant. He seemed to have lost all the ground made up in London, and she grieved at his wasted expression, the hopelessness in his eyes.

Twice she took him to the filming. Once in the run-down and unsettling area around the site of the Bastille, the second time in the great city market of Les Halles. They went at dawn, heard the broad provincial accents and saw the workmen, the onion soup, the brandy and the raw expressive French hands and faces. Joseph was collecting snippets of conversation, groupings, portraits, assembling, he hoped, a common Frenchness to intercut with one of Brassens's songs. Natasha could scarcely have been happier. This was a France she could embrace, the true France, she thought, France of the meat and the wine, of bread and earth. Joseph was impressively preoccupied, she thought, fussing but determined to get what he wanted, talking to the crew about every shot, dreaming of *Les Enfants du Paradis*. François was heartbreakingly happy, taken up by Alex, who let him look through the viewfinder, slap the clapperboard, carry completed rolls of film over to the assistant cameraman and help with the improvised cart which was to enable Joe to do a tracking shot. François was filmed sitting at a table, drinking coffee and brandy like a true worker. He was treated as an adult by these important English film makers. On that chilly morning the boy was as near the fulfilment of his life as he ever was to be and Natasha's heart ached to see it.

'We are at our wits' end,' said Véronique. She had invited Natasha to lunch at a restaurant near the church of St Germain, on the Boulevard St Germain. It was the sort of place Natasha had been taken to only on special occasions and yet she felt more at ease in its intact art nouveau interior than her stepmother, who pushed her food away hardly touched, impatient to get out a cigarette, nervous of this meeting.

'I think it is a mistake to ask him to do the baccalaureate yet again,' said Natasha.

'What else is there? He said he wants to go into the navy which is absurd, but even if he did, there would be more examinations and François cannot pass examinations. Louis tells me I must deal with it.' She lifted up her cigarette in a gesture which Natasha interpreted as untypically dismissive of her father. Véronique had never been so intimate.

'Had he nothing to suggest?'

'You know your father. If one cannot pass examinations there is nothing to be done.'

'Why don't you see if he can join a film company? Something very basic to start with. Something on the technical side, to do with cameras or sound recording or the lights. He would love that.'

'How can I organise that?'

'Doesn't my father know someone?'

'Not in the cinema. I think he stopped going twenty years ago! Of course he respects what Joseph does. He has always said that Georges Brassens articulates the French language as well as Charles de Gaulle himself.'

'I don't think Joseph knows any French film makers.'

'You and Joseph have done enough. I still think it was too much to give you the responsibility of François when you had just got married. How could I do that?'

'I was glad to do it . . .'

'The only suggestion Louis has made – and this was very reluctantly advanced – is that François go to the laboratory in Brittany and help there for some months. They have a little boat to collect specimens. They make experiments . . .'

'Why not?'

'What would it lead to?'

'It might make him happy,' Natasha said. 'It would give him time.'

'He has no more time.'

'How can you say that?'

'I don't like the Brittany idea . . .'

'She doesn't like Brittany,' Natasha said to Joseph as they finished their wine later, in what had become the crew café in the Rue de Seine, 'because she fears my father has a mistress there.'

'Crikey!'

'Why else were we always forbidden to go?'

'Tons of reasons. I can't imagine your father . . . with . . . anybody else.'

'Everybody does it, Joseph.'

'Everybody?'

'In Oxford, didn't you realise? Among the dons.'

'Do they?'

She liked to shock him.

'It isn't too terrible,' she said.

'Except if you're at the receiving end.'

'It's common in France. It's almost compulsory among the elite.' She smiled.

'Really?'

'They say it's the most sophisticated way to keep a marriage fresh.'

'How can that be?'

'I love you looking so bewildered, Joseph.'

Where did that take the argument? She often did that. Cut him off through a mix of flattery and put-down which confused him.

'Maybe it will work for François,' said Joe, recovering his equilibrium with difficulty. Her revelation and the authoritative appendices had lodged like a dart, '– just being away from home can help to set you up and straighten you out.'

'Did that happen for you?'

Natasha never looked away when she asked a question. He loved her directness; he was proud of it, it was yet more evidence of her singularity. It could, though, force him to own up when he would much rather have kept silent or fudged it.

'Not really.'

'First you had Rachel. By then you had friends and all the Oxford things. Then me.'

'François will find friends,' he said in diplomatic ignorance.

'Will he? I hope so. The easiest way to solve a problem is to think of what you yourself would do – not what the problem person could do. That is what you have done. Never mind. Let's see if we can get him to Brittany. All they want, all they have wanted for years, is to get him off their hands. I can understand my father and pardon him. Not her. Not his mother.'

She felt a shadow of sadness as they smoked and listened to the fragments of sound drift down the narrow streets; Paris turning out the lights. As she saw it, what she thought of as his surface achievements, the external magnets of his television life, gave him a carapace of character which was ebullient and full of fun and which he could not wait to share with her. Yet, she believed, this was not the real Joseph, not her Joseph, and not as nourishing of their joint life as when they sat in the opposing armchairs in front of the electric fire and read great literature; or discussed and tried to understand Antonioni in the tube on the way back from *La Notte*; or stared, with contrary reactions, at the mediaeval religious paintings in the National Gallery. It was at these times that she was absolutely convinced that she saw the real Joseph. She saw him as someone from the lower depths reaching up and out for more light, more inner knowledge. This external world of film crews and television deadlines and rushing around for 'stories' was not the Joseph she wanted. Nor was it Joseph at his best.

She knew how he saw her. He still shone with love. He also, since the first visit to France, counted her a prize, as someone not won but delivered by fortune. He loved to tell and retell the story of their so amazingly nearly not meeting. He could calculate the probabilities against that meeting in fractions until, he said, they reached infinity. She knew that he could not always contain his surprise at her pedigree and word of it leaked out to one or two of his friends. She forgave him that, but it was a pity. It did not help her. On this night, as they walked down the street towards the River Seine and looked over to l'Ile de la Cité, was she safe enough to let him go away, into his own new arena of activity and ambition? She had to: he would not go far, she thought, and soon he would come to know, once and for all, what she knew, that their lives would be fulfilled only with each other and doing what was most essential to them.

On the embankment they watched the waters of the Seine flow brokenly under the lights, watched in close silence. Natasha looked down onto the river bank itself and remembered how they had danced under the bridges of Paris. Not so long ago.

His audacity and his ambition could exasperate her. He took on a film about a classical conductor. For the rehearsals he was allowed four film cameras which he directed simultaneously through a sound link-up to each of the four cameramen. He worked from a score.

'What do you know about reading a score?'

'I learned the piano. I was in choirs.'

'But this is Mahler; and Stravinsky.'

'People help. You just rehearse it,' Joe said, doggedly, not wanting to admit his own growing apprehension. There were an awful lot of lines and an awful lot of notes on those lines.

'You played the piano as a boy. How can that be enough?'

'Well,' said Joe, cutting off her argument before it turned him to jelly, 'I'm stuck with it now.'

And after the film was transmitted and she praised him, he said, 'So there!' and laughed loudly and ringingly and she was lifted into his triumph like a kite by the wind.

She came with him on his raids into the bigger world; Peter rushed them down by train to see the declaration of the result of a crucial marginal by-election which, he prophesied, if it swung Labour's way, could be the harbinger of a long-awaited election victory. Anthony and Victoria invited them to post-Bloomsbury gatherings of extraordinarily well-mannered and intimately interconnected writers and painters. Edward took them to what he called 'a good old Soho dump of a pub' to meet some of the university iconoclasts ripping into the establishment in a new satirical magazine which had been founded in the Oxford of Joe's time there. James ushered them back to Oxford to hear a lecture by Robert Graves, the newly elected Oxford professor of poetry, whose historical novels Joe had gobbled up at school. They queued for Nureyev and sought out a performance by Ashkenazy and Barenboim and Jacqueline du Pré; and went to what was promised to be a Turning Point production at the Royal Court. Portobello Road on a Saturday afternoon seemed a unique market for someone seeking out cheap yards of battered but once finely bound editions of *The Lives of the Poets* or Walter Scott or Dickens. And in all this Joe in some way grasped he was blindly following the pulse of a new beat in the land, a new sound, a new promise in the old bulldog blood. It was not

249

Natasha's city but it beckoned to Joseph. There came a time when she was able to stay at home alone as often as go with him, unwilling to spend or waste the energy on what she sometimes saw as little more than the incidental aspects of life even though they were harvested by Joseph with scything intensity.

She began, in her search for safety, to turn loneliness into a sort of contentment. She needed a distance. There were nights in summer in the evening when they were in the West End and the humidity was too uncomfortable for her, the crowds too pushy, the air too fetid, the meaning of the noise too scrambled, when she would look at him and see him as an animal in the metropolitan jungle, open to it, charged by it, prowling the pavements like a forest floor, and in those moments she would wonder who he really was.

It went beyond London. He became infatuated, as Natasha saw it, with a boxer called Cassius Clay and in telephone calls to his father they would become hyperbolic about his qualities, using words, Natasha thought, that ought to be reserved for serious matters. He became friends with an Irish poet and novelist, a Proustian who told Natasha he envied her the French. His shy but secure confidence in the quality of his work from which he could quote was more mysterious to the fugitive, insecure Joe than the tomb of Tutankhamen. Joe admired the work and the man in equal measure. He taught in a school in Shepherd's Bush, near the television studios, and they drank together in the local pubs or spent the occasional Saturday afternoon at a football match. Joe would bring back to Natasha the man's sayings on writers old and new and judgements to which he submitted with a deference which annoyed her.

There seemed no end to his interests. The sex scandals set in Cliveden and the upper-class exploitation of call girls intrigued him, the struggles of the British Labour Party excited him, the glamour and tragedy of Kennedy's America and the fight of the Freedom Riders absorbed him. To Natasha's dismay he found a capitalist aesthetic in James Bond after he had seen *From Russia with Love* and when he read *A Clockwork Orange*, which she thought arid, he was, at least for a time, convinced it proved that inside the bloom of London the worm was devouring the bud.

His protean curiosity or, as she sometimes thought, his itch-greed for everything, impressed, exasperated and depressed her by turns but there was always the redemption. He would come back home and moments after he had delivered the news of the day, like a messenger in a Greek drama, it would be erased and the time would be theirs as it had been from the beginning. Or on Saturday morning he would go, with Natasha, but more often and with her permission on his own, and wander through the Gardens, out onto the towpath, up to Richmond and back along the Thames to return as cleansed, as Natasha saw it, as if he had been through the several rooms of the bath houses of Rome. They would have lunch, wash up together, sit around, read, write, talk and prepare to go out, or see their friends in Kew, which is what they did at weekends. If they were going to a party he would buy a bottle of Blue Nun at the off-licence next to the station. They would swap notes on the way back and on Sundays they would write and walk together beside the river, his arm slung around her shoulders.

The question came from such a distance and was so matter-of-fact that Natasha thought she might have imagined it. They were in bed, the curtains drawn back, the late summer night warm, the last aeroplanes homing across the sky, the last cigarette, the last moments before sleep. They had made love and lay naked in the heat under a single sheet, pillows propped, bodies touching, a time when they intermingled on the slide into sleep and wanted to stretch each minute to catch every last drop of this day. So she did not reply.

Nor did he, for some minutes, repeat the question. It had not been calculated. It came casually to his lips. It was innocent, a question out of Eden, natural, he might have said, and, once formulated, inevitable. Nor could it be withdrawn once released. It was the genie out of the bottle, it was the next hill that had to be climbed, the road they had to take. But he left the silence alone. It was good to lie quietly in the dark after making love. It was good to realise it was good. It was only when he had stubbed out his cigarette and turned on his side to sleep that he said again, 'Why don't we have a child?'

She had no idea how to reply. In the art college, to have a child, if considered at all, was a way of declaring that your ideals and ambitions had been put aside, permanently most likely. The notion of 'starting a family' was not on the agenda. It featured in none of the possible female scenarios for a future after the art college. The assumption was that a child would be the woman's total responsibility; so many examples of women artists proved that, and unless the life were immensely well protected or the mother intolerably selfish, the child would surely claim all the effort, focus and energy that belonged to the work.

More than that, for Natasha, there was an intimation of doom compounded of her knowledge of her mother's experience and of her need to seize this changing time with Joseph to stabilise herself. There was also a deep and tender regret that without, as she guessed, thinking much about it, Joseph wanted to bring to an end the life the two of them led. He wanted to close the chapter on their time of good fortune, a time that had turned both of them, in their different ways, she thought, to the sun, to a recognition of what life could give to them at their best. That would go. It might be replaced by better, but this miracle of respite and renewal, of just the two of them, would be over. So casually asked; and he did not wait for an answer. Soon she heard the deep steady breath of his sleep.

When they talked about it later she could not accept this mixture of casualness and persistence. There was a time in any marriage to have a child, he seemed to think; and now that they were settled in their own house, and with his regular job, the time had arrived. Was that all?

When she was alone, Joseph at work, back again on the routine of phoning her in the middle of the day but leaving her with reliable stretches of solitude, she tried hard to imagine life with a child. But the pictures she could summon up were troubling. These were days of unrest. She walked through the Gardens, under the Ruined Arch, towards the Pagoda, across to the lake to seek out the black swans, as if seeking for an answer, to rove among the redwoods, as if their ancient ancestry would bring her wisdom. She visited and revisited all her favourite places, as if it was here, in the cultivation of some of the extremes of nature, that a resolution would be offered to her.

252

Joseph did not pursue her. He did not make her feel that there was a deadline. Now almost thirty she went along with the assumptions of the day that her best child-bearing time was behind her and future uncertainty was already in view. But he did not need to stalk her. The idea itself did that.

Kew Gardens had in these three years wrapped around her until at last she felt that she was home. She loved to cross the river on the way back from London. Then she was safe. She loved the circumscribed unchanging gentle shopping parade, the silent ripple of the Thames which curled around and cradled the suburb, the trace of orchards and the comfort of sufficient means. Her three new friends had children and when she confessed that she and Joseph were considering this, all three smiled, all three warned her of the storms of change which would transform her life, of the tiredness and the depression. But she saw the look in the eyes, the expression on the faces of all three when a child was scooped up. They had taken that path and seemed to say, look before you leap, but leap you will.

But there was dryness in the throat and the impossibility of knowing what would happen to Joseph, to herself, to what had been . . . Did you have to have children? she wondered. It seemed unnatural to ask the question, even subversive. She realised it could be a question that Joseph would not be able to accept. In this he was still on the rails of his past. He saw it as an essential stage in the proper progression of their married life.

But did you have to? What greater power decreed it, now, in a world where many thought there were too many children, a civilisation, she thought, too preoccupied for children, her new country, one in which many people she had known seemed interested in divesting themselves as soon as possible of the presence of and the responsibility for the children they had. These points were made in a tentative way in the sentences they would exchange from time to time, Joseph waiting, Natasha like a wild horse on the end of a long rope, gradually tiring, gradually slowing down, coming closer and closer to his unmoving centre.

So they began to make love for a child. Natasha put away bad thoughts. These were urgent couplings. Somehow their sexual passion for each other became wholly uninhibited with the possibility of a child growing in the womb. The time came when Natasha conceived and, Joe thought, everything was as it should be.

—⟋ᘉ⟍—

Isabel arrived a week after the news reached France. Joe had expected she would stay at a hotel but she declared herself very happy to lodge at the house which she praised save for the bathroom which she deplored and the kitchen which she thought wholly inadequate. The Spartan spare room was judged to be perfectly good, even chic. The gardens front and back drew unexpectedly favourable comments and the mélange of furniture, pictures, books and well-spotted junk was described as quite suitable. The parade was agreeably English but she failed to understand why there were no real cafés. The Botanical Gardens were allowed to be 'superb' and she bought several postcards. She took her time: days passed by in lovely aimless gossip with Natasha, who proved to be, Isabel reported to Alain, a surprisingly proud guide to the glories of the suburb and Isabel equally surprisingly declared herself to be impressed by the way the English did things in their suburbs.

Eventually, as Natasha had anticipated, the time came to engage. Although it was a warm summer's day, Isabel preferred to be inside, the french windows open, onto the lush, rather unkempt garden. She was dressed for St Tropez, Natasha thought; the high silk pastel-coloured neck scarf, the beautifully cut cream silk blouse, the equally well-cut trousers, the sandals revealing toenails scrupulously painted to match her fingernails and her hair given some attention that morning ('She was not altogether terrible') at English hands in Richmond. Natasha was dressed rather floppily in a loose summer frock, boldly striped, green and white. Both women smoked. The intense silence indicated that the moment had come.

'You look well, my sweet,' said Isabel. 'You are not much disturbed by the event, are you? Alain told me that. He said the first few weeks were strange but not so serious.'

254

'Serious yes,' said Natasha, and laughed. 'Not strange. What is strange,' it was only to Isabel she could confess this, 'is that at times I feel truly excited. I walk with care, guarding the child.'

'And other times?'

'There are other times for everyone,' Natasha said and did not confess those times when it seemed an unyielding undercurrent would drag her away, into a predatory darkness.

'You look so very like your mother now, more than ever. When I lost your mother I lost part of my heart. It's true. I don't exaggerate. She was my special friend and my idol.'

'I wish,' said Natasha, in a measured tone, 'I so much wish I had known her.'

'Me too, my sweet.' Isabel drew heavily on the cigarette. 'Oh yes, Natasha: me too.'

Isabel did not know whether she had the right to say what she thought most needed to be said. She had the courage, but courage was easy, she had told Alain. All you had to do was to stop thinking. Did she have the right to tell Natasha everything about her own birth and about her mother's reaction to the pregnancy, at the time and her life afterwards? Did she have the responsibility? The pause was marked: Natasha felt a shrouding of apprehension.

'It will make your life difficult, this child,' said Isabel. 'Was it an accident?'

'No.'

'But it was Joseph who insisted.'

'Yes . . . but I agreed. He says it will make our life richer.'

'He adores you. You adore him. So to refuse him was impossible. What else could you do?'

'Say no.'

'It's not too late for that.' Isabel looked and then looked away and breathed out a stream of smoke which went unwaveringly into the shafts of sunshine from the garden, into the silence.

'You are a Catholic, Isabel.'

'I am. And I am a good Catholic. But you are not.' She paused. 'So there we are.'

Natasha felt dizzy. She waited for more.

'What are you saying?'

'I have said it, Natasha. And I have said it because it is you I must protect. Joseph is good but young: your friends are good but they know nothing about you. You know what I am saying.'

Natasha was too ashamed to confess that it had floated across her mind. Not uncommon, her doctor had said, not at all especially in the first weeks. You have been invaded, he said, and you want to regain your physical integrity: that is one of the inevitable reactions. His words had helped as had a conversation with one of her Kew friends which had confirmed what he said. But Isabel!

'Is that what you came to say?'

'Partly.'

Natasha felt the coolness turn to a feeling of dread.

Isabel lit a fresh cigarette.

—ɯ—

'But I said no more. I felt I had not the right to continue, Alain,' Isabel said, when she returned home. He went across to hold her as she began to sob, the stiff, awkward movements of the shoulders of one who so very rarely cried, whose stoicism was her character. 'How could I tell her when she was there in this little English house, so proud of her life and looking so well, Alain, more beautiful as pregnant women can be, how could I risk the destruction of that peace she said she had found in that love for Joseph?'

'It is better left alone,' he said. 'I have always said to you, let the past rest in peace.'

'But it is her past, Alain, and what if it returns to hurt her?'

'She has friends,' said Alain, holding her gently, knowing that there were so many layers, of Natasha's mother, of Natasha's childhood, of Natasha and Isabel and of Isabel's own thwarted longing for a child of their own. 'It is not your responsibility,' he said, 'if to anybody, that falls on Louis.'

'But he will do nothing.'

'Well then,' said Alain, 'the Good Lord was with you, my sweetest Isabel, because doing nothing is sometimes the best course of all and I

256

am proud that you did nothing and that you left Natasha secure.' He took her slender fingers and held them to his cheek.

—∭—

'You will forgive me,' said Isabel as they waited for the taxi.

'With you there can never be anything to forgive,' said Natasha. 'I understand why you tested me. Sometimes you have to be tested.'

'You are very precious to me, Natasha.'

'As you to me.'

'Why don't you come to live in France? Near by. In the sun. A writer is a gypsy, no?'

'Maybe. Some day, I hope. That would be good.'

Natasha went with her to the airport and stood at the departure gate for some time after Isabel had disappeared to catch her flight home.

—∭—

'She's so beautiful!' Ellen's eyes were almost wild, tear-washed, smile-deepened, full of wonder. She had scarcely been able to contain herself on the journey back home. Sam had to be fully informed.

'She's just the loveliest baby! She looks like a little girl already, not, you know, squashed up. And Natasha is so nice with her. You can see it. Joe complains of being tired more than she does! The birth wasn't easy, two days, but you would think it was Joe who had been through it! Oh, Sam! She's just wonderful!'

Ellen's a girl again, Sam thought, she's the girl I courted, she's the young woman I married, she's the woman who flung herself into my arms when I came back from the war.

'I want to go back right away. I would have stayed on but an aunt of hers was on the way from France. But I will go back as soon as I can.'

Sam thought she was going to dance around the kitchen. She was transformed.

'And I decided. We have to be nearer. Not London. I couldn't tolerate living in London. But somewhere nearer. They are so far away, Sam, and so expensive to get to. You have to get somewhere nearer to them.'

'Ellen! You? Leave Wigton?'

'But, Sam,' she burst out in tears of happiness and relief and pride, 'Sam – they're our family. She's our family!'

—ɯ—

'So here we are,' said Alain, reading once again from Natasha's letter, ' "She is like a rosebud. *Voilà!* I cannot believe she is with us. I cannot believe I have done this." You see! A triumph.'

'I will go again in two or three months.'

'You were right in what you did not say, Isabel. You were right to take the opportunity to say nothing.'

PART THREE
LONDON CALLING

CHAPTER TWENTY-THREE

'And always there is the fear that I do not do her justice,' he wrote, 'and always there is the suspicion that I take the easy way and merely condemn Joe.' There were only two other tables occupied in the glass front area of the café. He thought, but could not be certain, that he and Natasha had come here on their first visit to Paris. He could spread himself. The coffee and cognac for old times' sake; the pen and pad; and on the other side of the glass, thronging the pavement on this Holy Thursday where once there would have been pilgrims, there were now tourists, their secular descendants, guide books for prayer books, souvenirs for relics, worship unbroken. He was waiting for their daughter. She wanted to take him to Vespers in Notre Dame. She had lived in Paris in a retreat for a month. Now it was over. He waited for her with something akin to the anticipation with which he had waited many years ago for her mother.

'She is still here,' he wrote, 'in 2005, more than forty years on from that first visit. Sometimes I feel the city cobwebbed in our memories. I look for the spot where we waltzed along the banks of the Seine and I sang "Under the Bridges of Paris": it doesn't matter that I can't find the precise spot, it is the looking for it. I write this in a café in Rue des Ecoles next to the Sorbonne, and can see your mother arriving, as you will soon arrive, looking so like her now. You have matured into her, even similar gestures, how could you have picked them up so young? Your eyes lit with an inner delight or mischief, that rather long, rather serious face gentled into warmth by the flickering smile, the grace of you, of her, in Paris, in which we did not come to live . . . Should I have made that happen for her, for you, for me? I sit and wait for you and write in a café like a philosophical Frenchman, and try again to find the truth of it for you.

'Memory, Imagination and Language, those three, and the greatest of these? Together they make us what we are, perhaps even why we are, but the weak hold we have on them is never so exposed as when we try to write truth. Language, even that used by the best, is always an approximation to that changing, slithering, half-lit, half-understood complex of sensation and experience; grasping water. So many of these arbitrary expressions, perfect in their time, are eroded by time, by over-use, non-use, changed use, multiple use, burned out, quaint, dimmed, become opaque. Yet Language is at least accessible, through its nature. But Imagination? An almighty faculty which can take us back in thought to the beginning of the universe faster than the speed of light, which can lead us into ancient and alien cultures, into the hearts of strangers, into the minds of genius, and into those common sympathies which hold the world together, Imagination is like the ocean Newton saw undiscovered before him as he picked up a few pebbles of knowledge on the beach and which to understand, finally, might be to understand all things.

'But of those three it is Memory, for me, now, reaching out to you, that is the most tormenting. There is no possibility and no point in trying to remember "everything" about Natasha; nor is strict remembering the way of it for me. It is too fragmented, too unreliable, unshaped, a landscape without the definition of final meaning, undermined by shame, veiled by guilt. Your mother has to be fiction and yet she has to be attached to some of my recollections which rise up from the sea bed like monsters, or erupt into an unready mind like volcanoes or are frustratingly near yet ungraspable as they are today in Paris, in this café, with spring aching to be born, but the leaves still furled, hidden in the bough.'

You materialised quite suddenly.

'You were out of this world,' she said.

'You're early.'

'I don't want us to be late.' She smiled down on me. Her hair usually fell free and long: for this occasion she had braided it around her head. 'What were you writing about?'

262

'Mum. And me. And now you.'

You giggled. Once I had feared the sound, just a little, it felt too nervous to be good. Now I knew better; it was a ripple from that reservoir of joy you have made for yourself, despite everything, in defiance of everything, challenging everything.

'When can I read it?'

'When it's done.'

'What if I don't like it?'

'Then you will be its only reader.'

She nodded, rather gravely. In the silence our agreement was sealed.

'Did you and Mum go to Notre Dame?'

'Yes. But only once together. She hated it.'

But you loved it, didn't you? As I do and as I did so uniquely that Holy Thursday evening with you. You as an adult have found and deeply drunk in a faith I drowned in so happily, blindly as a boy and since have seen fade and drain away. But now and then it revives, sometimes fleetingly, even mockingly like the moon refusing to come out clean from behind the hills of clouds but sometimes plain, bold, as it was at Vespers in Notre Dame with you a few months ago.

I had never attended Vespers and so I expected it to be like the Anglican sung evensong observed in all the cathedral cities of Britain and executed by pupils from the cathedral choir schools, boys chosen for the beauty of their voices. Recently I had heard at evensong the choirs of Wells Cathedral and of York Minster and on both occasions been taken over by the song of the past and thoughts on the continuity and the mystery of things as those pure voices soared high into the stone ceilings, voices as they had been on these holy sites for centuries, plainsong uninterrupted in celebration and praise of God no matter what the assaults without or within the church, no matter even the indifference which produced a congregation on both those evenings fewer in number than the choir. Vast spaces of the cathedral were empty. Only the gallant few, as I saw them, huddled around the singers, as if for warmth, determined to bear witness.

By contrast, in Notre Dame even before the service began there was the full tide of a crowd. The area cordoned off for the Vespers congregation filled up steadily and you said we had better take care to find seats, which we did in, for me, the comfort of the back row. But as we waited what I was most aware of, more than the great rose windows or the candlelight which seemed to burnish the darkness, or the surge of the stone like a growth of nature, more than the animal whisper and shuffle of the tourists and non-worshippers in the darker regions of the cathedral, was your expression, which I glimpsed, I hope, without your noticing: stern and intent and enraptured.

The minister entered in his heavy white robes and his mitre and a junior cleric swung the incense which even reached out to us, about a quarter way up the nave. Then the organ began. I had not expected that. In our cathedrals it is often voices alone but here the great organ suffused the cathedral in sound made sacred by the place itself and I knew as I had done at times gone by that faith could be gained with no words spoken and music could be the voice of God.

And then she began to sing.

I had expected a choir. I had thought that the woman who stood alone and apart was about to read a passage from the Bible as, clad in a long blue cassock which looked like silk in the candlelight, she stood before a lectern which bore a book. But it was her book of songs. Her voice was crystal, single against the orchestra of chords from the organ, ringing to the vaults as might be of heaven, and she looked a little like you, more like your mother.

Soon I abandoned any attempt to translate the words and let the voice and the organ fill me with their sounds whose intention needed no translation. I saw, I believed, standing beside you in your belief, and seeing her sing, 'seeing' Natasha, a messenger. I was taken over by the sacred sound, the intimations and revelations which seemed magnetised by this sound. Later I remembered, as an adolescent, standing on a cliff edge in West Cumberland, looking over the sea at a rainstorm far off, knowing it would soon reach the land on which I stood and feed the streams which filled the oceans which fed the rain clouds and that simple circularity, naïf as it might now appear, struck me then, fifty years ago, as a defining insight into the wholeness of life.

Here, in Notre Dame, beside you, for those moments, if ever in my life I did, I believe that, in my seventh decade, I may have had a similar glimpse into the heart of things. That it was impenetrable and incomprehensible did not matter. There had been a beginning and we were still part of it and it is in us. Wherever you look in the old creation myths there is this assertion, this confidence. And when you look into the new physics of it, what is there but the same? The same Nothing Known which is also the heart of all things: fundamental essential particles as unseen as angels and archangels and all the company of heaven. It was as if I soared, I flew, for those few minutes I was resurrected and so was Natasha and through sensation I understood . . .

And then the music stopped. Why could it not go on for ever was a childish but, to confess, a true reaction. Why could it not go on for ever?

I did not tell you any of this then because you had your own thoughts, your own feelings which you did not want to reveal to me. Best at some crucial times not to talk. Silently, we left Notre Dame and came out to an evening calm and free, a darkening sky, the Seine flowing swiftly and I had a sudden sharp desire to eat and drink.

CHAPTER TWENTY-FOUR

On some days when Natasha went out wheeling first a pram and then a pushchair she caught a sight of herself in a shop window and wondered who this person was, so sedately pushing the child before her, so clearly one of the wife and child class of Kew Gardens, so irrevocably slotted into the expected pattern.

It was a club you joined and there was novelty in that for someone who had carved loneliness into a sort of self-sufficiency. But she was strange, this person reflected in the window of the butcher's shop, she seemed so calm and possessed, above all so complete, with the child, a woman fulfilled, surely? Yet what did it say about the Natasha who had just recently begun to feel confident on her own? Now she was two. Something had been given by her but something had been taken from her. What if the strongest of her had gone into the child, the best of her?

Her new friends in Kew had prepared her for the tiredness and the treadmill. Like all forewarnings, the reality had wiped the floor with the predictions and only now, more than a year on, was she beginning to recover her body fully, be more than a servant to its ceaseless demands. But they had not prepared her for this sometimes blankness of being. Who was the woman reflected in the big shop window? Was her time of being the individual she wanted to be over just as it had begun? She knew the thought was selfish but it was there and she was not going to duck it. Natasha felt that she had stepped through the glass into a different world. It was as if with and through the child she had set off on another journey entirely and discovered a way of life quite different, even alien to the one she had had, and there was no return. A solitary life had been ended and for ever. And she looked ill, spots on her forehead, pasty skin, saggy body: that was no help.

But nor had they truly foretold the moments of sweetness, the glimpses of joy, the first words presented to Joseph, the first steps delighted in, the assuming of settled features, the knitting together of a mind, a smile, a gesture, later a question, an action. Natasha could be entranced and quite suddenly thrown high in the air as she witnessed the blind, universal process of growing. She sketched her – there was a period of months when catching the mood of the child in the sketches was her work. It was as if she had to know in every way she could what this child was like. As if her drawn record was essential lest she lose her. Or be lost to her. The intense preoccupation proved to be some counterweight to the downward plunge, sometimes it seemed the freefall of her self-confidence.

For underneath everything was the drowning fear of not knowing. The birth had brought into her world not only her child but her mother, the mother who had left just after her own birth. How could she let that happen, get that ill, let go, leave me? There was about her own child sometimes a dread reminder of her own childhood. Yet there was hope, too, as if the baby was a messenger from out there bringing her news of what had happened, if only she could decode it.

Joseph slept lightly now, beginning to be unsettled, as she had once been, by the relentless trail of aeroplanes over their house: so the night feed was something of a relief for him, an excuse to be awake, and it let him feel useful. He could change a nappy as neatly as she could. On weekends he took charge in the mornings and went out to the park, into the Gardens or along the river, leaving Natasha in the empty house to breathe easily and alone for a few hours. When he came home through the week, he went immediately to their daughter and Natasha was only faintly jealous, glad that the love between daughter and father seemed so intense. His love for their daughter gave her a growing conviction that she was stronger, that between them they would always hold him.

In a year or so, she got back to her novel. Soon it became a refuge.

—✺—

267

After their daughter had been settled down they would eat supper and then sit for a while in the big battered armchairs either side of the electric fire. Unless there was something they liked on television they would read or, more rarely now, read to each other. They summarised the day, a routine which appealed to Joe at his most organised and was tolerated by an amused Natasha, who saw it as a parody of a bourgeois marriage – a description Joe had at first resented and still felt put down by.

'Ross says we should get an au pair,' he announced.

'Ross says . . .' She smiled and put aside her book. 'Ross says . . .'

'He is my boss.'

'He is your current Pole Star.'

'He's given me chances.'

'Only because he knows you can take them. It pleases Ross to be a patron. But he wouldn't do it if it didn't reflect well on him.'

'That's unfair.'

'He cannot do it for love, Joseph. There must be a reason. Vanity is more accurate. He is very vain. Don't bridle, Joseph! It can be attractive, even in a man.'

'You're so unfair! Ross McCulloch was a war hero, he did all sorts of things before he came to the BBC, he runs the whole Features Department now as well as the Arts Programme, he knows everybody yet he and Margaret ask us over to their house almost every weekend . . .'

'We are part of his court. His own children are too young to provide the court he needs. You always laugh at his stories . . .'

'His stories are great; he ought to write them down.'

'He never will, writing is a different cast of mind. You are enraptured by his war, even though Sam and his brothers and your grandfather and his brothers all went through wars, probably harder, probably more dramatic.'

'But Dad won't talk about it. Nor will anyone else.'

'Except Ross.'

'He won a medal for bravery, Natasha. Why are you so antagonistic? He likes you.'

'You should not have told him my background.'

'He likes you anyway. Margaret has been nothing but kind since the baby.'

'Margaret is not Ross. She is formidable.'

'She is a friend, isn't she? Like Claire and Anna. She is one of the Three Graces of Kew.'

'Sweet Graces.' Natasha's smile too was sweet. 'I am lucky with those three women.'

'So, what's wrong with Ross all of a sudden?'

'Partly that he is a man.'

'Natasha!'

'I'll concede that he had no say in the matter. But he is such a Man's Man, Joseph, such an Imperial Man, such a Polite to the Ladies Man, such a Superior Being. *Alors! You* are not a superior being.'

'He's who he is. Why should he change just because fashions change?'

'Not fashions, not fashions. It is a truth which has been emerging for generations and that truth is about women. It is an idea based on rational reality and it is the idea that is changing the times.'

'So we don't get an au pair. Why not? You get tired out. You get exhausted.'

'What inspires Joseph Richardson from the Blackamoor pub in Wigton to speak so airily about an au pair?'

'I was not speaking airily.'

'Don't sulk. I'll tell you. Last week when we went to the McCullochs' and he asked us and the others to bring something to read aloud and you very nervously read that beautiful section from this new novel of yours which is the first one that really works, what did he do?'

'He was generous.'

'He was patronising. And then he strolled over to those bookshelves, for all to see he was a Literary Gentleman, and plucked out *Sons and Lovers* and read a passage from Lawrence.'

'It was terrific. It's as good as anything he wrote. And Ross reads so well.'

'Why did he do that to you, Joseph?'

'He did nothing to me. We were all reading something and he read something. That's all.'

'I fear that you believe that. I don't. He tried to put you in your place. I told him so.'

'When?'

'Just before we left.'

'Told him what?'

'That he had taken advantage of your willingness to expose something raw and precious and he had tried to crush you, although,' she laughed out loud, 'it appears that he failed because you didn't notice! Oh, Joseph, I do love you.'

He felt irritated, as if he'd been patted on the head.

'What did he say?'

'He said, "You think that, do you?"'

'That's all?'

'That's all . . . and then, "Goodnight."'

Why could he not tell her how much pleasing this man mattered to him? How this pleasing of him was a pleasure because of his admiration for him but also a necessity if he were to retain this miraculous job which not only allowed him to make films but left him with the energy to write? Why could he not tell her that on some days in the office the fear that he might not be in favour with someone notoriously volatile in offering and withdrawing favours spread a panic about him which threatened to excite the violent waves of depression of his adolescence? Why could he not confess all these shameful weaknesses? Why could he not tell her that on some weekends it was impossible for him not to pass by the grand McCulloch house on the river on the off chance of seeing Ross or Margaret or catching sight of their children playing in the big garden and hope to be invited in? And that 'in' was safety and that this man a generation ahead of him served some inexplicable but desperate purpose? And as she, indisputably, knew so much about people, why did she not know this?

'What are you thinking?'

'Nothing.'

'That is what schoolboys say.'

He dived in.

'There's a girl in Caldbeck, she lives two doors along from the cottage we rented. You may remember her, very blonde, curly hair, rather small, Mary. When we were up over Easter her mother told me that she wanted to find a place in London because she has a boyfriend in Kent.

This boyfriend, she told me, had been in some sort of reform school near by but Mary had got to know him and she was pining for him, her mother said. So if I knew anybody who would look after her she would let her go because she couldn't bear her looking so unhappy. She's a "good little worker", her mother said, and "no bother, very quiet". She couldn't understand how she had got mixed up with a boy in a reform school, a delinquent, she said the word deliberately as if forcing herself to face the worst, but there we are. So Mary could come here.'

'Joseph! A Cumbrian au pair! Who could possibly resist?'

'Sometimes . . .' Joe stood up and mocked a threatening strangulation.

—⁓—

The stripper was in bed when Joe knocked at the hotel-room door and she had to repeat 'Come in' twice before he could summon the nerve to enter. When he did he was confronted by the sort of bedroom he associated with swish rooms in well-heeled films, more an unwalled apartment than a bedroom, the chaise longue, the dressing table as strewn with make-up as was the floor with clothes, mainly, it seemed to Joe at the briefest glance, specialist underwear, the open door to a large bathroom and, dominating the room, a four-poster bed and in the bed, head peeping over lilac sheets like a dormouse, 'Madeleine'.

'Over here,' she said in what sounded to Joe like a sultry and suggestive whisper and sent him into a confusion of responses. 'Sit on the bed,' she commanded, and a white listless arm fringed with blood-red nails patted the spot. He sat.

'I phoned,' he said. 'Four times.'

'The phone's too far away.' He looked down. It was at his feet. He nodded.

'They're waiting for you on the set,' he said.

'They can wait.' She twisted in the bed, revealing a breast he had seen before, and leaned down to the floor to pick up the Du Maurier cigarettes. She held out the box for Joe. 'Take two,' she said, in her unforgiving Yorkshire accent. 'Light mine.' She held out the lighter. 'I always think that's dead romantic.'

He did as he was bid. Marjorie Partington was her real name, fresh up from Barnsley, spotted by Tim Radley the documentary and feature films maker who was completing a movie, *Soho by Night*. Joe was making an arts process film about his working methods and he had been roped in to help in the setting up of a couple of sequences: including Madeleine the stripper whom Tim liked as much for her Yorkshire accent as for her amazingly proportioned and, as Joe had seen in the rehearsal, unusually supple body.

She tried and failed to blow a smoke ring.

'We're both from the North,' she said, 'so I can be honest with you.' She tried again and failed again and Joe could see that it annoyed her. Now she was propped up against the pillows, the sheet clutched over her breasts, her face completely revealed as fully made-up. 'I didn't run off to London to show my parts to a lot of dirty old men in macs.' She tossed her head; it was a well-rehearsed gesture and the thick blonde mane bounced back without hesitation. 'I'm not knocking the money,' she said. 'Money's good. But it's not me, Joe, not running between dirty little clubs watching dirty little men play with themselves. I want a career.'

Joe nodded and swallowed cigarette smoke and coughed until his eyes watered.

'You need something for that,' she said.

It was a little like a ventriloquist act, Joe thought. This beautiful woman, the blonde hair thickly waved, luxuriant, the features haughty, sexy, proud, but the voice straight from traditional Northern music-hall comedy.

'I know I speak common,' she said. 'You're thinking that, aren't you? But that can be worked on. I wouldn't be surprised if you didn't speak common yourself once upon a not very long time ago, my friend.'

'I did,' said Joe eagerly, in his new middle-media-class tones.

'Well, if you can get over it we all can, can't we, Joe?'

'Yes,' said Joe. 'Oh, yes.'

'I want a film making about me,' she said. 'Not just the stooge part in some dirty-minded director's little titivation. I can sing, me, and I can

272

dance. That's what I came here for. And when I saw you, Joe, yesterday, at what they called the rehearsal which was a free show to me, I thought – he'll do it; he'll make a film on me. Watch this.'

She hesitated for a moment and then said,

'Christ! Don't worry. You won't see anything you didn't see yesterday and you paid nothing then neither.'

She was magnificent! She sang 'Walking Back to Happiness'. The Northern accent was whipped off and replaced by an accurately mimicked Southern American soul drawl. And how she moved! Joe had seen the new women in the pop groups on television and Madeleine moved better than any of them, even though the lack of a dress might be an influence on his opinion. She gyrated like a stripper and strutted like a rocker. Though there was no band, her strong big rhythmic voice drove through the room.

'You were great!' he said. 'You really were.'

She was flushed.

'Really? You really mean it? Really?'

'Really. You were fantastic.'

'Do you think you can do something with me?'

'Yes. Or somebody can. Yes.'

'Why not you, Joe?' She walked towards him, as tall as he was, glowing, a slight sheen of sweat. 'I'd like it to be you.'

'I'll try,' he said. 'I'll ask.' Ross McCulloch? 'You deserve it.'

Why were his words choking in his throat? He stood up. She was all but on him.

'You won't let me down, will you, Joe?' Her eyes were blue and wide now and, he could tell, faking it, but that made no matter. 'I've been let down too many times in my life.'

Somehow from the thicket of his throat came words which, unscrambled, indicated that he would not dream of letting her down. She breathed very deeply, contentedly, her breasts rising and falling with satisfaction.

She looked over her shoulder at the bed.

'We could celebrate,' she said, 'our new partnership.'

'I'm married,' Joe said. 'I'm married.'

Marjorie smiled.

'I respect you for that, Joe.' She reached down and held him hard. 'But you can't deny an interest in the matter.'

'I'm married,' he said, gasping a little. 'Shall I wait outside?'

'While I put my clothes on?'

'Yes.'

'I think I'm going to like you, Joe, you daft bugger.'

It took him some time to disentangle that encounter. When he told Tim Radley how astounding 'Madeleine' was as a singer and a dancer the great man replied, 'We wondered what took you so long.' When he tried ways to honour his promise and get a film made about her, ways failed him and he broke his promise and felt bad. She haunted him. When he remembered what had happened he could not believe he had behaved like that but he knew that there was no other way he could have behaved and yet there was the undeniable fact of the erection.

A few months later, Tim Radley embarked on a project to do a dramatised documentary commissioned by Ross McCulloch on the life of Nijinsky and asked Joe if he thought he could write it. 'Ross told me that he'd heard you read some of your own stuff and it's quite promising, he said. He suggested I give you a chance.'

CHAPTER TWENTY-FIVE

He counted James as an old friend even though they had met only at Oxford. Joe was sparing in his use of 'friend' and considered it linked with length of time. But Oxford had been a new beginning and undeniably brought new friends, and James, surprising, Buddha-like, thoughtful, affectionate, James, like David, had become one.

'If you've nothing better to do we could meet for a drink,' James said.

'That would be great.'

'There's a pub in the street next to you, in Wardour Street.' He gave the name. 'I could be there by eight.'

'Thanks. Good. Yes.' When Joe put down the phone he realised that he was relieved. Natasha and their daughter had gone to Brittany that morning for their summer holiday. At the last minute Joe had been delayed because of the difficulties in the editing of the Nijinsky programme. It would be at least three days before he could join them and he had rung James, seeking help to fill in the unexpected prospect of an evening in London without Natasha. He would be finished in the sweaty little basement cutting room in Soho well before eight but strolling the streets in anticipation of seeing an old friend was a far better prospect than lugging himself back to an early night in the empty house in Kew.

'Fixed yourself up, then?' said Tim, who had affected to regard Joe as a 'randy sod' since his over-lengthy call on the stripper and her subsequent tokens of affection to him.

'Yes . . . a friend from university. Well, and since, actually. He's a writer, was, is, in the music business now, I can't quite fathom how he—'

'For God's sake, Joe, stop making excuses. The cat's away!'

Joe blushed even though he was innocent or perhaps because the innocence only papered over the disloyal desires for Madeleine.

'The problem with this movie is,' said Tim, 'how do we end this without giving it the full camp welly and if we give it the full camp welly how do we get to show it? How do we get it past Ross?'

Joe could weary of Tim talking like that about Nijinsky and Diaghilev, whose friendship, then brutal parting and Nijinsky's tragedy were, he knew, as moving for Tim as they had become for himself. But Tim had seen service in Malaya, and as he often said 'developed a First-Class Bullshit Detector', which meant that this heroic dancer, whose mental extremes of sensibility were awesome, and his lover, the great impresario of ballet, whose taste and patronage was on a level with that of the Medici, had to be discussed in barrack-room terms. When Joe hinted at that, he was given what Tim relished to dish out: an A1 bollocking.

Yet they got on well, helped by Tim's cheerful admission that he 'couldn't write his way out of a paper bag'. Nevertheless, he added, he knew what worked. Joe's script had been several times rewritten. It was limited in the amount of dialogue permitted in a docu-drama, but nonetheless it was a 'talkie', Joe's first.

Joe did not always make common cause with the total loyalty Tim demanded. When Ross McCulloch had come to see the first rough cut, Joe had been thrown by the man's dismissal of what he thought was a key scene; Nijinsky in his dressing room, naked (his back to camera of course) after the rift with Diaghilev, his master, his father figure (unfortunately Joe used that term: McCulloch was not impressed by psychoanalysis), and his clearly implied lover. Nijinsky was attempting to put together a sequence of what appeared bizarre steps as excerpts from his notebooks were spoken, interspersed with a rhythmic grunting and chanting. Tim had shot it in slow motion and put some bars from Stravinsky under it. Joe thought it expressed and encapsulated everything about genius struggling against madness to express originality all but out of reach. Ross said it was 'camp rubbish' and should be cut out completely. After the dust settled, Tim, to Joe's dismay, agreed with him.

Perhaps as a consequence, when Ross argued against a basic premise of the film, which was that you could intercut documentary techniques with dramatic scenes, that you could have a Nijinsky portrayed by real photographs and also a Nijinsky played by a young dancer, and Tim hit the roof, Joe said he could see some strength in Ross's point of view. When Ross had left the cutting room, after having surrendered on the issue, Tim said,

'You nearly blew it!'

'He has a point. As he said, a documentary is a documentary.'

'He always has a point. But that was a typical Ross establishment knee-jerk against what's new. And it was you he was attacking, you pillock. You wrote the dramatic bits. And not too bad, some of them.'

'But he still . . .'

'Bollocks!'

That was the end of it. Later Tim said,

'At least you're no dummy.'

And late that afternoon he said,

'Why don't you and Alison bugger off and have a drink. You've been ogling each other all afternoon. We'll finish this sequence.'

Alison was the young assistant editor, dark-haired, cream-complexioned, quick-eyed, rather like Rachel, Joe had thought from the start. She looked across at her boss, Gerald, the film editor, for his permission. Gerald nodded.

'He says the most terrible things,' said Alison when they were safely on the street. 'Ogling each other!'

'He's good, though. He knows his stuff. Ross thinks he's our best director.'

Joe had almost an hour to kill. He looked up and down the narrow busy scruffy sexy Soho street still sweating from the slowly setting sun. There was about this place a poison that made him nervous even as it exuded an erotic energy. Up and down the street there were tables uneasy on the dirty narrow pavements but clustered with drinkers determined to suck in the last of the afternoon heat.

'Quite continental, isn't it?' said Alison.

'Would you like a drink, then?' Joe asked. 'Just one. If you want to, that is. I've got to stay around for a while. You might need to go home. It's . . . I . . .'

'We could go up there,' she said, and pointed to a less crowded nest of tables at some distance. 'I'll have a dry white wine, please.'

As soon as they sat down, she offered him a cigarette, taking charge.

She told him that the sequence cut out by Ross was the best in the film. She told him that when he was not there, Tim made encouraging references to him. She told him she had loved his film on Brassens and especially the parts where he had imitated Renoir. Was it Renoir? She herself wanted to make films like Truffaut.

He did not quite understand how this came about but having clutched tight the secrecy of his novel writing, he told her he was on the final lap of the third draft of a novel set in Cumberland, in a place like the town in which he had been brought up. He told her about Faulkner and Bellow, whom he was reading just now, and Evelyn Waugh, and how odd it was to like Evelyn Waugh's novels so much when he hated his ideas and his personality so strongly. He told her he could not believe he had written a film for Tim Radley who was always mentioned in the same breath as the best new directors and playwrights and photographers. He told her he could not decide whether photography was a real art or not but when he had put that to Tim he had been informed he was just a literary snob, antediluvian, typically English, without any visual sense and so bloody arrogant he probably did not know how a film camera worked. He didn't. They had another drink.

When she left she gave him a warm kiss on the cheek which he thought only happened between theatre people. When he watched her walk away he realised he was studying the slim shapeliness, the twitch of the disturbing mini-skirted bottom, the length of exposed leg, the independent stride, the sexy freedom about her. He had drunk three bottles of beer on an empty stomach and his head was muzzy but pleasantly, welcomingly so, he thought, as he made his way to meet James at the rendezvous pub. The summer streets were mostly inhabited by young people, some extravagantly dressed in the new peacock fashions, all of them free and sexy, he guiltily admitted to himself, all of them with the world as their oyster. He too could go anywhere, he thought, on this evening, take any turn, go in any pub, he too was unconfined. Those few minutes following the absorbing appreciative conversation with Alison left him filled with a kind of helium of the moment.

'I find this pub rather noisy,' said James in the solemn, well-educated voice which was even more than usually at odds with his keen modern look. It was his clothes, Joe concluded; something very up to date about the clothes.

'I thought you might like the Buckingham Club,' said James, as they squeezed out and popped onto the pavement. 'It's gay but quite safe and I think it will interest you. Most of these clubs are dirty little fire-traps. The Buckingham thinks it's rather upper, but pretentious is a better description, though not at all kinky. I think you ought to be made aware of it.'

—∽—

Joe thought that it could have been mistaken for a rather run-down drawing room in one of those classy but cash-strapped town houses into which he had sometimes landed on his broadcasting quests. There were thickly textured armchairs and sofas, battered as if for extra style, Eastern rugs, well-stocked bookshelves along the panelled walls, real paintings, soft and flattering sidelights, little oak tables for drinks, ashtrays, newspapers and a clientele which, on the whole, looked as if it had been quite acceptably barred from the better London clubs, a couple of which Joe had also been invited to. The bar was a little item in a corner, as if an afterthought.

Joe's wary gaze was first attracted to a rich velvet plum-coloured jacket leaning heavily against the bar and containing a writer well known for his dashing bad-taste depictions of the lusts and intrigues of the upper classes.

'He's always drunk,' said James. 'If you talk to him you'll never get away. He loves the young working class, especially clever ones. Quite amusing but can be a bit of a barnacle.'

James steered him to a faded purple sofa in a particularly poorly lit part of the room.

'Busy but not at its buzziest,' James said. 'Yet not altogether dis-appointing.'

He signalled several times and at last a young man dressed in black trousers and a white shirt and even in the heat a tie, sauntered across.

'Two beers,' said James. 'Lager. One with lime.'

The young man sighed, put a small saucer of olives on the little round table and drifted away in the general direction of the bar. James addressed the situation.

'The first thing to grasp, though it may soon change from what we read, is that what is quite often happening here is still a criminal offence. Sodomites, as some of our judges like to call them, us, are sent to jail if discovered *in delicto*, usually in a public lavatory, and they trump up charges all the time, but in a club like this we're safe. The criminality only adds an extra frisson of dangerous excitement. Ah! I'd rather hoped he'd come in. That man, rather short, in the pin-striped, three-piece suit, is a QC, an utter shit and a hypocrite, a collector's item.'

James was silent for a while, looking the place over. Joe wanted to be a Chandler hero, quietly casing the joint, but it was all he could do to stay calm. As he began to decode the movements around the room, the questing of some, the posing of others, the soft voices and softer laughter, the soft strokings of the arm, the occasional kiss on the cheek, the intimate play over the lighting of a cigarette, he felt a rather erotic mixture of fascination and unease, alarm and attraction, a sort of breathlessness, and an unmistakable stirring of excitement.

'Oh, Lord, Rupert's coming our way. I'll head him off. I'll be about ten minutes. When he finds out you're straight he'll start boring you with his list of every queer in history from Socrates to Joe Orton. He also claims Shakespeare.'

Before Joe could respond, James was up, arm extended for a firm handclasp with a very tall, stooping, etiolated but elegant figure whose white hair was styled in the fashion of a junior public schoolboy.

Joe felt uncomfortably isolated and drank his beer too quickly. The young waiter glided over with a new glass and pointed at a small group of young men across the room. One of them waved, his hand dangling from his wrist, the cigarette dangling from his hand. Joe raised his glass and as he sipped he saw that the dangling waver was on his way towards him. His stomach clenched tightly. The excessively thin young man, a handsome yellow and white striped shirt open at the neck revealing a cross on a chain, flared trousers, long hair, was revealed as a follower of the latest foppish fashion. For the first time in his life, Joe was aware of the limitations of his sports jacket, grey flannels, checked shirt and tweed tie. The young man smiled warmly and sat down opposite Joe with proprietorial slyness.

'Joe Richardson,' he said. 'Fancy seeing you here.'

Joe paused and then it was as if a film in his head reeled backwards at the speed of thought.

'Paul,' he said. 'It's Paul!'

'It's Alexander now,' Paul said. 'Sir,' he nodded over his shoulder to where the tall white-haired man was talking at the bar with James, 'over there with your friend, I'm with him and he wants Alexander so Alexander he gets.'

Joe felt winded with the inrush of memories, a fierce jet of nostalgia. Paul in the gang of them together as children in the town, the adventures, the dramas, they flickered through his mind and with an almost dizzying intensity. Paul! Here!

'I've just been writing about Wigton,' Joe said. 'In a way. Those times. Our gang. Our lot. I thought *Our Lot* might be the title, at one time.'

'The old gang.' Alexander offered a cigarette, a Passing Cloud: Joe took one over-eagerly as if both to show and to confirm solidarity. 'Alan, Malcolm . . . Writing about Wigton, are you? I could give you Wigton, Joe. *The Lower Depths.* I couldn't wait to get out.' He offered a light from a slim gold lighter. 'Your Uncle Colin did me a favour.'

'He used to take you on his motorbike.'

'You could say that. I got money out of him at the end,' said Alexander. 'I made him pay: a no-squeal fee! He's terrified of your dad, you know. Absolutely terrified, he is.'

Joe parked all that: he could not cope, and besides, here was Paul–Alexander bringing, with evidence of Wigton, part of a past that Joe had been attempting to marinate in fiction, bringing a world which could so easily seem sealed off from his London life but the seal was broken as one of the actors in his past rose up in the Buckingham Club to drug him more strongly than the alcohol.

Alexander needed no encouragement. Gossip was his second trade. Joe was beguiled by his accent. It was still Northern, much more so than Joe's whose pronunciation had begun an inevitable journey south at Oxford, but softened, more like a woman's, Joe thought, one of the older women of the town, that was it, who talked in a stream of lilting heavily spiced sentences, almost a chant.

'Who's your friend, then?' Alexander asked after a heavy exchange on the darker incidents in the recent history of the home town. Joe explained. 'I've seen him here before. But you're straight, aren't you? Christ! Aren't you just! You're even blushing in the dark. I read something about you, I saw that television you did on the Northern painters. It made me feel very proud, Joe, to know you.'

He smiled, the smile emphasising the thinness of his cheeks.

'I'd better hop,' he said. 'Sir gets very jealous even when he's no need. Lovely to meet you, Joe. Take care. It's a wicked city, Joe, I don't think you know that yet.' He leaned forward, patted Joe's knee, and was gone.

'They make their own pasta,' James said. 'It's as good as anything I've had in Italy. And perfectly acceptable house red. This place has become rather a favourite with an in-crowd over the last year or so.'

They were still in Soho, in a small Italian restaurant presided over by a small, dark-haired, fleet-footed woman who reminded Joe of his mother. It was wall-to-wall young. Dandyism was de rigueur. Joe's sports jacket felt increasingly anachronistic.

'Largely the music business,' said James, looking around for a star or two to bear him out, 'or film,' he said, nodding at an actor just making his name, 'and television, I'm told.'

Joe munched the breadsticks greedily. There was blood-heavy, alcohol-fuelled, tension-charged congestion in his head and a vacuum in his stomach.

'Some of this crowd will be going on to the Shed.' James suddenly looked rather coy. 'You might like to come along. Tonight's when new groups showcase their songs.' He lowered his voice. 'To be honest, I'd welcome your opinion. One group is showcasing two songs I've written. The words. Howard did the music. He'll be there . . .' James smiled at Joe's expression. 'I met the group when I was working in radio,' he said. 'They're charming boys, and I thought, why not try? You had all the pop excitement young: in Hampstead we were actively discouraged. Jazz was about as far as it got, and, at school, a little soul music and the blues to show solidarity with the oppressed. Do you think it's all a bit absurd?'

'No,' said Joe, 'not at all. You were very good at translating poetry from Greek and Latin, weren't you?'

James laughed so loudly that people at nearby tables glanced across and smiled, some even laughed along with him.

'That was precisely what I wanted to hear,' James said, taking out a folded white handkerchief and dabbing his eyes. 'No. I mean it. Perfect.'

Joe could not decode that. Over the coffee, James said, 'I know it can all seem to be rather frivolous, the pop music scene. One ought not to be so deeply absorbed in it. How can one weigh it against the actions in Vietnam or the protests in San Francisco against the bombing or so much else of global importance? But there is a time when you have to follow your own instinct, I'm sure you agree.' James smoked small cigars. Joe was still trying to square the circle of this James, the pop man, with the James with whom he had shared rooms at Oxford, the cultivated and public-school James. Yet this increasingly original character, when he spoke about pop music, rather incongruously retained both the familiar tone of voice and the Oxford manner of careful discourse which Joe so much liked about him.

'For me,' James said, and sipped at the sambuca, ' "words alone are certain good", and the words describing the pop world now are very good indeed. Take scag, or speed and angel dust, and purple hearts, new coinages every day, rap and fab and freaking out and clubbing, vibes, switched on, bag, my bag, your bag, not my bag, those are a sort of proof of vitality, I think, culture grows where vitality is most virulent. I suppose it's rather sad to need proof, but there is certainly a new nerve here and it is ours, our generation, in truth a shade too old for us two. But damn that! No more than a shade! I think that what we think of as high and what was hitherto described as low culture are creaking and straining and coming together.' He laughed. 'You see how I have to dress it up! Let's go to the Shed. It should be a rave. I particularly relish "rave".' And this time he laughed gently, at himself, and called for the bill. As they waited for it he said,

'I hope that coincidence of meeting that old friend from your past is some sort of good omen. We pagans have neglected omens for too long.'

It was not easy to think of James as a pagan, Joe thought, as they took the few turnings to yet another building in Soho. Yet when they reached the Shed, a temporarily unleased underground car park, there was in the stridency of those congregated there and in the aggression of the music something orgiastic, bacchanalian, pagan, certainly in revolt against Christian Englishness.

'This is Sandra,' said James of a slight, blonde-cropped young woman in a loose red sweater and tight blue jeans, 'she'll keep an eye on you. I must find the band. We are on third. There are agents here. And publishers.'

As he went off, politely elbowing his way through the crowd, Joe had the impression of a man changing character. The Oxford poise of James, the composure and balance, was banished as his nostrils smelled the sulphur of success in this metropolitan nether world.

'Dance?'

'Oh yes. Thanks.'

But he couldn't. Not like her. Not like all the rest of them either. Joe had mastered ballroom dancing with his mother and honed it with Rachel and with Rachel learned the geometry of rock and roll: but this frog, this hully gully, this twist, this free flow was outside the life he and Natasha had led, a life without dancing. Sandra was patient for a little while and then simply walked away and danced in her own diameter. Joe was badly confused. He prided himself on his dancing. He loved it. He could dance till he dropped. He was making a film about a dancer! Now he stood 'like a bit of a plonker', said Sandra, his legs willing but frozen, his mind fuzzy but beating to the music, his body in a spasm of shyness.

'I'm no good at this,' he said when the band had crashed through its last long savage electronic apocalyptic chords.

'It's a knack,' said Sandra. 'Want a joint?'

'Well, I'd rather have a cigarette. Would you like one?'

'My friend says they're bad for you.' She was rolling the joint with show-off skill.

'Yes, but, I think, the devil you know, you know?'

'How come you know James?'

It was kind. About fifteen minutes later, James's group came on.

'The Moment of Truth,' said Sandra. They listened intently.

'The words, the lyrics, are really good,' Joe told James. 'And the music, Howard. The words and the music. Maybe the band was a bit raw.' Joe's voice only just registered above the noise.

'I thought they performed extremely well,' said James, loudly.

'Of course. But you asked me about the lyrics . . .'

'Fantastic!' shouted Sandra. 'Fab! A real turn-on. Best vibes of the night. Fanbloodytastic!'

'Do you really think so?'

'I did too,' said Joe. 'Yes. Real bite, I thought. Hard words – not hard-difficult, hard-tough, good.'

'The music,' said Howard, 'came first.'

'My legs were shaking!' said Sandra. 'But I made myself stand still. I bloody forced myself just to stand. Still. And listen.'

'We shall hear the professional judgements soon enough,' said James, grimly, looking around to search out the agents who were now, unnervingly, listening to the next band. Able to contain himself no longer, he slid back into the crowd and Howard followed.

'Darling!' Sandra threw her arms around a woman who, as far as Joe could see, was her twin. 'My friend,' Sandra said, loading the word, and whisked her onto the dance floor to perform a dance which prescribed that they hugged each other close and jumped up and down to the beat.

Joe was abandoned and, in the way of roller-coaster nights, quite suddenly and unexpectedly miserable. He leaned against the wall and wanted to leave. But there was one thing he had to do.

Eventually James came into view. Joe went across to him and above the big new band shouted, 'Look! Please don't get it wrong. I thought your songs were great. I really did. Difficult to talk here, that's all.'

285

'I much appreciate it,' yelled James. 'Don't worry. We can talk later. But I greatly appreciate your comments! There is an agent who seems quite interested.'

His smile was enormous: welcome, it said, to my new life.

Joe found his way to Wardour Street without too much difficulty. St Anne's Court, the address of the Sunset Strip, declared by the *Observer* critic 'the best strip joint in town' and the location for Tim's previous film and Madeleine's moment of stardom, proved less easy but eventually he navigated himself there.

'Madeleine isn't on the photos,' he said to the hefty doorman.

'They can't all be there, mate. "They're Naked and they Dance," ' he chanted in moderate tones to two men trawling past.

'But Madeleine was the star.'

Long tubes of neon lit up the narrow alley and gave it the glamour of a film set. Joe stood feet firmly apart, needing the balance.

'You were with the film lot, right?'

'Yes.'

'Thought I knew the face. It was good. Maddy was good. "They're Naked and they Dance." We lost her because of that.'

'What?'

'This film agent, said he was a film agent, picked her up off it, didn't he? Next day. Knobbed her, even bought the ring, I've heard. Said he'd make her a star, silly cow.'

'So she isn't there.'

'Cor-rect, my son. But the new ladies are even juicier, my friend.'

'Do you know where she is?'

'Don't make me laugh. Look, you coming in or clearing off, no offence? It looks bad you just standing.'

'So she's gone.'

'And never called me mother. In or out?'

Slowly Joe trudged away, wanting to hear once more 'They're Naked and they Dance' but the doorman didn't oblige.

He walked down to the Charing Cross underground, fighting the tiredness which now rose to possess him. And the guilt, the shame . . . and the traces of regret, the curiosity about paths not taken, the feeling, laughed at years later but real enough then, that Sodom and Gomorrah had lain before him and he on the brink swaying above the cesspits. And the traces of regret? Did he want to go back, go further?

The house was a sanctuary. The planes had stopped for the night. Mary had gone back to Caldbeck for her summer holiday and that night the small semi in Kew had a sacred feeling about it, of dedication, of ideals, of Natasha, his wife, and their child and the good life to come. He would telephone her in Brittany, first thing in the morning.

CHAPTER TWENTY-SIX

Natasha put down the phone and stayed a while in the comfortable chair, letting Joseph's words warm her mind, letting coils of affection rise from her memory and lift into her imagination. Her life to come would be a good life, a life she could never have led without Joseph. It did not frighten her that she was so certain. There was no superstition in Natasha, just as there was no religion.

Joseph could be used as a launch to let her fly to a place of light where everything would always be secure and, more usefully for Natasha now, to a place of darkness in herself which had to be attacked, now that she had the stability and confidence. It could not longer be cowardly avoided. It was possible at last to take all her courage and go into the depths of what she had been and why she had become as she was. It was, in prospect, exhilarating, she thought, as she took the pushchair and wheeled it over the fallen cones through the pine wood to the headland of this Breton fishing village.

She sat in the shade, the child asleep, and looked out to sea as so many women had done for centuries on this ground, had looked out for their men to return from perilous voyages. Her father had told her that, in order to be close for the return, the women had mended the nets near the shore. These were the 'Filets Bleus', soon to be comme-morated in an annual festival when sailors and their families from dozens of Breton ports would march through the town, the men playing pipes and drums, the women dressed in their traditional Breton costume, their embroidered dresses and high starched headdresses decorated distinctively village to village.

Now it was her turn to sit near the shore and look out to sea, waiting for Joseph who would arrive on the unromantic ferry in two days' time. He would embrace Brittany, she was sure of that. She smiled to herself as she took out a cigarette and focused on a dramatic bank of black rocks just a few hundred yards from the shore. She made shapes out of them, shapes which came out of the mass as here a lion's head, there a formation worthy of Braque, there the cruel teeth which had ripped into so many wooden hulls over the centuries.

Already she felt better. The sun, the sea, the sound of her own language, even the Breton whose crackling accent she enjoyed as much as the Provençal. It sounded a little like Joseph's accent, she thought, and the Cumbrian dialect he sometimes performed for her benefit. Years ago her father had bought this modest chalet house in the pine woods just above the town. It was furnished in a light summer style, bamboo chairs, and sofas, pine tables, a few colourful inexpensive rugs, the whole built for air, built to serve the large meadow garden which moated it to independence from the other few houses in what were called the 'Coat Pins'. It had no associations for Natasha and she liked that, no responsibility, neither a history nor a future invested there.

But for her father, what associations had it for him? What ties? She had met the woman on her one previous visit, in her teens, and been confused by her liking for the calm blonde rather plump sweet person whose reputation through the alchemy of gossip and rumour had been demonised into that of a scarlet destroyer. A woman more different from Véronique it would be hard to find. Later, to her surprise, Natasha had taken violently against her and even felt sorry for Véronique. Finally she had seen her father relaxed in the woman's company, playful, light, another man, a man she would love to have as a father, and her opinion swung back in favour.

Yet, was it true, this talk of infidelity? It was possible, she believed, to be platonically loving friends. The woman worked in the laboratory all the year round and lived alone in a small, extremely feminine house in the middle of the town. Natasha had gone there for tea and been introduced to some of her friends. Everything seemed so proper, so open and transparently without sin. Yet there was an affair, Natasha believed. Even the transparent amiability of a woman whom she might have welcomed, she thought, as a stepmother could not dispel that. And the signs from her father when he was in her company . . . signs of an affection she envied.

Yet, near him again now and once more in the ambience of the unlikely looking 'mistress', it was her father she puzzled over rather than the woman or the affair or the consequences it had. Why did she know so little about him? He never failed to respond when asked a question but the times spent with him were so short, so irregular. Natasha wanted to know more about Provence, her childhood there, his widower state, their life under the Germans, her father's reaction to that. She was sure that Alain had told her that her father had helped people escape, given money, provided contacts for the journey into the Alps beyond La Rotonde. But how much help and what had been the risk to himself? She wanted to dig into that past, that occupied territory. She wanted to talk about, perhaps to write about it, and he could help. But for now, Brittany was a haven, to be accepted for that, and the sea was a medicine.

Most importantly, she was with Louis and François and her daughter and no one else. Véronique had taken the children to La Rotonde. Louis would join them towards the end of the month. Natasha had come to Brittany to spend time with François. He was happily out on the sea now, with Sylvestre, the handyman from the laboratory, in a rowing boat fitted with a small motor, fishing for specimens for the laboratory, which Louis directed from a distance for most of the year. Louis's month's residence in the summer was much awaited. He was held in some reverence. Natasha had discovered that earlier in the morning when Monique, the pale-skinned Breton woman, a fisherman's wife, who came to clean and cook lunch, had given Natasha an encomium on the virtues and the value to the community of her father and the laboratory. Natasha had by proxy been flattered. She was moved at the prospect of days ahead with Joseph, their daughter, with François and Louis.

Monique, who had two children of her own, could scarcely keep her hands off the small, fair, merry English child and begged to be allowed to take her home for afternoons, to look after her, giving Natasha proper time to rest which, with sweet directness she declared, she so clearly needed, as all rich women did. It would be such a pleasure for her and for her children to have a little English girl from the Coat Pins. Natasha was practical. The prospect of such stretches of leisure was too tempting to miss and (she smiled to herself as she formulated this) it truly seemed she would be doing Monique a favour. There was happiness to be given, as well as leisure to be taken, an almost absurdly self-serving conjunction, but real, and too good to ignore.

The child woke up. Natasha re-entered into motherhood. It was as if she had been invisible while the child slept. So curious, she thought, this small person who was the two of them. Everyone said she was a lovely child. Natasha took her down to the beach where they would collect shells.

François saw that he was scaring the living daylights out of Joseph and so he strained to make the boat go even faster. It had seemed an innocent invitation. François's friend had told him he could use the tiny vessel. He had offered Joseph a trip despite Joseph's protests about knowing nothing at all about boats. All Englishmen were sailors, François said, as a challenge. Now he was stuck with it.

They had skimmed straight out to sea with a wind that had some of the other enthusiasts shaking their heads and holding on for calmer weather. The boat was very small. The sail was a clumsy thing, Joe thought. François's barked commands were largely incomprehensible. Land was soon out of sight. Would they ever turn back? They were alone on the ocean, it seemed, skimming very choppy water in a universe of sea. Joe fought hard to keep his fear down and the struggle took most of his attention.

It was when François began a series of tacking and turning man-oeuvres to bring them back to land that Joe's nerves began to show. Each turn, preceded by violent gesticulations and streams of obscenities from François, tipped the boat within centimetres of capsizing, nothing but the cold depth below, no one in sight to see the disaster, François yelling at him to lean out and keep the balance, lean right out, the sail all but dipping into the waves and Joe's confidence ebbing after every successful manoeuvre – it was bound to go wrong next time. It did. But only when, thank God, they were in sight of land. Joe's relief at the prospect of reaching terra firma had slowed him down and this time he sat frozen as the sail fell towards him, past him, and the boat capsized.

François commanded Joe's help to make several attempts to haul the sail up but its saturated weight defeated them.

'He didn't know what to do next!' François crowed as the three of them ate in the rather rough back alley crêperie François favoured. 'We were told all the English were sailors.'

'Sorry,' said Joe.

'He just didn't move!' François was triumphant. 'The sail began to come down, so,' he raised his right arm and brought it slowly down towards the table, 'and I waited for Joseph to move. He was like a statue.'

'I was.'

Natasha smiled. Joseph was giving François every gram of his moment.

'I was surprised,' said François, who took another pull of the Muscadet, burped, then speared an over-large forkful of the latest in the steady line of scorching crêpes which came hot from the galley kitchen. 'I thought he had done it before. But now . . .' François's frozen fork halfway to his mouth, body stiffened. 'A corpse. Nearly a corpse.'

'You helped him so much,' said Natasha, as they walked through the higgledy-piggledy alleys to the harbour front on which stood a few small restaurants, shops and two modest hotels. 'There's a French *mot*: "You missed a great opportunity to say nothing." You took yours and François was so proud – to show you up, to be superior to you, to be able to boast about it to me. And to all his new friends, I'm sure.'

'The fact is I was happy when it went over. All I had to do was swim and push the thing. I was. Really. Happy.'

Natasha joined in with his laughter.

'Why do we get scared?' he asked. 'Skimming along at a hundred miles an hour with a provenly safe boat under my bum gave me the near terminal jitters. Doing a sort of dog paddle over the same water was comfort itself.'

'It doesn't matter,' she said. 'You have given him enormous pleasure.'

She leaned across and kissed him on the cheek. It was such a fine night! Almost a full moon, the boats silhouetted in the harbour, the black-walled mass of the fortified old town out there across the causeway.

'Let's walk over there. Into the magical fortress.'

'You are always a romantic, Joseph,' Natasha said. They crossed the causeway in the silvery half-night. Once through the narrow gates they were drawn to the tables outside the sole open bar, its front wall slung with a dozen or so white electric light bulbs, beyond it the balmy darkness of a deserted street. Joe felt profoundly abroad.

Three men were earnest in dominoes at one table. At another a white-linen-suited, stylistically striking young man, English, Joe decided, from the battered Panama hat, was sitting disdainfully alone, sipping, what they heard on his re-ordering, a Kir, smoking a cigarette beautifully, as if it were his art.

'I'm glad François wanted to stay in the crêperie,' Joe said, lowering his voice to match the emptiness of the street. 'We're not alone much, like this, now, not enough, are we?'

'At home we are. When she is in bed.'

'But . . . out . . . being out is where there's life, isn't it?'

'Not only here. Nowhere has the monopoly. What is that line you so much like about reading?'

' "My days among the dead are spent." '

'Not so dead if you are reading the dead.'

'But . . . anyway . . .' The waiter brought cognac and coffee for him, coffee only for Natasha. 'I saw *Who's Afraid of Virginia Woolf?* in London,' he said. 'All of us did. All of us from the cutting room. After we'd finished.' He took a rather clumsy sip of the cognac. 'Margaret had told me that Richard Burton was particularly good. Ross knows Richard Burton. He says he's a "flawed genius".'

'Isn't everyone? That's too easy. Typical of Ross. It's simply said for effect. And you see, it worked!' She laughed.

Joe raised the glass of cognac to close down that subject.

'OK. But the film's about a man who is glued to his books. To the bottle as well. One reviewer said that every couple in London of a certain type went to see it to watch themselves on the screen. To watch two intelligent people in love tear each other to bits.'

Natasha made no reply. There was an unconscious overemphasis in what he said. It somehow connected with what she had thought of as a rather distracted, unsure look about him when he had come off the ferry.

'God, I love it here!' he said. 'So warm at this time of night, this bar, this fortress, the sea, you. I wouldn't trade this, this moment for anything, anywhere, ever!'

There was overemphasis again, but no dissembling, she could tell that. True as a bell, the words, and Joseph, and their life. The whisper of doubt faded as quickly as it had arrived.

'Isn't François in good form?' she said. 'I've never seen him in such good spirits.'

'He drinks plenty of them!'

'Joseph! He is proving himself a man among the men here. And the Brittany men are tough, they are strong, the fishermen, and François loves to go to their bars and cafés and Sylvestre tells me they like him. He has no snobbery. None. And they like his jokes!'

'He was telling me about the van, or is it a truck, he drives across to St Malo twice a week to send some of the laboratory's catch to other labs in Marseilles and was it Naples? He explained that what they can find here is unique.'

'You see? He knows what he is doing. *And*,' she smiled as if she had been vindicated, 'he is driving, not a lorry, but almost!'

'He's fine,' said Joe. 'I like him. Who couldn't?'

'Only his mother.'

Joe held back the cry for mercy: not Véronique, not on such a rare night.

'I think Father has adapted,' Natasha said. 'More or less. Or he ignores him now. Just someone else about the laboratory during the day and a son scarcely ever at home in the evenings. But Véronique . . .' Her face grew tense; he saw her make again for the unhealed past.

'Natasha . . . could we forget Véronique tonight?'
'She is . . .'
He sang, softly,

> 'She gets too hungry for dinner at eight
> Goes to the theatre but never comes late
> She never bothers with people she hates
> That's why the lady is a tramp!'

The sound of singing and in an American accent unseated the white-suited Englishman and imperiously he rose to leave. '*L'addition*,' he called, '*s'il vous plaît*.'

'One down, three to go,' Joe whispered, but one of the Frenchmen looked over and said,

'*Encore!*'

'This is you,' he said, and sang on:

> 'She likes the cool, soft wind in her hair
> Life without care
> She's broke, it's OK
> Hates California, it's cold and it's damp
> That's why the lady, that's why my lady, that's why the lady is a
>   tramp.'

The Frenchmen applauded. The proprietor beamed. 'Frank Sinatra,' he said, 'bravo!' The tall Englishman, with contempt in every stride, marched away into the dark reaches of the old town.

'You are so silly, Joseph,' Natasha said, when arm in arm they got back into the town. 'I love you when you are silly. You should be more silly more often.'

'It's hard,' he said, 'living with you.'

'Am I so serious?'

'Oh yes! So serious. Lovely and serious. Sea air makes seriousness sexy. Try saying that when you're sober.'

'We are happy, aren't we, Joseph?'

He stopped, faced her and kissed her.

Monique had achieved one of her goals – to 'kidnap' their daughter for the night. The next goal, she said, was to 'keep' her.

'Imagine,' Joe said, as they walked past the bulky laboratory and turned up the sandy path which led into the pine woods. 'Tonight we'll be on our own. No cries, no "alert". Just us.'

'We shall sleep the sleep of the dead,' said Natasha, 'in disbelief.'

—m—

A few days later she woke up early and lay on her side for a while, looking at Joseph in the early light. He was deeply asleep, one arm above his head on the pillow, the other stretched out towards her, his legs, she could see their shape through the single thin sheet, halfway towards the foetal position. She was reminded, by this pose, of the painting she had done, long ago it seemed now, of Icarus. One day she must collect it from Julia's cellar.

Joseph was already tanned. He liked the sun and in the first days, as always, he had taken too much and boiled red, lips blebbed, blisters on shoulders, but he stuck it out until he shaded to this gypsy brown which suited him, and brought out a deeper aspect of his character, she thought, something sensually unloosened, unmappable, less organised, and the richer for that.

She got out of bed and reached out for the black dressing gown she had worn since Oxford. She caught sight of herself in the mirror. Her hips had become heavy, her belly still sagged, the breasts still bigger, altogether too much of her, she thought, and knew she should try harder to regain her previous shape. Joseph would prefer that, however much he protested the contrary, what man would not? That was the result of the bone tiredness in her which had still not gone away. Why bone? she thought. She decided she must be the Empress of her own body and from this moment command it to obey her.

She went through to look at their sleeping daughter. Another love, a different love, flesh and blood now safely launched, a puzzle, she thought, so much out of me, the months in the womb, so little from Joseph and yet he was even more present than she in the face of this other self.

As she made a bowl of coffee she realised how little she understood

296

and did it help, even the little she understood? Or was the best way just an acceptance inside the inevitable?

She went into the garden, carrying the coffee, like a libation to the dawn; she could understand libations to the dawn. The rising of the sun must not have seemed inevitable on many a dark night. She went beyond the garden and further into the pines. She left behind her, in the wooden chalet, the four people she loved most in the world: Joseph, their daughter, her father, François – how could the one word, love, describe the nuances and the differences? Yet it served, she did not know how, to embrace tenderness, passion, respect, admiration, protectiveness, dependency, constancy.

There was the sea, calm on this morning of the Fête des Filets Bleus. The beaches were empty, the gulls held the rocks. Out there, when she narrowed her eyes, there were as always the small boats trailing the blue nets in the dark water. Soon enough the bands would arrive and the parade would begin, her heart would swell a little at the simple demonstration of continuity and victory over long voyages in unsafe waters, of the women looking out to sea, waiting for the homecoming, of the small community on this short strip of shore on the edge of the Atlantic celebrating its unity and survival. Joseph would romanticise about that.

He would also romanticise about the sea which was now beginning to sparkle as the sun's face moved higher from the east. He could go into states of almost instant exhilaration where she could not follow. Either in his nature, from his birth, or from those fractured boyhood experiences there had grown a religious, even a mystical feeling about the vastness, the unknowability, the interconnectedness of life and what sustained it, what moved it, a feeling almost entirely foreign to Natasha. Sometimes she could dream herself into a luxurious self-hypnosis, looking at the stars, looking out at the sea, but she was never far away from a more powerful sense of being puzzled or, more often, an overwhelming impulse to find out how it all worked. She was content with that, content as now with the fact that this was the sea and the morning light on the sea was beautiful in her eyes though to the fishermen it would just be work, to others an obstacle to cross or, as used by Joseph when he swam out to the rocks like an otter, a facility to turn happiness into health. What was really out there she did not know and such intimations as she had were no more than scattered showers on the fathomless indifference.

They would all be stirring soon. She took a final sip of the coffee, poured the remainder on the ground and walked back quickly, suddenly eager to be in the house, with them, with all of them.

—⏝—

Natasha kept clear of the main flow of the procession which took place under the midday sun, first along the coast road then marching into the town and finally across the causeway where troupe after troupe, pipes and drums skirling, walked between the waters into the narrow streets to the arena whose thick walls fronted the Atlantic. She took care never to let go of her daughter's hand. She had encouraged Joseph to go off with François and his friends whom she categorised as 'just like your friends in Cumberland'. Her father had said he would go his own way. Even on the day of the Fête he wanted to spend some hours in the laboratory and making arrangements on such a day of flux was pointless, he said. But, Natasha thought sadly, the other woman would share his time.

She remembered the day as a series of impressions. She knew the work of the Impressionists who had painted in Brittany near by. The broken daylight on the sea had provided the perfect subject. But so had the crowds, and those painters' interest in the movement of crowds could be both understood and realised, Natasha thought, in the gaudily clad marchers, the thronging spectators in holiday mood, the common open air, the constantly moving complex of light and people, of sky, sea and the gulls swooping along the shore.

Monique was in the procession and waved and both of them waved back, Natasha holding the child high in her arms. The tall Englishman in the white suit was joined by an equally tall young woman also in white and they stood on a wall, above the crowd, as if taking the salute. She saw Joseph several times, intent, smiling, shot through she could tell with the drama and the music, sometimes with François and his friends, sometimes alone. Her father was there at one point with Mademoiselle Benoît. She linked Louis's arm in an open companionable way.

Natasha eavesdropped on bits of the local broadly accented conversation which were like manna and made her homesick for the country she was in. When the sun began to sink over the wide sea to the west, mother and daughter walked quite freely around the town as most of the crowd had decanted into the fortress to watch the competitions of music, dancing, boules and to admire the intricate mediaeval hats and the densely embroidered aprons.

It was at this time, along the front, that she met François, drunk and alone, and she guided him protesting home and straight to his room so that their father would not discover him. He told her that his mother had said he had to leave Brittany and go south to Montpellier University in the autumn; that Alain had a friend there who had found a course he could do. He told her that he was going to run away and join the navy or become a hobo in America or hide in the houses of his new friends, anything to avoid university, he hated university, he hated everybody who went to university, they were snobs and phonies and they knew nothing and they were not pals like his new pals, they were all false.

He fell into a stupor of sleep as soon as he lay on his bed.

— ⋙ —

Isabel listened patiently. Alain had found an excuse not to attend what was clearly to be an emotional confrontation in the Prévost house in La Rotonde. Véronique was drinking her wine unusually quickly.

'She is intolerable,' Véronique stubbed out half a cigarette. 'She has always been intolerable. From the beginning of our marriage there was this glaring girl looking at me as if I had murdered her mother and stolen her father. She was never reconciled. When she went away to the convent school I thought, peace at last, but we had reports of her truancy and bad behaviour and Louis and I talked about her. We talked and talked, Isabel. We talked about Natasha more than all the other children added together, more than about ourselves. Natasha occupied our minds. We made plans for Natasha, we quarrelled over Natasha. We were exhausted over Natasha.'

'I know.' Isabel watched intently, nodded, waited.

'We had some respite when she went to Oxford although whenever she came back I felt her presence working against me. It was baleful. I was a criminal. But, I am sorry, Isabel, she was away in another country and I was happy, yes, I was happy, and then she married but what happens? She comes back again!'

'It is Joseph who encourages her to come, Véronique. It is Joseph.'

'But now with François! She telephones me. Louis telephones me. Natasha says he mustn't go to Montpellier. She sounds angry one moment and quite mad, we both know she can be quite mad, at other moments. She wants him to drive a lorry and live with the men who work on the boats or whatever they do. It will be amusing for a while but what of his life, Isabel? What of his future? And Louis is angry with me. Why is he always angry with me when François is the subject? He is our son, both of Louis and me. I know François is not a scholar as Louis wants him to be. He doesn't work, he is sly, he evades all his responsibilities, he has tormented me. Like Natasha. Why? And now the two of them together. It is intolerable, Isabel. It is insupportable.'

Isabel waited until Véronique had poured herself another drink. Her own glass was still full. She spoke quietly and slowly, in contrast to Véronique's rapid and agitated delivery.

'It is terrible for you, my sweet,' she said, 'it has been difficult from the very beginning. It was tragic from the beginning, Véronique, and there were faults on all sides, on all sides, my sweet, we cannot forget that. And Natasha was a child. We do not know what is inherited and she can be so very like her mother that I gasp, I say to Alain, "She is born again," but she was a baby who . . . Let us leave it there, Véronique. Time moves on. We move with it or we are lost. We are not in the confessional, we do not have to reveal everything to each other. We know what was in the past but she was the child.

'And now, with François, well, Véronique, it was you, I have to say this, who allowed or encouraged François to go to London and live with Natasha and Joseph because that is what he did, in effect, in the first year of her marriage. She gave him so much of herself – you told me that, Louis told Alain how good Natasha and Joseph had been for François and it cannot have been easy for them, a young couple, just started, neither of them at home in London, so different, those two, held together only by the grand passion or the idea of grand passion which is very fragile when there is nothing else to support it, no family, no common history, no common language, at the heart of it. Such a grand passion needs to be nursed. They did not know that. Joseph is very young and Natasha can be blind, her obsessions, this bad self-absorption – but they reached out their hands to François and they helped him, Véronique, and Natasha has become deeply involved with him and so there is no wonder. Is there?'

It was early evening. They were in the big room which was part of the old wall and faced east. There was a balcony outside the central window and from there a steep drop onto the rocks far below. The great stone walls kept the room cool. The two women sat face to face across a small card table. Isabel now sipped at her wine to take the dryness out of her throat. The silence built up and Isabel picked out from the next room the ticking of an old clock which Louis had inherited.

'You were always on her side,' said Véronique, savagely.

'That is not true,' said Isabel. 'You are upset. I understand. But it is not true. Yes! I love Natasha like a daughter. Yes! But she is not my daughter. And Louis I love and you, Véronique. I am not on anybody's side and I think, with Alain, that François should come to Montpellier at the end of next month, he should make one last attempt, here in a part of the world that he knows and it is so much less competitive than Paris. No Louis for a start! He needs to make friends in his own class. Natasha has gone too far. I will tell her that.'

'You will?'

'Of course. You have to draw lines. You and Louis are the parents. Natasha is obstinate.' She took out a cigarette but did not offer one to Véronique: each was smoking her own brand. 'But so am I.'

'So how do I tell you this? I don't want a long build-up, I don't want the action picture. It should be sudden, like it was. François was driving back from St Malo about two weeks after we had returned to London. It was late at night and I would guess he was at least a little drunk and he loved to drive fast, just as he loved to go as fast as possible in the boat. He hit a wall, smack on. They said the death would have been instantaneous. Natasha's grief was terrible to witness.'

CHAPTER TWENTY-SEVEN

Grief isolated her. She was so deeply drawn into it, so pulled into its apparently infinite darkness, that nothing could come near her that was not itself claimed for this grief. Even her daughter to whose needs she ministered dutifully, whose play and mere movements could strike chords of consolation, even she was best kept at some distance emotionally, best left out of this self-consuming struggle. Ellen came to stay and took the child off her hands for hours at a time.

As for Joe his quick and earnest sympathy was inadequate, he felt, although Natasha protested that he was helpful. He did not feel it. He could not follow her. The sense of each other through feelings alone became more faint and words failed. He felt pushed away. She needed to be left alone to inhabit this circle of grief and to save herself from it. For she felt the grief could engulf and extinguish her; so much guilt at what had not been done, so much sorrow at what had not been done, so much shame at what had been done to François, so undefended. Grief blighted her feelings.

Neither then nor later could Joe come to terms with a sort of jealousy. How could Natasha's grief make him jealous? That low, vile thing, a taint on such grief. Did it mean that he was jealous of the force of feeling displayed towards another man albeit her brother, her half-brother? That was plausible though not at the heart of it, he thought. It was the grief itself, the way it possessed her as love for him had never so fully possessed her. He saw grief as the fullest expression of her feelings, the most passionate, the most unqualified he had ever seen in her and it was not directed at him.

—ɯ—

They spent a weekend in Oxford with Matthew and Julia and Joe's anxiety dissipated by the hour as Julia's tender and teasing manner seemed to help heal Natasha. Joe was flattered at Matthew's curiosity about the metropolitan line he was following. He had assumed that his job was far below the high calling of scholarship, but Matthew displayed a close interest in it and Joe felt that what he did was acceptable. He was grateful for that. The weekend passed in undirected talk with the younger couple scarcely noticing the efforts being made by their older, wiser friends. Their daughter was commandeered by Matthew and Julia's children and she was delighted to be the little spoiled playmate.

They came back on an early evening train on Sunday, leaving Oxford in its May glory with regret: in Oxford both of them had sunk into nostalgia and Paddington Station seemed particularly grimy, soulless and unwelcoming. Joe saw that Natasha looked tired again, and the child, too, was weary, as if the weekend had been wiped out by that short journey from the university city. He decided against taking the underground. The taxi fare was just about within reach.

As they crossed over Kew Bridge, the Thames flowing softly beneath them, and came on Kew Green, the beautiful Georgian church, the cricket pitch just lately used, and swung alongside Kew Gardens towards home, Natasha's sadness sweetened. If only she could ignore the licence to unleash her implacable monsters that the death of François had given her; if only she could see what she had for what it was, fortunate in love, rich in daily life; if only she could see her life like that for more than a few illuminated moments and not look as she did at the outbursts of blossom, apple blossom, pear and most of all the cherry blossom, and think soon it will be gone, this blossom, this beauty, soon it will be dead.

There were three letters – all for Joe – from the Saturday delivery. After he had carried the cases upstairs and then carried the child up to her room and helped her into bed, and after Natasha had gone up to talk to her, as she did, in adult terms, which intrigued Joe, and he had put on the kettle for tea, made tomato and ham sandwiches and switched on the television, decided against it, found some music on the radio and flopped into one of the armchairs, only then did he open his mail.

He had been put into contact with a literary agency by Ross McCulloch. The agency had handed the unsolicited manuscript to one of the younger men. The two men had met in Soho for lunch. Eight weeks had passed since that encouraging lunch.

The letter said the novel had been accepted by a 'small but very respectable publisher'.

Joe felt that if you could have a blow to the solar plexus that caused a sickness of pleasure rather than pain, this was it. He read the brief but exuberant letter again. And then again. And when Natasha came down into the room he read it once more just to make absolutely certain.

He poured out two cups of tea. Natasha did not take sugar. They sat across from each other at the small table which was quite big enough for the small kitchen, still painted in cream and brown, unredecorated like the rest of the house. He offered her a sandwich and she took it but out of politeness, he thought, not appetite. He passed her the letter.

She read it, looked up with a quick full smile which swept all the fatigue from her face and then she read it again. 'It's good,' she murmured, over the letter, 'it's so good, Joseph.' He too smiled now: it was becoming more real. It was good, wasn't it? She handed it back to him and with rueful honest envy said, 'I've been writing for so much longer than you have. How did you do that?'

There was no appropriate response he could find and a vague guilt clouded his mind. If they lived in France she would have been published way before him. Writing in English handicapped her, yet her French style, she said, had become corrupted by the years of English speaking. 'Sorry,' he said, meaning it.

She forced down the competitive reaction which she knew was unjust and could see threatened to spoil his moment. Her tone grew warmer and more passionate.

'How can you be sorry? You must be very pleased. Aren't you?'

'Yes,' feeling anything but.

'It's wonderful,' she said.

'I'm sure yours will do better.'

'We have no wine in the house,' said Natasha.

'I'll take you out tomorrow night,' he said. 'Mary'll be back by tea time.'

'Congratulations,' said Natasha, raising her cup. 'Are you sure now that you like the title?'

'Don't you?' Joseph raised his cup in acknowledgement.

'Well . . .' she said, emphatically, 'the first title was more poetic, I think . . .'

'I'll change it back,' he said, smiling, relieved to give her something. 'To both of us.'

'No. To you, Joseph. To the success of *A Chance Defeat.*'

The cups touched carefully at the lip and they drank the tea.

The advance on the novel was one hundred and fifty pounds. The agent took ten per cent. The remainder was payable in two halves, sixty-seven pounds and ten shillings on signature of contract, the second half on publication. The first purchase he made with the first half of the payment was to buy Natasha a pair of tall church candlesticks, sworn by the dealer in the Portobello Road to be seventeenth century or earlier, Venetian, possibly spirited away. The candlesticks were embellished with small mirrors of a thick glass, allegedly, the dealer claimed, among the earliest of their kind. He put them on the mantelpiece where they looked absurd, Natasha thought, much as she liked their worn grandeur.

And yet they soon settled into the clutter that Joseph was accumulating. Everything – save the glorious antique candlesticks – scooped from the back of a junk shop or the final knock-down price on a late afternoon stall, a Papuan harpoon, a damaged Egyptian necklace of real age, rows of leather-bound, mostly split-spined books, a large oak chest described as an armour coffer decorated with rudely drawn men in high bowler hats, a gilded mirror lacking a fair bit of its gilding, scuffed oils, a faded kelim rug which, Joseph thought, brought in the romance of the East.

It was almost a tribute to her father's house, Natasha thought; yet in some way it was not in imitation but in competition with her father's scrupulous and admired collections. He brought her father closer than ever before, she thought, but on his own terms. This all-purpose unconscious competitiveness was an aspect of Joseph with which she could sympathise, though it annoyed him when she mentioned it. But from one or two of his remarks, she had also to consider that his collecting might be something else, an attempt, shoe-string as it was, to make a home in which she would feel at home. It had nothing of the cosy utilitarian efficiency of his own past. If this insight were correct, it was an homage; another example of his love, like the bunches of flowers, an attempt to treat her in a way which he thought befitted her.

What could she do? He got so much pleasure from these objects. To see his pleasure pleased her. To spurn these cheap but occasionally charming objects would be to spurn something in him. And yet it was again turning her towards a past she had thought herself well and for ever rid of. She put the candlesticks on the oak armour coffer. Joseph told her it made all the difference. She slung the kelim over the sofa: he said it made the room into a Turkish boudoir. His appreciation energised her. He insisted she hang some of her own paintings and covered the walls of the hall with her drawings of their daughter. She felt applauded. She painted the hall white, and then she painted the kitchen . . .

Joe had known from the beginning what he intended to do with the remaining thirty pounds of the first part of the advance. The certainty had arrived without forethought. It surprised him, it puzzled him, but he knew he would go through with it.

Often on a Saturday afternoon, Joe would head off alone. He went to the park with the child in the morning and after lunch walked on the towpath through Richmond, through Kingston, sometimes further, following the Thames upstream, boats passing by, a kindly English mystery about life on the river, its own world. This was the only time in the week he was fully alone. He would let himself rove for three or four hours and come back nicely tired, ready for an evening's writing or an outing. On Sunday afternoons they would go together all three into Kew Gardens, like the bourgeoisie of Paris, Natasha said, taking the air in the Bois de Boulogne. But Saturday afternoon had become his own time.

Recently his route had changed. He would catch the underground and go to Soho or Kensington or, most favoured, the King's Road in

Chelsea, an area still notable for its artists and bohemians but increasingly famous for its boutiques, its fashions, the new plumage, female and male plumage, which was tumbling onto the streets to the accompaniment of young cash in the pocket. Rock and roll and its progeny were on the jukebox and everywhere on the King's Road there was the mesmerising dazzle of a sudden power of Youth. The black and white of Joe's past was overlaid by this Technicolor; the establishment he had accepted was mocked or bypassed; the ubiquitous hat was increasingly discarded, replaced by ubiquitous hairstyles that were like hats. James had characterised it as the age of the poseur and the pill and of More: More sex, More liberty, More variety, More sensation, More music, More dancing, above all, More dancing.

Over the past few years, as this mushroomed around him in London though not in Kew Gardens, Joe had become infected by it, although 'poisoned' would later seem a more suitable word. He was increasingly like the boy with his nose pressed to the big plate-glass window of a shop full of toys and treats he had been told he must never enjoy and could never afford, fatally consumed by longing. Now the glass was melting.

To Joe, often weak-headed, easily recruited by manly marching bands as a child, a hungry audience for choirs, for drama on film or on the stage, this new drumbeat was the gut call of his generation, and to ignore it would be to miss out on its siren promises; of sinless pleasure, harmless excess, anarchy without effort. Natasha stood apart from all this as did her friends in Kew Gardens. They were as unruffled as Joe was ruffled. Outwardly, still the checked sports jacket, the regular job, the obedient day; outwardly a balanced conformist. Inwardly, increasingly an appetite for what was new which longed to be sated. To be in and of this time, his time, which called him into its rhythm. Not to answer would be to miss the uniqueness of his generation. It involved no surrender. No decadence. Nothing more in fact than appearances, a few clothes.

So here he was, in the King's Road, having walked the length of it trying not to look too lingeringly at the erotically charged underdressed girls, plucking up the courage to go into one of those clothes shops which bore so little resembalance to the rationed clothes shops of his youth. The sight and sound and smell of sex infested the city. Even shops were now, in this golden summer mid-afternoon, places of dark seductive disco dance-floor lights and the latest permissive hits from the charts, of crushed velvets and lace, brothels of dream garments.

He spun it out. He wandered from window to window, gazing at what were more costumes than clothes, disguises promising metamorphosis, a man could be made again merely by stepping through the door. It was as if in the sun-struck windows of the King's Road, Chelsea, London, England, a rebellion had announced itself and all you had to do to join in was to purchase one of the new non-uniform uniforms.

Did he see himself as freed from his past and unshackled, released into the air by changing in a cubicle? He could appear to change personality. He could become lawless. Perhaps the multiple opportunities of the metropolis demanded multi-personalities to meet and take up its challenges. That it might tempt him to invent a new, uprooted, liberated identity might also have stirred somewhere in his mind. But where would that take him? The apprehension which held him back would turn out, in retrospect, to be well founded. He ought to have averted his eyes.

There was something feverish about it, akin to the feelings he experienced in the Buckingham Club or when he became possessed by one of the new nerve-injecting pop songs; an atmosphere which called up impulses hitherto unknown or unacknowledged and produced a sensual and disturbing suffusion in his mind, a sensation without need of words, a freedom to change that dared him and stared him in the face. He had to enter. He knew he ought to walk away. This freedom had come too late for him. Married, treading softly into the thickets of middle-class England, with a child and a wife to support, mortgaged, with a steady job, with a pension, on the ladder, on the up. But there they were, the gears of change, respecting neither his conditioning nor his achievements nor his ordained ambition nor all the company of cautions. Did he realise that crossing this threshold would be his first infidelity?

—〰—

Sam and Ellen sat together in the pub kitchen after closing hours, after the helpers had left, the last cup of tea, the last dip into the novel for Sam, for Ellen the last daydream in front of the fire as she sat on the low stool, almost the last time this scene would be played out in this place.

Sam folded down a page, put aside *The Quiet American* and said, 'For one last time now, are you sure?'

'Certain.' She did not turn to him but gave the word to the fire, like a quiet oath.

'Remember when you came back after she'd just been born?'

'I do.'

'Well.'

'I thought it would be seen as interfering if we'd moved down then,' said Ellen, still not turning to him, 'it would seem that I didn't trust her. Natasha would have thought that.'

'She's turned out a good mother, hasn't she? When I've seen them.'

'Yes . . . yes . . . though she talks to her like a grown-up all the time. She'll explain things that I'm not sure a little girl can understand. Things that don't need explaining. They just need to be told – 'That's wrong,' 'That's dangerous' – but it's her way. It's Natasha's way.'

Sam's admiration for Natasha's patient explanations was unqualified. This, he thought, was the proper way to bring up a child, to pour in wisdom as early as possible, to take time to teach, to have nothing to do with the abrupt, imperious, unchallengeable cuffs and curt diktats of his own childhood and, to some extent, that of Joe.

'Proof of the pudding,' he said.

'Oh yes! She's lovely, isn't she? She's just lovely. There's nobody like her.' And now she turned to him and smiled deeply as images of her granddaughter came into her mind.

'So why now?'

'I've tried to tell you, Sam.'

Ellen's reply was an appeal. Sam heard it.

'Reading's just about an hour to London on the train,' he said.

'How far is the pub from the station?'

'There's a bus at the top of the road. Or you could walk. Either way fifteen or twenty minutes and then there's the tube at the other end.'

'An hour and a half, two hours at most.'

'At the very outside.'

Ellen had shown little interest in either the pub he had been offered or the district in which it was located. Sam was not piqued by this. She had come back from her latest visit to Kew Gardens utterly resolved and he had loved her for the steel in it. She had to be near them, she said, the sooner the better.

His landlord contacts had taken him to Reading. His qualifications, the account books he had taken and the references from the Cumbrian brewery's manager who recognised a mind made up, had struck lucky with the imminent availability of a run-down Victorian pub, the Builder's Arms.

It was in a very working-class area of Reading, he had told Ellen, who had nodded with relief: she did not want to go out of her league. Rows and rows of small terraced houses, more like the North than the South, he said, all going down to the Kennet which ran into the Thames. The rivers marked two of its boundaries and cut it off from the city of Reading itself: many of the residents of the area rarely went into Reading. Small shops galore, a place sufficient to itself and quite prosperous, with many of the women working in the big biscuit factory which loomed, like a castle, above the huddled terraces. He even mentioned the gasometers at the bottom of the street. In time he would become very fond of their perfect cylindrical shapes, the sinking and rising of their surfaces.

'It tickles me,' he said, 'that it's so old-fashioned down there.' He smiled, still taken with the discovery. 'You expect the South to be ahead of us, but it's like Wigton in the forties. It's quaint. There's still a Ladies' Only Snug. They come in, big women, half a porter, nicer people you could not meet. It needs a bit of work, but that's to be expected.'

'I've made up my mind not to miss Wigton at all,' Ellen said, 'otherwise I won't manage.'

'They have a ladies' darts team,' said Sam, 'the landlady has to captain it.'

'You'd better start giving me lessons,' she said.

'They're decent people, Ellen,' he said. 'A lot like here.'

—✴—

Joe had taken Charles, his agent, to the train. He walked back from the station under pinpoint-clear stars. He wished he could read them, although the wish was not strong enough for him to make the effort. His mother could do it but he had been too impatient to stand and be taught by her. Their presence was enough; the unknown sometimes being more attractive, he thought; perhaps to know would be to lose some of the provoking mystery; or so he reasoned in the euphoria of the evening. The late heat was always felt as a privilege by those from the North, a siren call from the warmer, easier South. The cigarette tasted good. The two or three glasses of wine over dinner sat comfortably, the taste and scent still a perfume, not yet a drug.

He had taken Charles to the train after a supper with five of their Kew friends that had gone exceptionally well. Charles, Joe had guessed, thought Kew a suburb in mind and class as well as location, but Anna's husband Harry had proved to be at Cambridge at the same time as Charles and off they had romped in the happy pursuit of mutual acquaintances. Claire had then confessed, during a conversation about the war in Vietnam, that her father had been a captain at Arnhem and won the Military Cross, which again reassured Charles. Joe watched Charles closely, wanting to impress this rather reserved upper-class stranger who had taken his career by the collar.

On the way to the station he had told Charles about Natasha's novel; he had told Charles about Natasha; he had told Charles too much and his conscience now twinged but it was only a twinge and the bigger fact was that Charles had been genuinely intrigued by her. Natasha, he said, was 'quite simply the most intelligent woman I have ever met'. Joe had taken that totally at face value and practically exploded with pride.

She was, wasn't she? She is.

And beautiful, he thought, as he meandered back home under the silvery moon.

He was so very lucky, he thought, and regressed to adolescence when he used to make so many lists. He ticked off his blessings.

There was Natasha; there was their daughter; there was enough money to live the life they wanted; there were friends, friends in Kew, friends at the BBC, friends from Oxford, friends back in Wigton, Natasha's friends in France; he liked his job; his novel had been accepted; he was English, in London in the middle of this young new noise. Oh, lucky man! Oh, Lucky Jim, he remembered, how we envy him.

As he reached the front door, what could well be the last aeroplane of the night whistled and screeched its way across the suburb, almost directly over his house. There were fewer at weekends, when the air controllers shared out the pain across West London and there were times like this when to look up was to see magic in the great bellied flying machine, lit up like a village. That was not without gain. And sky travel was the life of his time, the globe a mere journey, the heavens reached up to. So many lives to be lived was the reality of the bold and lucky ones in his generation.

He paused at the gate and let his proprietorial gaze sweep down the trim semi-detached avenue as if appraising Versailles. He thought of the wine – three bottles, and only half a bottle of the Yugoslav Riesling left. He thought of the pâté bought by Natasha, the French cheeses and the real coffee. He lit another cigarette and looked up at the universe as if inviting it to look down on him and administer a little pat on the shoulder. This was Living in Style! Who would have believed it?

Natasha had been too exhausted to go upstairs and so she gathered her strength in her usual armchair before the empty fireplace. Joseph came in glowing and immediately she felt better.

'There's a bit of wine left,' he said, 'want some?'

She shook her head. Joseph poured himself a full glass and took his usual seat opposite her.

'What did you think of Charles?'

'Oh, Joseph, I'm tired.' His disappointed expression made her rally. 'I think he has beautiful manners and he likes your work and he likes you and that is quite enough for a first encounter.'

'He was funny when he talked about Angus Wilson, wasn't he?'

'But don't you like Angus Wilson? *Such Darling Dodos*, you made me read it.'

'Yes. But he was funny about him.'

'He was funny against him. English humour is sometimes funny only to the funny English, Joseph. It can seem rather cruel to the rest of us. I was surprised at you.'

'Why?' Normally he would have felt a little dented by her disapproval but tonight he was on Cloud Nine.

'Well. Angus Wilson is a novelist you admire and so why do you like stories which show him in a bad light? You are not English as Charles is English. That cast of humour is not your cast. You were imitating him.'

'If you're saying he's a snob I couldn't disagree more.'

'Of course he is a snob. Harmlessly and charmingly. And he is confident in a world to which you come as a stranger. Stay a stranger, Joseph. It has great advantages. Stay outside. Sometimes you sound as if you want to be an initiate.'

'No I don't!'

She raised her right hand, as if to say 'pax'. His benevolence untroubled, Joseph took across a cigarette and kissed her on the forehead.

'That was really tremendous,' he said, 'the meal. The pâté. The wine. The – everything. Do you think it went well?'

'Of course.' He always wanted much more. She had found the formal dinner party rather a strain.

'Claire was a turn-up, wasn't she?'

'Claire is lovely. You make calf's eyes at Claire, Joseph!'

'I don't.' He did.

'You do. But it is you. You fall a little in love with everybody you like. Now it is Ross; now it is Charles; now it is Claire. It is an aspect of your character, Joseph, though sometimes I think it is a sort of giddiness like getting drunk too quickly on a few glasses.' She paused and looked at him with a tender seriousness. 'It is as if you need somebody all the time to be the fresh ground for your feelings, always somebody new and receptive and sometimes you become a little dependent on them for a while in the process, as with Ross.'

Joseph recognised, reluctantly, that there was truth in this but his wine-fuelled mood would not let him pause or answer: self-examination, never at that stage in his life a rigorous practice, was certainly not an option on such a night.

'You were wonderful,' he said, 'Charles said so. Charles said you were the cleverest woman he had ever met.'

Joseph decided he might as well finish the bottle: there was barely a glass left in it.

'Charles knows how to flatter. And by saying that he was flattering not me but you.'

'He meant it.'

'Of course.'

'I told him how great your novel was, is.'

'Joseph!'

Her annoyance was expressed and then withdrawn. He could be such a boy! Look at that ridiculous crushed-velvet suit.

'I pressume he told you he liked your silly suit.'

'As a matter of fact . . .'

'Why did you spend the money on clothes? You have never given me a satisfactory explanation. You were never interested in clothes. I thought you would buy books. Why did it all go on clothes? And not just for yourself!'

'She likes it.'

'It's dreadful!'

'She loves it. Especially the little gun. "Bang! Bang!" she says, "you're dead." '

'Why on earth did you buy her a cowboy suit?'

Because as a boy I'd always wanted one and there was no chance. Because I knew she'd love it and she does. Because it says 'Wigton' and not 'Kew Gardens', it says 'Daft' and not 'Tasteful', it says 'fun' and not 'fine'.

'I couldn't think of anything else,' he said.

'You haven't dared wear any of your new clothes for work yet.'

'I will.' He made the decision. 'On Monday. This suit. Want a bet?'

'You don't have to finish the wine, Joseph.'

He looked. More than half a glass left. His head was becoming the first turn of the carousel. He put the glass down.

She waited until he was steady and then said,

'You were so funny tonight, Joseph, when you talked about the Irish Horse Dealers in Wigton and mimicked them and then brought in James Joyce. It was very clever. We all loved it.'

'Even Charles?'

'Oh, Joseph. Especially Charles.'

'And did you? Did you?'

He beamed a drunken beam and she smiled.

When Joseph had gone to bed, she let the exhaustion overwhelm her like a swoon.

A small group from the laboratory had driven from Brittany to Provence for François's funeral. Among them was Sylvestre, the boatman with whom François had gone out most weekdays to look for specimens. Sylvestre, late middle-aged, a salt-and-sun-worn face, broad-shouldered, was uneasy in his black suit but well used to funerals.

With some skill he had manoeuvred Natasha apart from the others after the funeral, after the food and the wine.

He held out a nondescript box.

'I want you to have this, Miss Natasha,' he said. 'It's not much. It's shells. Plenty of the really little ones, the ones you can hardly ever find. They take a lot of digging out. François used to look out for them on the beaches we went to. He would hunt for them for so long sometimes that he came back blue with cold. He loved doing that.' He looked around. This had to be private. 'They're all washed and clean. Some of them are so small it was my wife who had to hold them to wash. She loved him too, Miss Natasha. We all did, you know. We want you to have them.'

It had taken Natasha some time to find a big enough jar, clear, solid, like the jars on the shelves of old-fashioned chemists. The shells filled the jar almost to the brim. At the top were the rather obvious ones, bleached beige-coloured, many tones of sand; below, those fugitive minute infinitely delicate little shells, so many shades of pale pink, a treasure, a wonder not broken.

She had put the jar on the oak chest between the two candlesticks. She could look at it for hours on end.

CHAPTER TWENTY-EIGHT

'I looked at Chris still asleep,' Natasha had written in her novel, 'death, I thought, gives you a taste for death, while life does not necessarily keep its grip on you. Love – and I looked again at the face of this man whom I had known for a bare six weeks and who slept so near – love does not necessarily have a hold on you either, provided you do not fear the absence of it.'

But I am beginning to think that I do fear its absence. Natasha sat back from the old typewriter and lit another cigarette. I do fear the absence of it, or rather the absence of Joseph which has become the same thing. I still do not fully understand how it all began with Joseph, with such a stranger. Was it an exhausted surrender? He took me over. Was there a moment? Moments? When was it clinched? Was it by him or by me? After Robert, did I merely see him as the receptacle into which I could pour myself and be safe?

So I need to watch him and watch over him, she thought. He must always be in my sights although he must never feel leashed. He must stay true to what I have found in him or both of us will be lost.

And now I can live for my own sake, she thought, and now I must, for her sake. I was becalmed in the shadows for so long they became my natural habitat. I liked to hide from the light, as if looking at the sun would burn me, as if exposure would reveal a terrible nakedness. I wanted to slip through the world in a shroud, as if constantly prepared for the end, even longing for it, drugged by the fumes from the corpses of my lost lives. Joseph led me out of that. He came into my underworld and took me from it but I was waiting for him, I must have been, I was ready to attempt to climb out of the darkness that had been made for me and by me and try with all my strength to live unhidden out here, in the sun, in the light for this brief life.

I want that now, she thought, I want to live all I can and for that I must guard Joseph and for that I must face myself, she vowed, however hard that is, not be a coward, pick off the scabs and look at the wounds. Maybe writing will help. Maybe writing will be enough.

She shuffled through the pages of the novel. Joseph had given her the title. He had made a film about Tennyson's *In Memoriam* and when they had discussed the novel, he had suggested *The Unquiet Heart*. She loved it. She had typed out two verses as the epigraph. It always reassured her to read them.

> I sometimes hold it half a sin
> To put in words the grief I feel;
> For words, like Nature, half reveal
> And half conceal the Soul within.
>
> But, for the unquiet heart and brain,
> A use in measured language lies;
> The sad mechanic exercise,
> Like dull narcotics, numbing pain.

'To write like that!' he had said.

Joseph often used that phrase. Ever since she had met him he would read out a passage and smile at its accuracy or its beauty and shake his head and say, 'To write like that!' She loved him saying that; the sense of awe, and of contest. And on he went. He plunged through setbacks as an animal in flight will plunge into a dangerous river, she thought, and then attempt to scale heights beyond his strength, dismayed, exhausted but always seeking the route. Joseph existed by saying yes. Sometimes she was fearful for him, but she would catch his fall. She was strong now, through her own life, through him. She trusted him utterly to take her as she was . . .

It was past noon. The planes, barely heard by her now, droned over. Mary had taken Marcelle to the shops. Soon she would be old enough to go to the crèche which Anna had established for her own children and those of her friends in the vestry of the nearby Barn Church. Natasha liked the name Barn Church. She liked its association with the remains of old farms, the orchards, the English pastoral which had once lapped here against the banks of the Thames. Kew would be her castle and within it she would be free. Through these few friends she was sufficiently part of it, as much as she wanted to be. Joseph's attempts to extend their circle and turn it into a place where they could know 'everybody' had been opposed by Natasha, often bluntly, often publicly, and earned her a reputation for rudeness. But Natasha had no anxiety whatever on that score. To be liked by mere acquaintances was not an ambition. To have to spend time with strangers was unsettling.

Anna had suggested that if she wanted to she could help out at the Barn Church one or two mornings a week, teach art to the children. That was worth talking about. Anna was a friend.

After lunch she would go and see another friend, Margaret, Ross's wife, who had revealed that she was in analysis. Natasha was intrigued. Julia had mentioned two of her friends in Oxford who had gone into analysis. Julia thought it a waste of time and money and humiliating public evidence of a lack of character. Natasha was not so sure. In one of Joseph's bulk buys off the cheap stall outside the Kew Bookshop she had found *The Interpretation of Dreams* and was overcome by it. Her attempt to apply it to Joseph had met with English empirical scorn, but she had expected that and infuriated him more by talking about 'denial'. Margaret had said she was getting a great deal from her analysis and had volunteered to recount the experience to Natasha.

There would be tea, there would be a walk in the Gardens with the child sturdily rushing over the shaven grass, bread to be remembered for the ducks, the two red-beaked black swans catching the eye as always, all so peaceful, English as she liked it. English that made no demands. For the heart of England she referred to the social and country-house landscapes of P.G. Wodehouse, to whose work she had been introduced by Matthew. 'Metaphors miraculous,' he said. It was enough to be in England, enough to live among it and write in it every day.

She looked again at the opening lines of the new chapter.

Brittany. Silver buckles on the men's shoes, lace bonnets on the women's heads. Tunny and mackerel fishing, in the old days large butterfly sails that roamed across the seas from Ireland and Africa, now engine-pulled ships with deep-freezes and radio contact still using the same routes. Yellow and black sou'westers, rubber boots, wooden clogs. Inland, the haystacks, the sour Breton cider apples, the naïfe village calvaries and the lichen-bitten steeples. Everywhere the granite stone of Brittany.

—⁂—

He was in a film, he was in scores of films and he was the star. It was called *Joe Richardson Hits New York*. Joe Richardson dances down Fifth Avenue. Joe Richardson helicopters among the skyscrapers. Joe Richardson sails past the Statue of Liberty and meets the Battery at the foot of Manhattan. He eats the deli sandwich the biggest mouth on earth could not bite whole. He sees the yellow cabs and takes one just for the hell of it and asks to be driven 'around the block, two or three blocks'. The black iron fire escapes cladding the grimy brick apartments in Greenwich Village in the dawn light are peopled by gangsters and private eyes, Forty-Second Street is shiveringly dangerous, sex the flaunt, the business, guns the law, hurry on, no eye contact, and the Hudson, the boat around the island, the nearness of the forests, home to Indian tribes from childhood matinées, and Central Park, the lung of it, tempting to test yourself against it after dark, safer to walk down the deep canyons of skyscrapers, bookshops open until midnight, MOMA, the Empire State, bars serving beer late, and the movie street names, Lexington, Grand Central Station, Wall Street, signs to Brooklyn and the Bronx, Madison Avenue, Manhattan, New York. In those few days Joe never failed for a moment to experience being in the celluloid dream, having been here before, his imagination film-fed from America since his childhood induction twice weekly at the Palace Picture House. Jazz, rock, blues America was his adopted soul.

He played the New London Dandy. The new Englishman abroad. His King's Road gear, still worn rather self-consciously and with discretion in London, was here, he thought, wholly appropriate. He was allowed to dress up for the part. Who cared? The bottle-green velvet jacket, the lacy cravat, the flared trousers and Cuban boots or, another day, the mock frock coat and striped trousers, the ruffle-fronted shirt, the hair daring to grow longer, cavalier, girlish, fashionable. It had never crossed Joe's mind until these last months that he would want to be fashionable, let alone enjoy it, let alone be able to afford it. But fashionable was expensive no more; not to the young. A mass market had commercialised and democratised fashion. And here was the Mecca of the mass market.

The land of Liberty! Joe thought he could see it in the faces on the streets. And of Democracy! He felt he could sense it in the poise, the conversations, in ordinary people who looked as if they owned the place. His darker knowledge, the Great Depression, McCarthy, union smashing, the genocide of the Indians and the racial intolerance of the blacks was blotted out by the energy he felt hit him from the openness and the beat of the city, from the gridded streets and the wide accommodating avenues, exciting energy, optimistic, ambitious new energy, where what was new was good.

He had been lifted out of drizzling London and flung across an ocean into another world, a world that, he thought, had been waiting for him as he for it.

'You are,' said Tim, 'like a fart in a trance. I am very surprised you haven't met yourself coming back.'

He raised his glass. They were in the Oak Room Bar in the Plaza. Tim had been given a double room overlooking Central Park. Joe was in a cubby-hole at the back. Joe had been an afterthought.

'So.' Tim was two sheets to the wind. But it was near midnight and what was a red-blooded Englishman new to the place to do but prop up a bar and drink Jack Daniels and put the world to rights. 'What were today's Adventures of the Cumbrian Candide? Jack Daniels on the rocks for my wide-eyed young friend. He wants to become a Success, you know, but he'll never admit it.' The barman, old, owlish, heavy-eyed, delivered a minimal nod and let loose the whisky.

Joe watched it waterfall into the tumbler and clenched his stomach. He'd already had a few beers. He tried to summon up a response which would entertain his friend. He owed Tim a lot. Including this. He liked him. Should he? Tim was wholly out for himself. Was he changing into someone like that?

'I,' said Tim, 'before you summon up the expurgated version of your day, will tell you about mine.' Once again he raised his glass. He was in a loop of toasts. 'Saul,' said Tim, 'good old Saul seems to want to go for it. He wants to make the movie. God knows why.'

'Why?'

'God knows.'

'He's always taken chances,' said Joe, sipping at the irresistibly sweet liquid, 'I looked him up. He's never really been a typical Hollywood producer. Even so.'

'Trust you to look him up. Even so what?'

'*Jude the Obscure.*'

'God knows.' Tim shook his head, gloomily even.

'He wants to . . .' It was too improbable even to articulate.

'He wants to make it. Low Budget but the land of Plenty, I tell you, my son, after starvation BBC television budgets. He'll produce it himself.'

'Well,' said Joe, winded. A feature film produced by Saul Elstein, who had since the war worked with legends – the word bobbed up into his brain, no other would do – legends.

'He's an Anglophile, that's why,' said Tim. 'Do you know he joined the Royal Air Force during the war? I bet you didn't look that up. And he ran a circus in Canada for three years. Then he married the daughter of Lord Whatsit – that will be in *Who's Who* even though they're separated; and he worked with Tennessee Williams and Brando and Olivier and such – I bet they're in the book. But this English thing.' Tim was puzzled. 'What he sees in us I do not know. But archetypal. *Jude the Obscure.* That's what he called it. Archetypal. Barman! A final replelli— replemish— Thank you.'

A feature film! Joe wanted to be somewhere alone. He wanted to fly. He wanted to start work now. Stop drinking. Remember Jude under the influence.

'His new lady loved the Nijinsky film. That's why we're here. His new lady. Here's to the new lady,' he said, for the umpteenth time. 'She's a big balle-o— ballet—'

'Balletomane.'

'Smart arse. Fancies Nureyev. Fat chance. Cheers!'

'When does he want us to start?'

'You know when he took us to that deli on Broadway and said he liked your script and his literary friend had liked your book?'

Joe choked on embarrassment and trusted himself only to mutter something that sounded like 'nnnhmm'.

'Well,' said Tim, 'he told me that had sort of clinched it.'

He held Joe's gaze in what he clearly intended to be a solemn and binding moment.

'That's why I asked him to fly you over here.'

'Thanks.'

'Don't thank me.'

Who then?

'He gave me this.' Tim pulled out a wad. 'A wad,' he said, 'I've always wanted to pull out a wad. Especially an American wad. This –' he thought he was lowering his slurred but still strong voice, 'is fifteen hundred dollars. Not on account, Saul said. For a few presents.' He picked at the notes with peering, finger-licking care. 'Three hundred for you. For you three hundred. You've only got tomorrow.'

'You needn't.'

'I know I needn't. Don't tell me I needn't. I know I needn't. When can you start?'

'Next week.'

'Won't Ross want more notice than that?'

'I needn't tell him. I'll just get on with it.'

'And still make the arts stuff?'

'Yes.'

'Do you have a routine? One more? Last one.'

'OK, then.'

'Martin!' The same barman came over patiently.

'We close in five minutes,' he said.

'Residents,' said Tim and looked at Joe triumphantly: not the slightest blemish in the pronunciation.

'You can move to the lobby, sir. Same poison?' He poured even as he asked the question.

'Room 211,' said Tim. 'Two–one–one.'

Joe braced himself for this 'last one'. But a swarming head and a restless sleepless sweaty night in his cubby-hole in hot New York were a small price to pay.

'What's your routine, then? All writers have a routine. It's their secret. Spill the beans.'

'I try to get up just before six, five days in the week, and write for a couple of hours before setting off for work. Doesn't always work out, but . . . anyway I try to make it. I go over it when I come back, write as much as I can at weekends. When that routine collapses I start to write after supper and go on until I'm knackered. Of course it's great that Natasha writes as well. It wouldn't work without her.'

'You've got to tell me what it's like being married to a Frenchwoman one of these days. Are you onto another novel? You are. I remember. Alison told me you were. Got your end away with her yet? Of course you have.'

A denial would be pointless. Tim would not be convinced.

'I'll put the novel aside,' said Joe, lying. He knew he would be incapable of not tinkering with it.

'Your funeral,' said Tim. 'I don't give a sod how you do it as long as you do it and it works. By their fruits you shall know them. Ross won't like it. You doing a film. He's OK, Ross.'

The check appeared on the counter at about the last moment that Tim was capable of seeing and signing it. He gave the barman ten dollars.

'Makes me feel good,' he said. 'Tipping. Over-tipping's even better.'

They walked to the lift slowly and circumspectly, as if considering every step along the way, as if thoughtful and abstracted, as if dead drunk. Before he stepped out to make for the minibar in 211, Tim said,

'Truth will out, my friend. I panicked a bit in London and wanted you to be here for when he got going on *Jude*. Saul knows his stuff, doesn't he?'

'He does. I'm a bit worried about what he said about the ending.'

'What'd he say? *Jude the Obscure*, he said, a story for our times, a story for the poor, a story for the immigrant, a story for those who dream. See. I remember. Bloody good, Joe.'

'Bloody good, Tim.'

—⁓—

Natasha had been waiting for this for some weeks. She wanted to make sure that she had the evidence. She wanted to give Joseph a chance to pull out of it. She wanted to feel less distracted by the pain in her back which had begun soon after the birth and lately returned with greater intensity. Her local doctor, a literary man, had waved it all away, prescribed painkillers, advised exercise and used most of their time together to give her his opinion of Chekhov's short stories. A couple of years earlier he had failed to spot that Joseph had an infected kidney, which was only discovered when he had undertaken a medical for insurance on the feature film. England, Natasha concluded, does not look after itself very well: it is *sauve qui peut.*

They were home where she most liked to be. It was late on a warm summer evening, the windows open to the garden, despite the growl of the planes. Joseph was sprawled in his armchair, *Couples* newly embarked on, the third revision of the film script sprayed about his feet, cigarette, glass of beer; and she herself, on the other armchair, his mirror image, her Nathalie Sarraute for his John Updike, her own novel at her feet, cigarette, coffee. The cushion in the small of her back helped the painkillers. The strain on Joseph's face had not eased for some weeks, nor would it, she thought, with the relentless redrafting of the script and the weekly grind of the new arts programme. If any time was right this was it.

She closed her book and waited until prompted by her action, Joseph obediently did the same with his. His eyes were not only tired, she thought: there was something else there, some misery. She could not unearth it but it fed her unease.

Like an overture, a plane braked overhead, unusually low, unusually screeching and loud. Joseph grimaced and glanced at the ceiling.

'How many's that, just since I came back?'

'You're tired.'

'A bit.'

'You're always tired these days.'

Joseph recognised the truth of that, resented it and said nothing.

'And it is here, in this house, where the consequences are suffered.'

Joe was miles away. He was worn out by the arguments over the shape and particularly the ending of the film script. The death of the children seemed to him essential. Saul and now Tim were not so sure. In television Ross was giving him increasing responsibility which was an opportunity but also a burden: he had been set to work on BBC2, a new channel which devoured programmes from a small and inexperienced staff. And then there was the pull of London, the temptation of sin, the greed for it all, the self-justification, the self-accusation. He took a sip of beer and remembered the Jack Daniels.

'Every time in the last weeks you have come back from work,' Natasha said, steadily, 'and into this house you have told me off or you have snapped at your daughter or at both of us. I understand that on occasion a marriage is and has to be the place where you are licensed to be your worst self, where you can be your opposite. But it cannot go on. Matthew would say you were a bit of a shit.'

'I'm not a shit. Am I?'

The word had caught him like a hook in the mouth and landed him.

'Yes.' Natasha wanted to smile at the stricken look on his face but she forbade herself that indulgence.

'We have a wonderful daughter and I know that you love her but for you she is always in the way. You are making her afraid of you.'

'Don't be stupid! How can she be afraid of me?'

'Because of your anger. You have become angry. Maybe it is because of the strain of too much work although you have done something like this before. Maybe you are finding it all much harder than you imagined and you are angry at yourself for not being able to force your way to succeed.' She paused but did not hesitate. 'I think it is deeper. There are factors I don't know about. But now you are making me fearful too.'

'That's ridiculous. That's awful. How could I hurt you?'

'I'm sorry, Joseph. I did not say afraid. You will never threaten me. But I am fearful of what you are becoming. I am fearful that you are being led towards the ruin of your former and best self because you think that it is too limited and too inexperienced and too provincial in this London world that you lust after, but you are very wrong, you are horribly wrong. Sometimes you are Jekyll and Hyde to me.'

'That's ludicrous. Maybe I have been angry. I don't know why but it isn't unusual, I would guess, among men my age trying to make their way. But Jekyll and Hyde!'

'Not very often. I exaggerated to make the point. But I can see the signs of it – and signs too that unresolved matters from your childhood are beginning to erupt into your mind and obstruct what you want to do now.'

'Please, Natasha. Not that.'

'Why are you beginning to do yourself harm?'

'I'm not.'

'I can see it.'

'But I'm not!' He felt that a net was being thrown over him and however hard he struggled he could not get out.

'I know you are.'

'How can you know me better than I know myself?'

'Oh, Joseph.'

'Oh, Joseph! What does that mean?'

'Sometimes the person outside can see more. With the eyes of love.'

'It doesn't sound like love to me.'

'That was lashing out. You didn't mean that. Look at your new friends. This Tim, for example.'

'Tim's fine.'

'Tim wants you to be someone else. He wants you to be his labourer. I can see you plain. You respect *Jude the Obscure*. Tim and the others are persuading you to act against your principles. They trade on your willingness to please and your pliability because you are so astounded to be writing a film script in the first place. They are tempting you to leave the path you have chosen and write a script of someone else's novel, which is against your better judgement and your better nature and you hate that and you want to hate them. But you cannot hate them as well as write their script so your hatred has to be released somewhere else and that is one reason why you are so angry with us.'

He stood up, hit, hurt, incensed. What she said was true.

'That's not true,' he said, he shouted. 'That's just not true! Everybody has to change things in novels when they turn them into films.'

'Not everybody. And not everybody wants to write films. And for you it is a torment because up until now you have only ever done what you believed in and that is who you truly are. That is why you will be good. But this film script! Tim! Saul! What do they matter?'

'Don't you realise? Don't you see?'

There was a sudden pain in Joe's chest, a stab, a sort of cramp, he guessed, but it made his right hand reach up and clutch the area around his heart. Natasha leaped up, held out her arms to him.

'Joseph. Please. I'm sorry. Joseph.'

The pain was already easing off. Her alarm was an affirmation.

'It's nothing,' he said, 'too much froth in the beer.'

She leaned into him and he put his arms around her. For a while they stood silently and then Natasha whispered,

'I love you so much, Joseph. They mustn't change you.'

How had this confusion in his head and heart so rapidly come on him? He held her more tightly. Everything was safe with Natasha and Marcelle, everything was as it should be. He knew that. In the end, he knew that.

—ᴍ—

Joe took the call in the only box room of an office available for private calls. Like all the offices, it held evidence of the preferred style of genteel bookishness which distinguished the BBC Arts Department. Pisan towers of hardbacks posted by publishers from all over London teetered on floor, desk and chairs, clearly signalling a fine excess, a careless cornucopia, something of the old college, something of the eccentric stately home. It was Tim, as he had guessed it might be, and as he had feared it was not good news.

'I wish we could have met face to face to talk about this,' Joe began, unprompted.

'I'm in Oxford.'

'I could get there in an hour or so.'

'I'm looking for locations.'

'I know. We discussed them.'

'Bloody good too, your suggestions,' said Tim. 'Look. Can't take all day. I've had another discussion with Saul . . .'

Joe waited; successive waves of fury and self-pity swept through him. How could they talk about the script, his script, when he was not there? What did they know about Thomas Hardy? Why had he not listened to them? This so-called scriptwriting was nothing to do with writing at all. It was carpentry. And even in this flash of compacted reactions he had time to remember that at school he had never been any good at carpentry.

'Are you still there?' Tim sounded urgent but unworried.

'Yes.'

'There are two or three what old Saul calls "intractables". I'll be quick. Sorry. It's starting to rain and I haven't been to – that place he ended up in yet.' Joe refused to help him out.

'Intractables?'

'The women. Beautifully drawn. The intellectual one, great character, and the sexy one, the two perfectly balanced. Perfectly balanced. As we discussed. As they are.'

'That's right.'

'That's wrong. Saul wants what he calls the sexual dynamic to play bigger.'

'But that would destroy the balance.'

'That's right. I said you'd say that. And all that business of Jude teaching himself Greek and so on.'

'We have to show that or where's the story?'

'I agree. Saul agrees. We've all been over this many times, Joe. It just takes too bloody long, old son. Somebody has to get in the scissors.'

'Unless you believe he's an obsessive autodidact the film's dead in the water.'

'Agreed. But we have to believe quicker. There are ways, Saul says, ways that old sweats, the old script doctors, learned with their mother's milk. And the ending.'

'The ending is the ending.'

'I told Saul you'd say that. Correct. The ending is the ending. The children end up dead. But it's no good sending everybody out onto the streets looking to top themselves.'

'Why should they? Tragedy has the opposite effect. It's catharsis. Look at *Madam Butterfly*. That's popular enough.'

'I told him you'd win the argument. But you know Saul.'

'I don't really. Not very well.'

'Look, Joe, bottom line: he likes you, you'll get paid, he's given it to one of those old fixers who I have to say has ironed out a few other problems as well.'

'Somebody else has already worked on it . . .'

'Joe. This is big-time. Saul asked me, Saul told me to tell you this. You're still on his list. He'll recommend you. You'll get more work. You're still on his list. Jesus, there's writers in Hollywood drawing their pension without getting a single script on screen. He likes you. OK?'

'Can't we talk a bit more? To each other?'

'Fait accompli, old boy. Kaput. Chin up. Call soon.'

Joe put down the phone very quietly. No one must see how thrown he was. No one must know about this until he was ready and prepared. He had failed. He had been fired. He had muffed his great chance. He was furious and ashamed. He picked up the phone and pretended to be listening in case anyone should look in. He should have walked off after the first confrontation. He should have gone along with them. He should have sorted out that ending but it was Hardy's ending, it was the right ending. He even moved his lips so that any gazers through the window would assume he was wholly engaged.

He could tell no one. He had to tell someone. Natasha would be sympathetic but, fundamentally, she would be pleased. She would see it as a providential escape. She would see it as proof of his integrity. She would see it as releasing time for him to get on with his own work, wholly his own, for to do that was the sole purpose of an artist's life. Even television, his livelihood, and hers, was only just tolerated by her, he thought. He had to hide this news from Natasha until the right moment. But how could he go back home now, early, so light still, and just sit and read and pretend? He could not bear the thought.

It was difficult to admit this even to himself but he did: he felt like crying with frustration. To be given such an opportunity and be found wanting. To fail and on such a project. How could he look anybody in the eye again?

He put down the phone, picked it up and dialled.

'Hello. I hoped you'd still be in the cutting room. Would you like – it's a bit short notice – in an hour or so, the Pillars of Hercules, just a drink, one drink?'

On several occasions, since the film, he had not got home until mid-evening and she was not yet disturbed by that. He was falsely cheerful when he arrived, she recognised that with dismay, and he held up a bottle of red wine. He said he wanted to watch the new Dennis Potter play. They saw it through in near silence. He drank most of the wine.

'That play was better than any feature film I've seen all year,' he said angrily. 'It was far more ambitious. And no selling out. Television's far more honest.'

Natasha tried to decode him but he kept the vital evidence hidden.

His anger festered for two days until finally he confessed the news about the script, still angry as if in some scarcely sane way she ought to have understood what was disturbing him without his having to say anything at all. It was a situation which would recur. He could not bear to admit failure or defeat or hurt to her, but he could not bear it that she did not somehow divine the problem and help solve it. She was glad, she said, after sympathising and agreeing that Tim was treacherous. He could spend more time on the new novel he had already begun.

She thought he had begun the new novel too soon, that he ought to have taken time off, time away from his fiction, time to dream, time to drift, but she understood. This immediate start was insurance in case the reception of *A Chance Defeat* was such that he would never summon up the confidence to pick up a pen again. Natasha sympathised with that and she was relieved that he was already doing what he should be doing. She was glad the film was dead.

Once more they would write together and Natasha would know they were safe. But only, she now knew, if she could be the guardian of their flame.

CHAPTER TWENTY-NINE

'We rarely took photographs of each other', he told their daughter. 'Neither family. Natasha's hoard was meagre, mine mostly school snaps. A camera was not part of our baggage, more's the pity. Of the very few we did take I can identify only one from this precise period when, looking back, our lives were eerily becalmed, like a targeted boat in a film, waiting for the killer whale to torpedo up from the deep and destroy.

'Natasha is sitting in the wooden shelter in the garden of the Builder's Arms. We fell into the habit (or I persuaded her, did she need persuasion?) of going down to Reading once a fortnight, sometimes even once a week. We would arrive early on Saturday evening so that there would be time for my mother to take her granddaughter out for some sort of treat. We would spend the latter part of the evening in the pub, invariably ending up singing "the old songs": "Goodbye Dolly Gray", "Pack up Your Troubles", "Tipperary", "April Showers", "California!", other Jolson favourites and a few from Bing Crosby and Sinatra, even up to Johnnie Ray and Engelbert Humperdinck.

'It was an old-fashioned company. Because of two Welsh women with high soaring voices, we always finished off with hymns – "Abide with Me", "For Those in Peril on the Sea" and "Bread of Heaven". Around closing time, the singing would draw in almost the whole bar although they were not as used to singing as we had been in the Blackamoor and there was no piano. Natasha was not as keen on the singing as I was. I itched to be down in the bar and help start it up. She would come down about half an hour from the end and drink little but in the end she did enjoy it, I'm sure of that. She grew to like the company and they her, her strangeness, and I can see her smile as she listened to the talk. Looking back it seems a curious thing to have done, and so consistently, for a year or so.

'Were these visits the need to reach out for a lifeline in my parents' marriage, something to hold onto? Or maybe it was a declaration of "Look; Kew Gardens is a lovely place, our new friends are fine, this life of theatres and mixing with the aspiring famous is OK, but it is here, in the pub, beside the canal next to the gasometers that I find lives to be part of, to be sustained by." Or was I testing your mother? We could have gone into London on those Saturday nights for the cost of the train fares to Reading and the drinks in the pub. "We should have gone to the opera more often," she said later, when we had separated.

'Or perhaps at its root was the desire to repay my mother. She had moved south, out of the life which had protected her and she had come, I knew, to spend her time with and to help her grandchild. The least I could do was try to match her generosity.

'It was on one of those visits that the photograph was taken. By me, I think, using my mother's camera which ate up about one roll of film a year.

'I remember from that time a conversation I had with my father. More, in fact, a monologue.

'He liked me to help him tidy up behind the bar before opening up on Sunday morning and I think I too liked it. It had seemed to be work when I did it with him as a boy; now it was play and I know it amused him that with my degree and what he called my 'Rolls-Royce job' and the writing of which he was so proud, he could still tell me I had not wiped the bottles clean enough.

'When we'd finished, we'd go out from behind the bar into the newly cleaned bar itself. My mother and Maude, who helped, and you, who got in the way to their intense pleasure, had moved on to attack the saloon bar. We'd sit and have a cigarette and he would burst with questions, believing that working for the BBC gave me access not only to everyone who mattered but the capacity to answer everything he wanted to ask. The force of it made me cringe or duck or it reduced me to shameful attempts at generalisations. I was not wise enough to understand the hunger nor sufficiently loving then to return interest with interest.

'This time, though, he spoke quietly. He still had about him that coiled, almost threatening single-mindedness which even then could make me physically afraid.

' "You've a good life," he said, "you've worked hard for it, nobody can take that away from you. You've got where you've got to on your own merits. Maybe there'll be more to come and it will get harder. You've some new friends, I like the people in Kew, very nice people. And your Oxford friends. You have a lovely house and most of all you have that child and there's Natasha. She's very special, Natasha." '

He paused. He now looked at his son straight on.

'I'll tell you this once. Natasha looks tired and she is not happy. I don't know what you're up to but whatever it is, you look after her. She needs help. I think she always will need help. And it's down to you. You didn't bargain for this but it's what you've got. And what she brings you – well, she's better than one in a million, Joe. There's nobody a patch on her. You look after her.'

And he looked hard at his son and forced him to meet the gaze and then he patted him on the shoulder.

'The photograph shows me what I failed to recognise or chose to ignore then. Natasha is utterly directed inside herself. She sits in the garden of the pub, her right leg over her left, a fairly but not fashionably short skirt. Her hair is thick and simply pushed back. She has a cigarette in her right hand and she is not looking at the camera. She was not, I think, looking out at anything in particular. She seems full of sorrow in the photograph, full of disappointment, but alert, stiff-backed (probably against the pain), trying to work out where our life or her life was going wrong and why and where she could seek the resources to repair it. She seems trapped, wounded and failing to find the way out. Perhaps she was thinking she had made a terrible mistake and yet was in too deep. I had sensed that before. Her eyes are clouded, peering, searching into the light. She seems immobilised in sadness and what I did was to take a photograph.'

—⟋⟍⟋—

The money for writing the film was, he thought, unbelievable. Joe had been put on the bottom rung but after the agent's percentage was paid and the tax clawback put aside, he was still left with three thousand five hundred pounds, almost three times his annual salary: bonanza. He gave two thousand to his mother to turn the scullery in the Builder's Arms into a proper kitchen; he put five hundred pounds into a building society and then he took Natasha on a squandering spree.

It paralleled his splurge in New York where he had bought what she thought of as rather unsuitable, trendy clothes for her, clothes that he wanted to see her in, and bulky toys at Bloomingdale's, to be shipped home, for Marcelle, silk scarves for his mother, a heavy silver-plated lighter for his father and still the dollars would not go. There had been a fever in the spending in New York, as if he had to get rid of the wad wildly and fast to match the city. There had been a giddiness in it, a high, a need for Jack Daniels on the rocks when it was done.

London was more decorous. A fine coat imposed on Natasha who had to surmount a lifetime's opposition to this kind of gift, a seventeenth-century oak dowry chest bought in one of the streets off the Portobello Road, and cushions, chosen by Natasha from one of the new boutiques, Indian, elaborately worked; she wanted one. Joe bought four. For Marcelle there was a bright pillar-box-red tricycle. It had a bell whose sound became a daily cheerfulness. After the spree Joe insisted on the Ritz for dinner: he smoked a cigar. Natasha decided that the whole affair was in the end an entertainment but even her teasing could not undermine Joe's pleasure at so extravagantly overdoing it. The cigar was too strong and too long for him, but he persisted.

And there had to be a party for their friends. But how could you word the invitation so that it told people not to 'bring a bottle'? It was always on the invitations for such herd parties. But the point on this occasion, as Joseph in his nouveau plutocratic mode explained to Natasha, was that bottles be not brought. He would supply the bottles. He had to supply the bottles. Good bottles. For their friends. That was the point.

Amused by the mixture of self-parody and benevolence, and this evidence that his naïf enthusiasm was intact, Natasha joined in and suggested that she would discreetly secrete the brought bottles and

Joseph could serve, without undue pride in the label, the inevitably more expensive wines he would import from the off-licence next to the station. She would also, she said, do more than nuts and crisps and olives for the buffet. 'Push the boat out,' he said, 'when it's gone it's gone.'

'You want to get rid of it,' said Natasha. 'You want to wash your hands of it. That's good.'

David always dropped them a card announcing his return dates in London and the party was arranged to suit him.

'You want to show off to him,' said Natasha.

'I don't! I like him, that's all. And he likes parties.'

'You want to gossip with him afterwards.'

'You keep telling me what I want to do.'

The invitation list was ambitious. All the new Kew friends, including Ross and Margaret; James, David, Bob, Roderick, Matthew and Julia from Oxford, Peter the politician and other new colleagues from the BBC, including from the World Service, Anthony and Victoria, Charles of course, and, after a deep breath, Tim Radley and his wife, a literary cluster including two literary critics he had met while doing a programme on L.P. Hartley, and an arts editor who had appeared in the programme he had made on David Jones. There was a novelist some years older already sporting a swagger reputation who had been sent an advance copy of Joseph's novel and, for reasons which Joseph could not quite trust, been keen to cultivate the younger man; there was the Irish writer already famous with a second novel which Joe thought was miraculously Chekhovian, the sculptor and his wife who lived locally, and finally an invitation to Saul Elstein, expecting an elegant refusal which came by return of post.

When they and a few others royally invited at the last minute piled into the small, overlit, semi-detached, furniture-cleared-to-the-walls, primed-for-party house, Joseph could have been Beau Nash supervising the great balls at Bath, he could have been hosting the salons patronised by Proust or feasting on the conversations of the elite at Garsington. He still took his wine too quickly and soon he was in that state just bubbling below full consciousness, a state of dreamily blurring euphoria.

Was it at this party that Natasha told the rather grand wife of the senior literary critic who held out her glass and said merely, 'Another drink' to 'Get it yourself, the wine's in the kitchen'? Was it on this occasion that Joseph had an overlong and damaging disagreement with the more junior literary critic, 'a rising star', that middle-class people like him could never really understand either pop music or football however hard they tried and anyway why should they want to colonise working-class pursuits when they had so many of their own? It certainly was here that Bob Romford explained the art of fly fishing and in particular the art of making artificial flies to the Polish Head of the European Service in such detail that the man declared he would do a programme on the subject to prove what the English were still made of. James bumped into a radio producer who left with the promise that he would listen to the demo records and see if he could get airtime for them and he did.

Joseph floated on what he thought of as a river of key cultural references. The names bobbed up like corks in a bath: Picasso, Norman Mailer, Harold Pinter, Philip Larkin, John Updike, Dennis Potter, David Mercer, Narayan, the Beatles, the Beach Boys, John Cage, the latest story about Kingsley Amis, the latest Bacon exhibition – he was as drunk on the names as on the glasses of wine. The older novelist with the swagger reputation was never to forgive Natasha after she told him that she thought he was a negative influence on Joseph after his attempt to flirt with her. 'It was the clumsiness,' she said, 'and the lack of tact which is typical of your negativity.'

Tim got drunk, 'like Jude', he said.

David helped with the washing-up and the three of them had a final glass.

'Perfectly satisfactory,' said David, 'it's so hard to give a really good party with such a quota of mere acquaintances if you know what I mean, but this one worked. The people from the World Service were distinguished and quite new to me, one doesn't meet them anywhere else. Matthew and Julia are stars of course and I liked Anthony, just outside my circle at Oxford. I know a little about his film-making, well spoken of. Only a couple from, as it were, the older families but they hardly seemed out of place at all. Charles is pukka and very personable.

Your Kew friends, charming, what else would one expect? Very glad to meet Tim Radley: disappointing in person but a real eye as a director. Ross McCulloch – much better than anticipated, much better, he listened, he did not seek to dominate, and your new television friends, fun, certainly. A good mix. As the only International Socialist present I can state that objectively.'

'So we passed the test?' said Natasha, laughing. 'Oh, David, you are so wonderfully absurd. Please don't ever change.'

David's return cannonade of laughter bounced around the room.

'You make me feel so deliciously embarrassed,' he said.

'And silly, I hope.'

'Silly?' The swirl of the large dark expressive eyes, the hands thrown up in surrender, the laughter commanding. 'For you, Natasha – silly.' He took a small sip of the Pouilly-Fumé. 'But a good party is hard to give. Don't underestimate that.'

'Do you really think so?' asked Joe, very near sleep and wanting only that the party be praised, interminably.

'I do. I really think so.' David looked at his watch. 'The last tube is at twelve-twenty. I've checked.'

'Of course,' said Natasha.

'You know me too well. I can't afford to miss it. Taxis to Kew are prohibitive.'

'I thought it got better,' said Joe, finding a swollen tongue an impediment, 'the longer it went on.'

'That new media kinship class,' said David, 'it's beginning to cohere. Perhaps around you two.'

'No,' said Natasha, firmly, soberly; and repeated, 'no. We don't want that.'

'Don't we?' Joe shook his head. 'Great crowd,' he said. 'Peter's great, isn't he? He'll be Prime Minister. Wait and see.'

'Some people go to these things every night of the week,' said Natasha. 'How can they?'

'Now, now, it was a good party.'

'It was a very good party,' said Julia as they took their nightcap, even though the journey back from London meant that they were running about two hours late on their unobtrusively observed daily schedule.

337

'I particularly enjoyed talking to the young poet – Edward Worcester. An intelligent man. He was up at Merton.'

'I thought the Tim character was terrific,' said Julia. 'So irreverent. He's making a film about *Jude the Obscure*.'

'Did you tell him your theory about the perfect balance between the two women?'

'I did. He said that had been taken into account.'

'The chap from the European Service, Konrad, Polish, impressive. We don't have his type in Oxford. More's the pity.'

'We do well enough here,' said Julia.

'They're rather a brilliant couple, no? He's come on well and Natasha was on good form.'

'I disagree,' said Julia. 'You always had a blind spot about Natasha. But to be fair she told me that she and Joseph, as she still insists on calling him, had had a sort of face to face in Reading, which in my view they visit far too often, and that it cleared the air somewhat.'

'They'll have their ups and downs. We had.'

He took out a cigarette. 'I feel the party as it were secures them in their position in their new society,' he said. He raised his glass.

Joseph wanted to have a final final drink in the garden. Natasha, temperate as always, sat with him to be the audience for his relief, pride and pleasure, but mostly, she knew, relief. Before the party he had been almost frantic with anxiety. He had threatened to walk off, to disappear, to cancel it. It was such an extreme mood, new in her experience of him and she needed time to extract its meaning. Why did it matter to him so very much, so viscerally? What was happening to him? And yet, when the party had begun, his mood had swung completely. Perhaps he needed the over-anxiety to stimulate the adrenal gland, she thought. Perhaps it laid his ghosts. But why was he so exaggeratedly insecure?

'No planes,' he said, having stayed silent a while. 'The night lifts the siege.'

'You'll soon learn to ignore them. The rest of us do.'

'That's what annoys me. The rest of you do. Or you say you do.'

He took a swig more than a sip of the warm white wine.

'Saying it often enough can help make it happen,' Natasha suggested.

'That's for babies, isn't it?'

'You were on good form, Joseph.'

'Was I? Really?'

'Yes. Matthew commented on it. He said you were rather brilliant.'

'Did he? Matthew. Really?'

Flattery, though sought for, fuddled him into silence. Natasha too, having diverted him, preferred silence. The night-time suburb, saturated in green, with heavy trees, thick bushes and lawns by the hundred, reinforced their own silence.

She wanted to think about herself. She wanted to continue a process begun years before but only now, in this marriage, allowed the oxygen it needed. She wanted to concentrate on her writing, her work, her art. She longed to become the artist she knew she could be. The time was right for it. Joseph had allowed that confidence to grow. He was broad-shouldered, indefatigable, flustered by the fray into which he was willingly led, bruised by the encounters he could not bear to miss, forever failing fully to grasp the danger of the new worlds that floated into his life, but going on, going on, obstinate and bull-like going on, she thought, and giving her all she could ever reasonably want from a man. It would not be too much to say he enabled her be free: and she must return that gift to him.

'You need have no fear, Joseph,' she said, and drew deeply on her cigarette. 'I believe you are innocent at heart and whatever you do that you think is a sin will not be a crime. It is the intention that makes the crime. Your intentions are pure and I will always be here.'

He said nothing. He felt X-rayed. He felt wholly understood by Natasha. Her certainty could disconcert and sometimes torment him but there was no mistaking the power her understanding exerted on him: or the subjection he felt in its grip.

'I do love you, you know,' he said heavily. 'I'll always love you. I always think I'm so lucky to be with you.' He nodded. 'Just imagine if we'd never met. What then? A life without you?'

CHAPTER THIRTY

'There was a willing current in our lives during the next year or two,' he wrote to their daughter, 'and mostly we went with it, we let it flow through our hearts and bear us along, striving to achieve what we thought was good. The friendships, the obligations, the love that was still there between us which was deepened through you was more than enough. It was rich when you looked around, when you made comparisons with others wherever, whoever they were. We were fortunate.

'Our friends in Kew were and remain good friends and their children were and are still your friends and all three of us knew that at the time. Your mother did teach and help on two mornings a week at the Barn Church. I joined the tennis club and was one of those convenient members below the average so that playing against me could be a useful warm-up and a fortifying victory. Natasha did some watercolours in the Gardens but the writing overtook the painting and her new friends urged her on. There were modest parties between the families, most commonly tea parties at weekends where all the children piled into the garden, the parents withdrew and for a couple of hours it felt rather like a kibbutz.

'I continued the forays into London on some Saturday afternoons, pollinated and unnerved by that buzz and a pressure of temptations and opportunities; sometimes it became difficult to distinguish between the two. Yet I was like a homing pigeon sent far from base, not in distance but in culture, always beating back south, across the Thames, safely home to Kew. Or like a kite which your mother played out until it soared unseen above the clouds and yet at the end of the day it would be safely reeled in. It must have been around this time that Natasha said, "You take all you want in London, I'll have Kew." The insight and the clever encapsulation were typical; but I'm sure I argued against the neatness of the division.

'For I too was deeply fond of the unintensive suburban pleasures of Kew and Natasha loved coming into London as long as it was with people she trusted. She trusted Anthony the drama director, a colleague at the BBC, and his wife Victoria, the painter. They had the kindly courtesies of their class, Natasha's class, at ease in their world, thoughtful, funny, surprising, and your mother took to them, and they to her, immediately and unreservedly. There was happiness in the theatre-going with them and occasionally the dinners afterwards in that rather louche club off St James's. And in Peter, too, she found a friend although she rarely failed to tease him about his political views. James of course, and David when he visited London and one or two others. There were many good days, calm days, days of equanimity and no outwardly visible drama, days when nothing much happened, maybe those were the best days, when nothing much happened save our lives lived together, life just trickling through the uncounted hours. Looking back it was a time of unacknowledged contentment.

'We went to La Rotonde in the summer and for one holiday we returned to Cumberland for a week in the cottage in Caldbeck and Natasha was fêted by my old friends, an exotic. And every morning you fed the ducks. Your mother and I wrote; we wrote and wrote. My first two novels had come out before Natasha finally completed what was to be her debut published work. Charles acted as her agent and there came the day when he sent her a letter, a publisher found, and her joy was deep. So was mine. She wanted it so much, I realised, when she got it: she needed it and now, armed with the publication of her first book, the object of desire, she felt finally equipped to take on her deeper, forbidden past.'

—꘎꘎꘎—

The restaurant was called Two Plums and Three Cherries and it had recently opened on Kew Green, near the church. Joe had heard it was

341

expensive and fashionable; perfect for his purpose. He arranged to meet Natasha there as he had work to do after office hours. This, though not habitual, was no longer unusual. The 'work' would be in a pub. The pub would be peopled with Edward Worcester and other young poets and novelists who hung around with him, partly from Edward's certainty of purpose, partly because of his powers of patronage as the producer of a literary radio programme. The work would be thirsty and Joe would float away towards the underground station wishing he had the time to walk home and clear his head. But it was not habitual, it did not much disturb Natasha. Nothing like as much as his sometimes dazed, imploded return from Saturday afternoon rambles in London. She saw the city clawing him down into its grip and knew that he was troubled by what he saw as a multitude of options that bewildered but also excited a sensibility that recognised them as dangers.

'It's great, isn't it?' he said, looking around the festooned restaurant when she arrived a few minutes later than him.

Natasha smiled and nodded: the nod was a cheat but it enabled her not to say what he least wanted to hear. The place was dreadful. Poor imitations of Impressionists crowded the walls, pink tablecloths, pink napkins, little red candles in vast brandy glasses on the tables, crystal glasses, posies, gleaming silver-plate cutlery, the quiet but unignorable thrum of fashionable droning quasi-mystical music and the smug air of being bang up to the new mood of the moment.

'I thought you'd like it,' he said. 'I've ordered something special.'

Joseph was a little flushed but it became him, she thought. It gave his tousled look the necessary youth. His velvet jacket and overlarge tie fitted the restaurant well; her quietly cut summer dress, bought for her publication party (sherry, olives, nuts, begun at six and all over by seven-thirty, fourteen people accommodated in the editor's office), looked rather plain in that company, she noticed. Two Plums and Three Cherries had drawn in the more fashionably conscious from a rich suburban catchment area. Or did her dress look rather old? Did she? Sometimes it seemed that Joseph was getting younger and the gap between them widening. The intermittent pain in her back made it hard to keep an ageing strain from her face; though she was not currently troubled. She had taken extra painkillers.

Two flutes of champagne arrived and Joseph beamed. It was such a smile! She was disarmed by his smile. It was wholly without guile or reserve, it was from the heart, even from the soul, she thought, it was the expression of a still untainted and innocent love which only Joseph had given her.

'To you.' He raised his glass and she took her cue. 'And to your great, great novel. It really is *great*, I was telling them in the pub. It's great! To success for it and long life and everything you want for yourself, Natasha.'

He reached out to clink glasses and so did she. For some moments she was overcome with shyness and silencing pleasure.

'Thank you,' she said, and then, 'and thank you for all this.' She looked around. 'It is a lovely place for a celebration.'

'Do you really think so?' The trace of anxiety revealed how much he must have fussed over its selection: matters like this always fussed him.

'Yes.' She reassured him and now she meant it. 'This is perfect, Joseph.'

This time his smile was more of a grin, cocky, confident.

'They do avocado with prawns,' he said. 'That's my starter.'

After they had ordered he brought her tales from the literary front. Natasha, still cherishing the smile and the true feeling behind this event, scarcely listened at first. She shielded that previous moment like a candle flame in the wind, wanting to watch it burn for every last second. She let him praise what he saw as these soon-to-be-famous young writers who met regularly now in that pub. He was dazzled, she thought, partly by what they said but more by the very fact of it, the literary clique in the London pub, the glamour of being with published writers, himself also a published writer, somehow in an exclusive court, recognisable only to initiates, special persons, chosen and distinguished by this rare and quite frankly rather superior fact of having a book published.

The writers he had just left drinking literature in the pub were, he believed, wise beyond their years, their words and works were weighed in the great balance of books and should be taken seriously. They had direct access to Creativity, they had Obsessions and their pronouncements were full of Fine Distinctions, they were Severe on Those Who Failed the Great Cause of Writing and Writers, the brotherhood. And they were fun, they were intellectuals, they were the metropolitan wits.

'Perhaps,' said Natasha, 'but I think they are no more intelligent or cultured than our Kew friends, none of whom has published a book. It is wonderful to publish a book, Joseph, but it is not an entitlement to automatic respect. Don't look crestfallen. It is just my opinion. I think in your heart you agree with it. I have heard you say the same about your friends in Cumberland. There are other matters of value, you know that, you tell me that. People have thought great thoughts and lived rich lives without writing a book: even, I remember you arguing with James, without necessarily reading a book. Sometimes I fear for you that you idolise these new friends too much. They are too cynical for me. But you will always accept it first before you regret it later, that is your way. Some of them are just playing the game of being writers. To be called a writer is their passport into society. They may be no worse for that, and it is a harmless game, but you are not like that, Joseph, and you would do better to keep your distance. They will never nourish you. And they live best in a world of criticism with which I know you find it difficult to cope.'

That final sentence was so accurate that he could dig out no reply. It was true, he hated the hostile criticism he sometimes encountered, it made him writhe. Sometimes because he thought it was justified, sometimes because it was wrong, always because it was a public humiliation and in an area in which the rules said that he was not allowed to fight back. To fight back which, in Wigton, was to prove yourself strong was, in London, to show yourself weak. And he writhed under the stupidity of that edict of turning the other cheek. He stuck to it but it demanded too much from him at this stage and for Natasha to refer to it was to stoke both shame and anger. Best if she had not mentioned it. The truth, being spoken, made him feel that not just Natasha but everybody knew of this weakness.

'There you are,' she said. 'I've spoiled it for you. Yet the criticism you receive isn't very severe, it isn't much at all, Joseph, and it doesn't matter. The good reviews outweigh the bad and people you respect admire what you do and they say so . . .' And all that was the case but the demons had been unloosed and she could see, through his transparent expression, the tussle he was having to thrust them away, not let them ruin her celebration and yet he wanted to brood on them and feed fantasies of revenge.

'You won that prize,' she said.

'What does that prove?'

'Some of your new pubby friends are vandals, Joseph.' She looked to jolt him out of it. The conversation was conducted in hushed tones, not wanting to disturb the pretensions of the restaurant. But here Joseph did raise his voice.

'Oh, Natasha! Vandals?'

'Artistic vandals.'

'What does that mean?' He took a gulp of the cold Pouilly-Fuissé, cheered up by what he saw as an exaggeration which could be disputed.

'They pull down what they can't appreciate. They prefer to destroy. They steal significance from art to enhance their own importance.'

'No they don't. They just don't. They write stuff. Sometimes good stuff. And they take it seriously even if they drink a bit. Writers drink, most writers, some writers, some of the time, they drink: and even if they do lash out at others, so what? Sometimes it's necessary, it's funny, it does no harm.'

'It does.' Natasha was firm. 'And you are straining to become one of them. It is not you. You once read out to me that D.H. Lawrence said that Pornography was doing the dirt on Sex. Was that it? Well, that kind of witches' kitchen does the dirt on literature.'

'That's rubbish! How do you know? They take it more seriously than anything. You've only met them once or twice. And they think you're terrific. Why don't you come more often?'

'You know that I would not rush into London at the end of an afternoon for a drinking session. Besides, it is a man's club. Women are welcomed but not equals. The conversation condescends.'

'That's just not true.' It was, he knew that, but he shook his head at her accusation. 'I like them,' he concluded, sturdily. 'And I admire the way that some of them are trying to make a living by just writing and reviewing.'

'That is admirable, I agree,' said Natasha, in her happiness too deep on this night to take any argument to the wall. She added, 'You should do that.'

'I can,' he said, feeling bold. 'I can afford it now.'

'You must.'

'The first two have come out in paperback in America and Germany and it all works out. I've calculated my pension fund comes to two hundred and seventy-two pounds and ten shillings and they'll let me withdraw that. There's the five hundred pounds in the building society. We've got enough for a year, living carefully.'

'You've been a business man!'

'I enjoyed it.' Her smile flattered him to the core. 'The guys said I might get some reviewing but the problem is that that's writing. The great thing about television is that it's the opposite of writing.' He took another mouthful of the white wine, most of which he alone had consumed. 'In television you're a team. Nobody can do it alone. In writing, being alone and doing it alone and on your own terms, finding your own voice, is the point. There isn't any other point. Whatever the result. That's the point.' His head was now pleasantly thickened by the cold sweet alcohol. 'So you see?' he concluded.

'When will you do it?'

Until this moment it had been a dreaming calculation, an itching reproach to a way of life he sometimes feared betrayed a lack of true commitment, even though his *Brief Lives of Contemporary Writers* told him that many novelists had harnessed their fiction to necessary remunerative work in the outside world. But the romantic notion, diktat, of dedicated isolation was a great temptation. Natasha's question was a gun to the head. He wanted to please her. He always wanted to impress her.

'Soon,' he said, out of alcohol and bravado. 'Very soon.'

'Joseph,' she lifted her minimally employed glass, 'to you. I have waited for this. To you.'

His glass was empty. She leaned over and poured him most of her wine and once more their glasses touched. He ordered a brandy and a crème brulée. Natasha had coffee.

He wanted to tell her the true reason why he had decided to leave the security and enjoyment of the BBC, but it would tilt into boasting. The fiction he was writing, set among people who had mostly been represented in literature, until recently, as servants, caricatures, objects of sentimentality, walk-ons, ciphers, fodder, had to be drawn with as much sympathy and complexity as those whose more privileged lives so powerfully commanded the heights of so much English literature. This task as much as the re-emerging lure of solitude needed more time and effort.

'Ellen once told me,' she said, 'that when you were a little boy, in the war, when your father was away, you would wake up singing to yourself, or whistling.'

'Did she? Did I?'

'I hope that is still inside you. I hope you never lose that.'

He deliberately turned the conversation away from the analysis he feared might be imminent.

'I liked whistling. Everybody whistled then. Why did it disappear? I'll whistle to you on the way back home.'

Though the Two Plums and Three Cherries slowly shed its customers, they stayed on. Natasha was determined to follow through her decision, taken earlier that day. It was as yet unrevealed to Joseph, drifting, sweetly drunk.

They picked at the past with the amused tolerance of parents looking down on the peccadilloes of their children. They spoke once again about the party thrown by Saul Elstein at the Georgian manor house he had bought in Oxfordshire and how Natasha had become so uncomfortable with the hugging, the kissing and the thronging of famous actors and actresses, big-name directors, writers, politicians, painters and a few star-struck aristocrats, that she had retreated to the fastness of the vegetable garden. She had been joined by another Frenchwoman, Sophie, equally on the run. Their native language and their native land cascaded over the neat English rows of good greens – 'I always wanted a country house and a vegetable garden,' said Sophie, '*et voilà!*'

The women talked rapidly as if engaged in a forbidden pleasure until both agreed with regret that they must return to a scene neither of them much liked. But, and Joe loved this, as Sophie Elstein explained, although she was 'the new wife' and of little importance in the world which came out of Saul's Technicolor past and his recently divorced connection with English high society, still she ought to be at her husband's side, 'although I am only French', when the guests came to say goodbye. 'Although I am only French' became a catchphrase between Natasha and herself for a while. The two women had met since then at Sophie's invitation, twice, for lunch in Mayfair. Natasha had enjoyed her compatriot's company but not enough to return the invitation.

Mostly, though, on this last lap, in the restaurant and on the walk back, his arm slung around her shoulder, and in the hush of their sitting room, Natasha wanted to talk about him and draw him out of the darker flash of mood in the restaurant. She feared his dips into depression: it was too much like herself; she saw it as her duty to save him from them.

She humoured him and recounted again his reaction in the little village church when she had refused to stand or kneel during Anthony's wedding but sat throughout, wilfully obtrusive and therefore unforgivably drawing attention to herself and to him, Joseph thought. Anthony said it made the wedding.

Or when, at a publisher's dinner, one of the older men had quietly, a whisper, complimented Joseph on his complexion and with utter naivety he had ascribed it in solemn terms to his mother. Even Natasha had joined in the laughter at his earnestness and the flustered expression of the questioner who had thought to slip in the compliment on the sly. Or when she had caught Joseph in their bedroom, dancing madly and alone to pop music from the radio – 'You looked possessed,' she said, 'like a shaman.'

Like his increased vanity, she saw it as a mere response to the mood of the moment, a tasting of the superficiality of the age, a passing self-indulgence. It was no more than a game to him, she thought, following a fashion of the times. He wanted to play many parts, as he wore several different costumes, one day a velvet dandy, the next a frock-coated parody of the city, the next a celluloid gypsy. As Natasha saw it he was play-acting, safe in anonymous London, and she understood his need to try different roles, to re-cast himself for this life, so full of temptations. But he was safe, she thought, he was strong. She rested on that. Whatever the costume, the character would not change. She relied on that. For the moment he wanted to bask in the shallows, to follow the running of the deer. And maybe simply to entertain her, to show off his paces. Neither of them sensed the dangers of this flirtation on the boundaries of his personality.

Just before they went upstairs she said what she had saved up for last. She came close to him and let him wrap his arms around her, benevolent, trancelike, and for a minute or two they rocked together, just a little, almost as if steadying themselves.

'Thank you, Joseph,' she said, focusing on his blurring eyes. 'Not just for the dinner. But for the book. Yes. Like the exhibition. And before that the examination. Without you I would not have written this book. With you maybe I will write more.'

'You will,' he said, uncomfortable with the intensity. 'You would have done anyway. You're the cleverest, the best, everybody knows that.'

She had left it too late. He would not even remember in the morning. She went up to look on Marcelle.

'And so for a while we flowed on with that current,' he wrote, 'which seemed good for us, easy to yield to, disposed in our favour, taking us from the remote and chance confluence of our first encounter, onto what seemed a plain of rich meadows with miles of life and miles of time all before us. To our friends, we could have seemed to lead a charmed life, Natasha and Joseph, now competing, now connecting, always spoken of as a pair, now in battle, now in concord. Joseph and Natasha. Ripe for the fall.'

For even as they had walked home on that night through the empty suburb, the last planes low in the sky, the grand houses in their lush avenues asleep and secure, Joseph taking a gallant shot at whistling the old favourites, the marching songs, 'Goodbye Dolly', 'Tipperary', the whistle rather diffuse, replaced by soft singing of 'La Mer'; even as Natasha rejoiced in the young man she had met at Oxford, still, she believed, unchanged, still at her command, still bound to her; even with the scarcely digestible reality of publication, of becoming a presence, however marginal, in the world of fiction in which they had wandered through others' books for years; and all that, and Marcelle, and friends, and all that; even then it is possible to say and with some certainty that the seeds of destruction were being planted.

Nor was this to be by any external force. They came from within, from the past, from the encounter with old selves, from the bold, possibly hubristic, attempt to stare out old terrors, old fears, suppressed depressions. Joe, energised by a determined but poorly thought through notion of where his future lay, was to leave routines which from a disturbed adolescence onwards had meant so much to him, done so much for him, kept his day in formation, his mind in discipline. He would attempt to fly free and alone. And Natasha, who meant to tell Joseph of her decision that night but delayed it because she sensed it would take away from the innocent pleasure of the celebration, had finally decided to go into analysis, to re-examine herself, to sink as deeply into her past as she dare, to claim it back, whatever the risk.

PART FOUR

THE FALLOUT

CHAPTER THIRTY-ONE

'At the time I thought I was living the dream,' he wrote, 'but I was stoking up the nightmare. The phrase "self-destruct" had just come into the language, old as an idea but new on the tongue, freshly minted for our day. There was a frenzy about what I did, like that type of sexual attraction which threatens madness denied physical satisfaction. I'm aware that I've said very little about sex. Difficult, to a daughter, and difficult to calculate its role in the scheme of things.

'My guess is that I took it for married granted and although I was very likely too stripling for her and although her exoticism was erotic, I had fantasies unsuitable for her and affronted her, from time to time, with an appetite for sexual experiments and adventure reaped from the more unbuttoned novels of the day. She must have longed for that sense of centred manhood she admired in the men who drank in the bar in La Rotonde, or in the confident and uncluttered sexual poise of a cinema hero of hers – Jean Gabin, a man without doubts about his manhood, a man to whom sex was calmly in its place. My guess is that your mother also took it for married granted most of the time. We thought it no matter of central concern.

'The passion and the will were concentrated on the work and the routine. "You'll have to get a routine," Ross told me when we met in the Kew Arms and I told him I was leaving the job. "Every artist I've met had a routine. It's either an amount of work a day or set hours, bank-clerk hours sometimes, night owl for others, that's the best advice I can give you – get a routine." Ross raised his half of bitter and smiled. "Then stick to it. That's the tough part. Otherwise it's the bottle or the bed. Good luck."

'I had at that time a very powerful inclination to seek out Ross for advice on everything, for reassurance, just for his mere presence, as if being in his company somehow validated my position in this strange broadcasting planet where work was not real work and privileged access was not earned and the playing fields of the artistic Etons of England were yours in which to roam at liberty. Or perhaps there was a simpler explanation: his uninhibited war-fired strength attracting my peace-coddled vulnerability.

'Yet that is not altogether true. He liked to call on me as an equal or at least a sounding board, a sparring partner at weekends, someone to drop in on. Perhaps he represented security and in that bountiful but alien world I needed it. Later I was to discover that he too in his youth had suffered depressive setbacks and so that could have been the cord between us. But when he said that I had to have a routine I followed his advice as dutifully as any official taking his instructions from the Emperor of China, as eagerly as a young acolyte bowing to an injunction from the Pope: it was the Law and it would see me right and I followed it with great hope.

'Your mother's routine, always easily assumed, her graceful style, was now interrupted only by visits to her analyst twice a week, late in the morning of Tuesdays and Fridays, half an hour or so on the tube into Central London. For her in the early months, the analysis was a deep pleasure, for me a drama from which I preferred to be excluded.'

For the first months, the only months, in truth, when it could be called fully operational, Joe's routine took him over.

He constructed it with care. He built it to last. Now that he was a full-time writer he would waste not want not for there was a living to be made, as well, and yet somehow he aimed to combine that with the liberating ambition of following his own star, writing out of his fullest capacity whatever the risk to livelihood and critical opinion. This would be his chance to be the free artist that Natasha had inspired him to be and the only way he could see it working was to lash himself to the oars.

He had a routine for writing, a routine for reading, a routine for exercise and a routine for family and leisure. With Marcelle it was an hour or so at the end of the day, Saturday and Sunday mornings to the park, Sunday afternoons *en famille*. With Natasha for talk it was the late evenings, usually after an hour or two of television. On Friday nights they went out, occasionally on Saturday nights too or they invited people round, especially Kew people where a well-knit interchange of babysitting was in place. Exercise was a brisk run-down to and around the park for about forty minutes every morning at seven-thirty followed by a cold shower to prove seriousness. If the others were up for it, breakfast together, otherwise on his own and always a boiled egg, an apple and brown toast. The day was set up.

After breakfast he went, he ran, upstairs where he had set up a card table in the bedroom and worked from nine until one, lunch, two until five, tea, Marcelle, six to seven-thirty, Marcelle bed, supper, read or television, chat, bed, and often a last sneak back to the card table. No alcohol save on Fridays and Saturdays and not much then.

The reading plan would later be remembered as puffed up, even absurd, but also as a salute to high-mindedness. He believed that the privilege of his liberty obliged him to seize the opportunity, and chose books of a nature more taxing than he had found time for in his previous pattern of life. Now was the time to test the best. He began with philosophy which had been part of his course at university – Aristotle, Hobbes and Rousseau had been what his tutor called 'the unholy trinity' on the history course – since when they had gathered dust. He began reading them once more and took on other philosophers.

The power of their minds daunted him; the difficulty of under-standing could give him a headache. Often as not he felt he was up against concepts he was not trained to grasp, but he soldiered on, thinking such strain was good, believing that what was difficult was important, pushing himself as hard as he could.

After eight weeks he felt as fit as he had ever been, brimful of purpose, a dedicated servant to the writing and proud that he was shaping so well this potentially wayward and lumpen thing, himself. After twelve weeks the first draft of the new novel was done, the twin exhilarations of achievement and toxic solitude were helium and he would chant, 'Better far than praise of men/ is to sit with book and pen.'

He was convinced that to write and to turn what it was inside his head into words and scenes imagined only by himself was his true calling. He felt good about the work, he felt good about Natasha and Marcelle, and about himself. All life was good. It must never change.

To counteract the noise of the planes he stuffed his ears with cotton wool which he soaked in Vaseline and when that proved only partially successful he dug around in the Portobello Road one Saturday afternoon and was eventually rewarded at a stall which specialised in artefacts for aeroplane buffs. He bought a pair of the ear protectors worn by the men who guided in the still-roaring aeroplane to its final berth. They helped but even so the planes had begun to interfere with his mind. Yet such was the spring of liberty, such the thrill of Being a Full-Time Writer, such the unexpected benefits which came in those early months just from being constantly in the same place as Natasha as in the old days in Oxford, and now with Marcelle, her gaiety, her perpetual affection, that the planes could be endured. They had to be endured, he told himself, others endured them, he should, he could, it was a price worth paying, a price always had to be paid. When on some days they switched the flight lines and passed the pain elsewhere the sense of gratitude for the peace was effervescent and that relief more than compensated, he told himself. Mind over matter, the old story.

Those few months were the happiest in the lives of the three of them. He would weigh them up, compare, take everything into account: yes, the happiest in their brief life together. Whatever happiness was, it meant Marcelle, growing bolder, more cheerful, naughtier by the day, himself on track, and Natasha heading home.

Natasha came to the couch a willing bride. Her analyst was an Austrian, Jewish, whose parents and remnants of her family had fled to England two years before Freud. She told her own analyst that as soon as

Natasha walked into her room, late because her navigation from Oxford Circus Station to Welbeck Street had been faulty, she had recognised 'a kindred spirit. It was quite extraordinary,' she said, in her clear metallic voice, 'I would almost use the phrase "elective affinity"; I knew that she needed what I had to offer. But I have to handle her with great care. I sensed that beneath the neurosis there might be a psychosis. In analysing her I find I analyse myself, which is perfect. Is it permitted to bring her into my own analysis?'

She herself was in the fifth year of what was still a tormented process striking deep into the horror of the mid-century madness and darkness of the Holocaust, the great wound.

When Natasha came in for the first session, apologetic but smiling, her social ease unassailable, the analyst merely indicated the couch and Natasha went to it with a nod of recognition. She lay down, looked at the ceiling, traced the worn cornicing around the large room, approved the rather threadbare character of the furnishings, and waited. She did not mind the silence, she found it comforting, an unconscious, unspoken overture. The analyst sat behind the couch, out of sight: Natasha had seen a green notebook.

But after some time – seconds, half a minute, a little more, time in this room would always seem askew or slippery – Natasha knew there was the expectation that she begin.

'I thought you would begin,' she said.

'You came to me,' said the analyst. 'To talk.'

'Where are you from?'

'It's better I remain as anonymous as possible.'

'Why?'

'I am only someone you know here in this room to help you. That is wholly who I am. Outside this room I have no existence for you.'

'How sad,' Natasha said. 'For both of us.'

It was a moment, the analyst later recounted, she would never forget. It was so heartfelt, she said, so simple yet so moving. This woman could simply reach out and touch her heart. She had to steel herself. Once again the silence.

'Say,' said the analyst, with some difficulty, 'whatever is on your mind.'

'But there is so much!' Natasha exclaimed. 'And how do I know what is most important? How can I use this time with you to the best advantage? I need to. I can only just afford it. And from what I read, sometimes the most important clue can be found in a small instance, as in a poem. Whereas if you look at it head-on it can yield nothing because it is all too big and blunt and impersonal. Is that true? I want to go straight to the depths but now I am lying here looking at your ceiling and I think, why am I here at all? I want to be here but why am I here? I know that really, I know the answer, but it is such a big answer I feel shy of speaking about it, but that is why I am here because something in me, something from my past – where else? – has made me unhappy even in the face of the happiness I now have at home, more unhappy in some ways or rather more fretful about the unhappiness as if it will endanger what has been achieved. Now that I know something of ordinary happiness, the inheritance of unhappiness is all the more damaging. It could snatch away what I have. I can see it for what it is now. It undermines the heart and infects life. I have to drive it away now, for their sake and mine, for Joseph and Marcelle also, or they will be drawn into it, won't they? Isn't that what happens? It is always there, clawing at me, and now I want to surrender to it so as to understand it. That is why I am here.'

'What you are telling me,' the analyst began, the slow probing of long-compacted grief and pain began; and Natasha listened as if her life depended on it and left exhausted, emptied but disturbed into the first inklings of compulsion, all but dazed as the empty midday tube rattled out of Central London and raced towards Kew.

Yet even as she crossed the river she was thinking of, even longing for, her next session.

—m—

'She began to keep notebooks,' Joe told her, 'sometimes she read them to me. Casebooks would be the more accurate description. She followed herself down labyrinths. Explorations, memories and assumptions were intertwined so tightly sometimes I felt I could scarcely breathe as I listened to them. She would sit in her chair, hunched over

358

the notes, so intent, smoking, her face drawn, what she was pursuing enthralled her. Those notebooks were the best things she ever wrote. Véronique destroyed all of them.'

—ɯ—

During the first three or four months of the analysis, which coincided with the first and beginning the second draft of Joseph's novel, Natasha experienced a slow burn of satisfaction. There were anxieties which had not been there for some time; there were sudden switches of mood which could be disturbing; and there was always the fear, but the fear could now be used to look into the darkness. The satisfaction grew the more she went to the analyst. As she learned how to use the fifty minutes so she moved closer, she was sure, to the nucleus of her fears. The analysis became her prime subject and she was strengthened by it even though from her reading she knew that there would be a period of weakening, a period of utter dependence, a danger zone in which her personality having been stripped down, unravelled, exposed as illness, would be encouraged to reassemble in health, re-form through pain to a new bearable wholeness. That was months in the future. For now she was in the honeymoon period and the exhilaration of discovery made her a zealot.

After a four-month stretch on his routine, Joseph emerged confused and disappointed in himself. He had thought that the routine would last for all time. That it stumbled and threatened to halt when he had driven through the first draft took him by surprise. What now? Revision had not the same dynamic and besides, the routine seemed arid, not as a way to write but as a way to live and surely you needed both. He could go for hours without receiving a phone call, for days without having a talk or even a chat with any like-minded group. He was proud of his dedication but the truth was that it took too much out of him. He badly missed working with others. After those first months his inner resources dried up, the book, an imagined account of the life of his grandfather in World War One, had taken more out of him than he acknowledged. He needed and wanted to drift, but he had not learned how to drift, and surely drifting was a waste, drifting could become a bad habit when you needed to earn a living, and drift where?

They were in the garden together in the middle of a fine autumn morning. Marcelle was at the nursery school. Natasha had been to analysis the day before and Joseph too had been in town but as yet not told Natasha why. The planes were numerous, noisy, a relentless procession across the London sky, every single one, Joseph thought, targeting their house.

'We don't have to live under a flight route,' he said, for the first time.

Natasha let the plane go over to be heard in peace.

'You're exhausted by the book,' she said, 'you never take into account that writing can be exhausting. If it is not hard manual labour then, in your view, you are simply not permitted to claim any sort of tiredness.'

'I was talking about the planes.'

'They are on the outside. They make a noise only if we choose to hear it.'

'That's barmy.'

'It is true, Joseph. It is inside our heads that the decisions are made about all of our senses and about all of our reactions to life. This noise is a nuisance but it is bearable if you choose to bear it. The important question is, why do you choose not to bear it? How does it threaten you?'

'Natasha! That's gobbledegook. I don't choose anything. Here comes another of the bastards!' The plane was flying low to Chiswick Bridge where it put on its squealing brakes to enter into the last lap before landing a few miles to the west. As it went over, Joseph opened and closed his mouth, miming speech, saying nothing. Natasha laughed.

'You looked so funny!'

He smiled and did it again.

'The plane is gone,' she said.

'My mind refuses to believe it.'

'It is fear, not noise, Joseph.'

'It is noise, Natasha. It is a horrible whining, braking, screeching, regular, torturing noise about which I can do nothing while I am in this house and I think, do we have to live under a flight path?'

'Marcelle doesn't even notice them. None of the children do.'

'That worries me. They should.'

'I'm afraid this is classic displacement, Joseph. Those planes represent if not fear then a threat.'

'To my sanity.'

'It is not the planes themselves which represent a threat to your sanity.'

'How do you know?'

'And sanity is too strong a word.'

'How do you know that, either?'

'It would be better for you to examine what is inside you. Especially the anger.'

'What do I do all day but examine what is inside me? Not much at the moment. Maybe not much, period. And anger. You can't examine anger. Anger just flares up and then it's gone.'

'You cannot deny that anger has origins in your character.'

'I don't want to know.'

'Why not?'

'I don't know.'

'You must.'

'Oh no I don't. There are things better not known – even if you could know, which I think you can't. I don't want to understand everything.'

'What do you want?'

'To find things out. Here comes another!'

Quite suddenly he stood, threw out the remains of the coffee from his cup and left, straight through the house, out, through Kew Gardens, onto the towpath, looking up to see what he was fleeing, the sky march of the planes, his head locked as in a cramp, everything wrong but why? everything out of kilter, why? as he pounded along beside the Thames as if driven by hornets. And why had she not asked him where he had been the other day? And why had he not told her he had gone to see Saul Elstein? And why was this novel no bloody good, would never be, who was to judge, whose judgement counted, how could they live on what this would earn, should that not matter? The heights, the calling? And what was Natasha trying to do to him?

Another plane crashed over his head as he passed two men fishing, oblivious.

CHAPTER THIRTY-TWO

'I'm sorry.'

'You look terrible.'

'I really am sorry.'

'What happened?'

'Nothing . . . I just couldn't stand the noise, it's stupid, I really will try, the rest of you cope, it's just stupid.'

'Don't look so depressed, Joseph. It is not a fault of character. It's not irresponsible.'

'I found a place,' he said, 'I walked to Richmond and then through the meadows and noticed that the planes don't go over the crest of Richmond Hill itself. So I went up there and wandered around until it was dark. There were no planes directly overhead. I could see them coming from Kew Gardens and see them heading over Richmond Green but they left the Hill alone, it's off the direct flight path, I asked the man. I rang up the airport authorities, they were very helpful.'

By now Joseph had sat down in the usual armchair. Natasha sat opposite him, considered but rejected bringing him a drink or making tea: she did not want to leave him alone. He had been out for hours; Marcelle had been in bed since seven; the autumn night was well under way.

'I wanted a drink but I went to buy a paper first, on one of the roads leading up to the top of Richmond Hill. There were these Small Ads and while I was waiting I read one, offering a room, in that street, just a few yards down the road, the man said, just beyond the pub. The room to let is in a small terraced house. It looks out into a bit of a yard and a wall. It's pretty grim, really. There's a shilling-meter electric fire, the carpet and the curtains are orange and grubby, there's a narrow bed, the whole place isn't much bigger than our kitchen but there's a kettle and a table I can work on so I'm going back tomorrow morning with my cheque book, two weeks in advance she wants. She's a rather shy old lady, she looks as if she's been very unhappy, and she didn't trust me an inch but she wants to let it to somebody, I assume, and it might as well be me. The thing is, there are no aeroplanes. I can work there in the day and then come back like I used to do from the BBC when the planes didn't affect me as much. I really am sorry.'

He got up and went into the kitchen, sank a cup of cold water, refilled it and brought it through.

'I should have phoned,' he said.

'It's all right.' She held out her cigarettes. He took one and then stood statue still and listened for the planes.

'Where are they?'

'They stopped,' said Natasha, 'soon after you left,' and her sweet giggle which might have been nervous, or tender, or both, shot through Joseph's mind like an electric taunt.

'They'll be back,' he said.

'Whatever comes to mind,' said the analyst. 'You must not feel you have to reach for the most significant things. They will reach for you. We must begin where you are now. We start from the now.'

'It's difficult,' Natasha said. 'I don't really know what the Now is.' She concentrated. 'The more I concentrate the darker it gets. There isn't one level is there, even in the Now? Surely you don't want to know about the journey on the tube or the cup of coffee I had on the way here, I was early, at that place where they have the coffee grinders in the window. Or before that taking Marcelle to the nursery in the Barn Church. And am I thinking about that or just cataloguing it for you? You want to know what deep feelings there are. Now. The feelings are covered with frustration because I cannot feel them. The real feelings. They are just little lumps of autobiography like stones on the bed of a clear river. I can see them through the water but they are dumb. It's making me angry trying to think what I am feeling, trying to find the feelings which will be of use to me. It's hard to think about me. Marcelle is so lovely in the mornings, she skips to the Barn Church. Joseph used to whistle when he woke up as a boy; Marcelle skips. He whistles. I want her to be like him. But he is troubled now.

'He is changing and he does not want to change and yet he does want to change but he wants to change in the wrong way. That makes him unhappy. He has mentioned a breakdown (he does not use that word) when he was an adolescent – I don't know how severe it was – he only mentioned it and regretted he had mentioned it but I fear he is not at ease with himself at all, change is not something he wants, not inner change, yet if he does not take up that challenge there will be some sort of deadlock. In some ways there already has been. I am sure he has been tempted sexually and perhaps even yielded but in such a timid and guilty manner that any satisfaction immediately turned into self-flagellation. I think he blames himself for me being here with you. I want him to tell me everything so that I can convince him I do not care. I may be wrong. It is difficult to know the truth about Joseph because he does not know the truth about himself. He is utterly faithful in the way it matters. I do not know him wholly, even though he seemed so open and simple when we met, both of us were blinded by our past when we met . . .' She stopped and waited.

'What you have told me,' the analyst said, 'with relation to your daughter is that you love the innocence which reminds you of the child in Joseph whom you love also even though you did not know him then, perhaps *because* you did not know him then. Maybe there is envy of your daughter skipping to school. You did not skip to school and you had no mother to take you to school to watch you skip . . . About Joseph you say things which are very like yourself. I see you in your description of him and I see a projection which may carry a truth about Joseph but tells me about you and your fears of change and of taking up the challenge . . .'

Sometimes Natasha returned from her analyst in a brood of silence, leadened. These were exhausted returns and, occasionally, for she was now an unswering disciple, she was dismayed that so little had been said or uncovered. On this day, though, she came back light-hearted, walking swiftly through the streets towards Oxford Circus, uplifted at the glimpse she had been given, of the sighting she had been privileged to witness, a sighting of herself, as Marcelle, as Joseph, as someone struggling to be reborn; good, that was good, and she wanted to be with them, at home, just to be with them, and at home.

———ɯɯ———

The room lasted for two weeks. There was a meanness about it which Joe could not live with. He tried. He told himself that he was lucky to have a room of his own in which to write. He told himself it was his sole decision to be there. He heard no planes. He made instant coffee and bought sausage rolls and tomatoes for lunch. There was no phone to interrupt him, no Marcelle to divert him, no Natasha just to be there – and he missed all three. In theory it was ideal.

After two weeks he had had it. He did not admire himself for this surrender. He had attempted to gain some imaginative currency from the miserableness of the place. He had attempted to gain some moral credit by rising above it. He had attempted to write and failed.

It was a rewrite but now that he returned to it outside the Spartan routine he saw gaps and repetitions which needed new work. More surprisingly, the release from the drilled days allowed a surge of fresh thoughts from the original inspiration, fragments and whispers which enabled him to write more directly about the men out there in 'occupied territory' as he had called it. Yet in that grim back parlour the fragments simply shrivelled up or he did, and without telling Natasha, he left.

He tried other locations. On some lunch breaks he had gone into the nearest pub and taken his pages and tried to get on with it as he had done, as so many did, in cafés in Paris. It did not work. He tried three pubs. None worked. He felt self-conscious in the pub and that made concentration impossible. It was in him or it was in the pub or it was in the customers or all three, but writing in an English pub did not work. English pubs cold-shouldered writing. Writers writing, not just drinking, were made to feel unpubby, doing the wrong thing in the wrong place. Pubs were severely communal and whether or not you joined in to be so obviously apart was not acceptable.

He looked for cafés. The best was a Tea Room just inside Richmond Park. But even here he was hobbled by the sense of being not only out of place but showing off by being out of place.

Finally, in the capacious gardens which fell down to the river from Richmond Hill he claimed a bench. Behind him, above the gardens, rose the white cliff-high houses on the Hill; below and in front of him the fat lazy wending snake of the Thames, open fields, westward-facing, big skies, big sunsets. He bought a flask and told Natasha it was easier to make his own coffee at home. He wrapped up in his coat and scarf. When the autumn air proved too much he got up and stomped around or made for the river and followed the towpath for a while or went into Richmond Park and looked for the deer. For more than three weeks he was content, absorbed in the work, jealous of his bench, quite pleased to imagine people thinking of him as an oddball, an outsider. He breathed in the benefit of a width of countryside, a prospect of landscape he had not experienced as fully since his long solitary walks back home before university.

The revisions were finally done, cold fingers, cold feet, his outward breath competing with the cigarette smoke in the cold air, a splendid isolation, enough people to distract and study, a few boats on the river, the Constable clouds, the Turner sunsets, the huddle of himself inside the coat, the hard bench, the book getting a life, the secrecy, the deep delicious secrecy, carried home every night in the autumn dark and hugged close.

It was finished in early December, finished in the short days, even some frost, good bedding for *Occupied Territory*, and after it went to Charles the snow came for a few days, Oxford, Reading, Kew Gardens, where he pretended he could now tolerate the planes and with all the children of their friends they enjoyed what proved to be something of a postcard-merry Christmas, their last in Kew Gardens.

In the New Year Saul Elstein rang again.

—〰—

'I've been suppressing this for weeks now,' he wrote to their daughter, 'but it recurs, it's like a good daydream that I want to recur, yet I don't know its value. You might find value in it.

'I keep seeing Natasha smile. There are so many variations of that smile which so transparently showed the character. Maybe the smile is the expression of the soul. I really can see it now, plain as I write these words to you, my dear Marcelle. It was so many smiles – it could flicker lightly at the edge of her lips, it could be quick and witty, a smile of applause of sudden happiness, it could be wide and held, full of agreement with the world. It could be much more and although it played on the mouth the music was always written in the eyes, such an appetite for the surprise of life. It breaks my heart to see it now.

'So how did I ever become separated from that smile, that soul? And how did I come to see the smile as mockery and the soul as a torment?'

Saul Elstein's offices were in Mayfair, in the middle of a street of shops trading in extravagant merchandise of impeccable pedigree, the envy of a Renaissance prince. When he walked along the exclusive street to the exclusive dining club Saul felt among the masters, his equals, a place in the sun for which he had fought hard; and he felt secure, no need to look over his shoulder, no police to ask for his papers, still now more than twenty-five years on from Vienna the wariness remained, the vigilance would never die. But this was London, a crystal-light day, films to be made, a young writer to lunch and a satisfying end to the afternoon assured. Saul was a heavy man, but his heels lifted sprightly from the pavements. As always he paused in front of the gun shop. Those who knew said it was here that you could purchase the finest sporting guns in the world. Saul liked to look at them and think, sporting guns, that was the England he loved, a place where the only guns you could buy were sporting guns and so well made.

'Joseph,' he said as he was escorted to his corner table, so placed that eavesdropping was impossible, 'punctuality I like. The courtesy of kings!'

He took Joseph's right hand inside both his, hugged it warmly and the big crinkled tanned heavy face emitted the smile which had charmed stars. Joe felt anointed. He ignored the large yellow teeth.

'You look a little tired,' Saul said. 'Where do you go in the winter?'

Without missing a beat, Saul realised that the question had no meaning for the young man and added, 'Mid-winter is the only time you have to have a break. Some prefer St Moritz, others the Bahamas. We go for the sun. You and your wife must join us on the boat. She made a hit with Sophie. Those French women like to stick together.'

The waiter arrived and hovered.

'For me the scallops and then the carpaccio as a main dish. Joseph?'

There had been time to make his selection.

'Avocado and prawns and a steak, medium, please.'

'We'll have a little wine.'

The waiter nodded, took the menus, bowed and went, leaving a pause while Saul surveyed the room, found acquaintances and inclined his head, a little smile. Then he concentrated on his guest, a concentration which Joe found rather hard to bear. It had something of the Inquisition about it, he thought; he was on trial. Saul recognised the nervousness and liked it. Nervousness was an indication of need, he thought, and ambition and modesty: he liked all three.

'How much do you know about David? King David.'

'David and Goliath?'

'That David.'

Saul waited.

'Well. Goliath of course and the sling and the pebbles from the river.' Joe remembered the stone fights he had had across the River Wiza in the Show Fields in Wigton, the boy gangs armed with pebbles sometimes collected by the girls, the day he had been struck so near his left eye he had nearly lost it and the bleeding which, it seemed, would never stop. David and his sling had been real then.

'Then there's King Saul,' Joe grinned, 'sorry about that, who wanted to murder him.'

'Saul was no good,' the great producer beamed. 'He had to go. Have no sympathy for Saul!'

'The psalms.' He must have sung most of the psalms of David in the church choir over those ten years.

'Wonderful psalms,' said Saul, gravely. 'From about 1000 BC. Your calendar.' The red wine came, decanted. The waiter poured a sip and Saul first put his nose deep into the glass, then sipped, then gave the most minimal of nods. 'The tragedy is we have lost the music.'

A thousand years BC, Joe thought, he had never thought of it as baldly as that, psalms composed in the passion and heat of Judaea still sung reverently in the cool of Anglican North Britain three thousand years later.

'Bathsheba?' Joe volunteered.

'Adultery,' said Saul. 'This is a problem. Are movie audiences ready for a hero who commits adultery?'

'He murdered her husband, didn't he?'

'Not proven. But her husband was killed, conveniently for David, this has to be admitted. I don't find that such a problem. Two jealous men, a beautiful woman, what the French call "*crime passionel*". That can be worked on.'

Was this the reason for the meeting? The first course came and while the dishes were placed on the table with some ceremony, Joe took flight to Israel. Now it seemed a possibility that Saul might make him an offer which would take him there, he could think of nowhere he would more like to go. It would be like America, another adopted country. Just the places: Jerusalem, Jericho, Judaea, Bethlehem, Nazareth, Gethsemane, Galilee, and before that the wars of the Kings and the Chronicles. Israel would be his Old Testament as New York had been the New. He could scarcely contain the rocketing of anticipation.

'I have hired a young Israeli writer,' said Saul, and named him. Joe had to shake his head in non-recognition of the name. He bent over his avocado. 'He fought on the Golan Heights,' said Saul, with pride, as if the young man were his son. 'What a victory, eh, Joseph? These boys will take over the world! At last the Jews are soldiers again – like David.'

He lifted his glass and indicated that Joe should do the same and they made a silent toast. He passed across the table the script he had brought with him.

'I want you to read this,' he said. 'Tell me what you could do with it.'

Joe looked at the title. *The Virgin Queen.*

'Are you stuck with that title?'

Saul shook his head and then raised his hand almost imperceptibly and from across the room a waiter began to propel himself to be of service.

'Is the movie audience ready for a virgin as a heroine?' said Joe, regrouping.

'We give them nothing else.'

'But one who died a virgin?' Joe asked.

'That's the problem,' said Saul. 'It's always the ending.' He smiled as the waiter bent to receive the whispered instruction to be carried to a far table. 'With you, Joseph, I have problems with the ending.'

'She did have suitors,' said Joe, wanting to help, wanting to work.

'It's a fine line,' said Saul. 'This feminism. It's strong in the States now. Maybe she would be an icon. Maybe better to reject all suitors. Die a virgin rather. And these men – they were weak.'

'I think her childhood's the most interesting part,' said Joe. 'She must have been terrified most of the time. And then she was so well taught, she spoke so many languages, she wrote poetry, she was probably the best-educated monarch we have had.'

'"We",' Saul smiled. 'I like "we". How do you know this?'

'University.'

'Oxford University,' said Saul, showing all the teeth. '*Oxford*. Don't be embarrassed. Oxford University got you a job with Saul Elstein in the movie business.' He was delighted with this. 'Why are you all growing your hair so long?'

Joe grimaced, shook his head, felt his hair flop and took one of Saul's minimal gestures as permission not to reply. He held up the script in both hands.

'I'll read it and make notes and get back to you on Monday.'

'Don't rush. This could be a big project. Dream a little, Joseph, think of this woman surrounded by men she could not trust and enemies at home and abroad who want to assassinate her. And she beat them all! That is a woman, Joseph, and an English woman. It is the Kremlin. It is the White House. How is the steak . . . ?'

The right move, Saul thought, as he strolled back down the street. *Jude the Obscure* had shown promise, Joseph's novel was well spoken of, the script needed a fresh eye and he would not be expensive. It was the Young today who carried the guns, Saul thought, and stepped out a little.

He had asked again for Fräulein Edelman. She was twenty-three and her techniques were intriguing. His driver should have picked her up from the Paris plane about an hour and a half ago. She would already be in the private suite he kept next to his office. *The Virgin Queen* was not a good title.

—ɯ—

Come on, he said to himself, after writing of Saul's peccadillo-infidelity habit. This cannot be a cover-up. This is not a Catholic confession, this is not revelation seeking absolution, but there has to be truth in the story and in the structure of Natasha's progress and there is an omission which could be of little account or it could be crucial.

According to Natasha infidelity was common among the dons in Oxford, taken for granted among the bourgeoisie in France, and not all that important, a sideshow, a minor digression, an unfortunate but assimilable fact of life, non-fatal, an admission that passing sex need not disrupt lasting love. That is what she said, although now, Joe thought, did she say it only to help me?

For Joe it was the descent into a pact with guilt which undermined him and could choke him with a sense of failure which tended to be released as anger at home. Innocence overthrown. It proved him weak, stained the undeniable love he had for Natasha and tied him in a knot; he knew it was of no importance and yet it could become the compulsive slaking of lust. It was greed or need or both and shame on both. It could be abandoned and replaced by their settled physical and domestic intimacy, but then it erupted again, needed like a fix. In no way was it 'worth it'. In no way did he see it threatening a marriage or a family. It could seem harmless as the woman, too, was secure in a marriage and of no mind to leave or damage her own arrangement through these occasional afternoon encounters.

But it let in deceit.

The mistake would be to leave this out of the story, especially as it happened before Natasha went into analysis and it has to be possible that the taint and web of lies, the disloyal tangle of feelings, the foreign element it brought to their marriage, the avoided look, the unanswered question, the fear of discovery, played a part, perhaps a key part, in her decision to go into analysis. Even though he would rush back to her after those occasions with his love for her heightened, beset by the fear he had damaged them irreparably and that she would leave him. Even though his affair ended a few weeks after she had entered into analysis.

It will not help to make it simple by constant breast-beating. Natasha sought analysis for her own reasons. She was always her own woman, was she not? A marital fracture may have triggered it but analysis and Natasha were like the *Titanic* and the iceberg. The tragedy can be seen as character, as destiny. Natasha needed to explore her past, and for that she wanted help, he thought, in desperate self-defence. No one could predict that the course of action she embarked on would lead to destruction. Yet why the betrayal, Joe asked himself, helplessly it seemed, when I had so much and valued what I had?

'You talk about him more and more,' said the analyst. 'You tell me you want him to be free because he must grow. But you fear what he will do when he is free.'

'I don't fear anything for Joseph,' said Natasha. 'I know how . . . I want him to understand he can change and make mistakes and he does not have to keep hold of his past and all its rigid values all the time. He refuses to grow away from it. After a while that has become very bad for him and for me also. He always wants to appear to me as a "good" man. He thinks that to admit being bad would rupture our world. Not to admit it could do that. I want to shake him and say, "Tell me everything, Joseph, don't be afraid, you can't be what you might become if you are afraid. I am not afraid of truth – not of my truth, not of your truth either" . . .'

The analyst made a note. She made very spare notes – three or four words – and expanded on them later. 'Herself through J,' she wrote. 'Again.'

'His mother told me that even when he went to university his first letters were so homesick that she wanted to write and tell him to come home. Her husband, Sam, persuaded her not to write.'

'I have to stop you there.'

'It won't take long.'

'I'm sorry.'

Natasha felt a weight on her. She had been about to shift something heavy from her mind and now she was left with it, a weight, too heavy to be held, a weight, straining until the next time so that she could continue . . .

'Until Friday, then,' the analyst said.

'Yes.' Natasha levered herself slowly from the couch and walked towards the door. She turned. 'Sometimes,' she said, 'I do not think this method works. It is too crude.'

'In ten minutes I have another patient,' said the analyst.

CHAPTER THIRTY-THREE

Natasha took up the novel she had abandoned before writing *The Unquiet Heart*. Her analysis called on resources kin to those recruited for fiction. To go back and along a trodden way enabled her to work and she needed that. The analysis threatened to become a sole passion. She read around the subject of psychoanalysis and embraced its revelations as warmly as any other believer in their faith. Her mind was being fed by an oracle, her fears explained, her hopes strengthened. These were the words, the laws and the prophecies which would make her whole.

Yet Natasha realised the danger that too fierce an embrace with her old self could drown both old and new. Work, as she had observed in Joseph, could be a refuge. She needed it. The analysis increasingly left her feeling out of control which, the analyst explained, was good, was essential. It was also frightening because not only was she losing control of herself faced by this new army of memories, half-memories, possibly false memories, rediscovered pain, shards from incidents agonisingly just on the edge of recovery, she was also, remorselessly it seemed, handing over control of herself to her analyst.

She was becoming dependent and since she so longed to find light in that darkness within her she hurled onto this listening woman all that she was, had been, wanted to be. Good, said the analyst, this is not weakness though you feel weak, this is strong although you will only know that later. I will carry you now, soon you are about to enter into the underworld, in which you will stay for who knows how long, but I will be there, guiding you, and the measure of the re-emergence is found in the completeness of your surrender: Natasha believed this.

But she could control the novel, and it was like coming up for air. The people on the page were hers, she was in charge. When she sat down with them and went into their world, her own receded: there were stretches of time when she dropped into this imagined world and she found deep refreshment there.

She had written and corrected about a half of it in Finchley when François had lived with them. The rest was only sketched out. François's death had taken her elsewhere in her work. On reading the as yet untitled earlier book she found that it still had life in it and if she blew gently at first on the embers they could be stirred to flame.

The first half was located in Provence, in an area around La Rotonde which she chose not to name. To do that, she thought, would have tempted her to be more autobiographical than she wished to be. Above all, she sought in the novel for distance from her past. It was set in 1944 and in that first part described the life of a family, the Palmets, in which there were two brothers, Aimé and Clément, one of whom, Aimé, was in the Resistance, the other, Clément, a simpleton, one who could have been described as a Holy Fool.

It began:

Some women expect to find all the innocence of a newborn child and the daring of a war hero in one man, and they rarely get what they are looking for. Madame Palmet was lucky to have around her three men, a husband and two sons, who were so different that between them they combined most masculine virtues and defects. They had to take turns with her and if she grew weary of one of them, she too could turn around and recover her good humour with either of the other two. Aimé, the eldest son, had always been able to fend for himself. Their father, Gilbert, was reserved by nature but he too could look after his own interests. She hardly ever stopped watching for what Clément wanted, what protected him best. He was meek and mild as a lamb, he was defenceless, a twenty-four-year-old child, worse off than he had been in the early years of his life, because others found it difficult now to guess how the fears and joys of a small boy could still inhabit his fully grown body.

Madame Palmet's focus was Clément. Her husband understood and tolerated it and helped her; her son Aimé understood but found it intolerable, was often inflamed with jealousy at the amount of loving attention given his brother, a jealousy which fed his anger.

But Madame Palmet was unable to prevent herself.

Clément was totally and absolutely kind, she explained: this could not be said of anyone else.

It took Natasha some time to re-enter this world. Now it seemed too clear to her in terms she had learned in the years since she had abandoned the book. Was Clément too near François? Was Aimé's jealousy and foul temper and daring too like Joseph? Was Gilbert the steady present father she longed for as she longed for a Madame Palmet, an all-embracing mother? At times she thought that all three men were Joseph. Perhaps she had made a diagram. Out of that she had built a boat in which she could sail safely out of her present. But the present had changed radically since the book's initiation. Maybe this resurrection was a mistake. She studied the story.

Aimé was with a Resistance group some distance away from the farm and the story in this first part was his determination to send Clément to a small camouflaged hut in the nearby hills for fear that when the Germans, who were combing the area, came to the farm and inevitably interrogated Clément he would just as inevitably tell them all about his glamorous Resistance brother of whom he was so proud, to whom he was so devoted. He went willingly to the hut, and once a week Aimé's wife, a schoolteacher, cycled from the village, hid her bicycle and walked up the hill to bring him fresh stores, bread, wine, fruit, a few treats and a letter from his mother. Aimé's wife had taught him to read and this long patient painstaking process now saw its reward. Clément filled out his diet by netting thrushes.

A priest arrived at Clément's hut, exhausted, badly wounded in the leg, incessantly incanting, 'Thou shalt not kill,' and Clément forgot everything that had been told him, boasted about Aimé and the Resistance, invited the man to share the small hut, fed him, nursed him and tended his wounds with the knowledge of herbs gleaned from his mother in the kitchen and his father in the fields.

Natasha remembered that when she had read that passage out to Joseph, as they did in those days, he had been impressed by her knowledge of herbs, indeed by her knowledge of the whole of that peasant-farming life so distant, he had thought, from the haughty life she had led in the big house. She smiled as she recalled how stung she had been by his insult. 'Haughty.' Though he would regret it and apologise immediately, he was not above a fit of venom about what he saw, sometimes, as her privileged background. But immediately he had praised, as he always did, her grace, told her how much he envied this ease with which she wrote so comprehensively about life, and gave her support. It was then that he pressed her on the reference she had made soon after they had met in Oxford, to the part her father played in the Resistance: had she not said that he helped people through the mountains on their way to Switzerland? That was what she had heard, she said, though not directly from her father.

'Either I have a total memory loss,' he told their daughter, 'or she simply did not talk, ever, about being a child in occupied France. Nor, just as astonishingly, did I press her to discuss that time. I can find no satisfactory explanation for this. Was I being tactful? Was she being secretive? Was I worried that I would find out something to her discredit? Was she? Was it simply a politeness, an unwillingness to re-open wounds? How we did not engage, at some time, in a conversation about what must have been the general shame and fear, the social condition of her life as a young girl in occupied France is beyond me.

'Yet I feel sure that she discussed this with her analyst. I have no means of verifying this but I am convinced that the two women, not very far apart in years, exiles both, intellectuals both, each one seeking reparation, would find in fascism, at its extreme and at its most insidiously acceptable, a purgatory in which to spend and redeem their time. Where had this taken Natasha? What scabs were unpicked and once unpicked could the wounds revealed ever heal again? And what safely buried fears were dug up as these two women excavated the grave of Natasha's past?

'None of that is known to me. Save through this novel. But fiction can be treacherous, especially when read as fact.

'Nor did I ask Isabel, or Alain, and nor did they volunteer information. Perhaps they wanted to leave the dead to bury their dead. And Natasha, too, maybe she could not face it. Yet my lack of curiosity at the least seems inexplicable. To have known Natasha in wartime, that would have been to have known something essential.'

—⁓—

The best part of the book, she now thought, the part she could build on, the part which rekindled her imagination, was that in which after the mysterious death of the priest, Clément assumed the priest's character and talked of his former self as 'Clément the son of Madame Palmet'. 'Clément' in his version of his new life was dead. His mother tried to hold onto him but failed completely. Natasha read what she had written:

> 'All I want to say is: this is your home, it will always be, and I am your mother, and I shall always be there.'
>
> 'Thank you, Madame Palmet.'
>
> 'You aren't alone, that's what I mean.'
>
> 'No one is alone. God is with us every day of our lives. God will decide. You have been very kind to me, Madame Palmet. I cannot be your son, Madame Palmet. Clément will not come back on this earth until the Last Day.'

That made it worth going on with, she thought. What finally happened to him? What happened to a mother so strangely and cruelly losing her beloved son? The father she could not fathom. Perhaps he would be discovered in the act of writing. He never was.

After a few days Natasha was settled enough to take it on. She would make it into two parts to match the break in her life.

She decided to set the second part of the book in 1954. She wanted to start it quietly, with the mother alone, an ordinary moment. She wrote quickly. The scene must have been gathering force over the days.

Madame Palmet stopped by the small mirror which hung above the bedside table. She sometimes paused in front of windows in the same way, freezing the pattern of her daily movements. There, at windows or mirrors, she found the familiar landscape which supported the mainstream of her inner thoughts. In such moments she tried to discover what mattered most, what was important, even what was missing, and what should be forgotten. Today, as she stood there watching the lines of her face, she experienced the strange sensation that not only the mirror, the bedroom, and her own features had met many a time but that the very content of her thought too was repetition. She had already lived through that very same morning, that was her impression. The feeling was clear and powerful.

She eased herself in the hard chair. On some days no amount of cushioning could draw the deep ache in the small of her back. She would look for some more painkillers later. She wanted to stay by the book, at her post. There was more to say about a mother's love. Meantime another cigarette helped.

Marcelle was nearly her own person. Natasha had ceased to make drawings of her and there were not many photographs, but the child was loved by the mother and studied every day. It was as if Natasha as a mother assumed the scientifically trained mind of her father and catalogued and classified the child. This external vigilance took some of the burden off her internal turbulence where what seemed an infinite love for Marcelle was unjustly, unsettlingly stained by a sense of envy that she had had no mother to watch over her childhood, of jealousy that she had no father as near and fond and physical as Joseph, that there was no shadow on the child's bold sweet gaze.

Natasha was inclined to let her run wild. She checked her rarely and then very lightly. Yet Marcelle was a tie, she had not featured in the student dream of the free and unfettered artist's life. Joseph had begun to talk of having another child, company for Marcelle, more like everyone else they knew, the expected next step, but she had resisted. She was in no hurry and in no shape, she thought, and judging by his moods, neither was Joseph.

Marcelle was so alive, climbing the fruit trees, and running free in the great Kew Gardens, spinning across the lawns fists full of bread for the ducks, perilously on the rowing boats at Richmond, so light, Natasha noted, so strong yet light, the child dancing above the waves, above the depths which reached up to claim the mother.

—◊—

There were many times when Natasha still saw Joseph clearly as in the early days, as through plain glass, all in view, nothing hidden, and then she felt safe. At other times, especially since he had left the BBC, she saw him through a prism, the single simplicity of the man who had taken her by storm was broken up into a spectrum of characteristics some of which seemed not to fit the man she knew. She did not like seeing several aspects of him. She loved the whole man, that direct full-heartedness which had played such a part in wooing her. It was not that he was becoming more complicated, she would have enjoyed that, he was becoming at times uncomfortably evasive. Sometimes she said to herself, 'Who are you?' or 'Where is the Joseph I met?'

But these were fears she knew that she exaggerated probably because in her analysis Joseph figured so strongly and very often appeared in an exaggerated role. There were still the calm stretches, the richly aimless chats which cement a relationship.

He told her about the Reading Room in the British Museum to which he had secured membership chiefly in order to have a base away from the flight path although being in that rotunda of famous scholarship, aware of the celebrated ghosts from the past who had sat on those seats, sneaking hopeful glances to spot those who would soon enough in their turn become celebrated ghosts, could depress his self-confidence. And it made him feel too solemn. When he had checked through all the research he needed for the script on Elizabeth I, he stopped going. He felt he had been an impostor. As he told Natasha, he thought that researching and writing a film script was not what the Reading Room at the British Museum was for. And the congregation of writers and scholars had proved claustrophobic.

Once again he tried the pubs and in the streets around the museum. Most of the shops there seemed mini-museums and Joe continued his magpie pickings with prints – Goya, Rembrandt, Degas, cheap, with no hope of future profit growth, but nevertheless real prints of Goya, Rembrandt, Degas . . . three small Egyptian statuettes, an oil lamp – Roman, first century. Surely in this place of all those in London there would be writing pubs but there was not one. Reading pubs, almost without exception. But writing still found no pub place even in the tributaries leading to the British Museum.

Back then to Kew Gardens where he forced himself to withstand the noise and some days found it tolerable especially as he walked every day for a couple of hours and headed off the flight path, and some days the traffic was light and there were days when the skies were empty, high days, holidays. Natasha had only glimpses of that struggle. She had so successfully suppressed her own disturbed reactions to what she had seen not only as an intolerably interfering noise but a threatening noise that she took it for granted that Joseph, stronger than she was in the matter of willpower, had also conquered it.

In Kew she saw him lovingly. He was relaxed with their friends, neither provoked into competition nor nervous to show off, just a friend among friends, often funny, making them laugh.

The visits to Reading were reduced: the habit of regular Saturday night outings into London was resumed. Natasha was grateful for such a reliable surface of life.

'Charles has just got me elected into the Garrick Club,' he announced one evening. Not only did Natasha look unimpressed, she was puzzled.

'I've told you about it. One of the great London clubs. This one was begun by the actor David Garrick, a friend of Doctor Johnson. It's for actors and lawyers mainly.'

'Then why do they elect you?'

'They take some writers and journalists these days.'

'What does it do, this club?'

'It's a dining club.'

'But we scarcely ever eat out and when we do we go to our friends' houses or out with Anthony and Victoria.'

'It's an amazing place. A Morning Room, a full-size Billiards Room . . .'

'But you don't play billiards.'

'. . . a unique collection of theatrical portraits. Best of its kind in the world.'

'Is there such competition?'

'You don't have to pay on the spot. Just run up a bill and they send it at the end of the month.'

'That's dangerous.'

'No lady members.'

'How sad.'

'But they can come for dinner two nights a week, I think, provided they use the back stairs.'

'Then I will never come.'

'And –' He smiled. He was by now enjoying her put-downs every bit as much as she was. '– there's a library. A small wonderful library. A pocket Oxford library. I can work there whenever I want to. Nobody uses it, Charles says. I'll have it to myself! It's perfect!'

Natasha let that one go, without realising what the deep silence of that small dark highly polished room signified for Joseph.

'Did they not object to your clothes?'

'Of course not.'

Though some of them had done, Charles informed him later. But the majority on the committee, especially a couple of aristocrats, had been keen to wave him in on that account alone. New blood.

'Is that where you met this Lord . . . whoever you told me about?'

'Yes. He's very keen on films.'

'Oh, Joseph,' she said, but she let it go . . .

On their eighth wedding anniversary he took her for a mystery day out. They went on the train to Oxford early in the morning and had a Cornish pasty and a half of beer at the Welsh Pony. A bus to Henley, another to Stonor and lunch in the Stonor Arms. It was a weekday.

There were only two other tables occupied but they noticed that just to approve it. They were less disturbed.

Natasha listened as he listed what had happened to them over the eight years and murmured and nodded him on because she liked the substance it gave their lives. It was a chronology which did well enough for a conversation, it was no more than a few notches in time but somehow, for Natasha, it provided a bass line on top of which she could safely play her own variations. His hair was longer than when they had married but otherwise there was little noticeable change in him, save he was so much more confident in that dining room than he had been eight years previously. She relaxed utterly and there came into her mind happy images of the years, a sighting of Marcelle here and there, an instance, a moment, their honeymoon entrance into this very room . . . staring away from herself, past and present merging into one, what she supposed could be called a waking dream, their life, lived seriously, she thought, his life, her life: together.

'What a lovely idea,' she said, 'to come back here, thank you, Joseph.'

He grinned, that cocky, confident grin.

He had intended to walk over to Fawley because of its association with Thomas Hardy but after a mile or so up the hill, through one haul of woods with another ahead of them, Natasha stopped.

'Do you mind?' she asked. The grass was thick and dry even though the sun was covered by cloud. 'I feel tired. My back.' She grimaced slightly and kneaded it with both hands.

They sat and smoked and looked around the Chilterns. 'It is so English,' said Natasha, 'and it is also us despite not being in Cumberland or Provence!' They listened to the near silence. 'No deer so far, Joseph . . . we were luckier last time with the white hart and the other deer.'

He nodded but he had been disturbed by a hornet sound coming closer, like a motorbike in the sky. Then he spotted it. A small biplane come to loop around, doing practice rolls and dives. Joe tried to block it out. It went directly above them and then it turned and set off back on its tracks only to crawl up higher and return in a series of graceful twists. He noticed that Natasha was looking at it but without much interest and with no irritation. Joe tried to be reasonable. Someone up there was having fun. Someone up there was not breaking the law. Someone up there was perfectly entitled to make this bloody awful racket which disturbed scores possibly hundreds of people to satisfy his own selfish pleasure and there was nothing anyone could do about it.

It had been such a lovely day. Natasha's face, the sweetest of smiles when he had led her to the Welsh Pony. Her silence so companionable, he thought, and so loving in the dining room of the Stonor Arms, at such ease together in the stroll uphill through the woods.

'We have to go!'

He jumped up.

'Sorry! I'm sorry. It's that bloody plane. It's stupid. I know it's stupid!'

Natasha stubbed her cigarette in the grass and stood up, carefully, stiffly.

'They ought to be banned,' she said.

'Oh, I don't know,' Joe said, feeling wretched at his lack of control, at spoiling the afternoon, at his weakness.

'I do,' said Natasha. 'They should be forbidden to destroy such a peace as this.'

By the time they had reached the road, the hornet had gone elsewhere. There was not too long to wait for the bus, and the journey home was a re-affirmation.

'Thank you,' she said, when they arrived home. 'What a beautiful idea.'

'Beautiful?'

'Yes,' she said, 'it was. Like you.'

Joseph was still not home and so Natasha, unusually for her, returned to the novel after she had put Marcelle to bed.

Clément's total change of character, his "madness" as described by an increasingly irascible Aimé, had finally proved too difficult for the cramped household to live with, especially now that Aimé had two children. He had to be taken to a local institution and after the examination and the final arrangements it was his mother who accompanied him there with the doctor who would then drive her back home. Natasha could see the car going through the bone-dry country-side, cutting through fields heavy laden with lavender. She saw it approaching La Rotonde and described the approach, but again left the village unnamed. Finally the car arrived at the asylum and Natasha found herself moved by what she next wrote about Madame Palmet.

> She found it difficult to speak without her voice trembling. 'I must say goodbye now, Clément my love' – she so rarely used that word – 'you'll be coming home soon, you'll be well soon, you'll be well soon. There you go now. There is the case. If you need anything you just let me know.'
> 'Goodbye, Madame Palmet, and thank you for your kind-ness.' Clément held out his hand. She took it. He would not have understood it if she had kissed him, so she did not. She would have been afraid to try because she would have cried against him and frightened him . . .

Joseph crashed in.

He was drunk but benign, she concluded, even before she saw him. 'I'll make coffee.'

'Good,' he said, and slumped in his armchair and sank back his head, exhausted. 'Saul goes on and on,' he said. 'He took me to the White Elephant. It's the flash film restaurant. How can you work in the White Elephant when people come across all the time and the waiters won't leave you alone? But he does go on and on. And on and on and on.'

Natasha returned bearing the coffee.

He took it with such gratitude that she found to her surprise that now was the right time to ask him.

'He likes the childhood bit,' said Joseph. 'He likes this terrified but brave girl princess in this threatening prison of a palace. He's not so keen on the teachers but that's all right. But about Dudley, oh God, he just goes on and on and on . . .'

She said nothing at all and gradually he talked himself out and arrived at an oasis of silence.

'Joseph,' she said, as carefully as she was able, and, unusually for her, not looking him in the face but staring into her coffee cup like a fortune teller, 'my analyst says that . . . she says that the only way . . .' – it was even harder than she had anticipated but she could not be a coward – '. . . for me to make real progress now is for you too to go into analysis. Not with her of course. But she believes that unless . . .'

'No. Please, Natasha. I don't want to.'

'She insists, Joseph, and she says that without it I will be able to go no further and,' she looked at him with a fear he had never seen on her face before this moment and it sliced into his conscience, 'I have to go on, Joseph,' she said. 'I do not know what I will do if I stay where I am . . .'

'But how can I help? I'd hate it, Natasha. You know I'd hate it. I haven't gone on at you about it, have I, but that's you, you're you, I'm me, I'd hate it. What for?'

'For me, Joseph. And,' she would never flinch, 'I think, to be truthful, for you, too. You are in some distress now and too often and because of what I am doing I cannot help you as I would like.'

'What distress? It's just work. Sometimes work makes you worry. Sometimes it drives you mad. That's all. I'm OK. Why should I go into analysis? I'd hate it, I'd absolutely hate it!'

She paused and her pride, her love for him, her sense of being fair and not exercising any sort of blackmail held back the words for a moment.

'Why should I?' he pleaded.

'For my sake, Joseph,' she whispered, and despite her resistance, tears threatened unbidden and she repeated, and firmly, 'For my sake.' She held the tears in check.

CHAPTER THIRTY-FOUR

Joe did not know why he was holding out against her but he would not give in. Like much else in his mind it was unexamined. He felt rather than understood his motives, and there was no compulsion to analyse them. The force of his obstinacy was proof enough of the rightness of the decision, he thought.

Joe was too uncertain to claim the superiority of 'instinct', nor did he think that the way he came to decisions and especially decisions involving feelings was better or worse than the ways of others but it was his way. He had built on it, and whatever it was that was now him had accrued through this lack of method, primitive though it might be. Over those weeks Natasha's suggestions, her arguments, her loving arguments, her steely suggestions seemed like crude siege weapons pointlessly battering the walls of his skull.

They were sitting in their opposing chairs, late at night, planes whining overhead, Marcelle in bed presumed asleep, Mary off for a few days. This domestic tableau had once seemed an idyll of intimacy. Increasingly Joe found it a time and a place to dread.

'It is about freedom, Joseph,' said Natasha, laying aside her book, RD Laing, *The Divided Self,* 'that is why it is so fundamental.'

Very reluctantly, Joseph put aside the Borges stories and once again entered into the lists. At the back of his mind he was timing the gaps between the planes.

'There used to be a man on the BBC who always said, "It depends what you mean by 'freedom' or whatever the word was." Well. It does. It depends on what you mean by "freedom".'

'I think you know.' Natasha gave that quick sweet smile which once upon a time automatically provoked a like response. Now it seemed to taunt him.

'I don't. Freedom means different things to different people.'

'Here it means,' Natasha paused, leaned down and put the book on the floor, 'first of all letting yourself admit all that you are, finding and admitting to the anger in you, the deep fear, the superficial anxiety and the jealousy and the envy – Melanie Klein is good to read on envy. You are both the object of it and subject to it.'

'What if I admit all that?'

What Joseph really wanted to say but could not, was, 'Why should I admit all that? I recognise it, my bad feelings, more than you know, but what I try to do is hold them down, I try to act as if they did not exist, as if I was not somebody with these terrible feelings. Just like lust in the streets, you have to suppress it, otherwise what would stop you acting on it? You have to sort it out for yourself and take the responsibility.'

'You will find it very difficult to admit all that. Bad feelings frighten you: you think they are the real you. Until you admit them you will suffer from them,' said Natasha and Joseph yet again felt that he was being X-rayed. But how could she be so sure? 'You see yourself as obliged to be seen as a good man, a good little boy, and so you conceal more and more of what you really are because you do not want to displease your mummy or anger your daddy, but the strain becomes too great if you do that. You distort your true self. You may even destroy your true self.'

'Oh, Natasha! How do you know what my "true self" is? How do I know? Why should I want to know?'

'We have to know ourselves if we are to take life seriously.'

'Lots of people take life seriously without knowing themselves in the way you mean it.'

'I'm not sure that's the case.' She lit a cigarette and Joseph hoped the pause would lead to a stop. 'And we must all start from where we are.'

'Don't we know enough of where we are for all normal purposes?'

'Not if we are harmed by what we have become.'

'How do we know we are harmed?' Joseph found that he was squirming in his seat. He made himself sit still. 'Maybe what you call harm is just experience and maybe that's inevitable and even good.'

'It is possible,' said Natasha. 'But not in your case. Nor in mine. We have to be as free as we can be to find the root of ourselves. That is the only way we can do our best work.'

'But how do you know this, Natasha? How can you know this?'

'You have to lose your inhibitions.'

'Why? Maybe you need them. Maybe they are what keep you together. Maybe what you call inhibitions are just ways of coping that you learn as you grow up, and different for everyone.'

'Freedom is the goal, Joseph, and you cannot deny that the past enchains you as it does me.'

'As it does millions of others.'

'The fact that you fight this argument so hard,' she said, with deliberation, 'proves to me that you need to accept it.'

'How can that be? That means there's no argument. What you say is circular.'

'The unconscious exists, Joseph, disabilities of personality exist, psychoanalysis exists to dispel these. It is your neuroses which make you fail to see or acknowledge your neuroses.'

He felt cornered, trapped, his opposition to her arguments tormentingly unavailing. Each time he pulled away from the knots of her argument they grew tighter.

'You're like a Marxist I knew at Oxford! Whatever you said about history he just insisted that all of it was always dependent on economic interests and if you said that was a limited view and argued with him he would say that was due to your immersion in economic forces. In other words, whatever you said, he was right. Same here. Another system. I don't believe we can be understood through systems.'

'Let us begin with your unhappiness,' said Natasha.

'I've been unhappy before. Most people are sometimes. Unhappiness is part of it. But you struggle your way out of it or something turns up and it lifts and passes. Maybe it's chemical. Maybe it's social. Why does it have to be psychological?'

'Don't you feel full of frustration and anger and anxieties at the way in which you deceive yourself? And me. How do you account for that? There has to be a reason and it has to be in the mind.' Natasha was vehement. 'The mind is all we have.'

'How do I deceive myself?'

'Joseph . . .'

'Joseph! What does that mean?'

'You know.'

'I don't.' The defiant tone of his previous answer guttered to misery.

Natasha looked at him with pity. He looked so tired. His face had an aspect of strain which was recent; you saw it most around the eyes in which Natasha had almost always looked for and found a comforting kindness; there was a paleness about his skin and his movements portrayed constant unrest. He lit a cigarette and she saw desperation even in the way he did that. He needed help, she was sure of it.

Joseph looked at Natasha with apprehension. Her looks were more as they had been when they had first met, hollow-eyed, so pale, her hair swept back again like Shelley but unkempt, and in her eyes a concentration so fierce that it unnerved him. If the analysis did this to her, she who was so accomplished at examining her own feelings, what would it do to him? He could no longer help her as once he had and that saddened him and made him feel that he had lost some of his purpose.

'You deceive yourself,' she said, 'because you think that you can surmount the difficulties you have and the changes which have been imposed on you without help, without even the help of your own acceptance and understanding.'

'Everybody has changes "imposed on them" as they get older, don't they? That's what happens. That's getting older. And what's so dreadful about the changes? I like what I do, I earn more than enough to live on, we have good friends . . .'

'Your lists sound less and less convincing. This life has wrenched you away from the paths you were originally made for.'

'Meeting you was the cause of all that!' He smiled.

'There are times when I fear it was,' she responded, gravely, missing the opportunity to take up his lightness of tone. 'When we first met I thought you were like an alien. There were days when I simply hoped you would go away.'

'Really?' Joseph was intrigued at this news. 'You really wanted me to go away?'

'Yes.' This time the smile came from her but it was thin, reflective, as if directed to herself rather than to him. 'I saw nothing in a future with you but the misunderstanding which inevitably follows a mismatch. And you seemed far too young.'

'I'm not that much younger than you.'

'There are many ways to measure the gap between us, Joseph.'

'I thought you were amazing,' he said. 'You were the alien. You were the one who came from another planet. I did not know that people like you existed. They still don't. Just you.'

'That is very kind of you.'

'It's true.'

'The truth is not often kind.'

'Well. We're fine. Aren't we?'

'You laid siege to me,' Natasha said. 'Julia thought you were far too persistent, it was even vulgar that you kept on when it must have been perfectly obvious . . . But you came with your flowers – you still do – and your "dates", everything you had to see in the cinema . . .'

'And I wore you down,' Joseph said.

'Yes.'

'Was it only that I wore you down?'

'Oh no . . . Oh no . . .' She stubbed out the cigarette and took another. 'I surrendered to you. A little here. A little more. Then I grew to love you. Not completely for one or two years but Joseph . . .' she lit the cigarette with care, collecting her thoughts, poised to say something she thought of key importance, 'if you had not rescued me I do not think I would be here now.'

She blew out a long thin stream of smoke.

'And so you see,' she said, 'I am laying siege to you in return.'

'Please, Natasha.'

'What do you fear?'

'I don't know.' Even as he said that, a sensation of panic seized his mind and he wanted to run away. He forced himself to stay.

'Why do you fear so much?'

'Do I have to?'

'My analyst grows more insistent. That is all I can say. She says that I will not be able to go where I must go without you being analysed too.'

'What does she know about me?'

'I have told her a great deal about you.'

'I wish you hadn't.'

'Joseph,' she said, 'we have talked about this matter for about a month now and always I give up. But she is insistent.'

'You sound frightened of her.'

'Not frightened. Dependent and increasingly so. Which is much worse.'

'So it's not really about me being Free or Facing up to My Demons or getting back to what I was when I bought flowers in the market at Oxford and tried to hide them as I walked through the streets. It's to help you.'

'It is all the other things as well. Please believe me.'

'But what it comes down to is this woman forcing you to force me to go into analysis.'

'Is that how you see it?' She looked defeated, and her face flooded with unhappiness. 'Is that how you see it?'

'It sounded cruel. Sorry.'

'It is one truth,' she agreed.

If he loved her this obstinacy was a torment to her. If he loved her then he would surely do all he could to help relieve the unhappiness that consumed her. He had to surrender. But how could he continue to protect her if he did that?

'OK, then,' he said. 'I'll do it.'

Natasha put her hand to her mouth and nodded. She felt such exhaustion.

'I am grateful,' she said.

'No, don't say that . . .'

'I am so grateful,' she said. 'And . . . maybe as your siege on my life was so good for me, I hope my siege over these weeks will prove as good for you. I think it will, Joseph. I'm sure it will.'

'They get to all you television people,' his doctor said, 'in the end.'

Joseph sat opposite him in the back room of a large semi-detached house which served as the surgery. He had come for advice. He wanted no one to know about it and he trusted the doctor to keep his confidence.

'What is it that makes you want to waste good money on talking to a psychoanalyst?' His large face, waxen, dolorous, bored save for the small blue eyes buzzing angrily.

Joseph was not going to tell him the truth.

'It's all a conspiracy, you know,' the doctor said. 'I had to do it at medical school. All they dish out is either common sense or mumbo-jumbo. Freud fleeced rich women with it and it's been a con ever since. When did you last sleep with your mother? Do you want to castrate your father? The cure, so-called, takes three years and the fact is, old boy, in three years just by living normally you can get yourself out of most mental fixes. And who needs it? Would Chekhov have written what he did if he'd been done over by a trick cyclist? Look at the way his father tried to destroy him. His father was a shit but Chekhov sorted his life out for himself. Maybe that's precisely why Chekhov was a genius. Psychoanalysis is unscientific, fashionable, mediaeval rubbish. Still. I've a friend in this game who isn't too much of a fraud. He's in Harley Street so take out your savings. I'll drop him a note although you look well enough to me, as well as anybody has any right to look if they write novels and work in the cesspit of telly.'

'I felt cheered up by that,' Joe wrote after reading the gist of that brief medical encounter which had taken place more than thirty-five years ago. 'His bombast reconfirmed my instinct and challenged Natasha's perspective. In the few days I waited for the call from Harley Street, I felt lifted by the saloon-bar bollocking of the pragmatic old-school English doctor. All I had to do was to remember that it was rubbish and nothing need be lost while Natasha's request would be honoured. More significantly he had admitted what I had failed to admit even to myself. For when he talked about Chekhov I remembered Ross telling me of Henry Moore who had begun to read a book which psychoanalysed his sculpture. He put it aside after a couple of pages, "I prefer not to know that," he said. What if whatever talent I had was the result of my own efforts to orchestrate internal contradictions, to make a coherent personality out of discordance, a work of art out of gradually shaping whatever I imagined, whoever I am? And what if it is intricate and unique to me and best cultivated in secret? How can anyone else possibly know the mind of someone better than the person who has lived with it all their lives?

'How could what is me be re-set by the application of a rule book of generalisations drawn from the experience of others whose experiences were probably far from my own? I resisted and disputed the notion that there was one magic bunch of keys which would unlock all personalities equally. Of course we are all born, we all grow painfully, want food, shelter, sex, security, children, happiness and then we die. But it is the nuances, the variations, the singularities, the fingerprints of our lives that make us individual, and that is what most matters. How could any one system apply to every different one of us?

'Yet as the day approached for my first visit to Harley Street, by way of Oxford Circus, like Natasha, but on Monday and Thursday so as not to bump into her on Tuesdays and Fridays, any buoyancy I had gathered from the doctor, any bravado I had garnered from my own rough-hewn recruitment of unanalysed heroes from the past, all the boosting of confidence and the exaggeration of contempt for psychoanalysis began to drain away. Natasha had embraced it. She said that she was already benefiting from it. But what would it do to me? I felt as if I were offering myself for some sort of intellectual lobotomy. What would happen when he tried to get at my mind?

'On the first visits I lay rigid on the altar of the sofa, sacrificing myself for Natasha, I thought in moments of self-aggrandisement, and wasting time, wasting money and wasting effort as I fended off the silent pressures for speech.

'"You don't want to do this, do you?" he said.

'"No."

'He waited until I cracked.'

—m—

Joe had managed to arrange the Thursday session for the late afternoon which disturbed the pattern of his day less than the morning time on Monday. The whole business, the tube, the walk, the session, the return, could take up to three hours and that did not include, as the process finally got under way, time for reflection or assimilation. After the session on Thursdays he went to the pub to meet Edward and the others.

Like Edward, Joe arrived there on the dot of opening time, five-thirty. The others turned up later. This day Edward was accompanied by the American poet Joe had heard about but not met. He knew she was a fine poet, an ambitious woman and the new girlfriend of the eight-year-married Edward. She drank water. They looked good together, Joe thought: Edward tall, rather square, broad-shouldered, called 'rugged' in a recent *Observer* profile, in looks and carriage more a countryman than a town wit; she blonde, leggy, her open health and beauty framed in confidence, new world, independent.

As soon as they had secured a table in an empty corner, Christina struck.

'I read *A Chance Defeat* and I liked it,' she said in her level gravelly sexy New England accent. 'Tell me. Do you believe the English provincial novel carries guns any more?'

Joe's smile took a little effort to sustain. He was intrigued and rather flattered to be such a close witness to this hot literary affair between Edward and Christina. He had adjusted himself to behave in an adult way, sympathetically, over the flaunted adultery. Despite the spilling of his entrails in Harley Street less than half an hour beforehand he thought he had put on the carapace of a man of the world. Christina punched right through all that and with a smile bigger and sustained at greater length than his.

'I mean when Hardy and Lawrence did their thing, Britain had an Empire and everybody listened. Everything that happens at the centre of an Empire is important both to those who want to join and those who want to beat it up. Even in the States we wanted to know what happened in Nottinghamshire and Wessex. Everything that mattered to you guys mattered to us guys. But will that wash any more?'

Joe nodded and then realised he was expected to reply. The daze in his mind which followed a session was usually anaesthetised in the pub by a few drinks with people who, like most (save the few in Kew to whom Natasha had unfortunately divulged it), knew nothing of the analysis. The shame at needing it had not lessened and he still feared that, publicly known, it would be the equivalent of having a card hung around his neck declaring him to be Unclean. Now, quite suddenly in the pub it was literary bare knuckle fighting.

'If writing's any good,' he responded, rather feebly in tone and emphasis, 'then it doesn't matter where it's set, does it?'

'Not in theory,' she said, crisply, 'I agree. And never in poetry. But the novel traditionally carries the news and what's the news from the English provinces today?'

Edward was happy to sip the stiff whisky, not a referee, not a contented spectator, more, Joe realised, a corner man wanting his own contender to land the telling blows.

'Same as usual,' said Joe, lighting up, 'same the whole world over, births, deaths and all that stuff in between.'

'I see what you're saying. And you're right, of course. But it seems to me that the novel has always tracked the power. I don't mean the political power necessarily although that counts. The best novelist alive could be in Finland but would anybody be as interested as the best novelist in America or Russia? No, the power I'm talking about is where the heat is. And it seems to me that you've had great novelists over here and we have too – look at Faulkner, just *look* at Faulkner! – who have quarried the provinces but it's time to move on.'

'People still live there.'

'I know. Oh, I know.'

'Things happen. Life goes on.'

'Oh, I know. You're right.'

'And what's a quarry got to do with writing anyway? Writing isn't an industrial process.'

'I agree with you,' she said. 'You say these things, then somebody comes along and writes a book that blows the thing clean out of the water.'

'But you must have said it because you believe it?'

'Yes. Sorry. I believe it.'

'So what next? In your system. Of perpetually and opportunistically moving on to pastures new.'

'Well, what next?' She took a steady sip of the water. 'Women writers – I know there have always been women writers but I mean self-consciously feminist writers – we are claiming more territory. The American Jews are riding high now. They're in the saddle. Next I think the blacks, in the States anyhow, they bring us news and news we can trust because it's fiction. Faulkner still has heat because of the blacks. Your old Empire, your Commonwealth has more and more writers demanding space for their experience. In the States the gays are gathering on the fringes and then there's genre writing. Crime's bigger than ever. I'm afraid the carnival's moved on from the English provinces.'

'Joe thinks you can find all human life in Wigton, don't you, Joe?' Edward's intervention was neat, amusingly delivered and just what was needed to save Joe and caution Christina.

'Too royal,' Joe said. 'A man's a man for a' that. Rabbie Burns, working-class poet, rare. My round.' He went to the bar glad to leave them.

Others came soon and the talking groups split and regrouped like amoebae until it was time for him to leave. He sought out Christina.

'I meant to say how much I liked the poems in *The Vanishing Point*,' he said, 'some of them were really good.' He quoted:

> 'Fragments of my past
> Shards of memory cut
> The days to ribbons
> Streaming blood before me.'

'I'm flattered, Joe,' she said. 'Thank you.'

'And I particularly like the seven set in Concord – *New England Blues*.'

'I grew up there,' she said. 'It's a kinda picture-book and historical-cut-out little spot but it was home, you know?'

'I do. Home's good. And very good to meet you.'

'You too, Joe.' She held out her hand. 'Read Robert Lowell. Good luck. I mean that. Good luck.'

Why did she say that? he asked himself as he zigzagged through Soho making for Piccadilly Circus. Does she think I need good luck? Do I look as if I need such a supportive send-off? And I've read Lowell.

He dwelled on the idea of his luck until he was almost home. It was, he thought, evidence of his exhausted mind that what was most likely a remark of passing American politeness he should seize so tenaciously. He used to thank his luck. A fortune teller in a fair on Hampstead Heath had once pointed out that his left hand was so criss-crossed with lines that even if he fell off at tower block he would land on his feet. He had believed her. But as the stripping away of the layers of his personality gathered pace in the analysis, he felt less sure of his luck. Had Christina intuited that? Her poems – those about mental break-down – certainly showed her understanding of states of disturbance. Maybe she meant that luck alone could cure what luck had caused. Edward was very brazen about her, he thought: quite rightly, much more honourable than hiding her away. A woman like Christina could not be hidden away. Her boldness reminded him of Natasha. It was a pity that Natasha never came to the pub. Perhaps if he told her about Christina . . .

On Mondays when the session was at 11 a.m. he made a day of it in London. His version of the script was now in its third draft and Saul had changed directors and brought in Tim whose *Jude* had not done too badly. Saul prided himself on spotting talent and on sticking with it, or at least giving it a second chance, and so far Tim and Joseph were shaping up well. Tim would keep it low budget, find good locations and not have to build expensive sets, and he would employ some of the brilliant new generation of English actors: they too were inexpensive.

On Monday afternoons Saul would hold court with Tim and Joseph, together with his accountant and sometimes his secretary whose touch, he said, was 'golden': 'If there was a female Midas Miriam would be the female Midas.' For Joseph these two or three hours swung between hell and an education. When they picked over every line of dialogue and asked him every question they could think up about the line, the response called for by the line, the response the line itself answered to, the necessity for the line, whether it should be two lines, or three lines, or no line at all, or a rewritten line and then they would all set to and 'rewrite' with arthritic spontaneity, Joseph would feel as if sawdust had replaced any remaining brain cells and the sawdust was being ground exceedingly small by a wheel of granite. Saul.

When, though, Saul would take out the long afternoon cigar and ease into anecdotes about the 'legends' he had worked with, Joe felt he had a ringside seat on history. Saul was generous with his stories, detailed, even pedantic in his descriptions of memorable scenes, the interplay between actors, a specific shot, what had been better by being left unsaid, the use of music. There was about him at these times the manner of a great teacher, rabbinical in scrutiny, worldly in reference, captivating and aware of it.

Afterwards, Tim would steer Joe to the nearest pub to spend half the time moaning that Saul would never actually sign off on the script, the other half moaning about the financial disaster resulting from his divorce.

Joe always walked through Hyde Park after that. He stopped now and then at a bench to make notes on what had been said. It did look as if this film would be made and with his script. He had to rein in his impatience. And Charles had hinted that parts of *Occupied Territory* would benefit from rewriting. He must not be impatient. How could you not rush, though, when there were no daily constraints of external routine? All the time in the world made you put extra pressure on yourself or you finished nothing.

He would watch the planes south of Hyde Park, still quite high in this part of the city, a tolerable drone, but every single one headed for Kew Gardens, for his house, the pilot's hand about to reach out to activate the screeching brakes.

He always arrived home irritated at his tiredness. Natasha would be eager to hear what had happened in the analysis and the strain of not telling her everything was something he could have done without.

It was late when he raised the subject. Perhaps he waited because, knowing there would be disagreement, he did not want to give it time to drag on. He knew that this would be no more than an opening shot but he had thought it through for months now and it had to be said. They had just watched *News at Ten*.

He waited until a plane had cleared over. 'Last Sunday,' he said, 'a plane woke me up before six. They say they suspend night arrivals until after six but they don't. After that I couldn't stop counting, wherever I was or wherever we were; in the house, out in Kew, on the towpath, round at Anna's or Margaret's, back in the house, I just kept counting. I was doing all sorts of other things as far as you or anybody else might have noticed but what I was really doing all day and all the time was counting the planes. It wasn't frantic but I couldn't get rid of it.

'Then I began to time the space between the planes so that I could work out when they might be coming and try to disconnect myself for those small spans but they vary even though they seem to come like clockwork, they vary as if to stop you predicting them. There were hundreds. There were pauses now and then and I thought – they've stopped. Then they came back. Two hundred and eighty-three aeroplanes went over our house last Sunday, flying low with brakes full on, and part of my mind spent all that day locked against the noise so that it didn't blow out my brains or make me run away again.

'Two hundred and eighty-three times I heard the plane, I braced myself against the plane, I tried to make whatever is inside this skull into a second layer of armour plating inside the bone and when the plane sound left, and as I imagined it sail over those great conservatories in Kew Gardens, across the Thames, I got ready for the next one. We ate meals, we went on a walk, we had tea in the garden at Anna's, we watched the play on television, we read, we wrote, Marcelle was seen and heard and for her and for you, I'm sure, it was a good day but for me it was two hundred and eighty-three aeroplanes ripping through my mind as they are doing now and Natasha, why do we have to keep living here?'

She saw a pleading face, puffy from the too much drink he took more regularly now.

'We love it here,' she began, fearfully.

'Yes.'

'Our friends, Marcelle's friends . . .'

'Yes.'

'Others . . .'

'I know . . . Others cope . . . I know.'

'Where would we go?'

'We could try Richmond Hill. They don't seem to pass over there.'

'No!' Natasha made an awful decision, obstinately held to. 'If you want to move, we move. Not just a few hundred yards.'

'It's further than that.'

'We have to think it over.'

'I have. Hundreds of times. Here it comes again . . . Why should we spend our life under a flight path when we could sell this place, buy another place and not be under a flight path?'

'This is where you brought me. This is where I have settled.'

'I know. I'm sorry.'

'You have settled here too.'

'I have.'

She saw the dejection but she was too occupied fighting her own alarm to take it into account.

'Can you not give it another try? Can you not go more to that library in the club?'

'I could. But I can't go every day. People don't. Don't ask me. They just don't.' And it's cut off there, he wanted to say, it becomes just odd sitting alone in a club library, in a beautifully furnished and polished room full of rare books I feel self-conscious, which is fatal. It's no place for me to write what I want to write and I'm not telling you this because you'll ask why it isn't and I don't know. And I always have to come home. There are weekends. And until midnight they're here most days, beginning again at six.

'I have to think about this.'

I have to talk to my analyst is what she really meant, Joseph thought, and said nothing.

'Please do,' he said and closed his eyes as another plane screamed over. 'Please. Do.'

CHAPTER THIRTY-FIVE

All their Kew friends seemed to take Joseph's side. 'Bloody nuisance, aren't they?' or 'Such a fantastic difference when we have a weekend off' or 'Friend of mine in a flat in Baker Street says they are getting worse even there.' But Joseph felt that he had been found wanting: even sympathy appeared critical. 'Don't blame you. Thought of moving ourselves' or 'If it weren't that the kids were settled in school here . . .' Joseph squirmed.

When their Kew friends were more than usually cheerful under the flight path he wanted to crawl into a corner. Even when an escapee from Kew said, 'It drove me mad too, get out before it traps you, get out before you're hooked,' Joseph still thought, but it's only him, look at all the others who endure it, look at what is being endured everywhere you look – what are a procession of noisy planes?

So again he tried to bear it. As his defences were being dismantled by his analyst so to prove his independence and his will he would test himself in Kew: holding out against the planes was the test. If he could stop counting them or act out indifference to that howl in the sky then he would be better able to resist the offensive of the analyst.

At the same time, they began the search for a new house.

There were times when he could not pass an estate agent's office without peering at the photographs of available houses and collecting sheets of information from all over London. For the rest of his life Joe could closely connect with many districts in London through the memory of visiting a house unbought. It was a journey to the interior of the middle-class metropolis and the more Joe saw the more cosy and hand-finished and neat their own house seemed in Kew. Years later he could still remember a large elegant double-volumed drawing room in Chelsea (too expensive), 'a gem of a place' (but no garden for Marcelle) perfectly situated next to the Kensington Public Library, a big end-of-terrace house near Notting Hill (but next to a pub), an excellent house in Chiswick but the planes came over almost as low as in Kew. So it went on for more than two months while Natasha worked on her book and Joe worked on the script and anxiously saw his novel through the proof stage and began to do a little more radio. Looking for a house became their way of life.

Natasha played fair. It would be unjust to make it simple and say that he rushed in with eager urgency and she somehow always found a way to block it. There were at least two houses she liked and said so and would have gone for. But at the back of his mind, Joe thought they were too show-off. They were too big a leap, too much of a statement, too uncomfortable to live with. It was Joe's vacillation in these two cases which passed by the opportunity.

His guilt at what he feared he was doing to Natasha made him read into her remarks and expressions an attitude which was not always there. Instead of accepting her willingness and building on her determined cooperation he kept looking for and, as he thought, finding the regret, the projected sense of loss, the sadness. It was Joe who extended the process and made it weary by misreading Natasha, by fearing too much for her, by letting his own never-absent guilt unnerve him. Joe who even at those two sunniest moments, when the way seemed clear, conjured up a shadow and drew back. Joe who decided after several weeks to make a further attempt to find a quieter place in Kew itself.

So again he walked the streets of the suburb logging the precise flight paths, and asked shopkeepers, landlords and even passers-by whether this precise flight path was frequently used, how it compared to one a quarter of a mile or two hundred yards away. He would stand still on the pavement, look at his watch and then look at the sky; make a note, move on. A surveyor of noise. Now and then there seemed hope – a cottage near the Green was a sort of island, a house towards Barnes seemed to stand between flight paths.

'There's a house in Kew Road,' said Natasha, 'one of those detached houses. Anna said she'd been in one and they are very well built, practically soundproof.'

'They're on the same flight path as us.'

'But they're Victorian, and they have cellars. You could work there.'

She smiled. She had not asked him the direct question. She had no need. She knew that he wanted to please her.

The cellars were large, windowless and cold.

'They are quiet,' she said when they went across the road and gazed at the house they had rather shyly looked through, feeling, as always, more voyeurs than potential purchasers.

'It's out of our range,' he said. 'I'd have to do another script.'

They stood, hand in hand, Natasha scarcely daring to look at him, Joseph not daring to say no. Was he to spend much of the rest of his life in those cellars? Well, why not? What did it matter where he worked? To make it harder, there were no planes that night and this broad and tree-lined avenue of solid middle-class grandeur, which led in a royal fashion to the Gardens, appeared perfect.

'The garden is so big,' she said, 'Marcelle will love it.'

'It is a real English house,' she said.

'We need never move again,' she said. 'Look how strongly it stands. Like a castle.'

Joseph's throat was dry. He had difficulty easing it. Recently, now and then, the mere drawing in of a breath had become a demanding exercise.

'Can we, can I, there's a couple more I'd like you to see, can we think about it?'

'It is perfect,' she said.

'Yes.' He swallowed with some effort. 'I can see it is.'

'You need not blame yourself for bringing pressure to bear,' her analyst said, speaking more slowly than usual, her voice matching the exhausted expression Natasha had caught sight of when she came in. 'Undoubtedly from what you tell me he is the sort of young man who will be putting pressure on himself in his analysis. He will perhaps still be ashamed of doing it at all, though that will go. He will fear it, of course. And he will fight to stay in control of the analysis, which of course cannot happen. The aeroplanes, I agree with you, are only a sign, they objectify the pain he is re-experiencing from his past. Nevertheless we must accept that for Joseph they are also real, and they are especially real at present and they must be respected.'

'Can I have two more weeks?' he asked her.

He based himself in Reading and looked for houses near the main-line railway station into London. Sam now had a car and drove Joe around for three afternoons while he sifted through the properties on offer. On two of the afternoons Ellen went with them.

'There's some beautiful houses,' she said to Sam after Joe had gone back to London.

'You've no idea, have you, until you see them. The money in those houses!' she said. 'I could've lived in any of them.' The well-tended, handsome Thames valley cottages, houses and mansions had been to Ellen like a vision from Hollywood. To think that Joe might live in one of them was not easy to assimilate. They were, no argument, a cut above.

'Natasha's not as keen as he is,' said Sam. 'She doesn't want to be in the sticks.'

'She doesn't look well,' said Ellen. 'Her eyes were as if she was running a temperature. They glittered. Didn't they?'

Sam had thought that Natasha was on the edge of tears.

'Joe looks as bad in his own way. He can't keep still. And did you see how he kept looking at her? It was as if he was a bit frightened of her.'

'What you've told me,' said Joe's analyst, 'is that to use your own expression you've entered into a phase of "chronic indecision". And I take your phrase "interiority complex". When you started looking for houses you said that you would have been happy to have taken the first one that fitted the bill but somehow that didn't happen. You don't quite want to blame Natasha for this but you do point out that it's been in your character to just take whatever turns up. And you believe that has worked for you. Yet you have always said that Natasha has better taste and more discrimination than you have. You fear she is imposing that to slow the process down or even stop it. Yet you also contradict that. Now you complain that you can't make your mind up at all.

'You tell me there's a possible place in Kew, there were two houses in Goring near Reading, quite convenient for London and one of them was "perfect", your mother said, in fact she told you that when you were very small and she cleaned houses – in the war – she used to take you to a house just like that. Now you say that Natasha seems to be losing interest and you don't have the strength to make the decision alone. You are afraid that she won't help you. You say it's the unstoppable noise that has "bled you weak" – your expression again.'

'He is taking so long to decide,' Natasha said to her analyst, 'that I can't believe any more that he wants to do it. If Joseph really wanted to move he would have moved by now. That is what he is like. There was one house we saw in Goring which was perfect. I would not have wanted to be stuck out there while he travelled into London, I would fear what he might do there alone, and we know no one at all in Goring. But the river is so beautiful and Joseph liked the fact that it is a small and cosy little town and it is near Oxford for me. But he kept asking me instead of making up his own mind.'

'Julia suggests we try Oxford,' Joseph said.

'Is this the last place? We've looked enough now surely.'

'Yes. This is it.'

'Of course you must come back to live here,' said Julia as she gave them tea. 'It would be lovely to have you here, you know Oxford and you like it. How could anyone not? I'm sure you can write as well here as anywhere else and people say the train to London is acceptably reliable. I've heard you can do quite solid reading on the journey.'

The one house in their range was a semi-detached in North Oxford occupied by five students. It was in an advanced state of disrepair and full of unsweet smells.

'It needs a total overhaul,' Joe said.

'Why don't you do it a room at a time?' Julia suggested. 'It could be fun.'

'Oxford,' said Natasha as they went to see it for the second time later that afternoon, 'is a place of good omens for us. I could go back to the art college part time. Julia says that there are several writers in Oxford, some of them dons, you won't lack for company. I'd feel safe here when you went to London or abroad.'

'But look at it,' he said as they stood across the road and gazed at the red-brick pile with its peeling paint and student sense of the transient. 'It would cost a fortune to make it decent.'

'You want everything too neat and tidy, Joseph! Remember that you are allowed to be a bohemian. We could leave some of the rooms for rent.'

'I don't want to live in a commune.'

'Where are your socialist principles, Joseph?' She laughed and later he thought that the laugh was a small flame he ought to have nourished. She had not laughed as freely and spontaneously as that for some time. But he ignored it in this time of chronic indecision. Perhaps her eagerness raised fears that she would meet young lecturers and artists when he was not in Oxford, that her status as a well-reviewed novelist ('Disciplines insight with a classically taut construction,' *The Times* had said of *The Unquiet Heart*) would see her into circles not as enthusiastic about him. It could be that a gust of jealousy blew out the flame . . .

Two weeks later they came out of the estate agent's in Kew Gardens having made their offer for the house in Kew Road. Natasha was radiant. The bloom on her face emphasised to Joseph the tension which had dragged her down over the past few months.

'Thank you, Joseph,' she said. 'From the bottom of my heart. I must pick up Marcelle now.' Her look of love and gratitude fortified him.

He stood there for a few minutes after she had gone, the small railway station, like a country stop, behind him, and in front the little plaza already tapestried in memory. The junk shop where they had bought much of their furniture, the bookshop and the little café which coyly put out a few tables on the pavement on hot days, the shops where Natasha was known now, the bank from which he still drew his modest few pounds of 'spending money' on Saturday mornings, the cigarette machine sometimes a last resort late in a night's writing, and in front of him, beyond the shops and the tree-lined road in which they would now live, the great Gardens, and beyond them, the towpath, the Thames, and around and about, their friends, and he knew that he was lucky and if Natasha's happiness meant some sacrifice it would be worth it. He felt good.

It was the right decision. He breathed it in and relaxed, let go, and just then, even lower than usual, what appeared to be a vast whale of metal ripped through the sky directly overhead and he thought that his head would explode with the pain of it, all tolerance instantly gone, all resistance worn down by now, brain lacerated raw, mind unhinged while sound possessed it, defenceless as the metal screamed west, and soon there would be further invasions and they would never stop.

He wanted to cover his ears with his hands but that would have made him too conspicuous.

—ɯ—

'I am aware of other lives going on untold,' he wrote to their daughter. 'They will have to wait for another time.

'For instance I have not told you enough about our friends in Kew who stay our friends to this day or the friends from work who made up a rather buccaneering meritocratic metropolitan gang at that time. We were engaged with both groups and there was seeding of what have proved long loyalties. I did not know then that two couples among our friends were having a bruising passage in the struggle of their young marriages or that fear of failure and failure itself were not uncommon.

'My guess is that they returned a good-mannered blind eye to us. We made efforts when with them and it is more than likely that being with them helped. It could be for a spell that it was our friends who kept us together.

'But there was a normal busy English suburban, privet-hedged, private-gardened life to be thankful for on good and on bad days. Although Natasha and I were sunk into real and assumed difficulties of being, the uncharted worlds of what we "really" were and what we might have been, I know that we played our parts in the central drama of that group in Kew Gardens, which was the parenting of the children, a job for which none of us was prepared, by which all of us could be exhausted, but in which most of us found some pleasure and no little achievement in getting through it. In Kew the children defined the group. In London the lack of children defined the group.

'Your mother increasingly regarded London with suspicion, as a corrupting, unprincipled force, but it was something I was part of and I always thought that, oddly, Natasha could have coped with it better than me, but she turned her back on it. She was certainly fêted by some of them – her brilliant but slightly idiosyncratic English, her rapidity of response whether sure of her ground or not, the amused anticipation with which she greeted people who were clever and threatening. Still, though less relentlessly, the films, the theatre, the bring your own bottle parties, still the feeding of the ducks, still the playground, the towpath.

'Surely to God it should have been enough.'

'Tea would be perfect,' said Matthew. 'Wine will be plentiful later, through and following the dinner. I think that our locally purchased sherry would rather dull the palate.'

'I thought a palate was to do with food,' said Julia, slowly stirring the tea leaves in the large floral-patterned teapot.

'I think one can get away with it.'

'Possibly.' She poured the tea carefully. 'You look quite dashing in your dinner jacket, Matthew.'

'Thank you.'

'It's rather a pity you don't wear it more often.'

'I would guess that Oxford colleges hold their own very well in the matter of formal dress for dinner.'

'I mean every night,' said Julia. She smiled brightly. 'I find it attractive sexually.'

'Then perhaps it's a good idea not to overdo it.'

'Your Feast Nights are quite pagan really, aren't they?'

'Or Roman.'

'They were pagan.'

'It depends on the period.'

'The better period.'

'I must be on guard tonight,' said Matthew, and took out a cigarette. 'I want your advice.'

'Ah. I ought to have suspected something of the kind.'

'Why?'

'That delicious mixture of flattery and aggression.'

'Don't be silly, Matthew. Sometimes you're too clever even for you.'

'A perfect illustration, if I may say so, of my point.'

'I bumped into Joe. Just after lunch. It seemed accidental but he was lingering around at the end of the road as if waiting to be bumped into.'

409

'How very curious.'

'Most odd. He came in and I gave him tea.' She paused. 'He was not himself. I found it disconcerting. He smoked a rather large cigar. He was over-elaborately dressed even by today's standards. I thought he looked rather like one of Augustus John's degenerate types. There was an air about him that was unsettling. Agitated is not quite the word. I would say upset.'

'About what?'

'One thing at a time. You have ten minutes. He said he had come to look again at the house they decided not to buy.'

'A wholly understandable act.'

'But he and Natasha have put in an offer for another house in Kew Gardens.'

'People behave oddly about houses.'

'Then he began to say how quiet our house is. He would stop speaking every now and then or say "listen" and smile at how quiet it is.'

'As indeed it is.'

'He mentioned the aeroplanes in Kew. Several times. They are directly under the flight path. He finds it painful.'

'Presumably that is why they are moving.'

'The new house is also directly under the flight path.'

'Julia. I quite enjoy being the audience for your Poirot or Miss Marple unravellings but I think a clincher is called for.'

'I think he is quite disturbed,' she said, quietly, 'and I think he feels trapped because Natasha loves Kew Gardens . . .'

'And he loves Natasha. A new twist on the fatal triangle.'

'I felt it was serious, Matthew. The question is, before you go off to eat your disgusting wild boar or your illegal swan, ought I to talk to Natasha?'

'Better not to.'

'I knew you'd say that. You always do. But what if I tell you that I believe there may be some danger? They are both in analysis, you know.'

'I didn't.'

'Yes. And it may be doing him harm.'

'It's outside my competence.'

'You're not to duck it. Shall I phone her and tell her that in my view for whatever reason this aeroplane-noise business is very serious for him?'

'It would be to interfere.'

'Yes.'

'And, with respect, not doubting your powers, you have not all the facts at your command.'

'No.'

'And they are adult, well married, intelligent, perfectly capable of working out their own lives.'

'Perhaps. Do you remember just before they met when Natasha was mistreated by that American painter?'

'The shit?'

'Yes. I went up to her room one evening to make sure she was all right and she looked so terribly hurt and in despair that I feared for her. Then Joe came along.'

'With some force!' said Matthew and looked at his watch.

'It is terrible to see those you love unhappy.'

'I must go.'

'He is calling on his parents on the way back to London. Once Marcelle is in bed Natasha will be in the house as it were on her own.'

'He may not wish her to know that he was here,' said Matthew as he stood up to leave.

'I've thought of that.'

'There may be other factors. After all they have lived in that place for a few years now.'

'That too.'

'You have to be very sure of your ground.' Matthew's tone was devoid of all levity.

'It was you who once said that to Natasha we stood in *loco parentis*.'

'I see you have solved the problem.'

'You'll be late for your sherry.'

'You never cease to impress me,' he said, and went to his college feast.

—ɯ—

'Hampstead Heath is the opposite of Kew Gardens,' Joseph said. 'It overlooks London from the north as opposed to sinking to the river level of the south. It's woody and hilly with small ponds, it's a pocket edition of the Lake District and kids love it – there are parks and pools, there's Kenwood House where we can go for tea and see the paintings. The Heath is vast, much bigger than Kew Gardens, you could be in the country, little paths, I used to walk there when we were in Finchley, and Parliament Hill where they fly kites.

'It used to be the haunt of highwaymen as the coaches hauled up the hill to get out of London. Dick Turpin operated out of Hampstead Heath. And Dickens used to walk up there and have a drink in Jack Straw's Castle. The pub is still there. Lawrence lived there, so did Keats and Orwell and Constable, Ted Hughes still lives there sometimes, Ben Nicholson, Al Alvarez, Margaret Drabble, it's partly an artists' colony really, the Everyman's the best art cinema in London, all the actors drink at the Cruel Sea, you'll love it, there'll be people we already half know and you'll just love it. So will Marcelle.

'And best of all for me, no planes, or so high you can't hear them. And best of all for you, a direct overground train to Kew Gardens, only twenty to twenty-five minutes, leaves three times in the hour.'

Her heart aching, her resolve firm, Natasha nodded and even smiled at the pleading and love in his desperately rehearsed salesmanship.

'I can't understand,' she told the analyst, 'why, now that we have moved, we have chosen the worst house we have seen. It is narrow and terraced and shoddy, and although it is in the middle of Hampstead most of the houses in that particular street are in sometimes dreadful disrepair. The garden is cramped and leads to a huge derelict garage. The house was previously let as bed-sitting rooms and going around it was like being a horrible capitalist about to evict people. There was an Australian woman, not young, with her mother, very old, where would they go? And one man who refused to talk or get out of his chair but simply sat there and hated us as the Irish landlady showed us around. Most of the houses in the street are like that – chopped up into single rooms, overcrowded, and so sad. Joseph thought it had the advantage of being near the middle of what they call Hampstead Village and being over four floors enabling us to have properly separate studies. Of course it is costing far more than he anticipated to make it even habitable – no damp course, no central heating, all rooms need redecoration, the builders are poor workmen and lazy. It is horrible. And Joseph knows it. He's already looking for other houses in Hampstead but they are so small, those we can afford. And we haven't the energy to move again. But he still talks to estate agents. I won't go with him to see them. We have to make the best of it.'

The analyst waited a while and then began.

'You are telling me that being ripped out of Kew Gardens is unbearable for you. You describe this house in terms so dramatic and even lurid that they cease to describe the house and instead they describe your own condition.' The analyst paused. She herself was very tired yet she needed all her resources to carry Natasha through this, the most important and dangerous chapter in the process. Natasha was almost wholly defenceless now and this move could not have come at a worse time. 'The nightmare is compounded by the act of love you have made. It is love that has provoked the nightmare. Your love for Joseph has been tested and not found wanting. You can hold onto that. His search for a new house is the result of shock. Shock can be a breakthrough.'

Joseph could not work out how he had blundered into this house. Over the months he had had options on several degrees of respectability, the chance more than once to be bold and take that splendid town house on a twenty-year lease or that freestanding house surrounded by garden in one of the loveliest streets in Hampstead – out of his range but not hugely – and surely a place that would heal and comfort instead of this which made him ashamed and then ashamed that he was ashamed. It was a bit rough but that was better than soft, or snobby, wasn't it? It grounded him, he thought, and that had to be good.

His mother had detonated the shame. 'It reminds me of Water Street in Wigton,' she said, and he not only saw immediately the run-down, cramped, crammed hovels which had in his childhood made up the poorest and the most feared street in the town, he saw it as the place in which his mother had once reluctantly and unhappily lived, and from which she had longed to escape. He saw dismay and disbelief in her look as she wandered up the shabby, dreary street and he could see her thoughts – how could he leave that lovely house in Kew Gardens for this? Or what about those beautiful houses we saw near Reading? How could he be supposed to be doing so well and end up here? – and her unspoken bewilderment and condemnation of his choice unnerved him. 'It's as if he's gone back to where we started from,' she told Sam. 'Back to Water Street. I can't comprehend it.'

Yet Natasha had come with him. He knew what that meant for her. And with all his might he tried to make it the place he had promised it would be. They walked on the Heath, he bought Marcelle a little boat and sailed it on one of the ponds; they wrote in their individual rooms. He became delighted with the back alleys and hidden little paths in Hampstead Village itself and on the Heath. He forced down his own dismay and attempted to crush the fear and shame the place brought on, he forced himself to bypass the foolishness of his agitated and wilful choice, and set his mind to start again and this time not to falter.

CHAPTER THIRTY-SIX

'Increasingly the past is breaking into the present,' he wrote to Marcelle. 'We two talk about Natasha much more intensely than before. The present reorganises the past. Memory changes all the time and is dependent not so much on past certainties stored securely but on present challenges: memory fortifies the day, it regroups continuously to accommodate the moment. So my memories of your mother change as I write. I trust a few facts – dates, the work we did, the houses, friendships – but all the ebb and flow of feeling, the flux that is life, has to be discovered and rediscovered. Some people say it is therapeutic, this exercise: I wholly disagree. If anything it is the opposite. Often the re-creation wounds deeply, it would be better left buried; it exposes old difficulties to new scrutiny which can be merciless; it brings the dead to life and between the death and the life there can be little but regret, mostly bitter, and blame for what still seems a crime more than three decades after the sentence has been passed.

'All this is a preparation for what is to come which seems at times a remote encounter with improbable insanity. As I write this, it is a summer evening, I am in an English cottage garden. Across a wheat-field, there is a marbled white horse standing under the lush umbrella of a group of maple trees, a red kite has flown by, gliding with oblivious grace, wood pigeons loud-throatedly coo from tree to tree, the door of the garage converted into my study is open to the garden, a thick row of lavender nods slightly in the evening breeze; why summon up demons, why reach out to the spirit world of the imagination? Why not be out in that English garden with a drink, with friends, with a book, with the Proms on the radio, with the day that is today and not spend life, waste life, on those dead days? What does it matter to anyone? Save you and me. But that is the point, isn't it? You and me. Save you and me.'

Joe hurled himself into Hampstead, sniffed it out like a pup in a new wood. He took Marcelle down the hidden ginnels and passageways, the alleys and all but secret paths which snaked up the hill towards the Georgian streets which topped the village and commanded views across the bowl of London to the Surrey hills. These narrow passageways were made for children, they wended behind churches, skirted private gardens, led to cottages hidden inside the muddle of unplanned clutter which was the character of the place. Joe thought that a knowledge of them would make Hampstead feel safe for Marcelle, while for him, unlike the open suburban order of Kew, it was a higgledy-piggledy reminder of the old alley-riddled centre of the town of his childhood.

Marcelle liked the school, a tall red-brick Victorian masterpiece of educational rectitude, and soon there were schoolfriends in the house and parents collecting them and costumes to be made for the Christmas play.

Natasha resolved not to make comparisons or lament the separation from their old friends and she stuck to it. The absolute nature of her resolve made Joseph feel the absence of complaint as an accusation. She tried very hard. While lacking the energy or the enthusiasm of Joseph who would come back with bullish comments of a 'great little Woolworths' or a 'real old-fashioned wood shop' or talk of Flask Walk 'full of old bookshops' and 'the Freemasons' Arms which has a terrific pub garden', she saw that given time it could be a place in which she could settle, in which roots could be put down even though its busyness contrasted unfavourably with ambling Kew, as did its competitive London culture with the quiet learning of Oxford. But there were quaint streets, good enough shops, a cosmopolitan character she sensed she would come to appreciate, and newspapers in many languages.

The truth was that she was tired out. The move had been frantic. The improvements in their new house had been banged up on the cheap and looked it. They had lived through its crude and stop-start metamorphosis and however Panglossian Joseph was about being lucky to have a house at all, to be in the middle of rubble and incompetence in your own home, your private inviolable space, was wearing. And she knew that Joseph's cheerfulness was false. He was every bit as tense, upset and disturbed as she was but he refused to show it save in recurrent irritability. It was as if she herself was being gutted, clumsily, carelessly, and always far too slowly and then being put together again just as clumsily, carelessly, like someone on a battlefield just stuffing back in the spilled entrails. To both of them, the house-home had become as close as skin.

And there was to her the alien nature of the street, young men mending motorbikes, older men struggling with old cars, evidence of loneliness and transience, evidence of bare pickings, evidence sometimes of a desperation that made her long even more that the house was finally theirs, which it did not yet seem, ghosted as it was with sad departures. And when one night, late, the man who had sat dumb in his chair and hated them came back drunk to his former address and banged and banged on the door to be let in; and when a loud young party across the street ended with sexual intercourse on the pavement outside their house; and when the flat of a woman three doors down caught fire and burned to death nine of her fourteen cats; and when the motorbikes roared up the narrow canyon of the street on a warm night so that Joseph asked her if he could close the bedroom windows but she said, 'No, this is the place you wanted, this is the sound you get'; then she wanted to run away, to run back to Kew, just to run. But she said nothing.

There was Joseph, pretending: she thought. Pretending that he liked Hampstead more than she was sure he did; pretending to like the house when she knew he hated it; pretending to find the people in the street 'real'; pretending to a fondness for the street itself, the shoddy tumble of a cheaply run-up Edwardian terrace.

Joseph was running out of himself. That which had taken him to university, to the marriage, to writing, to a family, to films and to money enough for him to be unloosed from a salaried anchor, was draining away. Or so he gleaned and assumed from his analyst. And so he noted from his tougher more successful acquaintances who laughed whenever the old Joe's naivety was exposed, who simply did not believe in his sometimes slow truths and gauche honesty. He needed recharging for the next lap. Analysis was at the core of it, he decided, and he was now in its grip to such an extent that when the analyst said that he was going away for a month's holiday, Joe counted the days, as he had done at Oxford when parted from Rachel, counted them down until they would meet again, counted them sometimes by the hour.

Yet on the surface, whatever it was that made him enabled him to get by. The final script on Elizabeth was delivered and accepted. *Occupied Territory* was received better than his previous novels. A television director bought the option to make it into a film. He went to a few literary launch parties and was always edgy which translated into too much quick drink followed by boasts or muted belligerence; but he coped. Tim told him to widen his experience and suggested strip clubs in the afternoons and dodgy bars in the evenings. Joe felt there were lives he was missing and yet the life he was leading was full. He smoked more. He was drunk more often. He went to football matches with Edward and the clasp of the crowd seemed the best thing on offer. His success led him to feel embattled.

Natasha dropped off Marcelle at the nursery school in Flask Walk and tacked up Hampstead High Street peering around her. Her eyesight was good but at times she could seem very short-sighted, peering, as if the world were too dangerous to be taken wide-eyed. She tried to get bearings. What would she latch onto? What would become one of those often unassuming spots which somehow make you feel safe and at home? She trailed up the hill scanning the unbusy street, glancing into the little courts and mews and walks, eventually turning right at the underground station and walking up Heath Street. On her left were some stone steps. She went up them as they twisted like an eccentric staircase and led her to the Mount, the top of the Hill, the little Georgian crown unordered but harmonious, not unlike La Rotonde. It was a place easy to love.

Why had Joseph not chosen the house here? They had looked at one but he had heard the boom of traffic far below from a main road and that had scared him off. These narrow traffic-free alley-streets soothed her and she followed one which led to an immense, once grand, now neglected, Victorian gothic churchyard. She could do watercolours here: that churchyard could yield a lot. But the distant noise deterred him, fatally.

Natasha came back into Hampstead by way of Mount Vernon and the Queen Anne splendour of Church Row, the sort of place where Ellen thought they ought to live and which they could have afforded, just, had Joseph not been determined to squirrel away some of his film earnings for a rainy day. The thrift was admirable but she wished he had been bolder. Yet Natasha applauded the common sense of what Joseph had tried to do and, more surely, she believed that an over-consideration of material circumstances was little more than an attempt to duck the real issues. So she wandered around Hampstead on that morning, a tourist, a stranger, trying to make it familiar, steadily suppressing the strong undertow of sadness for lost Kew.

'Natasha! How are you?'

She turned in the direction of the voice but recognised no one.

'Over here!'

Natasha focused. She was on the broad pavement at the High Street end of Perrin's Court, having just passed what she did not yet know was Hampstead's sole bohemian outdoor conversational venue, the Coffee Cup, a few tables under a permanent canopy outside a small restaurant.

'How are you?'

He had left his table and was in front of her.

'James!'

The name came to her with relief. James. And suddenly it was Oxford again and the early days in London, the magazine in Finchley, the beginning of James's wildly improbable but successful career as a writer of popular songs, a friend. They shook hands.

'Would you like a coffee?'

'Thank you.'

He ushered her to the small and uncomfortable wooden seats.

'Why are you alone?'

James smiled and felt a swell of warmth at her directness.

'Howard has just left. I stayed to pick up the bill.'

'Howard . . . he writes the music. We've lost touch.'

He ordered for both of them.

'Geography,' said James in that church voice Natasha so liked and liked all the more now that it stood at such odds with his vernacular popular lyrics. 'Underestimated. Geography is a great maker and breaker of friendships. But now that you live here we shall get together again. We've been in Israel for a few weeks. Howard has family there.'

'Joseph thought he might go there.'

'Everyone should,' said James. 'It's quite remarkable. One envies the kibbutz system without actually wanting to live on one. And Howard's friends – so intelligent. Do you like Hampstead?'

Natasha decided to avoid an answer.

'I've just been up at the top on the Mount,' she pointed.

'That's where we live.'

'Together?'

'Yes. We share a house, we share a job, but we don't share a life!' He laughed. 'A well-practised answer with the merit of being true. The house is small but it's somehow inspirational up there.'

Natasha nodded.

'I took *The Unquiet Heart* with me to Israel,' said James. 'Many congratulations. I loved it. I thought the young man was particularly finely drawn and Brittany came alive. It made me want to go there.'

'So the book had its uses.'

'It really is very good to see you,' he said, as the coffee was placed in front of them. 'How is Joseph? One reads about him now and then.'

'Changing,' she said.

'Don't we all?'

'No. Most of us grow older on the basis of what we are. Change is different.'

'I see it as inevitable,' said James. 'Especially if you move from one world into another.'

'Like you?'

'Yes,' he nodded. 'And Joseph.'

'But you have not changed,' she said.

'How disappointing.' His warm affectionate laughter reassured her.

'He seems . . . uncentred,' she said.

'I'm not surprised,' said James, 'when you look at the trajectory. But the last time I saw him, when he came to that launch just before our Israel trip – you couldn't make it, I remember – he seemed buoyant.' Even overexcited, James could have added, even hyper.

'Yes. He can't believe his life,' said Natasha.

'That could lead one to be a little unbalanced.'

'It leads to overconfidence and lack of confidence.'

'That's not unusual on the pop scene either,' said James, 'in fact I'd say it's characteristic. And in many ways Joe is very much part of that generation if not of that specific strand in it.'

'Is it so easy to sweep people up in the generalisation of "a generation"?'

'It is relevant,' said James, 'especially, I think, this one. Bright working-class boys, early success, coming up to London, the music thing, the drugs thing, the sex, the sense of the world changing from one's fate to one's oyster!' He laughed. 'Instant pop sociology has become rather a weakness of mine.'

'Sometimes I think that Joseph could have been homosexual.'

'What makes you say that?'

'When you study his background.'

'I see signs of a sort of pervasive sexuality, an erotic sensibility in some of his work and mannerisms, but I would describe that as feminine, not homosexual, and not uncommon, especially now.'

' "Especially now". Isn't it merely a boast to claim that we live in a "special" age?'

'Perhaps. All I can say is that this feels like one for me and for many others and across the old class barriers: it's the sort of bonding you read about in a war but this time it's a bonding in liberation of several varieties.'

'Hedonism,' said Natasha.

'I was rather perturbed by one remark he made when we met,' James said. 'He told me he wanted to go to Vietnam.'

'And you say he is buoyant? To go to Vietnam is a proof of buoyancy?'

'I took issue with him, of course,' said James, while still ruminating on Natasha's reference to Joe's sexuality, 'but he insisted he needed to test himself. I'm sure "test" was the word. I pointed out he would have no accreditation, he had no experience as a war correspondent and it could in one sense be seen as merely voyeuristic.'

'The voyeurism charge would check him,' said Natasha. 'Sometimes he seems to want to go into orbit or he believes he is already in orbit.'

That was enough, she decided. It was becoming disloyal and besides the cause of much of his recent uncharacteristic behaviour could well be tracked back to the analysis, she thought, which he was undergoing at her request and on her behalf. She must take on that responsibility and accept the consequences.

'We shall meet again,' said James. 'What a pleasant prospect.'

'You remember that song we heard on the Arab radio station,' said Howard, the moment that James came into their music room.

'The Egyptian one?'

'Yes. But listen.' Howard picked at a soulful melody on the guitar. 'Almost exactly the same. But what I've played is Gaelic.'

'How extraordinary.'

'Now if you sort of splice them together you get this.' Once again Howard played and this time for James images of remote islands in great seas, of Celtic crosses and god-haunted streams were superimposed on the deserts and dunes, the camel caravans and Bedouin of his romantic Arabia.

'It's not our usual style,' said James.

'Exactly.' Howard, already besotted by this composition, could not resist playing it quietly once more as they talked on.

'I've just seen Natasha,' said James. 'It could be her.'

'A woman alone.'

'A woman alone, in a pavement café; in Paris? At some crisis point thinking on life, how she arrived where she is, what choices she had.'

'I could slow it down a bit,' said Howard.

'No. That won't be necessary. We could give the song a name, the name of the woman.'

'It is extraordinary, isn't it?' said Howard. 'Egyptian and Gaelic.'

'Natalie would be a good name,' James said. 'When we meet her she's drinking coffee . . .'

———

Isabel and Alain liked to have 'les Richardsons' to themselves and this time they went for lunch to Roussillon where there was a serviceable restaurant and a large open-air public swimming pool to which Joseph took Marcelle immediately after the main course.

'She is adorable, your Marcelle,' said Alain as they sat back with their cigarettes and coffee. 'A little English rose.'

'For me she is completely French,' said Isabel, 'except for the language, but already she is learning. You should have made her bilingual, Natasha.'

'That's what Joseph wanted.'

'It is always the man who has the common sense,' said Alain.

'Don't be ridiculous, Alain. Were you asleep? It was I who suggested it. *Alors!*'

'Two languages can be a disadvantage,' said Natasha. 'They are to me. I feel frustrated. My English will never be good enough. My French is not necessary in London. I am between two worlds.'

'But Joseph tells me your English is superb,' said Alain. He indicated that he wanted the bill. 'He says the critics were marvellous.'

'But it is only in English!' said Isabel. 'When will it be translated?'

It had been rejected by three French publishers and Natasha was sore on the subject.

'These things take time, Isabel.'

'Patience, Isabel,' said Alain. 'Or read English.'

'Joseph's books are not in French either,' said Isabel, 'it's too bad.'

'I am going to see the swimmers,' said Alain.

'We will stay here out of the sun,' said Isabel, 'I have been waiting for you to go.'

'You see how I am treated by my wife?' said Alain. 'I am not appreciated.'

'Go away. I want to talk to Natasha.'

They watched his elegant figure saunter out of the cool restaurant, put on his English Panama hat and turn towards the swimming pool.

'Now then, *chérie*,' said Isabel, 'what is it . . .?'

Alain watched Joseph and Marcelle with keen pleasure. At this time on the hot Provençal afternoon the pool attracted only the hardiest, the town boys and girls, the sons and daughters of the peasant families, children and adolescents exploiting their freedom while parents took a siesta before calling them back to help with the perpetual work. Joseph seemed so at home there, Alain observed, and nodded to himself at that observation, proving as it did his theory of 'reversion to type'. He winced at the amount Joseph exposed himself to the sun but he was among equals in sun worship around the pool. Only Alain and a couple of others near his age took advantage of the rather tatty municipal parasols.

Joseph was teaching Marcelle to swim at the shallow end, holding her tenderly under the belly, telling her to kick out her legs, to pull with the arms, or Alain assumed that was the case. Then they would stop and he would hoist her onto his shoulders and stride into deeper water where he would throw her high in the air and she would shriek with joy, spread-eagled against the sky, seeming to hang motionless for a moment before falling down into his strong grasp and shouting, 'Again! Again!' They waved at Alain and he felt both sad and happy at the pleasure this surrogate family brought him.

'He swims like an otter,' he said to Isabel as they had their last drink before bed. The doors were still wide open onto the deep Southern warmth of Provence. The sound of the crickets cascaded into the room.

'She is not happy, Alain.'

'It will pass.'

'How can you say that?'

'The first forty years of marriage are always unhappy.'

'Alain!'

'Unhappiness may be our basic condition.'

'She sees a psychoanalyst.'

'That makes everyone unhappy.'

'You are impossible! Joseph, also, sees a psychoanalyst.'

'That,' said Alain and he paused, his tone changed, 'is not good.'

'You see!'

'Not the two of them.' Alain took a sip of the whisky. 'What did she tell you?'

'Nothing serious. What do you expect? For someone of Joseph's type, London is a box of chocolates.'

'He is young.'

'I agree. So does Natasha. Basically she feels that he is doing so many new things and fears he may be out of control.'

'He is having a success,' said Alain. 'Natasha may find that difficult. History repeats itself. Look at her mother and Louis.'

'I hadn't considered that,' said Isabel. She took another cigarette and shivered slightly. 'I hadn't considered that at all.' She drew deeply on the cigarette. 'Could you close the door, my sweet, soon there will be a breeze coming down from the mountains.'

At La Rotonde itself, the little fort on the peak of the village, Natasha and Joseph sat close and looked at the stars, bright, diamond, beguiling. It was time they meandered back down the hill but neither wanted to leave this Crusaders' rallying point. Joseph's mind was tired: it felt heavy as if he had a severe cold combined with a severe hangover; it felt deadened.

Natasha, the red tip of her cigarette the only point of light in the near darkness, was struggling against the feeling of loss at her absence from her analyst. She had not discussed this with Joseph. He did not take well to discussion of analysis but it would have helped if she knew that he too was suffering from this summer-vacation withdrawal. Her analyst had warned her she would, as on previous occasions, but it was worse this time. Natasha reasoned herself through it. They would be back in London in about a week and merely a week after that they would be back in analysis. One day at a time.

'Remember when I said we should stay here and live here?'

'Yes,' said Natasha. It had been circling in her mind too and she smiled at the coincidence: they could still be twin souls.

'We should have done it,' he said.

'Look at what you would have missed, Joseph.'

'We should have done it.'

'What do you say? "It's never too late."'

'But it is,' he said.

She could find nothing to say in reply.

—◊◊◊—

425

The first time it hit him with its full force was on Shepherd's Bush underground station. He had been to see friends at the BBC to discuss the possibility of working on a new arts magazine programme. Lunch in the bar had been noisy, beery, full of gossip with old pals, worlds away from his solitudes. He envied what he might have been had he stayed in the BBC and left the bar cheerful at the prospect that he might in some way rejoin that communal part of his past.

Shepherd's Bush Central Line station was all but deserted on the autumn afternoon. He did not have long to wait for the train.

As he heard it come closer through the tunnel it was as if a massive magnetic force began to pull him towards the edge of the platform, drawing him towards the tracks, overwhelming his resistance, and as the noise grew louder the strength of the pull grew and he found himself swaying, helpless, about to be taken fatally forward by it and then the train broke out of the tunnel and charged towards him. He backed away, he had to push himself back, against nothing but air but it took all his will, all his might to back away until he met the wall and pressed himself against it as the train braked loudly to a stop. The doors opened. He could not move. The doors closed. He waited until the train had gone. Keeping close to the wall he found the exit and took the stairs. The grey light of day made him blink. He would find a bus. He looked around at the strange world which was the same as the world before he had gone underground.

That was how it began.

CHAPTER THIRTY-SEVEN

There was only one course of action and he had to take it. He held onto that. He waited for the bus, saw it draw up, made no move, saw it pull off and then began to walk into Central London.

The city air seemed uniquely oppressive. He stopped at every crossing and looked right, left, right again, remembering the childhood code, and then he would repeat the movements and only when it was completely clear would he cross the road, carefully, like an old man uncertain of his balance. He walked slowly up the gentle gradient to Notting Hill Gate and then the length of the Bayswater Road to Marble Arch. He thought he might go into Hyde Park in the hope that it might begin the healing he had ascribed to the effect of the countryside which he had sought as an adolescent when in similar fear of being unhinged. But the space was too alien. He might find himself isolated. He sheared away from that. Here in the streets there were people everywhere who could be called on.

He passed Tyburn and tried to re-activate his shocked mind by remembering who had been hanged there after having been drawn and quartered and dragged out of the city in the Elizabethan golden age, but he could not call up the energy. He walked on, the gentle gradient now downhill as he went the full length of Oxford Street, until he arrived at Tottenham Court Road tube station. There, without breaking step, he went down, back into the underground. Sam would have told him he had to do this.

It was difficult not to scream.

The platform was much busier than it had been at Shepherd's Bush and he stood pressed to the wall, protected by those in front. The same

427

complete draining of himself occurred as the sound of the train came out of the black tunnel and despite the protective cordon of travellers he felt compelled once more to hurl himself onto the tracks. It was as if his mind disintegrated. He could feel it inside his skull. But he held on and when the doors opened he prised himself from the wall and went into the lighted carriage. He stood, by the door, rather than take a seat though several were available.

Hampstead underground station is near the crest of the hill and was said to have the deepest lift shaft in London. He remembered that.

The lift was already full and he could have waited for the next one or taken the stairs which is what he most wanted to do. A sense of claustrophobia came out of the lift as pungent as a smell of sulphur. He had not to be a coward. He squeezed himself in.

As the lift clanked its interminable out-of-date way up the shaft and the silent crowd of people pressed it seemed more and more anxiously against each other Joe thought he might suffocate. He seemed to have forgotten how to breathe. The lift went up slowly and Joe feared it might stop. Then what could he do? His mouth snatched small bits of the air. The lift would never arrive at the surface. He felt he might drown in dizziness. It moved so very slowly. He caught someone's eye and immediately looked away. They might see into him. He looked down at his shoes, head bowed, an attitude of prayer.

Never was London pavement more welcome but he did not know where to go. He was afraid of everything and everywhere. The Heath was too dauntingly empty and natural and he might go mad in what at this moment seemed its vastness. A coffee bar or a pub were out of the question: someone might talk to him. He was not fit to go home. He trawled up and down the High Street and Heath Street, walking slowly, making sure always to be near people, hoping he would meet no one he knew.

Above all he had to conceal this condition. Yet the strain of both bearing it and concealing it could crush him into a collapse he knew he must avoid.

Time devoted to writing her novel had become a sanctuary. Her analyst had suggested it was entirely a therapeutic activity. Natasha demurred although unusually she could find no substantial arguments to back up her objection and certainly when she told the analyst in any detail what she had written the subsequent silence had a quality of QED.

'Hector,' she explained, 'shares a room with Clément in the asylum. He accepts that Clément is now Father Lointier and adopts him. He becomes a self-appointed protector to Clément and claims him as his best friend. Hector has been an officer in the navy and constantly makes meticulous drawings of ships, scores of them, brilliantly accurate. But he is also obsessed by his wife who, he believes, drove him into the asylum. You said I might read you a passage if I wanted to. I thought that you wanted to more than I did,' Natasha smiled, a smile unnoticed, and opened the notebook. 'Hector has been talking about how at first he had missed his wife, and Clément – Father Lointier – says,' she read:

' "You missed your wife, Monsieur Hector, that's sad."

' "Sad, no! It was pure imbecility. She admitted, once on a visit, that she missed me too. 'Life isn't the same without you, I miss you, Totor,' she said, and it made me laugh. It isn't often that Coralie made me laugh, but that time, I laughed . . . Naturally, she could have been lying just to impress the nurse, but I think such considerations were well above her by then. I am fairly sure she missed me. No one to bully all day long, no one to persecute, well . . . she missed me and she absolutely hated me, so there we are . . . Nostalgia is just one of those human characteristics, which is not to say that Coralie was human . . . primates have human characteristics too, they peel bananas before eating them, for instance. Anyhow, that woman hated me and she missed me after packing me off to a loony bin, and I missed her although she had driven me out of my mind. Human failure, Father, that's what it is in my opinion. If you hate someone, they should disintegrate out of your consciousness altogether. If you hate a relationship, it should become a blank."

"You shouldn't hate anyone," Father Lointier said.

'That's enough,' Natasha said. 'I chose that passage especially for you!'

The analyst stayed silent for some time and in the silence Natasha thought she might have over-tempted providence.

'Why did I read that to you?' she said. 'I don't want to waste our time talking about Hector's babble. Now that I have read it I wish I had not. I wish I had kept it for myself alone. If we discuss it there will be nothing sacred to me alone and I need that. And yet it was I who brought it to you. I don't want you to talk about it. Yet I offered it to you. No one should know anything about it until it is finished and ready. I ask you not to talk about it. I have made a mistake.'

It was only rarely that the analyst permitted herself a question.

'Why do you think you made a mistake?'

'I think I used the wrong word,' said Natasha. 'Not only the wrong word, the wrong explanation. It is a gift. I have brought you a gift, possibly the most precious I could bring you. And you will want to know why I have brought you this gift, or any gift, although you are unlikely to ask another question. Gifts are partly to placate but I do not think I need to placate you. Gifts are gratitude and I am grateful but that is taken care of in the fee you charge. Gifts can be evidence of the richness of the giver and that might be the answer, to show you that whatever I bring you there is more that is just mine, beyond this place, beyond us.' She paused. 'I do not think any of those are right in this case,' she said. 'I think this gift was to cheer you up, to answer the sadness in your voice, the burdens of others you carry. It is my way to help you.'

Just as the analyst could not have observed Natasha's smile earlier, so Natasha could not observe the expression near to tears on the face of the analyst. She took her time.

'What you have said together with what you read to me are very important, Natasha.'

Natasha almost sat up and looked around. This was the first time the analyst had used her name.

'I will respect what you say about your novel. But you have told me that you believe I need the help of a gift from you. An important line has been crossed here. In essence, we will talk about this further in the next session, in essence you are becoming the analyst. This is a critical stage. You are now employing what you have learned in an apparently simple but a profound way in yourself but showing me directly how strong you are. This is a moment of turning. We have to be careful here. This is new and extremely fragile . . . I thank you for your gift . . .'

—〰—

'I spoke to the analyst about what had happened to me,' Joe told Marcelle, 'but no one else. I felt that Natasha was burdened enough. More likely I was embarrassed, most likely ashamed of it. In some ways I still am, more than thirty years on.

'Even to the analyst it was difficult to explain because the attacks quickly moved from being a series of incidents to become the prevailing condition of my mind. The specific and frightening incidents continued to happen: on the underground, or looking out of a window high up in a building, or sometimes walking along a traffic-heavy street, this tidal pull towards self-destruction. Each time it had to be withstood and battled through. Each time left me dizzy and weakened.

'But the spread of it, the way it infected all that I thought and did every minute was even harder to endure. It was as if whatever it was that held and contained the brain and protected it even against the skull had wept away.

'It would take another book, Marcelle, so let it rest on these points. The fear that I had forgotten how to breathe became more intense, especially at night. I would lie awake and force myself to breathe in and breathe out but that is not the whole picture, for the truth is that even when I forced myself there were times when nothing happened until a gasp of air would be inhaled or ejected by whatever that deeply planted biology within us is that will hold onto life until there is no hope at all.

'So there must have been some hope. It did not feel like it, for time and again, when I was in a script conference or discussing the new television series or in a restaurant with a few friends or in a theatre I would be aware most of all of this terror clawing at me, pulling me into its belly, this threat of darkness, closing around my mind. What I said and did on those occasions was so distant from what I was, I truly don't

431

know how I endured it. Whatever else I was doing, my fullest effort was to survive. At any moment, I felt I could crack up.

'Then there was another dimension. Time became so stretched, so unbearably extended. Five minutes could last an hour. This attack at night crawled like a snail. A night could take a month to pass by.

'As I remember, the analyst talked a lot about total control and losing control: I'm sure he said more than that but I find it difficult to remember. It is as if the struggle to conceal this condition from everyone but him and to continue though with far less energy to do the work I did was so difficult that it wiped out most of the resources of memory. More possibly, like any other fierce pain, once surmounted, it fades so that we do not carry anything like the full weight of it even in recollection. We need to be lightened and freed to move on.

'It went on at its most intense for months. Every day and most of the night. Years later when I was talking about this to James, who by then had become a psychotherapist, he said he thought that both of us, Natasha and I, around that time were in or verged closely on a state of what he called "clinical depression".'

Flailing about him as he struggled to hold Natasha, Marcelle and himself together, Joe decided to work Natasha's first novel into a film script. No one had commissioned it and he did not tell her about it in case he failed to complete it. *The Glory of Elizabeth* was in production and Joe was on standby to rush to the location and adjust the lines, but there was ample free time. His wish to start a new novel was strong but so far he had made pages of notes without arriving anywhere near a point of departure. His state of mind was too wounded and depleted to allow him to reach down into the wells from which the fiction might be drawn. But he had to work. Indeed the greater the fears and pain the more urgently he needed the structure and diversion of work however he felt when it came to do it. *The Unquiet Heart* was the perfect project and he still wanted to please and to impress Natasha.

They lay in bed trying to sleep. The windows were open although the night was not very warm and the noisiest hour in the street tended to be this, the post-pub run. But Natasha insisted the windows stayed open – 'This is where you moved and this is what you must live with,' she said, again.

Natasha lay on her back finding some comfort. The pain in her lower spine had not diminished and on some days she limped.

The comparative ease of her body seemed to release a flutter of thoughts, like a flock of rooks suddenly rising from a tree and spreading into the air. Her analyst had decided to take a longer summer holiday and broken the treatment earlier in the week. Natasha was already missing her and, as in much else, envied the better luck of Joseph whose analyst stuck to the old rules of vacation. She tried not to feel this longer break as a slight deliberately aimed at her and knew such a conclusion was foolish and yet she felt her resentment held some truth.

She tried to switch to thoughts on her novel. It would not be difficult to engineer the happy ending she wanted with Clément returning to the farm restored to his old self. Hector, she thought, could be her instrument in this. She must find something startling for him to do, something that would jolt Clément out of this adopted personality. He did not deserve an unhappy ending, he was too weak. Only the strong should suffer on their own account in fiction, she thought, tragedy was wasted on the frail.

These two lines of thought were not difficult to pursue. What most fascinated her were the little flashes of light – illuminations of memory or traces of insight, elusive, puzzling, each one a will-o'-the-wisp; a sheaf of lavender, the black swans in full sail, her father laughing with Isabel; but most of them so fleeting they did not even bring an image with them, mere pulses between the stars she could recognise, messages from the dark, infinitely small particles of energy which she longed to grasp and felt that once known could complete the puzzle of herself. Out of the dark, in the uneasy bedroom, Natasha said:

'How can psychoanalysis claim to know how the mind works?' She paused to make sure she had caught Joseph's attention. 'How can this one method with its few rules and systems based on so little logical evidence be so arrogant as to demand we accept that it has the key to life?'

'But we do accept it,' said Joseph, puzzled at her switch to arguments he had used against her zealotry. 'For the time being anyway, we both accept it.'

'Proust has a far better idea of how the mind works. Or the neuroscientists my father was telling us about.'

'Why are you suddenly so angry about psychoanalysis?'

'Why do you have to interpret an objection as anger?'

'You are putting your life in its hands.'

'That does not mean,' said Natasha, 'that I cannot criticise it.'

Joseph laughed gently and said no more. The laughter made them feel a little closer to each other, a condition becoming more rare. He wanted to tell her about the film script of her novel but held back. He wanted to talk on. 'When I was in Oxford Julia reminded me of the two paintings you did, for that exhibition, just after we met, the two you wouldn't sell.' He reached out for her hand.

'The two best ones,' she said.

'Yes. She still has them. Why didn't we ever pick them up?'

'I like to think of them there,' said Natasha. 'In that house. Like us. Like your head.'

'I looked at them,' he said. 'And I think that they've changed places.'

Natasha waited.

'The Icarus figure, sort of based on me, was also, I thought, supposed to be a warning to me. The other figure, based on you, being clawed into the depths was somehow your fears of the past. But it isn't like that any more.' He felt the closeness of her attention. 'You are Icarus, you are the one always going for the truth, flying as high as you can, taking risks with yourself. While I feel I'm being clawed down by my past, whatever parts of it I can produce in the analysis.'

'I disagree totally,' said Natasha. 'They are still as they were and they are also only paintings, not biographies.'

'But surely the meaning of a painting can change as circumstances change?'

'Not those paintings.'

'. . . it was just a thought.'

'Before I die,' said Natasha, 'I would like to know what thought is.' The conversation was over.

Miraculously soon, it seemed to Joseph, Natasha's breathing became deep and even. He felt alone. His throat began to choke dryly but he did not want to cough and wake her up. He swallowed, but in doing that the muscles inside his throat seemed to seize up. He opened his mouth and told himself to catch the air, out of the darkness, it was in the darkness, how could this invisible darkness make him live? His head prickled with multiple stabs of anxiety . . . He looked at his watch. Still only ten minutes to twelve. A night could take so long and whenever he woke there was still far to go.

CHAPTER THIRTY-EIGHT

When at last the morning came for her to go back to her analyst, Natasha realised how hard it had been to hold out. The melting together of so many sensations, provoked by this summer separation, had become a lumpen mass of anger, grief, resentment, dismay, disappointment, fear, fear above all, and it grew inside her, a weight, a ravenous feeder on energy, something that had to be removed before it took the life out of her.

She was early. She had taken care with her appearance. She was excited. The large uncared-for hall and the stairs covered with a faded navy blue carpet were home. She ascended to the first floor, slowly, to squeeze every ounce of pleasure from this imminent reunion. There was so much she wanted to say, so much, she had realised on her journey into the city, that she had achieved alone in that tormenting period apart. She had survived it, that was the main thing. And although she carried this burden, it would be dissolved when they talked. There was even a sense, as she took the curve in the grand staircase in what had once been a wealthy and fashionable town house, that this would be the beginning of the end, that her course was nearly run, that one more year would see her through and free and whole and with all her life in her hands at last.

The notice was pinned to the waiting-room door with a brass tack. In clear neat handwriting it read, 'Patients are asked to call . . .' followed by a number.

Natasha went down the stairs and onto the mid-morning early September London streets even relishing this delay. She was utterly calm, still buoyant in the mood of anticipated release. It was a dull morning but the clouds were high and still and the light grey colour suited these formal streets, she thought, these terraces of riches so placid, an insulated island at the heart of the seething city. She loved too the quietness of the people as they walked or more often strolled with a purpose but with no unsettling urgency. She too strolled until finally she discovered a phone box and entered its small and isolated little space with keen curiosity.

When she came out she was breathing deeply and with difficulty. She leaned against the wall and thought on how to pull herself together. There was a rose garden in Regent's Park not far from the northern end of Harley Street. With slow steps, almost faltering, she made for it. When she got there she found a bench, sat down with deep weariness, took out a cigarette and would have appeared to any onlooker to be looking calmly, this distinguished woman, and rather curiously at the rose bushes on which so recently so many flowers had bloomed.

Tim insisted that Joe give him lunch at the Garrick Club. One of Joe's reservations lay in the existence of a strictly implemented club rule that no business be done on club premises. Tim was meeting him for business, business which had been initiated by Joe. Joe was nervous, not helped when Tim arrived without a tie and expressed over-loud thanks to the porter who produced three rather shrivelled specimens, one of which Tim declared to be 'superb'.

They walked up the wide staircase to the bar and Tim insisted that Joe become guide and curator. He stopped in front of so many of the paintings that Joe feared they might arrive at the bar too late. The painting of 'Master Betty' intrigued him most especially when Joe explained, he hoped accurately, that this boy actor had been such a prodigy at the end of the eighteenth century that both Houses of Parliament had adjourned to allow the members to attend a performance. 'What a movie!' said Tim, and then insisted on looking at the cabinet of curios.

The bar was jostling full and friendly as always. Joe had entered the club not only at the bottom of the ladder but outside the pale. Now he

437

went in with sufficient confidence and the anticipation of courteous acquaintanceship from the fleet of Garrick lunchtime regulars. Tim ordered champagne because he had heard it was served in cool silver tankards. They were soon in conversation with a publisher and an actor whom Tim knew better than Joe did, as was the case with several of those they met. They talked the news of the day. Unconsciously, perhaps, the tradition of the original coffee house, which had begat this and other clubs like it two centuries before, was still carried on.

In the grand dining room, the Coffee Room, surrounded by Zoffany's portrayals of famous actors in famous plays of his day, they were taken to a side table. Down the middle of the room was the Long Table, glistening with polish like all the others, but reserved for members whose duty, Joe told a questioning Tim, was to talk to whoever they sat next to.

'You can't smoke until two o'clock,' said Joe as they sat down and, still in the character of curator, 'there has to be no sign of any business being done. No papers, nothing like that.'

'So the script stays on the deck.'

'Yes.'

'Who am I,' said Tim, 'to question the customs of centuries? But we can still talk turkey?'

'Yes,' Joe said. 'Hypocrisy is acceptable.'

'I like that! More like the old you. You've been a bit down lately.'

There was always now a gallop of impatience in Joe's head these days when he was in company. He wanted it to be over. But he held on. It had been fine so far – the familiarity and the unthreatening distractions of the club, the precise knowledge of what he could do in the next couple of hours and the known quantity of Tim had helped him to keep the threats at bay. To be told that he looked 'a bit down' threw him. No one must know.

'I'm fine,' he said.

'Probably not enough sex,' said Tim, newly hitched after his divorce. But Joe would not play. 'Sex sorts you out like nothing on earth. I've always thought you needed more of it. Being you. As I know you, that is. I'll start,' he said to one of the Garrick's uniformed waiters, Jenkins, who stood unsmiling, 'with your Morecombe Bay shrimps followed by your steak and kidney pie, all the trimmings.'

'Smoked eel please,' said Joe, 'and calf's liver. Thank you'

'The house red will do me,' said Tim.

'A carafe of the club claret, sir?' Jenkins looked at Joe who nodded. 'Isn't that the Foreign Secretary over there?'

Guardedly, Joe looked.

'He's with that journalist, what's his name, from *The Times*, what's his name? Corridors of power, Joe, this is where it all happens.'

Does it? Joe did not want to engage. Did it?

Already there was the pull which drew him from even such amiable banter. He needed solitude to see this attack through, if indeed he ever could get through it. Yet he also needed company. Every path bifurcated before him.

'The script of her book,' said Tim after the first course and two glasses. 'Shall I whisper?'

'Don't be daft.'

'It doesn't work. That is, it doesn't work for me. It feels too rushed but then I thought maybe it's too French. You've made it very spare.'

'She writes sparely.'

'But this is a script, Joe, it needs a bit of meat, a bit of colour, a bit of encouragement for the poor old director. Those shrimps were the best I've had for a while. What do you think?'

'Obviously I think it's OK. It will have to be worked on but what doesn't?'

'Maybe it's too continental for my taste. I like the location – who wouldn't want to shoot a film in Brittany? But the story's so . . . French. If you get very lucky somebody like Truffaut might do it, although he likes to do his own stuff, or one of the newer ones. It would have to be translated of course, but Natasha could do that.'

Joe wanted to put up a fight but it was beyond him.

'So you don't think it's worthwhile sending around?'

'Don't take my word,' said Tim. 'Mind you, I think you could have a good shot at it yourself. Saul might back you.'

'That's not for me.'

'Look. I don't think your heart was in it. It's too literary for what we do here. It might work in la France but who knows, and who knows how to crack the Frenchies? Sorry.'

It was as well, he thought, he had said nothing to Natasha. The gift would be ungiven and unmentioned. He knew he had not the energy to pursue it further. Maybe it had never been more than a gesture.

'Thanks.' The main course arrived. 'How's Elizabeth?'

'Elizabeth,' said Tim, 'will fly.'

Afterwards Joe decided to walk up to Hampstead. It would take him about an hour. The walk would do him good. He had nothing better to do. It was a fine early autumn day. No need to take the underground. There were even more excuses he made as he headed out of Central London thinking he might diverge through Soho, wondering why he felt he would disintegrate all the time, wondering how it had come to this.

—ɯ—

Natasha went back to copy down the phone number. Only when she was in the house, facing the stairs, did she remember that she had already copied down the number, it was in her coat pocket. But she stood there, looking up towards the high roof with its grubby cupola, the stairs winding in a gentle spiral, stood there as long as she dared, an intruder now, no place for her now. It was in its way a tribute, the silent lingering, a time of remembrance and pause before the terrible con-sequences enveloped her.

She wanted to go to Kew to see Margaret and the others or just sit in the Gardens but she needed to get back to pick up Marcelle from the nursery school. Perhaps after she had collected Marcelle they could go together. Marcelle loved seeing her Kew friends and the trip on the train was always an adventure. The relief Natasha felt when crossing the river was matched by the pleasure Marcelle took in rushing around her earliest haunts. When they left Kew, however, no matter how she tried, Natasha could not subdue a feeling of sadness and some grievance. Yet Marcelle was just as eager to return to her new place with the new friends. Joseph too liked Hampstead. It was only her.

As Natasha left the house in Welbeck Street for the last time and again searched out a telephone box she thought she might faint. She held onto a black iron railing while the swoon of weakness went through her. She supposed these were some of the symptoms of shock.

She phoned the number again and received the same information. She tried to prise out more, she wanted more detail, more facts, more background, information of any sort, but the kind and measured voice repeated that there was nothing more to say. She was the one who had to bring the brief conversation to a close. She told Natasha gently that she had to put down the phone. She did so and left Natasha stranded, phone in hand, the droning sound still compelling her to listen, at least the sound reminded her of contact.

The walk to Oxford Circus underground, the waiting for the tube, the change at Tottenham Court Road, the pretty red-tiled walls of Hampstead Station and the long clanking lift to the surface passed as in a trance. She could not bear to go home and took Marcelle to a small Italian restaurant, a favourite of Joseph's, where the waiters spoiled the little girl and teased her playfully as she battled with spaghetti. Natasha drank several cups of coffee and barely touched her food.

It was Joseph she needed, she realised, and needed him so much that it scared her to admit it. For he was distant from her now, on his own journey, a journey she had set him on. If she told him what had happened it would throw too much responsibility on him and besides there was in her that which did not want this fact known to anyone else in the world.

She was quieter than usual, the waiters agreed. Very deep, though, this one, a thinker. And with an outward mask intact and imperturbable, Natasha let days and then weeks pass as she sought to find a way out, afraid she was about to collapse but unable to cry for help. Why had the analyst not left her a message? Anything. Even just 'goodbye'.

On Tuesdays and Fridays she caught the tube into London at the same time as before. She found places to have coffee and tried to read books on psychology though her mind merely skimmed the page, taking in scarcely anything. Writing was even harder: writing in her state emphasised the isolation, reached into the same depths as depression and needed support from a wholeness to which she did not now have any access.

What a lonely woman despite husband and daughter and friends; what a disturbed, even distraught woman despite the material comforts, the knowledge she had, the life apparently available; yet she gave no outward sign, steady as a soldier under fire, telling no one, concealing most carefully from Joseph as he concealed his turbulence from her, telling no one, trying also to be steady under fire. So they lived in those few months approaching Christmas seeking to protect each other, seeking to protect themselves, together, apart, together . . . Further, further apart.

'When, much later,' he wrote to Marcelle, 'you by then already a woman, with your own vocation, you were questioning me closely, I told you of the death of the analyst. You were at first struck still and speechless and then you were possessed by fury.

'"Nothing after the phone call?"

'"Not that I know of."

'"Nobody to help her find somebody else?"

'"No. That I do know."

'"Just left her."

'You swayed as you sat, upright, clenched, but you swayed like a slender birch in a fierce wind.

'"Why did the analyst not pull out when she knew she was ill herself? She was no longer capable. She must have known. Why did she continue to treat my mother? Why did she not get help for her? Why did other psychiatrists not help her patients? Who are these people? Who are they to walk away from somebody they have dismantled just as much as a surgeon opens up a body? Would a surgeon just walk away halfway through an operation? Would he not get somebody else to take over? She above all people must have known that the mind and the spirit need just as much attention as the body. Oh, oh, my poor mum. What did she do to you? And what could you do?"'

'I have to tell you,' his analyst said, 'that Natasha telephoned me yesterday and asked if she could see me. She meant in a professional capacity. I had to explain why that was impossible. She wanted me to change my mind and she made a jolly good attempt at it. But it is out of the question. I hope you understand that.'

'Yes.'

Joe was puzzled but not enough to pursue it with the analyst, not enough to mention it to Natasha. It was her initiative, she would mention it if she thought fit. So he began once more to offer to the analyst what he always thought of as his inadequate evidence. But at last he needed to talk about what was happening to him, he needed this listener.

Yet even after this session, he thought, nothing of great consequence had happened, nothing new revealed, nothing solved, only this persisting sense of a fraudulent encounter. Even now he could not give the analyst what he knew he most wanted. He had produced only one dream. In it he had murdered and buried a girl very like the little girl he had befriended in the yard of minute cottages in Water Street where he had lived for his first few years. He had befriended this girl who had died of tuberculosis. In the dream he feared that the body would be discovered and then . . . But that could not be spun out further and besides it could lend itself to so many different interpretations, Joe thought – was it that girl? Could it be Natasha? – that it was of little or no use.

He walked quickly up to Regent's Park. He was relieved that the bench he had found after the previous session was again vacant. He sat near the middle and took out the small hardback edition of the *Faber Book of Modern Verse* edited by Michael Roberts. He had bought it in Oxfam for ninepence. Before he opened it he held it in both hands, closed his eyes and murmured:

'No worst, there is none. Pitched past pitch of grief
More pangs will, schooled at forepangs, wilder wring.'

He stopped there. He had to take it slowly. The next four lines were the hardest to remember. 'Comforter . . .' He had it! On he went. Each line remembered was a pebble in the dam he must build to stop this flood drowning his mind. The second stanza he spoke out loud:

> 'O the mind, mind has mountains; cliffs of fall
> Frightful, sheer, no-man-fathomed. Hold them cheap
> May who ne'er hung there. Nor does long our small
> ˙Durance deal with that steep or deep. Here! creep,
> Wretch, under a comfort serves in a whirlwind: all
> Life death does end and each day dies with sleep.'

He looked around the gardens, neat and ordered even in their autumn melancholy. No one was near him this mid-morning.

He had discovered the healing of poetry and crept under it, though how and why he did not know. Nor did he know how he had arrived at the decision to attempt to learn it by heart. Once that course was taken it was as if he made a vow to himself, a vow which to break would be to break him, that he must learn poems by heart. Only by forcing himself to hold these words in his mind could there be any hope of a recovery. The exhaustion of his resources was near, he thought: he could not much longer withstand the battery of panics and fears, this unleashed inferno, this laying waste. The poems would be a shield to hold over him, maybe even in some inconceivable future, to let him advance, but he dare not think about a future. To be the comfort that served in the whirlwind. Gerard Manley Hopkins knew. What a blessing that was, Joe had thought, when he had found it: thank God Gerard Manley Hopkins knew and thank God he wrote it down.

He turned over a couple of pages and found Yeats. 'An Irish Airman Foresees His Death'. It was short, like the Hopkins: it should be manageable. The real victory would be not only to remember the Yeats the next day but to be able to call up the Hopkins and the other poems also. He began to read.

> I know that I shall meet my fate
> Somewhere among the clouds above;
> Those that I fight I do not hate,
> Those that I guard I do not love . . .

Eventually he rose to go and walked north the length of Regent's Park, and up Primrose Hill where he stopped and turned and looked across London, such a broad and unperturbed sprawl it seemed even from this small height, nothing there to harm anybody. So why did it make him want to fly away? He opened the book.

> I balanced all, brought all to mind,
> The years to come seemed waste of breath,
> A waste of breath the years behind
> In balance with this life, this death.

On a weekend in late October, Joseph and Marcelle went to Reading leaving Natasha behind. She had a heavy cold which gave her a bronchial-sounding cough. She assured Joseph that he was doing her a favour. She would spend most of the two days in bed. The house was warm. She would take hot drinks and the medicine prescribed. They went on the Saturday morning.

All day she was in her dressing gown, unbathed, smoking, little food, coffee after coffee, in the evening hot whisky, one only. She sat on the chaise longue in Joseph's small study. It was the warmest room in the house and, Natasha thought, the cosiest: Joseph, she thought, had a real talent for making a place cosy, the clutter of it, a portrait of himself at his best, as she had loved him and still did in this frightening interlude, and still would when both of them came through.

Natasha rarely cried. Her griefs were dry-eyed, the tears buried too deep to be summoned. Now, as the evening closed in, as the room darkened and she did not put on the lights, as the bookshelves, the paintings and prints and curios turned to shadows of themselves, ghosting the walls, she felt the tears on her cheeks and the tears unloosed her.

Why had her analyst done this? Why had she not asked for help? She was her friend, she was trusted by her and trusted her totally. Natasha had put herself at her mercy and now she was without friend, confidante, analyst, healer. She had wanted to be like her, responding, helping, curing: that voice, disembodied, the voice which alone answered to her own depths, called out to her in her wilderness, was gone for ever. Now she wept more and bent her head over her knees and put both hands behind her neck, wrapping herself around, trying to hold back this eruption of grief. Her friend, her guide, her analyst, her hope was gone. How could she survive alone when so many truths and secrets and unfinished work had been ripped away from her? She had no right to leave her like this. She had not done her duty! And yet . . . Natasha now remembered the recent accretion of sorrow in her analyst's voice . . . she ought to have picked it up at the time and found a way to help . . . she remembered the strain of emotion in her words in those last sessions . . . Yet how could she not tell her? It was not right that she be abandoned without warning. It was unjust.

But, oh! She had loved her so much, the patience, the care, the reaching out; and always there, always ready for her, always there for her, trying to make her better. So much had been given. Poor woman. So unimaginably unhappy. So filled with unhappiness. Poor healing woman, dead.

'An overdose,' the measured voice on the telephone had said, and gone no further. 'An overdose.'

Natasha sobbed until she was utterly exhausted and stayed in the study throughout the night.

CHAPTER THIRTY-NINE

'What do you think of it?'

Natasha had been drowsing after reading Christina Rossetti and some of the poems in Christina Blake's new publication. Joseph had bought the book for her as a birthday present. He wanted to arrange a dinner for Christina and Edward with Natasha and himself. Natasha was not fond of Edward and Joseph had hoped the American woman's poetry would intrigue her enough to unfreeze an animosity which puzzled him.

He stood just inside the doorway of the small first-floor living room, comfortingly lit by the three artful side lamps Natasha had bought in the antique emporium in the High Street. It was a room at its best at night, she thought, when the curtains blocked out the street and the magpie purchases, the oak chest, the rugs, the scattering of small antiquities, the prints and paintings and the wall of books were harmonised through her lighting and gave off a sense of a settled, thoughtful life.

'Joseph.' She focused on him and her eyes half closed. 'You are preening yourself, like a cockatoo.'

'But what do you think of it?'

He patted the long dark brown leather coat, which fitted him so well it might have been tailored for him. The design was Italian, the style was totally of the moment, Joseph had never in his life owned or much wanted to own anything as contemporarily classical and absurdly expensive.

'You look like a mannequin,' Natasha said.

'OK. But what about the coat?'

'Fascist,' said Natasha.

'For God's sake! How can a coat be fascist?' He came into the room and, still coated, sat down on the armchair; Natasha lay on the sofa, cushions supporting the small of her back.

'I think I can smell it,' she said. 'It must be the rain.'

'Good leather,' said Joseph, repeating what he had been told, 'has its own aroma.'

'I am impressed.'

'No you're not.'

He stared at her and felt a surge of belligerence.

'It would do you no harm to dress up now and then.'

Natasha looked at the long navy blue skirt, plain, unfashionable, the white blouse for all seasons, the useful cardigan Ellen had bought her for Christmas. A hand went to her rather tangled hair. She wore no make-up in the house and very little at any time. Yet she thought it an odd remark.

'Do we care,' she asked, 'about appearance?'

'Do we care,' he mocked, 'about appearance?'

Joseph slung a leg over the arm of the chair and the long coat opened.

'Oh, God!' she said. 'Are those leather trousers?' and she giggled. On another occasion Joseph might have registered that this was the first expression of joy from his wife for several days and he would have welcomed and probably nourished it.

'What's so funny?'

'Have you been drinking?'

'That's it, isn't it? That's the total argument. If there's something I say you don't like it's "Have you been drinking?" End of interest. A few drinks and anything I say is discounted. You can think even when you drink.' Joseph smiled: the little rhyme tickled him. 'Thinking and drinking are not incompatible.' But the smile, Natasha knew, was not a warm smile and it was not for her.

'You have been drinking.'

'So what? So bloody what?'

Why could he not tell her that drink was medicine? Drink numbed him and he wanted to be numb. Drink gave him confidence, false? It didn't matter, any sort of confidence was good enough the way he was.

Drink slowed down his impatience, slowed down his mind. Drink made him unafraid. And loud and argumentative, yes, and it undid good and necessary constraints and things were said and done which ought to have been left unsaid and undone.

But for that time, that brief time afloat on alcohol, he was transformed into someone he had once been, even though a drunken someone, but not the frightened, timid, internally weeping thing he had become. Even though this someone he had been was a vulgarisation of his old self it was still recognisable as an old real self who was unafraid, who was prepared to take on the world and that was at least something. It was worth it. Even though it led to a sullen dead end and crashed through dear and valued life it was, he knew, for the sake of sanity, worth it. It changed his world and it changed his character and Joseph said amen to that.

'Why did you buy such clothes?'

'I didn't pay a penny for them.'

'I don't understand. They are expensive, aren't they?'

'Saul bought them.'

It had seemed so right, so much fun, they had been walking down Mount Street in Mayfair together and Saul had dropped into one of the new fashionable shops to collect some linen shirts and seen Joseph's expression – amusement, flavoured by slight but unmistakable lust. 'It is a beautiful coat, Joseph,' he said. 'But I expect, Mark, that its future owner thinks so too.'

'Its future owner,' said Mark, a new young success about town who took no trouble to disguise his East End accent, 'done a flit, Saul.'

'Try it on,' said Saul.

'Made for him,' said Mark. 'And there's trousers.'

'He treats you like a little boy,' said Natasha.

'He does not!'

'He takes you to dinner and uses up what you have learned, he leeches on you and takes your precious time and all you get is money we don't really need and now these childish presents that a man would never accept.'

He knew that what she said was true.

'That's ludicrous,' he said, loudly. 'It was just a whim. Why do you have to tear everything down?'

'That's unfair, Joseph.'

'No it isn't! It's just a bloody coat. It was a gift. What's wrong with a gift?'

Natasha paused and remembered her gift to the analyst.

'All gifts are not the same,' she said.

'Typical! Of course they aren't. But they are, as well. Aren't they?'

'Please don't shout, Joseph. It is bad when Marcelle hears you shout.'

'So I shout. People shout. She can't be wrapped in cotton wool. Cotton wool does more harm than shouting any day.'

'How do you know?'

'I remember Bob telling me, "Babies die in a sterile atmosphere." And he's a zoologist.'

'Have you eaten?'

'Yes. No. Yes. Would you like a drink?'

Natasha shook her head. Joseph got out the bottle of whisky from the oak chest.

'I need water,' he said and took the glass to the bathroom.

Natasha put the volume of poetry on the floor. Some of the poems were too painful. Others she thought crude: how could such an early and high reputation be gained on work like this? The more closely she observed the world of literary reputations the more disheartened she felt. She wanted it to be so much purer and better than it was. Great literature to Natasha, even more than great painting or music, ought to be sifted for without rancour, without jealousy, with fine judgement, setting aside what did not serve but doing so in a spirit that understood the difficulty of attaining truth, the value of trying one's best and failing.

The last time she had met Edward, just before he acknowledged Christina publicly as his mistress, Natasha had been depressed by what she thought of as the wicked pleasure he had taken in the political manoeuvrings of Robert Frost. A poet of such stature, she believed, ought to stand aloof, provide in himself an example of the art of poetry as heroes in war provided examples of soldierly courage and daring.

She knew this was a big demand. She knew she lived in times that loved feet of clay as much if not more than minds of crystal. She knew that just as the priest was fallible and would sin so artists were what the English called 'only human' and would scurry around demeaningly for advantage like any other group. She knew she was expecting too much and even denying the variety and richness of nature, its contradictions between frailty and strength, honesty and corruption, tragedy and comedy, its contrariness which was what she valued in much work. Yet her ideal of how the work should be regarded and the intention behind it was rigid and she would not yield, would not, could not. Literature should soar and so should those it engaged, it should seek the sun, nothing less would do. And Christina Blake, she thought, was too knowing, seeking favour and because of that even the celebrated and unarguably powerful poems of distress were a little less than they seemed. Yet there was no denying they were impressive. She wanted to discuss them with Joseph who was very keen on the poems but it would have to wait.

'We never talk now,' she said when Joseph re-entered, minus coat, the brown leather trousers tight-fitting and gleaming in the half-light, a high-necked black sweater, long hair, fatal glass in hand, a picture, she thought, of a romantic poet, a time gone by.

'We never stop.' Once more he cocked his leg over the arm of the chair. Once Natasha would have teased him about this attitude. It rather disturbed her. There was, she thought, a needless defiance in it, a pose unnecessary and unsuitable.

'We were so blind to each other at that crucial time,' Joe wrote to their daughter. 'How in God's name had we come to that pass?'

'We squabble,' she said, 'like old people who have nothing to say to each other but find some comfort in constant complaints.'

'Sometimes silence is better proof of . . .' He stopped.

'Can't you complete the sentence?'

Joseph raised his glass and took too big a sip, she thought.

'When we moved here you said there would be people like us we would meet and make friends with. Where are they?'

The shot of whisky had restored the anaesthetic effect.

'It takes time,' he said. 'You don't just march up and say, "Be my friend." '

'We could have a party.'

'I hate parties. I hate people coming into our house.'

'You used to love them. In Kew you loved them.'

'It's as if you license people to break into your home. Just to roam around and gawp. To spy everything that you are. It's voyeurism! No!'

'Joseph.'

She uttered his name with such despair that he was compelled to dismount from the alcohol-fuelled ride to stupor.

She looked pale and there was about her a pain he did not want to acknowledge because he had so much of his own and yet he knew he ought to reach out to her. His name, her chosen version of his name, was a cry he could not recognise, or would not, afraid perhaps that a full knowledge of her suffering would crush him and so he flinched away, turned tail like an animal evading danger. There was nothing he could say and his name hung in the silence.

'Your mother called my name and I made no answer,' he wrote to Marcelle. 'It would not be too much to say that my silence has run-down the years and has come back time and again as an accusation.

'But why did she not tell me that her analyst was dead and by her own hand? This is not to say that subsequent events might have been significantly different. There's no way of knowing. But not to say anything (and I have scoured the past for any evidence), not to allow there to be a hint, to give me a clue which might have set me off on a search to help her, why did she have to be so stoic and so self-harmfully stubborn? We still loved each other then. There was still no one else, that is no one I had ever for a moment thought of abandoning her for. We were being battered but the ship she had sometimes spoken of in the past, the ship of us was still intact.

'Perhaps in retrospect and because of my own times of helpless dependence, I exaggerate. It could be the case that she felt she had passed through the worst and was now capable of self-analysis. Others have benefited from that process and Natasha was certainly intelligent and determined enough to do it. I'm sure some of that went on. She had studied analysis and read about it widely, much more than I had. Yet I don't think that was the root cause. The total suppression and concealment of the fact of her analyst's death suggest that there was a more important motive.

'There was shame, I believe: that she had failed the analysis and the analyst even though the failure was not her fault. By contrast, as in other areas of our lives, I having arrived late still sailed on. There was fear, as when a small child loses its mother and is afraid of unimaginable punishment because it feels responsible for the death of the mother, even sometimes believing it has killed the mother. Above all, though, I now think there was dread. Something deeper than shame, even deeper than fear, a dread, a look into the void, a blanking out of being which says, "This must never be revealed because for the world to know this would destroy me."

'Or it was love. Her wish not to add to my own unspoken but all too obvious burden. A selfless and gallant act of love. That would be like your mother.'

Natasha began writing Joseph letters. She would leave them on his desk in the study. He replied, every time.

'Dearest Joseph,' she would always begin. 'You are so angry with me now and I can understand it. Your analysis must be in a crucial phase and it is so difficult to concentrate on anything else and yet you do, you work, you work. If only you could stop the work for a year or so, then we could find each other again as we were . . .'

'My dearest Natasha,' he would always begin. 'As once we were? When? I'm not being mean. I can't remember. I'm sure we've been happy. But I can't remember it now. Past happiness doesn't help when you really need it. More than that, I seem to forget it was ever there. And why do you want to go back all of a sudden? You were the one who was so keen to go forward . . .'

'Dearest Joseph. You must face your anger with me without guilt. I know that once we have come through this all will be well and I will follow you to the ends of the earth . . .'

'My dearest Natasha. I am not angry with you. I am angry. If I'm angry with anybody it's me for making so many mistakes. Why do you always tell me what I am? And I don't want to go to the ends of the earth! Here will do . . .'

'Dearest Joseph. There was some humour there which is hopeful. All I want is for you to disentangle yourself from these complications of your past and the undigested pressures of the last few years. I like it that you are learning poetry by heart. I'm sure that's good but even with that you blame yourself because your "target" of one new poem a day has not been met! You must let life flow through you. A real life is like a river. If we interfere too much it becomes a canal . . .'

'My dearest Natasha. I'm sorry I was so rude last night. Maybe I should go away for a while until all this stuff pours out of me but not all over you. But sometimes I fear that we are so far apart and maybe I shout and curse to draw attention and to call you back. I don't know. I have no idea about anything at all, Natasha. But I will try not to force myself to learn one new poem every one or two or even three days and I will, I promise, just be a river! Yet when I close the book and go through the poem and know that I have got it by heart I feel like someone who has been very ill and now takes a few unassisted steps. Of course I exaggerate . . .'

'Dearest Joseph. It is to yourself that you are being hateful although I feel battered also. Are you trying to goad me or have I goaded you? Perhaps we should go north, to the countryside, and begin again . . .'

Joe had suggested this to his analyst. Why don't I just go back to Cumberland, he had said, to the village we stayed in? We could buy a cottage outright. Village life could suit all of us. There's a bit in the bank. We could write, we could walk, in the Lake District we could get away from all the temptations and the greed.

The suggestion had been left hanging in the air and Joe had concluded that it was no more than an attempt to break loose from the analysis which would be cowardly, a retreat, a failure under fire in London and that too could not be lived with.

'My dearest Natasha. Maybe one day we will start again, in France, in Cumberland, somewhere free of this plague which poisons what should be, shouldn't it, a life of good fortune . . . or is our good fortune our bad luck?'

They wrote, sometimes two or three times a day, for dear life.

———∽∽———

He had never drunk so much in a single evening and yet even when they got back home and he sprawled in the chair with a final whisky and a cigar, he felt not only calm but sufficiently clear-headed.

'You look beautiful,' he said.

Natasha smiled. He had insisted that he buy her a new dress for the Gala Preview of *The Glory of Elizabeth* and she had gone for a simple classic line, had a hairdresser put up her hair, applied a little make-up and turned herself into –

'Class,' said Joseph, heavily.

In his hired dinner jacket, velvet bow tie now loosed, a flop of hair on his forehead, the white silk handkerchief ballooning out of his breast pocket, whisky in one hand, cigar in the other, he was a pretender, he knew that, uneasily but arrogantly out of his class.

'You look like a debauched young aristocrat,' she said, to tease him and to please him, and she was smack on the mark. He smiled uneasily, but also smugly. 'One of those young men who sow their wild oats but, what is it? Buckle down in the end. Buckle down.'

'Buckle down . . . you know . . . this is the best bit. This – talk. Now. This – is – the – best – bit.'

'You seemed to be enjoying all of it.'

'You see? You don't know me any more . . . It wasn't that I hated it. I didn't hate it. But I kept thinking I would explode like that puffed-up toad or shout obscenities especially when we were in the line and we all had to shake hands with Princess Margaret. Or when it started I thought I might be carried kicking and screaming out of the cinema – to be trapped in the middle of the row! – do you know that at every moment during the film, at every single moment, all I was thinking, *all*, was, how do I stop myself from going berserk? Calling up the poems.

Isn't that stupid? And sad? But it's true. Now is peace. But a couple of hours ago it was the worst ever. What's the analysis been for? My head just seems to crumble and bleed inside.'

'But you don't show it,' said Natasha, seeing his need for calm. 'Doesn't that make you feel good about yourself?'

He laughed. She was his analyst now. Maybe they were safe in those roles. He felt a sudden lift of confidence.

'What did Saul tell me you said to him? You'd liked the film but it wasn't as good as my novels. And what did he say?'

'He said, "You want him back, Natasha, all French women want their man under their control." '

'And you said?'

'I said, "That is just another fantasy which serves the infinite male ego." '

'That's right. That's what he said. "The infinite male ego." He liked that.'

'I like Saul. I think I understand Saul.' I think, she did not add, I may understand him a little better than you do; your hero worship and over-eagerness to please rob you of insight.

'Still, you shouldn't have said it. And you definitely shouldn't have told Tim's new lady that she was the spitting image of his wife.'

'She is.'

'There are things best left unsaid.'

'Not to Tim.'

'He likes you.'

'No he doesn't. Nor do I want him to.'

'Cheers,' said Joseph and felt the whisky sweet on the tongue. 'Then the party after the film!' he said. 'That was a bit better because I could move around.'

'I didn't,' said Natasha.

'I saw you sitting talking to that – who is he?'

She mentioned the name of a film critic.

'What did he think of it?'

'He liked it.'

'But will he write that?'

'I didn't ask.'

'What did you talk about?'

'Paris, mostly, he's a Francophile.'

'You should've moved around.'

'Why?'

'That's what you do at parties like that. You move around. Was he interesting?' Why was this happening? Why had she not responded to his confession of an attack of madness?

'Yes.'

'So *you* were all right, then.'

'Oh, Joseph!'

'Oh, Joseph.'

'What can we do to be happy again?' she asked and waited for an answer.

Joseph finished the whisky, made the decision not to have another and felt a welling of tears. He stubbed out the cigar.

'I don't know, Natasha. I wish I did. I really wish I did.'

'The film was good,' she said. 'The dialogue was very good. I told that to Saul.'

'Did you? Did you really? Anyway it's the acting that makes films. Not directors. I used to think that. Certainly not writers. The dialogue's . . . I don't know. A pastiche at best.' Suddenly he looked exhausted, she thought, too tired for the night, too tired for his years and for his life.

'You think actors are in control because you can't bear not being in control. That's why you are really a novelist. Novelists can be rulers. But, Joseph, why don't you believe me? You are too strange. When we went to the theatre last week you were angry with me and later you told me it was because of a bad review in the *TLS* which I had not even read. What is it?'

'I don't know,' he said. 'I wish I did . . . the actors make it. They always do. I used to believe in auteurs when we met.'

'You look like an actor,' she said, 'in that dinner jacket.'

'I wanted to be an actor once. Good place to hide.'

We are beginning to talk as we used to, she thought. Her yearning for him grew so strong she wondered that he could not feel the force of it across the silent sidelit room: but he was asleep.

457

For at least an hour Natasha sat and watched over him. She smoked. She scarcely took her eyes off him. She had to learn what had become of him and what he had become. He had become too important to her, she thought, and she must tread very cautiously not to scare him off. He was only a few feet away and yet miles apart from her. The task now was to reel him in. The task now was to meet again. Whatever the bruises she loved him. Whatever his faults and the casual woundings she saw her life in him. She examined him minutely and called up that which had been good between them, summoned up the successes of their past, felt less lonely than she had done for some time in this vigil, postponing and postponing again the time when she must wake him up.

'No worst, there is none.' He had read the poem to her and it was this phrase that looped in her mind. No worst? What if that were true?

PART FIVE

AGAINST THE SUN

CHAPTER FORTY

'Much later,' he wrote to Marcelle, 'Natasha's Kew friends were to say that she had told them that she had begun to like Hampstead. As well as joining up again with James and Howard we met Oliver, who lived in the next street, a friend from Oxford, a man with whom I had been on the university tour of *The Tempest* in Germany. He and his wife had a daughter the same age as Marcelle – that was sufficient for a reunion. Oliver's wife was Polish, a lecturer in East European Studies; he himself had gone into the Treasury. He was a tenor in the Parish Church choir, a trustee of the library. The four of us, or rather the six of us, could have made a unit, a nucleus, a beginning, the first building block, and Oliver, who had been born in Hampstead, was happy to take us into his relaxed, welcoming society.

'The friends in Kew said that although Natasha could have a look of sadness, which was not new, she seemed after two or three months to be reconciled, ready to get to grips with a new life though pleased to keep contact with the old. They knew no more than I what had happened to her analyst. She had shouldered that alone. My own analyst, when he finally learned the truth, said it was "the worst thing an analyst can possibly do to a patient". Yet Natasha found the strength to keep that to herself, which must have eaten away at her. The question recurs for ever. Why did she not let somebody know?

'As for me, Marcelle, I have stressed the drunken oaf and he was certainly one of me. Another was the shivering isolated wretch trying to keep sane through the poetry of others. Another was the man drowning in a lost embrace. But work got done, not with the effectiveness of before, but it got done, and life went on, from the getting up in the morning to the lying down at night, with Natasha beside me, often planets apart as we tried to rest in that bed, our lives on separate tracks and yet still side by side, still able to reach out and touch each other.'

—— ⁊⁊⁊ ——

'Come along,' said Peter, 'you might get some material.'

'I've been out of things for a while now.'

'It's exciting!' Peter Mills summoned his skills of persuasion, outstanding at Oxford when he had won the presidency of the Union, honed with the BBC where he edited a political programme, now finely tuned as he searched for a constituency in which he could stand as a potential Labour MP. But Joe was easily persuaded. He was wax to Peter's seal of purpose. It was as if his character was empty, waited to be animated. And this invitation promised protective company and a chance to slip out of the perpetual, exhausting, unmanly obsession with himself.

They had met outside Bush House where Joe had been recording the book programme on which he appeared intermittently, whilst Peter was revisiting his old department in which he had worked at the same time as Joe.

'Happy days,' said Peter as they walked quickly down the Strand towards Whitehall. Joe nodded. Peter was happy days. They had met several times since he had left the BBC, he had even at one stage thought he might buy a cottage near Peter's tenanted family cottage in Derbyshire, so positive and untroubling and outwardly beamed was Peter's company, so invigoratingly one hundred per cent his engagement with the times he lived in, so infectious his twinkle-eyed enthusiasm, even on this short walk as he all but skipped along, as open to the big wide world as Joe over the past years had made himself all but closed to it.

'We're off to tame the running dogs of capitalism,' Peter said, and giggled, with his rather goblin smile, which warmly split a long face made severe by the large nose. 'We're trying to set up a Royal Commission to look into the future responsibilities of television and, you watch! We'll do it!'

By the time they arrived at the House of Commons, Joe felt he had begun to shed one or two of his self-absorbed skins. The meeting was to start at seven o'clock and Big Ben began the strokes. Peter always cut it fine. Life had to be squeezed dry.

'They've given us one of the big committee rooms,' he said as they trotted through the St Stephen's entrance and along to the Central Lobby where they were directed to the broad stone staircase.

As they ran up the stairs, two at a time, Peter now muttering, 'These meetings always start late, TV people are never punctual, they always start late,' Joe wanted to look around this palace of legislation, this mother of parliaments, this forum of democracy and do as Peter had invited him to do, take notes or at least let something sink in. But they were now in full gallop and the notes would have to wait.

The committee room was crowded with people of Joe's generation and he felt enlivened to be among them. He felt as if he had walked into a lighted room after too long in the twilight. This was where his lot lived out serious, energetic, extrovert lives, far from the brooding, self-consuming inwardness of his own existence which seemed by contrast misguided, out of touch. There was a buzz, there was a feeling of important activity, there was a murmur of appreciation for Peter.

Joe felt that he had walked into a revivalist meeting. A vivid and noisy congregation of the faithful was gathered together waiting to hear the word. Issues which had once been alive to Joe were here again, full on, arguments over a social structure and a political system which could be changed and for the better and by them in this large committee room, windowed onto the Thames, about to be addressed by a Labour Cabinet minister.

Joe let much of it go over his head. He was more absorbed by the congregation than the preacher. Besides the shock of the normal winded him. These were the people he would have been part of had he stayed working full time in television. They were a new battalion, largely, he would guess, grammar-school-educated, like himself, many of them first-generation university graduates, scholarship produce delivered by enabling Acts of Parliament in the 1940s, and now bound together by the generational kinship David had spoken of.

They were young adults confident in their new identity and in the medium to which they gave their best energies and which increasingly was to give them an influence beyond their traditional class reach. But most of all, Joe thought, they were young people who saw themselves on a mission to unleash their high-mindedness through the new technology. It was as if he had opened a door in space and discovered a parallel universe which was also his own. These were his lot. It was a revelation and for a few moments he had no fear, no panic, no vertigo.

There was polite applause for the Cabinet minister which segued into a warm growl of expectation as Peter got up to speak. His friend was a fine orator, Joe thought, with something Gladstonian about his delivery. The Oxford Union had drilled Peter in the ways of parliamentary discourse but it was the man's own passion which gave the words their authority; and the laugh, even the giggle, which now and then both punctuated the speech and punctured any pomposity.

Peter's background was all but identical to that of Joe himself and he made a note to himself to write the outline of a novel in which someone like Peter would seize the opportunity, get onto the political ladder and slash and struggle his way to the top, to be Prime Minister and a Prime Minister whose 'peasant' past would never be abandoned. Loyalty to the past would be the charge to all his policies. Peter, he fantasised, was the very man to change a country so painfully uprooted from Empire and still bound in all the entanglements of increasingly redundant traditions. As he thought of the novel Joe smiled; it was at that moment, she said later, when she had first noticed him 'smiling to himself'.

'What we are here for may seem to some of small concern,' Peter began quietly. 'Those who rule over us want the status quo to continue in television as in so much else. They are the status quo. They want us to be grateful and obedient and uncomplaining and the greatest of these three is uncomplaining.'

As Peter swept on, Joe felt both impressed and daunted. How could you have the confidence to stand up and talk so fluently without notes to so many of your contemporaries, the sharpest judges? Peter seemed to have a control over a situation which would have been utterly impossible for Joe. He envied Peter's fluency. He flinched at the thought of himself being pressed into such service. Yet not long ago he could have made something of a fist of it. Again he saw the gap he had let grow between his immolated self and the world as it was for his lot.

'But television will not play their game. Because there's money in television. Because in its short life television has become the constituency of the people of this country and not the other way round. Because television is a truly democratic medium. And because people like you want to use television to make trouble for the powers that be and for the powers that should not be. We want to make the sort of trouble that brings about change and improvement to replace the change and decay we see around us now.'

Peter's voice rose; his eyes glittered. He laughed. 'Don't worry. No one is asking you to fight on the beaches. In the streets? Well. Demonstrate at least. Because they do not realise what you instinctively realise which is that the medium will not be a domestic pet any more. It is on the way to becoming a monster. A money-making monster and also a monster of hidden and not so hidden propaganda. All of us here want it to be another sort of monster. Our monster. A monstrous regiment for good. And for that we need the television channels old and potentially new to serve the Public Interest.

'That is why we are all here this evening. That is why we will press this government and future governments to set up a Royal Commission. That is why we will lobby and pester and argue our case. Those of us who make the programmes and who have the best interests of the viewers at heart will have our voices heard and if we are resolute and if we do not give in, our voices will prevail.'

Later in St Stephen's Tavern, there was an unattractive and long ringing sound. 'That's a division bell,' said Peter, rather proudly. 'The MPs can be drinking here and the bell goes for a vote and they can be in the lobbies within the allotted time.'

'*Division Bell*,' said Joe. 'Not a bad title.'

'I'm surprised there's nobody from Parliament I know in here.' Peter was a little disappointed. St Stephen's Tavern was not living up to expectations.

'I'm not surprised with your gang here. They've probably scared them off.'

'You are looking,' said Peter, gazing around with affection at the vivacious clusters of young media men and women raising the conversation in the pub towards a pitch of unintelligibility, 'at the vanguard of a new Britain.'

'What?'

'Just you wait,' he said. 'If you'd stayed in television you would feel it in your bones as I do. Hello!' He waved across the room and followed the wave. 'Back in a minute.'

His departure was too abrupt. Joe had, even in that brief time, become too dependent on his friend. Abandoned he felt giddy. But he could not, he would not let himself down. He felt suddenly physically feeble. The rapid transition unnerved him.

He steadied himself against the bar and sipped at the pint of bitter. The flush of engagement he had felt in the committee room had already waned and without Peter he found the crowd in the big bar, the unclouded faces and the wall of noise, intimidating. He focused on memorising the new poem. 'How do you know that the pilgrims track,/ Along the belting zodiac . . .'

'What were you smiling about?'

'Was I?'

'Not now. You're just muttering to yourself now. Back in the meeting. Before Peter spoke. You just sat there with a grin on your face.'

Joe tried to remember. He had begun to sink back into the well of himself and this interruption on top of the ever-increasing volume of the 'vanguard of a new Britain' disturbed him.

'It doesn't matter,' she said. 'I'm Helen, one of Peter's researchers. I know who you are. Peter talks about you.'

Joe held out his hand. The hand that took it was short but broad and strong. The handshake was a moment of pause. The eyes that met his were blue-grey, beautiful and calm. Her skin had the fair complexion that went with her blonde Anglo-Saxon hair, worn loose and long and flung back over her shoulders. Her mouth was entirely sensuous, curved like a bow, unsettling, he thought, until there came that open smile of unthreatening warmth and confident companionability. She was dressed in what Joe thought rather a student hippie fashion, a puff-sleeved cream blouse, a fawn waistcoat, a short fawn skirt, knee-length shiny brown boots. Later she would put on a white wide-brimmed hat; the hat suited her, and gave the outfit a charge: her own style.

'I saw your film,' she said. 'Not the Elizabeth one. I haven't caught up with that. The Nijinsky. When I was at school. Our music teacher used to take us to the ballet. I thought it was terrific. Especially the slow motion.'

I must go now, he thought.

'What are you researching?'

'I'm trying to set up a programme about different types of protest,' she said, frowning. 'The sit-ins, the marches, the usual picketing stuff, even letters to the editor signed by dozens. To be honest I'm not getting very far. There's not very much new except maybe the sit-ins.'

'Would you like a drink?'

'No, thanks. I've got one over there with my friends. Would you like to meet them?'

'Yes . . . but not now if you don't mind. I'm late home already.' She nodded, smiled and turned away. He watched her go and wished he had taken up her invitation.

He sought out Peter.

'I must go. It's been terrific.' He heard an echo of Helen's voice, the use of that word.

'A few of us are meeting at my place on Saturday morning to make placards for Sunday's women's march. It won't be a big turn-out so it's important we get as many people as possible.'

'I'll try.'

'Do.' Peter escorted him towards the door. 'It's good to see you again. We'd lost touch.' Peter nodded at Helen's group. 'All the gang will be there.' They were on the pavement. 'How's Natasha?'

'Fine.'

'I liked her novel very much. You're quite a cottage industry.'

'I suppose we are.'

'Don't forget us in the real world. And Natasha's very welcome, of course.'

'I'll see . . . Thanks again.'

Peter went back into the fray, leaving Joe at once relieved and vulnerable. All pressure unnerved him now. He decided to walk along

467

the Embankment to Charing Cross. He could catch the tube directly to Belsize Park. He had stopped going to Hampstead underground. There were fewer steps at Belsize Park. The walk by the river should steady him for the tube.

So she thought that the Nijinsky was 'terrific'.

———✺———

'Have you always been useless?' she asked.

Joe looked up. He was sitting on the floor leaning against the wall watching Peter's flat turn into a domestic factory dedicated to the artefacts of protest.

Helen was holding the two placards he had worked on. One had already come loose from its nails, on the other the slogan was daubed so ineptly that 'Equal Pay' had become 'Equal Pa'.

'I was never any good at carpentry.'

'OK. But what about this?'

'Or art.'

'Most of the paint is on your pullover.'

'It's old. I took precautions.'

'Can you make tea?'

'Definitely.'

'We're all parched,' she said, and swung her head in the direction of the kitchen. 'You aren't useless on purpose, are you?'

'Certainly not!'

'That's all right then.' She smiled and the smile activated him. He stood up and made for the kitchen, glad to be out of the mêlée.

After the initial fun of the start of the march, he began to look around him. They were walking through the City of London. Helen was holding her placard and, on command, joined in the chants of defiance which pealed through the empty City streets and rang around the empty offices. A few policemen walked grumpily alongside the marchers.

'You don't look up enough in a city, do you?' he said. 'Of course you don't often get the chance to walk down the middle of the road in broad daylight. But there are all sorts of styles and curiosities up there. Look at what they've done to that bank. It's just a bank but they obviously felt they had to give it authority by way of neo-classical architecture; why did that make it a better bank? I suppose it proved they had good taste and if they had good taste in one matter . . .'

'What do we want?' yelled someone at the front.

'Equal pay!' the marchers yelled back.

'When do we want it?'

'*Now!*'

Helen raised her placard and shook it at the bank.

'Joe,' she said, 'we're supposed to be on a march. You're embarrassing.'

'I'm sorry. Really. I'll shut up.'

'You don't have to shut up.'

'I'll join in the chants.'

'They're not chants.'

'I'll shut up.'

'Don't do that,' she said, and took his arm.

'OK.' Joe felt a rush of self-consciousness and said, stiffly, 'Do these demonstrations do any good? I mean equal pay's so obvious, can't it just be discussed and agreed?'

'There have been no advances in this country without protests.'

He nodded: she looked even better when she was serious.

'What do we want?'

'Equal pay!'

'When do we want it?'

'*Now!*'

'You joined in,' she said, and laughed.

'I'm a lifelong feminist,' he said. 'Ask my mother if you don't believe me. Of course the word was not invented then, but words often arrive rather late for the purpose. Some never arrive.'

'What *are* you talking about?'

'The real thing,' said Joe, 'ask Peter.'

'Peter never told us you were a bit bonkers. Ask your *mother*?'

Joe liked that. It was as if he had been handed a safety cushion. There was something cushioning about her lips. She was the real world.

Natasha had been pleased to see Joseph go off with Peter and take part in the march. It gave her two days in Kew. She stayed overnight on the Saturday and Joseph came down to join her and entertained them with stories of placards and the march in prospect and Peter's speech. He did not mention Helen. Natasha was happy to be with their old friends, old times, Joseph more in command of himself, talkative, funny. They slept together more closely that night than on any night for months.

—⟋⟍—

It seemed to have a course ordained. There was no straining. There was another march but mostly it was evening meetings with varying fractions of the gang. There was the worst meal Joe was ever to have in his life at an Italian restaurant in Westbourne Grove; a night in a traditional jazz pub where conversation was mime and semaphore; a couple of other evenings in pubs in and around Soho. It was in the Marquis of Granby, a rather plush-red-velvet pub in Cambridge Circus, in which they found themselves the last of the pack and had a quiet half for the road. Afterwards they walked towards Leicester Square. Joe decided he could not go down into the underground with Helen watching him so he hailed a taxi and he took her to her flat in Kilburn, a flat she shared with two other researchers. Her bedroom, he thought, was a cross between a library and a sitting room; the bed was pushed tight into a corner and covered with cushions to double as a settee.

—⟋⟍—

Some weeks later when Joseph came home late and subdued, Natasha said,

'We ought to talk, Joseph.'

'Yes.'

'You think it will hurt me to know.'

'Yes.'

'You hope it will just come and go without you having to say or to do anything.'

He paused. Whom would he betray?

'That's the hope.'

'But now you are not sure.'

'I still love you, Natasha. You and Marcelle. You're first.'

'I know that . . . Marcelle knows that.'

'Can't we not talk? I mean *not* talk.'

'I have to talk, Joseph. It is too difficult for me not to talk.'

Both of them smoked. Neither drank. The street was quiet, the things in the room wrapped them in their past.

'I don't know what to say. Well, I do know what to say. But . . . Natasha . . .'

'Yes.'

'We are together. Now. Here. Why does anything else matter?'

'Because we have to face the truth, Joseph. Then we can understand why we will stay together. What is hidden becomes dangerous. We both know that. We have to talk.'

CHAPTER FORTY-ONE

'There isn't just one truth,' he began.

'Joseph! This is a simple truth. It is not easy for me to say this, Joseph, but you are having an affair.'

'Yes.'

'It is obvious, and very painful for me.'

'Then why insist that we talk about it?'

'It would be even better not to continue with it.'

Better for you, Joseph thought, but dared not say.

'Better, that is, for me,' said Natasha. 'What is she like?'

'That's not fair.'

'Why not?'

He could not articulate an answer. But surely something and someone so private ought not to be hauled up for examination even by Natasha. The matter was supposed to be secret, secrecy was part of its potency, kept secret it could thrive and maybe harm no one, take away the secrecy and it came out of the dark into a light in which it would be destroyed or destroy.

'I'm sure you've told her what I'm like.'

He had.

'So this would be English fair play.'

'I said you were great. I said you were a wonderful writer and painter and much cleverer than I am. And that you looked . . . distinguished.'

'I believe you,' she said. ' "Distinguished".'

'It's true. And I did say that. All of it.'

'You are such a poor liar, Joseph, though you try very hard. But you are not lying now. Poor girl. I presume she is younger than you.'

472

'There's about a five-year difference,' said Joseph. 'About the same as between us.'

'So you are the one between,' she said. 'How did she respond when you told her I was a paragon?'

'Fine . . . Peter had told her much the same, she said.'

'Oh. She works with Peter.'

'She's a researcher.'

'What does she research?'

'Politics, usually; and social issues. That sort of thing.'

'Presumably she went to university and is full of life as the un-encumbered are and she wears a miniskirt.'

Yes to all three, thought Joseph, but he was damned if he was going to answer.

'I'll have one drink,' he said. 'Just the one.'

'Joseph. You are light years away from being an alcoholic. I have known alcoholics. You are an occasionally excessive and silly drinker, that is all. Drink what you must. I'll join you.'

'Why aren't you angry?'

'I like to surprise myself,' she said. And I won't cry. And I am very angry.

'Look,' he handed her the whisky, 'why don't we just let it drift?'

'Drift where? And what do I do while this drift of yours is going on?'

'I come back home, don't I?'

'Should I applaud?'

'So you are a bit angry.'

'Am I, Joseph? Do you want me to be?' She raised her glass. 'A la vôtre.'

'Just leave it alone, Natasha. Please.'

'What does she feel about it?'

'We don't talk about it. She doesn't push me.'

'That will be a relief to you for a while. In any case it is a good tactical position.'

'It isn't like that. Can we stop talking about it?'

'You admit infidelity. You expect acceptance. You plead for silence.'

'I wasn't pleading.'

'You are grasping at straws.'

'I'm here. You're here. Marcelle is upstairs. This is what is.'

'You're certainly pleading now. What you have just said is meaningless although you probably imagine it to be profound.'

'Is an affair the end of the world?'

'Our world? No. Not necessarily. Not at all. Except,' she paused, 'you have a fatal tendency to fall in love. This is usually shallow and temporary like a pang of infatuation. But I fear that this might be different. If you are really in love it is dangerous.'

'I am in love with you, Natasha. You know that.'

'I do,' she said and sipped at the whisky. 'And I believe that I will always know that. But I am not what I was when we met and, more dramatically, neither are you. Would you fall in love with me were we to meet for the first time tomorrow evening?'

'Yes.'

'Thank you, Joseph,' she smiled. 'I know you mean it. But would you? And would I? You had so many simple but important qualities then and sometimes I see that time and success have overlaid them.'

'You can't really talk about me having success, Natasha.'

'The television. Novels published. An important film made. It did not please all of the public or all of the critics but it was bold. I think we can say that Sam and Ellen and even your friends from university would use the word "success". But it has disturbed you, and uprooted you. It has made you defensive and belligerent, neither of which you were when we met, and left you marooned in your own no man's land.'

'You've always excelled at dissecting me. But other things have changed and some of them are liberating. Letting more life in and taking on as much out there as I could manage. You'd call it over-reaching probably, greed if you like; or even worse; I don't want to talk about that.'

'Do you talk about that with her?'

'No.' He hesitated. 'A very little. Very very little. When I feel a bit odd, she sort of tells me to take a couple of aspirins.' He smiled. 'Not really – but she has not gone down our route and when I say I talk very little about that I mean it, Natasha, I don't want to take it there.'

'So she is the comfort and the refuge. I am the confession box and the rubbish dump.'

'Why do you turn it against yourself? You've changed just as much as I have. You wanted to change. You went into analysis on purpose to change. Yet why is it that sometimes I think you haven't changed at all. When I see you smiling, even a little, even just trying to smile, I think, that's Natasha, that's her. And there's the inadequacy I feel in front of your serious sense of life. I've always felt that but it didn't much matter because there was a rough and ready equality between us. Not now. Your ideals soar above mine: so do your morals. And you are so deep in your analysis that I feel like an outsider. Your affair is with your analyst.'

Natasha wanted so badly to tell Joseph of the death of the woman into whose hands she had delivered herself but even now she held it in. It was a question of honour. To divulge that now would be to take unfair advantage. Pity must play no part in this. Neither of them should be the nurse to the other, she thought, and yet this reference to her analysis caught her unawares and almost threw her. It was daily more difficult to deal with that loss. Her best efforts had so far been unsuccessful. Joseph's reference brought panic into her throat.

'And I don't ask about that, do I?' he continued, seeing an analogy helpful to his case. 'I don't scrutinise you about your affair.'

'Joseph!'

'It's not so much different. Unless. Unless you believe that physical attention, well, sex is, of itself, vital. Then what you are saying is that to have sex is to be in love.'

'For you, Joseph, in this case, I may be mistaken,' she said, and stood up to go across for another drink, 'I think it is. When it isn't you dislike yourself for it. You don't dislike yourself now. You believe that love is central to sex, don't you?'

'It's what you believe that counts,' he said and held out his glass for her to pour a measure. She stood above him as she spoke:

'I think, although this might be changing in the present circumstances, but I think that I will always hold onto the conviction that the intention in our hearts is what most matters and you have no intention to betray me or to hurt me, I know that, and therefore sex elsewhere, I must accept, does not fundamentally matter however much pain it gives.'

475

'I could never leave you.'

'Are you sure . . . ? Are you really sure?'

The words came quietly, even dreamily, as if from some retreat deep within, from a life being led in darkness, away from the light of the day's events, a life which had begun to claim her in the analysis and one by which she found herself fearfully entranced, a landscape of dream deserts and oceans, of timelessness and ancient forests in which her mind seemed to roam through the history of the earth itself, a fugitive from the present.

'Of course I am,' he said.

'You sound like a true and stout-hearted Englishman, Joseph.'

They talked to each other more often and more clearly over the next weeks than they had done since the first few years when they had put together a life cut wholly to their best intentions. Sometimes in those early times it had seemed to him that while he was out at work she had been waiting and preparing all day for his arrival home, saving up for an intimate and lengthy discussion. Her preoccupation with him had been flattering and mostly he had been a willing accomplice. Now it was a strain, though still for him too a compulsion. The stakes had become much higher. The game being played out was serious. Yet in this combustible context for some weeks they talked on. Joseph drank sensibly, Natasha her usual restrained self, both smoked voraciously.

'I had hoped you would have come to a decision by now,' said Natasha after a month or so. 'You, I presume, hope that you will never have to come to one at all.'

He did not want to admit that this was true.

'What do you think love is, Joseph?'

'Oh, God!'

'Is it not a question you should answer?'

'How can you answer it?'

'You write about it.'

'That's different.'

'Evasion with you is a high art, Joseph. Why not risk an answer?'

'Caring for somebody, wanting to live with them, being attached to them physically, believing they think those things too.'

'Does that mean you love me?'

476

'Yes. You know I do.'

'But you prefer to be with Helen, don't you? You love two people now.'

'I'm with you, now, and every night.'

'Why should I love someone who prefers to be with someone else and only comes here to keep up appearances?'

'What appearances? Who cares, save us?'

'What we have been taught to do, that is what cares. Our past cares. What our parents might think of us or our friends, a little, but most of all what our own moral conscience thinks of us. You care about what you think of yourself, Joseph, and it's a great obstacle for you.'

'How do you know?'

'I don't,' said Natasha. 'I now think that all the knowledge we have of our essential selves is guesswork or mere acceptance of clichés or a work of the imagination. Of why we think what we think we know so little. We grope around. We look as your Bible says "through a glass darkly". I've always loved that phrase. One day it might all be clear: I wish I could have been born for that day.'

'You keep saying we know nothing,' said Joseph, 'but that is a sort of easy defeatism, isn't it? Look at what we have found out. Look at what we learn every day about other peoples and other cultures. Look at the moon landing and a hundred and one inventions that would have been thought miracles. Look at the discovery of DNA. You could say we know not too little but too much for us to take in.'

'Facts, yes; mountains of new facts. But what do we know, other than in the broadest brush strokes, most of which are just generalisations, what do we really know of what concerns us, you and me, now, of what we are truly thinking and feeling, matters that concern so many others who want to know about their feelings with precision. They need to know because it could be vital for how they lead their lives or whether they lead their lives. "To be or not to be, that is the question." It is always the question. Yet how can we answer it save in an unsatisfactory and general way? The poorest, most fragile human being can want "to be" so badly – I remember when you read to me the ending of *The Grapes of Wrath* when she who had only the milk in her breasts gave it to him who had nothing but hunger in his belly. Even in worse extremes of deprivation there are people who will fight to live. Yet there are others, who would seem to the poor and the starving to have everything that life could bestow, who will decide "not to be".'

As she said this, the hand that held the cigarette clenched and the cigarette broke. She gathered it and stubbed it out without losing a beat of her fluency. 'So how do we know what happens in our minds, how to answer that simplest question, to live or not to live, and why are there only individual answers and even then are we sure they are all the answer? So I maintain we know little of what we are inside us, Joseph, even though we know more and more about what is outside us. Love, truth, freedom, they are words but they are also slogans, often merely slogans and I am tired of all slogan words save one – freedom.'

'Tired of love, tired of truth?'

'At the moment, Joseph, yes. I can find neither although I believe you want to give me both.'

'How can I convince you?'

'By what you do.'

'I'm doing my best.'

'But it is not best for me, Joseph. At the moment and I believe it will only be at the moment, for a short time, she is giving you what I cannot give you. You will not admit that because you do not want to hurt my feelings but, Joseph, you hurt my feelings more by this silent stubbornness. Just as you have hurt them by your half-drunken rants on occasion – which often you forget completely overnight and for which when you remembered you apologised. But your anger is verbally physical. I am not used to that. It is a rage against all you think you have suffered. There are words that stay, words that scar. And now you plead silence.'

'How can I tell you when I don't know myself?'

'It is your duty to know. You have had enough time now.'

'But I don't.'

'You are either being stubborn or concealing something, both, I suspect.'

How could he say that when he was with Helen he did not feel that the world inside his head was going to collapse?

There was awkwardness when he was with Helen, a tug of reluctance, an unreality, the guilt at betraying Natasha, intensified by her knowing about it. This could poison his new-found land. Yet he knew that he loved Helen, but found it very difficult to say this to Natasha. When he was with Helen and her happily opinionated iconoclastic friends he often loved and missed Natasha. He missed her careful thoughtfulness, her singularity and he missed her respect for solitude in which to work through an idea. When with Natasha he could long for Helen.

But there was a tide, and it was the tide of the times, and Helen rode it and took him with her. With Helen the terrors of disintegration, which would never leave him as long as he lived, calmed down because of what they felt for each other and the radiance of Helen began to turn him away from that which wanted him to destroy himself and began to bear him out to a different sea.

'I am aware,' he told Marcelle, 'that this book will do little justice to Helen. When you write fiction, characters operate on their own rules in a world made for them. And in some cases, most of the energy is spent with no consideration of balance or fairness. This is for you, Marcelle, and it is about your mother.

'To describe the power of feeling that Helen and I developed for each other after a start which could have been casual but never was; to begin a new story that still goes on, a story you have watched and been part of, just as the story you most want to know about is in its final struggle, is too much for me and, I suspect, for you.

'But something serious happened with Helen, a gravitational pull in a direction away from your mother. It was as if Natasha and I, after circling each other so closely had been fatally jolted, flung off course like planets disturbed by a sudden shock attack. We were left without being able to find a sure way to keep together. We were wrenched, torn away from each other, pulled into what both of us feared but neither, finally, could halt.'

'I don't know what to say.'

Anything he said would disturb Natasha and he did not want that. Anything he said would betray Helen and he did not want that. His silence was helpless and Natasha recognised that.

'Well,' said Natasha, 'that is as near as you will get to being honest, I expect. So I thank you.'

She went for another drink, her third, unusual for her, and poured one for Joseph who sat looking miserable.

'Poor Joseph,' she said. 'To love two women! For you it is a sin. But really to love two women, as I think you may do now, and you are someone who can love well – that is hard.'

Natasha paused for some time and then, after a quick smile, she said,

'I will not bind you, Joseph, neither through guilt nor through a marriage ceremony. We met as free people and to be free is the most important thing of all. If you have the opportunity to be free then you must take it or what is life for? We are artists. Maybe we, maybe I am an artist mainly to be a free person and I found art because it is where great freedom is possible. In our marriage we have begun to lose our freedom, Joseph. Other matters seemed more important. But to me nothing is more important. I want my freedom and I want you to have your freedom. I cannot be free and wait for you every night like the wife of a sailor in Brittany looking out to sea for the return of her husband, always worrying that he might be dead. I cannot be free when my mind is filled with dreadful thoughts about you and this craving to live together as we used to. And I cannot be free if I feel that I am imposing on you, Joseph. Your freedom helps mine. So I will leave you now. I will leave this house and Marcelle and I will stay with our friends in Kew until you have made your decision in freedom. That is what you must do. I think it is your duty, even. And I will look for my freedom too and I will hope, my darling, that this freedom brings back a love that means more to me than all the world.'

CHAPTER FORTY-TWO

For Marcelle the return to Kew was as good as a holiday. She piled into the games, the park life, the last term of the Barn Church Nursery with the enthusiasm of a visitor and the confidence of an old hand. She slept on a camp bed in the same room as the two children who had been her best friends since friends had featured. Anna and Natasha kept the house cheerful at least when Marcelle was around. She did not hear the long late-night discussions, she saw no tears, she was protected by those good friends from the streams of sadness which could flow from Natasha.

Natasha wanted to exercise her new freedom immediately but she was hemmed in. The responsibility for Marcelle which she had assumed without much expense of energy when Joseph was around to help now bore down on her despite Anna's support. Anna and her family could not have been more supportive but the constant sympathy became stifling. How could she possibly complain faced as she was by such loyalty? But in order to make her new life work she had to find a way to carry out her determination to be a free spirit. And her back was getting worse. Sometimes she walked bent over. She wanted to hide away and rest, let it mend.

'I'm looking for a place to rent,' she wrote to Joseph. 'It is not a good feeling to go once again to estate agents and look at details of houses in Kew. It seems as if I am reliving a life that has passed on. I must find somewhere. Anna is so generous but this can only be a temporary resting place. And I must revise this novel. I have begun writing poems again and I want to return to painting but to take it more seriously now. I just let it go over the past few years and for no good reason . . .' I must be true to my old self, she thought, I must get back to the time before I met him. She did not write that down, aware it would hurt his feelings.

Joe first rushed through her letters and then re-read them very carefully, looking for clues. He missed her badly. He found it sad and strange to be in their house alone. Save for the occasional couple of days he had never lived in their house alone. He expected Natasha to let herself in at any time or Marcelle to be in the garden, on the swing. He walked warily from room to room glancing in to make sure they had not become occupied since he had last looked in. He did not like to eat there. Yet after a night with Helen he would still walk back, cutting a curve across north-west London, with the instinct of a homing pigeon.

'We could meet in Kew Gardens on Sunday,' he wrote. 'If you like I'll pick you up at Anna's in the late morning. We could take Marcelle into the Gardens or down to the boats at Richmond and find somewhere to have lunch and talk. Would that be OK?'

When they met he had trouble remembering why they had parted. What they did together was always what they had done together previously and the very repetition of the act seemed to carry the promise that life would go on as before because that was what was happening.

'It was so hard to leave you,' he wrote. 'When we came back to Anna's and you said "come in", I wanted to and yet something held me back. I walked to the station with so much of me, of my feelings, still with you and Marcelle. Even the planes seemed tolerable but then I was catching a train to take me away from them.'

Natasha tried not to plead with him to stay. She did though wish sometimes that he did not come to see them so regularly, did not come with that embarrassed eagerness which disarmed her, did not seem to understand that a distance had been established and ought to be respected. It was when he was with her that she missed him most. He was present and close but separate now, unbearably. She wanted time alone, she needed it to build this new life for herself. Even Marcelle could be an encumbrance.

'You must not feel guilty about Marcelle,' she imagined her analyst saying to her. 'You have told me how much liberty you give to Marcelle and how well she plays with the children of your friends and how pleased they are to receive her. Even so she is at this time a burden. It is not unusual nor is it unnatural for parents to find their children a burden although it is often very difficult to admit it. Procreation in our

482

society at let us call it your level has severed itself from many of the bonds of necessity. Yet protection and nurture are still essential. What you are really telling me is that Marcelle was your gift to Joseph's sense of securing a bourgeois life for which you had little inclination. Now that you want to go back to rediscover your single bohemian self much that Joseph has brought you seems a mistake. It gets in the way. Even Marcelle who is now your sole responsibility however often Joseph comes to see you.'

'You must not allow your love of guilt to get in the way,' she told Joseph. Marcelle was with friends in order to give them time together. On a wet autumn late afternoon there were few options. They had settled for the station café, almost empty at this time. They sat in a corner with tea and digestive biscuits. Joseph kept his voice low; Natasha spoke at her normal pitch which seemed loud in the rather bare utilitarian café.

'Guilt,' she continued, 'has dragged you down. You want to be bold and you have been bold but then guilt creeps in and snares you. You want to tell the truth and reap the cleansing that comes from that but by perverse thinking you fail to tell the truth because your guilt fears it will hurt me but you are the one who is hurt by these lies and that makes you angry, and angry with me, of course.' She smiled, that quick dart of smile which could still melt his heart. 'You are guilty because you are more fortunate than your parents and their parents, you are guilty because you are doing the work you want to do and not the work you have been made to do, and you are guilty because you think you are mistreating Marcelle and me and in one interpretation you are.' This time she laughed. 'That is the only guilt I can excuse. The rest you must banish.

'Your analyst should be giving you more help. Guilt has become a straitjacket. It seems to me that since you have few educational or financial or social barriers blocking you, this guilt has arrived to do duty for them all. Perhaps your peasant history is written so deeply inside you that you were made a creature of the habit of being oppressed by whatever circumstances. Your analyst ought to help you.'

'You keep fishing about my analyst,' said Joseph, taking the opportunity to switch away from her own analysis of his character before which he had always been in defenceless agreement. 'You know I don't like talking about it. I never ask you how your analysis is going, do I?'

Natasha nodded, drew on the cigarette, again let the opportunity for confession pass. That single reference opened up the sore. She stayed silent. She had to concentrate on Joseph.

'Look,' he whispered, leaning towards her, head bowed over his tea, not seeking out her glance, 'it'll be all right, really.' He swallowed to ease the sudden dry throat. Once again a mechanism in his brain had focused on the aeroplanes. 'I don't know what it is. It was good of you to leave and give me time on my own and I can see why you did it. Why should you put up with what I'm doing? I just barge on with my selfish life. And sitting here I can't work out why we're not together, Natasha.'

'Why do you always give me hope?'

'Because I love you. And you know that.'

'There are differences now,' she said. 'There are great differences and hurt that only great love or a wise tolerance can heal and make good. You need time alone to decide who you are, Joseph. I want time alone too.'

He sat before her, unhappy, on edge, vulnerable. She too found this meeting in the station buffet a strain, even a public humiliation, a place which forbade the intimacy they were most in need of.

'We have nowhere to go,' she said.

'Don't say that!'

'I mean here, Joseph, now, in Kew, nowhere to be privately together.'

'I thought that was what you wanted to have a rest from.'

'It would be good to be reminded of what we were and what we could be again. How long do you think this affair of yours will last?'

He found no response. The screeching of the planes, the pull inside him, now for Natasha and home, now for a different life and Helen, such huge forces they seemed to be, like two mingled oceans fighting to be separate. How could these forces seem so vast inside him?

'I don't know,' he whispered. 'But I do love you.'

'I know that, Joseph.' Her voice was steady. 'But that is not an answer.'

'A month or two?'

He wanted to leave. He wanted to run.

'Or three or four? Why two?'

'It'll sort itself out. I know it will.'

'Meanwhile . . .' she began and then checked herself. 'That is good for me too,' she said, resisting the temptation to talk more, to talk to Joseph as if he were her dead analyst. 'But there is sex. I miss the sex. And the warmth of intimacy.'

'Well, there's . . .'

'Poor Joseph. I cannot come back to Hampstead for sex and we cannot ask our friends to let us have a bedroom for an hour or so, can we?'

'Well, I suppose . . . it would be . . .' And suddenly the idea of making love to Natasha seemed like a solution.

'It will have to wait,' she said. 'And we are too old now to find places in the open air.'

'We used to.'

'You sought them out,' said Natasha. 'Sometimes on those walks I was aware that all you were doing was appraising the density of various hedges and bushes.'

'That was good,' he smiled. Life between them would be fine.

'You are such a romantic and such an idealist,' she said. 'But now that isn't enough.'

'Why not?'

'We need analysis now, Joseph, to repair the inevitable failings of idealism and romanticism.'

'Yours seems to be working much better than mine,' he said. 'All mine does is repeat back to me in a different version what I've already told him.'

Once again Natasha braced herself against the threat of telling.

'It is very important that you stay with your analysis,' she said, 'that, above all.' And with me, she thought, and with me.

It was always so awkward to part. Natasha wanted him to come back with her even though Marcelle would not be there. Joseph wanted to go with her but the prospect of intimacy was suddenly too difficult to manage. Natasha took on board the prospect of his eventual departure in front of others which was humiliating. She wanted to be with him, just to be with him. She knew that had she insisted he would follow her: he had done so before, but that kind of loyalty was not worthy of them, she thought.

In her mind's eye she saw him get on the overground train she herself had caught so often from Kew back to Hampstead, the first few friendly stations and then the grim industrial landscape around Willesden and she felt the pull of his reluctance, could imagine the power of his attachment to her still holding as he stared out of the carriage window and saw her walk through Kew to the house of their friends, a path taken so often by both of them. Yet somewhere on the journey he would not be leaving her but travelling to meet Helen. Each knew that the other was thinking like thoughts. In the manner of their parting they expressed an unmistakable and loving union and held onto that until the next time.

If Helen and Joe were defined by any one thing in their first weeks together, it was by dancing. Helen wholly embraced the music of her generation and the Stones, the Beatles, the Beach Boys, Credence Clearwater, Bob Dylan and others ignited her personality into a dancing, smiling happiness, and Joe came to this unthinking ambience of pleasure as to an oasis. She taught him the new dancing freedom. They danced in her room at the flat, they danced at the regular noisy weekend parties, they danced in the cheap discos some of Peter's gang would make for: dancing shaped them. It was the time when dancing apart from one another, separate and yet in communion, had become the fashion, an elaborate courtship ritual, curiously chaste in the new context of permissiveness, allowing each to weave variations, fanciful, parodic, camp, apart and yet together often by no more than an exchange of glances, dancing together even though entire songs could fly by without them so much as touching each other.

It allowed for public exhilaration without the curse of showing off. It allowed the music to flood the mind, to establish a chemical bliss of mindlessness, draw out all the inhibitions by its sweet marauding sirens of rhythm and melody, and in that dancing Joe's panic could find no place, his fragile confidence and damaged consciousness was soothed as if mesmerised through the music and the dance and steered towards a state of healing where the words he uttered were not poems hard learned and held onto like fingerholds on a rock face but the simple words of songs which came wrapped in singable melodies driven by a rock beat which pumped nerve energy.

Dancing became Joe's passion. Dancing was an escape from the old. Dancing began to mend him and the more flamboyant the steps and poses the more earthed he felt, at least for the duration of the dance. It did not end his fears. But dancing with Helen, it only worked with Helen, reintroduced him to high youthful sensations of being alive, of being him, on the planet, for these moments, a sort of static wildness such as he had experienced as a boy and even into manhood until the world he had chosen to reach out for with all his might had proved too much and closed over him. Now he had to get out of that. Freedom was dancing with Helen.

———ɷ———

At Christmas Natasha and Marcelle went to Oxford. Julia and Matthew's three children again adopted Marcelle as their little sister and competed for the attention of their young guest. To be released from perpetual vigilance and in the amplitude of this large and friendly house made Natasha realise how tense she had been over the past months. It was neither a religious nor was it a hypocritical household but the lack of a Christmas tree and general Victorian seasoning was compensated for by a spirit of good cheer, a Dickensian uplift of spirits which made its own Christmas with the exchange of inexpensive presents, usually books, the observance of a big meal on Christmas Day, and the undiscussed but collective decision to call out to each other on Christmas morning, 'A merry Christmas, why not?'

Natasha was given her former room. The daughter of the family, the only daughter, who was six years older than Marcelle, claimed her as a Christmas sister, and took her captive into her own bedroom.

Other au pairs had come and gone. The current occupant, who was German, had returned home for the holidays but despite the changes inspired by the years between her younger and her present self, Natasha soon felt the room to be her own again. She kept the curtains open. She looked over Oxford back gardens. She had brought her sketchbook and did some work. The bed was the same narrow bed. Julia had put flowers in the room. It was a room of such powerful memories that Natasha sometimes felt drugged on them and at other times lost in them, like a child in the dark forest in a fairy tale.

It was not in her nature to draw up lists or come to conclusions about how far she had or had not come since Joseph had first arrived at her door, not in her character to make calculations of achievement. To Natasha life was the fathomless and seductive past or a permanent present which hovered above it and which took all the attention she had to spare from the perpetual threat of a downward spiral into the dominating unrecoverable personal history that hypnotised her. So to Natasha the past and present in this attic room were seamless. She found sad pleasure in the overwhelming presence of Joseph and looked hard, as for months after his death she had looked at the jar of shells collected by François, at the two paintings she had brought up from the cellar, reading their lives in them despite her rational dismissal of such illogical fortune-telling ways. She found solitude there for hours on end and believed that it helped restore some equilibrium.

'She looks terribly tired,' said Julia.

'But not unwell, I think,' said Matthew, putting aside with some relief an article he was correcting: it ought, he felt, to be rewritten and his decision to put it aside for conversation with Julia confirmed that it would be.

'Do you think he's behaving badly?'

'Not really.' Matthew picked up his whisky but paused. 'I think that whatever has come between them is serious. Unfortunately these things happen.'

'I agree. But you never anticipate they'll happen to people you know. Or I don't. She talks about him ceaselessly, analysing him, I really should say, and torments herself about this Helen.'

'They are two serious adults with a dreadful problem,' said Matthew. He would begin the article again immediately, the following morning. Already he saw how he could both shorten it and make it more telling.

'She's moved into this awful little flat back in Kew.'

'She told me she rather liked it.'

'I asked her to describe it. It sounds godawful. And insanitary.'

'Ah.' He took out a cigarette. It could be rather effective, he thought, to begin the article where in its present form he had concluded it.

'I thought that he would be an old-fashioned, working-class sticker,' Julia said.

'I think that the adhesive of his class wore off some time ago.'

'But what about Marcelle? He has a duty to her.'

'Indeed. But in Marcelle one sees a very bright well-balanced child—'

'Which speaks volumes for Natasha—'

'I grant you that. But as we know once passion has its way nothing is too sacred to escape sacrifice. Literature is full of examples.'

'Literature is no guide to morality. I just want common or garden fidelity and if not absolute fidelity then the outward appearance and exercise of fidelity until real fidelity finds its way back which with these two I'm sure it will.'

'I admire what he writes and what he does,' said Matthew. 'I admire what she writes too. But in their work they stand well apart from each other.'

'Only if you read their fiction as autobiography which I cannot believe you do.'

'It can be a fine line,' said Matthew and held up his whisky. The pieces had fallen into place. If he still had the energy he once had he would have begun again now, even at this late hour.

'It is,' said Julia, 'impossible to help.'

'Except to provide shelter, if I may use that word,' said Matthew, 'which you, we, are doing now.'

'Thank you,' said Natasha at the railway station. 'I feel such a lot better.'

They were on the platform. Marcelle was still in thrall to her new 'sister' who had taken her to buy a comic to read on the train. There was some snow but not enough to excite the children. Oxford Station seemed designed for bleak partings.

'Don't you feel like just hitting him and telling him to come to his senses? I'm sure I would.'

'I'm sure you wouldn't, Julia . . .' Natasha smiled and for that moment Julia thought, yes, she is better than when she arrived, she will cope with this, she has the strength. 'He has to find and then obey his free will.'

'Isn't it rather dangerous to let him try?'

'There is nothing else that matters,' Natasha said, firmly, and suddenly Marcelle was upon her, waving the comic, flushed from the cold, brimming with life, holding out her arms to be lifted up.

Joe stayed in London for Christmas. Everything about it felt wrong. He had promised Helen they would go to a fashionable disco on Christmas Eve but he did not know any. The place he came across, off Bond Street in Mayfair, was empty when they arrived even though he had taken as he thought sophisticated care not to appear until after ten o'clock. They danced alone on the tablecloth-sized floor to the usual music but without any of the usual joy. The disco filled up slowly with a smart enough but by no means fashionable crowd, a few of whom danced but in the same subdued way as Helen and Joe as if this were simply a way to get through a rather desperate Christmas Eve. They lost heart and left just after midnight and took almost an hour to find a taxi which would agree a price to take them to Helen's flat where they drank too much wine, made determined but unsatisfactory love and slept the sleep of the drunk with hangovers waiting at dawn.

On Christmas Day they walked all but silently on Hampstead Heath. Joe felt utterly dislocated, aware that he was offering Helen a sad present which promised little joy. She ought to be with one of the gang he had met at that first meeting. She deserved a better life than he could give her. There would be no rest from the past. Joe felt wretched and vowed to himself that it was over. It would be better for Helen, only the family counted, he wanted to be back with Natasha and all the company and life they had gathered up together.

'What do you think? It's perfect, isn't it?'

Natasha looked at him as if she were showing off a desirable villa. They were in a street in Kew which curved from outside the tennis courts to Kew Green, a street of small terraced houses once inhabited by working families, now being sequestered by young professionals who saw a cheap chance to get on the property ladder in a desirable area. The cottages were originally two rooms up and two down, but time, hygiene and gentrification had brought additions to some of them – a kitchen and another bedroom stuck on at the back jutting into the small garden, an inside lavatory, central heating – and here and there, embellishments – new cornicing, the installation of a marble fireplace, and parquet flooring, which set off Eastern rugs to great advantage.

They went in. It felt to Joseph to be not so much unoccupied as abandoned. Grime ruled. The kitchen looked like a scrapyard. A worrying stink possessed the stale air.

'It's less than three thousand pounds,' said Natasha, uttering the sum of money very shyly. She had left all that to him, he realised. This simple utterance was said, he knew, to prove her new independence.

They stood in the front room which was bare and empty and yet cramped. Two cardboard boxes dominated the floor, the least distressing of the general litter. In the fire grate were a heap of ashes covered in soot. The light cord hung from the ceiling: light shade, bulb and socket had been removed. A floorboard in front of the fireplace had been torn up for no reason Joseph could comprehend.

'I would knock this wall down,' she said. 'That would make a double cube. Marcelle can have her own bedroom upstairs. The little room at the back faces north which is perfect for a studio. You can visit us here, you see?'

Her gaze was so intense that Joseph turned away and pretended to be interested in the windows.

'And if we . . .' Again her shyness – a new and heart-breaking characteristic – appeared in her words and she could not complete the sentence which he completed for her.

'. . . live together again,' he said.

'Yes . . .' What was stopping him doing it now?

'But, Natasha, I'm sorry, it's stupid, the planes, it's impossible. I'm sorry.'

'Well, until we are together again it will be somewhere for Marcelle and me to live. It would be so nice to have a home and not be with friends or in that flat with others. I know it is a lot of money.'

'I can manage. I'll remortgage Hampstead. Anyway, half of Hampstead is yours.'

'Could you . . .' and there entered into her tone and her expression a desperation and an embarrassment which Joseph had never seen or heard before, 'could you buy it all at once? So that we can be safe here. Is it possible to do that?'

'Yes.' Please don't plead, my darling Natasha, he wanted to say. Please don't try to get round me. Just ask. Why to God are we standing in this forsaken room discussing this and not together as we were and should be for always I don't understand, Natasha.

'I could pay for the changes. The alterations. I still have a little money left.'

'No. I'll . . . It'll be OK. I'm sure. Anyway.' He continued, 'But won't this make it more difficult for us? Wouldn't it be better if you stayed in that flat for a while longer until I sort it out?'

'I thought of that at Christmas when I was in my old room in Oxford.' Still the intent look, painfully expectant, 'and I thought, well, he has had several months now and I am very tired. I must be practical. I have my own work to do. Marcelle needs a base. We are safe in Kew, among our friends, we are safe here. And then I found this little house. Pissarro lived in this street when he came to London. So you see?'

He nodded. He could no longer trust himself to speak. How could he leave her when she needed him so much?

Fear of what would happen if he stayed. Fear of survival. Fear. Something was happening that would make an irreversible change; it was as if he could see a most terrible storm approaching but he felt paralysed. Why could he not find a compromise now, this day, this hour?

Suddenly she looked away from him and began picking at a white handkerchief she was holding. He realised what all this was taking out of her and went across to hold her. They stood as one.

'I miss the warmth of you,' she said. 'Just this.'

'It will be fine,' he said. 'Honestly, Natasha. I want it to be fine for us.'

'I know,' she said, 'I know . . . But for now, just hold me . . . Just let us be like this.'

CHAPTER FORTY-THREE

'Take whatever you want,' Joseph had said. 'I can be out all day if that will help. Take whatever you want.'

Natasha walked up the gentle hill from the station, Hampstead Heath to her right and on her left a row of Georgian cottages bright-white-faced in the mid-morning, mid-winter sun. She peered at the long lawned gardens which led to the pavement on which she walked. The triangle of pastoral playground reserved for younger children in which Marcelle had played, the tranquillity of the streets which led from the station up into the centre of Hampstead, the charm of this hilly colony made up a place which given time and peace she felt she could have come to like. Or was this sentimentality? She had made a hard decision. She had to steel herself to keep it.

Even their street was redeemed by the fine grey morning light and Natasha, who had not experienced the stain of Ellen's puzzled shame which had so unnerved Joseph, could find for the sad decline of an aspiration to gentility a certain melancholy affection. Morning light and absence laid many of the demons.

She went up the steps and found that her hand trembled as she put the key in the door. She twisted it one way and then the other without sufficient force and for a brief moment she feared that she had been for ever locked out. She saw herself as if in a painting on the top of five stone steps, a nervous woman in a long, black, rather Russian coat Joseph had bought her, a red woollen scarf slung around her neck, hair hastily brushed but appearing to be stylishly cut. Barred out? Breaking in? It could be a painting by one of the Camden School which would be appropriate, she thought, here in the Borough of Camden, and as she experienced the thought the key clicked, the door opened and she stepped into the narrow hall and shut the door very quietly behind her. Quiet was all around her. She let the brief and sad history of the house settle on her as she tried to slough off the feeling of being a trespasser. Would Joseph be there? She wanted him to be there.

'Joseph?' It was no more than a whisper.

Where to go first?

She walked towards the stairs and carried on up to the first floor and then up to the two small slope-roofed attic rooms. In one of them she had hoped to set up her studio. It was about a third the size of her attic room at Oxford but attics for Natasha were always a haven. Joseph had bought her a couple of posters. One of them was from the Tate Gallery, advertising the paintings of Turner and showing *Morning among the Coniston Fells* which, as well as being the Lake District and by the British painter Joseph most admired, showed, he told her, an ascent to paradise in a working landscape and she smiled at the memory of how he had deeply hugged to himself that combination of ordinariness and sublimity. The other poster carried a few lines from Wordsworth, printed big and in black against a hard blue sky streaming with white cloud.

> No motion has she now, no force,
> She neither hears nor sees
> Rolled round in earth's diurnal course
> With rocks and stones and trees.

She stared at it for a while and then reached out and took it down and rolled it up carefully. She thought she could hear him recite those words. Once upon a time he had liked to speak poetry aloud to her. It was a performance wrapped in self-satisfaction but nonetheless truly felt and she had been fêted by it. There was a terrified emptiness in her. What was she to do? Who would help her now? This house had been hers, his, theirs. There was a desperate hollowness, but what could she do, orphaned by infidelity.

She had already taken the easel and paints. There was nothing more she wanted to take from that room, nothing she wanted to mark for the removal men.

At the bedroom door she stood for some time but did not enter. The bed was neatly made, Joseph would have made it, but unslept in, she thought, for some time. She conjured up a picture of Joseph and herself asleep in that bed and shivered, she could not decide why. At the loss? At the memory of pleasure? Of pain? At the pretence of a love in marriage? It was such an ordinary bed. There was a pair of nineteenth-century French gilt mirrors on the wall, each bearing two candle holders; their elegance had caught her eye and their state of disrepair had made them affordable. Joseph had loved them and once or twice he had lit the candles and brought wine to bed. She had intended to take them but they made the room. She had not the heart to do it.

In Marcelle's room she marked all the furniture. But when she went downstairs to the living room the mood she had experienced in the bedroom caught her again. She tried to fathom it. It was as if the house had become a sacred spot, she thought, that was as near as she could get even though in her secular mentality the word 'sacred' made her uneasy. Yet here were the things Joseph had been so proud to amass: things which meant so much less to her; things, in truth, she could discard without a single backward pang of regret.

She went to lie as she had so often done on the long sofa, to ease her back. As she examined the room she appreciated more fully than ever before that Things, especially the Things with which he had furnished their home, meant a very great deal to Joseph. It was not to show off his money – some of the objects and the books were clearly inexpensive, even cheap. Nor were they to show off his taste – some of the objects were so naïf they made her smile – the homely hodge-podge was more like an eccentric pocket museum than any thought-through collection. But it worked, she thought, because it was Joseph and she could sense still the enthusiasm in the purchases. He was the integrating factor, it was Joseph plucking at new worlds and old, eager for all things, and at last these things were special for her because they were him. She left the room as she had found it.

She had not meant to go into his study. As soon as she entered it she knew why. Her apprehension had nothing to do with Joseph, despite the study revealing a yet more essential part of his life. She sat down and wished she had not come to the house at all. The memory of that final realisation in this room of the consequences of her analyst's death returned. She closed her eyes for a moment and then opened them, widely. Inside her head was a vertigo. Natasha knew that the loss and the passionate sense of being abandoned had not been resolved. Indeed it was intensifying. Thoughts of Joseph mingled with thoughts of the woman who had been there to heal her as she felt weakness possess her.

She ordered herself to stand up. On the mantelpiece Joseph had laid out his fragments from the ancient world. She went across and made herself examine them closely even though she knew them and even though such close examination was hardly necessary. She picked up the chipped and battered Egyptian necklace. Joseph had been told it was almost four thousand years old. It was the years rather than the object which entranced him. He had told her that one day they would go to Egypt and now she longed for that journey, just Joseph and herself. Her father had talked so much about Egypt, the Sphinx and the Valley of the Kings, Luxor and Nefertiti's Tomb, Champollion and the Rosetta Stone. He had made it seem the most desirable place on earth. This, too, was Joseph, she realised. Images of him as he had been, of them as they might have been. Why did she not stay and wait for him? Why did she not stay? He would surely return.

'Natasha is extraordinary,' said Julia. 'She's only had the house for ten minutes and she turned what I saw as a tip into an utterly charming little sort of salon and artist's studio combined. She's painted every-thing white. The furniture is from junk shops but it looks just right, far better than the clutter of the other place. She paints away and writes away and tells me she is meeting new people all the time. And Joe was there! He had come to help move in the last of the furniture and take Marcelle for an afternoon's outing which I thought rather sad but she then announced they were all three going off to Marlow for a few days!'

'We've talked about Marlow,' he wrote to her. 'Remember? At a time when you thought you could remember nothing at all about your mother, we talked about Marlow and you thought you could remember something. I wanted us all to have a holiday together. You would be just over five, you'd started in the junior school in Kew Gardens and I bought you a fishing net. Everything was so strained and out of joint that I play-acted as hard as I possibly could at being natural. It did not come easily. Perhaps you sensed as much in this over-hearty dad strolling along the banks of the Thames looking for a suitable fishing point, two fishing nets slung over his shoulder as if out for a hardened day's fly fishing, you with the jar for the hopeful catch, your mother trailing us, observing us, this Happy Family. Did you sense it was false and block it out?

'What you think you remember are the tiddlers. We struck gold in the Thames and shoals of tiddlers competed to be in our nets. Soon the jar we had brought was black with the tiddly fishlets fighting for water. We tipped them back into the river and then once again harvested those kamikaze tiddlers. And once again we tipped them back all in a high heat of daddy–daughter delight which for you I pray was real but for me looked, as your mother pointed out that evening, like an impersonation.'

Joe had gone to Marlow partly because Tim had recommended a fine riverside hotel which catered for children. 'There's two sorts of kids' hotels,' Tim said. 'One looks after the kids and is rubbish for us. The other looks after us and is rubbish for kids. This one does both. Don't ask me how.'

What it meant essentially was that couples could have dinner together while staff patrolled upstairs. Marcelle slept in a room connected to their own.

The dining room was full, low volume, and over-splendid for Natasha's taste. They had a window table overlooking the river now in full spring spate. Natasha ordered so quickly that Joe correctly concluded she had no interest at all in the meal. He was nervous on this, their first night, and he took his time.

'Wine, sir?' The waiter was old and bored, the shoulders of his dinner jacket powdered with dandruff.

'Number seventy-three.'

'A very good choice, sir, if you don't mind my saying so.' He bowed at Joe and bowed again at Natasha. 'Welcome to the Marlow Hotel,' he said.

'Do you remember Felix Krull?' said Joe after he had left. 'I've often thought it could be intriguing to be a waiter.'

'If you are Felix Krull. And if you are a creation of Thomas Mann,' she said. 'And if you meet a convenient prince.'

'A waiter is always playing a part,' he said. 'Slightly different to each table, different again, I imagine, in the kitchen. Always on parade.'

'Why should you like that?'

'Don't you sometimes want to lead the lives of others?'

'No. My own is difficult enough.'

'But your own life isn't one-faced, is it? We are all several people in one. We all contain multitudes.'

He talked on in this manner and she answered but her thoughts were a parallel monologue. Why are you behaving like this, Joseph? Why are you once again impersonating, this time an affectionate husband casually at ease with his wife? How can you? How dare you? Why do you want to preen here in public when at last we are away together for a few days on neutral ground and we could talk truth? You are frightened of the truth, Joseph. Perhaps you always have been. You insisted on buying me this silly dress in Marlow this afternoon and you do not realise that I conceded only because Marcelle was excited about it but the inexplicable thing is that you seem to think that it matters. What matters is us. Why do you evade that? You act as if nothing has changed. Everything has changed. You are across the table. You pour wine into my glass. We will go to bed together. You say you love me?

'I do,' said Joe. They lay in the dark, cigarettes alight, the slackness of love made bodies apparently at one. 'I do,' he repeated. He did.

'I believe you,' she said and paused a while; then laughed very gently. 'I am pleased,' she said, 'that you feel you do not need to seek the same reassurance from me. Perhaps you want to be a bigamist,' she said, 'that is not so unusual, neither in the past nor I guess today. But you will not permit that.' She turned away from him to stub out the cigarette. 'Marcelle told me that she loved going fishing with you. So you see. There is always another perspective.'

Joe's sense of the artificiality of the situation was exposed. 'I do love you,' he insisted.

'I believe the words. I would like to see the actions.'

'You said I could have time,' and the slackness in his body went away. He wished he were not there. He felt trapped – though it was he who had suggested it.

'You have all the time you need,' she said and lit another cigarette. 'I hope you are careful with it.'

'What does that mean?'

'She is young. Let us say she loves you. Let us say you tell her that you love her.' Joe froze. Natasha waited for a while and then relented. 'You must be careful you do not make her pregnant or that she does not make you make her pregnant.'

He had no answer. His admiration for Natasha's brave clarity added yet more to the power of the unanswerable question – how could he treat her like this?

'When we were at Oxford at Christmas,' Natasha said, 'the children put on a play. They wrote it for themselves and they wrote a lovely part for Marcelle. And who was the star performer? Marcelle. She takes after you there. It is a shame you did not see her . . . It is so very good to be together, Joseph, and I try every hour to understand, to hold to my belief in your freedom and mine. But it is tiring and sleep is no longer my friend.'

'They were in Marlow,' said Ellen, looking up from the postcard, 'and they didn't tell us.'

'I'm glad.' Sam picked up the river scene and read the brief note. 'They need time together to sort it out.'

'Will they?'

'They should be able to.'

'But will they?'

'If anybody can, Natasha can.'

'You haven't answered.'

'There's no certainty in these matters, Ellen.'

'I had a feeling even on their wedding day.'

'What can you say? There's rough and smooth, thick and thin, there always was. We'll see what he's really made of now.'

'And her. Not just him. Her as well.'

'He can't let somebody like her go,' he said. 'Nobody could. There's only one Natasha.'

—⚬—

Joe had been asked to do the screenplay for a novel set in Mexico and he went there for ten days' research. He had by this time been separate from Natasha for about nine months, and often he would tell her that he wanted to and intended to return. He had recently been sleeping most nights of the week with Helen, to whom he talked intimately much less but who understood that he was moving away from Natasha towards an eventually final separation. Each position seemed true when he was with each woman. Helen had endured Marlow though she had not been able to resist making a telephone call to him one evening when he and Natasha were in their room changing for dinner. She had supported his consistent visits to Kew and the weekend sightseeing trips into London that he now made with Marcelle.

He took Helen to Mexico half determined this would be the celebration of their union, half convinced that this would be the final few days with her, that by some process of reason she deserved this exotic trip: the paying of dues. He did not tell Natasha that they were going to Mexico.

They drove to Cuernavaca to look at the central location of the novel he had agreed to adapt. Their driver railed against the number of gods in Mexico – 'god o' the sun, god o' the rain, god o' the mountain, god o' every damn thing'. He spent the return journey attempting to persuade Joe to buy a gun from a thoroughly reliable friend of his. They went to markets and Helen bartered to Joe's embarrassment: the prices were low enough, the sellers too poor to begin with. They went on the boats in Mexico City and spent a long morning in the Museum of Anthropology, Joe stunned and suffocated by the sullen compulsion of the sculptures. Joe went to the communion service in the colossal cathedral across the square from their hotel.

They ate to the accompaniment of Mariachi bands and bought cheap jewellery for each other, rings and medallions for Helen and also for Joe, who soon looked like a playboy tourist. Every night they had a drink in a crowded piano bar with a long polished counter down which their glasses of tequila were skidded to them at high speed. Only towards the end of their stay did they realise that upstairs was a brothel. They drank too much tequila and suffered.

The climax of the visit for Joe was when they went to see the pyramids. He lingered over altars which had witnessed human sacrifice. Yet the most unexpected revelation was a central arena for ball games where, they were told, the finest young noblemen played for their lives. They found a sculpting of the Plumed Serpent and Helen took a photograph of him standing by it. She declined to have herself photographed there. Joe felt everywhere in Mexico pervaded and oppressed by both Aztec and Roman Catholic mysteries, Indian women squatting on the ground in markets, their eyes open wide but black, forbidding entry, and Catholic women in the cathedral, kneeling on the stone floor, their eyes closed in prayer, blind to the material world.

'It is always difficult to know what feelings were being experienced so long ago,' he said to Marcelle. 'But I remember strain in Mexico. I remember feeling betrayal that I was seeing pyramids with Helen and not with Natasha, but despite the loss that had bled so much from memory as well as from the life that followed it, I think Helen and I had some happiness there and we knew in some way we were trying to build a life there.'

Julia had challenged him. 'Why is it that you want to be apart from Natasha? What is it?' And he had said that when he was with Helen he did not fear that the world would collapse inside his head all the time. 'Then you have to hold onto that,' Julia had said. 'You must hold onto that.' And then, 'you ought to look after them.'

Yet at times he knew that by being with Helen and leaving behind Natasha who would have longed to be in Mexico he was doing the wrong thing. As he said it he meant it. What could explain this wrong course of action save love or weakness? But if there was something in him which simply would not do what was 'right', could that not mean he was wrong about right and wrong? This brought temporary relief on several occasions but could not, would never eradicate the stake-hearted conviction that leaving Natasha and Marcelle was wrong however many the excuses, however hard the course; he had failed himself and there would be no redemption. But he was with Helen. And despite all, he stayed with Helen.

Blind, blind, blind, he sent Natasha a postcard of the pyramids.

—ⅉⅉⅉ—

After lunch he had hoped to take Marcelle to Regent's Park where there was a children's boating pond next to a playground and the little girl could switch from one to the other. But August rain put paid to that. They went to a cinema in Oxford Street to see *The Yellow Submarine*. Marcelle called it 'Sumbarine'. The mispronunciation became a private joke.

They arrived in Kew earlier than usual and Joe telephoned Natasha to tell her that he was taking Marcelle to the Garden Café for egg and chips and she was welcome to join them which she did.

She was dressed in a sari, perfect, she said, for summer. Her complexion, always pale, was white. She seemed preoccupied and said little and drank tea while Marcelle and Joe dealt with their simple meal. Joe always ate very quickly and was finished way before Marcelle.

'Could I have one of your chips?'

'One,' she said. He took one.

'Hmm. They're really good. Can I have another?'

'One,' she said, enjoying the game.

'Hmm. They're really good. Can I have another?'

'Don't let him, Marcelle. Don't let him take everything from you. Say no! Say no!'

A small cloud of embarrassment made a temporary settlement on other diners in the café.

'It's just a game,' said Joe. 'We play it all the time.'

'I must take her home now. My back hurts.' Natasha picked up the cup, decided against the tea and put it down rather clumsily, not quite centring it on the saucer. Joe's eyes saw how fraught she was but there was that in him which refused to allow the observation to provoke help.

'What was the song?' he said.

In a clear, confident voice, Marcelle sang,

'We all live in a yellow sumbarine, a yellow sumbarine, a yellow sumbarine.'

CHAPTER FORTY-FOUR

Her struggle had begun in earnest and Natasha was aware of it all the time. In luxurious and dangerous dream-moods of fierce introspection she thought she was like a knight on a quest seeking to solve apparently insoluble riddles about herself, forced to encounter monsters, to meet with failure and to experience despair. Yet the quest could not be abandoned. Something that was essentially her needed to face these dark forces, never to be a coward, however ensnared and exhausted, never to give in.

She had thought that it would be painful but not too difficult without her analyst but that was a false dawn. She had been drawn into the sources of her fear by an analyst of great skill and experience sharpened to an even finer art by her own past and by her immediate and ever-deepening empathy with her patient. In one story inside Natasha's head the analyst could be seen as the temptress, who had lured Natasha by charms and spells into the centre of the labyrinth of the forest of her entangled memories, desires, rejections, pains, life traits. And then abandoned her. Natasha was the knight who had to rescue herself and there was no avoiding this task.

She noted this down as a summary of what was happening to her. But the story itself was all but lost in a haze, a veil made from random sensations and feelings which turned into not-quite-thoughts but were like innumerable spots of water which make up the swell of a sea, strong enough to move her to unnameable grief. Yet there was a voluptuousness too. Natasha could sit alone for hours, as she had done again and again in her adult life, locked into herself and though sad, not sorry for herself, though mourning, not self-pitying. At such times Natasha saw this interior complexity to be the best and richest way to live, the finest way to meet the impenetrable fact of this single accidental and meaningless life.

By sinking into her own mind she was connected with the dominating darkness out there, and with the fathomless galactic swirl. Inside the mind was all existence and attempting to observe and track the movements inside a mind enabled her, she believed, to be much more closely connected with the cosmos which was made of what she was made of. Was that not a purpose? Maybe the mind was the microcosm of the universe and its intertwined messages, its infinite secrets of space and time and motion as unlimited as the vastness outside. There was some relief in thoughts like these.

But for the external world she lived in Natasha knew that was not enough and to the building of a new world for herself and Marcelle in their new home she applied herself with all the energy she could call on.

She painted feverishly. She used oils, bright colours, reds and yellows in particular, paint slashed onto the surface with bold violence. Abstract though they were these paintings seemed to be moving also towards shapes recognisably cosmic – spirals, whorls, black holes . . . she was convinced this was new and strong and had to be seen. There were a few small galleries in the Richmond area which she intended to approach if the gallery just off the West End in which Victoria showed her paintings turned her down. It felt good to think of herself as a woman of action. Joseph had over-protected her, she thought, and consequently enfeebled her.

The novel had been accepted and was on its unhurried road to publication. Yet she decided that poetry was more important. Like painting, she ought never to have put it aside. Joseph's novel writing had been too strong an influence. Poetry, she thought, was how words could be best arranged, feelings and ideas most memorably expressed, human nature divined.

She returned for a while to teach at the Barn Church Nursery School even though Marcelle had moved on to the recently built junior school less than five minutes' walk away. She made friends with the Kew bookseller who was much attracted to her. She looked after his shop on occasions when he needed to be away on a buying trip. He said that the arrangement could be put on a more regular basis whenever she felt like doing so, but she did not follow it up.

Most visibly of all though, partly to show Joseph she could, was her success in forming a new circle. Her former friends in Kew were still close but, as if she wanted to show unquestionable proof of her new independence, her house became a meeting place for a number of artists or those aspiring to be artists. Natasha uncharacteristically, Joe thought, decided to embrace the current interest in Indian culture and mantras would be chanted, scented candles lit as they sat on the floor in a circle, cannabis would be smoked, hands linked. Those who attended what became soirées spoke of her Eastern perception and of being at the heart of things.

Joseph came across this new circle one Sunday evening when he brought Marcelle back rather later than usual. He resented them, all of them. He resented them being in Natasha's house. He was jealous of these strangers being so close to his wife. He hated the feeling they gave off that he was something of an intruder and certainly an outsider. He found it hard to cope when Natasha merely looked up, glanced at him, brought Marcelle into the circle, turned back to her company and let him stay or go as he pleased. He left the house in a confusion of anger. Why were they in that house? What did they all do there? Why was he so out of it?

On the train he tried to calm down and told himself he had no right to these feelings and vowed that he would not reveal them to his analyst but of course he did.

Natasha pencil-sketched Joseph obsessively, usually late at night, in her bedroom, propped up with pillows, not even courting sleep. Always his face. And then she would let herself be drawn down, pulled into those scarcely lit zones on the ocean floor of the mind, plunged at first with relief into the seduction of unoccupied territory.

'She lets Marcelle run wild,' Ellen said. 'The front window's left wide open and she comes in through that instead of the door. So do all her friends and they run about shouting and laughing up and down the stairs and in and out without a word being said to check them.'

'Why should they be checked?' Sam smiled. 'It sounds like a kid's paradise.'

'They shouldn't just be let do as they want.'

'Why ever not?'

'You always take her side.'

'Hang on. One thing at a time.'

'There's something overexcited about Marcelle and whatever you say it worries me.'

'She's lively, that's all. She's always been lively . . . What about Natasha?'

'She never stops talking about Joseph. At one point I thought she was blaming me for the way he was but I couldn't follow her. I had made Joseph like he was towards women, she said. She's getting hard to follow sometimes. Funny smells everywhere. She should have that back seen to properly.'

Ellen paused.

'She wants him back so badly but the way she's going about it . . . Anyway, I told her she was Number One to us. Whoever, whatever, she's always Number One to us.'

Joe invited Tim and Sarah, his new wife, to Hampstead for the evening. They began in the Flask, a pub frequented by a jostle of writers and bohemians he hoped would show off his area to advantage. Tim offered no comment while Helen and Sarah found a couple of seats at a table and talked to each other as if they met here regularly, Joe thought. He wanted to move up to the Cruel Sea, a pub which could boast serious stars, but Tim insisted on buying another round in the Flask and pub time ran out.

They crossed the High Street, went into one of the little lanes that knitted the old centre of the village together and arrived at the Villa Bianca, an Italian restaurant Joe considered the best in the area. In the short distance between pub and restaurant Joe unloosed an accolade to Hampstead, hyperbolic and hyper-tense as if his reputation depended on proving to Tim the outstanding qualities of the place in which he lived.

The waiter shook Joe's hand which reassured him inordinately and showed them to the bay-window table which he had requested.

'Where is it?' said Sarah.

'We didn't trust the Ladies' in the Flask,' said Helen.

'It's a pub with character,' said Tim, nodding at Joe, 'a real pub, a pub with a history. Women have no sense of history.'

'A man's pub,' said Sarah. 'A pub with funny ideas about women's little needs. They'd probably have made us stand up to do it.'

'Upstairs on the left,' said Joe.

Tim watched them. 'A blonde and brunette can never be bet,' he muttered as the two attractive young women walked through the restaurant and, after a backward glance, strode up the stairs. 'A new breed,' he said. He looked around and leaned towards Joe. 'Speaking of . . . Natasha phoned up two days ago. She wanted to see me. Immediately if not sooner!'

'And?' Joe provided the dramatic punctuation Tim needed.

'We had tea in Brown's.'

'And . . . ?'

'And,' another glance around, 'she tore me off a strip. She said I was responsible for the way you were. She said I had corrupted you. No kidding! Not just me – him – Edward – the poet – the two of us, had led you astray, and filled your head with cosmopolitan cynicism you couldn't handle and because you were so innocent you believed in it. She said we had taken no account of who you really were but just, what was it? 'idly undermined' you because you were such a plum target. Bad enough, Joe my friend, bad enough. But tea in Brown's is the afternoon rendezvous for the hushed voices of the English upper middle classes with a peppering of aristocrats at their most discreet. Even the clock whispers. And Natasha really let loose. Teacups were raised to shield faces. She belted it out! You had been corrupted!'

'Belted what out?' Sarah asked.

'Just talking.'

'Ah! Men's talk. Shall we leave the Males and go to powder our noses one more time?'

'Of course not.' Tim stood up and fussed with the chairs. Joe smiled and tried to push away what Tim had said. Corrupted? Clearly Tim thought of it as a comical encounter but Joe imagined the extremes that had driven Natasha to do it and he curled up with shame that he was part of what had brought her to this. The conversation around the table went on, largely driven by Tim. The women were more friendly more quickly than had ever been the case with Natasha (who would not, he thought, have liked Sarah). Helen, later in the meal, talked about her latest programme, which was to examine the origins of the Cold War. During all of it Joe spent the time thinking over why Natasha had done what she had done and what that said about her state of mind.

Had she done it to strike out at those she considered her enemies? Yet they were Joe's friends and always friendly to her. It might be that her analyst was now trying to move her even more deeply into Joe's life; to do that, she had to root out those closest to him – but why? What wound would that heal? Tim and Edward were at the very least OK. They could be cynical but no more so than many others and both of them had a kindly side, Joe thought, which he and Natasha had experienced. And why 'corrupt'? She would not have chosen the word carelessly. How had he been corrupted? What was it that she so strongly believed had been lost, a loss that had been instrumental in disrupting their marriage, staining whatever he had been? 'Poor Joseph,' he could hear her say, 'Poor Joseph,' and it maddened him.

They ate Italian, although both Helen and Sarah began with prawn cocktails, and praises were sung for the grilled vegetables, the ravioli, the penne, the zucchini, the Chianti, the ambience, the service and the guitarist who played and sang Neapolitan songs. Toasts in sambuca, black coffee, *arrivederci* and onto the street.

'Great,' said Tim. 'My shout next time. Great! And the girls seem to have clicked.'

'We girls are off to the Dorchester to see what we can pick up,' said Sarah.

'We went to the Dorchester two nights ago,' said Tim, swaying gently in the little lane. 'Into the bar. Prostitutes? It was a convention! I tell you.'

'He fancied some of them,' said Sarah. 'I had to drag him into the restaurant. Thanks, Joe, lovely night. See you soon, Helen. Come on, Tim, taxi time.'

'What can I do?' said Tim. 'I am under her heel.'

'Least said the better,' said Sarah and she linked arms with Helen and walked towards the arch which led to the High Street.

'One thing,' said Tim. 'Seriously. She, Natasha, she thinks you're going to come back to her. She says it's only a matter of time. Well?'

'I want to,' Joe said. 'Sometimes I sort of feel I've not really left her. Not really.'

'But you have. You and Helen. Helen and you. You have. Sexual Chemistry.'

'It's not like that. Well, it is like that, but it isn't just like that, not . . .'

'You have to make your mind up, my friend. The sooner the better. Take it from me. Now then, as the man said, *arrivederci*.'

Joe and Helen waited with them until a taxi turned up, waved them off and then, his arm around her shoulder, they walked back to his house.

'Sarah's good fun!' said Helen. 'What was Tim talking to you about?'

'Natasha,' said Joe. 'He was talking about Natasha.'

'It must have been painful,' said Helen and paused and then, 'Sarah's a copy writer in an advertising agency. She's very funny about the men,' and she laughed, recollecting what Sarah had said.

Fortunately it was Joe who picked up the phone.

'Hello.' The voice was uncertain.

'Natasha!'

Joe looked across the room at Helen who was lying on the sofa, making notes from Randolph Churchill's book on his father. She did not, or did not want to, understand his look.

'Have you some time to talk? A little time.'

'Yes, of course. Yes.'

Again he looked across at Helen. She smiled and then read on.

'Are you alone?'

'Yes. I'm alone. It's fine. We can talk. I'm alone.'

Now it was Helen whose look sought him out. He nodded, covered the mouthpiece with his free hand and mimed apologies. She gathered her notes and the book, without undue speed.

'Are you sure it's . . .?'

'It's fine. I'm just getting a cigarette.' He reached for a cigarette. 'Just a moment.' Helen went out. 'Lighting it. There we are. How are you?'

'Are you sure you're alone?'

'Certain! How's Marcelle?'

'Your lovely daughter gets better day by day. She is a delight. She misses you.'

'And I miss her.'

'Yes . . . Joseph, Ross and Margaret are having a party on Saturday evening and we have been invited. I've not wanted to go with you to the other parties but this one I want to go to and with you.'

'Yes. Good. This Saturday?'

'The invitation came here some time ago but I could not make up my mind. Now I have.'

Joe and Helen had planned to go out with Peter and the gang.

'Could I ring you back?'

'. . . I'd rather you decided now, Joseph.' Her voice was low, tired, needy.

'Of course I'll come. I had something. I'll cancel. Of course I'll come.'

'I would like us to arrive together. Marcelle is staying overnight with Anna. Could you be here at about seven o'clock?'

'Seven o'clock.'

'Thank you. I do thank you. You are not alone, are you?'

'Yes. No. No, I'm not.'

'Poor Joseph. I will see you on Saturday evening.' She waited a moment or two and then put down the telephone.

Joe felt eviscerated. Her stricken gentleness had crushed him. Helen wouldn't mind, would she? She had said something the other day about the limits of patience but he had not really taken it in. Now he did . . .

Natasha took four painkillers with a sip of whisky to ease her back.

The next step, the doctor said, would be surgery. But painkillers and willpower could do wonders for the short term . . .

—ᴍ—

She put on a dress which Joseph had bought her two years previously. It was at the height of the time when he wanted to buy her expensive clothes and see her in things he himself liked. It would have been churlish to deny him the pleasure but it was an act of loyalty on her part. The clothes were usually unsuitable. But this rather full dress, off the shoulder, satin, well cut, with something of the eighteenth century about it, suited her now, she thought, much better than when it had been purchased. Perhaps a slight but decisive turn of fashion had lowered its status and in doing so revealed its charm. And she was thinner now.

She felt like a character in a Russian novel fated to go to a ball. She put on a necklace and then took it off. The dress was sufficiently elaborate. She put on a little make-up to mask the severe whiteness of her face and brushed back her hair. Natasha had never been vain. It was Joseph who had a weakness for mirrors. But this time she did look at herself intently as if looking into a well, seized for the moment by superstition, hoping some message would come back to her from her image.

'You look lovely,' Joseph said. 'I'm pleased you're wearing that dress. You look really lovely.'

She was about to mock the surprise in his tone but she desisted.

'What beautiful flowers. Nobody else would bring me flowers like these.'

They stood in the front room which Natasha had neatened to his taste and lit with candles to hers. We are as awkward as a new courting couple, Natasha thought.

'I'll put them in water.'

Joseph was glad that she left the room. He needed a few moments alone. Her hair, fiercely swept back like Shelley, her shadowy form in the uneven illumination of the few candles, the fragility, the aura of yearning solitude had taken him back to Shillingford to their first encounter, to the woman silhouetted against the fire. The memory was so strong it produced a physical effect and he felt a convulsion in his throat, a pressure in his eyes threatening tears. How could it have come to this? How had it come to this?

She entered bearing the large ruby-petalled roses and offered them to him.

'The scent,' she said, 'is so rich.

'I bought some whisky,' she said. She held up a quarter-bottle. 'I've already taken a little but there is plenty left for you. I thought we should have a drink together before we left.'

'Thank you,' he said as she poured. 'Enough! I'll be drunk before we get there.'

'You look very handsome tonight, Joseph. Much better in that plain black suit. More like a man. *Santé.*' She raised her glass.

'*A la vôtre,*' he said.

'I should not have teased you so much about your French,' she said.

'I asked for it. I usually do.'

'That is because you take risks. Big, small, unnoticeable sometimes except to someone who studies you; but risks all the same.'

Joseph was moved. When she paid him compliments although his gestures shrugged them off they gave him a support available nowhere else.

'The room's different from . . . when I last saw it . . . with you and your friends.'

Natasha waved her cigarette in the air, a small dismissive gesture, but enough to dissolve at once all Joseph's agitation.

'I've almost enough paintings for an exhibition.'

'That's great. Congratulations. Can I see them?'

'Not yet. Not now. Let's just be here.'

Natasha did not want to leave Joseph, who seemed more open than he had done for months. It was almost as it had been at the start, she thought. There was a bottle of wine when the whisky ran out. Just to be with him, without interference, without his deadlines and her distress, without Marcelle and the pressure of Helen, just to be . . . To sit here, she thought, and let time knit them closer together, to begin the healing, that would answer.

'We'd better be off,' he said. 'It's nearly eight o'clock.'

They walked, arm in arm. They had split the flight routes for the Saturday evening so the planes were fewer. Even so after the first half-dozen, Joseph was unnerved at this debilitating reminder, but said nothing as they strolled like other well-married local couples to the blazing lights in the house of Ross McCulloch, on the bank of the Thames.

'I'm so glad you could come!' Margaret had flung open the door, releasing a warm chorus of conviviality into the night air. 'Natasha! You look marvellous! You could be on the way to Versailles.' She kissed Natasha on both cheeks and when she turned to Joseph she held his hands and looked at him with deliberation. 'It's so good to see the two of you together.'

Joseph felt himself clench. Margaret reminded him of Helen. The same corn-blonde hair unsullied by hairdressers, untroubled by curls; the rather round Anglo-Saxon face, eyes of a similar colour though without the defining grey of Helen, the same full smiling dash at life.

'You'll know most people,' she said. 'BBC, Kew, family, a few others.'

The 'others' were a selection from those Ross worked with. David Attenborough was talking to Ross himself, John Schlesinger and Peter O'Toole appeared, Joseph thought, to be talking to each other but simultaneously, Liz Frink he recognised, and Harold Pinter and Dan Jacobson, Ken Russell was talking with Tim, who waved and then bowed, an action clearly directed at Natasha. Most of the others were either the close brotherhood of BBC executives or producers from whom Joseph felt rather exiled. There were some old friends from the area and as the Kew contingent heard of their arrival both Natasha and Joseph were overwhelmed by the sympathetic and welcoming attention paid as to prodigals returned to the fold.

The buffet, laid out in royal style and rich portions, was served in the large room that overlooked the river. Natasha who wanted nothing to eat and Joseph who was tempted on all sides by the display of feast became separated. During the next hour or two he went from con-versation to conversation like someone in a gavotte. These circulations of conversationalists replaced the formal dancing which had once served the same purpose in a house such as this, he thought. They went from one new talking partner to another, a touch, a few para-graphs, a promise to meet again, another whirl.

Joseph soon found himself part of it. The talk stayed on the unchallenging slopes of the news of the day, or with BBC people dipped into the ever-fascinating topic of BBC internal politics; one or two people referred favourably to his work which he knew could have been little more than social politeness but nevertheless made him feel real as a writer. Tim said, 'We two can talk any old time . . . I've got a few more to get round. That Helen of yours is sex in boots. And bright.'

Sarah said, 'That was a great dinner. I've talked to Helen, we'll all do it again soonest. Is she here?'

Joseph kept an eye on Natasha. Much of the time she had sat talking to a man with heavy spectacles, a boyish haircut and a brown corduroy jacket that looked as if it had been passed down from his father.

'This is Jeremy,' she said, when Joseph finally got across to her. 'He runs the bookshop. I work there sometimes.'

'More times, I hope,' said Jeremy, who held out a soft hand for Joseph to shake. 'Pleased to meet you. I'm rather new, I've just taken the place over in the last few months.' Jeremy looked at Natasha whose gaze was fixed on Joseph. 'I think I need another drink. You?'

'No thank you,' said Natasha.

When Jeremy left them, Natasha stood up and said, a little too loudly, Joe thought, 'Why have you left me alone for so long?'

'Just . . . moving around. You seemed all right with Jeremy.'

'Sometimes just to be near someone who cares for you is enough. But I came here with you.'

'At a party like this,' Joseph adopted a whisper to try to influence and reduce the volume, 'aren't we supposed to mix?'

'Only if you choose to do. Which you did.'

'Well, we're together now. Did you have anything to eat? The food is delicious, especially that salmon.'

'Why do you talk about salmon?'

Joseph laughed.

'Natasha. Please. I'm sorry. I'm here. They've opened the french windows. Let's go outside.'

'What for, Joseph?'

We should never have come, he thought.

'Why did we come?' she said and her eyes blazed at him. But when he looked away she checked her manners.

'There is a large bowl of fruit salad,' she said. 'We could eat fruit salad.'

When the guests had finally gone and Ross and Margaret mulled over the evening he said,

'I overheard them talking. One of them will have to give in.'

'She looked beautiful,' said Margaret.

'I thought she looked exhausted,' Ross said. 'And he's in some sort of limbo.'

'I'm still glad they came.'

'I'm glad we went,' said Natasha when they got back to her house.

'So am I . . .' he said, and added, 'and it was good to walk there together and be there and now best of all come back here with a small history between us,' he said, loving her, and only a little drunk.

'Why do you still give me hope?'

She lit the candles and turned on the electric fire.

'I must phone for a taxi.'

'I must get some wine.'

Natasha poured out the wine.

'Thank you,' she said and raised the glass. 'I wanted you to take me there.' She sipped. 'It is curious, isn't it, that sometimes when people try to be kind and are kind and say kind things you could scream. I suppose that is what is meant when they say, "I don't want any pity." I felt rather a lot of pity tonight.'

'So did I. But they were, they are kind.'

'They want us to be back together,' said Natasha.

I wish I had more energy, Natasha thought. I am failing just as I want to be on my way to succeeding. Look at him. He is so nervous, ready to jump off that seat and run away at any second. Yet throughout the evening, both self-consciously and unconsciously he has been loving, his old self as the saying is.

His old good self. Not the self that seemed to grind me into his family's past as if I needed my nose rubbing in it! Not the self that now and then shouted and sometimes frightened me because he would have no better way than anger to resolve problems he had never thought to

515

meet. Nor the selfish self who could hurt so casually. But the self that always said and knew that he was sorry for that and could mend our lives at will. The self that had served and protected me. The self that encouraged me and cheered me on and tries hard to be a good father to Marcelle. The self that was just there most of, often all of, the time, content to go through life alongside me, expressing disbelief now and then that such luck should have come his way. The self that loved me enough to be with me. And there could be more of that, Natasha believed. She wanted to reach out for that Joseph at this moment and for him to reach out for her. It did not matter that he had fallen away from what he could be. What mattered to her was that he could still, she believed, be true to himself as she had found him. And true once again to her.

'Why,' he said, into the late-night, plane-free silence, in the cave of shadows promising resolutions which the candles conjured up, 'why did you not just come back to the Hampstead house? You and Marcelle. I kept thinking when I was walking home – they'll be there. And I didn't think, not once, Natasha, I didn't think – that'll be terrible, there'll have to be a scene, I just thought – they'll be there. Why not? The place was empty for months. They'll be waiting, I thought, time and again, the two of them. And when you weren't, I thought – why not? Why not just come back? What would I have done but accept it? We could have started again.

'I know you gave me my freedom. That was an amazing thing to do. That was you, Natasha. Only you. Nobody but you would have done that and so thoroughly. But you know I am in analysis, just as you are, and you know what that means and how weak it makes you. In one way I think it has the same effect as bloodletting for fever in the Middle Ages. The freedom you gave me was just too much for me. I'm not that good, Natasha, I'm not strong, sometimes this last year or two I've been jelly. And I'm not any sort of saint who was able to take this perfect freedom. It was too big a gift for me, Natasha. Or too big a test. Maybe that's nearer the truth. And I failed that test, Natasha. But, tell me – why didn't you just come back home?'

The tears which came to his eyes were not matched in hers because all her remaining resources were trying to hold out against the great tide of darkness which broke inside her sweeping away, it seemed, everything she had tried to guard. Why had she not done that? Simply that. And been saved? But now the wreckage of her life was swept down into depths she could not contemplate.

Joseph went across to her. She looked up at him with such sorrow. How could he bear to let her suffer such sorrow? She raised her arms to him.

'Can we go to bed?' she whispered. 'Together. I can't bear it, Joseph. And it will help me.'

After they had made love they clung to each other desperately like two people trying to force life to fire once again between them. Then he moved uneasily away from her and she knew he wanted to leave her. He was not brave enough. He had lost himself and now finally she must lose him too. Out of her darkness she said,

'You must go.'

How could he go? he thought, and she thought, how could he leave her?

As Joseph moved away, Natasha became conscious of her wedding ring. She turned away from him and as he dressed she tugged at the ring which seemed stuck fast but though it hurt her finger she persisted. When he came across – to kiss her one last time? To say goodbye? To apologise? To lie? – she turned, seeming quite calm, and held it out to him. He did not want to take it. She looked at him directly and with the courage that always moved him. He took the ring. She turned away and held on until finally she heard him leave the house.

CHAPTER FORTY-FIVE

'I think that there are some people who are driven by the Furies,' he wrote to Marcelle, 'and your mother was one of them. The Furies come out of an abyss to pursue you to your fate, they press your darkest destiny on you. Natasha whose need for me, as I was to learn from others, was turning into an obsession, came out of that visit like one hounded. Her only escape, it must have seemed to her then, was to rediscover and reclaim the person she had originally set out and sworn to be. Her only survival would lie in being unswervingly true to herself. The self she was before she met me.

'A few weeks later, without any preamble, divorce papers were posted to Hampstead. What did I feel? I am trying not to exaggerate but it is difficult not to. In the circumstances, given that I was by then living with another woman, some of my reactions were preposterous but they were nonetheless sane for that and even sincere, that treacherous word. I was outraged. I was hurt. I was blind furious. I was scared. I was out of my depth.

'I rang Natasha immediately and let loose – I am sure although I cannot remember a word – a hurricane of anger, and it was on that call, I am more sure of this, that I used a term which Tim had fed me and used in his own divorce – "A marriage does not mean you have security for life". There's shame. Natasha was not strong enough for that. Natasha had not been hardened to verbal violence. No mitigation has been able to redeem that. It was plain nasty. But to me divorce came like a threat to life, the unanticipated papers landed on the mat like a blow.'

—ɷ—

'I asked her not to pursue a divorce,' said James. 'She telephoned to talk to me and I went to Kew to discuss it with her. I tried to tell her it would do no good. You would not be able to cope. I told her I was sure you would eventually come back to her. Better not to push it. Better to wait at least until you had finished your analysis. I've known about that for some time, by the way. Natasha told me months ago and to return confidence for confidence, I am myself seeing not an analyst but a therapist once a week. I find it very interesting. But Natasha is totally determined to cut you out of her life and begin again. Yet she can talk of little else but you, you and Helen, with a terrible jealousy, you and her, why you are as you are, how you could change. It is very distressing to see how much she wants you back and realises what she has lost. That's the nub of it. And she believes that her life as an artist has been sidetracked. She is now in what I can only describe as a sort of frenzy of creativity.'

The more as her work did not prosper as she would have wished. Her second novel had been reviewed less well than the first, not an unusual experience but painful nonetheless. Victoria's gallery had declined to offer her a one-woman show and their suggestion that she might wait for a few months and take part in their summer show when six new artists exhibited had been turned down by Natasha in favour of a small gallery in Richmond in which the exhibition had been more a declaration of intent than the London launch of a new painter which she wanted. Joe had not been invited.

James's further efforts to recreate some goodwill on both sides were unsuccessful.

The phone calls between Natasha and Joe over the next weeks were on both sides acrimonious, unbridled, wounding to both of them. Frequently the phone would be slammed down and then picked up instantly after a bloodied interchange to offer an apology which as often as not fell once more into the rut of accusation often wild, always hurtful.

'You are angry at me,' his analyst said, 'because you see this process, this analysis, as one which, as you have just told me, has made you less guarded, less considerate, less able to be tolerant and "good-mannered", your phrase. You see that as a loss. You say you believe that had you not come to see me and were Natasha also not in analysis then the old defences and habits would as it were fudge or "insulate" –

your word – matters and see you through. But quite obviously the old defences and habits had had their day with you. They had ceased to be of much use, as you have indicated on several occasions, for the new situation in which you found and still find yourself. You worry about what her analysis is doing to her but of course you can't ask. Well, you could, but you won't. Perhaps you might like to talk about that here.'

But Joe found nothing to say. To talk to Natasha about her analyst seemed far away from what was between them now and besides she would evade even the slightest reference to her analysis.

'Do you have to be so root and branch?' Margaret asked her. The two women were alone in the drawing room, polishing the silver. Ross was taking advantage of a fine summer Sunday afternoon to take his own children and Marcelle to Hampton Court.

'What alternative is there?'

'Conciliation?'

'The time for that was given and is now gone.'

'Have you ever thought of talking to her? To Helen, I mean. I know it's not the usual route but when you and Joe are together you still seem, to me, you did at the party for instance, to have very much to offer each other. Maybe Helen doesn't know that.'

'I've thought of it,' Natasha said. 'I've thought about it often.'

She had lost weight. Curiously it made her look even more distinguished, Margaret reported to Ross, more foreign, more distant. 'At some moments she seems very shaky,' she said, 'at other times quite burning with a passion to follow her way. God knows what she's going through. But in the end she is always circling around Joseph.'

'I don't want you to take out Marcelle this Sunday,' she told Joseph.

'Why not? Last Sunday you said it was better for her to go out with Ross and his family on a trip he'd arranged and I could understand that. But not two Sundays in a row. What about Saturday?'

'Neither Saturday.'

'What is this?'

'You make her too excited. She has to be calm to make her life here. She mustn't have this circus every week. It unsettles her.'

'She seems not the slightest bit unsettled. Are you talking about her or about yourself? Marcelle and I have good times. I love seeing her.'

'I need to clear my mind, Joseph, and I need her to understand what is happening. You have to leave me alone. You make it difficult. So does Ellen.'

'What does my mother have to do with it?'

'She brings too many presents, she gives her too many "treats" as she calls them. This is no good for Marcelle. I've asked Ellen not to come here again. Until matters are resolved.'

'That's cruel.'

'I have to take the best decisions as I see them. I do not want you to take Marcelle on Sunday. Neither Saturday.'

'What if I just turn up?'

'Please don't. Please don't.' I could not bear it, she thought.

'I will,' said Joe. 'Sunday. Between half eleven and twelve. As usual.'

After he had put down the phone Helen came in and she went to hold him but the tension coming off him was so strong she retreated, sat on the long sofa, took out a cigarette. Joe looked out of the window onto the narrow street, his back to Helen, his feelings too turbulent to master, silence his only recourse.

'She says I can't see Marcelle.'

'I gathered that. I was outside the door.'

'I'm going down on Sunday. In fact I'll bloody well go down now.'

'Maybe it would be better to sleep on it,' said Helen.

'She can't do this. I mean . . . It's . . . Why should I not see her?'

'Maybe,' said Helen, carefully, having thought this through for some time, 'you ought to go back to her. Maybe that would be the best way.'

He turned and stood against the window, against the light. Helen could not make out his expression.

'Why do you say that?'

'You seem so unhappy. You're torn in two.'

'What about us?'

Helen did not reply.

Could I do it? Joe thought. Could I just walk out of here now not for Marcelle but for both of them? Could I do that and prevent the inevitable wreckage that waited on divorce, all of the ripping up of their life together? I want to: so much of me wants to. It would be hard, but Helen's offer had made it possible, and was not the alternative harder? It was harder to stay with Helen, his analyst had said. But what did 'hard' mean? It was not to be calculated on a list or a balance sheet of Advantages and Disadvantages. It had gone so far inside him, this decision and this indecision, that there was nothing but insistent uncertainty. Oh, how good it would be to return to Kew, to Natasha, to their daughter, planes to be endured somehow, back to the place where they had made a life worth living and rescue Natasha from the pain she was in and by doing the right thing begin to resolve the sleepless consciousness of wrongdoing which made him loathe what he had become.

But he could not. He could not. He could not leave Helen. Not even to save Natasha, not even to redeem himself. Even if he had to, as he would, pay for that for ever after.

'Let her have some time, at least,' said Helen.

Two days later a letter arrived from the solicitor asking Mr Richardson if he would desist from visits to his wife's house in Kew Gardens and until further notice desist equally for the time being from taking their daughter Marcelle away from her mother at weekends.

Once again Joe reached for the telephone but, mercifully, Natasha was not at home. Helen was out working on her film. Joe, alone at home, felt bound and gagged and trapped.

'I'm afraid of what he'll say,' she said to Anna, in whose house she had taken refuge. 'I'm afraid of him.'

'You mustn't be. He's upset just as you're upset. It's awful for all your friends to see you both suffering. But he would never hurt you.'

'I know.'

'I am convinced he still loves you. We all are.'

'I know that too. That's what gives me hope. His love gives me hope. And I know I will always live inside him. But what use is hope, Anna?'

'Oh, Natasha.'

'But I am afraid. I will go away. We will go away. Until this divorce goes through.'

'Why don't you shelve the divorce for a while? He doesn't want it. He's told us he doesn't want it.'

'But he must face it, you see. He has to see what the consequences are. I have to start again with everything clear. I want to go back in the dark and find my way, this time alone and safe.'

'She smiled,' Anna said later to her husband, 'and I don't know why but I wanted to burst into tears . . .'

— ɱ —

'But of course you can come and stay with us,' Isabel wrote back. 'Stay for summer? Stay for ever if you wish, my darling Natasha, and Marcelle too.'

But the house of Isabel and Alain was three kilometres from La Rotonde, quite isolated and, save for the two German shepherds who delighted Marcelle, there was no company for the child. She spent more and more time in La Rotonde where she soon found playmates. After a couple of weeks, despite Isabel's plea that Natasha still needed more rest and care from her, it seemed more sensible that Natasha and Marcelle move into La Rotonde.

Véronique gave them the bottom floor where the walls were at their thickest. It was cool against the heat but always rather dark. The windows were narrow slits. Sometimes Natasha felt she was in a dungeon.

— ɱ —

Joe was bereft. Bewildered, he trailed around the humid London streets as if looking for a thread which would lead him to the answer to all his questions. He was still working on the film from the novel set in Mexico and at least half the week was spent in morning 'script conferences' which lasted an hour or two and then left him high and dry. He did not want to go back to an empty house. Helen was working on her documentary. Sometimes he went into the London Library but its studious tranquility was unsuited to his oscillating, febrile mood. The external world was a shell he longed and threatened to break out of and yet strove to preserve intact.

He was surrounded by cinemas, galleries and museums which once would have been a refuge but now demanded too much energy. It was

523

hard for him to concentrate. The film script was effort enough and there he was helped by being with the producer and the director. He remained very nervous about travelling on the underground, still aware of imminent panic attacks. Although the self-imposed necessity to learn poetry had slackened he held onto it, kept at the ready like a well-cared-for weapon. And the sensation of blankness, of collapse could still overtake him. To walk the streets, however, to be a passing part of distracting, busy, city life proved to be a way to cope. Yet that summer the London streets seemed charged with too much intensity, so often on the edge of a thunderstorm.

He wanted Natasha. He wanted his analyst. He was like half a person aching, longing, crying for the other half, for the whole. Why had his analyst gone away? Why had Natasha? He felt inside her head, inside her pain, his pain; pain dominant.

The parting with wife and daughter was a brutal severance. The cut of it was raw. He reached out for them, and as he criss-crossed the West End of London, from offices to his analyst, to the library and the pubs, he was often so alive to Natasha and Marcelle that they seemed just around the corner, somewhere out there, waiting to be encountered. Yet he knew where they were and any day he could have joined them. But Helen was now his centre, however strained and bruising the effect of this separation.

Marcelle, he decided, must have a present and he came up with the idea of a hammock. It would be fun, he thought, for her and friends. There were two trees in the garden at La Rotonde between which it could be slung. He envied them the garden just as he envied them La Rotonde from the dirty steaming summer streets of London. He knew it would make Marcelle happy and a hammock was a big thing, it was something she could show off. He could see Marcelle in his mind's eye whenever he wanted to. Natasha's expression was so sad, her face more and more gaunt in sorrow, that he would turn away from it. He would remember the smile and that was unbearable. Again and again he thought that what he was doing was bad and wrong and yet he could not stop himself from doing it. He was then and would later be condemned for that.

A letter came from her, tender, brief. She was thinking of staying on after the holidays. Marcelle could attend the local school. Her back was hurting a great deal now and Alain had recommended rest in the warmth of La Rotonde and also he had prescribed strong pills which worked wonders. Would he object? Marcelle was flourishing and she told the other children boastful stories about her English father!

Joe was determined to respond well. It was good that she was in Alain's hands, he wrote, and Marcelle would surely benefit from being at a French school and they must stay as long as they wanted, until she, Natasha, felt completely well . . .

Natasha received it as the letter of a man who would rather his estranged wife and child stayed out of his new life, the longer the better.

—◁▥▷—

A friend of Helen's recommended a small hotel-pub in Cornwall, Journey's End, and they went for a few days towards the end of August. The train journey took longer than he had anticipated but it put both time and space between himself all that London had been and was, and he arrived in Cornwall in flight as much as on holiday.

The landlord who kept the bar in the deeply polished Jacobean premises was scarlet-faced and nose-purpled with rabid alcoholism. He boasted that if ever there was any untoward disturbance in his bar he brought out his double-barrelled shotgun and let loose at the walls and he pointed out several holes as proud proof. His wife, subdued and apologetic, made the place comfortable, and easy to like. Helen and Joe walked in the daytime, and after dinner went to a corner of the generally empty bar, where they played chess partly to avoid the conversational overtures of the scarlet-pimpled landlord.

Joe sent several postcards to Marcelle, on one of them asking if she had received any surprise from London.

They went for a final walk on the afternoon before they left. Perhaps it was the prospect of returning to London that jarred Joe but as they went up to the cliffs he felt unsettled and tried to draw ahead of Helen. He wanted space to resolve this. Helen, thinking he was in the mood for a more vigorous walk, stuck with him. She was still at his shoulder when they reached the top of the cliff path and the faster he walked along the edge the more Helen enjoyed the briskness of it, the feeling of her vitality being cuffed by the high wind and the warm sun and by the recently lost urgency which had returned to Joe's step.

He stopped and looked out to the horizon a while. Then he said, 'Do you mind if I go on by myself?'

'Why?'

'I don't really know . . . I just want to be by myself. I'm sorry.'

'What is it?'

Still with his back to her he said,

'What I really want to do is to join Natasha and Marcelle.'

'You traitor!'

He faced her. Had the word been used only mock-seriously?

'How can you say that?'

'You've made up your mind. You should stick to it.'

'It isn't like that, Helen.'

'Why not? It is for me.'

'I have to see them.' Her accusation had felled him.

'Well, do it.' Helen paused. 'But I'm not walking back by myself.'

As they went more slowly along the cliff edge and it curved inland on a path that would eventually loop them back to the hotel, it began to rain. Neither of them was dressed for it. Neither of them complained or even commented. Joe was fast in himself. Helen knew she could not reach him.

'I heard your mother that day,' he said to Marcelle. 'I can still remember it clearly. Such things had happened once or twice before in my life when I was young but they were long buried in embarrassment and anxiety at their over-strangeness. "Heard" will have to do although I know it summons up ideas of ghostly voices and mediums bringing messages from beyond the grave. But it is certain sure. As soon as I began to walk on that morning I felt that I had to go to your mother. There are many ways to explain it away and of course sometimes I believe that it was all my invention and not Natasha's intervention but all that I can tell you is that thinking on it again and again it will not be easily explained away and in the end what I experienced was your mother's calling me, calling me back. It was also physical, her hands reaching out to mine to pull me to her; I was consumed by it, it was as real as the rain, Marcelle. I offer it for what it is. But I did not go.'

They got to the hotel later than they had intended, still not a word spoken, and Helen went directly to one of the two bathrooms along the corridor. Joe undressed and perched his soaked clothes on the radiators. He dried himself down with a towel which he then tucked around his waist. When Helen returned he was asleep.

'We'll just be in time for dinner,' she said when she woke him, later. She had covered him with a blanket. 'I'll go ahead.' She held up the small travelling chess set. 'Shall I take this?'

Joe looked at her. She was calm, grounded, fresh-faced from the walk, her blonde hair shampooed. It was time to surrender to the fact that he was in love and unthreatened.

'Best of three,' he said.

'There was a period of time, towards the end of our marriage, when we wrote letters to each other by the score,' he told Marcelle, 'two or three times a day. As if speech had failed us or we did not trust it or we did not want to see on the other's face the effect of what we said.

'In France, Natasha began a frenzy of writing, sometimes poems or fragments of poems, mostly letters, all unposted. These are a few excerpts, fragments even, that might explain . . .

'She wrote to Ross's wife, Margaret, who had become more of a close friend to her since her return to Kew. "I am in France partly because I am so tired, my back, but mostly because in London I cannot bear people to know how much I love Joseph . . . I feel that it is only by accepting the idea of getting to the core I mentioned earlier that our relationship can be accepted again and the point is whether or not Joseph can bear it or doesn't want to chance it. It is also perfectly clear that unless I do extreme violence to myself, I could not stop loving him in a million years. Also I have to face up to the fact that my love for him is extraordinarily demanding as it goes on pursuing the deepest of his self as the most important part of him. This pursuit is rather obsessive perhaps, but I do not see myself pursuing much else with the same conviction as far as he is concerned. I would like to think that this doesn't make me a loser in other aspects of him. At the moment it seems to be so . . ."

'That was handwritten, clearly, neatly, early on. This, later, to me (only a small part of a "piece" which covered thirty-four pages), was much more loosely written . . . "I want to tell you how sorry I am about this time apart and how sorry I am too about all those hurtful things that have been between us. I wish I had never hurt you, that I had never failed you, that somehow I had been able to give you only happiness and good but I know I have not done that. I love you deeply, I miss you. I feel that everything I do is connected with loving you well, loving you badly, and somehow my mind and soul go in circles around you straining somehow to find answers, to stop asking questions, to love you and be your love. You have given me so much, you have given me life. I long to see our hands join in trust . . ."

'Quite abruptly the writing changes again and dwindles into a still neat but cowed small script. "I have not been well for a few weeks and I think it would be much better if I had a rest for two or three months . . . Perhaps we could meet then in a much calmer way. You are so upset and angry with me. My ambitions in life are to write and paint, mother my child and be with the man I love."

'There are poems. Mostly unfinished, lines slashed with corrections and changes. This, I think, is the last, written in a scrawling tormented script.

> 'Bewildered,
> Blinded by the lighting of grief
> Debreasted
> Neutralised
> I lay on the sand where heat had warmed
> Where earthy grain had never failed
> Even there I lost the last touch
> The ability to go to sleep.
> I saw you walk over the sky
> I saw you had gone.'

—ɯ—

The surge of acceleration took Natasha by surprise and pressed her into the pit of the seat. Her back hurt but only a little: Alain had prescribed well and given her ample supplies to reduce the pain over the next few weeks. She looked at Marcelle who had the window seat and was nose-pressed to it watching every moment of the earth sinking beneath her gaze. She had grown even in the two months in Provence, Natasha observed. She was practically self-sufficient now. Natasha did not look at her too intently or for too long. Tears were too near the surface for that.

When the No Smoking signal was gone she lit up. Véronique had tried to help by introducing certain disciplines – the most persistent and public of these was her insistence that Natasha give up smoking. The number of cigarettes she consumed was way beyond reason, she argued, and the ghostly pallor of her skin showed that those cigarettes had a visible effect on her health. Besides, Véronique argued, if she could exercise willpower in this matter, she could do so in others. Natasha had tried her best to go along with it, fearing to antagonise Véronique, even seeing in the diktat a kernel of real concern which moved her. But now she smoked, and ordered whisky.

The plane droned north. Her tiredness was beyond sleep. But the cigarettes and the alcohol, the presence of Marcelle and the security of the aeroplane brought to her tortured mind an interval of relief. And Joseph would be at the airport, waiting for her, she was sure of that. She had written to him. And then who knows? Who knows?

Soon the plane would pass over Paris and then swing west, over Brittany, and across the Channel to England to which she had fled so long ago now, too tired to work out how long ago. And met Joseph. And others. But Joseph who had loved her from the beginning and still loved her, she knew that, but it was difficult for him as it was difficult for her. Soon those difficulties would diminish and they would meet again and he would bring flowers.

When they came through Customs she restrained herself. It would not do to seem too eager. It would not do, and yet her heart beat faster and she could not wait until their suitcases arrived and they went into Customs and out the other side where Joseph would be waiting. She was so very tired now but the break would have restored his mind, of that she was utterly certain, as she had told him in the unposted letter. She knew him so well, she knew him because she loved him and he undoubtedly loved her.

There was a small crowd waiting for the passengers. It was not easy to pick him out. She must not be impatient. She stood for some time while the greetings and the welcomings went on all about her.

Finally when she was all but alone, she looked for directions to the train into London. Oh, Joseph . . .

———ɯ———

Margaret had gone to the house once a week and though rather cool it did not have a neglected air. The mail was piled neatly on a small table in the living room. There was a loaf of fresh bread and some fruit. She phoned Margaret to thank her and Margaret said she would come round.

Marcelle sniffed around the house to resettle herself and then went into Natasha's bedroom where there was a small television. Natasha was too weary to go upstairs. She shuffled through the post hoping: but there was nothing. She put on the electric fire and waited . . . A plane went over low, screaming, and she looked up, startled. What would it do? She waited. Another came, just as low, and she put her hands to her ears. It was such an apocalyptic sound.

She reached for the phone but before she dialled the number, she steadied herself. It took great effort. It would not do to seek pity. She sipped from the neck of the half-bottle of whisky she had bought on the plane. Then she dialled.

'Yes?'

'It's Natasha,' she said, and waited.

'Are you back?'

'Yes . . . Yes I am.'

'Good.' He turned to Helen and mouthed 'Natasha'. 'How's Marcelle?'

'Marcelle?' Natasha could find no reply. 'Joseph. You do think I am a good mother, don't you?'

'Yes. Of course you are.'

'You wouldn't lie, would you?'

'No. You're a wonderful mother.'

'Marcelle is like you. Even Isabel says so.' She paused. 'What are you writing?'

'Still the film.'

'You always wanted to write films, didn't you, when we first met? And so you have.'

'Natasha?'

'Yes.'

'Can I come to see you both tomorrow?'

'Tomorrow?' Not . . . now, now.

'Whatever suits you.'

'Yes.' She waited. 'Tomorrow.'

Another plane went over.

'Tomorrow, then.'

'Yes,' she said. 'Thank you.'

She put down the phone gently and sat very still. Joe said to Helen, 'I should go down to see her now.'

'You should,' Helen said.

'Yes . . . I should.'

But he believed tomorrow would be fine, would even be better. Yet he should have gone. Her life would have changed, would it not? If he had gone. And just to see her again. To be with her, her love, her great self, their unity again. He should have gone. For the rest of his life he should have gone.

He did not go. He does not go. He does not go.

Before Margaret left she said, two or three times, 'Why don't you come round and spend the night with us? It's always such a bother when you come back to a cold home at this time of night.'

But Natasha's mind was incapable of accepting such simple, kind help. Joseph would call back. And besides there were thoughts clouding her mind, thoughts or intimations of thoughts or echoes and calls and imprints from other times which she wanted to let possess her, be immersed in, float and fathom.

'Tomorrow,' she said, and Margaret kissed her cheek and went out, reluctantly.

Marcelle came down and ate some bread and half an apple and

then, cross at her mother's silence and tears, went off to bed by herself.

So at last she was alone. This was it then, this everything, this nothing. Particles of dreams, splinters of nightmare, colours of happiness, here, there, the slow swirl of it all so full of life, and that was all, that was everything, it was done. It was finished. The swirl quickened and became a tightening spiral pulling her down as she wept without feeling the tears and knew less and less, heard no calls of love, gone now. She went to her room and shut the door. There was no lock. She put a chair under the door handle and jammed it tight. That was for Marcelle, that must have been for Marcelle. And finally the fury.

—ɯ—

'It's Margaret.'

'No!'

'I'm sorry.'

'No. No! Please. No!'

Margaret closed her eyes and forced herself on.

'I'm afraid . . .'

'No. Oh, please NO. Don't say it. Please God. Don't. No!'

'Natasha's dead.'

'NO. NO. Please say she isn't. Please say that. Say she isn't. Please.'

CHAPTER FORTY-SIX

He took Marcelle into Kew Gardens later that afternoon. Margaret had given her bread and they went to the big pond to feed the ducks. It was here that he had imagined he would tell her what had happened. She had given no indication that she knew even though when Margaret had gone round in the morning she had found the bedroom door ajar. Joe watched her carefully but there was no sign of distress. Margaret had taken her away and she had spent the day with her children. Now the little girl stood at the edge of the water unafraid as the ducks crowded around her and clacked their hard beaks for the morsels she distributed: she liked to spin it out.

Joe sat on a bench. What would he say to her? It had seemed right, this open familiar place, and as he had anticipated there were not many people in the Gardens at this time on a weekday. But there were a few and even the few seemed to undermine his will. Another plane went over, the ducks clacked loudly, this was not the place after all, he decided, and when the bread was finished he took her hand and they walked towards Kew Green to the church which was empty and, after the outside light, quite dark. They walked together down the nave towards the altar. Now that he was here, now that there was no way out, Joe felt such a pressure of weariness that when he sat down he needed it, his life had drained away.

Marcelle wanted to explore but he put his hand on her shoulder and she stayed. The silence of the church crushed him.

'Marcelle,' he began, but at the mere mention of her name he thought he would crack. He could not stop now. 'Mummy has not been well. She's kept it secret because she did not want to upset you, or to

533

frighten you. She's, your mummy, is, I'm afraid that she died during the night. She's dead now, Marcelle. That means you won't, we won't, neither of us, ever see her again.'

The little girl looked up at him. She saw her father's face tremble against sorrow and her own face began to imitate his. It was too much for her to imagine, he thought. He let the silence be.

'Mummy was still asleep this morning,' Marcelle said finally. 'Before Margaret came.'

Margaret had told him that in one of what eventually proved to be several phone calls to people, Natasha had asked Margaret to come around as early as possible in the morning to look after Marcelle as she had to go into London.

Joe closed his eyes hard and waited.

'I shouted through the door and I tried to wake her up. So I went downstairs and then Margaret came.'

'She was fast asleep then, Marcelle.' And you missed the worst of it, he knew that, from everything about her; thank God for that at least.

'I couldn't wake her up,' said Marcelle and looked up at him, trying, he thought, to be helpful.

'No one could,' he said, finding it too hard. 'Nobody can wake her up now. She's gone.'

'Will she never come back?'

No. No. Though then and for ever he wanted it. No.

Joe could not speak but finally he shook his head.

Marcelle began to understand. She caught something of her father's grief. In the empty church they sat silently, his arm around her small shoulders. There was a violent strain across his chest as if it would burst open, as if his heart was forever broken.

Ellen had gone to London immediately. Sam waited until the day before the funeral. He would go in the afternoon, meet Ellen in Kew later and she would travel back to Reading, taking Marcelle. It had been agreed that it would be better for her not to endure the funeral, a decision Marcelle later thought a mistake. Ellen would look after her, Sam would go to the funeral. But before that there was one thing he had to do and alone.

Joe's instructions were clear. Turn right outside Richmond Station. After a hundred yards or so turn right into a crescent. The funeral parlour was on the right, impossible to miss.

'You are?'

'Her father-in-law.'

'Of course . . . your son telephoned.'

Sam was led to a door which was gently opened and after he had entered the room it closed gently behind him. The coffin was at the other side of the room, four tall unlit candles one at each corner, a chair beside it, just like in a hospital, Sam thought. He stood for a while, not wanting to approach it. He had a sudden desperate need for a cigarette, saw there were two ashtrays on the table and lit up. He had not anticipated what he might be in for but it was tougher than he could have imagined. He stubbed out the half-smoked cigarette and went across to the chair.

Her face was so white and looked so cold. Her hair, he saw, had thinned, making her high forehead even more prominent. Her closed eyes did not bring peace to her face.

'Why didn't you come and talk to me?' he said. 'I would have helped you. I would have done anything in the world for you. I'd hoped that somehow you knew that.'

Sam did not cry. Men who had led his life did not cry. His heart, though, ached, ached, as it had done from the moment he had been told. It was a pain that would never altogether go away.

'I wish . . .' he said, but stopped. There was nothing more to be said.

When Sam had collected himself he left quietly and nodded his thanks, not wanting to speak. Walking slowly, like a very old man, he made his way back to the station.

Ross and Margaret had made their house available for the day of the funeral. That was where the mourners would meet. After the service in the crematorium the congregation would be invited back. Natasha had told Joe long ago that she wanted to be cremated 'on a funeral pyre', she

535

had said, 'while you sail on'. Joe was seeking permission to place the urn behind the altar in the church on Kew Green.

Louis and Véronique came an hour earlier than everyone else. Isabel had taken ill at the news and could not travel and Alain would not leave her by herself. Of the household Joe had met at Natasha's aunts' house only one person was still alive and she had followed Louis's advice that the journey would be too taxing for her. Véronique had thought it better that the children did not come. Louis was the only one there of French blood.

Margaret brought them coffee in the small sitting room at the front of the house. She left them, Louis, Véronique, Joe. This was the first time they had been together since Louis's and Véronique's arrival late the night before. Véronique, Joe thought, looked much more distressed and anxious than he had thought she would. Louis was grave. He had embraced Joe when they had met and Véronique had kissed him on the cheek but Joe felt that he was about to be charged with the death of Natasha. There was no defence.

After the explanations about Isabel and the others, after the appreciation expressed for Ross and Margaret, Louis said, in his careful English, 'Natasha created a hostile world.' He looked at Joe so directly that Véronique might have felt excluded. 'Ever since she was a child it was the same. Of course her mother dying when she was still a baby had a great effect. That was very unfortunate for her. But when I married Véronique it did not get better. It even got worse. It was always Natasha against the world.'

Joe recognised that the core of this held part of a truth he would have recognised but he found that he wanted to challenge what Louis said and question it. Yet as Louis went on developing the point as he would a thesis, Joe checked himself. This was Natasha's father who had known her much longer and presumably much better than he had. This was a burial day.

'So you see,' said Louis, 'at some time or other it was inevitable that she would feel that the world would turn against her even more strongly than it usually did. All that was missing was a crisis.'

No, thought Joe, she was not such a victim. She was not weak. And there may have been a hostile world but she also had a world of friends whom you will see, people who thought she was marvellous, beautiful, unique. As I did. As I do.

'It will be very difficult for you to go into her house for the next few days,' said Véronique. 'If you give me the keys I will go there and put it in order. I remember Natasha saying that you could get annoyed at her untidiness and even such a small thing can be distressing at such a time.'

She held out her hand and Joe handed her the keys.

The crematorium was packed. The service, too short, too plain, Joe thought, was yet charged with such grief and loss that few dared catch another's eye. The reception in Ross's house was by contrast an affair of support with their friends, from Oxford, from Kew, from Joe's work, from Natasha's recent acquaintanceship. There was a hum to it, and life was even now beginning to move on. Joe could not bear it. He sought out Ross.

'I want to say something about Natasha.'

Ross looked at him closely as if he were inspecting one of his men before battle.

'Are you absolutely sure, old boy?'

'Yes. It's as if . . . it's as if there's something to be ashamed of and I don't want it to be like that. It isn't, it shouldn't be like that.'

You are the one, Ross did not say, who is ashamed.

'OK. Have a drink. I'll give you two or three minutes, then I'll give you the signal.'

The speech was not good.

'I remember only a little of what I said,' he told Marcelle. 'I felt a hundred angry eyes and cries of shame and disgrace only barely withheld. But this was not the parting for Natasha. I wanted to tell them what they all knew about her but which was being excluded because of the terrible nature of her death. I hope I said how wonderful she was and how much can be made even of a short life and they all knew that, they were here because of that and I told them how much she knew they had given her. I remember that I said . . . I said I had loved her very much and still did. And then I just choked and stopped and no one said anything until my father, whom I had not noticed standing behind me, tapped on my arm and I followed him to where the drinks were. People left us alone together for a few moments. He poured two whiskies, handed me mine and looked at me so intently that I feared the blow. "That took guts," he said. He raised his glass an inch or two. "There's marriages break down without it leading to this," he said. He saw I needed help. His own grief had to wait, his true judgement for ever buried.

' "She deserved so much better," I said. "I was not good enough for her. Or strong enough, you would say." '

Sam did not reply.

'I should have looked after her,' Joe said. And that was the seal on it, the guilt determined and, he thought for ever after, undeniable, and, as it proved, crippling.

James hung around to travel back to Hampstead with Joe. He would go to Reading in the morning to pick up Marcelle.

The two friends took the overground train as Joe and Natasha had done so often. They said very little but Joe was grateful for the company. Yet it seemed so strange, Natasha's death, the familiar stations, still there. He was still shaken from what had not been said, but what he had imagined they were thinking in Ross's house. Opinions were on the loose. Edward Worcester had said it was 'an act of revenge'. Saul's wife had said that Joseph had 'killed Natasha' . . .

They got off at Hampstead Heath and walked up towards Joe's house where Helen would be waiting.

'Why don't you come in?'

'If you don't mind,' said James, 'I'll pass. It must have been a hell of a day for you.'

'Yes . . . thanks.'

They stood at the bottom of the steps that led up to the house which was thrown into dramatic relief by a nearby streetlight. Joe was reluctant to lose James, his long friendship, knowing Natasha from the start, his link with the day of the funeral. In the back of his mind Joe had believed the funeral would point towards an ending. It was starting to dawn on him that there would be no ending.

'There are so many ways to look at this,' James said, his words rather tentatively offered, his style even more formal than usual. 'One is to say that Natasha has let you go. She always wanted freedom for both of you and now she has given you yours. I think that could be called an act of love.'

It was offered to give more ease. It was received like the final and finishing punch. They shook hands and Joe slowly levered himself up the steps of his house to Helen. How could anyone live on after such an act of love?

—∭—

Joe raged with hunger to talk about Natasha. He wanted to know what she had been like before him, without him, how she had seemed with him, what people had thought of her, what she had said about him, how his relationship with her had been perceived. The perception of their marriage to his frantic mind and guilty soul sometimes seemed as important as the reality of it. He wanted to know everything about Natasha and what their friends had thought about himself and Natasha. Yet he was and remained throughout his life only occasionally able to raise the courage to ask about her, even with good friends. But in the beginning he forced himself to talk with them: brief conversations, embarrassed summaries, but attempts which met with sympathy though little that could ease the pain for more than a few minutes. It always came back to the conversation with himself and the pain would have no end.

He feared above all that he would be thought of as someone merely seeking acquittal and there was a truth in that. He wanted everyone who had ever known Natasha to tell him that he need not feel this guilt, that it was not wholly his fault. He longed for absolution and yet would have accepted none. Shame and guilt branded his character from then on. He had, he thought, helped bring about an unnatural act and there was no natural way in which he could be absolved. How could he have done that to such a woman? He thought of writing to her analyst but his own analyst advised him against it. Soon it would be time for him to leave the analysis. That too pulled him down but he would leave, he decided, he would not cling on. It was time to let go.

He struggled hard to keep up a front, to deliver, do things, be anaesthetised by activity. But his success was limited.

Julia invited him to Oxford. She specified lunch when Matthew would be in college. They ate frugally in the dining room and she offered Joe white wine although she drank none herself. Afterwards they went upstairs into the living room, scene of almost all her late-night conversations with Matthew.

She built up the fire, accepted his offer of a cigarette, poured coffee and said,

'You look absolutely terrible. That's no surprise.'

'Yes,' he said, rather slurred, she thought, already, 'it's been . . .'

'I didn't approve of what you did,' said Julia, 'the split-up, but these things happen. We have friends in the same boat. Natasha was always extremely difficult. But I did not approve. There was Marcelle to consider. I thought you behaved very badly.' There was no accompanying smile to soften what she said.

'I could tell . . .' He took a sip of the coffee and then returned to the wine. 'This house is very quiet,' he said. 'It's always seemed extra quiet.'

'Yes. They knew how to build. But what Natasha did was wrong. She should not have done it. What she did has blighted your lives, both you and Marcelle and Helen. It has blighted all your lives.'

He could find no response. If it were true, it altered a balance and by making her less white made him less black. But if it were true it was a lifetime's curse.

'I thought she might attempt this before. Before she met you.'

Joe waited.

'It was an adolescent thing. Perhaps I ought to have taken it more seriously. I want to tell you that both Matthew and I are of the opinion that through you her life was extended.'

Joe could not take that in. Not then, not ever and yet like a cross touched by the faithful for some hope, he would reach out for it throughout his life.

'Do you think so?'

He meant: 'Could you please say that once again.'

'I do. We both do. I thought I had so much to tell you,' said Julia. 'But I've considered it so often that I've as it were boiled it down to essentials. The chief thing now is for you to look after yourself so that you can look after Marcelle. At the moment you are letting yourself go

540

rather badly, in my opinion.' She sipped her coffee. 'Which train are you catching? I could always run you to the station.'

'I'll walk. I like walking.'

'I remember Natasha used to complain that you walked too quickly for her . . .' She smiled a little, but the sadness would not be denied. 'How did it come to this? You were so wonderful together . . .'

—m—

'To be rather brutally honest,' David said and looked around, although there was no one in the Morning Room of the Garrick Club this early in the evening, which was why Joe had chosen it as a location for their meeting, 'I was surprised when you got together in the first place. Don't get me wrong. I loved Natasha. Better to say I "adored" her: she was one of those sorts of people who provoke those sorts of statements.' He smiled, sadly. 'Perhaps only in me. Gosh!' He sipped at his gin and tonic. 'What a very grand room this is . . . that's Thackeray in the corner, isn't it? I remember reading somewhere . . . he was a famous member, wasn't he? And Dickens? It's very like a stately pile, isn't it, a rather grand country house that's seen better days and been tugged into London as its last berth. I must say it's a style I admire enormously although being a good socialist I ought to frown on it.'

David was just back from Mozambique and before Joe could head him off he delivered what at another time Joe would have devoured and admired as a brilliant résumé of the condition of that country.

'. . . and it was that which caused me to miss the funeral,' he said. 'I'm told it was very moving. Of course it would be.'

'Why,' Joe drove himself to say, 'were you surprised when we got together?'

'Well now. I could see how Rachel fitted into your life. I suppose I could see that it had to end although I don't know enough about these matters and it always struck me as rather odd that when she as you say "finished it", you didn't sooner or later go back and reclaim her. That could be to do with the working-class virgin thing. But Natasha? Yes, you were very much in love but it was a mismatch. You were chalk and cheese. She was Cartesian and of the mind; you, well,' he paused for effect and his manner was roguish, 'let us say you are religious and of the heart.'

'But as you say,' – Joe wanted more: anything would do – 'we did love each other.'

'Ah well,' said David, 'what is this thing called love?'

'The thing is . . .' even to David this was hard to say, 'I think that I did it. I can't get it out of my mind. Whatever anybody says or whatever excuses are offered up, I believe that I am to blame.'

'Blame,' said David, very firmly, 'is not the issue. If you had stayed together it could have been even worse. I am firmly persuaded that you would both have perished. I would go so far as to say that you intuited that and it was for that key reason that you dared not go back to her. It was basic self-preservation on your part, I believe. Natasha had a pact with death. That is a real consideration. Her will was very firm and so is yours. Separation was probably the only option. Unhappily, tragically, it triggered a series of consequences in Natasha which overpowered her while you managed to survive.'

Joe was silent and for some moments. He was being offered a prospect of eventual resolution: but it was too late.

'Natasha telephoned me just before she went to France,' David said. 'She asked me to go to the French Embassy with her for their Fourteenth of July party. I assume she was on the list because of her father and I know you've been several times but I hadn't and of course I wanted to help. She dressed beautifully, something rather courtly, I thought, decidedly at odds with the Fourteenth of July, but absolutely right for the French Embassy. It was there that she said to me, "You have a face that has suffered so much, no one will want to hurt it again." That is the last thing I remember her saying. And after an hour or so I noticed that she was peering at the room, you know, of course you know how she half closed her eyes. I needn't have been there. And I thought – she's bored with life, she gave off unmistakably a cosmic ennui.'

Joe let himself absorb what David had described and then said, 'But why? Who had pushed her there?'

'It's possible to know only a part of the picture,' David said, 'the part

542

you knew is so important to you that you think it is the whole picture but it never is.'

'But to . . . to . . .'

'Kill herself.' For the first time in Joe's experience of him, David took a substantial drink and then set on the table the glass which he always liked to have in his hands. The playfulness, that long smile which seemed a release from the captivity of a man staked out against hurt, was replaced by an expression of such severity that it was as if a mask had been pulled off. 'You want to be helped,' he said, looking straight ahead but not looking directly at Joe. 'And I want to help. So I will tell you this. The only person I've told this to is my very best and closest friend whom I met at school.' He paused, but only for a moment. 'Both my parents committed suicide. My father just after I was born, just after he got out of Germany. My mother eight years later. I have always blamed myself and it has been a waste of life. And sometimes when I am alone, I feel as I know you feel, that I must follow them. But it must be resisted. Blame is not the issue. It is not the issue. It must be resisted.'

After taking Marcelle down the street to the primary school at New End, Joe came back to make his breakfast. Helen had left for work while he had been out. He made the toast and coffee and carried them from the galley kitchen up into his study where he could look out at the strip of garden. There were three letters, a telephone bill, a note from his publisher and a letter from the solicitors who were dealing with Natasha's affairs.

'As you are aware, your wife made no will despite our best efforts and this has occasioned and will continue to occasion delays. However we consider it quite proper in all the circumstances to forward to you the enclosed letter, addressed to yourself, given us by your late wife some four months ago . . .'

The writing on the envelope was not as firm as her usual hand but it was perfectly legible. 'To my husband,' it read, 'Joseph Richardson. To be sent to him on the occasion of my death.'

So how could he open it? Tell me, Natasha, he said inside his mind, tell me how I can open it? Four months ago. Before you went to France.

'Dearest Joseph,' it began and his eyes blurred.

In the event of my death I know that you will be a good father to Marcelle. I know you love her and I can rely on you without qualification. She is a lovely child who loves you dearly. But I must ask you to ensure that she keeps in contact with our friends and their children in Kew. These are people who know and love her deeply and it is important that she keeps in close contact with them.

As for me, at this time I do not feel well, Joseph. My back is a continuous drain of my strength but more than that my analyst took her life almost a year ago and I fear the effect on me has not been good. It is tiring without her. While without you it is an abyss.

Yet my love for you is unimpaired. You brought me great happiness and I am grateful for that. What will happen now is beyond me.

Natasha.

CHAPTER FORTY-SEVEN

'I asked my analyst if I could stay on with him a while longer,' he told Marcelle. 'I was fearful of everything again, of being alone, of crowds, of the underground, of loud noises, of an imminent liquefaction of my brain. Work helped; work could blot up feelings and wipe out thought for a while; work had become such a habit in my life that thankfully it could continue on a sort of automatic pilot and even though the results reflected that, at least it was work, it annulled some of the hours, it was time spent with matter unconnected with what was really happening. Helen was always there, bracing herself against her own shock, loyal, loving. And there was you. You were the heart of it now, for all of us. We watched over you.'

They were in La Rotonde. Joe and Helen had brought Marcelle there every summer. She would stay with the family, Joe and Helen would find somewhere in a nearby village and come across to La Rotonde now and then. Every year Louis had been as welcoming to both and as interested in discussion as he had always been. Véronique, although uneasy with Marcelle, had accepted the arrangement with resignation. For Alain and Isabel it was the crux of their summer.

Decades passed by; more than thirty harvests of lavender; the village was reclaimed by heritage, La Rotonde restored, the Crusaders' Tower transformed into a chic rendezvous for seasonal concerts of early baroque music. A studio for pottery and ceramics opened and flourished; the bakery closed down. Yet the place itself, even tidied up, never lost its unique attraction, Joe thought, and even though he still walked in sadness up the pathways between the houses carved out of the mountain's rock, there was still the charm of the place, an unfailing melody.

Louis and Véronique were dead. Alain had suffered a long time from lung cancer and died at Easter. Joe had been filming in America, unable to get to the funeral. Now in the summer they had come to see Isabel. It was too much trouble for her to accommodate them. Marcelle stayed with an old childhood friend, who was married with two children. Joe and Helen also stayed with friends some kilometres away near Bonnieux.

Isabel had said firmly that she would like to have lunch with them on their last day. The evening before, they went to her house for drinks, a tradition introduced by Alain, who called it 'the *bon voyage* farewell to our dear English friends' and at which he always, with a little pomp, served champagne.

The local taxi brought Isabel into the village for lunch. She came every weekday. It was her main meal. At the weekends she ate what had been prepared for her by the housekeeper who had been with her for more than thirty years. As usual, Isabel looked beautiful: old, arthritic in the hands, but still slim, upright, a stick to make doubly sure, fine make-up, clothes, hair, perfect, as she strolled from the taxi, the dogs obedient beside her. She had that great beauty which never goes however far it fades.

Bertrand's was now the only place to eat in La Rotonde. Isabel came late, partly because her morning took time, partly because Bertrand preferred the place to be emptying when she came to her corner seat with the two German shepherds. As often as she could she ate outside under the awning where there were only two tables and from which she looked up into the village.

After the coffee had been served, after Bertrand's two staff had gone home and he himself was taking a siesta, Isabel asked Joe, Joseph she called him, to move a little nearer to her. Helen looked away across the lavender fields and gave them the intimacy Isabel wanted. Isabel lit a cigarette and sipped a little coffee. For a while there was nothing said. Then she looked away and held out her left hand. He reached out to hold it. She spoke as always in clear old-school French, and did not rush, for Joseph's sake.

'You see,' she began, 'I do not want to live now that Alain is gone. It is only for the dogs. They have been faithful to me for so many years. If they were to go . . . My life is over now. It is not important. I am very old, and

Alain was the love of my life. But you should know some things. Now. Too late. You should have known them years ago. We make mistakes.

'You must know that Natasha's mother, who was my dearest friend, whom I adored completely, was determined to be the equal of Louis. And in those early years she was. They were so fine, they worked together in the laboratory, we all knew how important their work would be. And then Natasha was born and it was not an easy birth. A few weeks after the birth, Sophie died. She did not take good care of herself. She was in a terrible depression. She believed that the beautiful partnership between Louis and herself was at an end. She could not be convinced this need not be so.

'Louis, poor Louis, was distraught and he took a housekeeper, what else could he do? She came from the next village, Banon. Janine. She was a malign person. She was young, a peasant, pretty enough and when she saw she could not get Louis she turned on Natasha. This was discovered when Natasha was five years old and Alain was treating her. But it was too late. The damage was done.'

She released his hand to take another cigarette.

'Véronique was good for Louis but not for Natasha. Natasha was extremely difficult. They sent her away to convents and she would run away. She refused to take her examinations. She accused Véronique of mistreating her. She made terrible accusations against Véronique. Alain said they were intended for Janine. I loved Natasha, but for Véronique, and when her own children came, it was too much.

'Louis? Louis was doing what Louis always did. He arrived on the scene, he announced perfect solutions and he went back to his laboratory. He was the man he was and Alain said he had never met anyone whose memory was so perfect. I once told Louis that he should have been a monk. I was serious. The relationship between Véronique and Natasha became so intolerable that they could not be in the same room together. And when Natasha went to England, Véronique rejoiced. It is a stepmother problem, Joseph, and your *chère* Helen will know that. You are strong, and so is Helen and so now is Marcelle. But Natasha . . . They let her go to England.

'After some years in England Alain and I believed that Natasha had found her way. And when you arrived, Joseph, we thought she was safe at last. She truly loved you and we saw that you truly loved her.'

She turned to him, for the first time. For some moments she held his faltering gaze and then she smiled. 'You were our hope, Joseph, and for some years she was very happy, and so were we, Joseph; so were we. Thank you for that.'

She turned away again to hide the emotion and Joe held her hand more tightly.

'You have to know what happened when she came here for that last summer. Alain thought she was very ill. Not just the terrible back which he said should have been operated on years before! Sometimes she could scarcely walk. But it was her whole psyche, Alain said. But there was Marcelle to occupy which helped her and even in that gloomy room Véronique gave her she could rest. She talked about you, Joseph, she talked to Alain and me about you night after night after night, and sometimes of Helen of whom she was unbearably jealous, so jealous she tried to avoid mentioning her. But chiefly it was of you, not criticising you but explaining you, saying what you had done together, making plans for what you would do again when what she called your "madness" passed.

'But there was the terror of you also. She thought you might not give her any money. She thought you might abduct Marcelle. When you sent a parcel for Marcelle, she would not go to Banon, the post office there, to collect it because . . . she said it might be a bomb. Alain collected it and then she was overcome with pleasure that you had sent Marcelle such a present, but what she wanted, Joseph, was a letter from you saying you wanted to live together again. She wrote all the time in her notebooks, and letters to you, which she was afraid to post. What she longed for was for you to arrive, just like that, to come to La Rotonde out of the sky and I can see her now, standing on that balcony and looking out into the countryside as if by looking alone she could bring you back to her. It broke my heart.'

Isabel stubbed out the cigarette.

'Véronique made her give up smoking to strengthen her character, she said. I thought that it was stupid. Then the time came when Alain had to return to his laboratory in Marseilles, Louis and Véronique had to go back to Paris. I said I would stay with her but Véronique and Louis considered that Natasha would be better in England and certainly Marcelle would be happier with her friends and it was time for her to return.

'Louis and Véronique were our dear friends, Joseph, and they remained our dear friends until their death but they were wrong. The night before the flight Alain and I came to La Rotonde and tried to change their minds. Our voices were so loud that Marcelle must have heard us and poor dear Natasha sat between us, looking from Louis then to me and then back to Louis, so sweetly, trusting us. I think now that her beautiful soul was broken. She was helpless. We should never have let her go, poor darling. We abandoned her . . .'

She let go of his hand and now Joe turned away. His chest ached from holding in the sound of sobbing. Natasha . . .

'There is one final matter,' said Isabel. 'I collected some of her writings after she left, to keep them safe for her. Many of them were illegible or unfinished. And all of them in English, Joseph: for you.

'But they were too sad, I thought. I gave them to Véronique who, I think, destroyed them. Save for a few lines. They are in this envelope. I have waited for the right time. Now it has come.'

She handed him one of her elegant envelopes, well sealed, and then, without fuss, embraced both Helen and Joseph and wished then '*bon voyage*'.

After Isabel left, Joe and Helen walked leadenly up through the spiralling village towards La Rotonde, where he had agreed to meet Marcelle. Helen left him alone and went to buy some lavender.

The sky was blue and without cloud from horizon to horizon. The men playing boules nodded as he passed by and he sought out a quieter path, outside the mediaeval wall, and with increasing weariness he walked up the hill through the cypress trees. Isabel's words had felled him. Natasha was everywhere about him in La Rotonde. The village seemed to hold her spirit and at every turn on this terrible walk away from Isabel, he dreamed to see Natasha, alive, the smile. 'Please be there,' he asked her, 'just for one moment together.'

'When I reached La Rotonde I sat where Natasha and I had last sat together, one night, so many years ago now. As I waited for you, I got out my notebook. There were very few people around at this hot time in the afternoon but I wanted to cut myself off and I knew that if I seemed to be absorbed in writing, I would not be disturbed.

'The notes made there are the basis for these final sentences. I have tried my best to bring Natasha home to you who now look so much like her. Many times I feel that I have not done justice to her, to a life so much purer than mine. Time is said to heal all wounds. Well, it doesn't always, Marcelle; in some cases it deepens them. I wanted you to know what I know about your mother, my wife. This account is yours, to do with as you wish.

'The biggest thing of all is loss. Not to see her again, never to hear her, to be alive when she is not alive . . . Time is passing faster for me now, year by year more quickly, and sometimes I find I say, "It will not be long now."'

He sat in the shade on the steps of La Rotonde and waited. Eventually he saw Marcelle down the path in the distance, the sun behind her. He closed his notebook. She looked up, saw him and smiled and then she waved as she walked towards him and brought Natasha with her.

He got up from the bed and went across the cool tiles to the window and looked again at what Isabel had given him.

Natasha had copied out some lines from Christina Rossetti. They were scrawled in uncharacteristically hectic loose handwriting.

> Remember me when I have gone away,
> Gone far away into the silent land;
> When you can no more hold me by the hand,
> Nor I half turn to go, yet turning stay.

And then the scrawl slid into a violent tangle of lines and shapes, wordless; nothing but pain.

The shutters were ajar. He opened one of them wide and looked at the diamond stars, the fathomless darkness, and listened to the night sounds of Provence.

She is out there now, he thought, in the infinite and unbearable space of memory.